MW01233587

What four West Point authors have to say about *Grip Hands:*

"An amazing collection- *Grip Hands Thru the Shadows* is two centuries' worth of West Point literature masterfully assembled."

Jason Kasper, USMA '81 USA Today Bestselling Author of the *Shadow Strike* series.

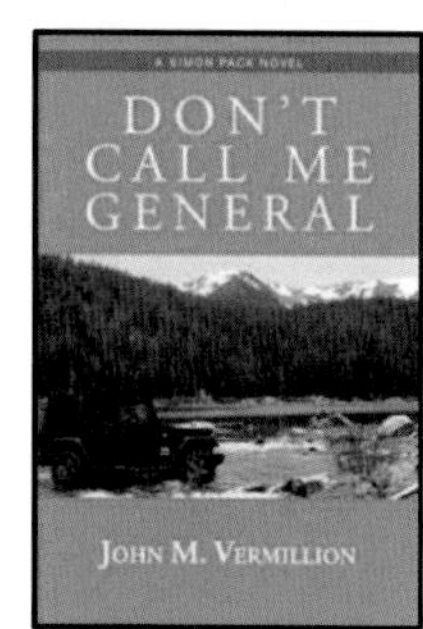

"This beautiful, well-researched (500+ pages) book exceeded my expectations. For anyone interested in fiction either by West Point authors or involving the Military Academy, this book is the indispensable resource. Once upon a time, I might've used this as the start point for a doctoral dissertation. I'll find a trove of new novels to explore from these pages. Congratulations, sir, for making this excellent work available."

John M. Vermillion, USMA '70, Author of *The Supe* and eight follow-on Simon Pack thrillers.

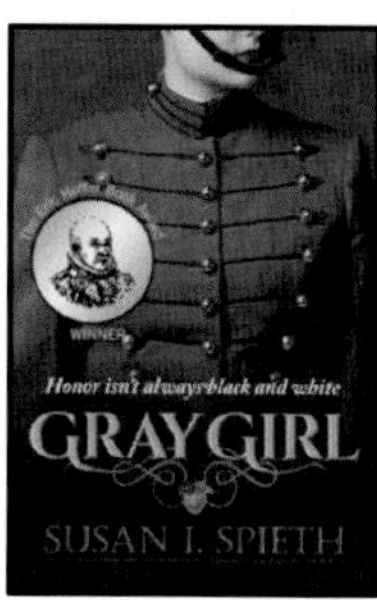

"Who knew there were so many books related to West Point? Ed Blomstedt has compiled a comprehensive collection of West Point fiction into twenty-four chapters on topics ranging from *The Cadet Experience, Paranormal, Supernatural & Futuristic, Women at West Point, The Cold War*, and many more. This weighty volume (pun intended) is a must-have for all supporters of the United States Military Academy—cadets, officers, employees, alumni, family and friends. Thank you, Ed, for this herculean task of bringing the *Soldiers of Fortune, Paladins, Miscreants and Rogues* all together in one place!"

Susan Spieth, USMA '85, author of the Gray Girl Series. Winner of two Eric Hoffer Book Awards for *Gray Girl: Honor Isn't Always Black and White*

This is a grand work of love by Edward Blomstedt, a remarkable author with intimate knowledge of West Point, its ancient lore, and its countless stories. I*n Grip Hands Through the Shadows,* he has impressively and even improbably written reviews of 200 years of fictional works about West Point, that fabled institution whose historical truths can sound like myth. It's a great read that keeps giving and belongs in every Army, Academy and patriot's bookshelf.

Augustus "Gus" Lee entered West Point with the Class of 1968 but left before graduating. He served as a non-commissioned officer, later completing his undergraduate and law degree at the University of California.

Grip Hands Thru the Shadows

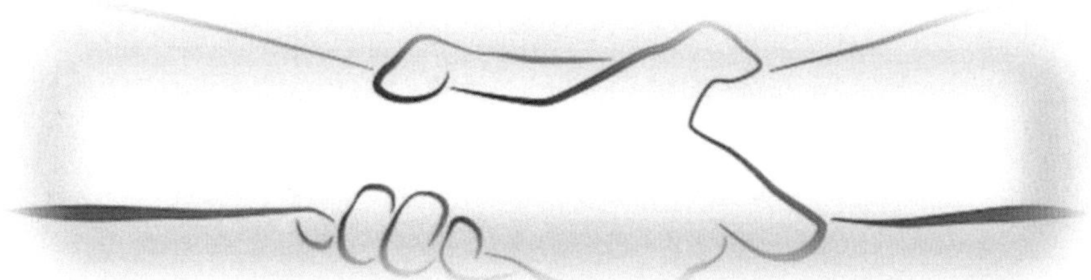

Two Centuries of West Point in Fiction

Honoring the West Point Class of 1998

Edward A. Blomstedt

Grip Hands Thru the Shadows

Edited by Joyelle Soucier

Cover design and illustration by Kristi Ramsey and Sara Dudley

Barton Cove Publishing
78 French King Hwy
Gill, MA 01354
413.230.2500
bartoncovepublishing@gmail.com

Printed in the United States of America

ISBN: 978-0-9819555-4-4

To the Reader

This is a catalog depicting the works in a collection of historical fiction about West Point which the author accumulated over the span of twenty-five years. It includes novels, stories, plays, movies, poetry, pulp fiction, and some memoirs, all written from 1835 through 2023. There are about 600 items, many of them written by West Point graduates featuring cadets, graduates, candidates, girlfriends, wives, sports, mascots, Army life, service experience, as well as a few scoundrels and rogues.

This work is dedicated to my wife, Margaret (Mae), who, during our 50-year journey together, delivered hundreds of small packages from our mailbox to my place at the kitchen table.

"What are you going to do with all those books?" she once inquired.

I probably mumbled something about West Point, but now....

"Well, dear, this is it!"

Ed Blomstedt
Spring House, Pennsylvania
June 2023

Table of Contents

Honoring the Class of 1998

"Make no mistake. You will serve in perilous times. The history of the United States will be written with the blood of your classmates. That has been true since 1802. Your class will not be an exception."

General Dennis J. Reimer, Army Chief of Staff
Addressing the Class of 1998 at their Graduation Dinner

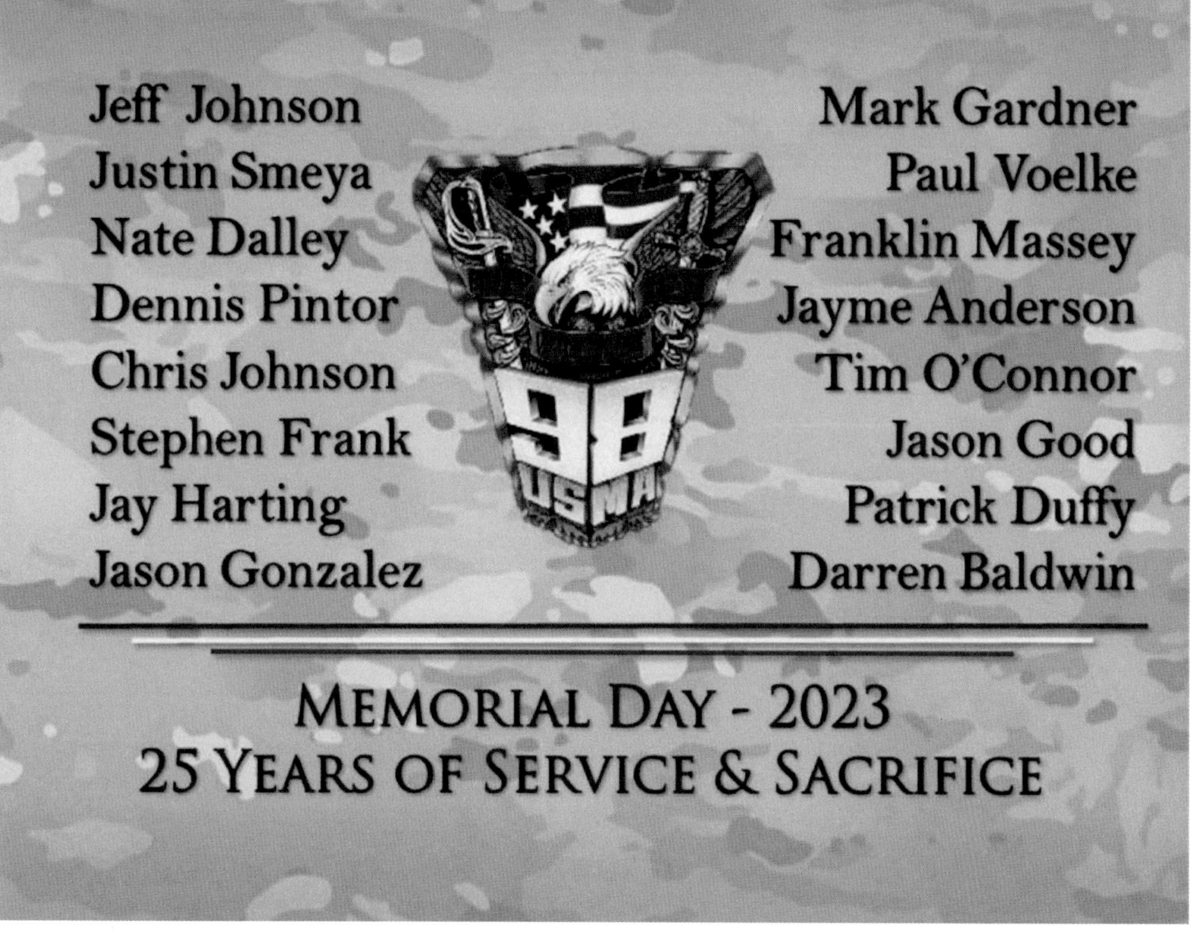

Why "Grip Hands?"

The phrase comes from a poetic hymn written for the United States Military Academy by West Point Chaplain H.S. Shipman around 1902. The hymn expresses how the current cadets gather strength from their predecessors. It is sung at graduations, memorial services, funerals, and alumni gatherings.

THE CORPS! THE CORPS! THE CORPS!

The Corps, bareheaded, salute it, with eyes up, thanking our God.
That we of the Corps are treading, where they of the Corps have trod.
They are here in ghostly assemblage. The ranks of the Corps long dead.
And our hearts are standing attention, while we wait for their passing tread.

We Corps of today, we salute you. The Corps of an earlier day;
We follow, close order, behind you, where you have pointed the way;
The long gray line of us stretches, thro' the years of a century told
And the last man feels to his marrow, the grip of your far off hold.

Grip hands with us now though we see not, grip hands with us strengthen our hearts.
As the long line stiffens and straightens with the thrill that your presence imparts.
Grip hands tho' it be from the shadows. While we swear, as you did of yore.
Or living, or dying, to honor, the Corps, and the Corps, and the Corps.

Introduction

In the Beginning

The first books were acquired for the author's reading pleasure when his son enrolled at West Point in 1994. Starting with Lucian Truscott's *Dress Gray,* Rick Atkinson's *The Long Gray Line* (not fictional), James Agnew's *The Eggnog Riot*, Russel Reeder's *West Point Plebe,* Norman Ford's *Black, Gray, and Gold*, and Gus Lee's *Honor and Duty*, the collection blossomed. By 2008, the author considered writing a novel about the ghosts of that Long Gray Line rising from the cemetery to engage in some sort of debate with the current generation of cadets. Alas, the muse failed to ignite a suitable plot. Instead, the author turned to preparing a picture book on the cemetery highlighting hundreds of its occupants. The result, *Be Thou at Peace*, was published in 2013. By then this collection had grown to 300 books and the author was retired. What to do? Keep collecting and reading, of course, between rounds of golf and travel.

During a visit to West Point in 2012, I stopped in the archives office which was then located adjacent to the Visitor Center. In response to an inquiry about their works of fiction, the librarians pointed to two shelves containing maybe 40 books and magazines. I turned to the ladies and said, "There are lots of books on eBay that should be in this collection." They responded. "Oh, we know, but we don't have any budget to acquire them." Considering that for a moment, I stated: "Ladies, I have the budget and am building a grand collection for you. It may take a few years, but you will have it." They thought that would be wonderful. Now, the time has arrived!

Why Do This?

The sands of time eventually bury us all in anonymity, except for the truly famous or infamous. When our grandchildren pass on, we and our times are lost to history. The same is true of popular culture, although that does not usually take two generations to fade away. How many under the age of forty in the year 2023 can recall anything about Henry Arnold, Mary Pickford, Neville Shute or Andrew Mellon? How about Tommy Dorsey, Charles Evans Hughes, the Cuban Missile Crisis, or Zimmerman telegram? All were prominent personalities or events in the pageant of American history. Lost, except for academic niches of inquiry.

The history of America is well reflected in the story of the United States Army officer corps. Not all Army officers graduated from West Point by any means, but the spirit of the officer corps from West Point and the history of the Army over two centuries has been captured by writers celebrated and obscure. West Point with its motto of "Duty, Honor, Country" established a spiritual and moral foundation for many literary efforts. In those novels and stories lay a wealth of history, psychology, the humanity of American soldiers, their families, and the times in which they lived. By pulling together this collection, presenting it to the West Point archives, and preparing a catalog, the author expects to keep that grand story from fading entirely into historical oblivion.

Did I get them all? Of course not. There are dozens, maybe hundreds of more stories out there, especially in the pulp fiction magazines, that I just never discovered. My apologies to those authors and their families if they have been overlooked in the collecting process. If you have been overlooked, consider donating a copy of the "missing" work to the archives at West Point.

Selecting the Books

The initial criteria were straightforward: The book had to be fictional with a plot featuring West Point, the cadets, or a graduate. Any novel by a West Point graduate also qualified for inclusion. That held for the vast majority of works in the collection. However, gray areas soon arose. How about memoirs by the wives of graduates who endured and recorded Army life and times, particularly in the 19th century? They were added as were books describing Army mascots and other animals, as well as novels and stories on the paranormal, supernatural, and futuristic. Then I discovered many West Point related stories in comic books and the pulp fiction magazines from the first half of the 20th century. Poetry, drama, and film could not be denied.

The collection grew steadily. "Mission creep," you say? Certainly, though I think of it as "securing a better perimeter."

A Literary Buffet

Challenge: How to best present the collection so that a reader will see it as more than "a large pile of old books?" Displaying them alphabetically by author leaves the reader with little more than a card catalog with pictures...and not much insight. A chronological presentation based on publication date would give the reader some sense of the evolution of writing style and the significant events that motivated their writing. However, it is a long slough of reading from 1850 to 2000 on a wide variety of subjects to glean some framework that characterizes the body of work. Few readers would care to do that.

The reader must come first, not the books, so I pondered how to present the collection in reader-enticing chunks – perhaps a literary buffet – with West Point as its centerpiece. It would be especially appealing if the reader could leave a chapter to locate and read one of the books then later "return to the buffet with a fresh plate," taking up a book from another chapter that piqued his or her interest. Eureka!

I had found a "literary taxonomy" grouping books with a similar plot focus together. Fortunately, the history of West Point and artistry of those who wrote about it provided an abundance of primary topics – from cadet life to the Civil War, winning the West, Army life and Army wives, and then the mascots and the supernatural. I am thankful for the many authors who put their minds to work, their pens to paper, and scratched out so many stories for our reading enjoyment.

Though the collection comprises books, magazines, pamphlets, and miscellaneous articles, for simplicity they will be referred to as "books" or "works."

Housing the Collection

In 2023 the collection will be presented to the archives of the United States Military Academy as the **"Class of 1998 Collection of West Point Fiction."** The archives are being relocated to a renovated Cullum Hall in 2024. Access to the collection will be governed by the Academy's rules.

Built in 1896, **Cullum Hall** was originally designed to memorialize the service and ultimate sacrifice of West Point graduates who died in war. The grand ballroom upstairs with its oil portraits, commemorative plaques, statues, and cannon trophies, is a tribute to the achievements of West Point's notable graduates. The main level is a memorial hall opening to a wide terrace that overlooks the Hudson River. Cullum Hall's paintings, under the care of the West Point Museum, are among the most significant memorial portraits at the Academy. The lower two basement levels, which currently house various Cadet Clubs, will be completely renovated to serve as the new home for the USMA Archives.

Source: https://www.westpoint.edu/USMA-2035/academic-infrastructure/academic-building-upgrade-program

Looking to Acquire a Specific Book?

Currently – in 2023 – most of the books are available through used book websites (eBay, Alibris, Abebooks, Biblio, Goodreads) or on Amazon and Barnes & Noble. The oldest books (pre-1930) can be expensive (over $60) or in poor condition. A dustjacket in acceptable condition will double or triple the price. If you only care to have a reading copy, the price is more reasonable. However, copyrights of the older books have expired, so many are being reprinted. Reprints may lack the charm of the original, but the text is the same and may be more readable.

The books in this collection, with some exceptions, are from the original printings, but not necessarily first editions. Dozens bear the author's signature.

Creating this Catalog

Classifying the Books

The table of contents lists twenty-four chapters into which the books have been placed. Many books could be included in multiple chapters, but choices had to be made. Some of the books, particularly those in an author's series of works merited mention in more than one chapter, and so they have been – with a reference to the primary chapter.

Chapter Organization

Each chapter begins with its own introduction differentiated from the ensuing book descriptions by inclusion in a gold-shaded box.

As a rule, the books are presented within the chapter chronologically, not by publication date, but by era – e. g. "before World War II and after World War II." This approach maintains a historical progression, while allowing the reader to compare the perspective of authors from different generations.

Proceeding through the chapter, the cataloger's commentaries on the grouping of books or adding a historical perspective are also encased in a gold-shaded box.

About the Authors of These Books

Readers often enjoy knowing about the book's author. Many of the authors were graduates of West Point. Others were prolific writers of dozens of novels and/or hundreds of short stories. "Writer's block" did not seem to plague them. An appendix includes a complete listing of authors and their works in the collection.

It took considerable effort to ferret out their biographical information if it was not included on the dust jacket or book cover. For some writers no biographical information could be found. Possibly they were pseudo names. Others had extensive write-ups in Wikipedia or their own websites. In this rapidly evolving digital world, one does not know how long the internet entries will be accessible, but source information is noted in the Source References appendix.

Author biographical highlights are enclosed in a gray box for most entries. Notations have been placed at the end of each author block to indicate the source for the author's biography.

About the Authors

Items in the Collection	624
Authors in the Collection	336
Works by West Point Authors	184
Female Authors	69

** West Point graduate
(?) Maybe a graduate

These twenty authors produced 29% of the works in the collection.

John Wesley Howard	(31)
Lt. John T. Hopper **	(18)
Charles King **	(17)
Jason Kasper **	(12)
P. G. Allison (?)	(11)
Jeff Shaara	(11)
Brian Haig**	(9)
Janet Lambert	(8)
Russel Reeder **	(8)
Robert Sidney Bowen	(7)
W.E.B. Griffin	(7)
John M. Vermillion **	(7)
Henry "HAP" Arnold **	(6)
William Chamberlain **	(6)
Lt. Frederick Garrison	(6)
Beverly C. Gray	(6)
Ed Ruggero **	(6)
Paul Malone **	(6)
Richard H. Dickinson **	(5)
Tom Willard	(5)

Presenting Each Book

Each book's summary information follows a standard format: **Title, Author, Publisher & Date**. Also included is a "Tag" in italics to identify the primary topics addressed by the author. For example: *Civil War, Romance, Cadet, Sports, WP (West Point) Author.* Most books have multiple "tags."

The **Text Description** for each book came from one of the following sources:

1. A scan from the book's dust jacket (when available) or the back cover for paperbacks. This is the most common source for the books in this catalog. These descriptions have been identified with the notation – "**DJ**" or "**BC**." Alternately, a blurb by the publisher in the front piece is referenced with – "**FP**." Minor editing was done to remove effusive praise supplied by the publisher.

2. Few books published before 1930 had the descriptive dust jackets or back cover that are prevalent today. Rarely, the publisher inserted a front piece with a description of the plot and characters that could be scanned and used. This cataloger had to read the

book and prepare a synopsis, often a tedious exercise. The writing style prior to 1910 was excessively flowery with parenthetical asides and sometimes confusing antecedents. Those descriptions have been identified with the notation "**EB**."

3. Stories from the pulp magazines had only the briefest of blurbs along with an introductory drawing to entice the reader. The cataloger read the story and prepared a synopsis or extracted a few paragraphs from the beginning of the story. Those descriptions have been identified with the notation "**EB**."

The **book pictures** are scanned from the actual works in the collection. The older ones usually did not include a dust jacket or illustrated cover. Instead, the book cover or title page was scanned. Pulp magazines are presented with a composite picture of the colorful front cover and the black and white illustration that introduced the story.

External references for a book or author are noted with a superscript (e.g., [1-01]). The sources are identified at the end of the book in the Source References appendix.

Book Reviews and Commentary

Other than presenting a brief summary of each book's plot, I did not rate, rank, praise or deprecate the individual books. Among the almost 600 books in the collection, there are many great reads, some poor ones, talented authors, and others less accomplished. The readers are left to form their own opinions.

Chapter 1

The Cadet Experience

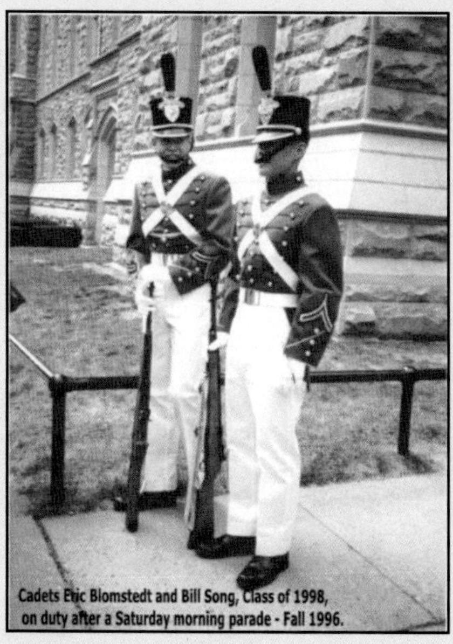

Cadets Eric Blomstedt and Bill Song, Class of 1998, on duty after a Saturday morning parade - Fall 1996.

The cadet experience today is grounded in customs and traditions that date from the Academy's earliest days, though it certainly has evolved over two centuries. On the other hand, the literature about the cadet experience dating from the 1860s was decidedly formulaic well into the 20th century. That changed dramatically only since World War II. The distinct literary shift had much to do with the changing tastes of a more worldly reading public and authors responding to those expectations.

A perspective on the earlier works was presented by Major Aloysius Norton, USMA Class of 1944 in a master's degree thesis at Columbia University in 1948 called, "The Customs and Traditions of West Point in the American Novel."

> "In the rare book room of the United States Military Academy rest some twenty-two novels that deal with cadet life at West Point. In any other library, these books would scarcely gain space in the juvenile section, largely because the books are "dated." Yet these novels offer pictures of the living past, but they have value for West Point…[and] value for all America…for they faithfully record the customs and traditions that provide for West Point's success."

Norton points out that the authors invariably chose, "cadet life as the subject because of the almost exotic nature of its being by focusing on three fundamental tenets of the cadet development: equality, the fourth class [plebe] system, and the honor system." He asserts that the authors succeeded in that respect.

> "Inasmuch as life at West Point differs considerably from that in civilian colleges, any cadet novel, unfortunately, will involve explanatory notes on all the detail. These elaborate asides often reduce the novels to role of glorified guidebooks that can scarcely be called literature…
>
> "Ironically, the novels thwart the possibility of becoming acceptable fiction [for modern tastes] solely because…in the accomplishment of that purpose, they do not go far enough…
>
> "Cadet life presented solely as a matter of shined shoes, brass buttons, and parades, only touches upon the subject. To tell only of fantastic rescues, strained honor violations, and

victorious football games results in romantic idealization. The novels are honest photographs; but, like photographs, they reflect little more than…obvious details."

> "A more serious failure in the West Point novels manifests itself in the 'characterizations.' Primarily, the protagonists are just too moral and exceedingly capable, overcoming a variety of diversity to rise to the top of his class by graduation…If the authors had increased the breadth of their characterization, they would not have been forced to rely as heavily on stereotyped plot action.
>
> "The authors fail to produce the best possible novels, and they also fail West Point by ignoring the obvious human appeal of character change or development through equality, the honor system, and the plebe system. If West Point's mission includes the molding of character, that mission should operate in the novels, for all reading audiences are interested in character change and development. Because the characters of these novels are consistently all good or all "flawed", West Point [of the novel] can do nothing for them. They are unreal simply because the authors fail to apply the missions of the Academy that are necessary to West Point's existence."

Of the twenty-two novels reviewed by Norton, he identified only one as coming close to demonstrating character development in the protagonist. That is the one that follows: "Cut: A Story of West Point."

> "The characters of Roe's "Cut" actually undergo change and development. West Point can do something for them. Their actions are not those of super-cadet."

In this chapter we present individual novels about specific cadet experiences. The plot in some may span more than one year, but usually not. Two works (*Tin Soldiers* and *Dress Gray*) represent the transition from the older to the modern. They were controversial because they departed from the "tried and true" but were far more engaging to modern readers.

Cut: A Story of West Point

Cadet, WP Author

G.I. Cervus J.B. Lippincott (1886)

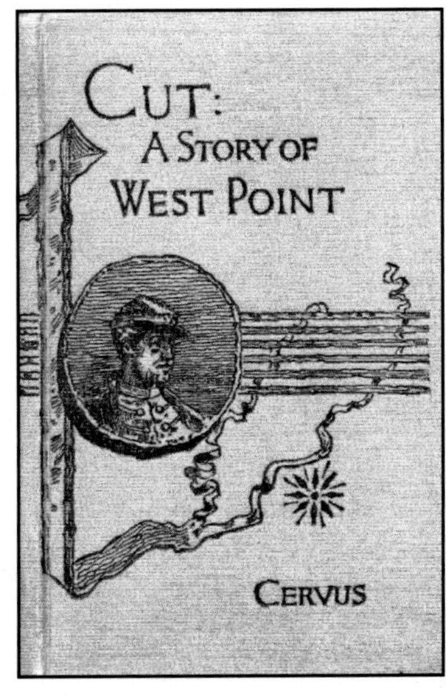

Cadet Kenyon is aggrieved that Cadet Wilmarth has used his position of authority to put him on report excessively. He raises this issue with Wilmarth but is rebuffed. Kenyon then reports their disagreement to the Commandant. Wilmarth is outraged and proposed they settle this affair of honor in a fight. Kenyon refuses to fight. Other cadets propose that Kenyon be "Cut" or shunned/silenced by the class for his obduracy and tattling to the commandant. Kenyon's roommate narrates what ensued:

"Chapter XIII, Cut by the Class"

After this day, while we were cadets together, except on matters of duty, I never spoke again to Wirt Kenyon, nor he to me. The last words, other than those of military formality and ceremony, had been "You can do nothing for me."

When Hasler, with no pretense at disguising his satisfaction, told of what Kenyon had said to him in the mess hall, I was, if not foremost, also not last to join in the hue and cry that arose forthwith. Perhaps he had been wrong; perhaps I might have done something for him. Now, looking back across the years that intervene, I seem to hear the still, small voice, that then only ticked a tiny treble all unheeded sound like the deepest tones of a cathedral bell.

"He says he won't fight," said Hasler, addressing the excited group of our class when we broke ranks. "Cut the coward, then!" cried Wilmarth and even the best men in the classmen who held their charity high as they held their honor–fell in readily with the views of the outspoken majority. That very night a class meeting was held. Due notice was given in the mess hall, for what purpose all by this time knew.

Kenyon was not there. No doubt he knew well what he would be called upon to undergo. At this time, I was resolute as the rest, convinced, not against my will, but inclination, that my duty was plain. The moving spirits—those who felt the deepest animosity or who held in highest esteem the dignity and credit of the Academy --laid all their plans deftly, and the meeting in Barlow's room, on the first floor of the fifth division, was called only for the purpose of putting in due form the sentiment -- now unanimous -- of the class... [EB]

Cervus was the pen name of **William James Roe** (1844–1921) Class of 1867. He served in the artillery but resigned his commission in 1869. He took over the family business, experienced a failure, and built several other businesses. Roe took up writing as a hobby and published seven novels using various pen names. The later ones reflected his interests in fantasy and the occult. [1-01]

Cadet Days: A Story of West Point

Cadet, WP Author

Charles King Harper & Brothers (1894)

Georgie Graham, 'POPS,' had really been in the army all his life, since his father was a post surgeon out in the Rocky Mountains. He traveled with the cavalry troop and was contributed greatly to rounding up some renegades. But his big chance--the chance he hardly dared to dream of—came when he received his appointment to West Point. It is an exciting and adventurous story -- the story of Pops' four years, from the time that he was a lowly plebe until that memorable graduation day when he was in command of the classes, with his mother and father and Buddy looking on. His story following graduation continues in *To the Front* by Charles King. [DJ]

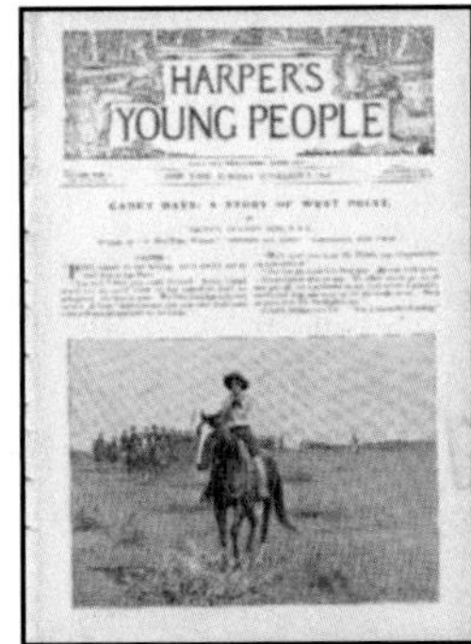

This serialized edition of the book appeared in "Harper's Young People Magazine" during 1893.

Charles King (1844–1932) graduated from West Point in 1866 and served in the army during the Indian Wars under George Crook. He was wounded in the arm and head during the Battle of Sunset Pass forcing his retirement from the regular army as a captain in 1879.

He wrote over 60 novels, mostly about West Pointers and army life in the late 19th century. The chapters "Manifest Destiny" and "Army Life and Army Wives" feature a number of his works and an expanded biography. [1-02]

Short Rations

Cadet, WP Author

Williston Fish Harper Brothers (1899)

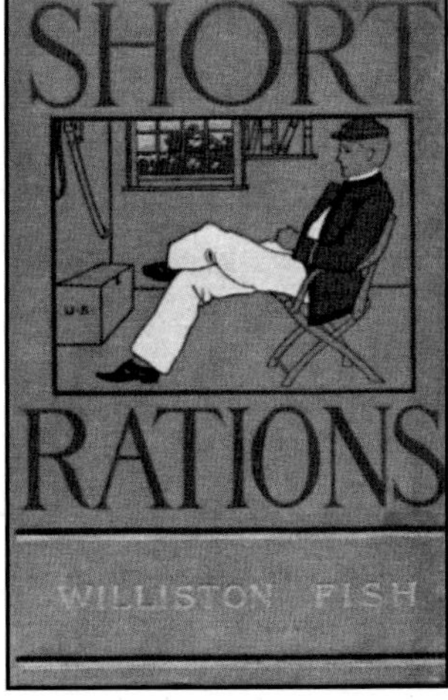

"Introduction to the Garrison"

"In another month Mrs. Colonel will catch chills and fever in her cold stone house, and Mrs. Mother-in-Law Major will be nursing her as if she were her very own mother. And as to Mrs. Colonel, why, she is only playing with the Second Lieutenant, just to assert her womanly self-respect, and before Spring she will marry him to one of the Major's daughters, and she take as much interest in the match as though young Miss Major were the little girl of her own who died in a damp casemate lodging eighteen years ago."

The army of the United States occupies an anomalous position among the military forces of the world, for which the statutory limit of its size is in part accountable. The army is practically without at staff corps, and in time of peace they are lacking proper facilities for the broad study of the soldier's profession. Against the time of war there are miserably inefficient laws for increasing the size of the army, and, for another provision against the time of war, there is the vicious practice of political promotions and appointments.

As matters now are, it follows from the insignificant size of our army that the garrison of a United States fort…is a garrison in name only. Soldiers enough to mount guard and a meager complement of officers are assigned to each one of the antiquated forts. [EB]

Williston Fish (1858–1939) was an American poet, novelist, and short story writer. He attended Oberlin College and West Point, Class of 1881, following which he spent 6 years of service in the United States Army. He then went into law, becoming a successful attorney in Chicago. He published 2 novels, and hundreds of poems and stories. His other novel *Won at West Point* is included in the chapter, "West Point Romance." [1-03]

West Point Colours: Life at A Military School

Cadet, WP Author

Anna B. Warner James Nisset & Co. (1903)

"Introduction To This Tale of a Possible Cadet"

SOME of my friends in a certain cadet class beset me to write a West Point story; promising me incidents at will, a plot, a name, and a tactical officer for "the villain." Perhaps it was because I declined this last sensational detail that they backed out of all the rest and having given my boat a shove into deep water, left me to row and pilot as best I might.

However, help came from other men, in other classes. I was cheered on in my work, and given story after story, with full leave to use them as I chose; and so, it falls out that my book is quite true. Not that all the happenings ever came to any one cadet, or within the bounds of any four years' course. But they have almost all, at some time, been part of somebody's life at West Point. With what men, or in what years, it does not matter: the last decade of the nineteenth century nearly enough covers the whole.

I have tried hard to have the small technicalities quite correct. Yet as rules do vary now and then, even at West Point, everything may not always seem right, to this or that graduate. And, of course, I may have blundered here and there. Certain points in cadet life I was especially asked to handle; and if once or twice I have told only what might have been, even there I had the warrant of cadet opinion.

As for the fancy names, it was so hard to find plain ones that were not down in some Army List or Visitors' Book, that I made up a few, choosing rather to give caps which nobody would put on than others quite sure to be appropriated. Truly, I did not name Miss Dangleum: a young officer did that, and Cadet Devlin was also dubbed by one who knew.

Since certain words of my story were written a few changes have come in. The cadet classes have pledged themselves to abolish hazing; the Hundredth Night (in its old wild glee) has been forbidden; the Cadet Howitzer is spiked. The shady nooks along "Flirtation" have been cleared up; Fort Clinton is a memory, the tents are brown, and Dade's white shaft now stands in the gayest and sunniest of all the thoroughfares. But human nature survives, and "boodle," and the girls, so that my book is declared to be still "absolutely true." [FP]

Anna Bartlett Warner (1827–1915) was an American writer, the author of several books and poems set to music as hymns and religious songs for children. From 1837 until the beginning of the 19th century, Susan and sister Anna lived on a farm on Constitution Island across the Hudson from West Point. They were quite religious, published many books, and frequently invited West Point cadets to attend prayer meetings and relax away from their post on a Sunday afternoon. The sisters are both buried in the West Point cemetery. Their home is preserved and may be visited by taking a boat from the dock at West Point. [1-04]

The Long Gray Line: Black Knights of the Hudson, Book IV

Legacy, Cadet

Beverly C. Gray Self-published (2013)

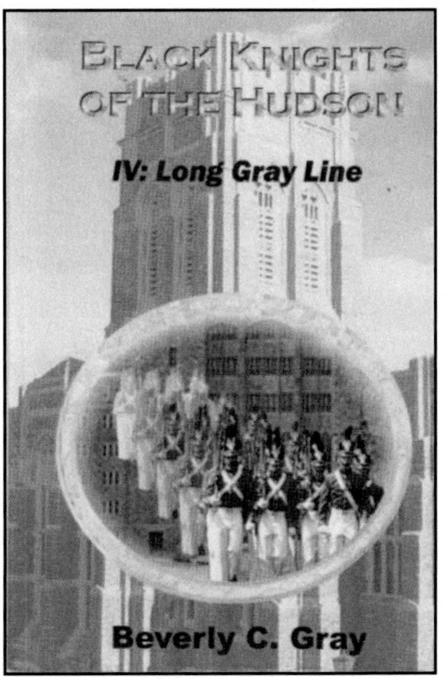

This is the fourth book in this sweeping family saga of the MacKendricks; who live by West Point's motto — Duty, Honor, Country. The war with Spain is over and the United States has moved beyond its continental boundaries. With new inventions on the horizon, the United States at last takes its place in the world order and the MacKendricks are quick to answer the challenge. Cousins Fitzjames and Jackson Lee MacKendrick arrive at West Point to assume their own places in West Point's fabled Corps of Cadets. Jackson Lee, classmate of the impressive Douglas MacArthur, demonstrates a quiet competence and is marked closely for later advancement by the senior officers. Fitzjames, son of a legendary officer of the United States, barely survives the tender mercies of the Yearlings in 'Beast Barracks' when he is hazed brutally for his effrontery in bearing such a famous name. In *Long Gray Line*, the MacKendricks march forward to greet the new century. From the football field of the annual Army-Navy game, where the canny Charlie Daly leads the Cadets against the Midshipmen, into the growing clouds of a world war, Jack and Fitz assume their fathers' mantles as the next generation of West Point's famed Corps of black knights. Attractive, engaging, from a background of wealth and privilege, the MacKendrick cousins prove to be fair game to the Army brats, college girls, New York society women, and English Ladyships who seek to join the equally important line of Army wives who have taken Milton's words as their own motto: 'They also serve who only stand and wait.' [BC]

Beverly Gray has written a six-book series, *Black Knights of the Hudson*, about the West Point journey of the MacKendrick family from the Civil War to World War I. See the "West Point Legacies" chapter for more on the series. [EB]

The West Point Boys or *Learning to Be a Soldier*

Cadet

Col. J. Thomas Weldon   Street & Smith (1910)

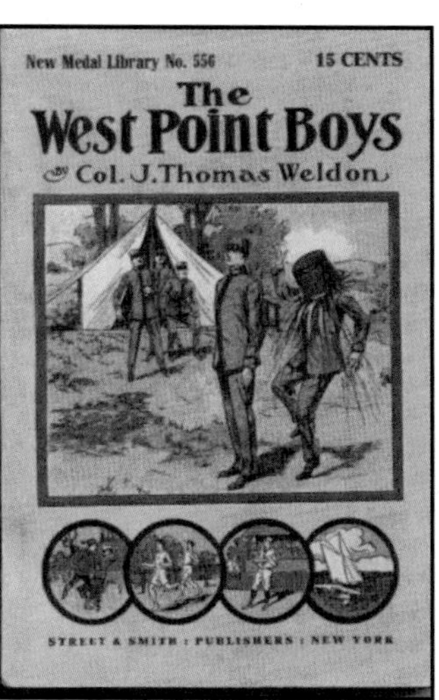

From the chapter "Hank Harrington's Triumph"

"It was a terrible situation the four plebes found themselves in. They were on a narrow ledge of rock with a precipice below them, and no method of reaching the top. Above them were their deadliest enemies, for once completely triumphant.

The yearlings might try any method of torture they chose; they might drop stones upon their victims' heads. They might leave them there all night; or they might pass them a rope to climb up by and take them prisoners, one by one as they came. After that the victims could be pummeled at the captors' leisure.

Altogether, therefore, it was a most unpleasant state of affairs. The only possible hope lay in the chance that the gallant Oracle, with the aid of his timid comrade, might succeed in driving off those four powerful yearlings.   It was a very slim chance, however..." [EB]

No biographical information about this writer could be found.

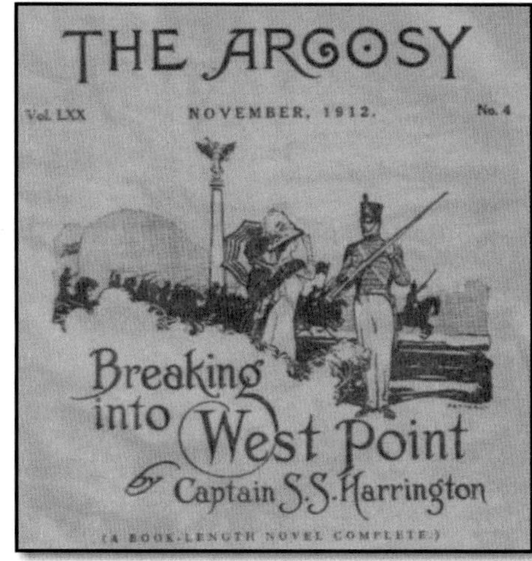

"Breaking into West Point: A Romance of the Military Academy"

Cadet, Pulp Fiction

Capt. S. S. Harrington   Argosy Magazine (Nov. 1912)

"The Congressman's Callers"

Of the ten or twelve million young men in the United States, probably one-third of them are annually seized with an ambition to go to West Point and become defenders of the nation.

Since, however, the average size of the entering class at the United States Military Academy is limited to about 125, there are bound to be disappointments. In short, the chances of any aspirant, barring the accident of the political pull of a famous general for a grandfather or Presidential favor, have been computed as about fifty thousand to one.

A long shot of the long shots was Russel Bartlett. He was just one of the "plain people" -- a stalwart, broad-shouldered chap with a mop of reddish, brown hair, a pair of keen blue eyes . . .

His "previous condition of servitude," as they say at West Point had been that of a teamster in a brickyard, though he was high school educated.

With the unexpected bankruptcy of the brickyard and loss of that job, Russel found himself called upon to seek some new occupation; and it was at this juncture that the idea of donning the cadet gray suggested itself to him…

His sole cash asset was twenty dollars savings since the plant had been in arrears in its payroll, but he had a tremendous store of self-confidence; his was the obstinate Missouri temperament which demands to be shown.

Since the appointment he coveted lay in the hands of Congressman Jones, his only course, as he saw it, was to go directly to Jones and make known his desire...but Jones was in Washington and would not return to his district for weeks.

Russel Bartlett did what needed to be done. He boarded the train that night for Washington, D.C. [EB]

Captain S. S. Harrington is almost certainly a pseudo name. No biographical information could be found, though his stories appeared in several issues of Argosy from 1912 to 1925.

"Hazzard of West Point: Part 2 of 3"

Cadet, Crime, Pulp Fiction, WP Ex, Panama

Edmond Lawrence Top Notch Magazine (November 1912)

The story is serialized in several issues of Top-Notch Magazine. This is a summary of the first installment:

Roderick Hazzard, a cadet captain at West Point, while acting as officer of the day, interferes when a masked cadet tries to run the guard by intimidating a "plebe" sentinel. The masked man knocks Hazzard down and escapes, vowing to get even with him for interfering. Hazzard is lured outside the lines at night by a ruse, and before he can get back to quarters the reveille gun is fired—a favorite trick of mischief-makers. He is captured and accused of firing the gun, and reduced to the ranks, Cadet Buell Guernsey Bucknell being appointed captain in his place. He is ordered to appear before a court-martial, and when he prepares to report to the court, his side arms are stolen from his tent, and he appears before the officers without his sword—a matter of affront to his superiors.

Hazzard's chum, Dion O'Hara suspects Bucknell of causing the trouble, and fights him, but is whipped. Later, Hazzard catches Bucknell hazing the plebe, Robin Blair, and challenges him to a fight. He thrashes Bucknell, but later he is summoned to the cadet court of honor; his coat has been picked up near the scene of the fight, and some articles of jewelry found in it which had been stolen from cadets. He refuses to answer to the disgraceful charge, and the cadets sentence him to "Coventry"—no cadet may associate with him or speak to him, except in the discharge of duty. Hazzard is crushed by the humiliation, but he resolves to bide his time and try to forget his woe in strenuous football training. . .It doesn't work out that way, though." [EB]

Edmond Lawrence was a pen name used by **Lemuel Lawrence De Bra** (1884–1954) in his early writings. The "Hazzard" series ran through six novels. [1-05]

Tom Taylor at West Point

Cadet, WP Candidate

Frank V Webster Cupples & Leon (1915)

As a West Point aspirant:

"So am I, Mother, particularly as we need the money. But I think I can find something else to do. Business is picking up a little. I'm going to be on the lookout. Something is sure to turn up. And I do hope it will be something worthwhile, so I can, by some means or other, get enough ahead to go to West Point."

"You haven't forgotten your ambition I see, Tom," said his mother, as she vigorously plied her needle, taking advantage of the last hours of daylight.

"Forgotten it, Mother? Indeed, I haven't, I never shall. I intend to go to West Point and become an army officer." Tom straightened himself up as he said this, as though he had heard the command: "Attention!"

But the only sound that came to the ears of his mother and himself was the distant hum and roar of the little city, on the outskirts of which they lived.

Mrs. Taylor sighed. Tom was folding the bills into a neat little package, enclosing within the silver coins. It was a small sum, but it represented much to him and his widowed mother. "I don't like to think of you being a soldier, Tom," said Mrs. Taylor, as she stopped to thread a needle.

"Well, I guess there isn't very much danger," Tom laughed. "There aren't any vacancies from this congressional district. So, I understand, and the appointments have all been filled. And even if there was a chance for me to get in, I couldn't do it, I guess. It takes about a hundred dollars to start with, but of course after that Uncle Sam looks out for you. But I sure would like to go!"

His mother said softly: "I can't bear to think of the war. It is so cruel!"

"Oh, just because I want to go to West Point and become an army officer, doesn't mean there will be a war, Mother. . . . But the best way not to have a war, is to be in the finest possible shape to meet it if it does come...the United States Army does a lot of things besides shooting and killing," Tom said. Look at the officers and men -- see what they have done in the Panama Canal zone...in spite of the fact that they are trained in the arts of War. [EB]

Frank V. Webster was a Stratemeyer Syndicate pseudonym used for the **Webster** series of stories that resemble the writings of Horatio Alger, Jr. Unlike many pen names, a conscious effort was made to present "Frank V. Webster" as a real person. A 1911 Cupples & Leon ad to the book trade, likely written by Edward Stratemeyer, made the Alger connection. [1-06]

"Fred Fearnot at West Point" or "Having Fun with the Hazers"

Cadet, Pulp Fiction

Hal Standish   Work and Win Magazine (April 23, 1915)

Fred "Fearnot" Durham is an adventurous young man who can clearly fend for himself in difficult situations. His brother Phil, an identical twin is a plebe at West Point and badly set upon by upperclassmen. Fred and Phil arrange an exchange of places to give Phil a break and Fred an opportunity to build respect for his twin. . . .

On Wednesday, when Phil Durham returned to West Point, he found Fred in full uniform down at the station waiting for him. There were other cadets there who were looking for friends. As he stepped off the car Fred rushed at him and the two shook hands like old friends who had been separated a long time. The cadets looked at them and noticed the very marked resemblance to each other. . . .

They went up to the hotel where Phil registered under the name of Frederick Durham.

Up in the room, they quickly exchanged suits. and Phil was once more in his uniform. "What kind of a time have you had, Fred?" Phil asked him.

"I've had a grand time old man. But it is too long a story for me to tell you now. There have been more than a score of attempts made to haze me."

"Great Scott! I was afraid of that, Fred. But how did you come out?"

"Beat them every time, and I'm blessed if I believe any of them could be hired to try it again. I've written the whole thing out for your guidance, to save you from being caught in a trap. You are good at boxing yourself; understand fencing, and all about the ammonia guns, and the little rubber stench."

"Great Scott! Do you mean to say you used those things?"

"Yes. And I had the fun of knocking out fifteen of them at one time, and I tell you, the skunk created a sensation. They were the sickest crowd you ever saw. You'll find the whole story in manuscript in the inner pocket of your coat; so, if you get caught it will be your own fault." [EB]

Harvey King Shackleford (1840–1906) wrote over 300 dime novels between 1869 and his death in 1906. About sixty of his novels appeared in the "Fred Fearnot" series, stories which revolved about the adventures of a young man of that name. These were signed "Hal Standish." After his death, the series continued under the authorship of several others, although they still used the "Hal Standish" name. [1-07]

Classmates

Cadet

Walter F. Eberhardt Grosset & Dunlap (1924)

"If every inspiring thought of Americanism were to be contained in one story, that story would be that of West Point."

This was the declaration of a man who was one of the greatest statesmen of his time: but, until now that story has never been written. In fact, West Point has been singularly neglected by novelists and fiction writers, a deficiency that is all the more deplorable because of the wealth of adventure, romance, and drama enacted in the daily lives of the cadets, officers and graduates of the Academy.

Classmates is a story that centers around West Point. It gives an intimate, always interesting and strongly dramatic pen picture of the life of Uncle Sam's future army officers during their training course. It brings out for the first time in book form, the rigid system of discipline to which a candidate for an officer's commission in the US Army voluntarily submits themselves. It accentuates the inspiring inviolability of the Honor Code as practiced and enforced by the cadets themselves. The story carries beyond the four-year course and shows how the strong bonds of friendship, bred at the Academy, are perpetuated afterwards.

Classmates was presented as a play by William de Mille on the New York stage in 1904, and a movie in 1924. [DJ]

Walter F. Eberhardt (1891–1935) was a publicist who worked for a number of film studios and later as the director of publicity for Electrical Research Products, Inc. (part of Western Electric). In 1932 he turned his hand to mystery writing, producing the novels *Dagger in the Dark* and *The Jig-Saw Puzzle Murder*, in addition to two earlier film novelizations. [1-08]

"Recognition"

Cadet, Pulp Fiction, WP Author

Lt. John T. Hopper Argosy Magazine (June 4, 1927)

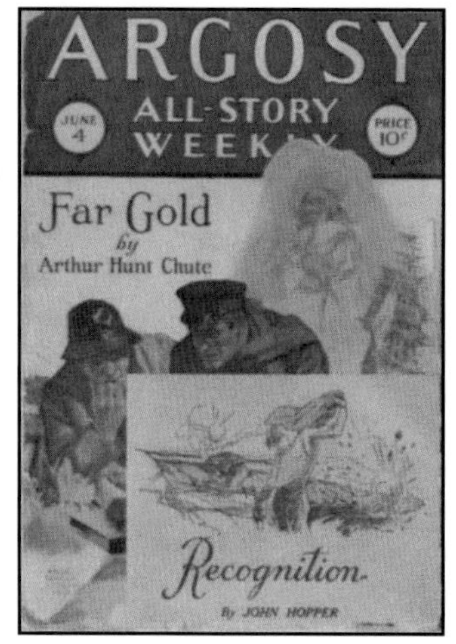

"You'd better snap to, Mr. Randall. This is June Week, you know. Now beat it."

Glad to be released, Dave Randall ran down the hall of the fourth floor to his room. As he slammed the door behind him, he flung his cap upon his green-topped, steel table.

"What's the matter, Dave?" drawled George Horton in his lazy, Tennessee voice. "Jimmy Brice been getting on you again?"

"Yes -- damn him!" quivered Dave, his face distorted with anger.

"Guess I'd feel that Way about it, too," contributed Jack Longan, the sentimental roommate from California. "If a man stole my girl as plain-as Brice stole yours, I'd be hankering to punch his face in."

"Oh, come off of it, you two!" cried Dave. "It's not Jimmy Brice, nor his stealing my girl, as you call it, that has anything to do with it. I'm just sick of this place, that's all. Just sick of saying 'Yes, sir' and 'No, sir,' and jumping here and running there for everybody who says so, just because he happens to be an upper classman."

But deep in his heart, Dave knew that the place was all right. It was just that bitterness had been eating into his soul for the last couple of months. Bitterness because Jimmy Brice was gaining favor in the eyes of the girl whom Dave Randall had worshiped since way back in their high school days.

What made it doubly hard was the fact that Dave himself had paved the way, provided an introduction to Miss Peg Burton, for Brice. Plebes were not allowed to attend hops and, when Peg came down to visit Dave, he had arranged that Jimmy Brice take her to a hop, never thinking that it would be natural for the girl, to be attracted to the care-free, experienced, upper classman, and that he, in return, should go on further than it was intended for him to go, and fall in love with the girl.

Since that time Dave had been growing more and more bitter, taciturn, and rebellious. He was rapidly losing his reputation of being the "best plebe" in the company. George Horton drawled again: "Dave, you make me tired - going around here with a face like a sour lemon. Forget all this nonsense. Why, June Week is almost over! To-morrow night comes Graduation Parade and Recognition. Stick it out with good grace until then, my boy. After Recognition you will be an upper classman yourself." [EB]

"Texas Comes to West Point"

Cadet, Pulp Fiction, WP Author

Lt. John T. Hopper Argosy Magazine (August 4, 1928)

"Ride'im, cowboy; ride'im!" The familiar cow-puncher cry had just been shrilled by one of a half dozen cowboys who leaned against the iron bars enclosing the big corral of Griffin's ranch, watching a horse and its rider raising the dust inside.

"Whoop-ee," cried a second cowboy.

It was a sight worth watching, worth the yells of the beholders. The horse was of the variety known as "buckin' broncho." The rider was a calm, masterful youth of about twenty years. The dust of the battle royal shaded the horse and rider. It was evident that something was due to be broken in the outcome of the battle, either the horse—or the rider's neck.

"Danged if I don't think the Kid'll do it" said one as he wiped the sweat from the band of his sombrero with a red bandana. The Texas sun was very hot. "He said he'd bust thet danged hoss a'fore he went to West Point, or the danged hoss would bust him, sure' nuff."

"Thet's jus' like 'im" said another. "He's jus' like his ol' man. The Kid has tried t' bust that devil hoss 'fore now. Las' time, 'member, he got a busted arm outen it?"

. . .

And yet, Old Jack hesitated about sending his son off to an "Easterner" college. He had heard and read (too much about them). He thought, with fear in his heart, of his son returning to him thin-chested, pulling at a long cigarette holder, and receiving lavender-scented notes from girls—flappers—left behind him in the East.

One day the senior Griffin had returned home from a cattlemen's meeting at the county seat. His face was aglow. His Congressman had told him of a wonderful college in the East - a man's college. There the Kid would imbibe the blessings of a college education, and yet be subject to none of the dangers. It was a hard school, where life was more difficult than a cowboy's life. None of its students had time for "lounge lizardry" or flappers. They must exercise their bodies in becoming proficient in the arts of manhood: becoming expert in the use of rifle, pistol, saber, boxing, command of men, and -- riding.

That last item had sold Old Jack. Any school which made its pupils ride must be all right. And so, the Kid was duly appointed to West Point. Now, the time was at hand when he was to make the long journey northeast to the United States Military Academy at West Point, NY. [EB]

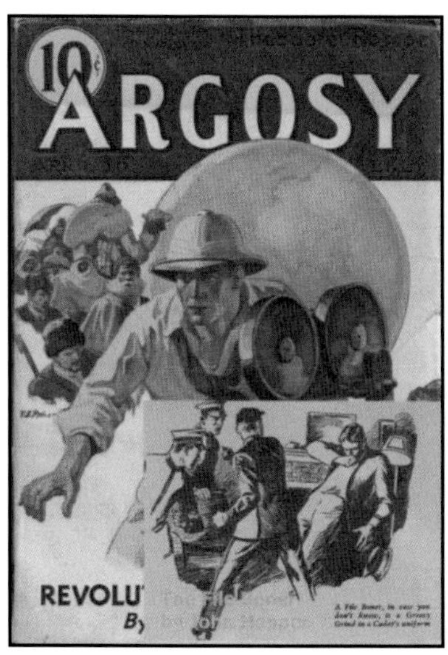

"The File Boner"

Cadet, Pulp Fiction, WP Author

Lt. John T. Hopper Argosy Magazine (April 10, 1937)

A File Boner, in case you didn't know, is a greasy grind in a cadet's uniform. Binker was awakened by sounds of movement in the next alcove. He raised himself on one elbow in his upper bunk and listened, trying to determine what was going on. He decided finally that it must be John Davis. Binker looked at the windows. Outside it was still completely dark. Blinker's ire rose. What in the dickens was Davis doing, moving around, waking people up before reveille?

"Hey, Davis!" he called in a low voice, in order not to wake Bill Treadway, who was still asleep in the bunk directly beneath Binker's. "What're you doing? What time is it?"

"It's pretty near time for reveille," came a low answer from beyond the partition between the two alcoves. "I'm making up my bed."

"Say!" broke in Bill Treadway sleepily. "Why don't you guys go and debate someplace else?"

"The file boner," said Binker bitterly, "is at it again. He's making his bed before reveille."

"Well, I won't have time to make it after reveille," John Davis snapped back.

Just as Davis finished speaking, enthusiastic bursts of noise were un- leashed upon the United States Corps of Cadets in their beds. Bells clamored in every hall of barracks. Drums beat and bugles blared. First call for reveille. The day had officially begun at the United States Military Academy at West Point." [EB]

John Hopper (1903–1970) graduated from West Point in 1927, then resigned his commission in 1930 and took up writing for pulp fiction magazines. There are eighteen of Hopper's stories in this collection distributed through several chapters. See the "Army Sports" chapter for more by Hopper. [1-09]

A West Pointer's Honor

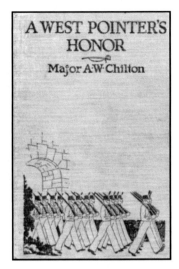

Cadet, Cuba, Mystery, WP Author

Maj. Alexander W. Chilton Harper & Bros (1928)

Three cadet roommates are looking forward to a ten-week furlough before beginning their 2nd Class year. Two of them travel to Cuba to meet a family acquaintance and enjoy some beach and fishing. Their elderly host entrusts them (one is an electrical engineer) with his design for a secret weapon, but they are bedeviled by foreign agents eager to obtain the design.

Back at West Point, the cadets arrange to continue development in the lab with the blessing of an officer in the War Department with whom they have shared the secret. The foreign agents are bold and pursue them even into West Point. In trying to secure the design, one cadet must go AWOL to deliver it to safety. The issue of honor arises because he has sworn not to reveal the nature of the design except to their contact in the War Department. He cannot reveal the justification for leaving the post. [EB]

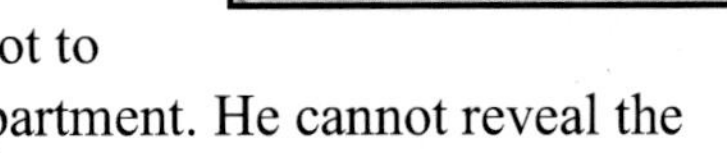

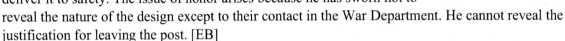

Alexander W. Chilton (1884–1985) was then the oldest living graduate of the United States Military Academy when he passed away on September 17, 1985. He spent much of his career as an educator. Chilton penned his own lengthy, but modest, obituary for the Association of Graduates Memorial page. It concludes:

"… Like every man who writes a book, I have acknowledgments to make. I am grateful for sensible parents, who in my boyhood, made for me a life of disciplined freedom within a large family. To West Point, I owe my thanks for a training of the body, of the intellect, and of the will, which training, though it has not placed me among the Academy's great, has at least ranked me among her useful…." [1-10]

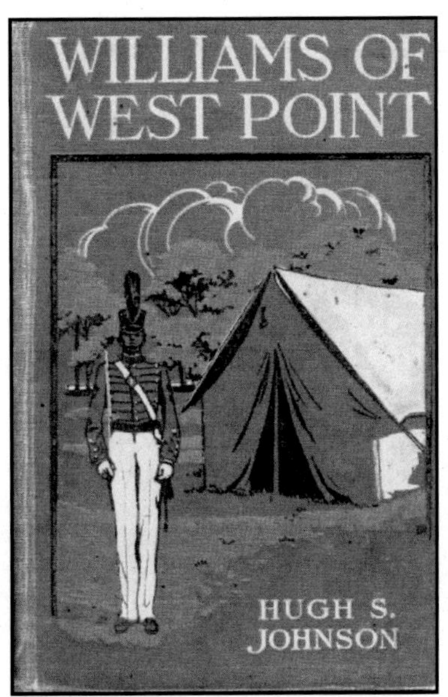

Williams of West Point

Cadet, WP Author

Hugh S. Johnson Hearn Dept Stores (1934)

This is the story of West Point, just as "Tom Brown" is the story of Rugby and Oxford. It tells of Bob Williams, who comes to West Point and by sheer force of hard work and manliness gains a position of leadership in his class. He has a rival in Brinsley Bartlett, a brilliant young fellow whose head has been turned by popularity. Bartlett succeeds in involving Williams in a quarrel from which, according to the West Point code, he cannot honorably withdraw without fighting. For reasons which the cadets do not know, Williams has to follow something higher than West Point code; in his particular ease he does not dare to permit himself to fight.

This brands him as a coward in the eyes of the cadets, who refuse to listen to his reasons at first, and later Williams is too proud to explain. He is "sent to Coventry" and enters upon a life whose peculiar hardships would not be sanctioned except in a place where a man charged with cowardice is as utterly and universally despised as he is at West Point. Williams is a thorough man, however, and he wins out, in a series of most interesting incidents. At the end a stirring football game is played between the Army and Navy in which Williams removes the last trace of the blot that has rested upon his reputation. [FP]

Hugh Samuel Johnson (1882–1942) was a U.S. Army officer (West Point '03), businessman, speech writer, government official and newspaper columnist. He is best remembered as a member of the Brain Trust of Franklin D. Roosevelt from 1932–1934. His other book, *Williams on Service*, is included in the "Far East" chapter. [1-11]

Three Plebes at West Point

Cadet, WP Author

Paschal N. Strong Little, Brown (1935)

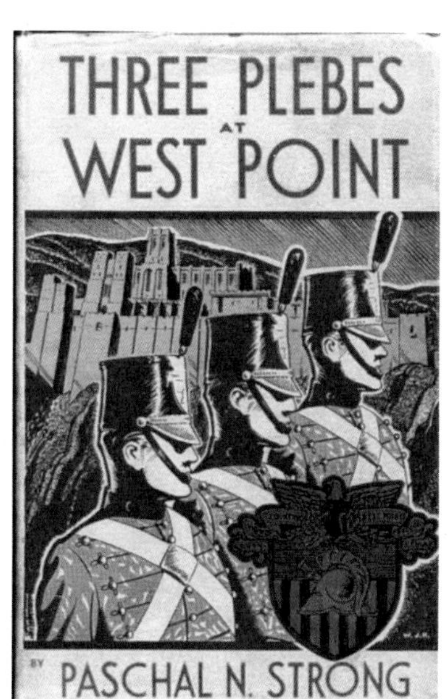

This is the story of three typical West Pointers in the making. Walter Layman, a poor Southern lad, Hale Baxter, from a Colorado ranch, and Cortlandt Vandeberg, of the rich Albany Vandebergs, are roommates during their first year at the United States Military Academy. Van's arrogance and certainty of his social superiority get a quick jolt when he finds they count for less than nothing at West Point; Hale's pride resents the hazing which is imposed on plebes by the upper classmen; Walt's fear of a horse wins for him the unwarranted stigma of "yellow."

There is fine officer material in these three boys and plenty of excitement in the story of their development as Walt overcomes for all time his fear of horses, as Hale defeats the upper-class champion, and Van conquers his overbearing manner.[DJ]

Lieutenant Strong knows his West Point and all its traditions. *Three Plebes at West Point* is in every way the equal of his previous book, *West Point Wins*.

Paschal N. Strong (1901–1988) graduated from West Point in 1922 and served until 1954 when he retired as a Brigadier General. During these years, Strong was a prolific author. Five of his books are in this collection. See the chapter on Army Sports. [1-12]

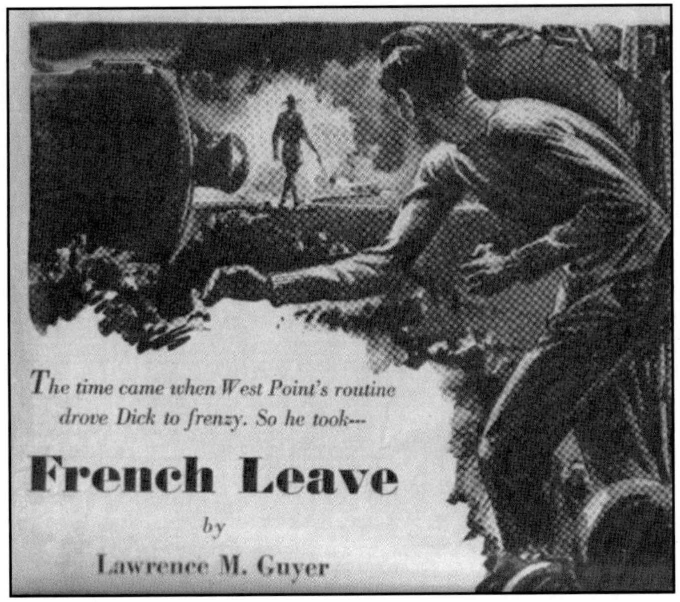

The time came when West Point's routine drove Dick to frenzy. So he took—
French Leave
by
Lawrence M. Guyer

"French Leave"

Cadet, Pulp Fiction, WP Author

Lawrence M. Guyer
American Boy Magazine (April 1936)

"THAT'S funny," whispered Thurston Stone, as he stood on the only chair in a tent at the West Point summer camp and hesitated in the act of drawing on his stiff, white-starched, cadet trousers.

"What's funny?" asked Bill Holliday with an irritated sigh. "Listen, Pebble Stone, if you don't get off that chair pretty soon, there's going to be some—thing a lot funnier around here. Maybe somebody else wants to put on his pants.

"Me, for instance," chimed in Peter Wentworth.

"Have a heart, Pebble."

For answer, Pebble Stone withdrew the one leg he had already thrust into his pants and flashed his two tent mates a severe glance. "Big things are happening in this tent, and you two don't even see it."

"See what?" Wentworth asked. "Anything to get you off that chair". Pebble nodded his head toward the opposite side of the tent where sat "Colonel" Dick Calhoun.

Wentworth and Holliday nodded soberly. They knew as well as Stone that Dick Calhoun was the model of all West Point cadets. Number Three in his class in academics, Eastern Intercollegiate gym champion, and number one in his class in discipline! You could have hidden all of Calhoun's demerits beneath a small dress-coat button. He was always and forever shining up his equipment. The perfect soldier. And now, to see Calhoun surrounded by his shining materials, yet not shining! Wentworth blinked, incredulously. Holliday stared, entranced, as Pebble Stone jumped down from the chair and bounded over the floor to Calhoun's side.

"What are you doing?" he demanded, abruptly.

Calhoun looked up and chuckled. "Nothing," he said, "just drawing."

Dick Calhoun was certainly out of sorts and had been ever since a fall from a high trapeze had left him with broken ribs and a month in the post infirmary. There was a hop tonight in Cullum Hall which most cadets were eager to attend, but not Dick. He was intent on taking "French Leave" making an unauthorized exit from the encampment for a cooling swim in Delafield Pond. When his three tent mates left for the hop, Dick stealthily sneaked past the sentries and ascended past officer homes to Delafield Pond. He removed his shoes....and then something totally unexpected occurred..." [EB]

Lawrence McIlroy Guyer (1907–1982). The son of an Army officer, he was raised in the service and spent his boyhood at many Army camps and stations, mostly in the old west and in Alaska. He graduated from West Point in 1929, 61st in a class of 301. During the first 14 years of his service, General Guyer was an artillery officer in the Coast Artillery Corps. In 1943 he shifted to the Army Air Corp, retiring in 1959 from the Air Force as a Brigadier General. In 1942 as an artillery officer, General Guyer put on a diving helmet and went down into the sunken USS Arizona, in Pearl Harbor, to ascertain if, from an artillery viewpoint, the two aft 14-inch gun turrets could be removed from the battleship and installed on land. The conclusion was affirmative, and the job was later done. [1-13]

Cadet Derry, West Pointer

Cadet, WP Author

John Berchram Stanley Dodd, Mead & Co. (1950)

Against his will, though there is Army blood in his veins, Steve Derry enters the United States Military Academy at West Point and is embarked upon a career in the Army or Air Forces.

Mindful of his family's deep interest in his success at the Academy, Steve tries hard to suppress his resentment toward both the Army and West Point. Helping him along his way are a roommate, a friendly upperclassman, and Coach Frank Hall. But Steve does not get along with his other roommate, although football makes the first year bearable.

In the three years that follow Steve reaches stardom in football at the same time that he is learning much about the Academy and its mission of training young men for service as officers in the Armed Forces. An involvement with the famed honor system of the Academy, a gambler who takes advantage of Steve to alter odds on a football game, and an airplane crash serve to change Cadet Derry's outlook toward the Academy; but the final decision as to whether or not he should accept a commission in the Army is hard to come by.

In the end Steve finds his doubts resolved and proudly joins the ranks of men who have helped make great the Armed Forces of the United States: the graduates of West Point. [DJ]

After West Point, **John B. Stanley** (1910–1999) served in the infantry at various posts around the country and Central America. With the outbreak of World War II, Colonel Stanley was assigned to the War Department in Washington until early 1945, when he was sent to the European Theatre of Operations. He has written other books that are included in this catalog and had his stories published in *Boys' Life* and anthologies. [1-14]

As mentioned at the beginning of this chapter, two books by West Point graduates altered the tone of literature on the cadet experience. The novels became more character-evolving rather than just dramatizing the typical event sequences of cadet life. Here is the first of the two books. For exposing the darker side of cadet life, *Tin Soldiers* was not well-received by the "Old Corps." It may have undergone efforts to suppress its circulation, since it is a hard-to-find book.

Tin Soldiers

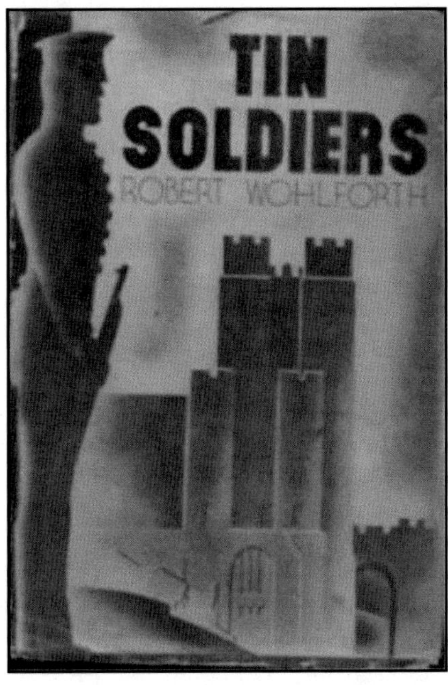

Cadet, WP Author

Robert Wohlforth Alfred King (1934)

This novel of sensational disclosures about the cradle of the army is the first realistic portrayal of what life at West Point does to a cross section of young Americans...The author is himself a graduate of the academy. Here, amid the cruel torment of four years of intensive, monk-like training, two boys, who have fallen in love with one girl, learn to become generals as they forget to be men... It is a novel of great sacrifices, betrayals, romance, comedy, failures, and the making of future generals. [DJ]

A review from NY Times June 17, 1934:

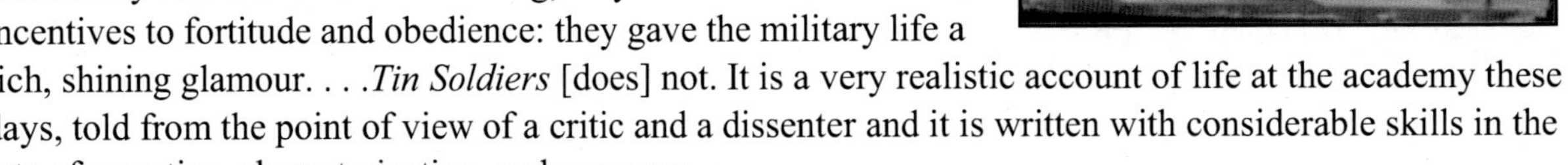

...boy's books about life at West Point used to be pretty heady stuff. They told tall tales about hazing, they contained sound incentives to fortitude and obedience: they gave the military life a rich, shining glamour. . . .*Tin Soldiers* [does] not. It is a very realistic account of life at the academy these days, told from the point of view of a critic and a dissenter and it is written with considerable skills in the arts of narrative, characterization, and exposure. . . .

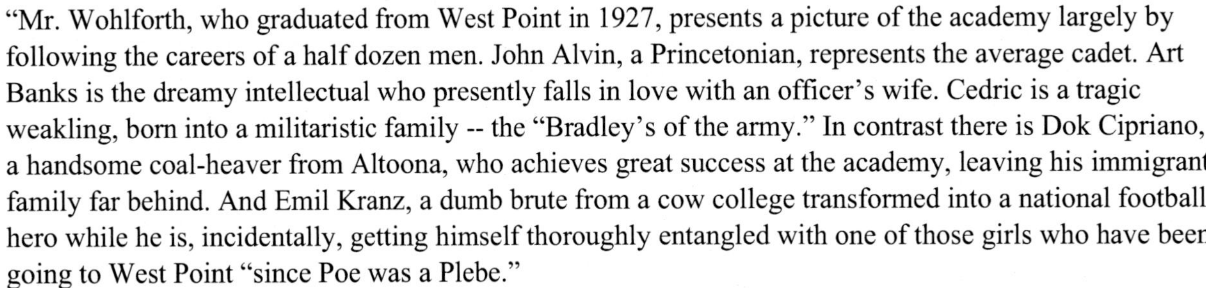

"Mr. Wohlforth, who graduated from West Point in 1927, presents a picture of the academy largely by following the careers of a half dozen men. John Alvin, a Princetonian, represents the average cadet. Art Banks is the dreamy intellectual who presently falls in love with an officer's wife. Cedric is a tragic weakling, born into a militaristic family -- the "Bradley's of the army." In contrast there is Dok Cipriano, a handsome coal-heaver from Altoona, who achieves great success at the academy, leaving his immigrant family far behind. And Emil Kranz, a dumb brute from a cow college transformed into a national football hero while he is, incidentally, getting himself thoroughly entangled with one of those girls who have been going to West Point "since Poe was a Plebe."

The best single portrait in the book is LePere, the Chicago Negro who is inexorably forced out of West Point by the system: not by what people say to him but by their never saying anything to him at all; by a slow torturing ostracism that even those who would like to be friendly are following. Paul Copley, a football player who never gets into a game, a would-be aviator who gets deathly sick the first time he goes up, who sacrifices his own interests so that Emil Kranz may shine, is made to carry too heavy a load of contrived irony to be a real character.

There can't be many "angles"... that Mr. Wohlforth fails to illuminate. The harsh hazing of the "Beasts" when they first arrive, the weary monotonous round or duty, the hops and the rare leaves, the troubled questioning of the philosophy that makes them warriors, the swarming crowds of sightseers who feel, as taxpayers, that they own the place, the special care that athletes get, the camps and drills and the ceremonies are all here.

Robert Wohlforth (1902–1997) enrolled at Princeton but left in 1923 to enter West Point. He graduated with the Class of 1926. In the late 1930s, Bob became a newspaper reporter and writer, which led to work with congressional committees. In 1939 he was appointed to the antitrust division of the Department of Justice. During WWII, he headed an investigation of economic connections of the Nazis. In 1952 he became associated with a new publishing group that became Farrar, Straus and Giroux. Bob married Mildred E. Gilman in 1930. Mildred was a well-known novelist. [1-15]

The second of two ground-breaking books that shifted the reading public's understanding of cadet life and their development was *Dress Gray* by Lucian K. Truscott, IV. Published in 1978, it is a shocking tale of a murder at the Academy and includes graphical sex scenes. While hardly unusual in literature of the 1960s and 1970s, it was a first for West Point and not well received by the Academy and the "Old Corps." Because the novel focuses on a crime and its resolution, it is included in the chapter "Mystery, Crime, and Intrigue."

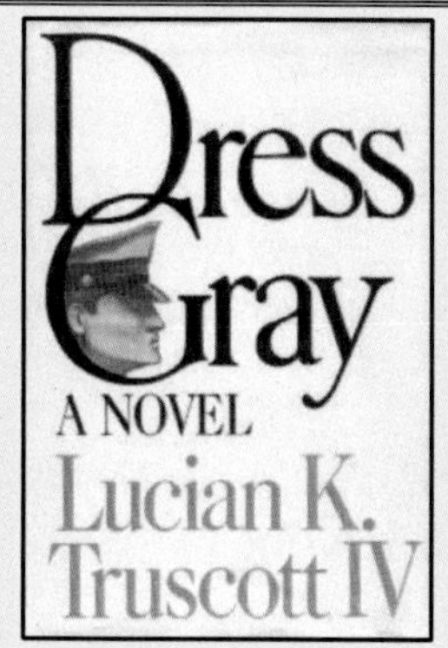

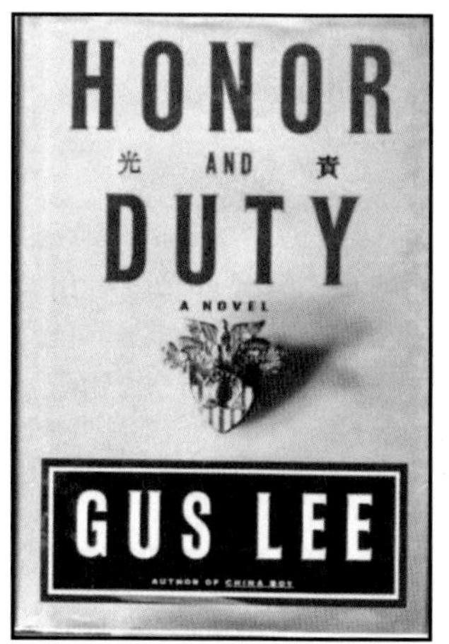

Honor and Duty

Cadet, WP Author

Gus Lee Knopf (1994)

In a stunning new novel by the author of the widely acclaimed China Boy, provocative issues, from the American military to racial stereotypes to identity—both national and cultural—come together to create a literary tour de force about the Chinese-American experience.

Kai Ting is a cadet at West Point in the 1960s. He comes to the military academy from his turbulent San Francisco boyhood with the hope of honoring his father, a former officer in Chiang Kai-shek's army who never came to terms with his new life in America, where he was stripped of his native culture; of escaping his stepmother, a stern, uncaring American woman; and above all, of becoming firmly and undeniably American. And he leaves behind Uncle Shim, his confidant and friend, the person who had served as a Chinese conscience throughout Kai's youth.

But as one of the very few Asians at the Point and with the shadow of Vietnam hanging over the cadet corps, Kai, enroute from plebe to upperclassman, must walk a precarious tightrope over a lava pit of prejudice and preconceptions. Kai is intelligent and eager—but he is not surefooted. And when he plummets into the heart of a cheating scandal, his very survival depends on his ability to learn -- and learn fast -- a new code of behavior, a new tribal etiquette.

Gus Lee has written a powerful novel about the force of tradition—about a young man's struggle to bring together his double heritage and to find his way between two often contradictory concepts of honor and duty. [DJ]

Augustus Samuel Mein-Sun "Gus" Lee (1946–) entered West Point with the Class of 1968 but before graduating, he served as a non-commissioned officer, later completing his undergraduate and law degree at the University of California. He returned to Army service from 1974 to 1977 as a Command Judge Advocate. Subsequently, he has held many legal, educational, and business positions focusing on the promotion of ethical thinking and behavior. His first book, *China Boy* (1991), and his third book, *Tiger's Tail* (1996) are included in this collection. [1-16]

Of Honor and Dishonor

Cadet, Viet Nam, WP Author

David Crocco PublishAmerica (2002)

West Point's true character was revealed in winter when, alone with itself, it became a monastery for men of action who were too energetic for the contemplative life and too passionate to live carelessly among the hawkers and workers of the everyday world. They created their own world, with its own language and rituals, its own trials of the flesh, its own shibboleths, its private standards of honor and dishonor.

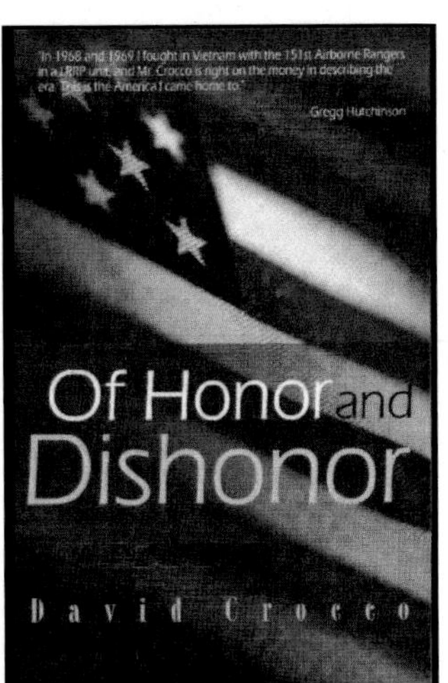

In July of 1969, fourteen hundred men entered the United States Military Academy at West Point. Against a backdrop of the Vietnam War, the Peace Movement, and anti-war protests that tore families apart, they learned the meaning of duty, honor, and country. This is the riveting story of that tumultuous year as seen through the eyes of Phil DeAngelo, a naive mid-western youth who has wanted to go to West Point since he was nine years old. The crucible of the Plebe year forces him to come to grips with a wider world where good and evil often co-exist, and where each man must find his own, often lonely, way. [BC]

Like many boys in the fifties, **David Crocco** spent much of his Western Pennsylvania childhood playing army. He attended West Point in the late 1960s, was honorably discharged and later graduated from the University of Pittsburgh. [BC]

The Days: A Novel

Cadet, WP Author

Kevin R. Manos Infinity Publishing (2003)

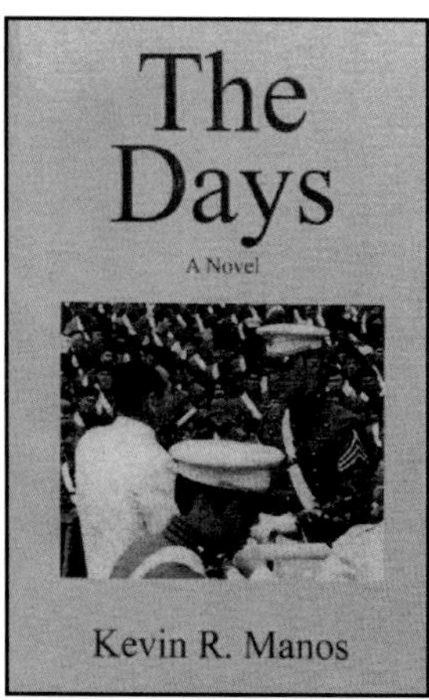

Robert "Sonny" Stuart reported to West Point in the summer of 1977. After the rigorous basic training known as "Beast Barracks," he landed in a West Point company known as "The E-2 Dogs." Now, entering his last year at West Point, Sonny is facing graduation, his own coming of age, and the moral dilemmas that his choices have left him with. If he is to survive and graduate from West Point, he will need the help and support of his fellow E-2 Dogs, his new fiancée, his family, and the other people who have helped shape his experience. [BC]

Kevin R. Manos is a Class of 1981 West Point graduate and an E-2 Dog from Atlanta, Georgia. [BC]

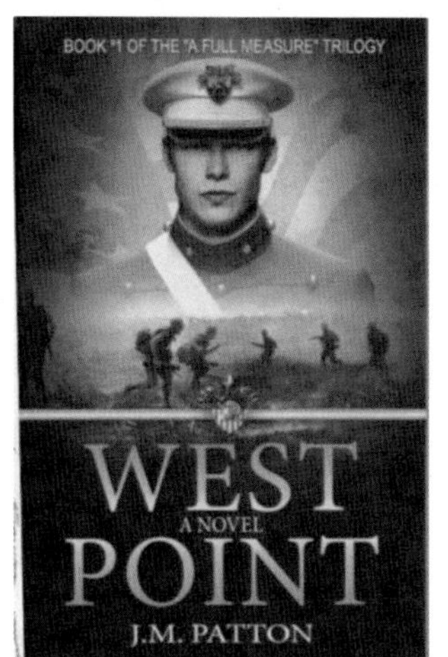

West Point: A Novel

Cadet, Vietnam, WP Author

J. M. Patton PublishAuthority (2020)

The trilogy, *A Full Measure*, is a tale of love, and conflict for those reconstructing the U.S., of the Vietnam War era, and the decades following as terrorism emerges in enemies foreign and domestic. The setting brings to life the turmoil faced by his civilian peers in a hostile antiwar environment, and the evolution of a current-day mission.

West Point takes the reader to the United States Military Academy (USMA) to step into the humor and heartbreak of the daily life that slowly develops the panache of a West Point leader of the Vietnam era. Of the same development came the likes of Lee, Jackson, Grant, Bradley, Eisenhower, MacArthur, Patton, Schwarzkopf, and many more from the ranks of the Long Gray Line. Graduates receive their degree, but unlike a college, there is but one mission, and that mission is to produce outstanding officers in the combat arms.

John Paul "Jake" Jacobs and Patrick McSwain build an unbreakable bond as they overcome the challenges of West Point. Anyone even remotely interested in military fiction will enjoy this captivating read. The reader is likely to laugh, be exhilarated by the tale, and maybe shed a tear or two. [BC]

Mike Patton (1951–) after two years at New Mexico Military Academy entered West Point with the Class of 1973. He was given a medical discharge after his yearling year. He continued his education and earned a degree in mathematics at Baylor University. After successful years with a large U.S. computer company, his career evolved to various management positions in finance, banking, and securities. [BC] His other two books in the "Full Measure" trilogy are included in this collection.

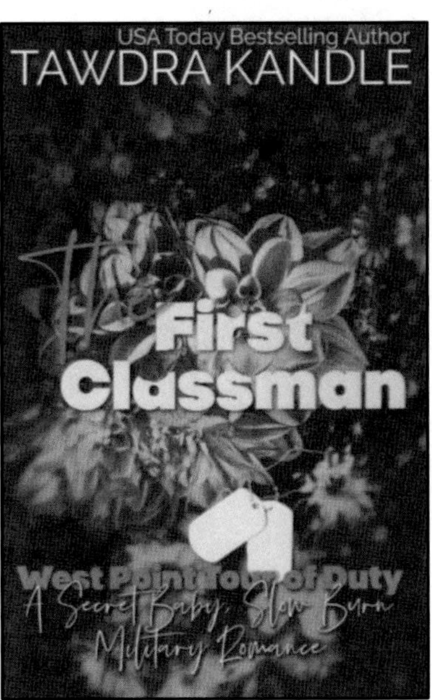

The First Classman: West Point Tour of Duty

Cadet, Romance

Tawdra Kandle Self-Published (2023)

Willow: I only knew his first name. The night we met we were only having fun. It wasn't serious. It was one last fling before real life took over. I knew I wasn't ever going to see him again.

But I was wrong.

Dean: I didn't ask for her last name. She was a spontaneous night of fun right before I went back to West Point and football. We were only together for a good time. I knew we couldn't have anything real beyond that one night.

But I was wrong.

And when we meet again in the most unexpected way, I find out that one night of fun could cost me my career and all of my goals. It could mean the end of her dreams, too. [BC]

Tawdra Kandle is the daughter of a West Pointer (Class of 1965) and married a West Pointer (Class of 1987). Also writing as Tamara Kendall, she has penned over 100 romance novels starting with her first full-length novel in 2008. Except for this novel her series "West Point Tour of Duty" is in eBook format. [1-17]

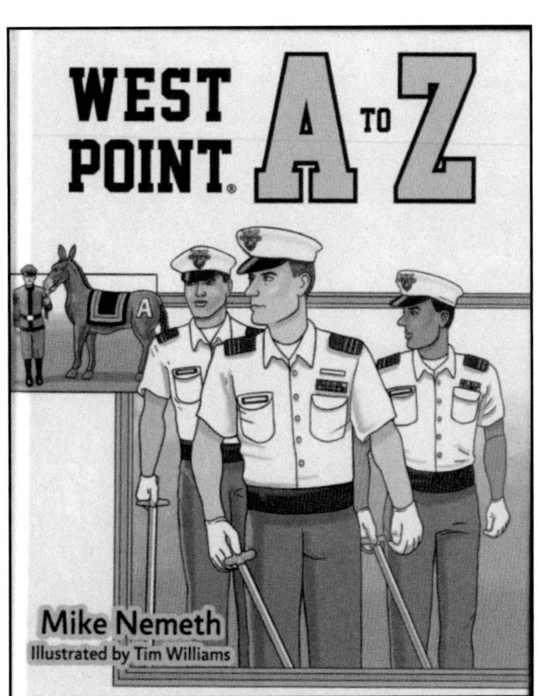

West Point: A to Z

Cadet, Children, Satire, WPAuthor

Mike Nemeth Mascotbooks (2013)

This illustrated book is light and satirical, not really fiction but an entertaining view of West Point for children. From Eisenhower to Room Standards and Black Knights to the Long Gray Line, experience historical West Point from A to Z and everything in between. [BC]

Mike Nemeth is a 2004 West Point graduate. He wrote a popular weekly series of satire articles and videos about cadet life called "Center Stall." While a cadet, Mike only marched in two parades, wrote the jokes used for his class graduation speech, convinced the Secretary of the Army to grant him a lifetime reprieve from morning room standards, and only walked twenty-five hours (far less than he should have walked). He hopes one day to receive the Thayer Award but will settle for a Distinguished Graduate Award. [BC]

The next two works satirize the cadet experience. Both were the creation of cadet Michael Conrad for "The Pointer" magazine at the end of the 1970s when women were first admitted to the military academies. A third work by Conrad is included in the "Paranormal, Supernatural, and Futuristic" chapter.

The Adventures of Peter Parsec Space Cadet

Cadet, Futuristic, Satire, WP Author

Mike Conrad

MikeConradArt.com (2002)

"Peter Parsec first appeared in issues of *The Pointer*, a collegiate magazine produced by cadets of the United States Military Academy at West Point. Running from 1976 to 1980, the satirical adventures of Peter and first-captain Carrie Sabres poked fun at comic books, science fiction and Academy life, and helped many classes of cadets get their minds off of the combined pressures of a heavy course load and countless military duties and regulations." [1-18]

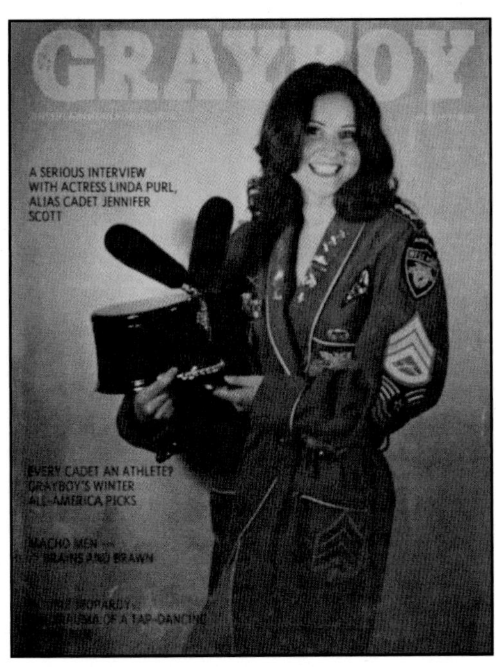

Grayboy

Cadet, Satire, WP Author

Michael Conrad MikeConradArt.com (1979)

"This was a special issue of *The Pointer*, the magazine published by cadets at the United States Military Academy at West Point. In 1979, the Academy attempted to co-opt what had been traditionally an entertainment and satire magazine created by cadets for the cadets' own enjoyment and use it as a platform for official information. The result, after two or three issues, was a steep decline in readership, many cancelled subscriptions and angry letters from cadets and graduates all over the world, which showed that such a magazine would not reach the audience for which it was intended.

In a bid to restore faith in *The Pointer*, the staff proposed a more even balance between satire and serious features. However, there was much ground to be regained, so to signal the return of humor to the publication, they brainstormed to come up with something big, eye-catching, and above all, fun.

At the time, *Playboy* was riding high among the readers of the same demographic and was already controversial in the public mind. So, a parody of that magazine was a natural. With the relatively new presence of female cadets in the Corps, this issue was sure to ignite some controversy of its own, but to ensure that the women were not totally relegated to the role of cheesecake, the pictorial section featured male cadets in fictionalized profiles that were designed to turn the idea of eye-candy on its head.

The ploy worked like a charm. Soon, subscriptions were up, the world was fun again, birds were singing, and Plebes took big bites. There was even a request from Playboy to send them an issue, which was featured in that magazine's "The World of Playboy" section." [1-19]

Mike Conrad (1958–) is a freelance artist/writer/designer working in Orlando, Florida. A self-taught artist, he graduated from West Point in 1980 and served as an army officer until 1988, when he decided to make a career out of his art. He counts among his clients Disney, Universal, SeaWorld, Busch Gardens, Lockheed Martin, Kennedy Space Center, and the Orlando Science Center. His illustrations have won many awards at SF and fantasy conventions. [1-20]

The final item in the chapter is a graphic, interactive depiction of the cadet experience. This board game complements the Ransom House Landmark Series book # 70 - *The West Point Story*. The book, written by Russell "Red" Reeder, was published in 1956. It is a surprisingly realistic simulation of cadet progress from Plebe to Firstie in that era.

The West Point Story: A Game

OBJECT OF THE GAME

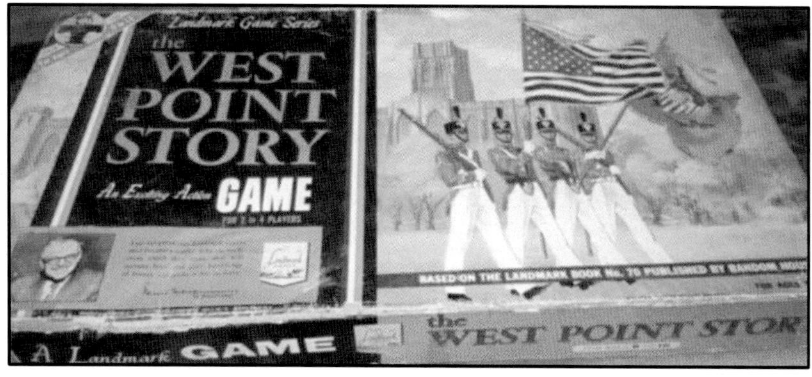

Enter the United States Military Academy at West Point as a plebe and be promoted, when a 1st classman, to the rank of Brigade Commander.

To advance to Brigade Commander a player must be promoted in grade from plebe to 1st classman by the achievement of scholastic points and also advance in rank from Corporal to Brigade Commander by accumulation of Tactics, Sports, and Popularity points - and use of the Promotion Spinner. First player to accumulate 150 points in Scholastics, 50 points in Tactics, 50 points in Sports, 50 points in Popularity - and achieve promotion to Brigade Commander -- WINS THE GAME!

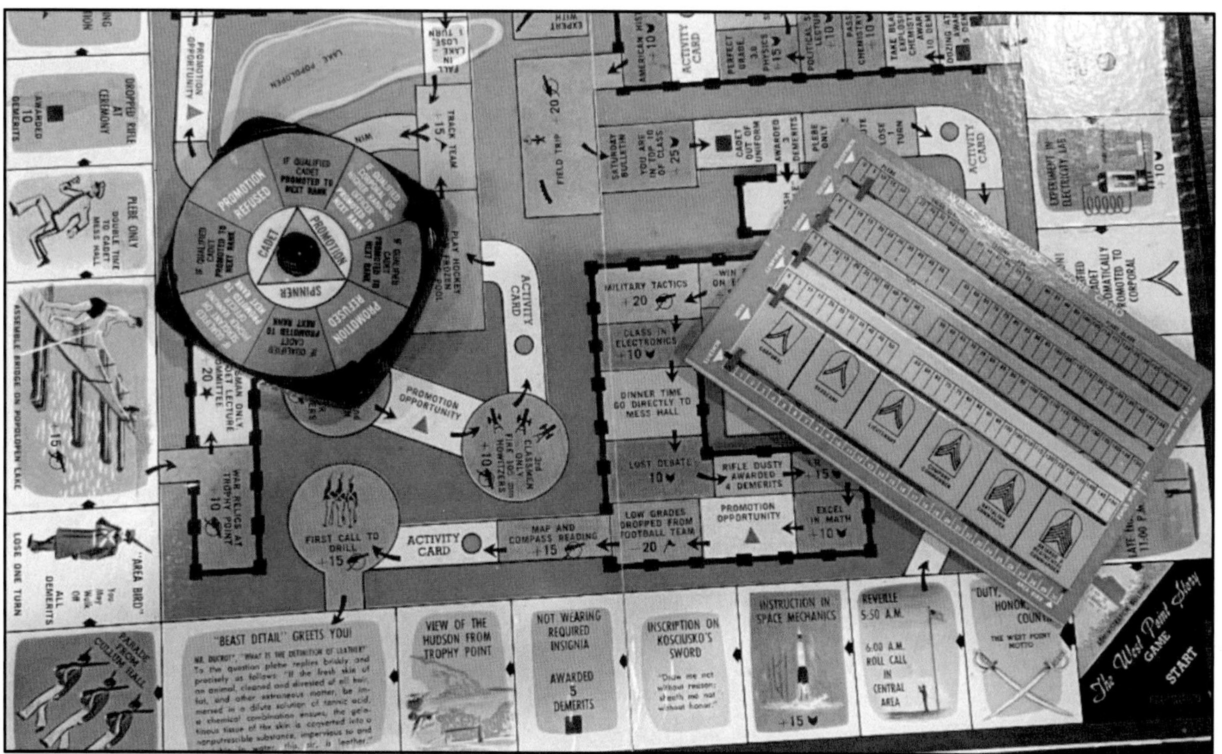

Chapter 2

The Cadet Series of Books

West Point and the cadet experience captured the imagination of the reading public from the 1890's through the 1950's. Books and pulp fiction stories appeared annually. These were directed at youth who might be inspired by military affairs and consider joining the U.S. Army. Several authors capitalized on this elevated interest by writing a series of books following one individual through their West Point years. . . and thereafter. This peaked in the 1950s with Russell Reeder's six volumes and the television series, "West Point" which appeared from 1956 to 1957. The 1960s and the Vietnam war changed the general public's interest in the "West Point experience" and the genre went dormant.

Another factor was present. The books were consistently formulaic, lacking serious character development, and ultimately unappealing to modern tastes, as Aloysius Norton USMA 1944 points out in his thesis on the "Customs and Traditions of West Point in the American Novel." See the introduction of Chapter I for an elaboration.

A "cadet series" of books did not re-emerge until the second decade of the 21st century with a surprising twist—they were about women's passage through West Point. The books addressed the challenge of character development that was missing in the earlier series.

The first two authors of these series adopted a pseudo name, then appropriated a military rank to add credibility to their writings.

Cadet Kit Carey Series

These books cover more than Cadet Carey's West Point years. Starting with his struggle to get admitted as a cadet, the series concludes with Captain Carey fighting the Indians at Pine Ridge.

Lieutenant Carey's Luck

Indian War, Cadet Series

Lt. Lionel Lounsberry David McKay Company (1899)

Following graduation from West Point, Kit Carey is assigned to a cavalry unit at Fort Forward in the Dakota territory under the command of his old patron, Col. Crandall. On his way by stagecoach to the fort, Kit aids in fighting off bandits and is handed a package of documents by a dying passenger to be delivered to the Colonel. When he arrives at the fort, he finds two officers who had borne him much enmity during his passage through West Point.

Before he can arrange delivering the critical package to the Colonel, Kit leaves the fort with several hundred troopers to bring justice to the marauding outlaws. Having spent his youth living with an elderly hermit in this territory, Kit's familiarity with the terrain and Indian ways enables him to avoid or defend the soldiers from certain annihilation by huge bands of Sioux and Comanche tribes.

He returns to Fort Forward a hero, to the chagrin of the two hostile officers, and then leads another force to round up the outlaws and bring them to justice. This assures Kit Carey of a promotion to 1st Lieutenant.

There is a romance involving the Colonel's niece, Kate Osmond, and two officers who are both showing interest in Kate. Kit's "secret" document reveals that the suitor Kate greatly dislikes is brought into disgrace thereby freeing her to marry the one she very much loves. [EB]

Henry Harrison Lewis (1863–1947) was an editor and author— often using the pseudonym, Lt. **Lionel Lounsberry** (and others) in his pulp fiction stories for boys. He worked for the publishers, Street and Smith 1893–1898, where he wrote a *Lost World* novel and *The Treasure of the Golden Crater* as Lt. Lionel Lounsberry, in which treasure hunters in South America discover a prehistoric race. He edited "Army and Navy Weekly" from 1897 to 1898. Lewis must have gathered some military insights there, since the Cadet Carey books were all published in 1899 shortly after his departure. [2-01]

Cadet Mark Mallory Series

Lt. Frederick Garrison David McKay Company (1903)

From the introduction of *Off for West Point*: "Every American boy takes a keen interest in the affairs of West Point. No more capable writer on this popular subject could be found than Lieut. Garrison, who vividly describes the life, adventures and unique incidents that have occurred in that great institution—in these famous West Point stories."

Frederick Garrison was a pseudonym employed by the prolific early 20th century "muckraking" author and political activist **Upton Sinclair** (1878–1968). He is most well-known for his exposure of the meatpacking industry in The Jungle. While enrolled at Columbia University after 1897, Upton supported himself and his family by writing boy's adventure stories for magazine and book publication, including this series on West Point. He wrote nearly 100 books as well as many magazine articles, jokes, pamphlets, and pulp fiction stories. He ran for political offices as a socialist in California but never was elected. He won the Pulitzer Prize for Fiction in 1943 for *Dragons Teeth.* [2-02]

The early years of the 20th century saw the emergence of a new breed of authors for the Cadet Series. They were graduates of West Point and served with distinction in the regular Army, thereby imparting credibility to their written words.

Cadet Douglas Atwell Series

Winning His Way to West Point

WP Candidate, Philippines, WP Author, Cadet Series

Maj. Gen. Paul Malone Penn Publishing (1904)

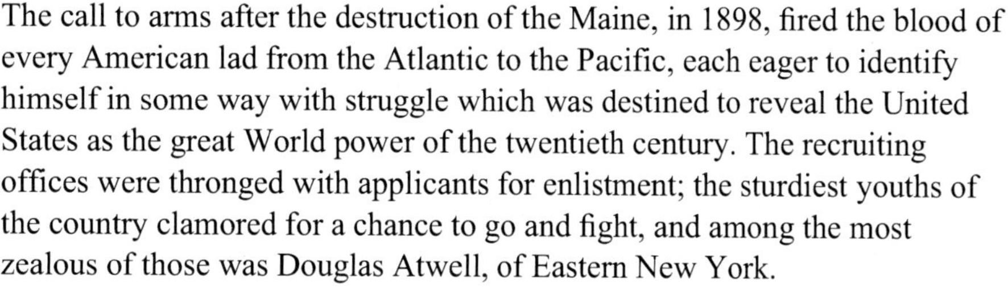

The call to arms after the destruction of the Maine, in 1898, fired the blood of every American lad from the Atlantic to the Pacific, each eager to identify himself in some way with struggle which was destined to reveal the United States as the great World power of the twentieth century. The recruiting offices were thronged with applicants for enlistment; the sturdiest youths of the country clamored for a chance to go and fight, and among the most zealous of those was Douglas Atwell, of Eastern New York.

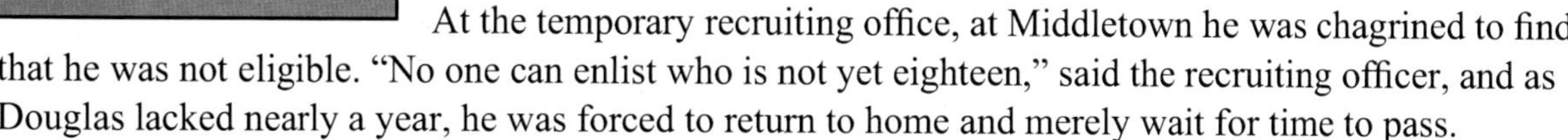

At the temporary recruiting office, at Middletown he was chagrined to find that he was not eligible. "No one can enlist who is not yet eighteen," said the recruiting officer, and as Douglas lacked nearly a year, he was forced to return to home and merely wait for time to pass.

It was not, therefore, until the war clouds began hovering over the Philippines, the following year, that Douglas was permitted to begin his eventful career in the United States Army.

As a recruit of but three days' experience he saw the first hostile shots flash out across the San Juan River on the night of February 4, 1899, and the next day he participated in the memorable charge of his company on blockhouse, N0. 14.

The story of Douglas Atwell's service in the campaign through the jungles of Luzon is told in this volume. Atwell follows a code of honor and ethical behavior. He earns the respect and friendship of everyone except Pvt. L.C. Jackson, who becomes a bitter enemy when Atwell uncovers the man's cowardice. For his gallant conduct in that fearful muddy ordeal of jungle warfare Atwell received a Presidential appointment to the United States Military Academy. [FP]

A Plebe at West Point

Cadet Series, WP Author

Capt. Paul Malone Penn Publishing (1905)

Imagine a strong, well-built, self-reliant lad, who has spent his youth upon an obscure farm on the Shawangunk Mountains of eastern New York whose opportunities for education had been limited by the curriculum of a district school possessing less than a dozen pupils.

Such a lad was Douglas Atwell when he reported at West Point to become a cadet at the United States Military Academy. The privilege of entering this institution. The Alma Mater of Grant, Sherman, Sheridan, Lee, and Jackson had been sought in vain by thousands of the best-trained boys of the country while Douglas has found the honor thrust upon him. For gallant conduct in the campaign in the Philippines the President had appointed him a cadet at large, thus opening to him the possibilities of a great career in the service of the government.

These pages narrate the experiences of the soldier-cadet in his first year at the military academy. Unfortunately, Atwell must again cope with his nemesis, L.C. Jackson, who also obtained an appointment to the academy through the political influence of his wealthy father. [FP]

West Point Yearling

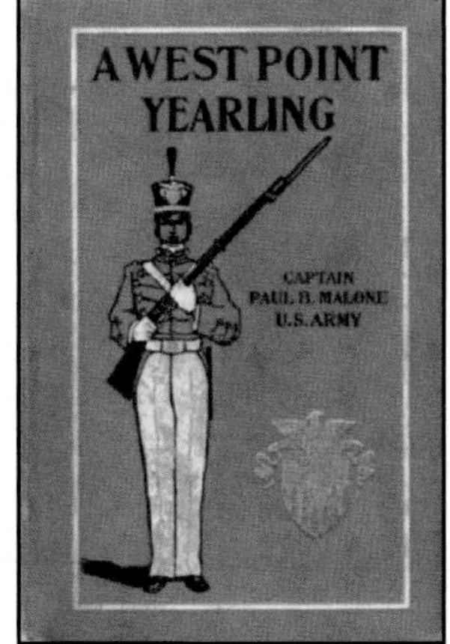

Cadet Series, WP Author

Capt. Paul Malone Penn Publishing (1907)

During the period covered by this volume, hazing had become a serious menace to the discipline of the military academy. The efforts on the part of the authorities to suppress the vice met with but little cooperation from the cadets who believed that no plebe could be inspired with the proper sense of instantaneous obedience except by the so-called system of hazing which had been practiced for many years at the academy.

So strong, honest and deep-seated was this belief that the cadet who opposed it was subject to suspicion as a sycophant and "boot-lick."

Among the opponents of the system, however, was Douglas Atwell, President of the yearling class, a recognized and stalwart leader among his comrades. In these pages an effort is made to trace his struggle against the growing opposition of his class: in a word, to follow out the system of hazing to its logical consequences.

The early experiences of our hero had admirably fitted him for the crisis with which he soon found himself confronted.

As a poor country boy on a lonely farm, he had acquired that hard "horse" sense which recognizes the fundamental and rejects convenient theory; as a soldier in the US Army in the Philippines, he had trained his fearless nature to ignore consequences, and as a plebe at West Point, he had seen the folly of the "system," the injustice of the "Code," and now with his whole heart he resolved to oppose many of his classmates.

There is a suggestion of romantic interest with the occasional presence of Alice Dryden, daughter of a wealthy New York businessman. This continues sporadically through the remaining books in the series. [EB]

A West Point Cadet

Cadet Series, WP Author

Capt. Paul Malone Penn Publishing (1908)

While never a brilliant student, Douglas Atwell has always been a hard worker, and has won his way through many difficulties. His determined stand against hazing has made him unpopular with some cadets, but nevertheless, he has many warm friends and has commanded the universal respect of the Corps. Douglas has also had several triumphs as a football player. As this story opens, he is nearing the end of his cadet days, and looking forward with confidence to a useful—and happy life. [FP]

West Point Lieutenant

Indian Wars, WP Author, Cadet Series

Capt. Paul Malone Penn Publishing (1911)

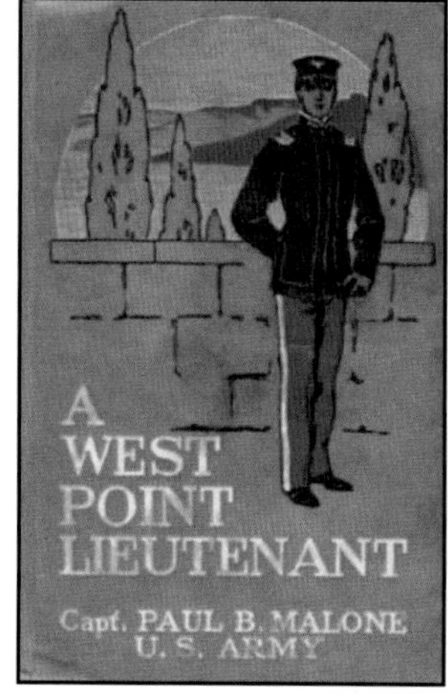

Several years have elapsed since Douglas Atwell's graduation from West Point. He is now a lieutenant stationed at the Presidio in San Francisco, living with his mother and sister, who he transported from the East. Atwell is supervising in the Army's quartermaster office.

Alice Dryden reappears in this book, travelling with her father from New York. She displays an upper crust callousness which Atwell with this poor country boy heritage finds most disturbing. But the romance stumbles on.

Atwell is offered an enormous bribe to fix a contract in favor of a business consortium. He is righteously indignant and pursues actions to expose the corruption. This becomes the main plot line in the book. He eventually succeeds, but in doing so exposes Alice Dryden's father as the ringleader.

Of course, Atwell's world implodes…but then something amazing occurs! [EB]

Author **Paul Malone** (1872–1960) graduated from West Point in 1894 and joined the 13th Infantry. As a staff officer of Wikoff's Brigade, he participated in the Battle of San Juan, when twenty-five percent of his Regiment was killed or wounded in the assault upon the block house on the crest of the hill.... In 1899, First Lieutenant Malone left San Francisco for the Philippines to participate in the campaign against Aguinaldo. His book, *Winning His Way to West Point*, is based on his experience during the years of fighting, followed by civil reconstruction. [2-03]

Dick Prescott Series

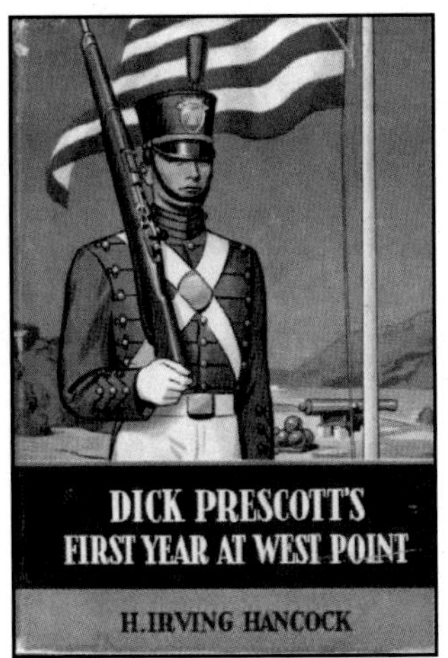

Dick Prescott's First Year at West Point or Two Chums in Cadet Gray

Cadet Series

H. Irving Hancock Saalfield Publishing Co (1910)

Dick Prescott and Greg Holmes looked around at their room. At one end was a double alcove separated by a wall. In each alcove was a bare-looking iron bedstead. There were two washbowls, two chairs, and two desks that looked as though they had served the needs of generations of cadets. There was a window that looked out on the quadrangular area of barracks.

"Well, we're actually here, anyway," breathed Dick, his eyes sparkling. "We're halfway through the ordeal of becoming new cadets at the wonderful old United States Military Academy!" This was the beginning of a thrilling year for the boys, a year filled with a new and different sort of living. But at the end when the plebes were ready for their "yearling" camp, Greg remarked: "I'd sooner tote the water bucket at West Point than own a steam yacht and an automobile anywhere." [DJ]

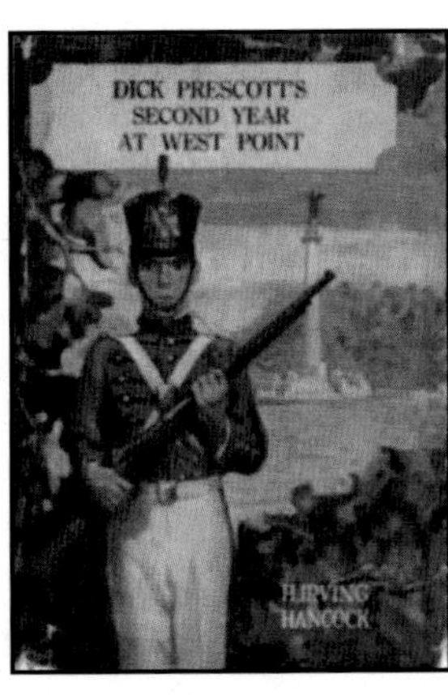

Dick Prescott's Second Year at West Point or *Finding the Glory of a Soldiers Life*

Cadet Series

H. Irving Hancock Saalfield Publishing Co (1910)

CHAPTERS

- I. The Class President Lectures on Hazing
- II. Plebe Briggs Learns a Few Things
- III. Greg Debates Between Girls and Mischief
- IV. The O.C. Wants to Know
- V. "I Respectfully Decline to Answer, Sir"
- VI. Greg Prepares for Flirtation Walk
- VII. The Folks from Home
- VIII. Cadet Dodge Hears Something
- IX. Spoony Femme--Flirtation Walk
- X. The Cure for Plebe Animal Spirits
- --XI. Lieutenant Topham Feels Queer
- XII. Under a Fearful Charge
- XIII. In Close Arrest
- XIV. Friends Who Stand By
- XV. On Trial by Court-Martial
- XVI. A Verdict and a Hop
- XVII. "A Liar and a Coward"
- XVIII. The Fight in the Barracks
- XIX. Mr. Dennison's Turn is Served
- XX. A Discovery at the Riding Drill
- XXI. Pitching for the Army Nine
- XXII. Greg's Secret and Another's
- XXIII. The Committee on Class Honors
- XXIV. Conclusion

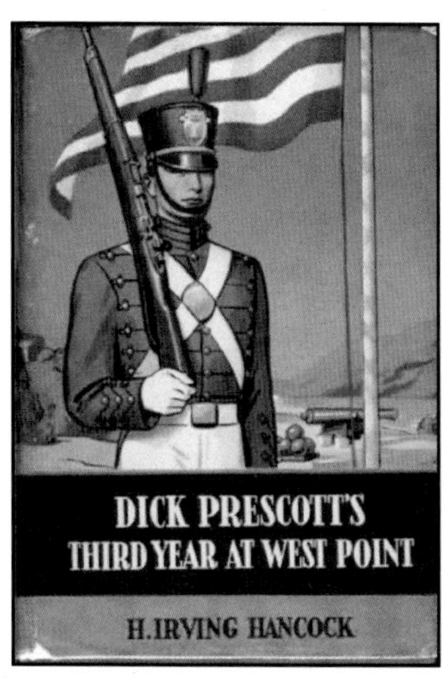

Dick Prescott's Third Year at West Point or *Standing Firm for Flag & Honor*

Cadet Series

H. Irving Hancock Saalfield Publishing Co (1911)

Dick Prescott spends a pleasant summer at home on his furlough, then he goes back to West Point -- a Second Classman.

There follows another year of work and play. An accident in the riding hall sends Dick to the Cadet hospital with an injured spine that threatens to put an end to his cadet days. His greatest joy comes on Commencement Day when the medical examiners tell him that there is no question about his full recovery.

"My, but you look like the favorite uncle of the candy kid!" mutters his chum, Greg Holmes.

"Why shouldn't I?" retorts Dick; "My spine is all right, and I'm to stay in the service. Then besides, Greg, old fellow, think what we are now. First Classmen! Only a year more to the "glorious" old Army!" [DJ]

Dick Prescott's Fourth Year at West Point or *Ready to Drop the Gray for Shoulder Straps*

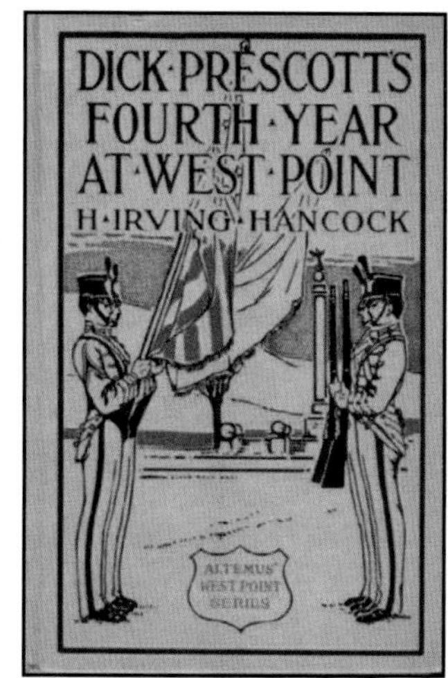

Cadet Series

H. Irving Hancock Saalfield Publishing Co (1911)

CONCLUSION

The graduating exercises at West Point had finished. The Secretary of War, in the presence of the superintendent, the commandant and the members of the faculty of the United States Military Academy, flanked by the Board of Visitors, had handed his diploma to the last man, the cadet at the foot of the graduating class, Mr. Atterbury.

Dick had graduated as number thirty-four; Greg as thirty-seven. Either might have chosen the cavalry, or possibly the artillery arm of the service, but both had already expressed a preference for the infantry arm…

Five minutes later the young graduates were laying aside the gray uniform for good and all. Cit. clothes now went on, and each grad. surveyed himself with some wonder in attire which was so unfamiliar…

That evening the class was to meet, for the last time as a whole, at one of the theaters in New York. And the late cadets would sit together, solidly, as a class. Friends of graduates who wished would attend the theater, though in seats away from the class…

Then one morning each received a bulky official envelope bearing the imprint of the War Department at Washington. How their eyes glistened, then moistened, as each young West Point grad. drew out of the envelope the parchment on which was written his commission as a second lieutenant of United States infantry.

Their instructions called for them to start within forty-eight hours, and to wire acknowledgment of orders to Washington. The Forty-fourth United States Infantry was at that time in the far West, in a country that at times teemed with adventure for Uncle Sam's soldiers.

H. Irving Hancock (1868–1922) was a journalist for the *Boston Globe* from 1885 to 1890 and served as a war correspondent in Cuba and the Philippines during the Spanish American War. As an author his works included westerns, detective stories, and historical adventures.

Much of his writing was in a series of "Boy's Books" initiated by the famous Stratemeyer Syndicate. Their assumption was that "boys want the thrill of feeling 'grown-up'" and that they like books which give them that feeling to come in a series where the same heroes appear again and again. Hancock authored a dozen series including the Motor Boat Club, West Point, Annapolis, High School Boys, and Uncle Sam's Boys. [2-04]

The next series is by Florence Kimball Russel an Army 'brat' and Army wife. She takes Jack Stirling from a West Point candidate with the cavalry out West to his arrival at the Academy in *Born to the Blue. In West Point Gray,* she presents Stirling and his friends as "plebes" and "yearlings". *From Chevrons to Shoulder Straps* she carries them up to the day of graduation.

Jack Stirling Series

Born to the Blue: A Story of the Army

Indian Wars, Western, WP Candidate, Cadet Series

Florence Kimball Russel L.C. Page Company (1906)

"BANG! That was the reveille gun. Up flew the garrison flag; the bugles sounded sharp and shrill; and then, almost drowned in the strains of the "Star Spangled Banner," came a little cry—not feeble and wailing, but vigorous and strong - the first cry of a wee baby boy who stole into the house with the earliest peep of day on that glorious Fourth of July.

It was just as the band started on its patriotic rounds about the garrison, dispensing national airs and hymns, which were greeted with uproarious delight by the younger members of each family and a disgusted jamming of pillows over the ears of older ones.

And all day long the popping of firecrackers, the firing of salutes, the joyous screams of children, and the distant music of the band, floated in through the half-closed blinds, as impossible to keep away as was one rebellious stream of golden sunlight, which flickered in through a loose slat, and danced in an ecstasy of delight when old Nurse Groghan vainly tried to bar it out.

But neither noise nor sunlight seemed to disturb the little soldier lying placidly on his mother's arm, with one pink fist curled up under his chin, and the other tightly clasped around a tiny flag which had been sent to him by one of the garrison children. Such a strong, sturdy baby as he was, a veritable Fourth of July boy, with the national colors well reproduced in his very red skin, his blue eyes, and his mop of fine white hair. "You're born to the blue, Jack!" his mother whispered delightedly over and over again. "Born to the blue!" . . . [EB]

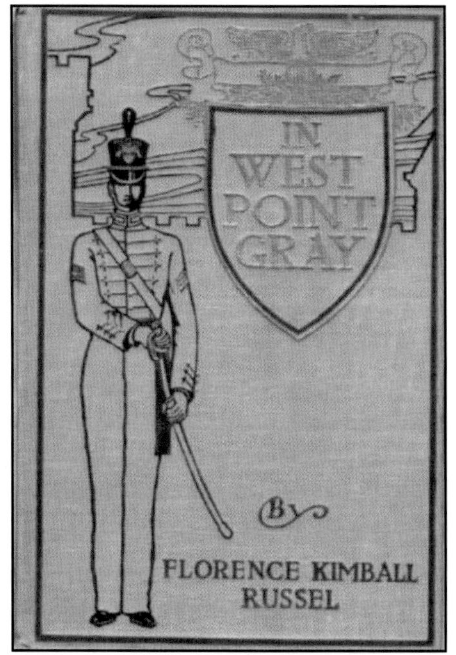

In West Point Gray: As Plebe & Yearling

Cadet Series

Florence Kimball Russel L.C. Page Company (1923)

Guard-mounting over at Fort Union, the trumpeters shrilled their way back to the guardhouse where the old and new officers of the day made their inspections, verified the number of prisoners, and then reported to the commanding officer, who relieved the one from that particular duty and gave the other his instructions for the next twenty-four hours.

It was a small cavalry post in Arizona, and everyone there from Maj. Stirling, the officer commanding, down to the newest recruit in the barracks, which turned out each morning at eight o'clock to witness the pretty ceremony.

"It's our theatre, circus, and Atlantic City boardwalk rolled into one," the first sergeant of K troop remarked as he slipped off his belts and loosened an uncommonly tight blouse. "At other drills and parades, barrin' the ladies on Officers' Row, we're all actors instead of audience, but once a day, at least, most of us gets a chance to see how we look from the other side of the footlights."

"Sure, and it was Jack Stirling himself that used to love the military formations," commented a little Irishman whose bunk adjoined the door of the first sergeant's room, "and it's the truth I'm telling you, Donnelly, that I miss the lad as if he'd been gone a year! Why, it's taken the very soul out of all our drills, not seeing his bright face looking on, and sometimes I get that blackhearted with the loneliness that I most wish the President hadn't appointed him 'at large' to the Military Academy."

Sergeant Donnelly threw back his head with a characteristic movement, much as a restive horse might toss its mane. "And what's our loneliness got to do with Mr. Jack's career?" he demanded truculently. "What's his father's and mother's loneliness got to do with it? Though, to be sure, you'd never have guessed to see the Major and the Major's lady sayin' goodbye to the boy at the station last week..." [EB]

From Chevrons to Shoulder Straps: A Story of West Point

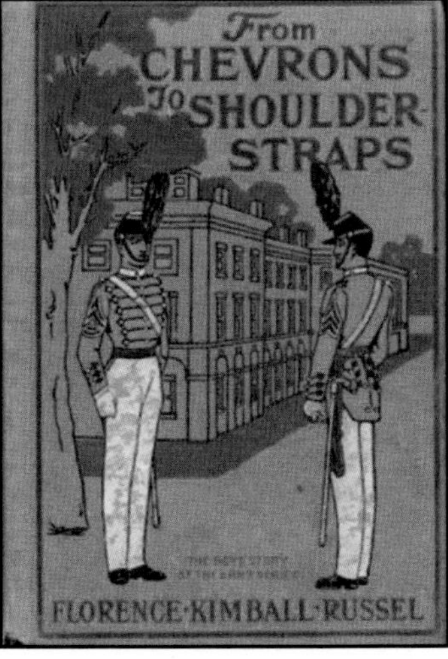

Cadet Series

Florence Kimball Russel L.C. Page Company (1914)

In the present volume, as in the previous volumes of the series, the author describes the West Point of twenty-five years ago when, in her own words, "football was an unknown quantity, and baseball played so seldom that the average score might be summed up briefly as a broken nose on one side to a dislocated thumb on the other . . . camps, drills, and riding-hall experiences replacing the athletics of other schools. But in spite of this lack of valorous intercollegiate rivalry, the life at West Point was not without interest, the very fight for standing in the section-room having its romantic side, while no crack players on the modern football eleven or baseball nine are more looked up to than were the men wearing chevrons in those old days."

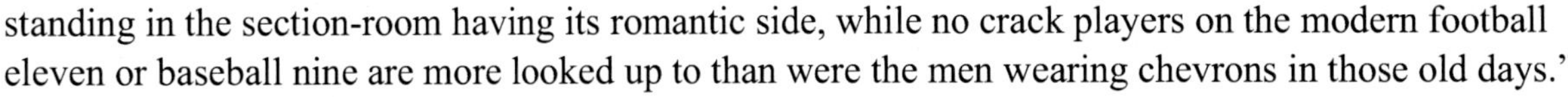

The development of a raw "plebe" into a manly, self-reliant young soldier is depicted, and many incidents show the high code of honor among the cadets, and how discipline and the glorious traditions of the Academy are maintained, quite aside from the Tactical Department and Academic Board.

True to its conservatism, the West Point of today is the West Point of twenty-five years ago, save in the matter of sports, so Mrs. Russel's book may well be called an accurate picture of life at the Military Academy. [FP]

Florence "Floss" Kimball Russel (1873–1963) was in every sense an "army woman," the daughter of an officer, born at a frontier post. Her earliest recollections are of the army, and throughout her life Florence's connection with it was never severed. She was the wife of Maj. Edgar Russel and the sister of another army officer. Many of the incidents which she wove into *Born to the Blue* were taken from her own experiences, and the climax of the story is based on a personal experience of her brother. [2-05]

In addition to the Jack Stirling Series, Kimball Russel authored a popular memoir in 1909 titled, *A Woman's Journey through the Philippines,* about her experiences when her husband was posted in that far off land. That book is included in the chapter, "In the Far East."

The Argosy Series

A series of stories appeared in Argosy Magazine in 1937 and 1938. Although each story is stand-alone, featuring a different cadet, they are a continuum recounting a typical cadet's passage through the academy.

"West Point Fourth Classman"

Pulp Fiction, Cadet Series

Paul R. Morrison Argosy Magazine (July 1937)

Time: Mid-July Place: West Point Weather: Hot

CADET CROSS COSTIGAN'S face dripped with perspiration. As a Fourth Classman—the lowest ranking class at the United States Military Academy, he was paying the penalty for his latest transgression. An eagle-eyed yearling had spied him slouching at the dinner table. Dinner at West Point, you know, is at noon, and about this time in mid-July the sun is sucking the last molecule of moisture from the Plain.

"Mister Dumbguard," the yearling, Third Classman Mambus, was instructing him with great patience, "pull your backbone up out of your tron! Bend forward at the waist! Now, hold it while you heave out on your chest! And get your chin back inside your collar!"

First Classman Reynolds, cadet lieutenant of B Company, glanced up from his plate long enough to observe, "If there's anything I hate to see more than anything else, it's a plebe with a chin."

"Mister Ducrot, did you hear me? I said get your chin back inside your collar!"

Fourth Classman Milton Wakefield, who sat beside Costigan, could hear Costigan his roommate, breathing hard. For the last two minutes, every upper classman at the table had been taking turns working over Cadet Costigan ....

He kept on muttering while he got out of his all-white uniform, which had been the order for dinner, and climbed into his own hiking outfit. He scowled as he adjusted his O. D. hat with the West Point black and gold hatband.

"You look positively handsome, Costigan," observed Wakefield with a broad grin. "You'd make a good cowpoke for Dad's dude ranch out home."

"Don't be funny!"

While Costigan finished folding his clothing away, Wakefield leaned against the tent pole and watched the barren top of Crow Nest, a mountain to the northwest of that point of land that juts eastward out into the Hudson River—West Point. On Crow Nest one might see the terrific ravages of exploded shells and pick up bits of metal shell casings and shrapnel. Rocky, treeless, the mountain top made an excellent target for the West Point artillery batteries.

As Wakefield looked, a thin rainbow of white smoke streaked up from behind the westward hills and plunged, comet-like, down upon Crow Nest. There was a puff of smoke just before the rainbow was completed—bursting shrapnel. Another little higher, farther beyond. A third almost directly in the center of the two previous bursts. The explosions reached his ears—dull innocent sounding but blasting a deadly cone of slugs upon the ground beneath, leveling anyone who might be there.

But no one would be beneath. Cadets stood guard to all entrances and here and there regularly enlisted men warned persons from the danger zone. An upper classman strolled down the street, and Wakefield ducked back inside. . . . [EB]

"West Point Third Classman"

Pulp Fiction, Cadet Series

Paul R. Morrison Argosy Magazine, (November 1937)

Time: Autumn Place: West Point Weather: Chilly

CADET CORPORAL Baird Quinton clicked through the guardhouse vestibule and halted to inspect the white-gloved, white cross-belted cadets of the punishment squad. He glanced along the wide-spaced, single file that tramped wearily back and forth across the graveled ground in front of the guardhouse—West Point's famous area.

It was not the late afternoon, autumn sun that set a frown on his face; rather, it was the sudden realization that as an officer of the guard it was his duty to report his friend, Ward Michaux, for talking in ranks. Ever since Quinton became a third classman with corporal's chevrons, and Michaux—his predecessor by one year—second classman with a clean sleeve, a coldness had grown up between them, blighting a friendship that dated since boyhood.

In a low voice, Michaux threw the traditional information to a plebe, who, under compulsion, strutted exactly six paces ahead. Michaux said, "The AB degree, Mister Dumbguard, may be acquired at West Point at any time before graduation. Even by a blasé plebe like you."

"Yes, sir!" Plebe Stuart Cruse, III, from Boston, acknowledged in a throaty whisper.

"But" Michaux continued, "in the case of a plebe—especially a wooden one like you, the degree of Area Bird may not be earned without conscientious effort." [EB]

"West Point Second Classman"

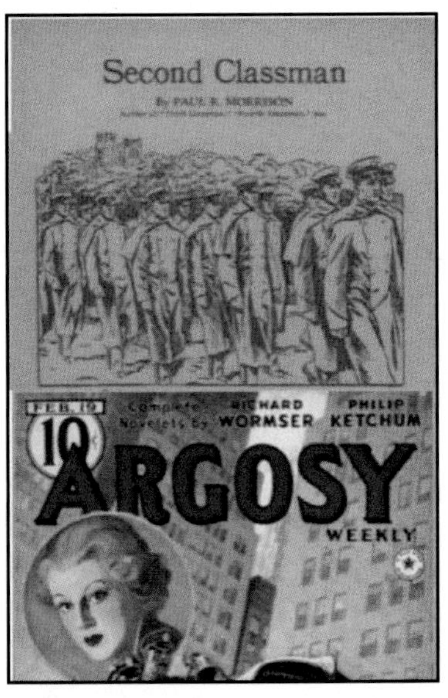

Pulp Fiction, Cadet Series

Paul R. Morrison Argosy Magazine (February 1938)

Time: Winter Place: West Point Weather: Below Zero

"Who's that plebe out of step up there?" the West Point yearling's voice was guardedly low, heavy with the responsibility of upholding the ancient military academy's grim traditions that come to third classmen. "Look! -- look at his head bob!"

"By the cube root of minus one!" First Classman Julian Blanchard gasped. "It's not a plebe—it's Cliff Knight. Imagine that of a second classman with two and a half years---"

"Why don't yuh apes lay off Knight?" Timothy Mead's words slurred with the ingratiating accent of the South. Mead was a second classman, too, and Clifton Knight's roommate. "Can't you see—the guy's so homesick he doesn't know what he's doing."

"Homesick?" Blanchard scoffed. "What's that?"

"Nostalgia, my priceless wooden soldier," Mead drawled. "Seems to be a pretty real illness—to Knight anyhow."

"Who's talking in ranks?" A cadet lieutenant dropped back down the line.

No other noise than the measured tread of the Corps crunching through the snow to Grant Hall for supper.

Inside, Blanchard took his place at the head of the table, on his left another first classman, on his right blithe Timothy Mead; then two yearlings and, finally, three plebes rigid under the casual but all discerning scrutiny of their seniors..." [EB]

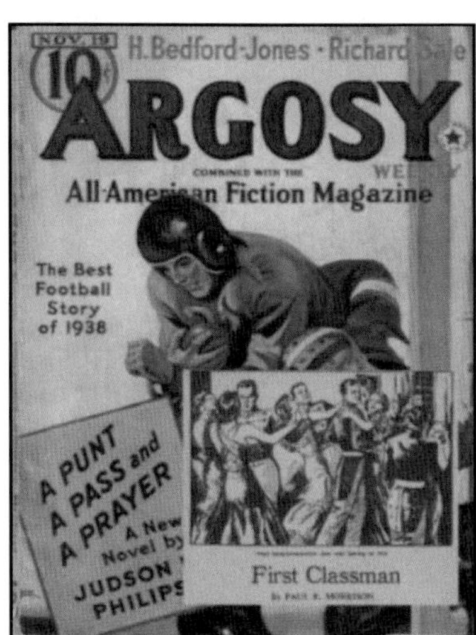

"West Point First Classman"

Pulp Fiction, Cadet Series, Romance

Paul R. Morrison Argosy Magazine, (November 1938)

Time: Spring Place: West Point Weather: Increasingly warm

This story is about two cadets, their dates, and a West Point hop in their senior year.

If you haven't heard of *terpsichophobia*, you haven't heard of Terry Hudson. That's what Parker Freem dubbed Terry's morbid fear of dancing. And Parker, confirmed social addict, should know. He'd been Terry's roommate four grinding, West Point years.

Terpsichophobia? The dictionaries don't help much. You have to know Terry Hudson. Or Marion McKee, who, long before she graduated from Vassar, came down to West Point's Saturday night hops. Maybe others of that brilliant assemblage, girls from Wellesley and Smith and Bryn Mawr. Marion was Parker's fiancée. Their engagement dated from the day that Parker completed his sophomore year at Harvard and got his appointment to the military academy. Marion was then Vassar's most unorthodox freshman.

This Saturday evening Terry stirred uneasily about his room, casting furtive glances at Parker, who hummed tranquilly while he rubbed a last-minute polish on the brass buttons of his full-dress blouse. Terry hadn't yet deduced how Parker had trapped him into going to the dance tonight at Cullum Hall. [EB]

Paul R. Morrison's biography could not be located, though there was an ex-cadet of that name in the Class of 1920. So, maybe it is he? [2-06]

The post-World War II "Baby Boom" generation of youth was given the most popular of all the cadet series books, written by a remarkable graduate of West Point— Russell "Red" Reeder (1902–1998). The series takes the traditional format of one volume for each year of the Clint Lane's West Point experience. Reeder followed it up (like some of his predecessor authors) with two books on Clint Lane as a company grade officer during the Cold War.

The Clint Lane Series

West Point Plebe

Cadet Series, WP Author

Col. Russell Reeder Duell, Sloan, Pearce (1954)

Clint Lane, football player and "army brat" from California; Chugwater Austin, trick-roping champion of the world; Joe Flynn, son of a Maine lobster fisherman -- these three are roommates in their first year at West Point. The story of that plebe year centers on Clint, but together the three roommates struggle under the pressure of the "Beast Detail," assigned to whip the plebes into line, and together they buck the problems and share the excitement of the year.

Clint's first big problem is math, which can keep him from the football he loves. His next big problem is Sue Sims, his home-town girl who is crazy about athletes, and cadets. On sentry duty during the Plebe Hike, Clint runs into real trouble for the whole Corps. The combined efforts of Joe Flynn and a Canadian Minister of Defense are required to extricate them -- and to beat Navy in the annual football game.

Here is a rousing, intimate, hilarious picture of the life of a plebe today, by a man who is himself one of the famed "men of West Point." [DJ]

West Point Yearling

WP Author, Cadet Series

Col. Russell Reeder Duell, Sloan, Pearce (1956)

Everyone who reads *West Point Plebe*, with its rousing, intimate, hilarious picture of plebe life, will be thrilled to share with Clint Lane and his classmates in *West Point Yearling* the even greater adventure of their second year. Attention continues to center on Clint Lane, football player and "army brat" from California, though his friends Chugwater Austin, trick-roping champion of the world, and Joe Flynn, son of a Maine lobster fisherman, come in for their share of attention. So do Boy McCoy, who is something less than a friend, and others. Their experiences make lively and entertaining reading as they learn—if they did not fully realize before—that training to become an officer is serious business. Clint is taught a lesson in leadership on night maneuvers and learns that orders are orders even when one's best girl is calling long distance, and McCoy receives a sharp reprimand for hazing plebes.

But combat maneuvers, night patrols, demerits, calculus, and psychology must share the days and nights with cadet parties, football, fishing and the many other forms of entertainment and sport cadets enjoy—including the three mysterious and "uninvited guests" from Mexico, who are strictly "off-limits": Injun Joe, James Bowie, and Admiral Nelson. [DJ]

West Point Second Classman

WP Author, Cadet Series

Col. Russell Reeder   Duell, Sloan, Pearce (1957)

Clint Lane, football player and "army brat" from California; Chugwater Austin, trick roping champion of the world; Joe Flynn, on of a Maine lobster fisherman -- these three are roommates in their first year at West Point. The story of that plebe year centers on Clint, but together the three roommates struggle under the pressure of the "Beast Detail," assigned to whip the plebes into line, and together they buck the problems and share the excitement of the year.

Clint's first big problem is math, which can keep him from the football he loves. His next big problem is Sue Sims, his home-town girl who is crazy about athletes, and cadets. On sentry duty during the Plebe Hike, Clint runs into real trouble for the whole Corps. The combined efforts of Joe Flynn and a Canadian Minister of Defense are required to extricate them -- and to beat Navy in the annual football game. Here is a rousing, intimate, hilarious picture of the life of a plebe today, by a man who is himself one of the famed "men of West Point. [DJ]

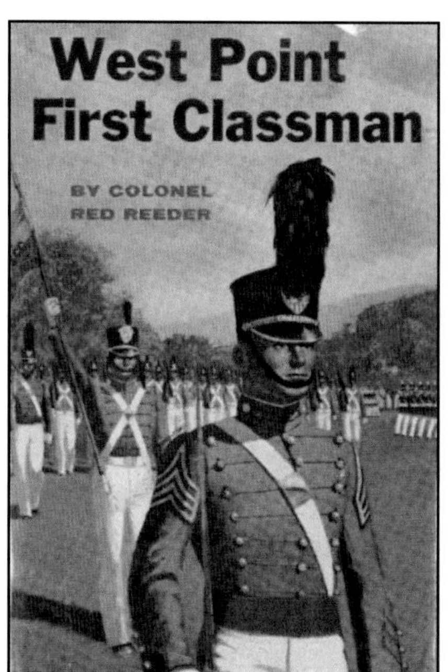

West Point First Classman

WP Author, Cadet Series

Col. Russell Reeder   Duell, Sloan, Pearce (1958)

Clint Lane's final year gets off to a fast start. Assigned to Beast Detail as acting company commander, he proudly witnesses the traditional ceremony at Battle Monument when the New Cadets are sworn in—and late that same summer day stands before the Tactical Officer under suspicion of hazing Plebes and in danger of court-martial.

From that moment the story moves about as fast as Clint himself—nicknamed the California Comet—can move on a football field. He finally wins his stripes as Cadet Captain, he accepts new responsibilities and masters new skills, makes new friends—including some remarkable ones among the Plebes—and shares the work and excitement with such old pals as Chugwater Austin, Joe Flynn, the Bull Elephant, and Roy McCoy. He meets Navy head-on in football and baseball, and those two games weren't all glory either.

There are one or two very special events in his year as a first classman—the ordeal of rescuing a squad of men in a forest fire with the aid of the astonishing Hambone from Boston, and the wonderful occasion of the Ring Hop at which Betty Willard is his guest. Both of these special events lead to special rewards when the year ends —for suddenly, all too soon, the year is over and it's farewell to West Point. [DJ]

Clint Lane: West Point to Berlin

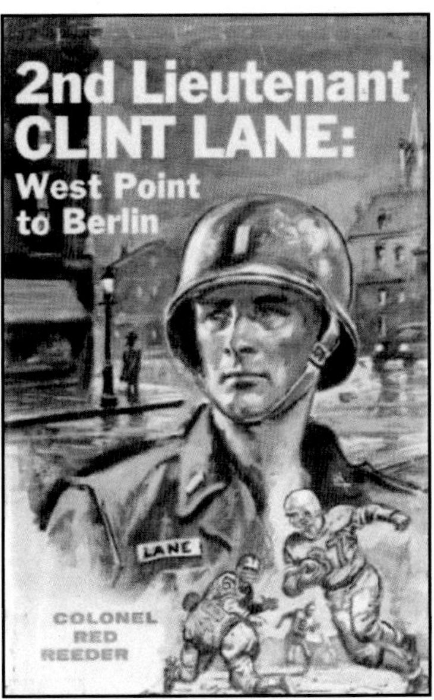

WP Author, Cold War, Cadet Series

Col. Russell Reeder Duell, Sloan, Pearce (1960)

Colonel Red Reader, in this story, tells of the adventures of 2nd Lieutenant Clint Laue in Europe. Although Red was once a second lieutenant himself, and expertly knows that life, he traveled recently in Germany and France to make certain that this story accurately portrays the life and problems of today's modern Army lieutenant. . . .

One reason why second lieutenants are so important is that they are the officers in closest touch with enlisted men, who make our Army great. I particularly admire, as will you, the two sergeants whom Clint gets to know and rely upon in this book; he is fortunate to break in with such experienced, helpful, and interesting non-commissioned officer leaders. [DJ]

Clint Lane in Korea

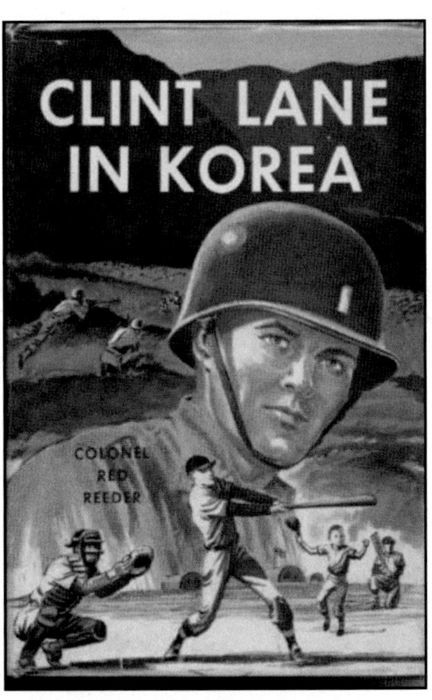

WP Author, Korea, Cadet Series

Col. Russel Reeder Duell, Sloan, Pearce (1961)

First LIEUTENANT CLINT LANE took his first look at Korea with mixed feelings. He was worrying about the safe delivery of a top-secret message for General Carter, but he was excited to know that First Sergeant Bingo Burns would be at the dock to welcome Clint to the Land of the Morning Calm.

Clint Lane's first hour in Korea was anything but calm. It was as mixed up as his own feelings about the place. At one minute he and Bingo and two Marine guards and their driver were faced with a wild, howling mob; next minute, Clint and his companions were enjoying the quiet and shelter of a typical Korean home. It was there that Clint Lane met Jim-Joe Bong, "the best boy in Inchon," who was destined to play such a large part in Clint's life, just as Clint did in Jim-Joe's.

With its picturesque background and unusual, exciting twists, this fast-action novel is the most interesting of the famous Clint Lane stories. From start to finish it is a story of dramatic contrasts, of sudden and violent action erupting to jar the long, silent vigil of the watches on the Communist front, of intrigue and treachery menacing the peaceful lives of families and villages. Clint Lane does get a limited chance to play once more in a great football game and in an even more dramatic baseball game, but mostly his is the hard life of the soldier manning the Korean ramparts. Clint's struggle to save Jim-Joe, who becomes his adopted son, turns into the biggest and most challenging fight in Clint's life and not until the very end does Clint know if he's going to win that big one. [DJ]

Russell Reeder played football and baseball while a member of the West Point class of 1926. In 1944, Reeder took command of the 12th Infantry Regiment which landed on Utah Beach on D-Day. On June 11, 1944, Reeder was hit by a shell that almost severed his left leg. Among his decorations were the Distinguished Service Cross and Silver Star. After leaving military service in 1946, Reeder became the athletic director and baseball coach at West Point. He retired from the Army in 1967 to author many books military non-fiction in addition to the "Clint Lane Series." In 1997, Reeder was awarded the Distinguished Graduate Award by the Association of Graduates of the United States Military Academy. [2-07]

The *Guardians of Honor* series is a pioneering work of Christian fiction that examines the moral and ethical dilemmas faced by believers in the intelligence community as witnessed through the eyes of female officers and cadets serving at the US Military Academy at West Point and beyond. [BC]

Details on each book may be found in the "Women at West Point" chapter.

Guardians of Honor - Casey Sullivan Series

By J. E. Bandy, Jr. Westbow Press

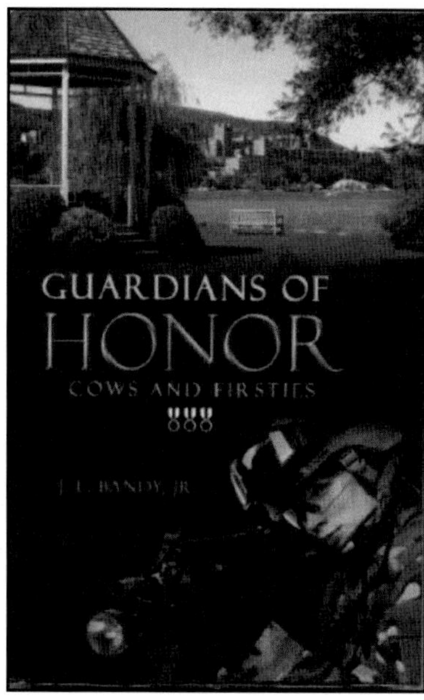

J. E. Bandy, Jr., is an Intelligence Analyst with the United States Government and a former Naval Intelligence Officer. He is also an evangelical Catholic who hopes to inform, entertain, and inspire through his novels. [DJ]

The *Gray Girl Series* depicts authentic experiences of the early years when the United States Military Academy first admitted women cadets. Jan Wishart is both heroine and troublemaker. She and her friends sometimes create their own dilemmas but mostly solve the larger issues they face while at West Point in the early 1980's.

> "Long before the 'Me Too' movement, I entered West Point on July 1, 1981-- a day that will live in infamy in my mind. The first class with women graduated in 1980, so we were still very much a novelty. Even then, I knew that I would someday write about those experiences of being in the largest fraternity in the world…" [2-08]

Details on each book may be found in the "Women at West Point" chapter.

Gray Girl Series

Susan I. Spieth Amazon – Kindle Direct Publishing

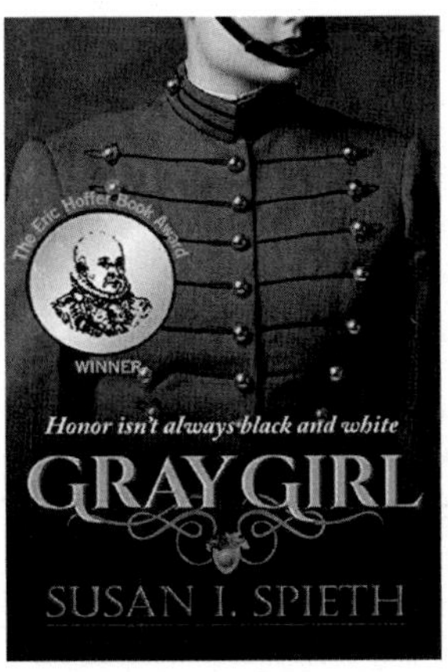

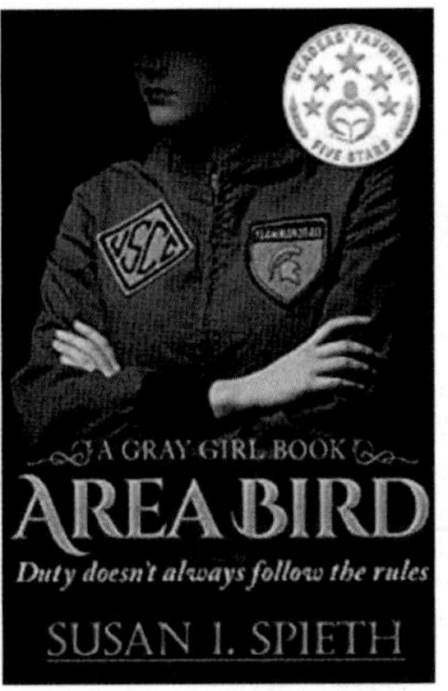

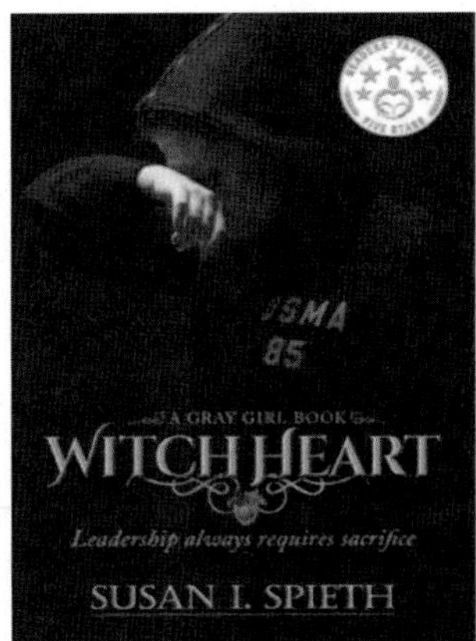

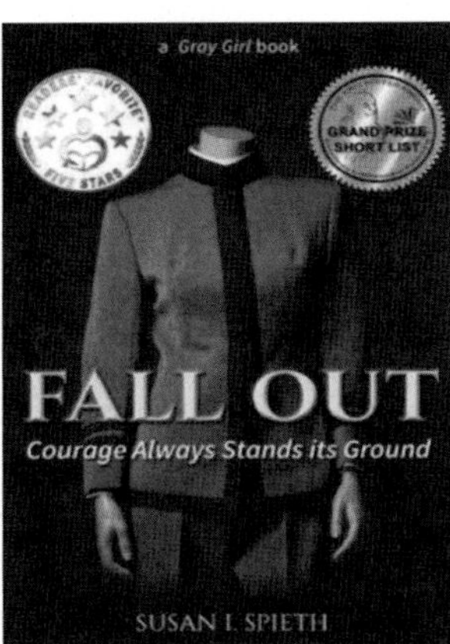

Susan I. Spieth graduated from West Point in 1985 and served five years in the Army as a Missile Maintenance Officer. After completing her military service, she attended Seminary where she earned a Master of Divinity degree. She is an ordained clergywoman in the United Methodist Church. [2-08]

Chapter 3
West Point Romances

There's something about a man in uniform that catches many a young lady's eye...

Much of the fiction about West Point from the 19th century through World War II was centered upon the romantic interests of cadets and young ladies. The stories are replete with summer encampments on the Plain, Saturday night hops, June week visits, and weddings. Even many of the novels and stories of West Pointers on the frontier included a sentimental romance. That focus faded after World War II as the fiction became more directed at West Pointers in their active-duty careers.

This chapter presents novels in which the romance is at the center of the plot. The first part of this chapter presents novels about West Pointers in the 19th century. We finish with the novels about the very different realities of late 20th century.

Artwork: From the program of "The 100th Night Show" of the Class of 1936 by Arthur William Brown '36.

Tactics or Cupid in Shoulder Straps

Romance, Satire

Hearton Drille Carleton Publisher (1854)

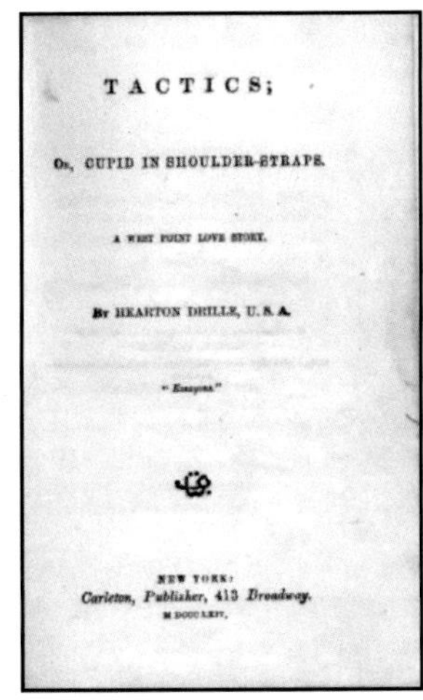

TACTICS;

OR, CUPID IN SHOULDER-STRAPS.

A WEST POINT LOVE STORY.

BY HEARTON DRILLE, U. S. A.

NEW YORK:
Carleton, Publisher, 413 *Broadway*.

Saturday on West Point! ... Enchanting spot, on that day! The hearts of three hundred cadets bounding at the thought of release from duty. Their joyful prospect of meeting loved friends from abroad! The calls to be made -- all so glad to see them. The strolls over the beautiful hillsides; the paradisaical walk on the riverbanks -- Flirtation Walk. The putting into practice all they have learned during the week; Modes of attack—means of defense—making slow and quick marches, and the 'Manual of arms,' in which all are versed. For example:

"ATTENTION" then "SQUAD"

At the second word the recruit will take a position in front of the eight-by-nine looking-glass and arrange his hair.

"SHOULDER" then "ARMS"

He shall sew on his new chevrons.

"LOAD" He shall polish his forty-four buttons, put on his coat, button it tightly to the throat.

"PRIME!" At this command, he shall adjust his cap very far forward on his head, a little to the left.

"READY" One time and three motions. The recruit advances to the front, and inspects the Plain, to ascertain if there is an enemy to be seen. He descends the stairs, grasps the tail of his coat, gives one energetic pull toward the heels.

"FORWARD" then "MARCH"

The recruit will retake a step of twenty-eight inches, until he reaches the hotel. On arriving, he will execute rapidly the several commands. . . .

Elsewhere. . .

Lieutenant Saberin, going to his room, sat down to plan what he would do in the city. He drew his vade mecum, as he called his *porte-monnaie*, from his pocket to make an entry, when out fell a little note he had received that morning. It was written in a lovely little hand. Lieutenant had been for years rather in the flowery toils of a sweet village maiden. She had been a schoolmate when he was a beautiful ingenuous boy. … He could not afford to marry so recklessly, though he loved her -- heaven only knew how dearly -- he regretted the necessity of such a course, but was it not kinder to drop the correspondence between them? He had gently checked her warmth by not writing to her, but within the past few months, some sweet little pieces of poetry had come to him through the mail, in which, though prettily disguised, he could trace the graceful Italian hand. [EB]

The title page above indicates that **Hearton Drille**, the author of this flowery satire of romance at West Point, was an Army officer. Possibly so, but there was never a West Point attendee of that name. It is certainly a pseudo name employed by some sharp-eyed observer of the romantic goings-on at the Academy.

The Rose Croix

Adventure Abroad, Western, Romance, Masonic

David Tod Gilliam Saalfield Publishing Co (1906)

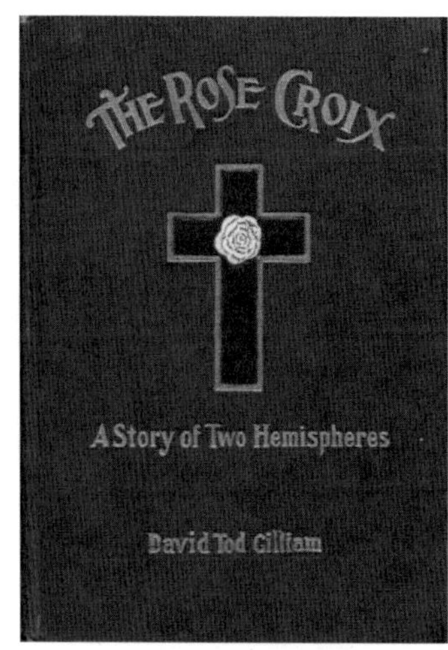

From the publisher's flyer:

> The romance of Zena, the beautiful daughter of the opulent Señor Zavala and the dashing young American officer, West Pointer Lieutenant Sylvester, a thrilling tale of love and war.
>
> It records the struggle of Texas for independence. the most tragic page in American history. There never has been a more vivid portrayal of the utter annihilation of the defenders of the Alamo, a picture so vivid that it seems as though at least one had escaped to tell the story. Here fell Davy Crockett, Colonel Bowie and others whose names are dear to American hearts. The Rose Croix is the moving element of the story, and yet so natural are the sequences of its subtle power, that the reader scarcely takes note of the cause. It lies over the heart of the hero, nestles in the bosom of the fair heroine, and is emblazoned on the accoutrements of the "Little Chevalier," a mysterious personage whose feminine beauty and valorous deeds electrify the grim patriots of the Texan Army. How the "Chevalier" comes between the lovers and the complications and tragic denouement are written in words that burn. The Rose Croix is very different from the conventional novel and will be enjoyed on that account. [FP]

David Tod Gilliam (1844–1933) was an American doctor who served the Union in the War. He had a long career as a gynecologist, obstetrician, and a pathologist in many cities, inventing new instruments in this sphere. He published several medical books and two novels. [3-01]

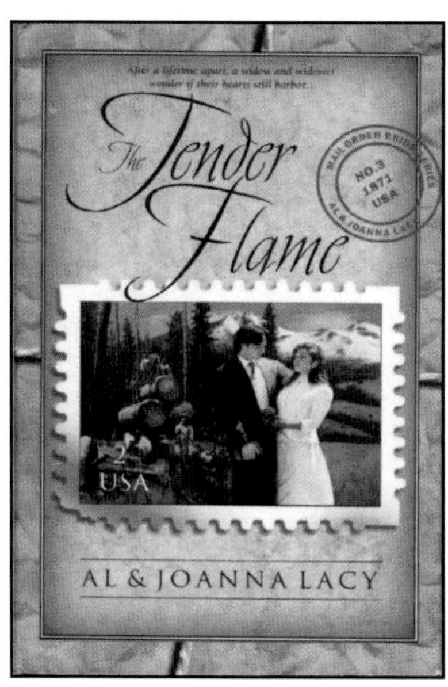

Tender Flame

Romance, Faith, Mexican War

Al & Joanna Lacy Multnomah Publishers (1999)

Grant Smith is 16 and Lydia Reynolds is l4 when they first fall in love. Their "tender flame" continues to burn and, as Grant approaches graduation from West Point, he asks Lydia to many him. Wedding preparations are postponed, however, when President Polk announces war with Mexico and Grant is called into battle. Lydia is grief-stricken when she is informed that Grant has been wounded and believed dead.

But Grant returns two years later, after escaping from a Mexican prison, and is devastated to learn that Lydia has married another. Should he let her know he is alive—or give up his own hopes for happiness?

Captain Meredith Marshall St. James had a West Point education, a general for a father and an attitude that didn't meet with Major Bannister's approval. But if Ace didn't like her attitude, he sure liked everything else about her—which taught him that on the battlefield of love, unconditional surrender is sometimes the only option! [BC]

Al Lacy is an evangelist and author who has written more than 100 Western and historical novels that include the series "Mail Order Bride," "Angel of Mercy," "Journeys of the Stranger," "The Orphan Trains Trilogy," "Hannah of Fort Bridger," and the "Frontier Doctor Trilogy" among others. There are more than three million of their novels in print. **Joanna Lacy,** who had been collaborating with Al for years, is a retired nurse. [3-02]

Mildred's Cadet

Cadet, Romance

Alice King Hamilton T.B. Peterson & Bros (1881)

From the front piece: This is just such a novel as readers, especially the ladies, have long been looking for. It is a light, breezy love story...Mildred, the heroine, is an only daughter. Her father, a wealthy and ambitious Pittsburgher, and her mother, a vain, silly woman desires her to wed a man many years her senior. Of course, Mildred dislikes and despises her venerable suitor. Her parents take her to West Point to pass a few summer weeks, and there she immediately falls in love with a cadet. This brief inkling of the plot is sufficient to show the drift of the tale… [EB]

From the publisher notes: "The authoress, **Alice King Hamilton,** is the wife of a United States Army officer, and has all the details of West Point experiences at her finger ends, indeed, her acquaintance with the innermost details of life at the famous military academy is astonishing. The book is beautifully illustrated with scenes characteristic of the cadets and West Point."

Flirtation on the Hudson (Journey of Cornelia Rose)

Cadet, Romance

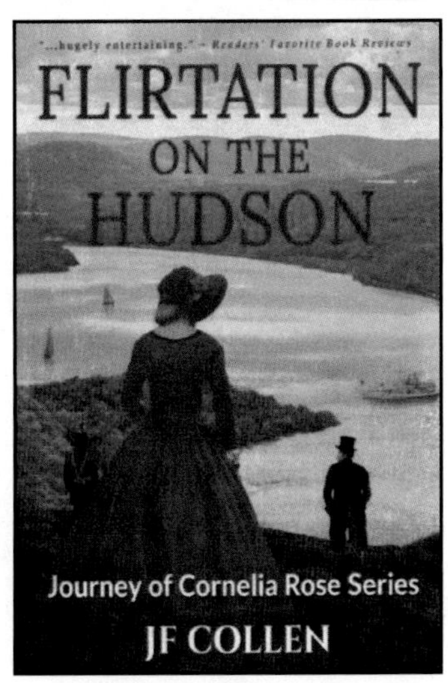

J. F. Collen Evolved Publishing (2019)

Cornelia Rose decides early in life, almost instinctively, not to allow anyone to limit her to the few choices available to women in New York in the 1850s. Marry well and become a proper lady—is that all I can do? She surreptitiously pursues learning 'not meant for young ladies,' and begins the journey to become a midwife.

Flirtations and sexy, Cornelia attracts suitors everywhere she goes. Flooded with invitations after her unofficial debut, her courtships take a dramatic turn when invited to the West Point Military Academy as the guest of a cadet. Will her romantic escapades compromise her choices? Who will decide her future?

Shivers of delight raced through Cornelia's entire body as she thought, "Strolling Flirtation Walk with my escort, unchaperoned? How could this be permitted, much less condemned?" [BC]

Jane Frances Collen has spent years practicing as a lawyer, but always wanted to be writing novels instead of legal briefs. She has written award-winning children's books, though her real love is history. Collen's books depict modern dilemmas in historical settings, with a touch of humor. Much to her husband's dismay, they still live in New York. [3-03]

Won at West Point: A Romance on the Hudson

Romance, Satire, WP Author

Williston Fish Rand McNally & Co. (1883)

Chapter I. Introduces a choice selection of heroes; relates various conversations which go to show the surpassing deference paid to plebes by their superiors; and awakens the interest of the reader.

The Narrator: With no other warning, Gentle Reader, than a friendly admonition to brace up, I introduce you boldly to the cadet mess hall. You will observe that there is some noise, some little confusion. You wish for more silence, and presently you have it, for a youth of majestic appearance rises from the select table near the inner door, and remarks:

"Battalion, at-t-en-t-i-on!"

Narrator: Now you have silence enough and to spare; you long for a cemetery, or the alleged store-that-does-not advertise, to infuse new life into your petrified being. You look at the youth who has risen. He is about to speak. He is the first captain. And you don't know it? What shameful ignorance! See how well he knows it! There is certainly no fact with which he is better acquainted. He has impressed it thoroughly on his own mind and now he desires to impress it on the mind of beholders. To this end he glares down toward the part of the mess hall where "D" company regales itself. Immediately afterward, he glares upon "A" company, at the other end of the hall, and his fell gaze is intended to wither the little fellows in the intermediate companies of "B" and "C". . . . [EB]

Williston Fish (1858–1939) - pen name Fush - attended Oberlin College and West Point, Class of 1881, then spent six years of service in the United States Army. He became a successful Chicago attorney and railroad executive who enjoyed writing. He published 2 novels, and hundreds of poems and stories. His other novel *Short Rations* is included in the "Cadet Experience" chapter. [3-04]

A West Point Wooing: A Victorian Romance

Cadet, Romance

Clara Louise Burnham Houghton, Mifflin (1899)

Excerpt from the book:

Near a window in the library at West Point a young woman was sitting. She held in her hands a book, but her eyes often wandered from the page to the smooth green lawn without, or absently sought the faces in the large paintings which line the dignified room.

In truth the life of a girl at West Point is so far more interesting to her than any effort of the fictionist, little wonder that the spell of the latter is feeble to hold her. She cannot spare time from the engrossing heroes and heroines in her actual surroundings to those who have not the pleasure of her acquaintance.

Of course, there are stars of varying magnitude in the picturesque orbit of the post, and this brown-haired young woman in the library was a bright particular star of the present summer. Even many of the plebes -- those downtrodden, wing-clipped butts of every upper classman's ugly or merry humors knew her face and name. Two of them were in the library now, a forlorn Damon and Pythias, companions whose friendly bond was born of their common misery. [EB]

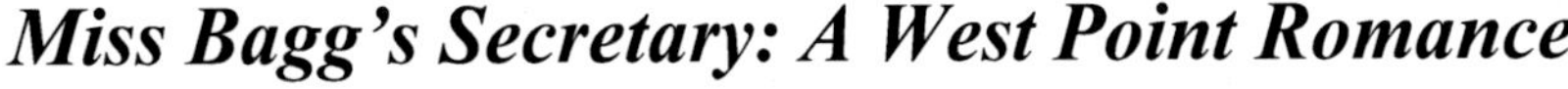

Miss Bagg's Secretary: A West Point Romance

Cadet, Romance

Clara Louise Burnham Houghton, Mifflin (1892)

In New York City, the wealthy, aged, Jotham Bagg passes away wifeless, childless and intestate. Several cousins all had expectations, some more than others. One was Max Van Kirk, a recent graduate of West Point, who was persuaded to resign his commission in anticipation of assuming the role of managing Mr. Bagg's affairs.

Alas, not so. The lawyer executor of the estate determined that the spinster daughter of Mr. Bagg's brother was to inherit the lot, leaving others very unhappily out in the cold. Now, Miss Lydia Bagg, living outside of Boston in very humble circumstances, was largely unknown to the rest of the family. She was stunned and totally unprepared to assume the mantle of enormous wealth.

Max Van Kirk takes the "high road" with no expectations and escorts Miss Bagg to New York City to meet with the executor -- after arranging with great effort -- that Lydia had garments more suited to the big city. Miss Bagg moves into Jotham's mansion and not knowing who else to trust, persuades Max to manage her affairs -- and become her Secretary. Not having other prospects, the young man assents to the shock of the other relatives, but with the great approval of her lawyer/executor.

Now romance ensues (not between Miss Bagg and Max), but with another woman enticing the very eligible Max. It reaches a climax during a visit to West Point to take in the scenery and the cadet's summer encampment on the Plain. Miss Bagg is fascinated with West Point and pays for everyone to stay at the Cozzen's Hotel on the Point for several weeks. In the end, true love triumphs, and Lydia extends great generosity to the family. [EB]

Clara Louise Burnham wrote 26 novels between the years 1881 and 1925. Three of these were Christian Science themed fiction: *The Right Princess* (1902), *Jewel* (1903), and *The Leaven of Love* (1908) are often referred to as her "Christian Science trilogy." Clara's short stories and novels were widely read, and several of her books were adapted for stage and screen. [3-05]

As a Soldier Would

Romance, Mystery Intrigue

APUSA Broadway Publishing Co. (1911)

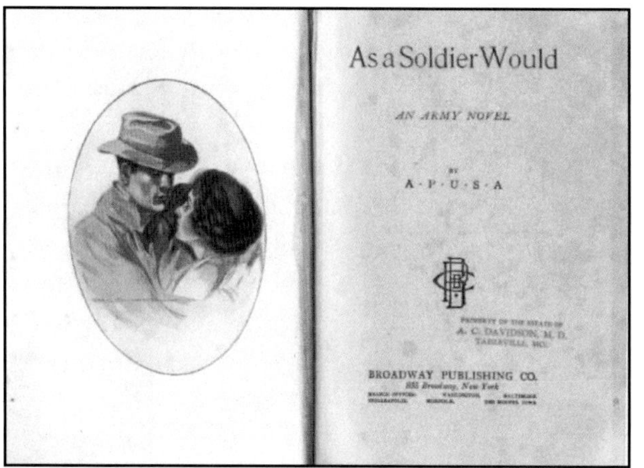

After several summers apart, three Class of 1879 graduates reunite at a resort in New York State. Romance is encountered as well as scoundrels out to upset their respective courtships. The story continues with a visit to West Point for the end of the summer encampment and the final summer hop. The course of true love does not run smoothly for Lt. Vorne. He overcomes a father's disfavor with his heroic actions in New York City and Idaho. [EB]

No authors were identified in this anthology of stories.

Chevrons: A Story of West Point

Cadet, Romance

Bertha Lippincott J.B. Lippincott (1901)

Table of Contents

Bertha H. Lippincott Coles (1880–1963) was a Philadelphia socialite who devoted much of her time to caring for off-duty and wounded or convalescing soldiers. She was one of the founders of the United Service Club, a recreational club offering lodging to soldiers on leave, and was very active in related organizations. [3-06]

The Underside of Things

Romance, Officer Wife, Army Life

Lilian Bell Harper Brothers (1896)

Table of contents

Lilian Bell was the pen name for Mrs. Arthur Hoyt Bogue (1867–1929). She was an American novelist and travel writer. Her works included *The Love Affairs of an Old Maid, At Home with Jardines*, *Hope Loring*, *Abroad with the Jimmies*, *The Interference of Patricia*, and *The Lilian Bell Birthday Book.* [3-07]

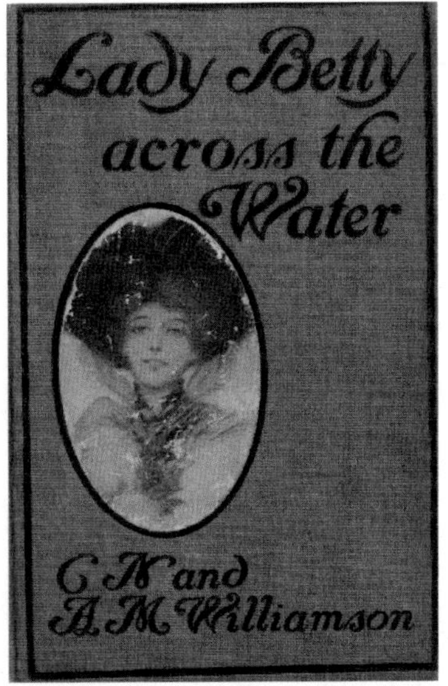

Lady Betty Across the Water

Youth, Visitor, Cadet

C.N. Williamson & A. M. McClure Phillips & Co. (1906)

Lady Betty, a young English woman is invited to visit America with her aunts. One of the stops is at West Point. She has a delightful ride up the Hudson, often commenting on strange American customs, but upon her arrival at West Point:

"I was a great deal more interested in the youths, who were the first classmen, I was told, and would be second lieutenants next year.

I never could take much interest in Eton boys, the few have seen, for they look such children that one would be positively ashamed to bother with them; but the Point cadets (though one couldn't exactly take them seriously like regularly grown-up men, perhaps) fascinated me from the very first glance.... They looked as if they thought a lot of themselves, and the girls they were with had the air encouraging them to think it. I wondered what kind things they said to girls and secretly longed to find out.

It seems that in summer the cadets leave their barracks and go into camp, which is a time of year that the girls visit West Point and those whose fathers are there, like very much. We had a glimpse of them from the long street of the officers' quarters; and we had visited a few technical things in which I was polite to show that I was hardly interested, we strolled over to where we could see the little white pyramids gleaming under the Stars and Stripes. I had been afraid that all the cadets would have gone away to Flirtation Walk, with girls, but to my joy there were plenty left in camp. On chairs under the trees two or three ladies were sitting with some white-butterfly girls; and a crowd of cadets were talking to them.

"There's a great pal of mine, Mrs. Laurence," Captain Collingwood said, "She would love to know Lady Betty. Do you mind if I introduce you to each other?"

I replied that I should be delighted to meet Mrs. Laurence, and a few sample cadets, if any could be provided for the consumption of an enquiring British tourist. Mrs. Laurence was delightful and kind. We chatted for a bit responding to the questions which Americans all seem to have about England. Then she introduced me to five cadets.

I was terrified for a minute, because until I left home my entire (youthful) male experience consisted of one brother, three cousins, and two curates, dealt with separately with long sleepy intervals between. I began to wonder how I could possibly manage five tall youths all at once, and to rack my brains for the right kind of conversation; but before I should have had time to say "knife" to a curate, I found myself chatting away with these cadets as if I had grown up with them. I never once stopped to think what I should say next, and neither did they."

The ensuing tour and evening hop were a grand success for Lady Betty:

"Although I didn't get to bed till after two, I was up early next morning, because I had promised my best cadets that I would be at morning parade, or whatever they call it, to say good-bye. Sally went with me, and it was quite an affecting parting. I shall never forget those dear boys if I live to be a hundred, though I can't remember any of their names, as after all I lost the card I meant to keep always." [EB]

British authors **Charles Norris (C.N.) Williamson and his wife Alice** collaborated on many novels and eventually films before the Great War. She did most of the writing, apparently. They used West Point as a background in another novel in this collection - *A Soldier of the Legion,* which is included in the chapter, "Soldiers of Fortune, Paladins, Miscreants & Rogues." [3-08]

A Girl of the Guard Line

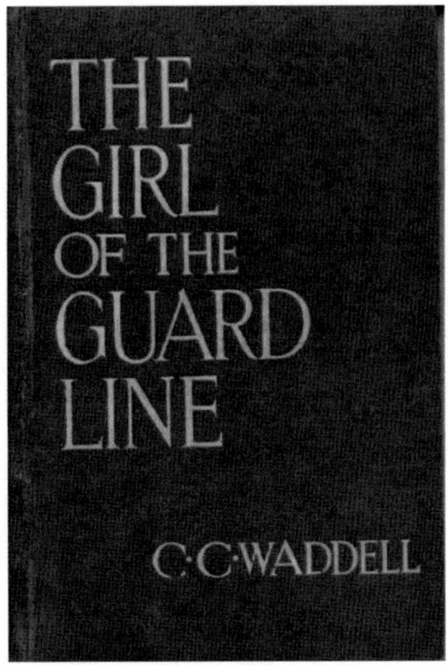

Cadet, Romance

Charles Cary Waddell Yard & Co (1915)

Chapter 1: At Post Number Three

"Halt! Who's there?"

The challenge tore sharply through the August night, and Burr Beverly, West Pointer, bringing his rifle to a sudden "port," peered searchingly up the road that skirted the northern edge of the cadet encampment.

Unless he were greatly mistaken, he had spied a moment before, a stealthy figure flitting almost shadow-like among the trees along this forbidden way which serpentines out past Kosciusko's monument and thence around the brow of the promontory in the rear of the tented Corps. Ah! There it was again.

"Halt! Who's there?"

A second time, and even more emphatically, Beverly voiced his challenge; but as before there was no response. Yet, as he strained his eyes through the darkness, he caught once more that movement of a furtive advance. . . .

290 pages later...

...[Burr] was hardly startled to see a graceful, slender figure making its way toward him through the trees. Nadia was coming in search of him. Playfully, the lieutenant threw his walking stick to a "port." "Halt! Who's there?" he challenged.

But this time she did not seek to run away. Straight ahead she came and, after a little mock struggle between them, drew the walking stick out of his hands. "But I have the countersign this time," she announced triumphantly.

"Give it, then."

"Well, close your eyes," she commanded, and raising herself on tiptoe, kissed him.

"You are right, sweetheart," murmured Beverly, catching her in his arms. "That is a countersign that will always pass you anywhere that I have power to let you go."

"Ah!" Her musical laugh rippled out. "That is no news to me, Señor. I discovered it that night two months ago, the very first time you ever challenged me." [EB]

Charles Carey Waddell (1868–1930) graduated from Marietta College (OH) then spent the first half of his career as a newspaper reporter, editor, then owner, publisher, and eventually mayor in Chillicothe, OH. Waddell then moved to New York City and took up writing, contributing more than 400 serial "adventure" stories and novelettes to various magazines, often collaborating with his wife and sister. [3-09]

Flirtation Walk

Cadet, Romance

Siri Mitchell Bethany House (2016)

Lucinda Pennyworth, the daughter of a con man, is trying her best to leave her father's sordid past behind her. When he dies unexpectedly, she takes the opportunity to move to West Point to live with her aunt, ready to take on a new life and determined to marry a respectable man, a West Point cadet, to impress her relatives.

Seth Westcott, a cadet at the academy, is proud to be at the top of his senior class. But when his mother dies and his sister loses their inheritance to a swindler, Seth wants nothing more than to head West to track down the con man. But the army will only send the cadets at the bottom of the class to the frontier. . .which leaves Seth with some tough choices.

When a woman trying her best to be good meets a man determined to be anything but, can there be hope for love, or will two lonely hearts be condemned to casual flirtation? [EB]

Siri L. Mitchell writes romantic, general, and historical fiction; she has also used a pen name (Iris Anthony) to write some of her work. She has lived all over the world (places like Tokyo and Paris) because she is a military spouse. She graduated from University of Washington, getting her business degree, and has worked in various levels of government. Sixteen of her novels have been published to date. [3-10]

"A Soldier's Honor"

Sports, Romance, Intrigue, Pulp Fiction

Captain S. S. Harrington Argosy Magazine (October 1917)

In 1916 Kerr Mosely had left West Point and his football career to work with his brother on an engineering contract in China. The political intrigue was all-consuming involving his enticement by a scandalous woman, then he was grievously injured when an earthquake collapsed his home.

"Farewell now to any hopes of returning to West Point; Farewell, likewise, to the continuance of his career in China. Worse than all, farewell to the dream of ever winning Marian Long. He had seen her swift recoil at the revelation of Prince Chu, the look of aversion and contempt with which she regarded him. He would never be able to convince her that he acted innocently in the premises; She would always believe him a cheat and a deceiver."

November again, and Thanksgiving time. A crowd at the Polo Grounds in New York which, for color and size and tensity of excitement and official recognition, can be matched on no other occasion. It's the annual football contest between the Army and Navy.

But that day things were going hard with the Army. Like an irresistible wave the Navy line had crashed into them again and again to beat them back, and now to add to the climax of a series of misfortunes, Ventable, the chief dependence of West Point, was so seriously injured just as the first half was ending that he had to be ordered out of the game. The score stood 15 – 0 in favor of the Navy. Already the cold, chilling sense of certain defeat had gripped the ranks of gray.... Then some inspired soul on the Army side of the field suddenly raised the cry: "Mosely! Mosely Give us Mosely." In an instant it was taken up all over the grounds. Ten thousand voices were chanting it, twenty thousand feet were stamping the stands. . . . Then something amazing happens. [EB]

Captain S. S. Harrington is almost certainly a pseudo name. His stories appeared in several issues of Argosy from 1912 to 1925. Otherwise, no bibliographical information could be found.

"West Point Girl"

Cadet, Romance, Pulp Fiction

Ruth Anderson Thrilling Love Magazine (May 1933)

Colonel Jimmy laughed.

"Carolyn's pet cadets will be here any minute. They clutter up this place every chance they get and pour out their troubles to a listening ear. Since Carol's outgrown her sweetheart of the army days, she has become the mother-confessor."

Mrs. Jimmie made a face at him.

Thoughtfully, Faith repaired her make-up and brushed the golden helmet of hair that cascaded into soft ringlets at the base of her neck. She didn't change her dress. It was very effective, a slimly tailored thing of black wool, emphasized by white galyak. Looking in the mirror she saw herself as she hoped a pair of very blue eyes would see her, a slender poster-like figure of black and white and gold.

She ran lightly down to the living room from which came the sound of voices. Several uniformed young men stood at attention. With a sense of disappointment, Faith saw that Dixie Crane was not among the cadets. [EB]

Ruth Anderson wrote romantic stories for several pulp fiction magazines in the 1930's including *Thrilling Love* and *Thrilling Ranch Stories*.

Summer of Dreams

Cadet, Romance

Elizabeth Camden Bethany House (2016)

Evelyn White, the daughter of a powerful army general, dreams of attending college and vows she will never marry a man in uniform. . . which is why West Point cadet Clyde Brixton presents a problem. Clyde's brilliance in the new field of electrical power has him poised for a promising career in the Army's Corps of Engineers, but his penchant for racking up demerits threatens his chances for graduation. Evelyn and Clyde feel instant attraction toward one another as they spend one magical summer together. As their lives become more entwined, their friend Romulus's begins to come undone. When faced with helping Romulus at the expense of his own future, which one will Clyde choose? And when nothing turns out the way Evelyn planned, where will that leave her own future? [BC]

Elizabeth Camden is a research librarian at a small college in central Florida. Her fascination with history and love of literature led her to write inspirational fiction. Her eighteen novels (so far) have won the coveted RITA and Christy Awards. Elizabeth has published articles for academic publications and is the author of four nonfiction history books. [3-11]

No author depicted romance at West Point better than Janet Lambert. She wrote several series of novels about Army families and their children's coming of age. Some of the very popular Penny Parrish books are presented below.

Star Spangled Summer

Army Life, Romance

Janet Lambert E.P Dutton (1941)

Carrol Houghton, charming, lonely daughter of a wealthy eastern businessman goes to visit her friend Penny Parrish at Fort Arden in Kansas. Never has Carrol enjoyed herself so! She cannot believe there actually are parents like Major and Mrs. Parrish.

Swiftly, from one gay diversion to another, moves this appealing story. There is a scavenger hunt, a junior hop, a picnic, and best of all a horse show that brings special thrills to the Parrish family. Then Penny's great "treat" for Carrol—a visit from no less person than the austere Mr. Houghton himself -- threatens to spoil everything, but actually adds the crowning touch to this truly star-spangled summer. [DJ]

Dreams of Glory

Army Life, Romance, Cadet

Janet Lambert Grosset & Dunlap (1942)

Here again is another story of the adventures of the irrepressible Penny Parrish and her delightful family.

By one of those happy accidents best known to fiction, Major Parrish has been transferred from Fort Arden, Kansas to West Point, where all concerned can keep an eye on David, the family's cadet. And happily, Penny's friend Carrol Houghton lives in an enormous barn of a place not far up the river from the Point. So it is not surprising that the two girls are together constantly.

There's excitement from the very beginning when the Parrishes visit the Houghtons at their New York penthouse and attend the Army-Notre Dame football game. Penny -- who can get herself into more jams than anyone else -- gets herself lost in the crowd, and by chance meets a famous actress. This adventure definitely decides Penny on a career in the theater. And it does seem that this time Penny's mind is really made up!

There's near tragedy for Penny's brother David, which luckily ends happily. But besides that the winter for Penny is a delicious whirl of hops at the Point, a trip to Florida with the Houghtons, and at last June week – and romance. [DJ]

Glory Be

Romance

Janet Lambert Grosset & Dunlap (1943)

In GLORY BE! Penny and her friend Carol encounter more serious grown-up problems, but they never lose any of their charm, wit, and sense of excitement with life.

The story opens with Penny's eighteenth birthday party, which is followed by a shopping trip into New York with Carol. The carefree time of the girls is interrupted, however, by the tragedy of Pearl Harbor. From that fateful day, events move fast for the Parrish and Houghton families. The lives of the girls are suddenly transformed and they need all the character and courage they have built up to face the uncertainties and heartbreaks that war brings. With a unique understanding of a young girl's heart, Janet Lambert shows how the girls meet tragedy and come through with a deeper maturity. [DJ]

Miss America

Cadet, Romance, Army Life

Janet Lambert Grosset & Dunlap (1951)

Tippy is Penny Parrish's younger sister.

A year in another country can be a very, very long time, and Tippy Parrish is not at all sure she is going to like the changes time has wrought on this side of the Atlantic.

For one thing, pretty clothes cost much more than they did a year ago. And people have changed too: Bobby, unpredictable brother Bobby, wants to leave West Point to go into advertising; and Alice Jordon, Tippy's beloved "Alcie," seems just a shade distant, with a secret she doesn't care to share. But most painful of all to Tippy is that her dear Peter Jordon keeps getting lost behind a smoke screen of memories raised by handsome Lieutenant Ken Prescott whom she left behind in Germany. Tippy is frankly bewildered. Then out of a clear sky, war in Korea looms, and the entire Parrish clan is forced into making some pretty important decisions. [DJ]

Don't Cry Little Girl

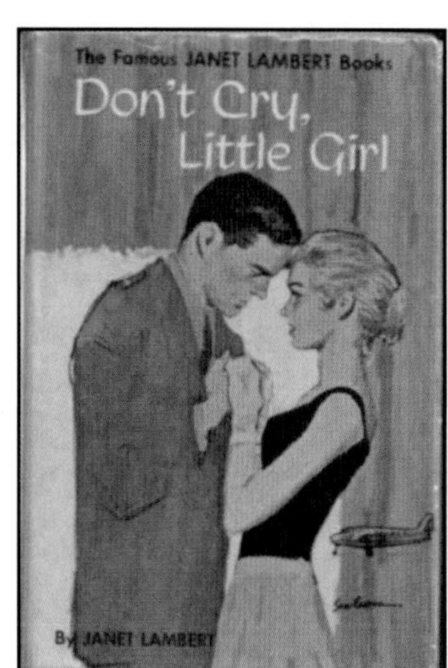

Officer Wife, Army Life, Romance

Janet Lambert   Grosset & Dunlap (1952)

WHILE TIPPY PARRISH eagerly awaited the arrival of Ken Prescott, she dreamed of love and marriage. And when she found his sentiments to be the same as hers, her happiness bubbled over.

Then, quite suddenly, Ken's leave was cancelled. With a heavy heart, Tippy put away the lovely tablecloth she had purchased for their game of make-believe at being married.

As Tippy bravely saw Ken off to Korea on the morning plane, she gave some serious thought to the months that lay ahead. She would learn how to knit, to sew, and to cook, against the day when they would be reunited once again. She would write him regularly, and look forward to receiving his precious letters. Busy with school -- with comforting Peter Jordon and the weekly hops at West Point -- time did pass. But one day, the world almost came to an end for Tippy, and all her hopes were shattered. . . . [DJ]

That's My Girl

Cadet, Romance

Janet Lambert   New York, Dutton (1964)

Parri is convinced that if her cousin Davy would just confide in her she could help him solve all his problems. Davy, who is now a plebe at West Point, is just as convinced that interference by Parri is the last thing he needs.

Davy's roommate is a moody, unhappy young man named John Robinson, the son of a United States senator. Davy has just about given up trying to understand John, but when John decides to go AWOL, Davy feels that it is his duty to stop him from making a mistake that could ruin his life.

And to Davy's amazement, who should come along at exactly the right moment, but Parri proves her usefulness in other ways, and Davy begins to think that his young cousin is not so bad after all.

Parri, of course, has her own active life, playing a leading role in the high school play, which her producer-father, Josh MacDonald, directs. She attends a West Point plebe dance, and is becoming quite the budding belle. [DJ]

Candy Kane

Army Life, Romance

Janet Lambert E.P. Dutton & Co. (1943)

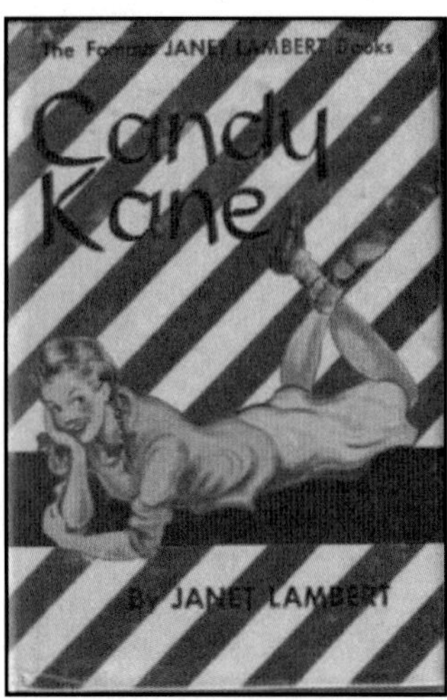

Candy wasn't as pretty as her sister Leigh, but she had a wistful little combination of something else in her make-up that made people love her and trust her and want her to be around. At Fort Benning, for instance, where Major Kane was stationed, Candy was absolutely essential to the success of every party or outing. Leigh and Mother, however, were of another stripe, and made the going rather difficult for everyone . . .especially for a certain young soldier. Later on, in fact, when it was much too late, they discovered their mistake and from a distance Candy could smile her quiet, small, happy smile. [DJ]

Janet Lambert (1893–1973) was an actress before marrying and authoring 54 young-adult fiction titles for girls from 1941 to 1969. Lambert's life experience as an Army wife provided the background and settings for many of her books. Lambert's best known works are the Penny and Tippy Parrish series, which focused on the lives and coming-of-age choices of the wives and children of U.S. Army officers during World War II and the Korean War-era. While West Point figures appear frequently in the lives of her characters, her husband did not attend West Point, gaining his officer training through the National Guard and Army specialty schools. [3-12]

West Point Nurse

Romance, Cadet

Virginia B. McDonnell, RN McFadden-Darnell (1965)

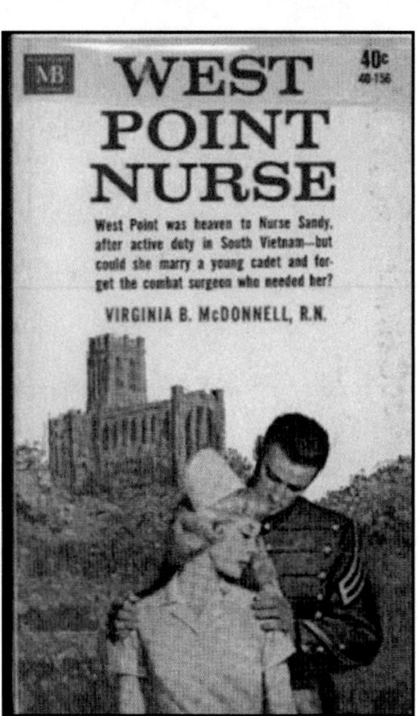

ONE LAST DANCE . . .

"You have it all wrong," Cadet Bob Thompson told Nurse Sandy as they danced at a West Point hop. "I have no intention of leaving the Army—ever!"

"But ever since you were a little boy, your father has hoped you would practice medicine with him," Sandy protested.

The last dance was over! Had she turned Bob against her? Would she ever see him again? She knew she was in love with the headstrong cadet, the son of the man she had promised to marry! [BC]

This book is also included in the chapter "Army Medical Service Corps" with author biography.

Weekends at West Point

Of course, there were untold numbers of young women who journeyed to West Point for the Saturday night "Hops," to enjoy the pageantry, and meet cadets.

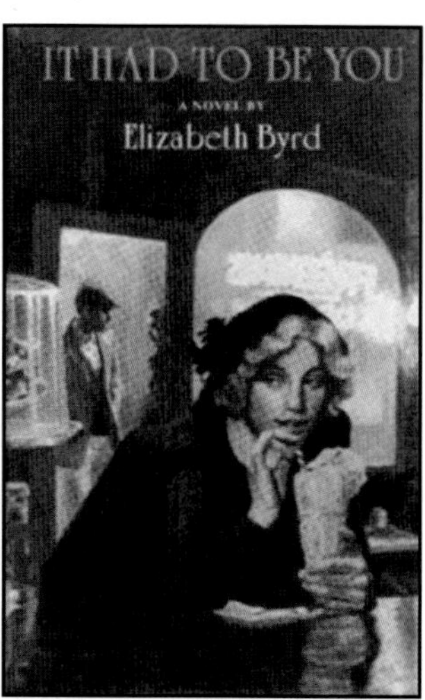

It Had to Be You

Romance, Visitor, Cadet

Elizabeth Byrd Viking Juvenile (1982)

Only a romantic sixteen-year-old like Kitty Craig could see New York City during the Depression through rose-colored glasses! Buoyant and irrepressible, Kitty tells of her only dream: being Johnny Aiken's girl. Nothing—including an exciting weekend at West Point could make her forget that it had to be handsome and aloof Johnny who won her heart. [DJ]

Elizabeth Byrd (1912–1989) was an American radio journalist, literary agent, and author. Her main body of work is historical fiction, and her most successful novel is *Immortal Queen,* a historical romance about Mary, Queen of Scots. Nine of her thirteen novels were published while she was living in Scotland. [3-13]

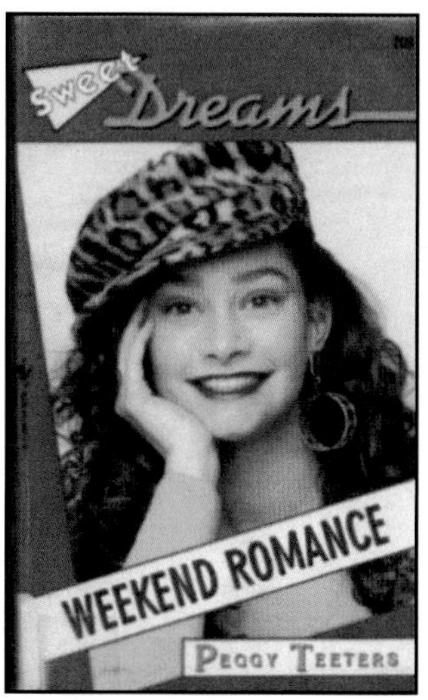

Weekend Romance

Romance, Visitor, Cadet

Peggy Teeters Bantam Books (1995)

"Army brat" Katie O'Connor has always dreamed of a romantic weekend at West Point. But when her older brother, a plebe at the Point, arranges a date for Katie with his roommate, she hesitates, thinking of Scott McA1lister, her boyfriend at home. But Katie's friend Melissa convinces her that a West Point weekend isn't really a date — it's an event. She's sure Scott will understand...won't he? [BC]

Peggy Teeters (1919–2011) authored "how to" books for beginning writers, and this one in the Sweet Dreams Series. The series had over 230 numbered stand-alone young adult romance novels that were published from 1981 through to 1996. Each teen novel dealt with the usual high school drama and romance; first dates, first love, conflicts, etc. Cover designs were real photographs using models that best depict how the heroine of the novel looks. [3-14]

"Advice to the Ladies Who Come Up in June…"

To marry or not to marry—that is a question which faces many cadets and their femmes. On the part of the cadet, he is usually overwhelmed with all sorts of advice from fellow members of the Corps, and from officers telling him what he should do and what he should not do. On one side, they point out to him the heavy responsibilities of marrying a girl, taking her out of her home environment, and trying to live on a rather small Army salary while he is getting established in a profession. On the other side, even the severest and most confirmed non-marrying adviser has little argument with a man who has fallen in love.

If a romance has reached this stage, no one is going to heed the advice anyway. And if it's "really love," the marriage will overcome the material obstacles that will confront young people in their early years together—either in civilian life or in the service. But there are some considerations which a girl should honestly face when she considers a life in the service at the side of her husband who has dedicated himself to a career in the Army. The Army life is a happy one and is generally one of great contentment if a young woman can readily make the few adjustments that such a life requires.

Perhaps the most difficult problem for the civilian girl who may have lived most of her life in a closely knit community and circle of friends is the problem of picking up every two, three, or four years and moving her family to another station.

But when the orders come, and all has been done that can be done, they must be obeyed, which may mean that the Army wife is left with the children and a move to make without the aid and assistance of her husband. It is seldom a move completely on her own even in these circumstances, for the assistance of the Quartermaster and "the outfit" is usually at hand.

Now the last thing on your mind when you are young and enjoying the hops at West Point and the happy days at Camp Buckner, is retirement. But the rich and happy associations of an Army life can always be looked back upon with enjoyment and fondness. Financially, the Army retirement is an annuity which an Army family can look forward to with some measure of comfort.

From **Mary Quayle Bradley**, wife of General of the Armies Omar Bradley.
Pointer Magazine April 18, 1952

And here is one very young gal who came up to West Point in June for her uncle's graduation and wedding.

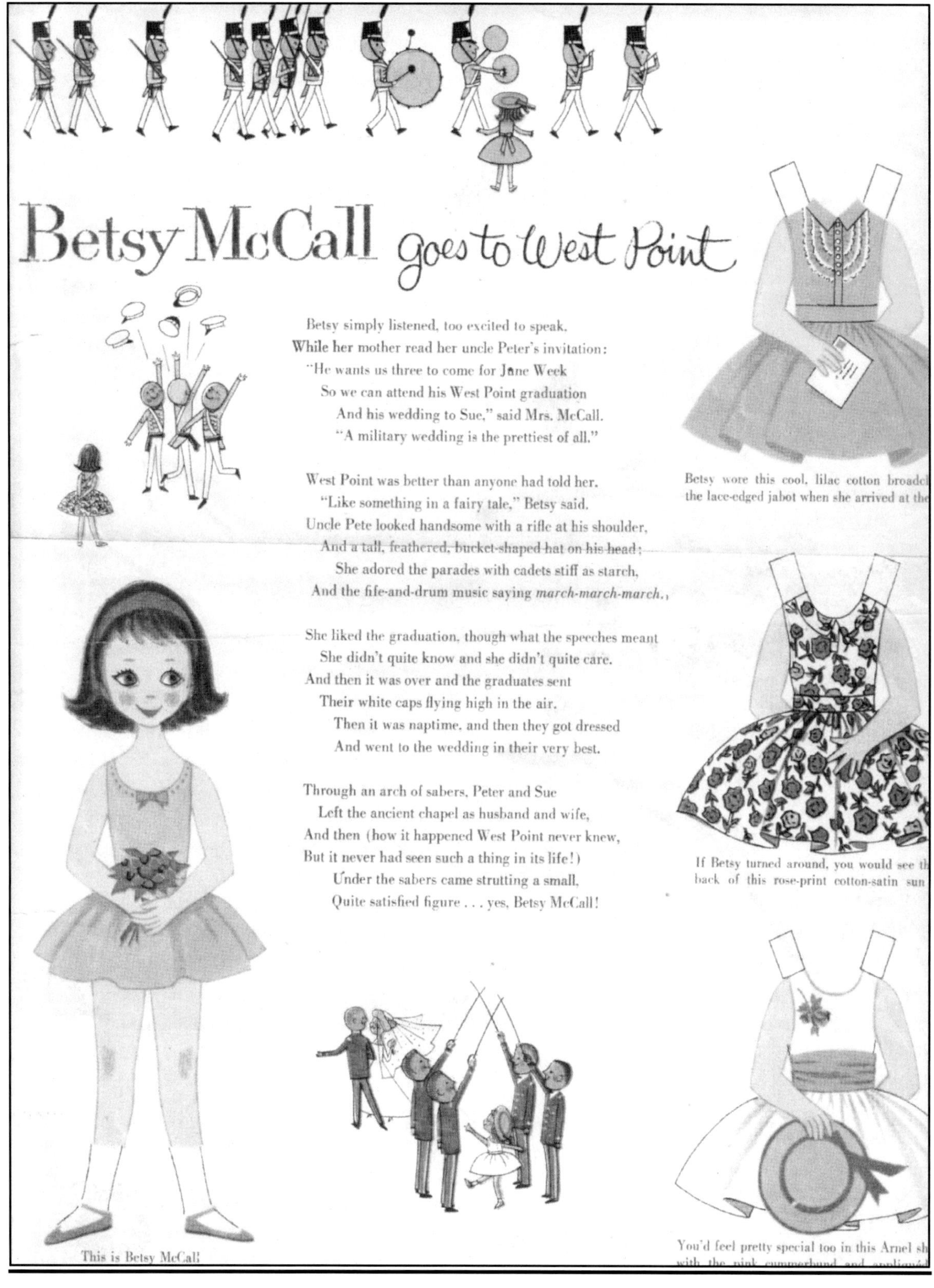
Betsy McCall goes to West Point

Betsy simply listened, too excited to speak,
While her mother read her uncle Peter's invitation:
"He wants us three to come for June Week
So we can attend his West Point graduation
And his wedding to Sue," said Mrs. McCall.
"A military wedding is the prettiest of all."

West Point was better than anyone had told her.
"Like something in a fairy tale," Betsy said.
Uncle Pete looked handsome with a rifle at his shoulder,
And a tall, feathered, bucket-shaped hat on his head;
She adored the parades with cadets stiff as starch,
And the fife-and-drum music saying march-march-march.

She liked the graduation, though what the speeches meant
She didn't quite know and she didn't quite care.
And then it was over and the graduates sent
Their white caps flying high in the air.
Then it was naptime, and then they got dressed
And went to the wedding in their very best.

Through an arch of sabers, Peter and Sue
Left the ancient chapel as husband and wife,
And then (how it happened West Point never knew,
But it never had seen such a thing in its life!)
Under the sabers came strutting a small,
Quite satisfied figure . . . yes, Betsy McCall!

Betsy wore this cool, lilac cotton broadc
the lace-edged jabot when she arrived at th

If Betsy turned around, you would see t
back of this rose-print cotton-satin sun

You'd feel pretty special too in this Arnel s

This is Betsy McCall

West Pointer romances certainly do not conclude with June week. Here are a few involving serving West Point graduates.

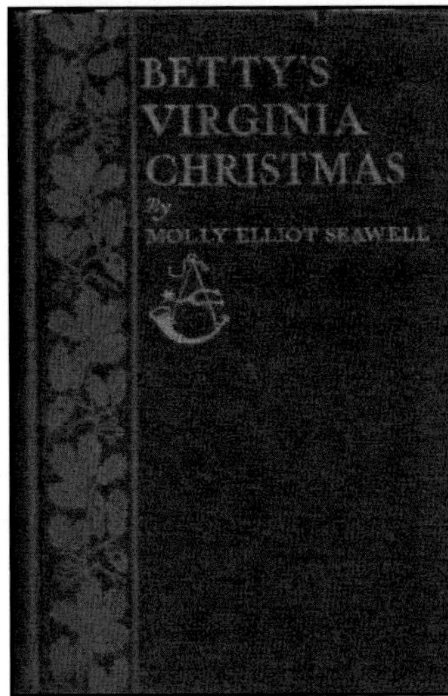

Betty's Virginia Christmas

Romance

Molly Elliott Seawell J.B. Lippincott (1914)

In the decade following the Civil War, Betty Beverly, a belle of 20, lives with her elderly grandfather and two servants at the Holly House cottage near the Tidewater region of Virginia. Up the road a mile is their former home - the Rose Hall plantation. Betty's father and grandfather, West Point graduates, fought with the Confederacy during the war in which her father perished. In the hard-times that followed, the Beverly's were forced to sell Rose Hall and locate to the modest cottage. Despite living in genteel poverty, Betty is a cheerful coquettish lass enjoying the many picnics, parties, and fox hunts of her peers.

The new owners of Rose Hall are a wealthy northern family who are rarely in residence. However, shortly before Christmas, their son, West Pointer Lt. John Hope Fortescue pays visit to Holly House and manages to save Betty from a nasty fall while she was hanging Christmas decorations from the rafters. Fortescue was there to request permission for a group of his soldiers to camp nearby in the Beverly's woods that Spring while conducting a survey for a fort to be built some distance down the river. Old Colonel Beverly, though resentful of the Fortescues, had no grudge against Union soldiers and was rather taken by the handsome lieutenant. He gave permission while rejecting any form of compensation. Listening to all this, Betty was hoping to at least acquire funds for a new gown or two.

Fortescue received invites to the Christmas Eve ball at a nearby plantation as well as the traditional Christmas fox hunt. Betty is an accomplished rider, but the Beverly's have no suitable mount for the hunt. Fortesque comes to the rescue with a very capable horse form his father's stables. And the romance ensues with assorted advances and retreat. . . .

It is a delightfully cheerful tale of Virginia country life circa 1880. There's a sequel with Betty some years later, married to now Col. Foretescue, as they weather a winter at cavalry post, Fort Blizzard, in the far Northwest. [EB]

Molly Elliott Seawell (1860–1916) grew up on a Virginia plantation, taking up writing at the age of twenty. She was widely read in her time and, at the beginning of the 20th century, was included in standard reference works on American writers. Her literary production included forty books of fiction, collected short fiction, non-fiction, and numerous political columns from Washington for New York dailies and essays. [3-15]

Beyond the Cloud

Romance, Officer, Aviation

Emilie Loring Bantam Books (1964)

When Delight Tremaine joined her brother in an Alaskan air base, she was warned that the young officers there were starving for the company of an attractive girl. She promised to just be "Best Friends with all of them." But she did not reckon meeting Lt. Bill Mason, so handsome and yet so maddeningly aloof. Neither did she expect to meet Captain Steele, who was hard as his name. Delight suspected that the hatred between these two West Pointers was deep. Was it a girl? Was it a passed up promotion? [BC]

Emilie Loring (1864–1951) was a prolific American author of romance novels. She began writing in 1914 when she was 50 years old until she passed away in 1951. Much of her work was published posthumously by her sons who had her unfinished material completed by another author. [3-16]

Illusive Lover

WP Female, Romance, General Officer

Jo Calloway Dell Publishing Co (1983)

An officer - and a lady - West Point graduate Susan Vance was determined to do her duty. But she would not succumb to her dashing new Conmmander in Chief.

First the playboy general promoted her to the rank of major; now he claimed her as his own. General Beau Valentine was deflnitaly out of order when he took her in his arms. She tried to say no, but he invaded her heart with a single incendiary kiss. It was a war of wills, a call to arms, passionate combat of the most dangerous kind. She thought she knew the enemy and could outmaneuver him in his own territory—until she discovered the traitor within. [BC]

Jo Calloway authored 22 romance novels in the 1980s. It may have been a pseudomym used by the publisher Dell Books. [3-17]

Major Attraction

WP Female, Romance

Roz Denny Fox Harlequin Books (2000)

TOP GUN MEETS HIS MATCH!

Major Ace Bannister hadn't survived life on the mean streets of Texas or worked his way up through the ranks by being a "softie." No, it had been hard work and discipline that had gotten him where he was today, and he wasn't about to change -- not even for an alluring and sexy female captain who believed in a "new" army.

> Captain Meredith Marshall St. James had a West Point education, a general for a father and an attitude that didn't meet with Major Bannister's approval. But if Ace didn't like her attitude, he sure liked everything else about her—which taught him that on the battlefield of love, unconditional surrender is sometimes the only option! [BC]

A secretary by trade, **Roz Denny Fox** (1939–) began her writing career in 1986 by free-lancing a series of self-help articles. She sold a short story to a magazine in 1987. After much prodding from her then high school age daughter, Roz tried her hand at writing a contemporary romance. Roz began writing full-time in 1995. She has had dozens published through 2017. [3-18]

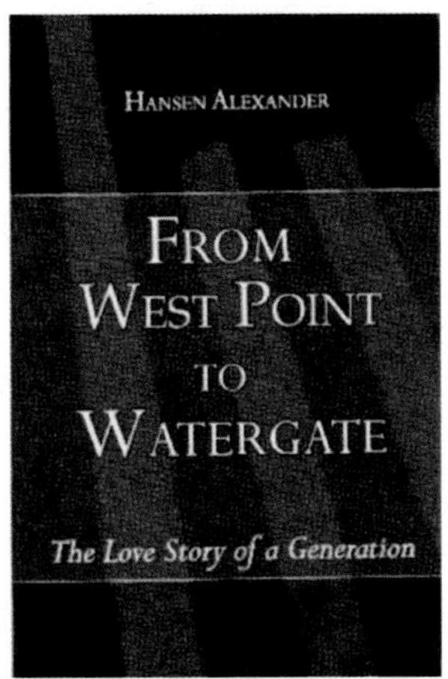

From West Point to Watergate: The Love Story of a Generation

Romance, Sports, Vietnam

Alexander Hansen PublishAmerica (2006)

Wayne Riley must overcome the haunting failures of his cursed family. His great great grandfather and Civil War veteran lost a chance to play major league baseball when he broke his leg in a saloon brawl. His uncle lasted exactly sixty-nine days with the Boston Red Sox. His father was kicked out of West Point for cheating and was killed by his wife in a murder-suicide for his adultery. Wayne is groomed by his beloved grandfather to atone for the family's honor, to go to West Point, play football and become a general. He makes a good start. He becomes the leading rusher in Army football history and leads a helicopter squadron in Vietnam.

But then the high promise of youth becomes unraveled. He is seriously wounded in Vietnam, eroding his confidence and diminishing the possibility that he could return to football as an alternative career. He marries badly and suffers a traumatic divorce, which includes his wife's adultery and a public accusation that he is a homosexual. He gets back with his first love, Lynn Black, a graduate of New York Law School who is elected to Congress. But then her breast cancer is discovered just as she is wrestling with the possible impeachment of President Nixon as a member of the House Judiciary Committee.

The novel portrays the great social changes of the time, particularly the changed role of women. Wayne's body heals slowly and he begins the painful and difficult comeback to play professional football after he quits the Army in frustration. He plays a major role in the Super Bowl for the Washington Redskins as the game against the Kansas City Chiefs moves to overtime and the sun sets over Miami's ancient Orange Bowl. [DJ]

Alexander Hansen (1953–2020) was an attorney and writer, penning over a dozen reference books, biographies, and novels. He also edited The Middle Class Review, a literary journal, with his wife and published several pieces within the Florida Times-Union newspaper. [3-19]

The Mayor's Daughter

Cadet, Romance, Crime

Mary Alice Gernert iUniverse, Inc. (2012)

Baby Boomers Beware...The book is pure fiction. The author pulls out every stop to keep the reader turning pages with loads of love, hate, desire, revenge, jealousy, and passion. Background music is supplied by the Great Depression, World War II, Washington Politics during Harry Truman's Administration, with Bess and Margaret in the White House, and most importantly, West Point's challenges for the cadets and their sweethearts.

It was a rough ride for Laura Jackson and Bill Bentley who fell in love in college. They knew they were meant for each other. She was the girl of his dreams. She believed that intercourse would take place after the wedding bells sounded loud and clear. He wanted her for his wife, his partner for life.

Their love was secure until Bill's serious problems at West Point interfered with writing to Laura, who was still a student at Brown State University. The mistake Laura made was worse. It was a deadly one that changed everything. They had to go in different directions. The bright flame of love in their hearts was reduced to embers, but it refused to die.

Years later, when both were married to others, they were blackmailed and falsely accused of infidelity and murder. They were forced to work together with the police in order to catch the criminals red-handed. [BC]

Mary Alice Gernert (1917–2013) attended Bowling Green State University. While there, she met and fell in love with Bill Gernert a cadet at West Point. They married on his graduation day in 1942. As he moved from pilot training to B-24 training she made the first few of the 27 moves during his 28 year Air Force career. Mary Alice wrote children's books as a young mother and published several semi-autobiographical novels while in her nineties including this novel shortly before her death. [3-20]

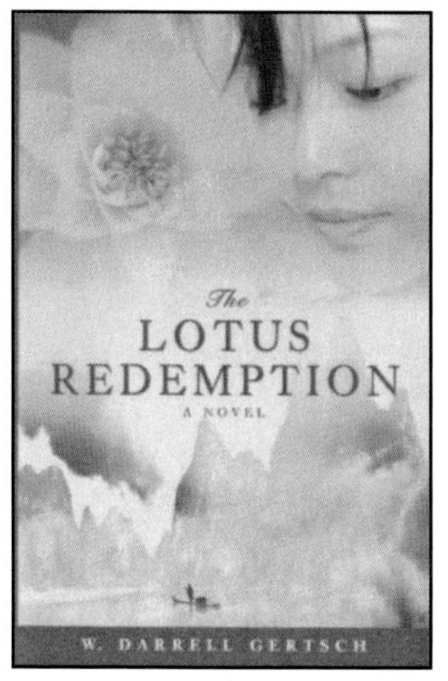

The Lotus Redemption

Aviation, Viet Nam, Romance, WP Author

W. Darrell Gertsch iUniverse, Inc. (2007)

After Frank Gerard graduates from the United States Military Academy at West Point, he's commissioned in the U.S. Air Force and becomes a B-52 pilot. For many months of his eight years in service, he flies bombing missions during the Vietnam war from his bases in Guam and Thailand. Years later, he's an internationally renowned energy consultant, but he wants more than anything to return to Southeast Asia and revisit the landmarks of his past.

One of Frank's colleagues introduces him long distance to Le Chi, a woman from North Vietnam whose own family was involved in the decades of resistance and war with the French, the Japanese, and the Americans. She agrees to set an itinerary and accompany Frank to visit some of the most horrendous battle sites in Vietnam.

Leaving his wife and children behind, Frank begins a fantastic three-week odyssey with Le Chi. Together, they develop an understanding of each other's perspectives on the many years of war in Vietnam. But when a powerful bond emerges between them, Frank encounters difficult contradictions between exotic romance and his own traditional values. [BC]

W. Darrell Gertsch graduated from West Point in 1962 and served as a U.S. Air Force navigator. He earned a master's and a doctoral degree at the University of Washington and was on staff at the Los Alamos Scientific Laboratory, Georgia Tech, and the University of Oklahoma. [3-21]

For Love Through Tears

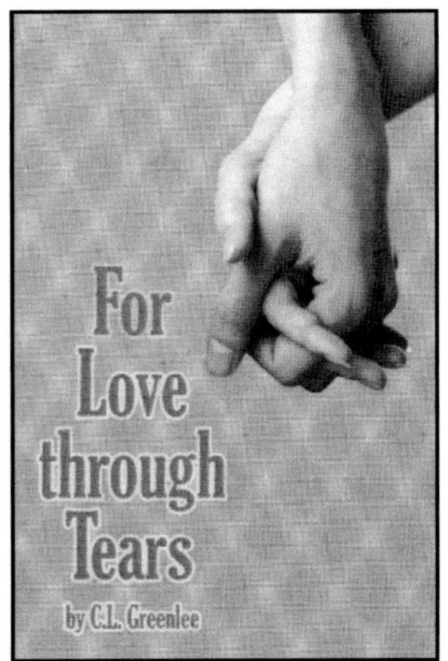

Romance, Balkans War

C. L. Greenlee AuthorHouse (2007)

Joe and Betti as children were neighbors and best friends. The two attended different colleges, he at West Point, she at UCLA, but still bonded by friendship. Joe becomes aware of his feelings and knows his heart, but keeps his tongue.

The night before he is to fly to the Balkans, they become passionate. Does he come home for the delivery? Will he stay? Joe may know his heart, but Betti struggles with hers. While trying to find her love she comes across Derrick. He seems too good to be true. But is he? She is never totally there, as part of her heart is with someone she may have lost to an accident. Who will she walk down the aisle with? [BC]

C. L. Greenlee is originally from Pennsylvania but her husband of 20 years is from Georgia. "We are retired military. Once I had decided to write, it had taken a few years to finish this one due to the nature of the military. Now that I have finished this one I began writing my second still untitled but almost finished. With all my books the ending will always be a wedding to me that is the best part. [BC]
Later released in 2013 with a different title: *Promises Under the Stars.*

Chapter 4

Army Sports

Physical development is one of the three cornerstones, along with academics and military training, in turning a West Point cadet into an Army officer. With the advent of the pulp fiction magazines in around 1900, tales of Army sports were a regular topic. The demise of the pulp fiction magazines in the 1950s limited the outlets for authors, but hardback novels appeared in the 1950s and '60s, then largely died out after 1970.

The stories are mostly about football, but also feature basketball, baseball, track, lacrosse, and fencing. It's notable that several writers chose to re-visit Army sports again and again.

Dick Merriwell's Battle for the Blue or *The Yale Nine at West Point*

Sports, Pulp Fiction

Burt L. Standish Street & Smith Publishers (1912)

From Chapter I. "On the way to West Point"

The northbound train on the West Shore line bore a lively company of Yale men on their way to West Point with the Yale nine. The members of the nine and substitutes, and the Yale coaches with Dick Merriwell at their head, occupied a parlor car, in which were a few other persons, two of whom were in the trim gray uniform of the United States Military Academy.

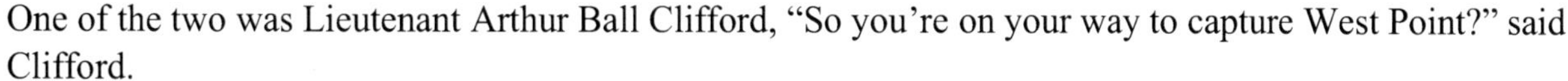

One of the two was Lieutenant Arthur Ball Clifford, "So you're on your way to capture West Point?" said Clifford.

"We expect to have the defenders of the old academy worried about this time tomorrow," Dick Merriwell returned, with a smile.

"We've got a good nine this year," urged Clifford, "and we're on our own grounds."

"To be on its own grounds is an advantage that West Point has every year, if it is an advantage."

Bill Brady drew himself up lazily, and laughed. "It isn't a regular prison pen over there, you know"...The first two years of a cadet's life he isn't permitted to leave at all and even after that the amount he gets isn't going to hurt him." [EB]

William "Gilbert" Patten (1866–1945) was best known as the author of the Frank Merriwell stories, with the pen name Burt L. Standish. His sporting stories in the Frank Merriwell series began April 1896, for the publisher Street & Smith. He produced one each week, at a length of twenty thousand words, for twenty years. The series, which appeared in Tip-Top Weekly, was immensely popular, selling some 135,000 copies a week. [4-01]

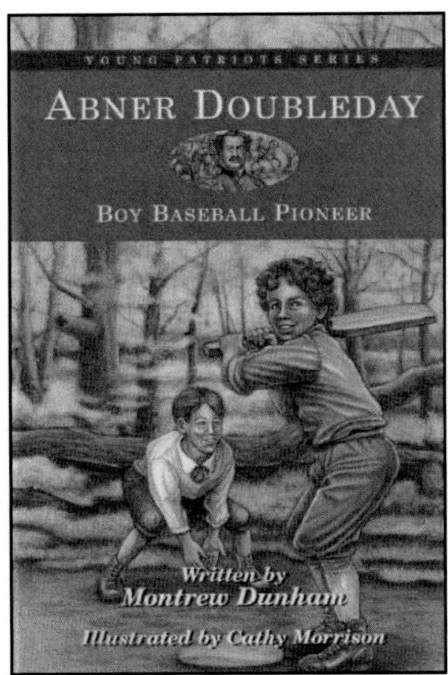

Abner Doubleday: Boy Baseball Pioneer

Sports, Youth

Montrew Dunham & Cathy Morrison Patria Press (2005)

Who invented baseball? Some say Abner Doubleday but most say America invented baseball. Abner grew up to become a famous Civil War general and hero at the Battle of Gettysburg, but as a boy he was never happier than when he had a bat and ball in his hand. Share young Abner's love of the game in Volume 1 in the Young Patriots Series.

The baseball field at West Point is named after Abner Doubleday. [DJ]

Montrew Goetz Dunham (1919–2017) was a longtime resident and historian of Downers Grove, IL. Dunham received degrees from Butler and Northwestern University. She wrote several of the series books, Childhood of Famous Americans, including *Neil Armstrong*, *Langston Hughes*, and *Ronald Reagan*. [4-02]

Abner & Me

Sports, General Officer

Dan Gutman HarperCollins (2007)

Cannons are blasting! Bullets are flying! Wounded soldiers are everywhere!

Stosh has time-traveled to 1863, right into the middle of the Civil War. In possibly his most exciting and definitely his most dangerous trip yet, Stosh has decided to answer the question for all time: did Abner Doubleday, a Civil War general, really invent the game of baseball? It's all here: big laughs, dramatic action, fast baseball games in the middle of a battlefield. [DJ]

Dan Gutman (1955–) has written dozens of books directed at youth. His philosphy, "I want reading my books to feel effortless. I'm trying to write stories that are so captivating that kids will look up after an hour and feel like they'd been watching a movie in their head." He has writen twelve books in this "Baseball Card Adventure" series where a young lad time travels to meet baseball stars of yesteryear. [4-03]

No individual wrote more stories about Army sports than Lt. John Hopper.

As observed by Samuel Wilson in a 2016 pulp fiction blog "...there are sports stories, and then there are Army sports stories, a subgenre Lt. John Hopper may well have had to himself. To illustrate the whims of posterity, Hopper is pretty much forgotten today."

A dozen of Hopper's stories are distributed through several chapters in this catalog.

"That Army-Navy Combination"

Sports, Cadet, PulpFiction, WP Author

Lt. John T. Hopper Argosy (Nov. 26, 1927)

"COME on, Army!" A strident voice dragged out that imploring call. The white stone semicircular stadium was dumb except for that one break from the anguished soul of a supporter in gray.

Near the northern goal posts two teams, serious, businesslike, crouched opposite one another. It was the Army team's ball. The maroon-jerseyed opponents had just lost it, after taking it, by a chain of rapid forward passes, almost the length of the field to Army's last ten-yard line. There it had been regained by heroic defense and seemingly inextricable piling up of the two lines.

The game had not been going very well for West Point. Expecting little opposition from this almost unknown college from the South, it had been taking life easily until two touchdowns to the credit of the enemy, and a desperate attitude on their part to give the Army none, had startled the team and the observing corps of cadets into the nervous realization that here might be a lost game, a blot on an otherwise clean schedule.

For three whole quarters the first team—the "Big Team"--had done nothing better than tie the score. Now, late in the last quarter, it looked as though a tie score -- or worse, would have to be accepted, unless the bewildering rain of forward passes of the Southern team were fathomed. Army's ball, and not any too soon! Clearly, in the brooding silence of the field, upon which November shadows already were beginning to fall, the quarterback's crisp, sharp signals could be heard.

"12-18-32-4!"

The ball was passed back. A black figure plunged by the quarterback, received, and tucked the ball in his arm. Maroon and black mingled. The fleet back hit unyielding tackle, bounced off, sped parallel to the line, and skirted toward end, eluding grasps of unsettled linemen.

The corps, in a series of gray waves, beginning at the front row of benches, rose to its feet. So too did the varicolored crowd which stretched away on either side of the solid block of gray... [EB]

“Army's Ball”

Sports, Cadet, PulpFiction, WP Author

Lt. John T. Hopper Argosy Magazine (October 1931)

Blood flowed in the hardest of all fought Army-Yale games, when West Point halfbacks risked life and honor to keep their promise to the Corps. [EB]

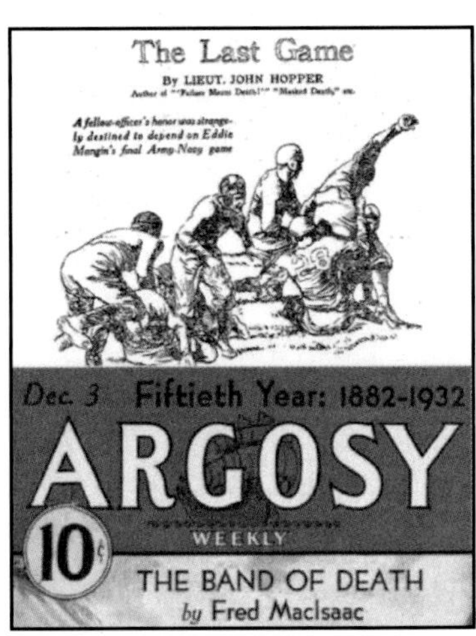

“The Last Game”

Sports, Cadet, PulpFiction, WP Author

Lt. John T. Hopper Argosy Magazine (December 1932)

A fellow-officer's honor was strangely destined to depend on Eddie Mangan's final Army-Navy game.

Chapter 1. “Idol of the Crowd”

The field judge's stopwatch was ticking off the seconds with fatal rapidity. The game was in its final moments, and the score was Notre Dame 7, Army 6. The Yankee Stadium, New York City, where this grim, relentless struggle between football giants was being fought, was packed with seventy thousand people. The dull, gray November day was fading with the ending game, and the air was bitter cold.

The two teams faced each other on the Army's twenty-eight yard line. They were bruised, battered and weary. The Notre Dame eleven reminded the seventy thousand watchers of a tired, tenacious bulldog that had already secured its bone and was grimly determined to hold onto it. The Army team looked as tired, but it was desperate. Desperation was written in the tense faces of the linemen behind the ball, in the strained voice of the quarterback calling signals, in the anxious, crouching postures of the backfield. It was Army's ball, first down. Time was flying; the last quarter was almost over. There was time for one more set of downs. . . . [EB]

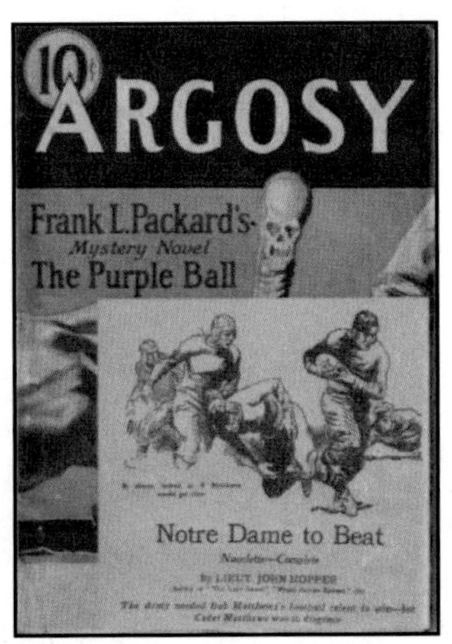

“Notre Dame to Beat”

Sports, Pulp Fiction, Cadet, WP Author

Lt. John T. Hopper Argosy Magazine (October 1932)

The Army needed Bob Matthews's football talent to win, but Cadet Matthews was in disgrace.

Chapter 1. “Rising Star”

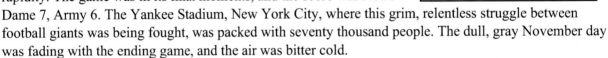

Early in the season, at the Army-Harvard game, fifty thousand people saw a new star rise in the football firmament. He was the quarterback of the black and gold team of West Point, playing in his first big game. For the previous year he had been a plebe, and therefore had not been eligible for the varsity. His name was Robert E. Lee Jackson Matthews, but his classmates and friends called him simply Bob. . . .

The Matthews being a proud and distinguished army family (his father was a major general in the Regular Army), it was but natural that young Bob Matthews should come…to West Point. It was a vindication and a relief to the new and youthful coach of the Army team, First Lieutenant Hugh Ford, when Bob Matthews went into the game as substitute quarterback, so changing an almost certain defeat into a decisive victory. The only person in the vast stadium at Soldiers Field, Cambridge, Massachusetts, who refused to admit the flowering of football genius, was Harvey D. Jones, the replaced quarterback. Jones was the team captain, and was playing his last year. [EB]

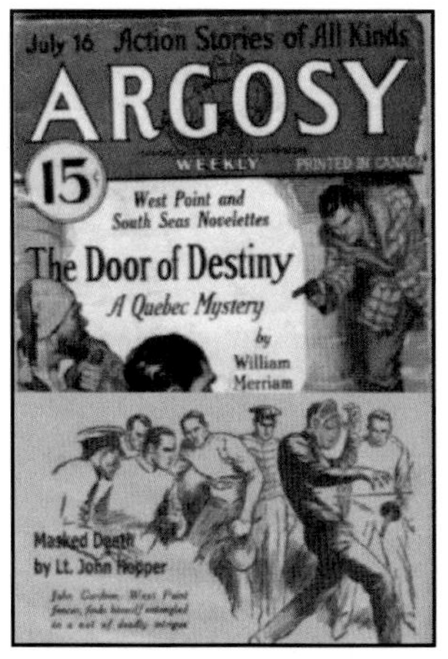

"Masked Death: A West Point Fencing Story"

Mystery, Sports, PulpFiction, WP Author

Lt. John T. Hopper Argosy Magazine (July 1932)

Señor Juan Hernandez seemed to be waiting for someone, listening impatiently -for the sound of the door bell. This conduct was most unusual for the señor. Night after night he sat alone, almost hidden from sight in the depths of his big arm chair. Motionless for hours at a time, he would stare at the logs which blazed both winter and summer on the hearth of the massive fireplace. The firelight, flickering through the gloom of the room, would play on Hernandez's face, sometimes finding him lost in reverie, but more often finding his features set in a mask of intense hatred. Hernandez's hair was thick and dark above an olive skinned, characterful face, in which a pair of flashing, black eyes were deepset. A superficial glance at that face would show it to be remarkably distinguished and handsome, but a more careful scrutiny would discover cruel lines in the high, thin nose and the narrow, tight-lipped mouth.

Usually the señor's living room was illuminated only by the red glow from the fireplace. But tonight every bulb on the circular, wrought iron chandelier, which depended from the lofty ceiling was glowing brightly… [EB]

"Puck Shy: A Complete West Point Hockey Novel"

Sports, Pulp Fiction, Cadet, WP Author

Lt. John T. Hopper Popular Sports Magazine (February 1939)

Cadet Johnny Glasgow, Army's hockey goalie, licks overpowering fear in order to bring triumph to his Coach father -- and to West Point.

West Point is shooting for an undefeated hockey season, but a lone loss to Williams dashed that hope. Only one chance remained to make a grand season - the traditional game against R.M.C. - the Royal Military College of Canada. R.M.C. had triumphed over Army for 13 years in a row. [EB]

John T. Hopper (1903–1970) graduated from West Point in 1927 but resigned his commission in 1930 to pursue a writing career. Hopper was noted for his pulp fiction magazine stories, particularly in *Argosy* (over 70) from 1926 through 1939. In 1938, Hopper reportedly sued Paramount Pictures for ten million dollars, believing their popular film *The Plainsman* was based on his 1933 *Argosy* novelette, "Blood Across Kansas." The outcome is not known. [4-04]

Herb Kent, West Point Cadet

Cadet, Sports

Graham M. Dean The Goldsmith Company (1936)

This is the first story about husky, likeable Herb Kent, who had a football physique with a brain attached, and his experiences at West Point Military Academy. It is an exciting story of Academy life and adventure.

BIG NEWS

Herb's mother suddenly found tears welling into her eyes and a high flush mounted on his father's cheeks. "Oh, Herb, I'm so happy," cried Mrs. Kent. "You've worked so hard to win the appointment. What did the telegram say?" Herb had to admit that he didn't know exactly what the telegram did say, except that he was going to the military academy. [DJ]

Herb Kent, West Point Fullback

Cadet, Sports

Graham M. Dean The Goldsmith Company (1936)

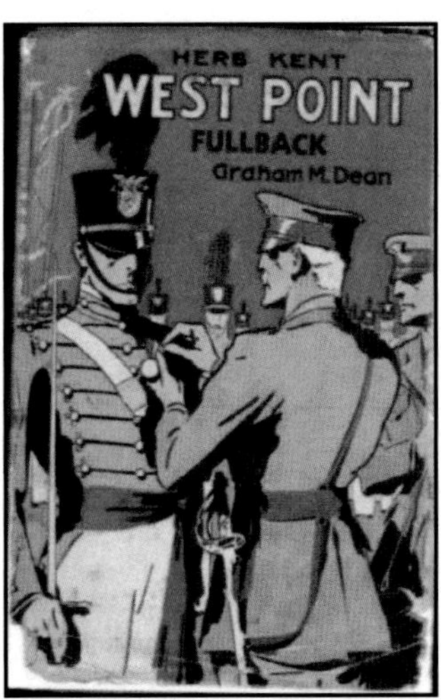

This is the second story of the experiences of Herb Kent as an Army fullback at West Point Military Academy. A great mystery is unraveled which takes Herb Kent thru many thrilling experiences and exciting incidents before he finally wins his position of fullback on this famous Army eleven. [DJ]

In the 1930s **Graham M. Dean** (1904–1974) wrote seventeen novels targeted at youth. Besides West Point, Dean's works included news reporter/detective mysteries, westerns, and aviation stories. As a newspaper editor living in cattle country (Iowa then California) he had first-hand knowledge of his subject matter. [4-05]

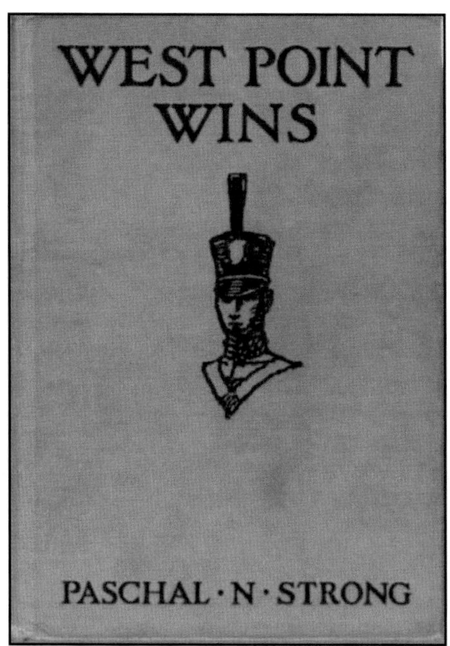

West Point Wins

Sports, Cadet, WPAuthor

Paschal N. Strong Little, Brown (1930)

Mr. James Wadsworth Leslie enters West Point from North Carolina, awkward in carriage, callow in manner and an untried youth, but with a sense of honor and a fighting spirit; and gradually, through the gruelling experiences of sentry duty, the "slug", the officers' masquerade, the Air Corps, baseball, and football, he shows that "Cadet" Leslie is a man and that in him the true West Point spirit lives and wins.

Lieutenant Strong, himself a West Point graduate and member of the Corps of Engineers, tells of the present daily life, the traditions and ideals of our old and honored Military Academy on the Hudson. [DJ]

West Pointers on the Gridiron

Cadet, Sports, WP Author

Kennedy Lyons (pen name of Pashcal N. Strong)
Saalfield Publishing Co (1936)

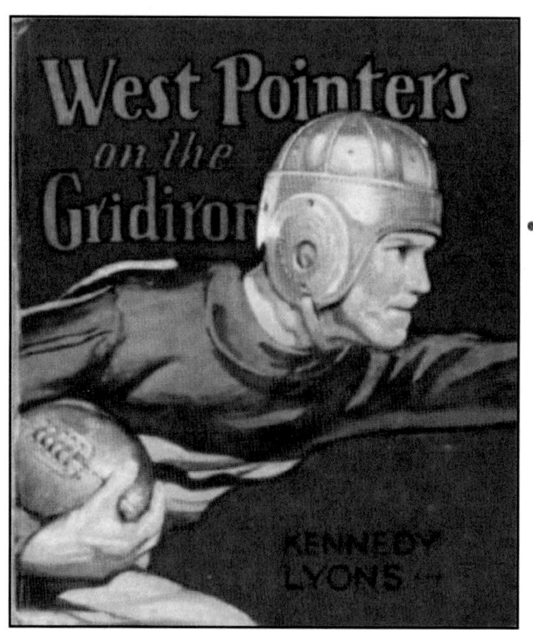

...The file-closers -- cadet sergeants who marched in rear of each platoon -- exhorted the plebes in muffled whispers to try to march like upperclassmen for once. The first platoon swung along in faultless line past Visitors' Row. Larry's mind, however, was on the practice field where he had labored each afternoon for the past month. Today was to have seen the last scrimmage before the opening game. Now there was the game tomorrow, and it was rumored that the coach was going to give each prospective back a chance to show his stuff. Larry's heart jumped at the thought of it, even as his platoon snapped their eyes to the right as they swung past the reviewing stand.

Perhaps tomorrow his dream of years would be realized. Perhaps he would be a full-fledged back on an Army team. . . . [EB]

The West Point Five

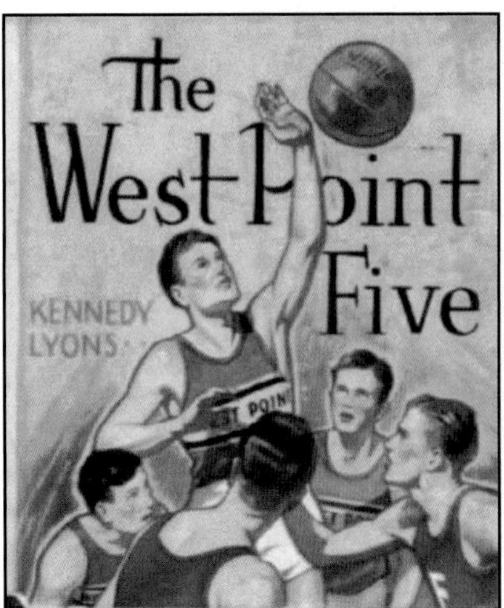

Cadet, Sports, WP Author

Kennedy Lyons (pen name for Paschal N. Strong)
Saalfield Publishing Co (1937)

"Sir, there are four minutes until assembly, sir!"

...Doug steeled himself for the moment when he must fling off the covers. Something tingled in his half-awake brain. He knew, vaguely, that this was a big day. It was a day he had looked forward to for many weeks. What could it be?

Ah! Now he remembered. Basketball! Today was the opening game of the season. There were other things not far away, such Christmas furlough and final exams, which were the highlights for the other cadets, but for him the beginning and end of existence was centered in what happened today. He would get his chance to show what he could do in big-time basketball. In varsity basketball, on an Army team!

"Sir, there are two minutes until assembly, sir!"

Basketball! Would he, could he, do half as well as his roommate Larry had done on the gridiron the past fall? Would he even make the team? Army was supposed to have a strong team this year, with a wealth of good material left over from last season." [EB]

Teenage Sports Stories – "The Land Torpedo"

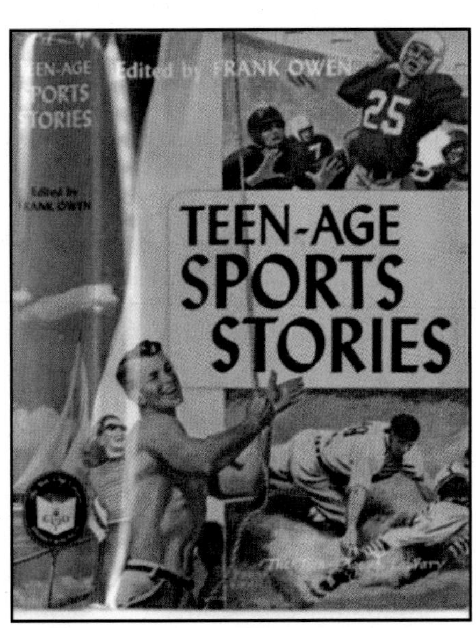

Sports, Cadet, WP Author

Paschal N. Strong   Grosset & Dunlap (1946)

A short story about lacrosse at West Point from the era when they were a national powerhouse in that sport.

Bret's stick flashed like a rapier and snagged the ball out of the air. He spun and and dashed toward the crease. His man was waiting grimly for him, and to Bret he looked as big as a mountain. His large defense stick, tightly gripped resembled a huge battle mace, and he crouched there, a ferocious giant waiting for the Killer.

Bret didn't feel like a giant killer just then. As he dashed in he prepared for one of his swift sorties to the flank if the other Army forward, Mayfield, wasn't free. Anything to avoid crashing his slight frame against that husky defenseman. In the nick of time Mayfieid broke away and Bret flipped the ball to him. Then, safe from danger of a body check since he no longer had the ball, he flashed past his man toward the net.... [EB]

Paschal N. Strong (1901–1988) graduated from West Point in 1922 beginning his Army career as an engineer. He served until 1954 when he retired as a Brigadier General. His most notable assignment was overseeing the blasting of tunnels in Corregidor in the 1930s before managing the development of infrasture crtical to the the war effort in the U.S. and in Europe. During these years, Strong was a prolific author. Using his own name and a pseudonym, Kennedy Lyons, he wrote seven novels for boys and dozens of stories for Boys Life and the Jack Armstrong radio serial. Five of his books are in this collection. [4-06]

"I've Got Army in My Blood"

Cadet, Sports, Pulp Fiction

Herbert L. McNary   Popular Sports Magazine (Winter 1950)

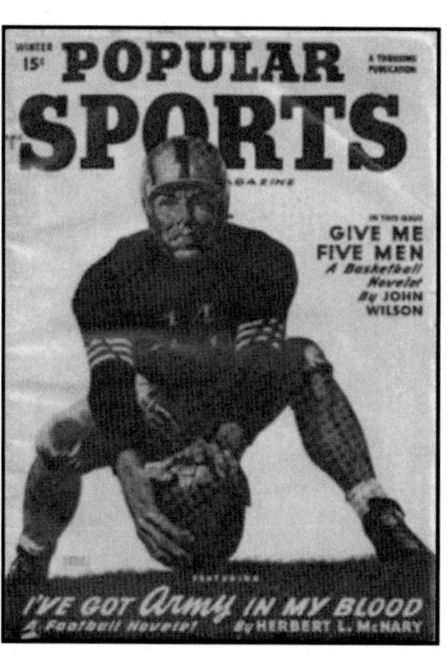

Darrel Layne was the best back that West Point could put on the field -- but he had to prove to his teammates that he was a real soldier.

Darrell Layne stood again on the turf of Michie Stadium, the cleats of his shoes pressing hard in fulfilment of a dream. As a boy, long after the littered stands had been cleared of spectators and famous gridiron heroes of his had departed, the tow-headed son of a math instructor had stood on this muddied field and had dreamed another self streaking for the distant goal posts with pigskin in his grasp.

Today was not complete fulfillment of that dream since he was only a Plebe. You played for Army only when you made the varsity—the big team. But that would be only a year away.

Layne clutched nervously for a blade of short grass. In a few seconds Columbia Freshmen would kick off against the Army Plebes. Layne had won a starting assignment as halfback. There had never been any question of that in his mind, or, seemingly, in the mind of others. Practice had quickly demonstrated that his line-splitting runs of high-school and California days had been no press agent's dream. [EB]

"West Point Bombardier"

Cadet, Sports, Pulp Fiction

Herbert L. McNary   Exciting Football Magazine (Spring 1942)

Triple threat man Dike Cummings didn't want to go to West Point -- but when he began tossing passes, West Point didn't want to let him go. [EB]

Herbert L. McNary was a regular contributor to pulp fiction magazines from 1930 to 1950. Sports was his most common subject, but he also penned mysteries and adventure tales. [4-07]

Although *Bringing Up the Brass* is a memoir, not a novel, its relevance lays in documenting the physical training that was critical to the Corps and the teams depicted in this chapter. For that reason it is included. This is one of the rarer books in the collection, if one can judge by the asking price on used book sites.

Bringing Up the Brass

WP Author, Sports, Memoir

Sgt. Marty Maher with Nardi Reeder Campion
David McKay Company (1951)

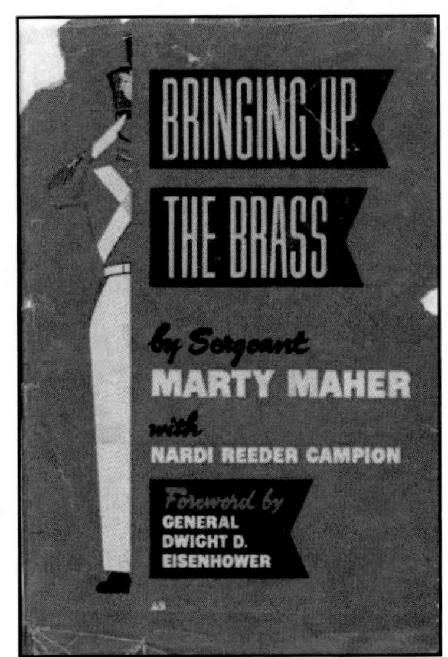

Marty was born in County Tipperary in 1876. He left Ireland when he was twenty because, in a small argument, he pulled the wrong end of his boss's necktie and almost killed him. During Marty's fabulous career at the Military Academy he has served as waiter in the Mess Hall, custodian of the Cadet Gym, and swimming instructor to the cadets. Among other remarkable tales, the book explains how Marty taught swimming for thirty years without being able to swim a stroke himself. Marty has also held down several positions in the Army Athletic Association and worked in the training room, where he has helped care for three generations of Army athletes. Through Marty, the reader gets a close-up of famous figures in sports, such as Knute Rockne, Jim Thorpe, and Red Blaik. [DJ]

Bringing Up The Brass is a book that could have been written by only one man — the famous **Sergeant Marty Maher** of West Point. The United States Military Academy was 150 years old in 1952. Marty had been at West Point for 55 of these 150 years, and his character was woven into the fabric of the Academy's history. [DJ] Marty Maher (1876–1961) and his wife are buried in the West Point cemetery.

Nardi Reeder Campion (1917–2007), a graduate of Wellesley College, was the sister of prolific West Point author and athletic director, Russell 'Red' Reeder. She authored nine books of non-fiction and historical fiction and also had humorous articles appearing in *The New Yorker, Sports Illustrated* and other periodicals. [4-08]

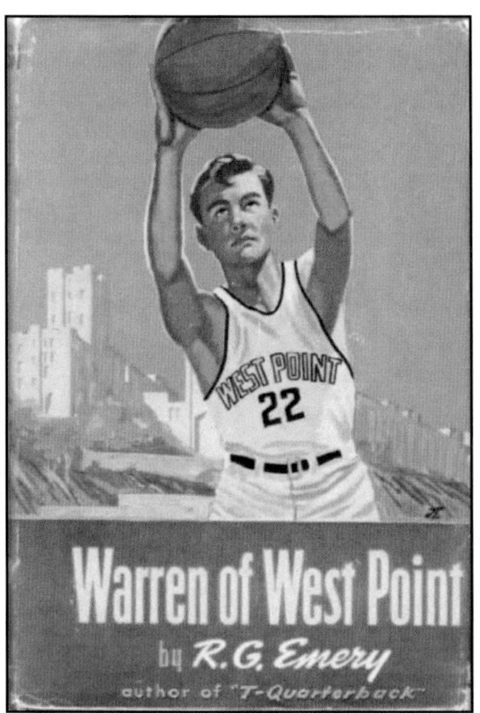

Warren of West Point

Cadet, Sports, WP Author

R. G. Emery Macrae Smith Company (1950)

An exciting, action-packed basketball story, written around life at the West Point Military Academy, with all its traditions, glamour, sports, and studies. Warren, who arrived at West Point a gangling youth from the Midwest, unsure of himself and his capabilities, was brought face to face with the problem of overcoming his handicaps to meet the exacting demands of the Academy.

His two roommates, boys more successful and more mature, recognized in Larry Warren the abilities that he had neglected to use. With the help and understanding of his instructors, his friends, and the methods by which this great military school develops the very best in its students, Larry began to make a place for himself both in sports and in the classroom. It was not until a real struggle had taken place that he found his part in Academy life and became a star player on the basketball court. [DJ]

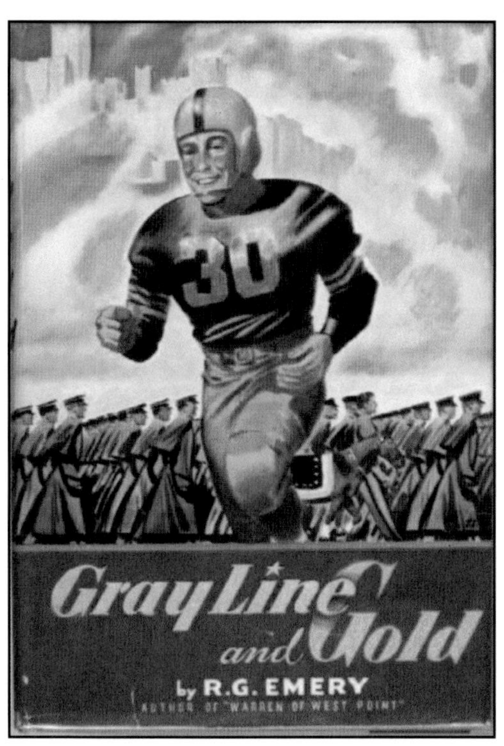

Gray Line and Gold

Cadet, Sports, WPAuthor

R. G. Emery Macrae Smith Company (1951)

The colorful and spirited cadet life at West Point does not completely absorb Joe McMinn during his final year. Joe's brilliant success on the football field makes him a national figure and spreads his popularity among influential people outside the Academy. His roommate's sense that his interests are diverted from cadet life, while Joe is dazzled by impressive offers of money to play professional football. There is also pretty Cinda Holden, who has come to mean much to him.

But the four vigorous years at West Point have not gone by without leaving their impact on Joe. With the help of his roommates, Larry Warren and Knox Parker -- whom the reader will remember from *Warren of West Point* -- Joe McMinn realizes that the motto, "duty, honor, country", has a special meaning for him—and that he has to fulfill an obligation both to himself and to the Long Gray Line of West Point men that has formed through the years since the Academy was founded. [DJ]

Rebound

Cadet, Sports, WPAuthor

R. G. Emery Macrae Smith Company (1955)

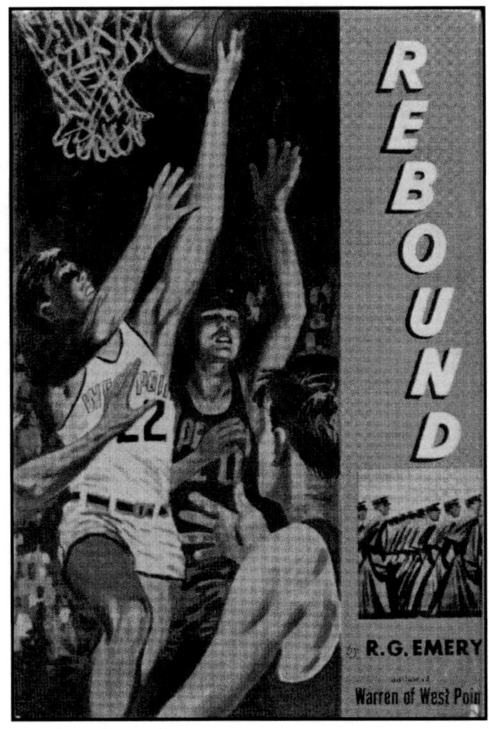

Aware that since his plebe year he has added almost an inch to his already towering frame, Larry Warren begins to feel conspicuous among his classmates. Although advantageous on the basketball court, Larry winces at even the friendliest jibe and lets a sense of inferiority lead him into trouble. But under the demands of Academy life he matches his physical stature by equal growth in mind and spirit.

Here is the well-paced sequel to *Warren of West Point* in which Larry almost ruins his Academy career. How he reacts when he hits bottom and how he fights his way up again to reach a new level of accomplishment and honor are the ingredients of this story set against the excitement and color of West Point and the basketball court. [DJ]

Russell Guy Emery (1909–1964) graduated from West Point in 1930. He excelled in boxing at the Academy, coached the 1936 Army Olympic Boxing Team, and accompanied the American Olympic Team to Berlin in the same year. In 1940 his first book was published – *Wings over West Point*, also in this collection. In January 1945, as a commander of an infantry regiment in Luxembourg, he lost a leg and won a Silver Star for rescuing one of his own men from a minefield.

Following the war, he concentrated on his writing, published a mystery novel, *Front for Murder*, wrote many magazine sports stories, and a series of boys' books with a West Point background. All the while, he attended the University of Virginia Law School then returned to West Point as Professor of Law. Later he had a notable career as an attorney specializing in military law in Washington D.C. He died suddenly at home in 1964 and is interred at West Point. [4-09]

West Point Wingback

Cadet, Sports

Joe Archibald Macrae Smith Company (1965)

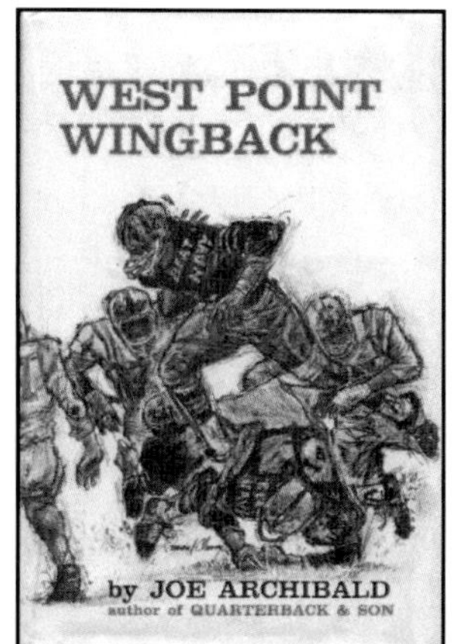

Ronald Ellis Burritt had it coming to him. Born and raised in the pleasant rolling hills of Brantwood, Pennsylvania, the only child of patient parents, he had always sought -- and found -- the easy way. But at West Point he finds there is no easy way…. He wanted out. The plebe football coach gave him a start by kicking him off the squad for lack of effort.

But fate and an institution long known for the making of men had other plans for Ron. In a spirit of retaliation, the rebellious plebe was involved in an accident which injured the Go-Co team's valuable fullback, in a year when Army was determined to break Navy's domination of the annual classic. With resentment against him at an all-time high, Ron was goaded into offering himself to the B squad, the rag-tag punching bag of the first team. He was the sacrificial lamb. Cut out from the pack and pounded, he took his lumps silently while discovering that he could kick a football a country mile and run faster than most. He had to - in order to stay alive.

Gradually, the crucible of pain brought an understanding that he must extend himself fully, to believe in something bigger than himself. The corps had ushered another boy into manhood… [DJ]

Joe Archibald (1898–1986) is best remembered today for the numerous juvenile sports fiction books he wrote, especially his baseball titles. He served aboard a naval sub-chaser during the First World War and continued to write during his time in the service—working as a cartoonist for military publications. From 1955 to 1974, Joe Archibald was one of the leading authors of juvenile sports fiction. His first book was published in 1947 (*Rebel Halfback*) and was followed by more than 50 titles through the '40s, '50s and into the 1960s. [4-10]

"Army Brat: A West Point Track Story"

Cadet, Sports, Pulp Fiction

Moran Tudury Dime Sports Magazine (April 1940)

Cadet Robert E. Lee Jones was a very proud young man. He walked across the parade ground and turned off toward the gym, and his gray tunic swelled with pride. Today a great many West Point yearlings would report fearfully to the Army track coach but not Cadet Jones. He walked straight and stiff like a color sergeant on review.

After dressing down a plebe cadet that crossed his path, Cadet Robert E. Lee Jones went on to the gym, smiling at the world. A plebe was a very low animal and must be kept in his lowly place.

The gymnasium was crowded with the cadets. Some were upper classmen from last year's track team...but Cadet Jones did not join them. He was not self-conscious and awkward. He did not have to be. His father was a brigadier general in the Army. Cadet Jones had been born at West Point, and last year had captained the plebe track team. He could afford to be proud. . . .

[Later] Desperate, spent, Cadet Bob Jones fought to the last grim straightaway, toward the hard-faced man who had told him—"If a good guy slips, it's one of them things. But when a bum like you don't deliver, the Corp doesn't forget...never." [EB]

Moran Tudury (1901–1954) authored stories for many pulp fiction magazines from 1930–1940. [4-11]

"The West Point Whirlwind: A Touchdown Outlaw"

Sports, Philippines, PulpFiction

Curtis Bishop Football Action Magazine (1945)

"People will talk about West Point as the place where Happy Hooligan played football," Hooligan bragged. Silence was his answer -- grim bitter silence. The cadets had decided to break this line crusher who sought to stage a one-man show on a no-star field.

The Colonel's car pulled to a stop in front of the temporary bleachers. A trim, smiling youth in the uniform of the United States Military Academy leaped to the ground as soon as the big automobile had stopped rolling and ceremoniously handed out a slim, dark-haired girl who rewarded him with a flashing smile. A similar-clad youth made a motion as if to lend the same assistance to a red-faced, white-mustached officer.

"Colonel. the officers at the club told me your team didn't have a chance," teased the girl. She was his daughter, Myra.

"Hmph!" snorted Colonel Mike. "You spend too much time with those air corps whippersnappers. I tell you, we got a boy. . . hey, there he is!"

A group of football players were trotting toward the field. The usual formalities of a football game were missing at Clark Field, Philippine Islands….The spirit of competition was there, however. The Sixth Air Force was boasting all over the islands what it would do to the Thirty-Third Infantry. "Just a bunch of thick-headed foot soldiers," they said about the infantry. "We'll take 'em." "Yeah!" the infantry snorted back. "Wait 'til Hooligan gets a hold of you panty-waists. You tea-sippers! You gold-bricks!"

"We'll give 'em, a ball game," grinned one of the players. He was a tall, broad-shouldered giant with sandy hair and light blue eyes. "Sure you will, Hooligan," cried the Colonel. "You tear into those fair corps boys and show 'em what a rough-and-tough infantryman can do."

"Are those orders, Colonel?" grinned the big man.

"Those are orders," snapped Colonel Mike. "We can't have fun poked at the infantry. We've won every war this country has ever fought and we'll win the next one. They can take their infernal flying machines and be damned."

Curtis Kent Bishop (1912–1967) was a newspaperman and author. During World War II Bishop was with the Foreign Broadcast Intelligence Service in Latin America and the Pacific Theater. On his return he became widely recognized for his books on sports and for his western novels, at least six of which were made into motion pictures. He wrote more than fifty books on teenage sports fiction and western lore as well as hundreds of magazine stories. [4-12]

The Rivalry: Mystery at the Army-Navy Game

Sports, Mystery

John Feinstein Knopf Books (2010)

Stevie Thomas and Susan Carol Anderson are teen sports reporters. In the first book in this series, *Last Shot*, they won a writing contest and were invited to report on the Final Four tournament. They also solved a mystery involving a blackmail attempt, and the two keep getting invited to cover big sporting events, even though trouble seems to follow them. In this, the fifth book in the series, Stevie and Susan Carol are part of the coverage of the annual Army-Navy college football game, which is being played in Washington, D.C., and will be attended by President Obama.

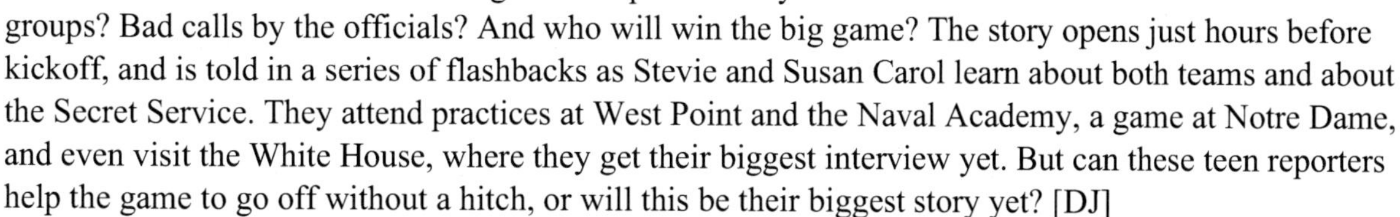

It is not immediately clear in The Rivalry what the main mystery in this book will be. Is it the threat against the president by hate groups? Bad calls by the officials? And who will win the big game? The story opens just hours before kickoff, and is told in a series of flashbacks as Stevie and Susan Carol learn about both teams and about the Secret Service. They attend practices at West Point and the Naval Academy, a game at Notre Dame, and even visit the White House, where they get their biggest interview yet. But can these teen reporters help the game to go off without a hitch, or will this be their biggest story yet? [DJ]

John Feinstein (1956–) has written 44 books. His most famous, *A Season on the Brink,* chronicled a year in the life of the Indiana University basketball team and its coach, Bob Knight. In 1995, he authored a best seller, *A Good Walk Spoiled*, about a year on the PGA Tour as told through the stories of 17 players. Feinstein has also written a sports-mystery series for young adults in which main characters Stevie Thomas and Susan Carol Anderson are reporting on major sporting events including the Final Four, US Open (tennis), Super Bowl, World Series, the Army–Navy Game, and the Summer Olympics. [4-13]

And then there is the darker side of collegiate football. West Point has not been immune. The following three novels depict the measures that administrators, coaches, and their alumni undertake to skirt NCAA rules and trample their institution's academic values in pursuit of championship teams. Interestingly, these were all written by West Pointers to highlight their observations of the corrupting influence of big-time college football.

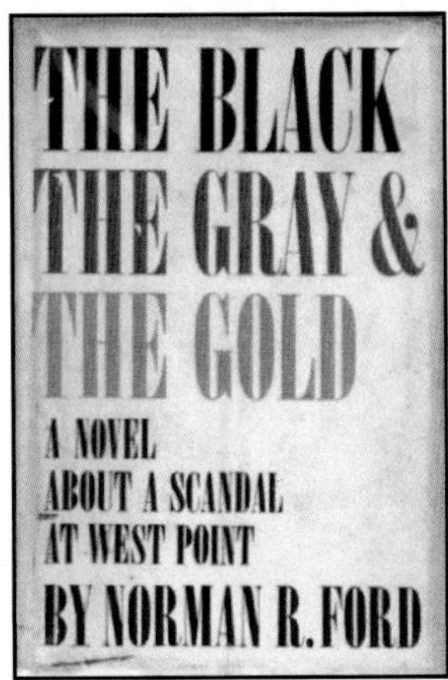

The Black, The Gray & The Gold: A Scandal at West Point

Football, Scandal, WP Author

Norman R. Ford   Doubleday & Company (1961)

Many of the cadets received identical white envelopes at breakfast. A hush fell over Washington Hall as each turned pale. It was no longer Corps rumor: a committee was to investigate reports of widespread cheating. What happens at a revered institution like West Point when one of its most basic codes, the Honor System, is threatened by scandal? Norman R. Ford brings such a volatile situation to life in a strong, vivid novel which tells a startling story.

Luther Philipbar, once a model cadet, now a ruthless, posturing colonel, heads up the Board of Inquiry. George Landseer, also once an outstanding cadet, had long ago lost face with the Corps by revealing—as the Honor System demanded—-a merciless hazing by Luther. Now a major, he, too, is on the board. The relationship between the two officers is further intensified by Charlotte Philipbar, who is the major's love, but the colonel's wife. Attracted to Luther, she became involved with him in a tangle of misunderstanding, rape, a common love of acting—on and off stage—and because she needed him to maintain her status as an Army lady.

Here is the fictional behind-the-scenes world of West Point, from the cadets' quarters to the officers' homes. Here, inside the barracks and the hallways, outside on the parade grounds, and up at the large estate which looks down on it all from the hill, you will meet: vast, hulking Clem, who in half innocence almost throws the investigation into a riot; the son of the Philipbar's gardener, for whom West Point is a real step ahead; a maid who uses her obvious charms to work her way into the secure social world of the Army; and a housekeeper who has the task of revealing to Cadet Adam Philipbar the truth about his parentage.

The Black, The Gray & the Gold telescopes many days of many lives into the hour-by-hour suspense of the investigation and ultimate decision and loyalties that swing swiftly from honor to compromise, he unfolds a powerful drama. [DJ]

Norman R. Ford, West Point Class of 1932 aspired to be a novelist. In the following years he worked at the various odd jobs that seem almost mandatory for a struggling writer. He later served in the Navy. He spent the better part of his life writing, despite steady rejection by publishers. Once, to get his work in print, Mr. Ford wrote short books, printed them page-by-page on a hand press, stitched them by hand, and sold them by mail. His most widely read work was *The Black, The Gray & The Gold.* [4-14]

Ringknockers

Cadet, Intrigue, Sports, WP Author

Keith A. Bush Diezel Press Inc (2000)

Ringknockers reveals West Point's untold inner circle—the Old Grads. A brotherhood bound by their class rings, this covert society of military, political, and financial icons tends the fate of their proud alma mater. Led by multimillionaire entrepreneur T. Buckminster Sterling, seven Old Grads pool their wealth, ingenuity, and fanaticism to resurrect West Point's tarnished image. Fueled by American sports mania, Sterling blazes a path of bribery and racketeering, building an Army football dynasty on the shoulders of star quarterback, Cadet Cody Straup, a prodigal athlete with a checkered past. But as Army's football season climaxes, Straup's personal problems threaten to reveal the Old Grads treachery, sparking a controversial suicide—or is it? Only the quarterback's best friend, Cadet Joel Gerardi, and a brilliant plebe, Cadet Thorne, dare to seek the truth. Together, the pair wages war to appease Straup's memory and preserve West Point's honor. [DJ]

Keith A. Bush (1975–) attended the United States Military Academy at West Point for two years before graduating from the University of Pennsylvania in 1998 with a degree in chemical engineering. *Ringknockers* is his second novel. [DJ]

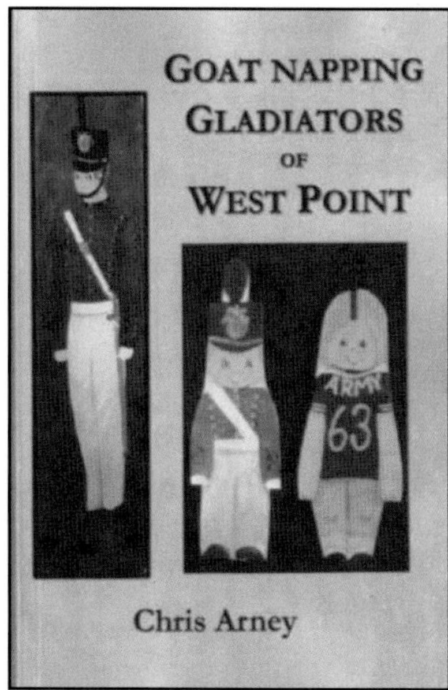

Goatnapping Gladiators of West Point

Sports, Football, Satire, WP Author

Chris Arney Patriot Publications (2022)

Goatnapping Gladiators of West Point is a satire revealing misguided priorities of the Academy's leaders involving football, honor, and education. The story takes place during eight weeks of a football season at the U.S. Military Academy in West Point, NY. In their effort to garner football victories, generals lead the Academy into a tangle of misplaced masculinity, misogyny, spying and counter-spying, and much more. At the center of the tumult is the clueless Superintendent who uses his power to corrupt followers and attack foes. Gritty cadets and faculty fight back to save their Academy.

Author Chris Arney with over 30 years at the Academy weaves a tale of amusing absurdities and zany follies. The title's *Goatnapping Gladiators* is a parody involving special operations performed, not by green berets, but by cadets to steal the Naval Academy's goat mascot. [BC]

David "Chris" Arney (1949–) Class of 1971, is a retired Army officer and a West Point emeritus professor of mathematics. Arney authored numerous technical articles and books on the history of science and mathematics. He employed the pen name Alan Firstone for a number of works including his only other novel, *Son of the Silvery Waters*. [BC]

Chapter 5

Mascots & Other Army Animals

Mules, of course, but maybe a Bear?

The Army mule has been the mascot of West Point football for over a century, but it is not the only animal sent forth to inspire Cadets at an Army-Navy game.

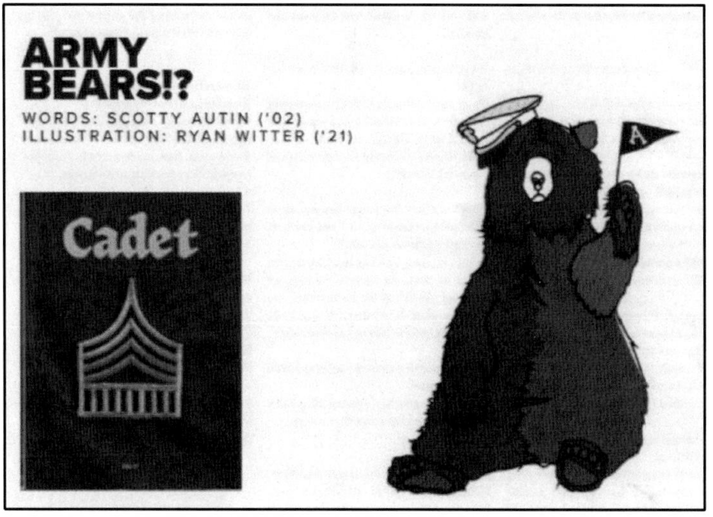

ARMY
BEARS!?
WORDS: SCOTTY AUTIN ('02)
ILLUSTRATION: RYAN WITTER ('21)
Cadet
A

"Army Bears!?"

Mascot, WP Author

Scotty Autin
Cadet Magazine Vol. IV (2020)

In a 2020 article from *Cadet* magazine, the writer narrates an unfortunate series of events initiated by Superintendent Hugh Scott before the 1907 Army-Navy game. Hoping to impress President Teddy Roosevelt at the game in Philadelphia, Scott directed a subordinate to "find a bear." And he did, albeit, a small cub, then arranged for it to be leased - including the trainer, and travel to Philadelphia - using funds from the Cadet Mess.

It did not go well. On Game Day the President had pressing matters that kept him from attending the game. The small bear's appearance was underwhelming, cowering before the Navy goat, and Navy trounced the Army team. Then it got worse. A scandal erupted over Col. Scott's authorization for leasing the bear. A significant number of irregularities were uncovered when the Cadet Mess fund was audited. The oversight officer went to prison for embezzlement. Finally, Teddy Roosevelt is said to have greatly disliked the whole "Teddy" bear craze. [EB]

Scotty Autin, West Point Class of 2002, is an avid USMA memorabilia collector according to the brief bio in this article. LTC Autin is currently serving at the Joint War College in Chesapeake, VA. [5-01]

No more bear mascots, but some famous bears did visit the Military Academy. Even today bears are occasionally reported in the hills around West Point. Possibly looking for a large goat to intimidate.

Roosevelt Bears Visit West Point

Children, Animal

Seymour Eaton Barse & Hopkins (1916)

"Dressed and ready for hours of fun,
With cavalry horse or battery gun."

The day was fine and the Bears were free
To take a River boat to see
The Palisades and Tarrytown
And to view the Hudson up and down.
A request had come from a young cadet
Of West Point school, whom the Bears had met,
To dine at the West Point Army Mess,
And to see the boys in their army dress,
And to sleep on an army barracks cot,
And to try their luck at a target shot,
. . .
At West Point landing the Bears were met
By a double carriage with the young cadet
And a cavalry mount to escort them round
To see the buildings on the ground.
They drove about for an hour or less,
Then went to their barrack rooms to dress
In soldier suits for the evening mess.
TEDDY—B said he'd be Colonel's aide
And inspect the boys on dress parade,
While TEDDY—G said he'd march or stand
As leader of the soldier band.

The parade dismissed and the supper through,
The Bears had nothing else to do
But to roll themselves in barrack wraps
And to put out the lights at the sound of taps
At reveille at six next day
They were wide awake and bright and gay
And dressed and ready for hours of fun
With cavalry horse or battery gun.
The boys had fun when TEDDY—B
Rode a cavalry horse down a shute to see
How to jump the walls and the hurdles take
Without a tumble or balk or break. . . . [EB]

Seymour Eaton (1859–1916) was a Canadian-born American author, journalist, educator and publisher. He wrote a series of illustrated children's books on the travels of the "Roosevelt bears," earning him the credit for popularizing the name "teddy bear." [5-02]

The Army Mascot

The tradition of mules as mascots for the Army dates back to 1899, when an officer at the Philadelphia Quartermaster Depot decided that the team needed a mascot to counter the Navy goat.

Mules were an obvious choice, as they were used as haulers of Army gear for generations. They symbolized endurance, strength, and determination.

Not much is known about the "official" mules at West Point until 1936, when Mr. Jackson (named for Thomas J. "Stonewall" Jackson), a former Army pack mule, arrived from Front Royal, Virginia. He served for twelve years, presiding over two national championship teams. Starting with Mr. Jackson there have been seventeen "official" Army mules through 2019, only one, Buckshot, being female. [5-03]

The West Point mules are trained by cadet Mule Riders, a part of the Spirit Support Activity of the U.S. Corps of Cadets. They present the mules at many of West Point's athletic events, parades, and other ceremonial activities. [5-04] The mules serve not only as West Point's mascot, but also as the mascot for the entire United States Army.

Aging mules are "retired" to live out their lives on an alumni or Academy booster's farm. Replacement mules are traditionally donated to the Academy by alumni.

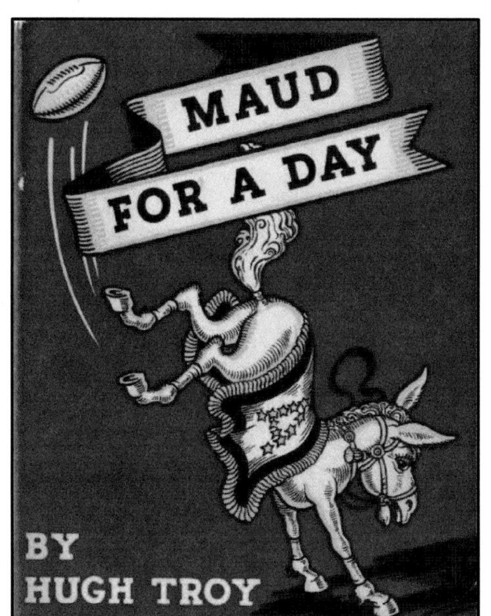

Maud for a Day

Sports, Animal

Hugh Troy Oxford Books (1940)

Maud was ill! The honor of the United States Army was at stake. How could the Army-Navy football game be played without the Army mascot --Maud the mule? Faced with this dreadful situation the General, ever resourceful, was not more than temporarily baffled. He had rushed from a nearby coal mine a gentle, pleasant little mule named Marigold. No one but those directly connected with the affair knew about Maud's illness so, unknown to the thousands who cheered her, Marigold became Maud for a day.

It was a momentous day. Marigold, groomed and polished as she had never been before, played the role of Maud with distinction. In fact, she won fame for herself and the Army. [EB]

Hugh Troy, Jr. (1906–1964) was a Cornell University graduate. He made a living as a painter, illustrator of books and magazines, and author of several children's stories. He is reputed to have been a great practical joker. [5-05]

***Maud for a Day* is one of the prizes in the whole collection.** A great children's story, superbly illustrated by the author, worth re-reading every December before the Army-Navy game. And it's hard to find a copy. The book should be re-issued, if one can track down the copyright holder or wait until it expires in 2035. I tried, but the publisher, Oxford University Press, had no record of it. It would be wonderful if surviving kin of Hugh Troy might have a copy and get it reprinted.

"The Murders on the Range"

Western, Animal, Pulp Fiction

Paul Annixter Argosy Magazine (October 1934)

O'Leary, the four-footed hurricane of a mule, didn't really want to turn renegade—it was just that he got in with bad company.

The fight was not of O'Leary's seeking. He had been moving down toward the lower pasture that morning as was his wont, with nothing but friendliness in his heart or eyes. At the little stream he had stopped to drink, and as he stood knee deep in the current, the cool water dripping from his big jaws, a muffled bray, of sheer well-being escaped him.

And up on the hill across the stream Stawano, the big spotted gray stallion, had heard it and came prancing toward the sound... O'Leary dimly sensed what was coming, but it never entered his thick-jug head to flee. He felt no anger nor hatred for the oncoming stallion; certainly, he was not nervous. Nerves had been left out of the recipe when the mule tribe was planned… [EB]

Howard Allison Sturtzel (1894–1985) was an American author of popular children's equestrian books he wrote with his wife, under the name **Jane and Paul Annixter.** In addition, the couple also penned over 500 short stories. [5-06]

Capitán: The Story of an Army Mule

Animal, Youth

Lucy Herndon Crockett Henry Holt & Co (1940)

Lots of people do not know that Army mules live a long time. Some of them see as much service as the most veteran soldier. So, when Capitán, young, frisky, black, but even then, with a keen eye and an observing habit of mind, was first mustered into the service, he had a long career ahead of him. He tells the story of his life just the way you expect a mule to do, and his story is a mule's-eye picture of the Army and of the men in it through many campaigns and in many lands. [DJ]

Lucy Herndon Crockett (1914–2002) was an American novelist and artist who illustrated her own books. She grew up on military posts and served in World War II with the Red Cross, spending five years in New Caledonia, Guadalcanal, the Philippines, Japan, and Korea. [5-07]

"Major, Here's the Mules"

Animal, Tennessee, Pulp Fiction

Sam Carson Argosy Magazine (July 12, 1941)

Pvt. Cowpoke, who didn't know a general when he saw one, hadn't heard about the Army being mechanized. But he had the strategy to out-maneuver flood and storm and chaos.

Seven inches of rain in three days, a row of bad breaks affecting contractors and the deadline for early summer maneuvers at hand, qualified Camp Maylon for a Grade A headache. Here was the cantonment—created to house some seventy thousand-odd guardsmen for weeks and located for convenience to Tennessee flat land between hill country and mountains—most completely outflanked by the weather.

Yes, it had rained, and was raining again.

> "And if it does," Major Robbins told Captain Holland, his undisturbed adjutant, "we're sunk."
>
> "We have twenty-four hours left," he said. "Then we welcome four trainloads, plus two brigadier-generals. And, he added, "including Horsley." What officer didn't know that warhorse! Major Robbins groaned. "The fire chief in person," he muttered. "Look, Holland. Lacey yards are choked with material. The branch line is soft, and the wooden trestle is unsafe in the bargain. With this pressure and the Salina rising. It's eight miles, and a mountain climb to the Waller mine branch. So that leaves us the concrete to Lacey, and a bridge with weak abutments."
>
> Major Robbins continued his monologue, till he saw a six-footer, in high-heeled boots, wide-brimmed hat and oiled raincoat. The man had a guitar case strapped across one shoulder. Atop the other was a blanket roll, rolled astride a horn saddle.

"Howdy, Cap'n," he announced, addressing the major. "Reckon this is the place to sojer. The name is Setters, but folks mostly call me Montana. Account of its my home—Montana. Been dude ranching, if yuh know what that is."

Major Robbins glanced at Captain Holland. Sergeant Wiggs winked slowly at an open-mouthed orderly. "So, you brought your riding gear along, eh?"

"Shore. Reckon yuh got hawses in the field artillery. Never heard tell anything else. Sa-a-ay, what goes on down in this country? Dry as powder hack home. Reckon if you'll tell me how to find the stables, I'll put away my plunder."

"Brother," Sergeant Wiggs spoke grimly, "There ain't any more horses. Not in the artillery. They're mechanized outfits now."

But horses were badly needed to resolve their dilemma and Montana was there to help. [EB]

Samuel Carson was a pulp fiction writer par excellence. Hundreds of his stories were published between 1920 and 1950, almost one a month, in dozens of different magazines: Peoples, Argosy, Ace High Westerns, Super Sports, Battle Birds, Thrilling Stories and Fantastic Universe and more. [5-08]

Missouri Canary

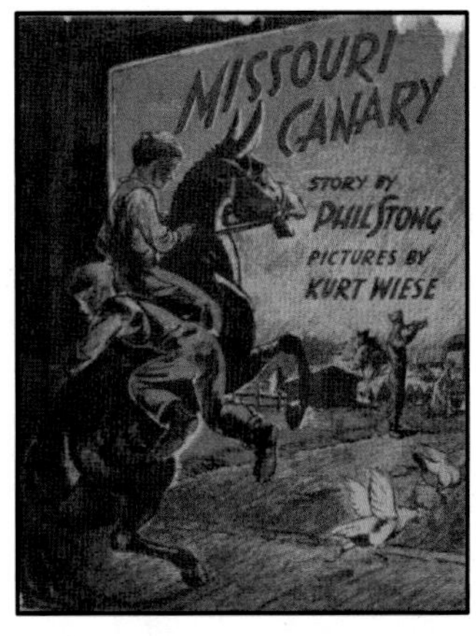

Animal, WW2, Youth

Phil Stong Dodd, Mead & Co. (1943)

Chuck and Bob were a little too young, at eleven and twelve, to join the Army; also, they were engaged in essential farm labor with their favorite mule, the Missouri Canary.

The Canary had a voice something like Lily Pons and something like Chaliapin but mostly like the bugling of Private Kaminsky, who had to peel a bushel of potatoes whenever he blew a false note. He was several thousand carloads of potato peels in debt when Bob took over his musical education.

Kaminsky, his sergeant, and several hundred soldiers came into the boys' lives when two Army forces from Des Moines put on practice warfare down the Des Moines River in Iowa.

This fast-moving, funny story tells how the boys' knowledge of the country and particularly their terrific charge on the back of the Canary as "irregular" cavalry had a devastating effect on the "enemy" during the Battle of Mudcat Creek, resulting in Bob and Chuck being decorated with all the hot dogs and sodas they could hold - with oats for the Missouri Canary, that original, alternating NON-GO . . . NON-STOP model of a military jeep! [DJ]

Philip Stong (1899–1957) was an American author, journalist, and Hollywood screen writer best known for his novel *State Fair.* It was adapted as a film (1962) and Broadway musical in 1996. [5-09]

Sgt O'Keefe & His Mule Balaam

Animal, Youth

Harold W. Felton Dodd, Mead & Co. (1962)

In 1881, the U. S. Army Signal Corps' weather station atop Pikes Peak was in the capable hands of one Sergeant John Timothy O'Keefe. Ably abetted by his durable Army mule, the tall Irishman saw that weather reports went out to the waiting world.

But it was the strange events that took place up there near the foot of heaven that really challenged the jovial Sergeant and Balaam. There was the time all the snow melted, and they had to whitewash the Peak. And molten lava fair threatened to make an end of the two of them, until Balaam's ears were put to astounding use.

The sugar-eatin' rats caused considerable trouble, too, and the night the blizzard came—well, even Sergeant O'Keefe himself wouldn't have believed it if he hadn't been there at the time. [DJ]

Harold William Felton, (1902–1991) born in Nebraska, was an American writer and folklorist, an author of many children's books and books of American tall tales. Among them were Paul Bunyan, Pecos Bill, John Henry, and Mike Fink. He worked for the Internal Revenue Service until retirement (1933–1970). [5-10]

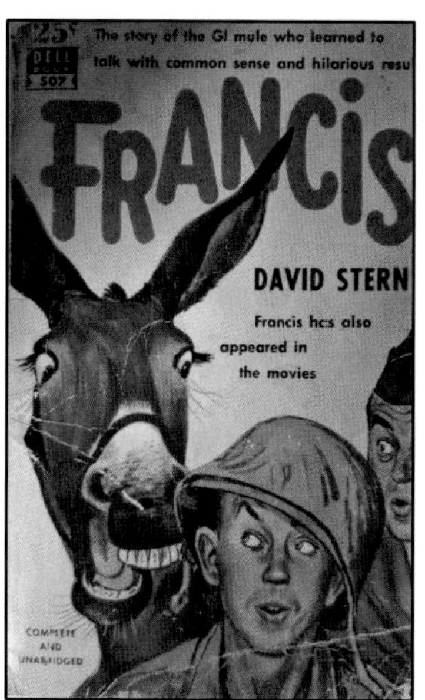

Francis the Talking Mule

Animal, Youth, DVD

David Stern Dell Comics (1946)

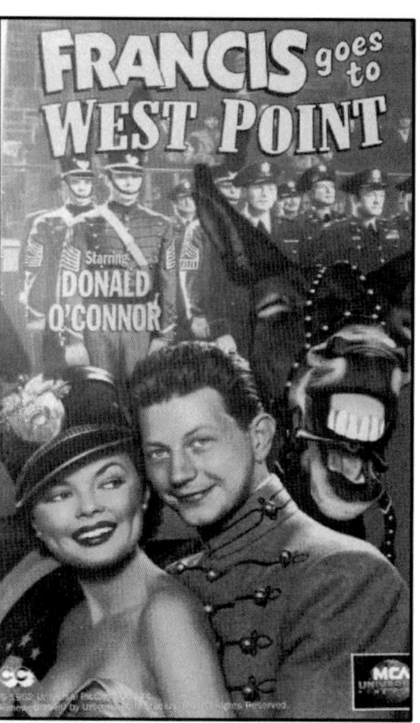

"Francis" tells of a soldier lost in the jungles of Burma who encounters an old army mule...who happens to talk! 2nd Lt. Peter Stirling finds himself in a mental hospital after he tries to explain to his unbelieving superior officers that a talking animal rescued him from behind enemy lines. When his four-legged friend appears with plans of heroic action, the U.S. Army faces one of its biggest - and most stubborn - challenges.

The book later became a film series starring Donald O'Conner in the role of Peter Sterling. The mule who appeared on-screen was a female named Molly, selected because she was easy to handle. The distinctive voice of Francis was provided by veteran character actor Theodore Childress, also known as "Chill Wills," with his deep, rough voice. [EB]

David Stern III (1909–2003) was an American iction author and scriptwriter, sometimes under the name Peter Stirling which was the name of the human lead opposite his most famous character, Francis the Talking Mule. During World War II as an Army captain working on military newspapers, Stern conceived a story about a talking mule in the Army. [5-11]

Hemi: A Mule

Animal, Youth

Barbara Brenner Harper & Row (1973)

Hemionus, a mule, grows up in the barn yard under the watchful eye of his mother and the sharp tongue of Hen. His life is pleasant but hardly fulfilling until the day the new farmhand arrives. Melville and Hemi become fast friends and Melville tells Hemi of his plans to buy a farm that they can work together. But one day Melville goes off to agricultural college and Hemi is sold to the Army to serve as mascot for their football team. Jackson, an old Army mule, prepares Hemi for the quiet, easy life in the Army. But Hemi is a restless mule. He wants more out of life than a green pasture and a warm barn. So Hemi starts the long journey west to find Melville. [DJ]

Barbara Brenner (1925– ?) is an award-winning author, specializing in works of both juvenile fiction and nonfiction educational material that deals with animals, nature, and ecology. [DJ]

Two authors in this chapter – Fairfax Downey and Helen Orr Watson, certainly enjoyed composing animal stories, especially about Army mascots. Seven of their stories are presented below.

Army Mule

Animal, Indian Wars, General Officer, Youth

Fairfax Downey & Paul Brown Dodd, Mead & Company (1945)

This is a novel about the mule, Proverbio, and his young packer, Stephen, during the 1870s Indian Wars. The historical pack-master General Crook, famed for the quality of his mule pack-trains, is a main character and the story draws on his experiences.

The campaign against the fierce Apaches in the 1870's is the setting for this exciting and likable story of a U. S. Army mule. He led one of the remarkable packtrains which carried ammunition and rations for the troops in hard marches through the deserts and mountains of Arizona to corner and conquer raiding tribesmen.

The mule Proverbio belonged to a veteran pack master, Fray Luis, who, buying him to save him from a former owner's cruelty, won the man's enmity. In this grudge and in encounters with Indians, Proverbio played far more than a passive part. He possessed a large share of the keen intelligence of his kind and was gifted in the use of that natural weapon, his heels. He was as devoted to his master and to his young packer, Stephen Flint, as they were to him and shared magnificently the perilous adventures they met. That smart and sturdy animal, the American mule, helped win the Indian Wars, as this tale relates. [DJ]

Mascots: Military Mascots from Ancient Egypt to Modern Korea

Animal

Fairfax Downey Coward-McCann (1954)

This book recounts thirty-one stories of military mascots, including ten from the U.S. Army divisions since the War of 1812 including "Mexique – U.S. Army Mule."

> "One day in 1832, a young lieutenant strode through an army camp in Alabama. He was William Tecumseh Sherman, who in the Civil War would become a famous Union general and fight his way through the heart of the Confederacy to Atlanta and on to the sea. Now, as he passed the stables, he stopped to look at a big sorrel mule tied outside on the picket line. The mule lifted his head and brayed. That long, raucous heehaw of his was inherited from his donkey father, as were his long ears, while his body was like that of his mother, a mare.
>
> Sherman stood admiring this splendid specimen of army mule. Such a strong fellow would surely pull more than his share in a team hauling a heavily laden supply wagon mile after mile, and he could easily carry on his back a pack weighing two hundred and fifty pounds or more. Sherman called the stable sergeant, to question him about the animal. Yes, the sergeant agreed, the mule was a wonder, although he was no longer a youngster. Why, some veterans in the garrison said that this mule had joined the army away back in 1818 during General Andrew Jackson's campaign against the Seminole Indians in 1830…"

Other Army mascots were "Wahb – U.S. Infantry Bear," "Young Abe – Eagle of the 101st Airborne," "G.I. Joe – U.S. Army Pigeon," and "G.I. Jenny – Fifth U.S. Army Donkey." [EB]

Fairfax Downey (1893–1990) was a writer and military historian. After graduating from Yale, he served in the U.S. Army as a captain of the 12th Field Artillery in World War I, receiving the Silver Star for gallantry at Belleau Wood. In the Second World War he served in North Africa, retiring as a lieutenant colonel. Several other of his books appear later in this chapter. [5-13]

Shavetail Sam: U.S. Army Mule

Animal

Helen Orr Watson Houghton, Mifflin & Co. (1944)

Sam was a mule with a great deal of zest and a mind of his own. The leader of all the mule foals on the farm, he did learn how to plow, through Elmer's patient training, but he enjoyed outwitting his master at every chance. Yet when Sam was auctioned off on Mule Day, Elmer felt sad, for he knew Sam was an unusually capable and clever mule.

The United States Army bought Sam and sent him to Front Royal Remount Training Depot. His name soon became Shavetail Sam, and he was taught how to be a pack mule and was broken to a rider. Sam proved his ability was unusual by conquering his instinctive fear of water and by taking such an exciting part in a fox hunt that he was sent to West Point as a mascot.

Shavetail Sam's West Point career, however, was cut short by his being mistakenly sent overseas. He saw England and arrived in the midst of the Italian Campaign to take a heroic part which brought happiness to Italian Tony, and by a strange coincidence, to his old master, Elmer. [DJ]

Helen Orr Watson (1892–1978), Army brat and wife of an Army Colonel, brought a thorough knowledge of Army life and a great love of horses and mules to the writing of her stories. Three of her books are in this chapter: *Shavetail Sam*, *Top Kick Army Horse*, and *Trooper Army Dog*. She also wrote a story about a U.S. Army carrier pigeon. [DJ] [5-14]

The Army Mule, and Horses Too!

Both animals were essential for Army mobility throughout the 19th and into the 20th century. Each had advantages over the other, depending upon the mission.

Mules are considered the tougher, stronger through the feet and legs, and generally able to pull and carry heavier loads. Moreover, they tend to be healthier and more disease resistant. Mules use less feed and survive on lower quality feed than horses. Mules have a longer working life. They are less likely to be spooked. Finally, mules, though noted for stubbornness, are quite safety-conscious, and will balk if uncertain of the wisdom of proceeding. [Drawing by Frederick Remington]

Horses are more agile, swifter and more compliant than mules. Horses were also used to haul artillery and wagons, but they were superior to mules as cavalry and officer mounts. [5-15]

Top Kick: U.S. Army Horse

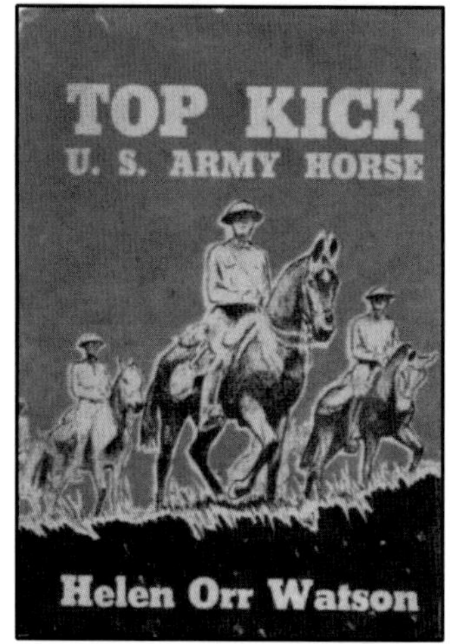

Animal, WW2

Helen Orr Watson Houghton, Mifflin & Co. (1942)

From the time he was old enough to stand up, Top Kick was an unusually lively and smart little colt. At the Army Remount Depot where he began his life, he astonished the stable sergeant by jumping over the pasture fence when he was only two weeks old, thereby earning the name he lived up to ever after. The first two years of his life Top Kick spent in growing, playing with the other colts, and getting into mischief. Then he began the long, careful training necessary to make a good cavalry horse, and under the wise guidance of Lieutenant Bayley and Muggins, the Colonel's daughter, he became the best jumper at the fort. His training completed; Top Kick went with Hayley to the Philippines for peace-time maneuvers on Bataan. Then bombs fell on Pearl Harbor, and Top Kick went into active service. In the days that followed, both horse and rider had opportunity to prove themselves true soldiers. [DJ]

"Horses for the Cavalry"

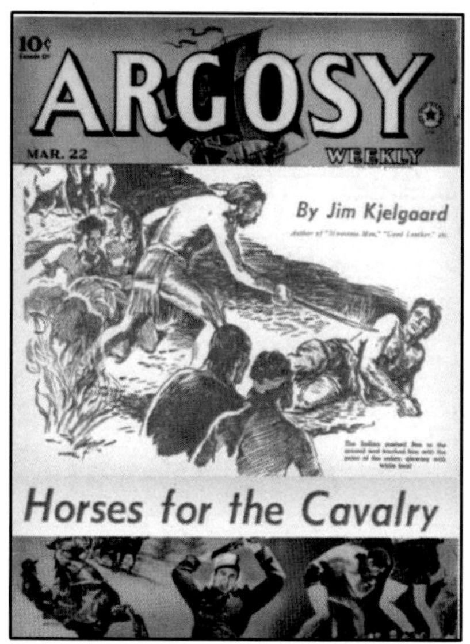

Western, Animal, Indian Wars, Pulp Fiction

Jim Kjelgaard Argosy Magazine (March 22, 1941)

In all the old West there's only one who can have his feet where his head ought to be and still win hands down. It's the Kid. Send him out with a stallion to deliver, and he comes back with a load of scalps. Threaten him with a Sioux, and he turns up with stew...

The thirty horses strung out in single file and walked at a fast pace. Trailing them by ten feet was a huge pinto stallion with a black head and a mean eye. He wore a rope hackamore, and from it a rope strung to and tied around his right front foot. That held his head down and kept him from running. Ten feet behind the stallion Ben Egan sat on a stubby black horse with the reins loose on his neck. Beside Ben, the Kid rode a bay pony. His chubby face was rapturously alight. This -- going out and buying horses for Tooker's cavalry -- was part of the high adventure he had come West to seek.

The holster flap of the elaborately carved pistol that swung by the Kid's side was buttoned back. They were near Indian country, and there was nothing like being ready.

Suddenly the stallion, holding his head low and running with a hopping little gait, ran ahead into the horses. He reared and sank his teeth into the neck of a little black mare. The mare squealed and fell out of line. Pivoting, the stallion singled out another mare. Ben dug his heels into the sides of his horse and rode forward, his rope swinging. The end of the rope hissed about the stallion's flanks. He kicked, laid his ears back, and snorted. Then he resumed his place in the rear. The Kid watched.

"Why'd he do that, Ben?" he asked.

Ben shrugged. "He run on Timly's ranch for many a year. He was head boss of eleven of the mares we got here. We buy the bunch from Timly an' they get a new boss. The stallion don't like it."

"What would he do if you let him go?"

"Reckon he'd cut his eleven out of the bunch an' cut back to Timly's. He's a troublemaker. Law lurnmy! I don't blame him. But he'll make an officer's mount. Shouldn't be surprised but what we can sell him for fifty, sixty dollars."

"Are all stallions like that?" the Kid pursued.... [EB]

Jim Kjelgaard (1910–1959) was an American writer of juvenile fiction, young adult, and children's literature stories. Kjelgaard wrote more than 40 novels. His books were primarily about dogs and wild animals, often with animal protagonists and told from the animal's point of view. Kjelgaard also wrote short fiction for several magazines, including *The Saturday Evening Post*, *Argosy*, and *Adventure*. [5-16]

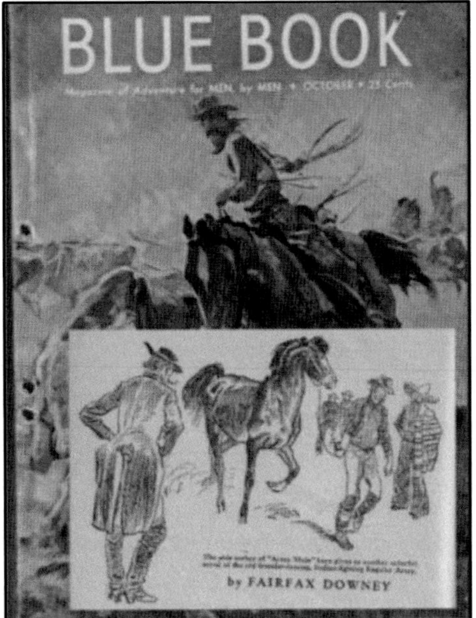

"Cavalry Mount"

Animal, Western

Fairfax Downey Blue Book Magazine (Oct. 1946)

He was black as night, except for his near foreleg with its "stocking" of gleaming white, so short it might almost be called a sock. He stood a trifle over fifteen hands high, and his conformation was good though a trifle short-coupled. But the feature of the horse that caught and held an observer's eye was his crest. Crest was the word for that neck proudly arched and head held high. His eyes were alight with spirit and intelligence. His ears, pricked up alertly, were small and set rather close together. Had his mane been roached, his crest would have been the very image of the horses' heads the ancient Greeks sculptured, or of the black night of a chess set. Somehow you could not picture him as ever crestfallen.

The horse, led by a lanky loose-jointed man through the single street of a frontier town to be watered in the stream beyond, stepped springily and tossed his head. Men turned to look at him. It was curious that he should attract any attention. In the Texas Panhandle in 1870 only extraordinary horses drew more than a passing glance…

And it was evident that the lanky man leading the black meant him to be noticed; his air of unconcern was a shade too elaborate. After he had walked the length of the street, he appeared to recollect some pressing errand at the store at the other end. Swinging himself onto the horse's back, he trotted back to the store, slid off and entered, while his mount stood patiently. The lanky man then emerged and rode back toward the stream. In the course of this performance, he had succeeded in demonstrating that the black horse possessed not only a stead walk, an even trot, and a swinging canter, but a fast running-walk and a smooth single-foot which made his rider seem to be comfortably seated on an air cushion. Here was a horse with five gaits. . . .

When man and horse had passed, two spectators followed—a grizzled, gray-bearded Major of cavalry and a stout, swarthy man, part Mexican, part Indian, to judge by his features. Twice the latter's beady black eyes had gleamed while he watched the horse: Once in admiration of the smooth single-footed gait, and again—and brighter— at the sight of the horse's one white leg. . .

The Army man strode to where the black horse was being watered and ran appraising eyes expertly over the animal. In the traditional manner he opened the bargaining. [EB]

Comanche

Animal, Youth, Custer

David Appel World Publishing Co. (1951)

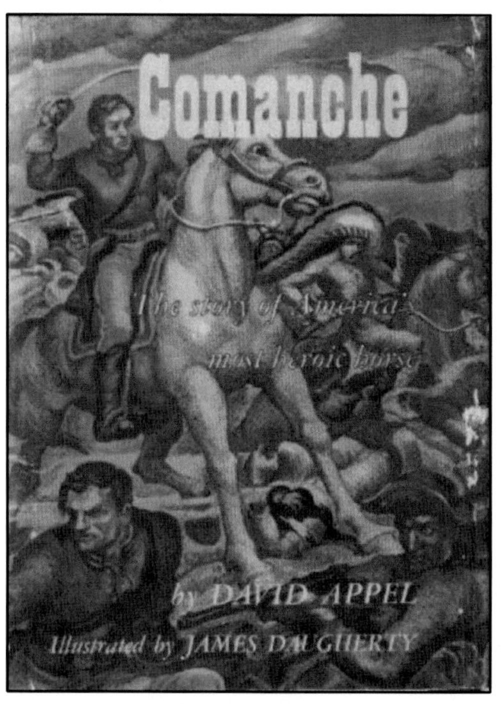

From Custer's Battle of the Little Big Horn, fought to the bloody climax known as Custer's Last Stand, there emerged one lone, badly wounded survivor: the ugly duckling army horse Comanche. Told by himself, this is Comanche's true story—the story of a man and a horse, a tale of drama and high courage in the West and on the battlefield. Comanche would never have won a blue ribbon at a horse show — but he was "all horse," just as his master, Captain Myles W. Keogh, General Custer, and others of that gallant little band were "all men." Here, in a story that recreates in miraculous fashion the atmosphere of the Western frontier and the tragic conflict between Indians and Federal Troopers, are some of the heroes of the West as well as some of the famous Sioux chieftains — Sitting Bull, White Bull, Crazy Horse, Rain-in-the-Face — who made life such a dangerous adventure for the pioneers. The horse Comanche belongs in the gallery of immortal Americans and famous horses. Sensitive and lovable, he is the hero of a story filled with action, drama, and suspense — an important part of the most exciting history of our country. [DJ]

David Appel (1910–1984) was the long-time book editor and feature editor of the Philadelphia Inquirer. An avid student of American history, he was fascinated by the character of George Armstrong Custer and the Battle of the Little Big Horn. [5-17]

Other Animals in West Point and Army Lore

The Seventh's Staghound

Animal, Indian Wars, Western, Custer

Fairfax Downey Dodd, Mead (1948)

The legendary General Custer and the gallant 7th Cavalry he led in the Indian Wars live again in the pages of this dramatic story. Following history closely, it rises to a stirring climax in the Battle of the Little Big Horn, presented with all this fine author's skill in combining fast action with a depth of feeling.

Primarily, this is the story of a staghound, one of those magnificent breeds of great dogs originating in the Highlands, dogs also called the Scottish deerhound or shaggy greyhound. Bran was a member of the pack of forty dogs with which Custer hunted buffalo, elk, and wolves. Just as dogs followed the Crusaders and staghounds were mascots of Scottish regiments sent to America and Canada, so favorite hounds accompanied Custer on his campaigns, including his last march against the Sioux and Cheyenne. Since the saga of a dog must also be that of the master he loves, this is also the tale of Trumpeter Peter Shannon.

Paul Brown has made the superb drawings of troopers, dogs, and horses, as in Fairfax Downey's five preceding historical novels of soldiers and the animals gallantly serving them. [DJ]

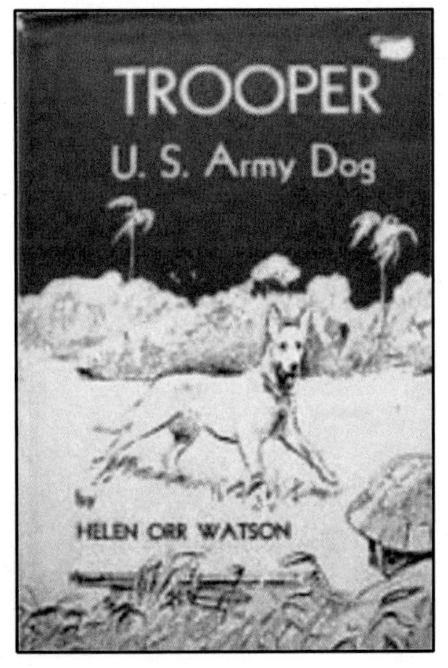

Trooper: U. S. Army Dog

Animal, WW2

Helen Orr Watson Houghton, Mifflin & Co. (1944)

U.S. Army Dog is rather more detailed routine of training of K 9's, however, and boys and girls who are considering the possibility of lending their pets for the duration [of the war] will find plenty of answers to questions as to what happens to them in this text. It is the story of Trooper, a white shepherd dog, who eventually gives his master full value for his sacrifice by discovering the brother reported "missing." [DJ]

Johnny Mouse of Corregidor

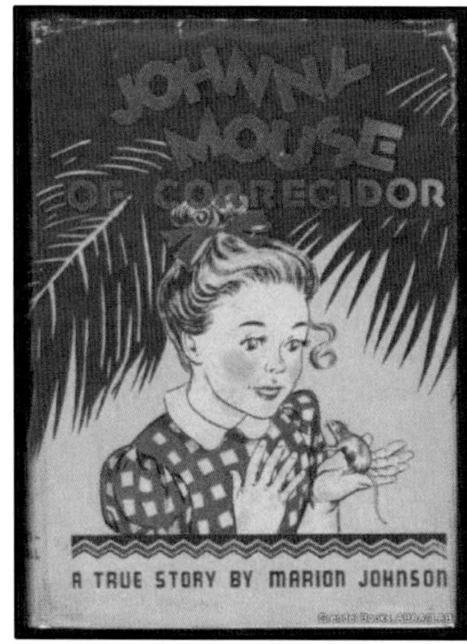

Youth, WW2, Philippines, Animal

Marion Rolfe Johnson   Bobbs-Merrill Company (1942)

Dedication:

To all the Army boys and girls whose fathers were on Corregidor December 7, 1941

Author's Acknowledgment:

The character "Johnny Mouse," which delighted me as a child, was originated by Johnny Gruelle, an author of popular children's books in the 1920's and 1930's. My Johnny Mouse was named for him. In this true story of my own little mouse, it seemed unthinkable to give him any other name than his own. I told the Johnny Gruelle Company how I felt, and they were friendly and understanding. The use, in this book, of the name "Johnny Mouse" is with and by full permission of the Johnny Gruelle Company. I earnestly hope that it may serve as tribute to that original Johnny's creator. . .

Marion Johnson aka **Janet (Jacquelin) Dietrich** grew up as an "Army brat," and her books reflect that life experience. In 1942, thousands of American soldiers were trapped by the Japanese on the Bataan Peninsula which motivated her to write this children's book. She also wrote two novels of life as an Army wife in the years before World War II. They are described in the chapter "Army Life and Army Wives." [DJ]

Wesley the West Point "Wabbit"
Freddy the Would-be Field Mouse
Rufus the West Point Squirrel

Animal, Children

Mary Elizabeth Sergent
Self-published between 1966 & 1976

Each of these extensively illustrated booklets – about 35 pages each – tells the story of a small animal observed on the Academy grounds.

Wesley was from a large family of West Point "wabbits." He lived in a borough near the Reveille gun. And he was terrified every time the gun went off "wham" morning and evening. . . .

One day at 10 a.m. Gen. Omar Bradley came on post. That meant nineteen "whams" as the saluting battery welcomed the Academy's only living five-star graduate. Wesley was a wreck when it was over, but worse was to follow. [EB]

Freddy was a barracks mouse. He lived in the cadet barracks at the United States Military Academy, West Point, NY, up the chimney in a room on the first floor of the old First Division.

He eats boodle which has been hidden up the chimney. And through a bizarre set of circumstances earns his parachute jump wings with a cadet at Ft. Campbell. [EB]

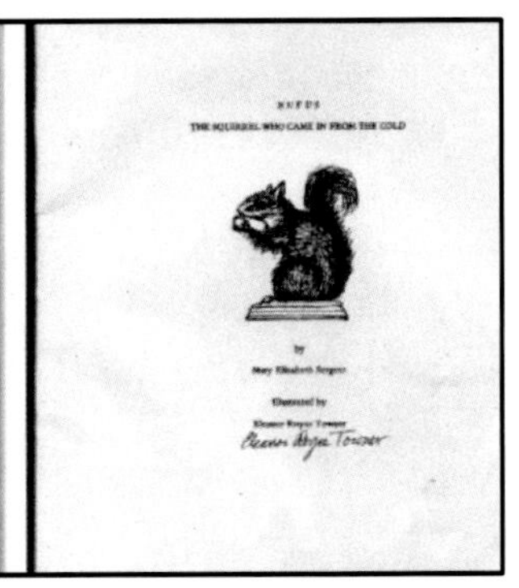

Once upon a time there lived a little gray squirrel named Rufus on the grounds of...West Point – in an oak tree on a hill half-way between the Catholic and the Protestant Cadet Chapels. Rufus came from a very ecumenical family.

He also came from a very old family. They were F.S.V's – First Squirrels of Virginia – though Rufus wished his ancestors had stayed in Virginia because it was very cold at West Point in December.

Long before the Army-Navy Game, Rufus began figuring out ways and means of keeping warm. Since he was a squirrel, and since any squirrel is one of the most diabolically intelligent of all creatures this was no tax on his brain. In fact, if he had been a human, he would have been a West Point graduate...with a doctorate from MIT. [EB]

Mary Elizabeth Sergent (1919–2005) grew up in Hudson River Valley and her father taught at West Point. She was active in the schools and historical societies of Orange County and authored these three children's stories in paperback between 1966 and 1976. Her other works include two non-fiction books on the West Point Class of 1861, May graduates - *They Lie Forgotten* and the Class of 1961, June graduates - *An Unremaining Glory*. Both were published by Prior King Press, 1986 and 1997 respectively. [5-18]

The book drawings were by **Eleanor Royce Towner** (1893–1979), a noted American illustrator living in the Hudson River Valley.

Chapter 6

Paranormal, Supernatural & Futuristic

"The terms 'paranormal' and 'supernatural' are often tossed around to mean the same thing—something we don't understand. They are actually two separate terms. Though "Paranormal" refers to something that's not understood by current scientific knowledge; there is the potential that something paranormal will someday be explained scientifically, and a likelihood of a good, natural explanation for it. "Supernatural" refers to a phenomenon that is beyond our capability to understand now, and simply forever, because it just doesn't operate under our rules." [6-01]

Paranormal at West Point

The Academy, with over two centuries of history, is fertile ground for the paranormal! Certain "haunted quarters" and the cemetery are the principal locations as you shall see.

On October 31, 2019, **Michelle Schneider**, a frequent author of articles in the *Pointer View* on events at the U.S. Military Academy, posted an article on supernatural occurrences at West Point at https://www.army.mil. Her article, which follows, serves as an excellent narrative for the Paranormal section of this chapter. So, we begin with it. [6-02]

> The U.S. Military Academy's buildings are covered with textured granite, turrets and perched gargoyles that gaze over cadets as they go about their day. Inside the large wooden doors, they walk through dimly lit hallways with triangular stone arches and wrought iron windows.
>
> Cadets over the years said they have a shared feeling as if they were being observed by an unseen presence just to find no one there, while others have reported encountering apparitions in the middle of the night. This was frequently documented during the 1970s when a ghost visited the barracks.
>
> In 1972, West Point experienced an explosion of national inquiry and publicity because of a well-documented apparition that attracted famous demonologists, ghost hunters and psychic mediums of the last century to investigate, but that is just one of West Point's ghostly tales. The stories below were sourced from more than 40 years of correspondence, articles and book excerpts collected by USMA historians.
>
> Lt. Col. Timothy R. O'Neill gave a thorough perspective in his book, "Shades of Gray." The following story was inspired by details from his research.

Shades of Gray

Paranormal

Timothy R. O'Neill   Penguin Publishing Group (1987)

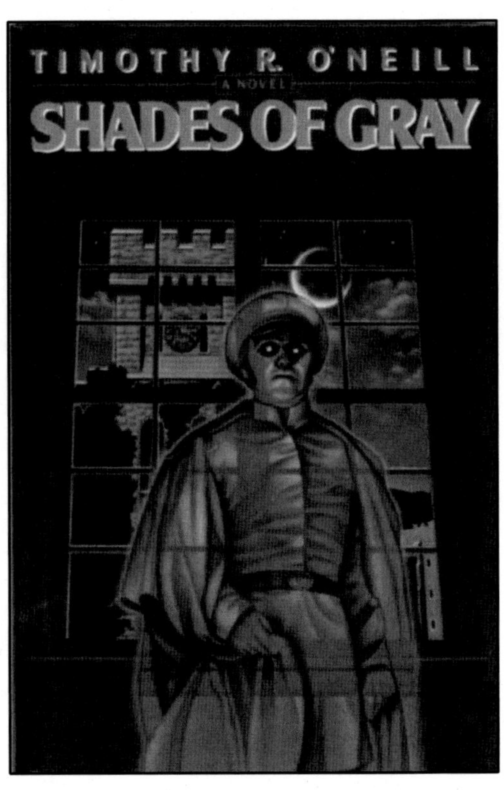

The dream would start with the high-pitched sound of a child crying, and with that would come the cold, frosting the windows of the old barracks room in the 47th Division at West Point. Cadet Barstow would wake then, and the gray shape would be there, the lights of its eyes shining on him with infinite sadness. Barstow thought he was going crazy. One morning, visited again by the dream and its spectral attendant, he disappeared.

When faculty psychologists Sam Bondurant and Liam FitzDonnell are consulted in the Barstow case, their job is to keep the episode quiet—at least until the Army-Navy game—and to find some reasonable explanation for whatever the hell is really going on in that room. Sam and Liam are friends who rarely see eye to eye, but together they're fit for the task—Sam with his rationalism and faith in sophisticated equipment, Liam with his own painful grasp of the demons to which the mind is vulnerable. Their investigation is willfully joined by Sam's scholarly and fanciful wife, Maggie, who gradually uncovers evidence of not one ghost but several, bound together in the warp of time by a fatal fire in 1830.

What none of these protagonists realizes is the awesome power of the supernatural – the power to clutch at the living from the other side of death. *Shades of Gray* offers the reader many satisfactions: a colorful and amusing portrait of West Point and the people who spend their lives there, a resonant psychological theme, stylish and intelligent writing. But, most of all, Timothy O'Neill's novel makes the power of the supernatural real…and terrifying. [DJ]

Timothy R. O'Neill (1943–), a graduate of the Citadel, served in the United States Army for 26 years, and on the faculty at West Point for fifteen. At the US Military Academy, he was director of the engineering psychology program. Since his retirement from the Army, he has served as a business executive, trained foreign special operations units, and worked as a defense consultant. He is the author of several novels. [6-03]

Article by Michelle Schneider (continued)

Room 4714 & The Pusher

In October 1972 at 2 a.m. in Room 4714 of the North Barracks' 47th Division, two male cadets were sound asleep when a ghost Soldier manifested in front of the younger cadet and the closet against a wall. The Soldier stared with menacing eyes made of light that stirred the cadet to consciousness. Upon waking, the cadet screamed, and the Soldier immediately vanished. The cadet's roommate did not see anything but said there was an otherworldly coldness in the room.

The ghost was described as a middle-aged Soldier donning an antique uniform from the 1830s, a musket, shako hat and handlebar mustache. The ghost earned his nickname "The Pusher" because his ice-cold presence forced other victims to lay immobile until the pressure of his hazy, glowing physique disappeared.

According to The New York Times, The Pusher appeared a second time in an area known as the Bureau. One cadet they interviewed shared that the ghost walked out amidst a group of cadets which caused them to scream, clutch each other and say the rosary. Reports of seeing him were sporadic over the following years, but The Pusher has not revisited where he first appeared.

Room 4714 is no longer occupied by cadets; the room was converted into a study area and seemingly exorcized due to no other paranormal accounts being documented since 1972. The building has since been renamed Scott Barracks.

Ghost Hunters: True Stories from the World's Most Famous Demonologists

Paranormal, Anthology

Ed & Lorraine Warren St. Martin's Press (1989)

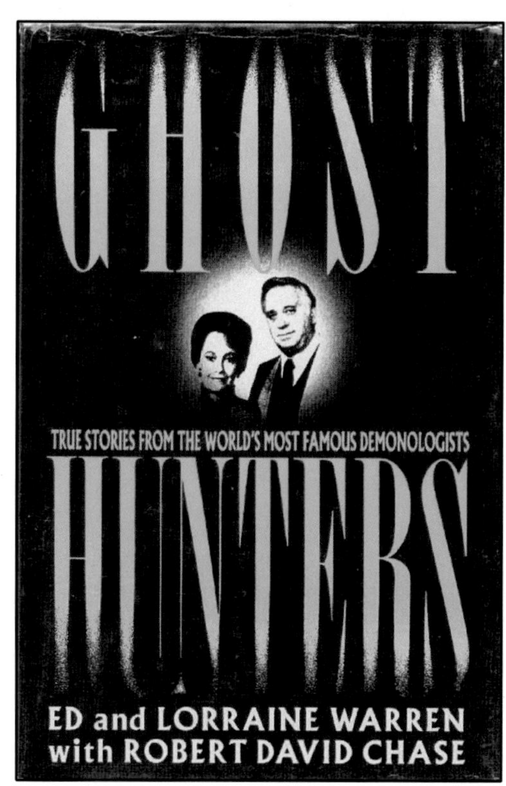

The year was 1972. At the time, Lorraine and I had a manager who helped to schedule our speaking engagements. Before hearing anything about ghosts at West Point, we had been scheduled to speak there at the request of staff and students alike. We were flattered. Like most Americans, we have great respect for our military academies. So, it was a special thrill to be asked by such a group to tell them about ourselves and our work. We accepted the invitation at once and were told that on the appointed day, a military car would pick us up at our home.

Few speaking engagements make us nervous -- we've become accustomed to sharing ourselves with audiences, but both of us admitted to a little bit of apprehension as the day approached. This was, after all, West Point!

Lorraine smiled to herself when she saw the "car" that had been dispatched from West Point. This sort of limousine was something she had seen previously only in movies... Over the next few hours, we passed through some of the most beautiful land in the nation, rural hills and valleys fiery with hot October autumn....

As the limousine topped a hill, Lorraine caught her first glimpse of the military academy. She literally caught her breath. She had rarely seen anything so beautiful. Set on part of a 16,000-acre military reservation and situated on the bank of the Hudson River in New York. West Point gives the impression of being a vast fortress of stone, brick, and mortar isolated from all civilization. In fact. the academy is only fifty miles from
New York City. . . .[EB]

Edward Warren (1926–2006) and **Lorraine Rita Warren** née Moran (1927–2019) were American paranormal investigators and authors associated with prominent cases of alleged hauntings. Edward was a self-taught and self-professed demonologist, author, and lecturer. Lorraine professed to be clairvoyant and a light trance medium who worked closely with her husband. [6-04]

Article by Michelle Schneider (continued)

Quarters 100-Molly & Greer

Over 217 years have passed since West Point opened its doors as an Army institution of higher learning, but the land hosts a complex history that comes with an abundance of stories. One can imagine there are plenty of other haunted areas on post besides the barracks.

The superintendent's house is known as Quarters 100. For paranormal believers, it serves as a supernatural hotel given the variety of spirit personalities that come and go. Based on several reports, there are two permanent ghost residents to this day.

Former Superintendent Lt. Gen. William A. Knowlton invited married clairvoyants Eric and Lorraine Warren to perform a psychic investigation and séance at the house in 1972. The wife revealed her psychic impressions of those living in another dimension as she toured the rooms of Quarters 100.

The superintendent noted detailed accounts of Warren's psychic impressions that she picked up during her investigation. They included descriptions of the spirits and energy present in each room. He wrote them down in a memorandum to the librarian requesting them to search West Point archives and find evidence that supported her claims.

Warren described a woman who could be the ghost named Molly, an Irish cook who served Sylvanus Thayer. She is known to rumple bed linens and knock wine bottles to the floor in the kitchen.

"She is not old, very domineering, athletically inclined, and really not quite a lady. I get a feeling of no man; if she had a husband, he was dominated while at home," Warren said.

Others who've worked at Quarters 100 have said that although mischievous, Molly does not mean any harm and is more playful than hurtful in nature.

Another ghost that struck Warren with a strong psychic impression was an African American man named Greer. She shared that Greer is the one responsible for moving objects throughout the home. One example was written in Knowlton's memorandum.

When the former superintendent of the Coast Guard Academy and his wife stayed at the house as guests, they woke up early in the morning and found a wallet that belonged to another occupant in the home carefully placed between them in bed.

Warren described Greer as tall and slender in a gray uniform, that he was an orderly to a superintendent and communicated that he carries a deep burden of guilt and sadness from committing murder.

In the librarian's response to the superintendent's request for verifiable information, archivists were able to find documented evidence of several African American men who came through West Point with Greer's name. One of the descriptions that potentially best fits that of the ghost Warner encountered was Lawrence Greer, a Buffalo Soldier who turned out to be a criminal.

"General prisoner Lawrence Greer was definitely black, formerly a private in Troop C, 9th Calvary. He escaped from confinement at Fort Leavenworth in June of 1931, and was apprehended the following April near Albany, New York. He was brought to West Point and court-martialed for his escape and subsequent desertion," Chief of USMA Archives Stanley Tozeski said.

Found guilty, he was sentenced to 2 1/2 years of hard labor. However, the sentence was disapproved by command of Maj. Gen. Connor because the prisoner was judged insane at the time of his trial. We have no record of what happened to Pvt. Greer after these events.

The librarian seemed motivated, but he said most of Warren's descriptions would require an extensive search of reminiscences from past superintendents which are not part of the archive's holdings. Today, West Point archivists can provide memories from past graduates and professors when they lived at another haunted house.

Fright to the Point: Ghosts of West Point

Cadet, Paranormal

Maj. Thad Krasnesky Schiffer Publishing, Ltd. (2011)

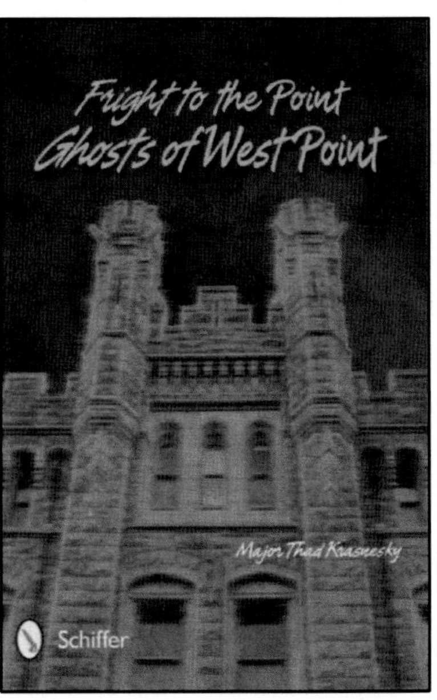

The United States Military Academy at West Point houses more than cadets; there are ghosts aplenty to harbor your imagination and pique your curiosity about the country's oldest continuously running military base. This collection of 13 spooky ghost stories is focused on apparitions that make their home at West Point right along with the living souls who march the halls of patriotism every day. Within these pages meet Vivian, a mourning ghost at the Morrison House, but be careful not to lose your head over her (literally). The playful, but lazy, spirit maid of Washington Hall may take your wallet, or you may be surprised to see the Lady in White at the Catholic Chapel floating at nearly 100 feet above your head -- just before she plunges to the ground and disappears. What will frighten you at West Point? [BC]

Thad Krasnesky retired from life as an active-duty Military Intelligence Officer and settled down to his new life as a children's author. "During my five deployments, I took time out to write and work with children. I have always enjoyed telling stories to my daughters." [6-05]

Article by Michelle Schneider (continued)

Quarters 107B & The Lady

It was reported in email correspondence between several former cadets and the Association of Graduates that a ghostly occupant named "The Lady" resides at Quarters 107B on Professor's Row, a home overlooking the Hudson River.

A professor once lived there with his young wife, but their story does not end happily ever after. The couple was struck with tragedy when she became fatally ill in the 1920s. To help ease her sickness and keep the house tidy, her mother came to live with them. The story goes that the professor and mother shared an attraction that grew into love which devastated the wife; perhaps her untimely death arrived even faster due to a broken heart.

They say "Hell hath no fury like a woman scorned." She made her husband pledge not to remarry her mother, but once she took her last breath, he took vows shortly after with the mother anyway.

The ghost was left by a man she was in love with for her own mother, and their affair began in the same home she was bedridden in. Some mediums say her intense emotional distress began while she was alive, but keeps her soul gripped to this world from a lack of finding peace. This is what has prompted chaotic paranormal activity over the years.

It was reported that items were thrown and turned upside down, a clock that was frozen for years abruptly chimed to life and a former tenant said they heard "horrendous sounds in the night like someone riding a big wheel across the wooden floor overhead." The haunting was so frequent the post engineer had to seal the ghost's bedroom off at one point because she scared people out of it, but the room was eventually reopened in the 1950s.

Although these disturbing actions were not very lady-like, the ghost received her name from the 8-year-old daughter of a Class of 1960 graduate. The family lived there between 1971-75 and the little girl and her younger sister occupied the haunted room during that time.

The girl woke her parents up in the middle of the night on multiple occasions. They heard their child having a conversation, but after getting out of bed to check on her, they discovered she was not speaking with anyone they could see. When the parents asked her who she was talking to, she called her The Lady.

Aside from West Point's most famous spirits, there were reports of other paranormal activity throughout the installation. An extra head in a cadet's group photo peered in from a MacArthur Barrack's window. Frightened pets barked at nothing in officers' quarters. A cleaner on the night crew quit his job after being thrown by a malevolent spirit in Building 606.

While this concludes Michelle Schneider's narrative, the supernatural sightings at West Point were covered in a number of other publications from the 1970s on.

"The Haunting Hussar of West Point"

Cadet, Paranormal, Comic Book

DC Ghosts Comics, #20 (November 1973)

For nearly two centuries, the United States Military Academy has turned out men of iron courage, gallant in battle, fearless in the face of death, so why do the cadets at West Point panic when they encounter The Haunting Hussar of West Point?

The plebes first saw the ghost on October 21st, 1972. [EB]

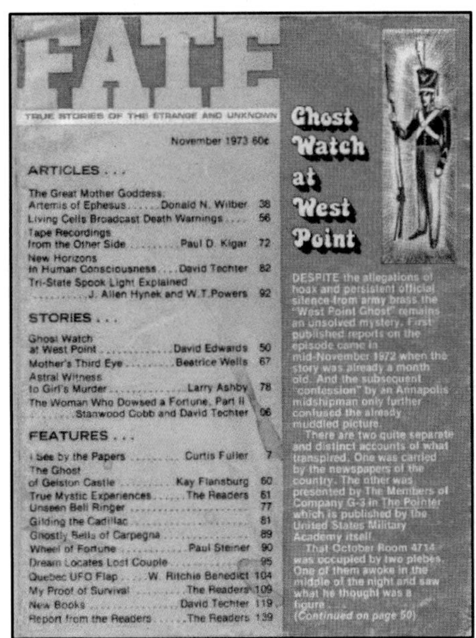

FATE

TRUE STORIES OF THE STRANGE AND UNKNOWN

November 1973 60¢

ARTICLES . . .

The Great Mother Goddess:
Artemis of Ephesus . . . . . . Donald N. Wilber 38
Living Cells Broadcast Death Warnings 56
Tape Recordings
from the Other Side . . . . Paul D. Kigar 72
New Horizons
in Human Consciousness . . . . David Techter 82
Tri-State Spook Light Explained
. . . . J. Allen Hynek and W.T. Powers 92

STORIES . . .

Ghost Watch
at West Point . . . . David Edwards 50
Mother's Third Eye . . . . Beatrice Wells 67
Astral Witness
to Girl's Murder . . . . Larry Ashby 78
The Woman Who Dowsed a Fortune, Part II
. . . . Stanwood Cobb and David Techter 96

FEATURES . . .

I See by the Papers . . . . Curtis Fuller 7
The Ghost
of Geiston Castle . . . . Kay Flansburg 60
True Mystic Experiences . . . . . . The Readers 61
Unseen Bell Ringer 77
Gilding the Cadillac 81
Ghostly Bells of Carpegna 89
Wheel of Fortune . . . . Paul Steiner 90
Dream Locates Lost Couple 95
Quebec UFO Flap . . . . W. Ritchie Benedict 104
My Proof of Survival . . . . The Readers 109
New Books . . . . David Techter 119
Report from the Readers . . . . . The Readers 139

Ghost Watch at West Point

DESPITE the allegations of hoax and persistent official silence from army brass the "West Point Ghost" remains an unsolved mystery. First published reports on the episode came in mid-November 1972 when the story was already a month old. And the subsequent "confession" by an Annapolis midshipman only further confused the already muddled picture.

There are two quite separate and distinct accounts of what transpired. One was carried by the newspapers of the country. The other was presented by The Members of Company G-3 in The Pointer which is published by the United States Military Academy itself.

That October Room 4714 was occupied by two plebes. One of them awoke in the middle of the night and saw what he thought was a figure . . .

(Continued on page 50)

"Ghost Watch at West Point"

Paranormal, Anthology

David Edwards Fate Magazine (1973)

Despite the allegations of hoax and persistent official silence from Army brass the "West Point Ghost" remains an unsolved mystery. First published reports on the episode came in mid-November 1972 when the story was already a month old. And the subsequent confession by an Annapolis midshipman only further confused the already muddled picture.

There are two quite separate and distinct accounts of what transpired. One was carried by the newspapers of the country. The other was presented to the members of Company G-3 in the Pointer which is published by the United States Military Academy itself.

That October, Room 4714 was occupied by two plebes. One of them awoke in the middle of the night and saw what he thought was a figure coming through the door of their room . . . [EB]

"The Werewolf of West Point"

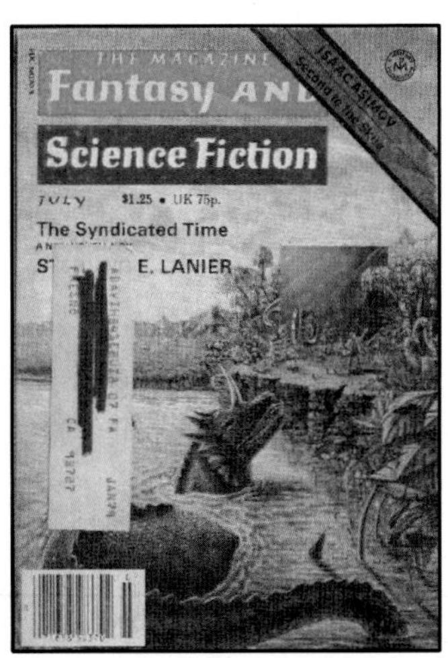

Paranormal, Anthology, WP Female

Paul Dellinger Fantasy and Science Fiction (July 1978)

The U. S. Military Academy at West Point, New York, might seem an unlikely setting for such an encounter, unless perhaps you've been there during the dead of winter and seen its gray Gothic architecture looming in silhouette against a mist rising off the Hudson River. That's how it looked the night I was walking across the reservation back to the enlisted men's barracks, after my usual frustrating few minutes with the beautiful Bingo Barbetta of the incomparable face and the impossible figure.

I suppose any guy who lets himself flip for a West Point cadet deserves what he gets (which isn't much, considering corps regulations about public displays of affection), but Bingo was something special. She'd come in with the more than 100 Bicentennial broads who, after 174 years of male exclusivity, broke the academy's sex barrier, and she was one of the few who'd made it through their plebe year. Now she was less than a year away from graduation and a second lieutenant's commission, and what could be sillier than a lowly Specialist 4 myself lusting after her . . . [EB]

Paul Dellinger tells us that he graduated from Roanoke College, Va., in 1960, spent the next three years in the Army, being assigned during the last two years to the Information Office at West Point and eventually as editor of its post newspaper, which is where he got the background for this story. 6-06

"West Point Werewolf"

Anthology, Futuristic, Paranormal

L. C. Stephens Lee's Publishing (1998)

This tale appears in a collection of short stories about the supernatural.

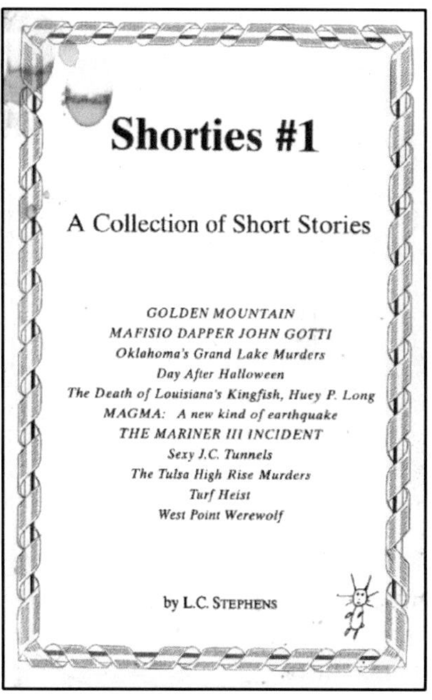

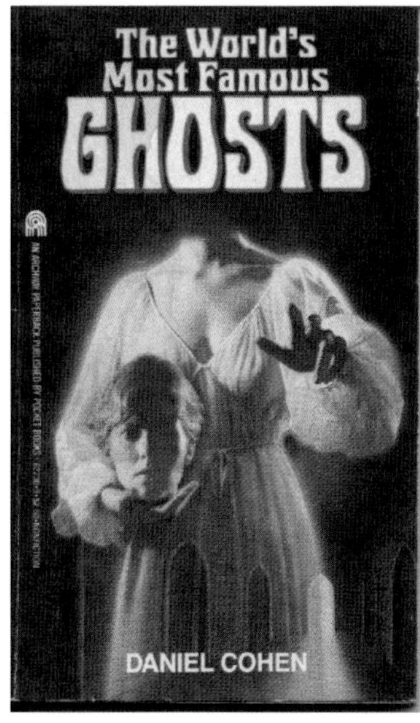

The World's Most Famous Ghosts

Paranormal, Anthology

Daniel Cohen Pocket Books (1979)

Table of Contents

Daniel Edward Cohen (1936–2018) was an American non-fiction author who wrote over one hundred books on a variety of subjects, mainly for young audiences. Cohen was well known for his books about UFOs, ghosts, psychic phenomena, cryptozoology, and the occult. He also fought for justice for the death of his daughter and the other 269 victims of the terrorist bombing of Pan Am Flight 103 over Lockerbie, Scotland. [6-07]

To conclude this section, here is a novel that might well be classified both as "Paranormal" and "Supernatural." It is a bizarre tale with many scenes of winter on the Hudson between the communities of Newburgh and Garrison, NY. It's about the days following the disappearance of Cadet Richard Cox in 1950. See the chapter, "Mystery, Crime & Intrigue" for stories about his disappearance.

Hard to Die

Mystery Intrigue, Supernatural

Andra Watkins Word Hermit Press (2016)

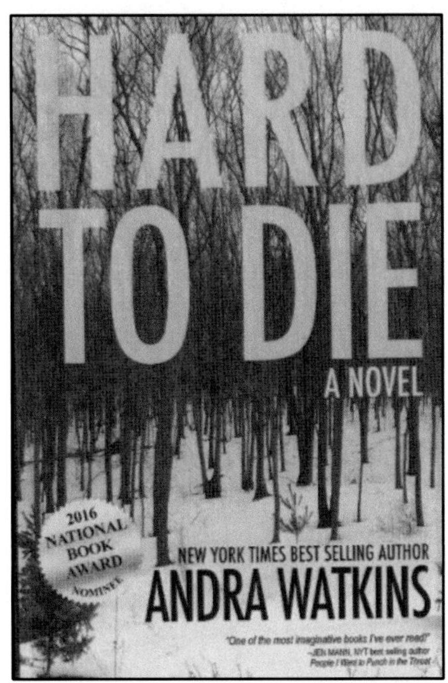

This speculative fiction time-warp combines elements of history, the paranormal, and suspense to breathe fresh air into Theodosia's (daughter of Vice President Aaron Burr) forgotten life and story. She encounters, Richard Cox, the cadet who mysteriously disappeared from West Point in January 1950 and was never seen again. The surprising sequel to her debut novel, *To Live Forever: An Afterlife Journey of Meriwether Lewis*. [DJ]

Andra Watkins (1969–), though a CPA by training, she now devotes her time to writing and public speaking engagements. She is the author of five books and counting. She has received a National Book Award nomination.
6-08

Supernatural

Now we turn to novels with plots and characters that are simply incredible. The laws of our natural world do not encompass the transformations we see here, but readers may certainly savor the fantastic stories.

P. G. Allison created a dozen novels (so far!) about two supernatural women that attend West Point.

The *Missy the Werecat* series depicts a girl growing up with no pack, no pride of other werecats and no Alpha for guidance. Missy exhibits fantastic abilities to do great things in today's world among humans. She can convert herself to a female werecat [mountain lion] when called upon by her handlers in the U.S. Government. Later in the series, Missy spends a semester at the Naval Academy as part of the cadet/midshipman exchange program.

Allison's second series of three novels features Tracy, an Army brat and a Fire Witch, who attends West Point. She aspires to be a helicopter pilot. [EB]

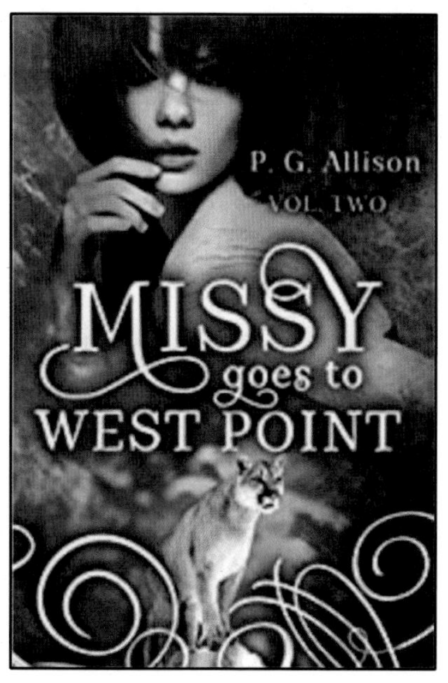

Missy Goes to West Point

WP Female, Supernatural

P.G. Allison Create Space Independent Publishing (2014)

The US Government's Paranormal Branch has learned Missy's secret and followed most of her activities. They have her FBI friend join their team, telling him that other super naturals also exist but Missy is the only female werecat. They want Missy to go on to West Point and tell him that, "being a vigilante is not what we want for this girl."

What had started out as her simply trying to help protect another teenage girl eventually led to her being targeted by both the East Boston and New York criminal organizations. With some help from her FBI friend, she copes with crime bosses while finishing high school and starting out at West Point. She also gets some help from her new friends at West Point but makes some enemies there as well.

Even with all this help and her enhanced senses, Missy sure has her work cut out for her! [BC]

Missy's First Mission

WP Female, Supernatural, Afghanistan

P.G. Allison Create Space Independent Publishing (2014)

The US Government has avoided using super naturals in the past, concerned that public knowledge of their existence will pose greater risks than any benefits. But, after Missy agrees to help her Paranormal Branch buddies and one thing leads to another . . . the question then becomes whether Missy can somehow provide assistance during an international crisis, without the world learning about her supernatural powers and abilities.

Meanwhile, when Missy interferes with the sexual harassment at West Point by going around and putting everyone there on notice, she becomes the target. Controlling herself . . . doing things in plain sight which almost look humanly possible . . . that just might be her greatest ability. [BC]

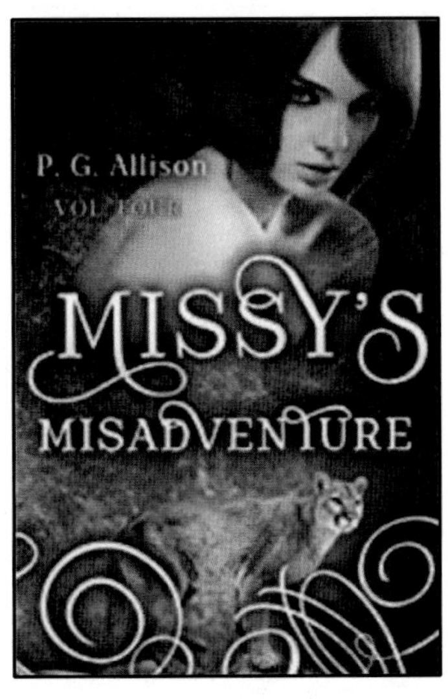

Missy's Misadventure

WP Female, Supernatural

P.G. Allison Create Space Independent Publishing (2015)

Missy has returned to West Point, only to find she must once again rush off to help her buddies at Paranormal Branch. This time, her friend Tracy goes along. One thing leads to another and soon the girls are dealing with international crime organizations and terrorists. They also, of course, must then explain a few things to their boyfriends!

Missy and Tracy certainly have many friends in high places at the U. S. Government, but those friends are finding it harder and harder to keep all the supernatural activities by these girls a secret. And will any of Missy's adventures affect her career at West Point? [BC]

Missy Makes Mayhem

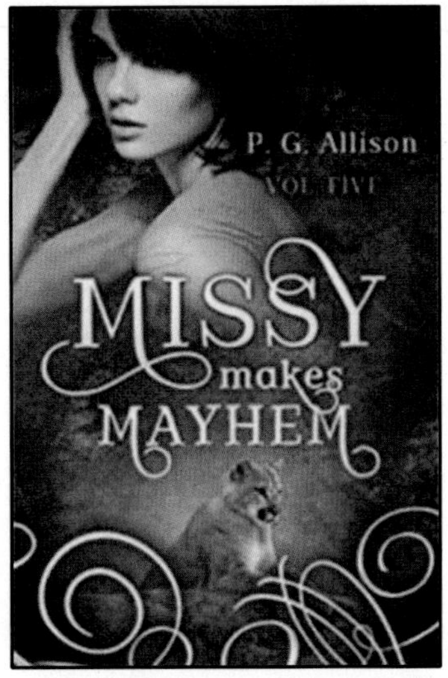

WP Female, Supernatural

P.G. Allison Create Space Independent Publishing (2015)

Missy and her friends have convinced government officials that using super naturals can indeed be managed. Such activities must of course be disguised or kept secret. The greater concern now is whether any enemies of the U.S. might have super naturals and, if so, how to deal with them.

Meanwhile, Missy enjoys day-to-day life back at the academy until learning a mob war puts some of her friends at risk; she once again confronts the local crime boss only to end up helping him. Thank goodness she has discovered a new and unique special ability which she can use. Then, that ability becomes especially needed when terrorist threats against some target cities in the U.S. are discovered. [BC]

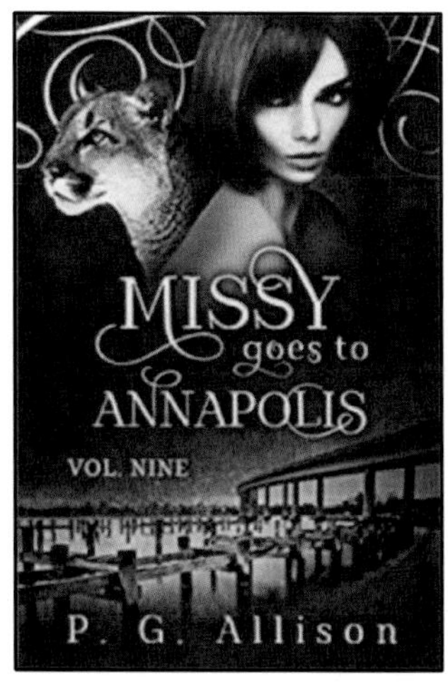

Missy Goes to Annapolis

WP Female, Supernatural

P.G. Allison Self-published (2021)

After her second year at West Point, Missy returns to her Special Forces A-Team in Afghanistan for summer training. That soon leads to her being deployed into Iran and Syria. Her boyfriend Mike tells her that's getting a little too real since she's not just training over there.

Then, for the first semester of her third year, she heads over to the Naval Academy to participate in the Service Academy Exchange Program. The idea is to make better leaders by promoting professional, academic and social experiences.

But there are those who have other ideas about her being there. Can she handle all the responsibilities the Fates have given her, hide all her supernatural abilities and cope with those who are planning to destroy her? [BC]

More Missy Adventures at Annapolis

WP Female, Supernatural

P.G. Allison Self-published (2022)

Missy is halfway through her semester at the Naval Academy, and all is well. Or is it? Those mobsters she warned not to mess with her are ignoring her warning. Soon two of her friends will be dating spies working for those mobsters.

Meanwhile, over in Iran, the investigation continues as to how U.S. forces are somehow learning so many secrets and interfering with planned attacks. Eventually, that investigation will lead back to Missy. How will she choose to handle that?

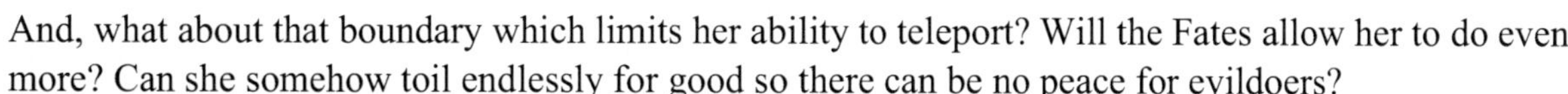

And, what about that boundary which limits her ability to teleport? Will the Fates allow her to do even more? Can she somehow toil endlessly for good so there can be no peace for evildoers?

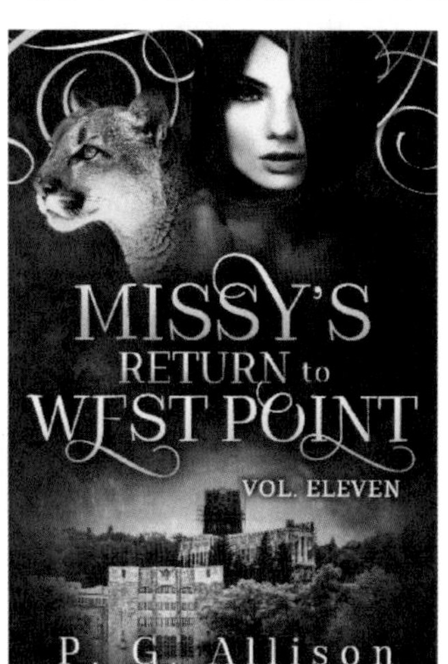

Of course, the really big question is: who will win the Army-Navy game? [BC]

Missy Returns to West Point

WP Female, Supernatural

P.G. Allison Self-published (2023)

Book XI Missy returns to West Point after her semester at the Naval Academy. Things all seem to go nicely at first. Her mobster buddies are no longer causing problems. Things in the Mid-East are winding down and the U.S. will be withdrawing its troops later that year. Everyone is watching how the new administration in the U.S. will be handling things.

The transition team does have concerns, however. Once they discover supernaturals exist and how some of them have been helping defend the country, their initial reaction is to seek some rules for engagement. Missy is so powerful they consider her to be a weapon of mass destruction which must be controlled.

Then, the new Defense Secretary asks Missy to use her teleporting ability to do some more spying. What threats might there be from secret nuclear programs being carried out by their enemies? What will she find? And ... what will she be asked to do about it? [BC]

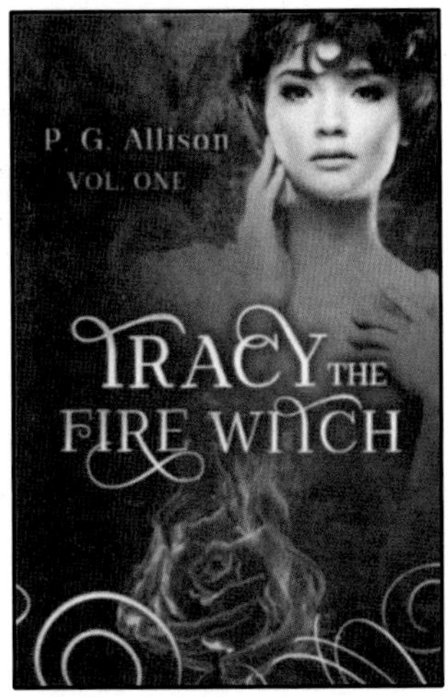

Tracy the Fire Witch

WP Female, Supernatural

P.G. Allison Self-published (2019)

When a nightclub in Munich is bombed by terrorists just days before Tracy starts her spring break vacation from West Point, the U.S. government's special task force asks her to join the team they're sending to Germany. They're hoping to stir up those terrorists and make them scramble. Having Tracy along will provide them with some added firepower. When she asks her soulmate John if he's okay with going with her, he replies, "Germany? Werewolves? Maybe some terrorists? What's not to like?" [BC]

Tracy Plays Demon

WP Female, Supernatural

P.G. Allison Self-published (2021)

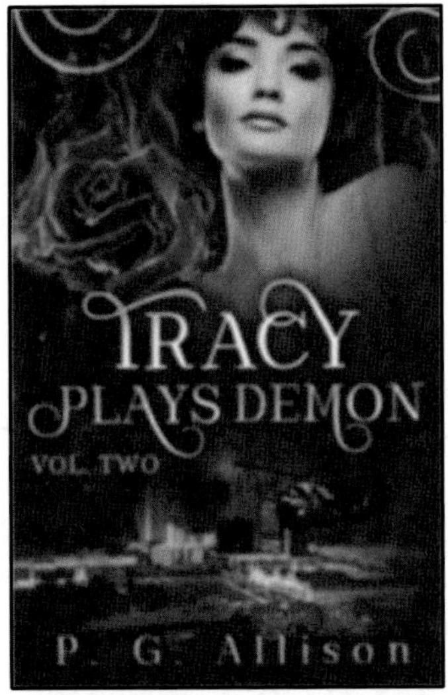

After her second year at West Point, Tracy is headed to Ft. Rucker for a few weeks of training; she hopes to become a helicopter pilot someday. But before she even arrives, there's a murder. This will affect her assignment while she also makes some new friends.

Meanwhile, some prisoners released because of the U.S.-Taliban peace deal have vowed revenge against the U.S. military and are also headed to Ft. Rucker. They're getting support from WIJO and there's a warehouse filled with explosives they can use.

Her government friends will help but they'll also need a few werewolves before this is over. And, what about those new powers and abilities which Tracy has been gaining? [BC]

P. G. Allison has always loved stories about female characters with special powers (Supergirl, Wonder Woman, Bionic Woman, Batgirl) along with stories about witches and werewolves. Biographical information about the author is not readily available. She has an exceptionally detailed knowledge of cadet daily activities and customs. One suspects she attended West Point or has a close friend or relative who assists her with describing Missy's cadet activities.
6-09

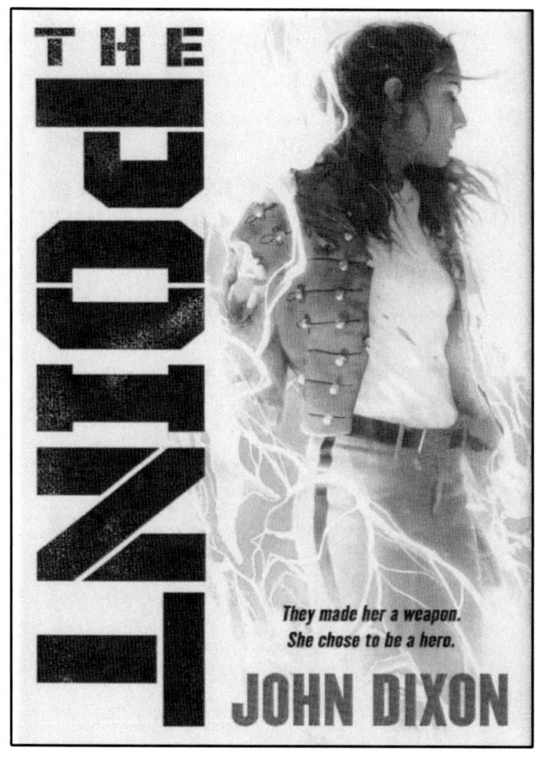

THE
POINT
They made her a weapon.
She chose to be a hero.
JOHN DIXON

The Point

Cadet, WP Female, Supernatural, Satire

John Dixon

DelRey Books/Penguin Random House (2019)

This place, West Point, this granite fortress beneath the bluest sky Scarlett had ever seen, rattled her irreverence. She could feel the academy's proud history coming off the gray stones of its buildings, which reminded her of castles, the realm of American knights. She was surprised to feel a glimmer of pride within her. This was absurd, of course. She didn't belong. She hadn't earned her way here. How could she measure up? How could she possibly keep up with these fiercely attentive recruits, this gathering of valedictorians, sports stars, school presidents, and Eagle Scouts?

And then Scarlett joined the flood of cadets leaving the auditorium, grinning with unexpected excitement. Maybe she could do this. . . .

"Welcome to the Point, future leaders of the Posthuman Age. New Cadets, society is not ready for you. The oldest, fiercest fear is ignorance. The general population would burn you at the metaphorical stake. Here, you will train alongside other post-humans. You will learn to control and maximize your powers and to use them for the greater good. You will discover camaraderie and purpose. You will become a part of something bigger than yourselves: The Long Gray Line."

Scarlett Winter has always been an outsider, and not only because she's a hardcore daredevil and born troublemaker -- she has been hiding superhuman powers she doesn't yet understand. Now she's been recruited by a secret West Point unit for cadets with extraordinary abilities. Scarlett and her fellow students are learning to hone their skills, from telekinetic combat to running recon missions through strangers' dreamscapes. At The Point, Scarlett discovers that she may be the most powerful cadet of all. With the power to control pure energy, she's a human nuclear bomb - and she's not sure she can control her powers much longer. Even in this army of outsiders, Scarlett feels like a misfit all over again, but when a threat that endangers her fellow students arises from the school's dark past, duty calls and Scarlett must make a choice between being herself and becoming something even greater: a hero. [DJ]

John Dixon's first two novels, *Phoenix Island* and *Devil's Pocket*, won back-to-back Bram Stoker Awards and inspired the CBS TV series, *Intelligence*. A former boxer, teacher, and stone mason, John lives in West Chester, PA. [DJ]

Futuristic

Leaving the 20th century and the Hudson Highlands, we advance forward in time and into the cosmos and the future - the realm of science fiction. Actually, that is a relative matter, because several of these books were written five to seven decades ago, anticipating a future that might have coincided with the novels *1984* or *2001 - A Space Odyssey.*

The protagonists in the following books are often graduates of West Point.

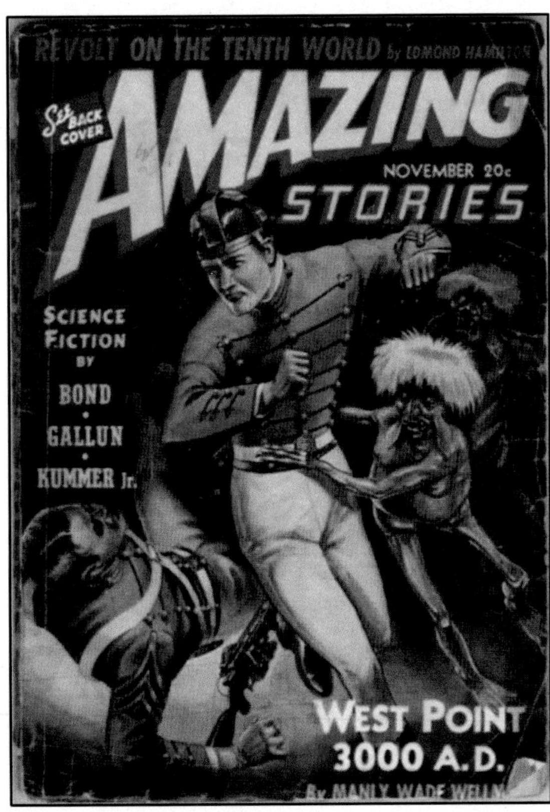

"West Point 3000 A.D."

Futuristic, Comic Book

Manley Wade Wellman
Amazing Stories (Nov. and Dec. 1940)

Trapped in the Underways as Martian revolt flames, Garr Devlin discovers the real meaning of West Point's honor and of a thousand years of tradition.

In the first installment, Garr Devlin, strong of build, dark, purposeful, was kidnapped from the Underways by police of the Upper Town, after his father had been shot down for his "crimes."

The oppressed creatures of the Underways, never allowed to see the sun, tended Upper Town's great subterranean heat, light and water plants. But one among them, Garr Devlin's father, determined his son should grow up strong and healthy, had stolen precious vitamin rations and sunray lamps from the Upper Town.

His lot had been—death. Taken to the Upper Town, young Garr Devlin was impressed into service at Earth's military academy, West Point. At first bitterly rebellious, his defiance gradually weakened under the sympathetic interest of Nola Rakkam, daughter of West Point's superintendent, General Rakkam.

Suddenly a devilish plot on the part of a Martian military faction to seize control of Earth boiled over. The scheme was to employ Martian cadets at West Point as fifth columnists, arouse the Underways with promises of freedom and loot. Now enmeshed in this treachery because he had been assigned by General Rakkam as an Intelligence student to share the same quarters with Bexlann, a Martian cadet, Garr Devlin is torn between his duty to the Point and his hatred of the Upper Town for its treatment of the Underways. [EB]

Manly Wade Wellman (1903–1986) was an American writer. While his science fiction and fantasy stories appeared in such pulps as *Astounding Stories*, *Startling Stories*, *Unknown* and *Strange Stories*, Wellman is best remembered as one of the most popular contributors to the legendary *Weird Tales*, and for his fantasy and horror stories set in the Appalachian Mountains, which drew upon the native folklore of that region. Wellman also wrote in a wide variety of other genres, including historical fiction, detective fiction, western fiction, juvenile fiction, and non-fiction. He once estimated his output of stories and articles at about 500, of which about 80 were in the fantasy & science fiction genres. [6-10]

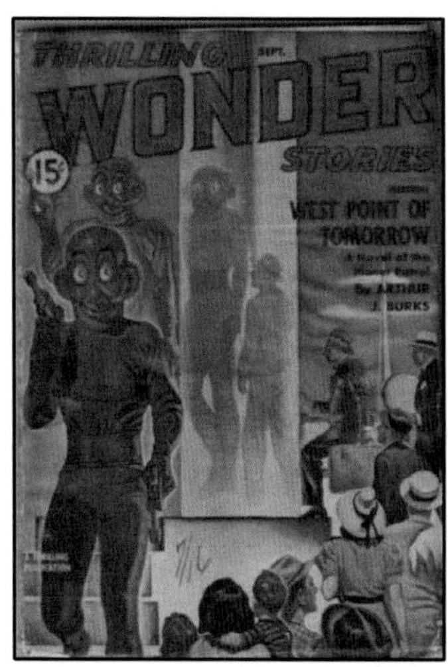

"West Point of Tomorrow: A Novel of the Planet Patrol"

Futuristic, Comic Book

Arthur J. Burks
Thrilling Wonder Stories, Vol. XVII, No. 3 (Sept. 1940)

CHAPTER I The Master Ship

There was no great surge of pride in the breast of Jan Van Reese with several hundred other newcomers to West Point, he was being conducted through the Catacombs of the Spatials. For the last five hundred years, since the Year of Our Lord 3676, in fact, there had been a Van Reese at West Point. Every last one of them—each a direct forebear of Jan—had attained command of the Polestar.

Jan had never seen the Polestar. What's more, he didn't care whether he ever did. He had heard three generations of Van Reese's talk about it until he knew everything there was to know about the ship. He could have drawn every nut and bolt of it without a single mistake, on a big blueprint. Jan Van Reese came from a military family, a fighting family—-but he was thoroughly sick of the whole business of war. Tradition was all right, yet after five hundred years of other people's bloodshed and Van Reese glory, it was time a Van Reese got tired of the profession.

Just the same, listening to the "ohs" and "ahs" of the other plebes, he couldn't keep down an involuntary surge of emotion that rose and clogged his throat. His father, grandfather, great-grandfather, great-great-grandfather, and their fathers, had each walked this way before him. And each, he must always remember, had commanded the Polestar. He did remember. They would never let him forget. [EB]

Arthur J. Burks (1898–1974) was an American pulp fiction writer. He served in the United States Marine Corps in World War I and began writing stories of the supernatural that he sold to the magazine, *Weird Tales*, in 1924. In late 1927 he resigned from the Marine Corps and began writing full-time. He became one of the "million-word-a-year" men in the pulp magazines by virtue of his tremendous output, writing 800 stories for the pulps primarily in the genres of aviation, detective, adventure, science fiction, boxing, and weird menace. He returned to active duty in World War II and eventually retired with the rank of lieutenant colonel. [6-11]

"Earth's Last Citadel: The Eleventh Hour of Terra"

Futuristic, WW2

C. L. Moore & Henry Kutner ACE Books, Inc. (1943)

The plot takes place during World War II but introduces a futuristic side-trip for the protagonists.

During World War II, four twentieth-century human beings are stranded in the Tunisian desert. These four are Alan Drake of U.S. Army Intelligence; Sir Colin Douglas, a distinguished Scottish scientist that Alan has been assigned to protect; and two Nazi agents -- the beautiful spy, Karen Martin, and a former American gangster named Mike Smith.

"Don't shoot," a girl's light voice said from the darkness. "Weren't you expecting me?"

Drake kept his pistol raised. There was an annoying coldness in the pit of his stomach. Sir Colin, he saw, from the comer of his eye, had stepped back into the dark.

"Karen Martin, isn't it?" Drake said. And his skin crawled with the expectation of a bullet from the night shadows. It was Sir Colin they wanted alive, not himself.

Underbrush crashed behind her and another shape emerged from the bushes. But Drake was watching Karen. He had met her before, and he had no illusions about the girl. He remembered how she had fought her way up in Europe, using slyness, using trickery, using ruthlessness as a man would use his fists. The new Germany had liked that unscrupulousness, needed it—used it.... He was, he knew, in a bad spot just now, silhouetted against the brilliance of the thing from the sky. But Sir Colin was still hidden, and he had a gun.

"Mike," Karen said, "you haven't met Alan Drake. Army Intelligence—American." ....

They come upon a monstrous, strangely brilliant sphere that appears to have risen out of the sand, and they are compelled by some irresistible alien power to open the door in its side and enter. Once inside they fall into a drugged sleep. They are transported in the sphere to a strange, gray, slowly dying world of many centuries ahead. Faint in their memories, as they awaken and step out of the sphere, is a fearsome and shadowy force that they know only as the Alien. [EB]

Catherine Lucille Moore (1911–1987) was an American science fiction and fantasy writer, who first came to prominence in the 1930s writing as C. L. Moore. She was among the first women to write in the science fiction and fantasy genres. Moore's work paved the way for many other female speculative fiction writers. Moore married her first husband Henry Kuttner in 1940, and most of her work from 1940 to 1958 (Henry Kuttner's death) was written by the couple collaboratively. They were prolific co-authors under their own names, although more often under any one of several pseudonyms. As "Catherine Kuttner," she had a brief career as a television scriptwriter from 1958 to 1962. She retired from writing in 1963. [6-12]

A serialized version of the book appeared in *Argosy Magazine* from April–July 1943.

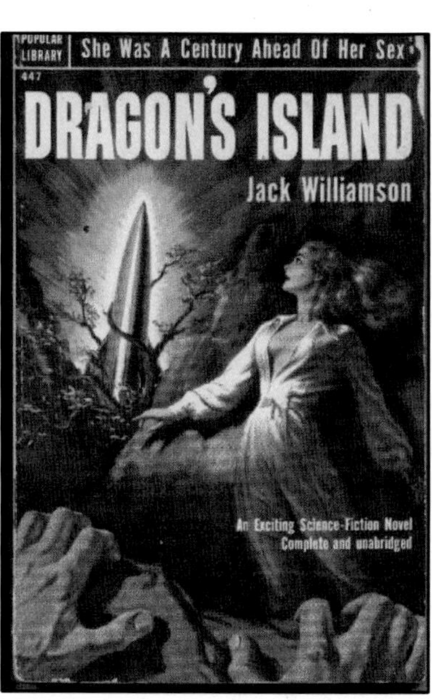

Dragon's Island

Futuristic

Jack Williamson Popular Library (1951)

This is not the typical science fiction story of far-off planets and far-future eras. The time is our century, only a few years from today; The setting is New York City and the jungles of New Guinea...

There were a young West Point cadet's quite workable plans for setting up a military dictatorship in the United States; An Alcatraz prisoner's homemade H-bomb; a madwoman's accurate prediction about the future; a child's valid refutation of quantum theory.

Such was the evidence the pain-wracked private detective has shown Dane Belfast. Evidence to support his strange story of a warped, superior race - the not men -concealed among humans, threatening to supersede mankind. [BC]

John Stewart Williamson (1908–2006), who wrote as Jack Williamson, was an American science fiction writer, often called the "Dean of Science Fiction." He is also credited with one of the first uses of the term "genetic engineering." By the 1930s, he was an established science fiction author eventually publishing 30 novels. The teenaged Isaac Asimov was thrilled to receive a postcard from Williamson, whom he had idolized, which congratulated him on his first published story. Williamson continued writing into his 90s. The Jack Williamson Science Fiction Library at New Mexico State University is one of the top science fiction collections in the world. [6-13]

"Tommy Tomorrow: Origin at the West Point of Space"

Cadet, Futuristic, Comic Book

Lee Elias Showcase Comics (Nov–Dec 1962)

Planeteers! The heart of every youth in the solar system soars at the sound of that name! To serve with those planet-hopping lawmen is their boldest dream! But for the most skilled and daring of them all, young Tommy Tomorrow, that dream turns into a chilling nightmare as he becomes the center of a frame-up at the planeteer Academy.

Tricked into a personal feud that permitted the criminal Chardu to steal the all-powerful Stone of Gazda, Cadets Tommy Tomorrow and Lon Vurian vow to capture him and clear their names. But when the Academy ships return for the students, their unit sergeant has other plans for the two cadets who "helped" Chardu become The CRIMINAL WHO COULDN'T DIE. [EB]

"Tommy Tomorrow of the Planeteers: The Brain Robbers of Satellite X!"

Futuristic, Comic Book

Lee Elias DC Showcase Comics #42 (February 1963)

Chapter 1: Fledgling Lieutenants Tommy Tomorrow and Lon Vurian of the Planeteers are fresh out of the Academy, full of enthusiasm and raring for interplanetary action! But, instead, they draw the dullest assignment in all the solar system! How can they know that this desolate district will shortly become a fantastic testing ground for The Brain Robbers of Satellite X?

Chapter 2: At gunpoint, Tommy and Lon are forced into the great building where a fantastic sight awaits them, Masters of the Asteroid Brain.

Chapter 3: As the group of newly freed brain-slaves follows silently behind him, the grim-faced scientist leads them into a work room, where a large diagram of fantastic design hangs! And then the tired, reedy voice of the scientist unfolds a story of gigantic and nightmarish import - The Doom Factory. [EB]

Lee Elias (1920–1998) was a British-American comics artist best known for his work on the Black Cat comic book in the 1940s. Elias' work on comic strips included a two-year stint as an assistant to Al Capp on Li'l Abner. His best known comic strip was "Beyond Mars," which ran from 1952 to 1955 and was co-created by Elias and science fiction writer Jack Williamson. [6-14]

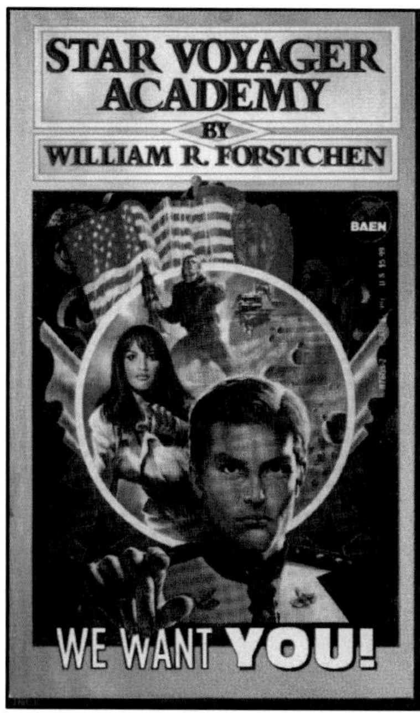

Star Voyager Academy: Wing Commander

Futuristic

William R. Forstchen Baen Publishing (1994)

It's 150 years in the future, and times have changed. For one thing, the long-stalled space program finally went private and got off the ground. For another, the U.N., courtesy American military muscle, managed to pacify all the feuding mini-states that sprang up following the demise of the evil Soviet Empire. So, Peace at Last, right? Wrong: In the future, as in the past, there will be war and rumors of war.

Right now, the big issue lies between the United Nations of Earth and her erstwhile colonies on Luna, Mars and in the Belt. No longer dependent on Earth supplies for survival, they want their freedom and true to the age-long tradition of mother countries, the U.N. doesn't want to let them go. It hasn't come to war yet -- not yet -- but as with West Point before the Civil War, this split threatens to tear humanity's only unified military academy apart, as brother is set against brother, and lovers become foes at Star Voyager Academy. [BC]

William R. Forstchen (1950–) is an American historian and author of numerous popular novels and non-fiction works about military and alternative history, thrillers, and speculative events. His three alternate novels of the Civil War were co-written with politician Newt Gingrich; two also had the participation of writer Albert S. Hanser. He and the other two men have also written three novels about General George Washington during the American Revolutionary War. [6-15]

Hocus Pocus

Futuristic, Satire

Kurt Vonnegut Putnam (1990)

Hocus Pocus is the fictional autobiography of a West Point graduate who was in charge of the humiliating evacuation of U.S. personnel from the Saigon rooftops at the close of the Vietnam War. Returning home from the war, he unknowingly fathered an illegitimate son. In 2001, the son begins a search for his father and catches up with him just in time to see him arrested for masterminding the prison break of 10,000 convicts.

Using his famous brand of satire and wit, Vonnegut captures twenty-first century America as only he could foresee it. In Hocus Pocus, listeners will find a fresh novel, as fascinating and brilliantly offbeat as anything he has written. [DJ]

Kurt Vonnegut (1922–2007) in a career spanning over 50 years, published 14 novels, three short story collections, five plays, and five nonfiction works, mostly satire and gallows humor. Born and raised in Indianapolis, Vonnegut attended Cornell University but withdrew in January 1943 and enlisted in the U.S. Army. He was deployed to Europe in World War II and was captured by the Germans during the Battle of the Bulge. He was interned in Dresden, where he survived the Allied bombing of the city in a meat locker of the slaughterhouse where he was imprisoned. After his death, he was hailed as one of the most important contemporary writers and a dark humor commentator on American society. [6-16]

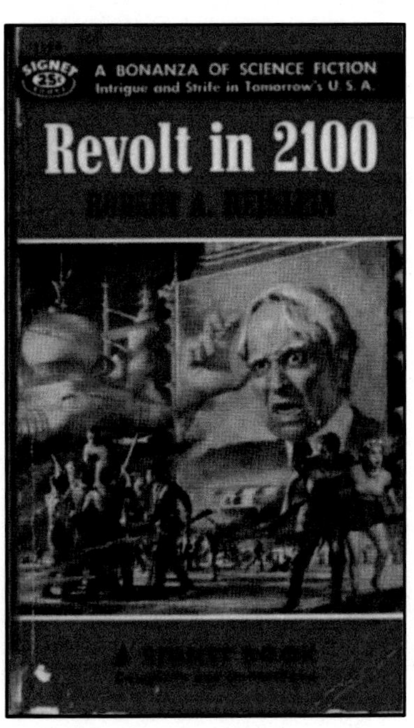

Revolt in 2100

Futuristic, Naval Academy Graduate

Robert A Heinlein Baen Publishing (1981)

It wasn't the communists who got us after all...

A great change came over the nation in the last part of the 20th century: Nehemiah Scudder showed up at the height of America's secular decadence, bearing the rod and the wrath of the Lord for those who opposed him, the promise of heavenly bliss for those who followed. Under his banner, America was transformed into a high-tech version of a medieval theocracy -- a religious dictatorship that was to endure 100 years. But nothing lasts forever.

"If This Goes On—" John Lyle had been a believer all his life. When he turned 18, his uncle had prayed an appointment for him to the

Military Academy at West Point, which perfectly suited the young man's temperament and hopes for the future.

John was not a brilliant student, but upon graduation—because of his consistently high marks in piety, no doubt—he was assigned to the personal guard of the Prophet Incarnate, the Angels of the Lord. Life at New Jerusalem did not turn out to be quite as he imagined, however. To his shock, he discovered that priests and ministers of state did not spend their days contemplating matters of faith, but rather scrambling for power and favor at the hand of the Prophet. He found himself surrounded by intrigues; even the officers of his own corps were corrupt. But when he spoke of such things to his more worldly friend, Zebadiah Jones, Zeb just said that John was extraordinarily naive and would grow up sooner or later.

The process began sooner, in a manner John never expected. It was while walking guard duty that he chanced to meet Sister Judith, one of the Holy Virgins consecrated to the Prophet. In the normal course of events they'd have passed each other by without a glance. But they were both so young and lonely. . . and that night duty, and the Inquisition, were easy to forget.

Suddenly overpowered by feelings he'd long denied, John realized that there was no place he and Judith could ever really be together in the Prophet's America. Yet there were those who dreamed of a new society, and they needed men and women of courage and vision. So, John Lyle, devout Angel of the Lord, set his life on a new course—dedicating himself to the fight for freedom. [BC]

Robert A. Heinlein (1907–1988) was an American science fiction author, aeronautical engineer, and naval officer. He was a 1929 graduate of the U.S. Naval Academy. Sometimes called the "dean of science fiction writers," he was among the first to emphasize scientific accuracy in his fiction. His published works, both fiction and non-fiction, express admiration for competence and emphasize the value of critical thinking. He was one of the best-selling science-fiction novelists for many decades, and he, Isaac Asimov, and Arthur C. Clarke are often considered the "Big Three" of English-language science fiction authors. [6-17]

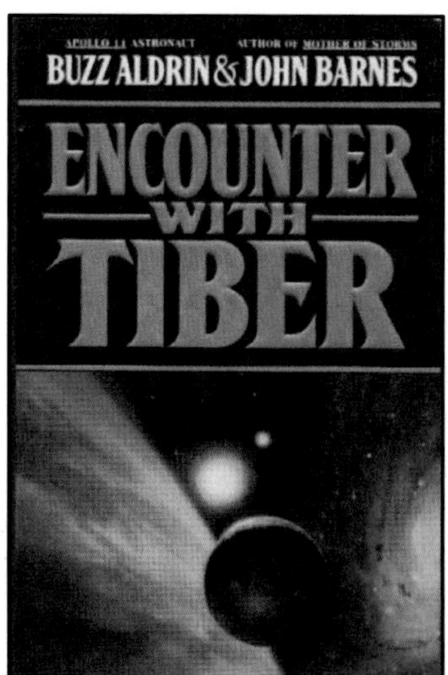

Encounter With Tiber

Futuristic, WP Author

Buzz Aldrin & John Barnes Grand Central Pub (1996)

It is a chronicle of two grand quests, two dynasties of heroes. A new space race is sparked by a bitter feud between scientist-astronaut Chris Terence and visionary entrepreneur Sig Jarlsbourg: two enemies determined to claim the frontier blazed by the Apollo pioneers. A radio beacon from deep space, from a world called Tiber, will bring both men together—and lead one to his doom. Solving the Tiberian mystery becomes a legacy, driving Chris's son and Jarlsbourg's heir, Jason Terence, to found the first city on Mars, and leading their descendants beyond the confines of the solar system.

Encounter With Tiber is the saga of another family as well. Its heroes were brave, desperate, ancient beings who learned all too well the precious fragility of lives and worlds. Beings who did indeed come to our ancestors in chariots of fire—and who proved to be anything but gods. [DJ]

Buzz Aldrin (1930–) is an American former astronaut, engineer and fighter pilot. Aldrin made three spacewalks as pilot of the 1966 Gemini 12 mission, and, as Lunar Module Eagle pilot on the 1969 Apollo 11 mission. He and mission commander, Neil Armstrong, were the first two people to land on the Moon. Aldrin graduated third in the class at West Point in 1951. He was commissioned into the United States Air Force, served as a jet fighter pilot during the Korean War flying 66 combat missions and shot down two MiG-15 aircraft. [6-18]

Metaplanetary: A Novel of Interplanetary Civil War

Futuristic

Tony Daniel Harper Voyager (2001)

The human race has extended itself into the far reaches of our solar system—and, in doing so, has developed into something remarkable and diverse and perhaps transcendent. The inner system of the Met—with its worlds connected by a vast living network of cables—is supported by the repression and enslavement of humanity's progeny, nano-technological artificial intelligence—beings whom the tyrant Ames has declared non-human. There is tolerance and sanctuary in the outer system beyond the Jovian frontier. Yet, few of the oppressed ever make it past the dictator's well-patrolled boundaries.

But the longing for freedom cannot be denied, whatever the risk.

A priest of the mystical religion called the Greentree Way senses catastrophe approaching. A vision foretells that the future at our bitterly divided solar system rests in the hands of a mysterious man of destiny and doom who has vanished into the backwater of the Met in search of his lost love. But the priest is not the only one who grasps this man's importance. The despot Ames is after the same quarry -- and until now there has been no power in the inner solar system willing to oppose Ames and his fearsome minions.

But now a line has been drawn at Neptune's moon Triton. Roger Sherman, a retired military commander from Earth's West Point and a Greentree ally, will not let Ames prevail. Though dwarfed by the strength and wealth of the Met, the cosmos under Sherman's jurisdiction will remain free at all cost—though defiance will ensure the unspeakable onslaught at the dictator Ames' wrath — a rage that will soon ravage the solar system. A rage that will plunge all of humankind into the fury of total war. [DJ]

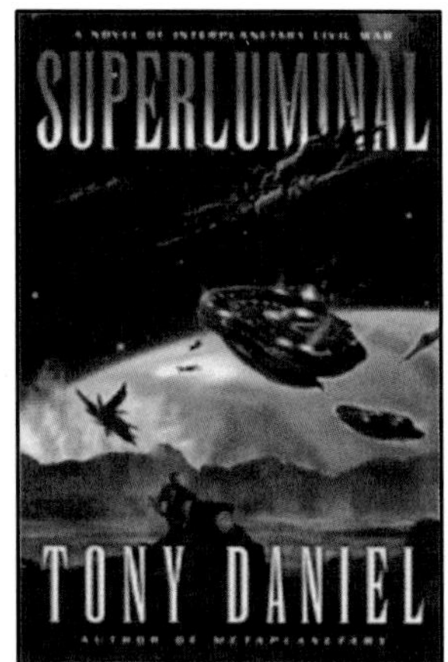

Superluminal: A Novel of Interplanetary Civil War

Futuristic

Tony Daniel Harper Voyager (2004)

Tony Daniel brilliantly dreamed this future in his groundbreaking *Metaplanetary*, and now continues with *Superluminal*. It is a time when individuals take astounding forms and live astonishing lives. But it is also a future at war for humankind's very soul. Civilization has extended itself far into the outer reaches of our solar system -- and in so doing has developed into something remarkable, diverse, and perhaps transcendent. But the inner system -- its worlds connected by a vast network of cables -- is supported by the repression and enslavement of humanity's progeny, nanotechnological artificial intelligences. Now the war for human civilization shifts into high gear. A pogrom against the A.I. "free converts" moves toward a Final Solution, even as the elite super-beings, called LAPs, are co-opted into Napoleon-like Director Ams' all-encompassing, all-powerful personality. Superluminal flight is being secretly developed, and with it a weapon that promises utter victory for Ams. But hope remains alive in the outer system with General Roger Sherman and his Federal Army. From the tattered remnants and fleeing refugees of a dozen moons and asteroids, these contentious, democratically minded warriors have been forged by the fire of battle into an effective and adaptable military force. Given time, the Federal Army stands a fighting chance to beat Ams. But the nanotech-driven war-machine of the Met is in full production, and time is the one commodity the forces of freedom lack. It is total war for humanity in all its myriad shapes: war between the vast cloud ships of the outer system and the deadly armada of the Met; between massive regiments of soldiers equipped with almost unimaginable firepower. Most of all, it is war within the hearts and minds of every human being. For this is the fight that will decide, once and for all, what form -- and which way of life -- humankind will take to the stars. [DJ]

Tony Daniels (1963–) has authored eight books, numerous short stories and poems, as well as literary criticism and reviews. The novels *Metaplanetary* and *Superluminal* are part of a series, based upon the novella "Grist," while the third installment of the trilogy has yet to appear in print. [6-19]

The Claus Effect

Futuristic

David Nickle & Karl Schroeder Tesseract Books (2002)

It's the 1990s. The Cold War is over, the Soviet Union is down for the count — and the Free World is getting ready for its first nuclear-free Christmas in decades. Only one thing in the world can ruin it - SANTA CLAUS.

The Claus Effect is a continuation of "The Toy Mill," the 1993 Aurora-Award-winning story about a malevolent, post-industrial-revolution Santa

Claus and Emily, the little girl whose wish to be a Christmas Elf nearly destroys the world. The Claus Effect takes up eight years later, when events propel teen-aged Emily and West Point cadet Neil Nyman on a breakneck journey through suburban shopping malls, Ontario cottage country, and the frigid northern wastes of the former Soviet Union — battling displaced Cossacks, blue-blooded cottagers and homicidal, down-sized elves along the way. Finally, they must face down the terrifying truth: about Christmas, the New World Order — and The Claus Effect. [BC]

David Nickle (1964–) is a Canadian author of horror, science fiction and fantasy novels, *The Geisters*, *Rasputin's Bastards*, and *Eutopia: A Novel of Terrible Optimism*, and co-author of *The Claus Effect*, with Karl Schroeder. [6-20]

Karl Schroeder (1962–) Canadian science fiction author and a professional futurist. His novels present far-future speculations on topics such as nanotechnology, terraforming, augmented reality, and interstellar travel, and are deeply philosophical. [6-21]

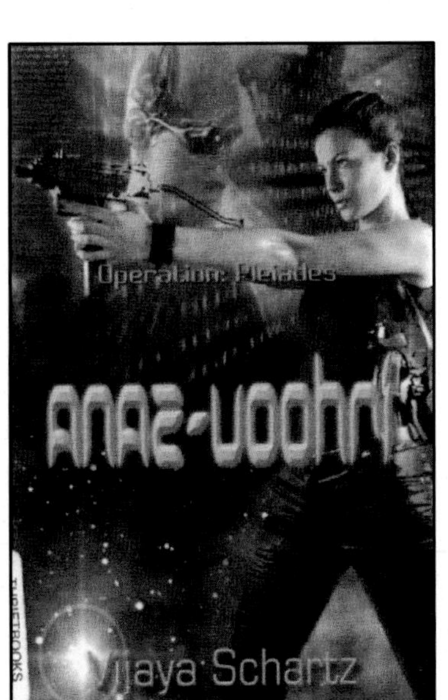

Anaz-Voohai: Operation Pleiades

Futuristic, WP Female

Vijaya Schartz — Triskelion Publishing (2006)

Tia Vargas was the best of the best at West Point, and when her schooling was over, had been assigned to oversee the conditioning of a special unit of soldiers. Unaware of the mission they faced, she strove to make sure these men could handle any situation with no questions asked. She excelled at all weaponry, all weather survival, and could handle herself in battle. The only thing that challenged her was her occasional nightmare, filled with strange, disconnected images of an arid unknown landscape which left her shaken and filled with dread. One soldier defied her at every turn but proved to be her greatest ally. When he told her of their impending mission, all her nightmares came back with startling clarity. Could her mother's ramblings of alien abductions be true? [BC]

Born in France, award-winning author **Vijaya Schartz** never conformed to anything and could never refuse a challenge. She writes about strong heroines, brave heroes, and cats. She likes action and exotic settings, in life and on the page. She traveled the world and claims she must be a time traveler, since she writes with the same ease about the far past and the far future. With almost thirty titles published, Vijaya Schartz writes action adventure laced with sensuality and suspense, in exotic, medieval, or futuristic settings. [6-22]

"Batwoman: Seven Years Ago"

WP Female, WP Ex, Comic Book, Crime

Greg Rucka Detective Comics, Vol. 59 (Jan. 2010) and Vol. 60 (Feb. 2010)

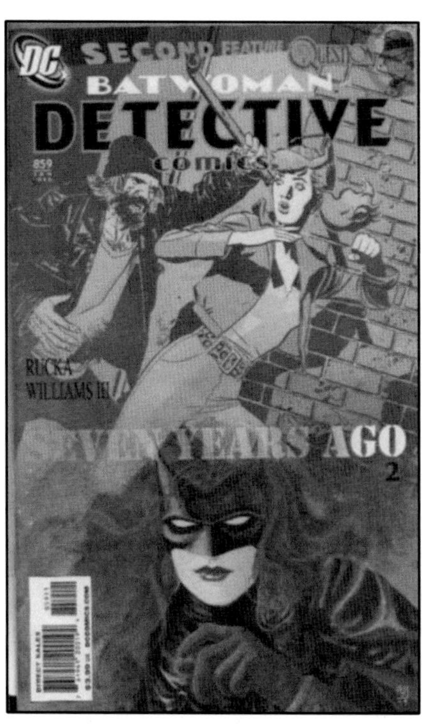

This comic book series depicts the transformation of Kate Kane into Batwoman following her resignation from West Point. She chose not to lie about her sexual orientation.

Kate Kane never planned to be Gotham's new vigilante. Three years after Batman mysteriously disappeared, Gotham is a city in despair. Without the Caped Crusader, the Gotham City Police Department was overrun and outgunned by criminal gangs. Enter Jacob Kane and his military-grade Crows Private Security, which now protects the city with omnipresent firepower and militia. Years before, Jacob's first wife and daughter were killed in the crossfire of Gotham crime. He sent his only surviving daughter, Kate Kane, away from Gotham for her safety. After a dishonorable discharge from military school and years of brutal survival training, Kate returns home when the Alice in Wonderland gang targets her father and his security firm, by kidnapping his best Crow officer, Sophie Moore…

But Kate is a woman who's done asking for permission. To help her family and her city, she'll have to become the one thing her father loathes — a dark knight vigilante. With the help of her compassionate stepsister, Mary, and the crafty Luke Fox, the son of Wayne Enterprises' tech guru Lucius Fox, Kate Kane continues the legacy of her missing cousin, Bruce Wayne, as Batwoman…Armed with a passion for social justice and a flair for speaking her mind, Kate soars through the shadowed streets of Gotham as Batwoman. But don't call her a hero yet. In a city desperate for a savior, she must first overcome her demons before embracing the call to be Gotham's symbol of hope. [EB]

Gregory Rucka (1969–) is an American comic book writer, screenwriter, and novelist. He is known for his work on well-known comics such as *Action Comics, Batwoman, Detective Comics*, the *DC Comics* miniseries "Superman: World of New Krypton".[6-23]

The following comic book is a sequel to the original Peter Parsec, Space Cadet which Mike Conrad wrote for *The Pointer* while a cadet, class of 1980. The original is in the "Cadet Experience" chapter along with Conrad's bio.

Peter Parsec, Space Cadet - Raiders of the Lost Dark

Cadet, Futuristic, Satire, WP Author

Michael Conrad MikeConradArt.com (2002)

Something is wrong with the Universe, and it's up to Peter Parsec to save it. When Colonel Parsec gets the call from General Carrie Sabres (who happens to be his wife) at the Hexagon, he is all set to depart from his post as Commandant at the United Space Military Academy and take the mothballed Starship Aintnoprize into action. But while he's getting his things together, a group of cadets led by his son accidentally launch the ship. Not one to shy away from a mission -- or a chance to get off post for a while -- Pete Junior and his co-first-captain Rusty Barrels end up leading the charge, accompanied by the partially mechanized Cy Borg, saucer-riding Alienne Gray and martial-arts instructor (and evolved giant panda) Yin Yang. There is no time to turn back; indeed, it seems that time is turning back on itself, and these half-trained cadets are the galaxy's only hope. [6-24]

The Future is Here! West Point has played a significant role in the U.S. space program dating back to the Gemini launches in the early 1960s. More than 20 graduates have served as astronauts, among the best known are Buzz Aldrin and Michael Collins (Apollo 11); David Scott (Commander of Apollo 15); Ed White (who perished in an Apollo 1 launch pad fire along with Virgil "Gus" Grissom and Roger Chaffee); and Frank Borman (Commander of Apollo 8, and first to orbit the moon).

Class of 1998 graduates Drew Morgan and Frank Rubio are active astronauts and have served on the International Space Station. [6-25]

Chapter 7

Women at West Point

Women were first admitted to West Point and all other service academies in the summer of 1976. The first class of females graduated in 1980. Those difficult early years have been recounted in memoirs authored by graduates including Carol Barkalow (*In the Men's House*) and Donna Peterson (*Dress Gray*). Both were published in 1990. The accounts of their challenging West Point years should surprise no one. The fictional accounts that follow Peterson's memoir relate the same experiences but are seasoned with intrigue and suspense.

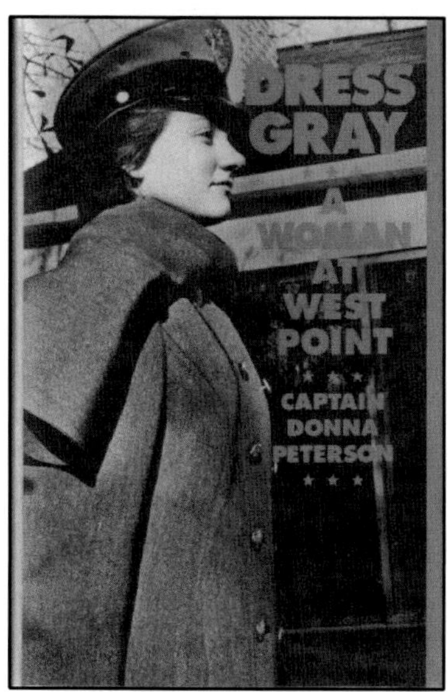

Dress Gray

Cadet, WP Female, WP Author

Donna Peterson Eakin Press (1990)

As a member of one of the first classes that allowed women into the hallowed grounds of West Point, Donna Peterson ran into many roadblocks. The arrogance of male cadets, officers/instructors, and even alumni who didn't believe that a woman should attend West Point would be enough to discourage any cadet male or female. But Donna Peterson persisted. Now she takes us behind the scenes of how the institution works, examines some of the arcane rules and rituals still maintained, and gives the reader a better understanding of the academy as not only a military training ground but also a center for learning and obtaining a college degree. Being very proud of the institution and her service career, Captain Peterson opens up this man's world with a remarkably candid and insightful look from her unique perspective. She eloquently details the ins and outs of the system and how women struggled to achieve their place in the Long Gray Line.

> "So, tell me, Miss Peterson, just how much money did your daddy have to pay to get you in here?" Pay? How degrading! I had worked harder than many of the other cadets for my appointment. I didn't know anything about getting a West Point nomination. My parents were hard-working, middle-income Americans struggling to raise a family of four children. What did this cadet know about what I had to do to get here? "You really think it's fair that you took the place of some deserving young man just because your father could pull a few strings?" he continued. "But that's just your style, isn't it? Let a man do all your work for you. That's your style." That was not the first time I had shed a tear during Beast, though it was the only public display. On the fifth night I was at the Academy, I remember tears falling on my pillow for several seconds before I fell asleep. Before then, I was probably too tired at night to stay awake long enough to cry. [DJ]

Donna Peterson (1959–) graduated from West Point in 1982 with a degree in general engineering. She went on to become a helicopter pilot, a maintenance test pilot and the Chief of Protocol for the free world's largest military installation, garnering numerous awards for her performance along the way. She has been honored as an "Outstanding Female Veteran of Texas" and has been presented honorary memberships to both the Korean Veterans of America and Vietnam Veterans of America for her support of veterans' groups and veterans' rights… [7-01]

Women at West Point

WP Female, Cadet, Drama

Juleen Compton Unpublished Draft (1978)

This document is a first draft of a screen play written by Compton. It was turned into a made-for-TV movie *Women at West Point,* directed by Vincent Sherman and starring Linda Purl, Leslie Ackerman, and Jameson Park.

The story of the first women to enter the U.S. Military Academy at West Point, and how they--and the school--faced the resultant problems.

From a review by "taylorje" on IMDb in 2006:

> "Linda Purl plays Jennifer Scott, who is among the first group of women admitted to the United States Military Academy at West Point. She and the other women can't wait to meet the male cadets, but soon discover that they will not receive special treatment just because they are women. Many of the cadets and faculty resent their presence and go out of their way to make life miserable for them; in particular, J.J. Palfrey, played by Jameson Parker. Every time Jennifer makes a mistake, J.J. is there to scold her. As "plebes" the women are subjected to endless scrutiny, criticism, and the same physical fitness regimen as the men. One hilarious scene is when a cadet conducts a surprise inspection in Jennifer's room and pulls a bra from a drawer. He is momentarily speechless and embarrassed; the women laugh, and he starts yelling at them. The already small group of women begins to dwindle. Jennifer is lonely and succumbs to the advances of an older cadet named Doug Davidson, played by Andrew Stevens. Plebes and cadets are forbidden from being friends or dating, so Jennifer and Doug risk harsh discipline by meeting in secret. Unfortunately, J.J. catches them kissing and turns them in. They are both disciplined but Jennifer gets the worst of it. Her friends feel it's not fair, that Doug was older and knew better. Jennifer and Doug break up and Jennifer feels she cannot complete the academic year. She contemplates leaving, but somehow finds the inner strength to stick it out and complete the extra physical training that is part of her punishment. Just when you think things can't get any worse for Jennifer, the school year ends, and she is no longer a plebe. Even J.J. Palfrey seems less of a villain."

Juleen Compton (1933–) was an American independent filmmaker, writer, and actor. She is best known for *Stranded* (1965) and *The Plastic Dome of Norma Jean* (1966), which she wrote, directed, and financed. [7-02]

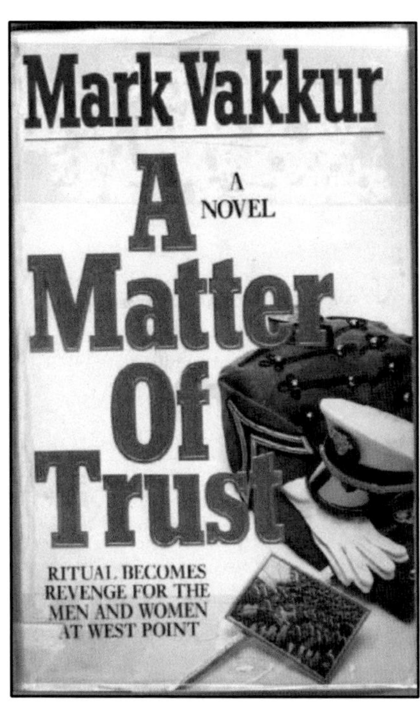

A Matter of Trust

WP Author, Cadet, WP Female

Mark Vakkur Harper Prism (1990)

Point of No Return

Cocky new cadet John Waleski is waging his own horrific war at West Point. His adversary is sadistic upper classman Clarence Wiggins. The explosive conflict drags even the best and brightest into its destructive whirlwind -- from a tarnished all-American hero to a brutally abused female cadet, from well-meaning peacemakers to leatherneck warriors.

Amid all the revelry and romance, pomp and circumstance of the fledgling military life, Waleski's and Wiggin's war soon exceed the horrors of hazing and plunges them into a dark psychological pit from which neither will emerge unscathed.

This is the real West Point as seen through the terrorized eyes of the new cadet. [BC]

Mark Vakkur (1964–) is a Distinguished graduate of the Class of 1986. He attended Duke Medical School and practices psychiatry in Decatur, GA. His other published novel is *Rites of Passage*, depicting the trials of attending medical school. [7-03]

Indomitable: The First Women at West Point

WP Female, WP Author, Cadet

Ben Spiller Pikes Peak Pub. (1989)

Col. Ben Spiller's *INDOMITABLE* is a fact-fictional story of how the 170+ year old all male institution's wall crumbled down to receive its first coed class. It will show the character's indomitable armor as they combat the stress of academics, psychological "hazing" and walking the area, and still have time to retaliate with a few combative plays of their own. [BC]

Col. Ben Spiller (1918–1993) graduated in the Class of 1941 and was the fourth person in his family to attend the United States Military Academy. [7-04]

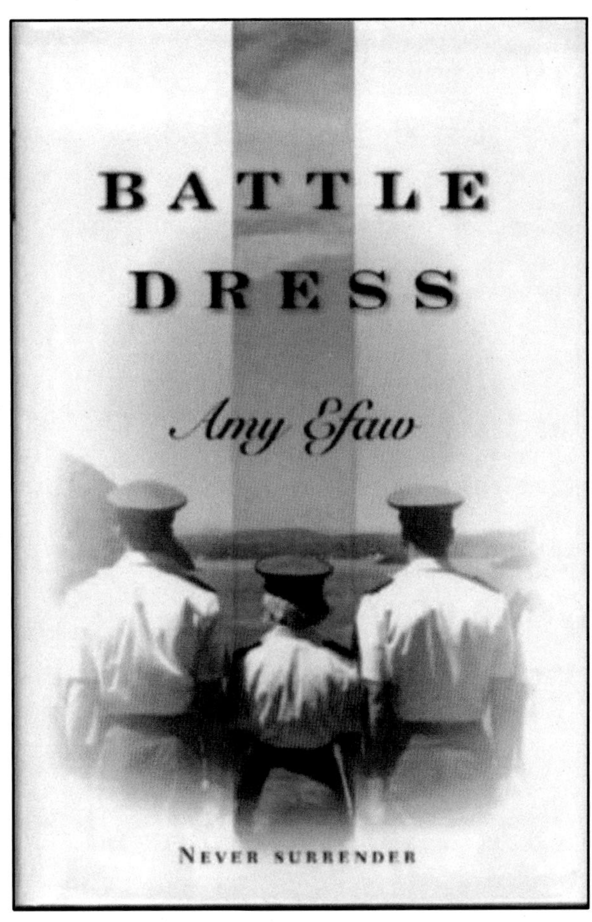

Battle Dress

WP Author, WP Female

Amy Efaw Harper Teen (2000)

Andi Davis is looking for an escape from her disorganized, dysfunctional home life, and West Point seems the only logical way out. Andi figures that given everything she has had to put up with at home, West Point will be a breeze. But nothing could have prepared her for the first six weeks of cadet training, better known as Beast.

Andi is screamed at, belittled, and worn down during the long, grueling training that is designed to break cadets and then rebuild them into soldiers. The upperclass cadets bark orders so fast that her head spins, and the fact that she is one of only two girls in her platoon makes things even more difficult. But Andi decides that anything is better than going home, anything. [DJ]

Amy Efaw is a 1989 graduate of West Point, the mother of five children, and a self-described "soccer mom extraordinaire." A former Army officer and now a freelance journalist, she's written two novels for young adults and plans on writing many more! [7-05]

The following is a slim volume of poems and recollections from 80 women who attended West Point between 1977 and 2007. Because most of the entries are poetic, this book is also included in the chapter Poetry, Drama & Film.

Athena Speaks: Thirty Years of Women at West Point

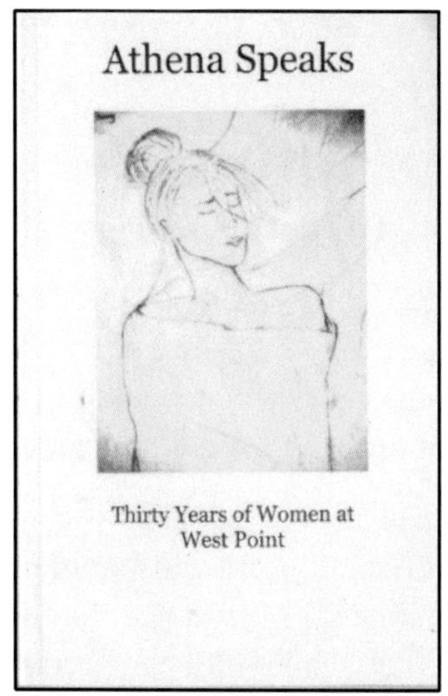

WP Female, Poetry, Cadet, WP Author

Abbey Carter & Marya Rosenberg, Editors
The Margaret Chase Smith Foundation (2009)

From the Introduction by Dr. Katherine Goodland, Class of 1980:

"Athena Speaks...

The title of this collection, "Athena Speaks," conjures a complicated history of the relationship among poets, warriors, and women. Athena, the goddess of war, whose helmet emblazons the West Point crest has, for most of her history performed the role of silent muse rather than agent on the battlefield…This symbolic elision of the agency of women in the unfolding of history and war is a longstanding myth of Western civilization, a tradition that continued in this country until, in 1976, the academies admitted women to their… Athena stepped down from her elevated place and walked through the gates of the United States Military Academy...

Some of the writers in this collection express dismay and even resentment that they are now burdened with the difficult choices that we, the first class of women to graduate from West Point, made available for them. They wonder, as I have, how their expected roles as wives and mothers can be reconciled with the option of becoming soldiers. This difficult choice is a necessary aspect of being a citizen in a true democracy…. The following essays, poems, photographs, sketches, and paintings bear witness to the necessity of confronting difficult truths through artistic expression. The tradition of the warrior poet is as old as Athena herself and probably older…

Artistic expression affords the most precise form of philosophical inquiry and contemplation…

Athena speaks. Let us hear what she has to say."

"The Gray Skirt"

"Someone was pulled off the Mess Hall stairs by the back of their skirt." Why do I feel so strange listening to this discussion? I am anxious and almost scared. My heart begins to race. They are talking about incidents for *Stronger Than Custom*, a book about the entrance of women to West Point. It has been over twenty years since 1976, when I was a plebe.

The girl wore a skirt at lunch formation. She was pounding up the stairs. "Good afternoon, sir." The Cadet Battalion officer grabbed her by the back of her skirt and stopped her from moving forward. She turned, and he screamed, "How dare you wear a skirt in my formation?"

"No excuse, sir!"

He yelled for what seemed like a lifetime—she could no longer hear his words. "Good afternoon, sir," she said as he left. It seemed like thousands of people were staring. She wished she could disappear.

She turned and pounded up the stairs. An officer stopped her and asked what she did. She fought back tears as she said, "No excuse, sir." He told her to talk freely.

"Sir, I wore a skirt in formation."

"The regs say you can do that."

"Yes, sir."

"Why did he stop you?"

"Sir, I do not know...Good afternoon, sir." She went to her table with a thousand eyes on her.

The girl was questioned by her Tac, by the Regimental Tac, by all the upperclassmen. She could not figure out what she had done wrong. The upperclassmen sneered at her and told her if anything happened to the cadet who harassed her, she would be gone. She was the victim but somehow, she became the criminal. The Academy pretended the event never happened.

I could not believe this was me. I had steeled my resolve, hid my tears, and had not thought about it again for twenty years. How could this have happened, and I had no memory of it until now? Not even a glimmer. The pain, the humiliation; they all came pouring out. Years of anger at West Point and the military came into perspective. I made a vow no woman in the military should be mistreated for her gender, especially those who were the youngest and were cadets at West Point. On that day in 1976, there was an attempt to intimidate and make the girl conform to being a male cadet, to become a man. Instead, forged in steel, the girl became a woman. Now years later and years from the pain, the event is part of the tapestry of the woman I have become. The attempt to make me male solidified my differences and made me a strong woman.

Marene Nyberg Allison, 1980

Abby Carter, Class of 2009, and **Marya Rosenberg**, Class of 2007, compiled and contributed poems to this anthology.

Katharine Goodland, Class of 1980, is a professor in the English department at the College of Staten Island (CUNY - Staten Island).

Marene Nyberg Allison, Class of 1980, is currently the Vice President and Chief Information Security Officer at Johnson & Johnson.

The Guardians of Honor - Casey Sullivan Series

The *Guardians of Honor* series is a pioneering work of Christian fiction that examines the moral and ethical dilemmas faced by believers in the Intelligence community as witnessed through the eyes of female officers and cadets serving at the US Military Academy at West Point and beyond. [DJ]

Guardians of Honor: The Plebes

WP Female, Mystery Intrigue, Cadet Series

J. E. Bandy, Jr Westbow Press (2013)

In the fight against terrorism, there is a thin line between what is criminal and what is necessary. After discovering through clandestine informants that a group of home-grown extremists is attempting to use West Point as a training ground for its future leaders, the army fights back. To do so, the Academy recruits an unlikely heroine-a shy but strong-willed female cadet named Casey Sullivan.

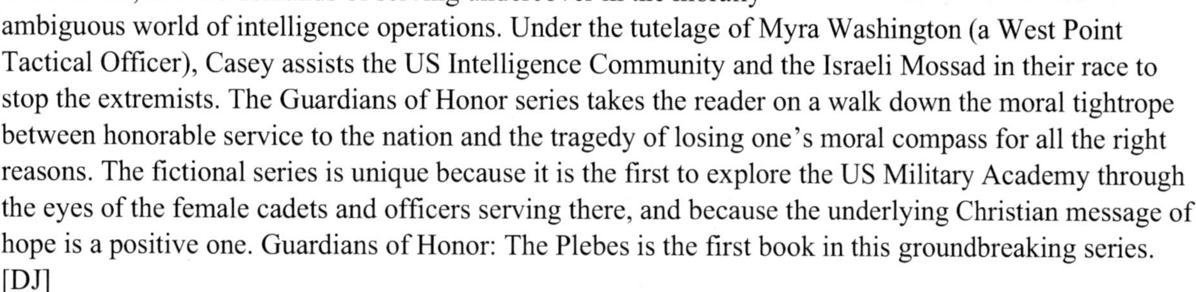

Throughout the operation, Casey negotiates an ethical minefield between the high standards of the West Point Honor Code, her Christian convictions, and the demands of serving undercover in the morally ambiguous world of intelligence operations. Under the tutelage of Myra Washington (a West Point Tactical Officer), Casey assists the US Intelligence Community and the Israeli Mossad in their race to stop the extremists. The Guardians of Honor series takes the reader on a walk down the moral tightrope between honorable service to the nation and the tragedy of losing one's moral compass for all the right reasons. The fictional series is unique because it is the first to explore the US Military Academy through the eyes of the female cadets and officers serving there, and because the underlying Christian message of hope is a positive one. Guardians of Honor: The Plebes is the first book in this groundbreaking series. [DJ]

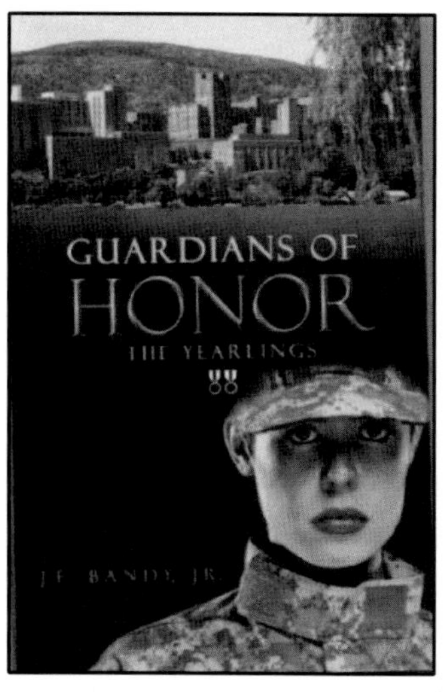

Guardians of Honor: The Yearlings

WP Female, Mystery Intrigue, Cadet Series

J. E. Bandy, Jr Westbow Press (2014)

When old enemies form alliances with new and more treacherous adversaries, Casey Sullivan's undercover assignment becomes more complicated and more dangerous in part two of this exciting Christian thriller. With Casey's help, the United States Military Academy scored a major victory against right-wing extremists attempting to infiltrate West Point during the previous academic year. However, unknown to the academy's leadership, its victory only strengthened the enemy's resolve.

In Guardians of Honor: The Yearlings, the US Intelligence Community and the Israeli Mossad become increasingly aware of a larger and deadlier plot against the American homeland, a plot with deep roots and international implications; a plot that Casey learns has a name--Operation Patriot. Once more, Casey finds herself engaged in a delicate dance between her Christian values and operational necessity, and between the high standards of West Point's Honor Code and the murky chasm of moral relativism. Casey gains mentors in unexpected places and on opposite sides of critical ethical issues, edging her closer and closer towards a dark night of the soul. [DJ]

Guardians of Honor: Cows and Firsties

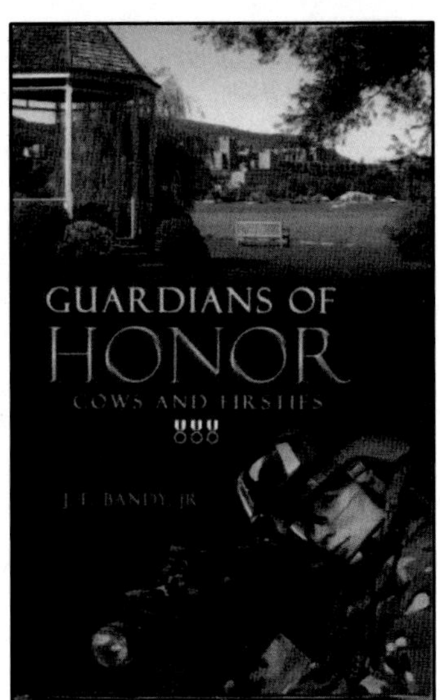

WP Female, Mystery Intrigue, Cadet Series

J. E. Bandy, Jr Westbow Press (2016)

In a desperate race against time, the US Military Academy, Federal authorities, and the Israeli Mossad again enlist the assistance of Cadet Casey Sullivan in their covert war against right wing extremists seeking to use West Point as a springboard for the commission of unspeakable acts of terror against the American public.

Casey, after two years of undercover work and hoping for a measure of normality, returns to complete her final two-years at West Point only to find that the radical Operation Patriot is bigger and far more deadly than anyone had imagined. Casey reluctantly agrees to continue assisting the authorities, but soon discovers she is in more danger now than she has ever been. As her confidence and skills as an undercover operative increase, the ethical and spiritual challenges facing her also increase, and Casey discovers that she has a new and illusive enemy; an enemy bent on her personal destruction. [DJ]

J. E. Bandy, Jr. is an Intelligence Analyst with the United States Government and a former Naval Intelligence Officer. He is also an evangelical Catholic who hopes to inform, entertain, and inspire through his novels. [7-06]

The Gray Girl Series

The *Gray Girl Series* depicts authentic experiences of the years when West Point first admitted women cadets. Jan Wishart is both heroine and troublemaker. She and her friends sometimes create their own dilemmas but mostly solve the larger issues they face while at West Point in the early 1980's.

> "My books contain many authentic situations we faced as cadets--with a bit of mystery and suspense thrown in. They are fictional stories, based on truth. Because sometimes truth is stranger than fiction." [7-07]

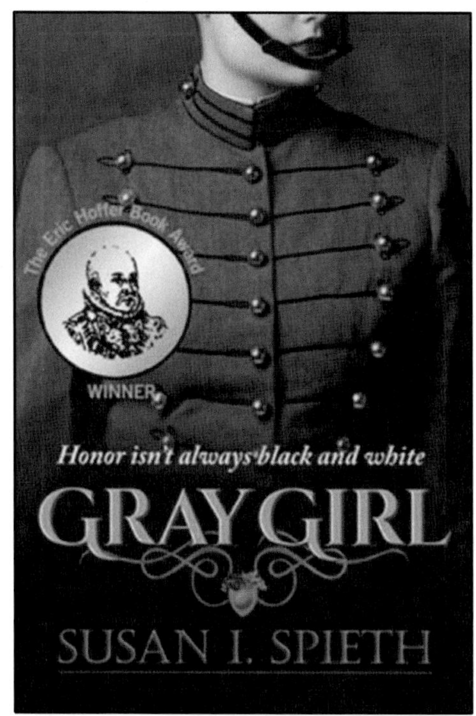

Gray Girl: Honor Isn't Always Black and White (Gray Girl 1)

WP Female, WP Author, Cadet Series

Susan I. Spieth
Amazon – Kindle Direct Publishing (2013)

Ten men for every one woman.

Those odds are stacked against Jan Wishart as a freshman at West Point. The first year at the military academy is harsh, with exhausting physical and mental demands which beat everyone down. But the women cadets also endure body shaming, sexual harassment and contempt from those who want to see them fail. Charged with an honor violation, Jan must defend herself before an all-male cadet jury. She's convinced that her accuser is likely the predator who violated a friend. The battle for justice will rage, not only for Jan, but for the victims of the predatory cadet. And one night will change everything--for better or worse. The grayness of West Point is not only in its buildings and uniforms. Even honor isn't always black and white. Relying on her wits and a few friends in the hostile environment of the U.S. Military Academy, Jan discovers the value of friendship, the genuine marks of leadership and her own inner warrior. [DJ]

Area Bird: Duty Doesn't Always Follow the Rules (Gray Girl 2)

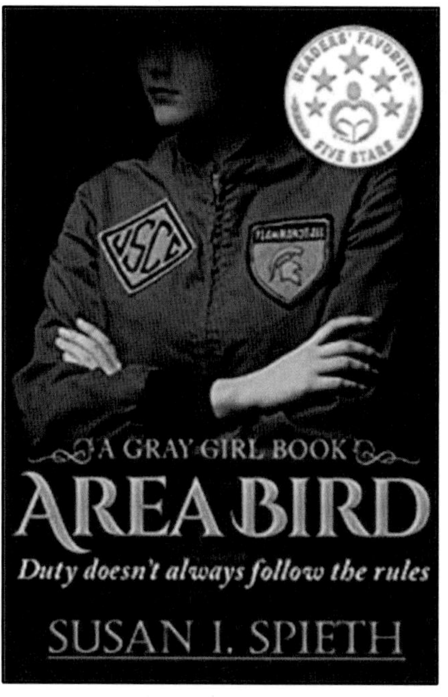

WP Author, WP Female, Cadet Series

Susan I. Spieth
Amazon – Kindle Direct Publishing (2015)

Change is coming to West Point!

Jan Wishart is back in her second year at West Point. Triggered by her former roommate's sudden resignation, Jan's mission becomes finding out what's happening to women at the academy. She discovers a systemic problem that has been ignored and perhaps cultivated at the highest levels. In order to fulfill her duty, Jan must break with tradition and the longstanding culture of the United States Military Academy. Her coming-of-age year is thrown into further chaos by the death of a classmate. Yet not everything is as it seems. Once again Jan's world view is about to be upended by the secrets of West Point. [DJ]

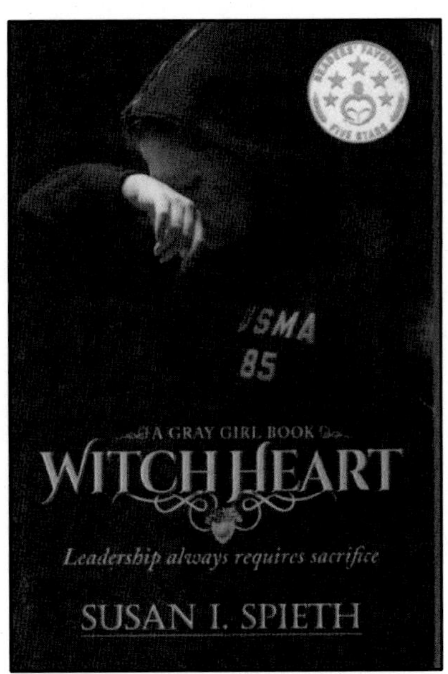

Witch Heart: Leadership Always Requires Sacrifice (Gray Girl 3)

WP Author, WP Female, Cadet Series

Susan I. Spieth
Amazon – Kindle Direct Publishing (2016)

Meanness only makes her stronger!

What does a witch, a night stalker and a recurring nightmare all have in common? After a deadly accident in Airborne School, Jan Wishart returns to West Point under a cloud of suspicion. Branded a "witch" by some at the military academy, she becomes the recipient of creepy markings and objects. Jan also loses the precious commodity of sleep due to a masked nighttime intruder. Or is that just another one of her nightmares? Furthermore, she's trying to save a freshman woman from the influences of her classmate, a bad seed. But he's not the only threat. There's another, more deadly foe who's trying to take her out. Jan Wishart's third year at West Point may literally be her last. What doesn't kill you...can still cause a lot of damage. [DJ]

Fall Out: Courage Always Stands its Ground (Gray Girl 4)

WP Author, WP Female, Cadet Series

Susan I. Spieth
Amazon – Kindle Direct Publishing (2019)

She's in over her head this time...

She wears a saber, a red sash and the infamous "crass mass of brass and glass," the United States Military Academy ring. The Army-Navy Game, the 100th Night celebrations, spring leave, and the highest of all cadet days, graduation, await Jan Wishart's final year at West Point. It should be the best one in her notable cadet experience. But graduation and commissioning as a Second Lieutenant in the U.S. Army may never happen for Jan. Instead, she might be sent to the Consolidated Brig, for female military convicts.

Her friendship with Dimitri Petrov, a diplomat's son and a rising star in the Soviet Army, may derail everything she's fought so hard to achieve. When their relationship takes a dark turn, Jan becomes embroiled in something that will test her stamina, her faith and her friendships, as never before. But like honor, duty and leadership, courage always stands its ground. [DJ]

Susan I. Spieth graduated from West Point in 1985 and served five years in the Army as a Missile Maintenance Officer. After completing her military service, she attended Seminary where she earned a Master of Divinity degree. She is an ordained clergywoman in the United Methodist Church. [7-08]

Missy the Werecat & Tracy the Fire Witch Series

This author has created a dozen novels about two women with *supernatural powers attending West Point.* The first woman is Missy from Massachusetts who can convert herself into a female werecat. She aspires to serve in the Special Forces. While at West Point, Missy undertakes a variety of missions against evildoers at the behest of the government. Later in the series, Missy spends a semester at the Naval Academy as part of the cadet/midshipman exchange program.

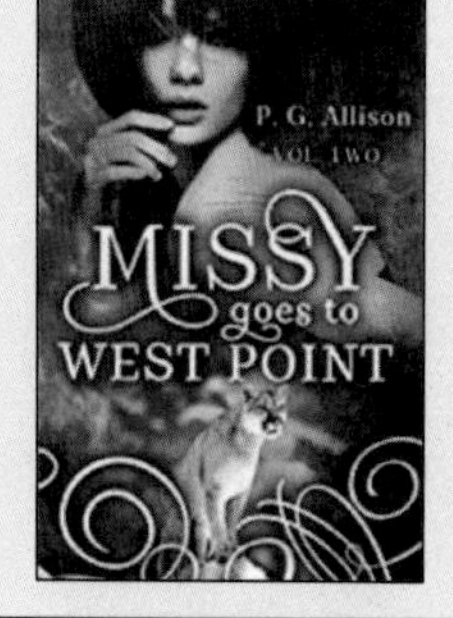

Allison's second series features Tracy, an Army brat from Texas, a fire-witch who hopes to be a helicopter pilot. Missy and Tracy are roommates the second semester of their plebe year and share their secrets.

Bizarre fiction! The descriptions of these books can be found in the chapter "Paranormal, Supernatural, and Futuristic." [EB]

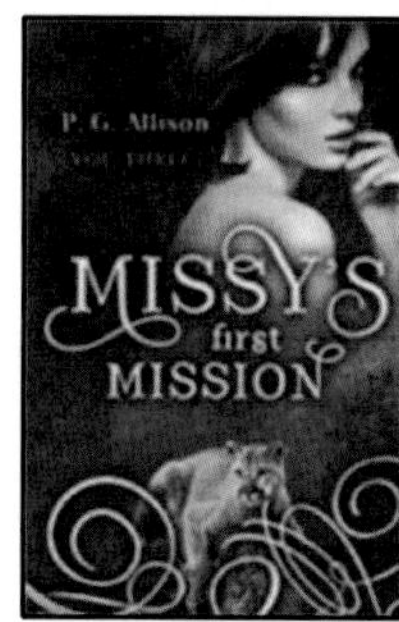

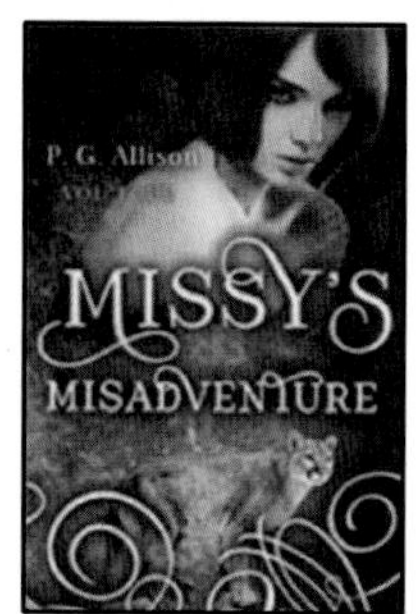

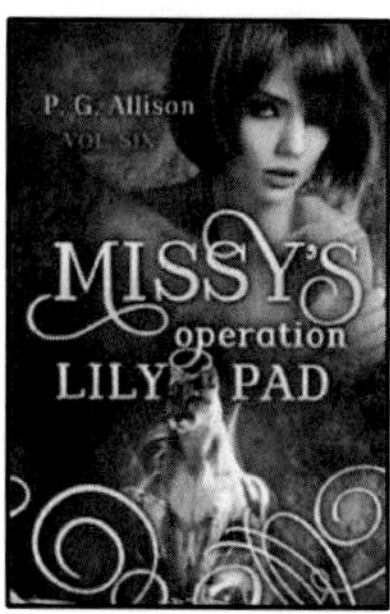

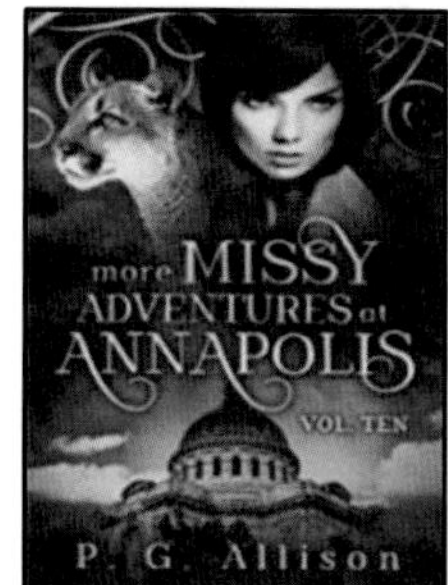

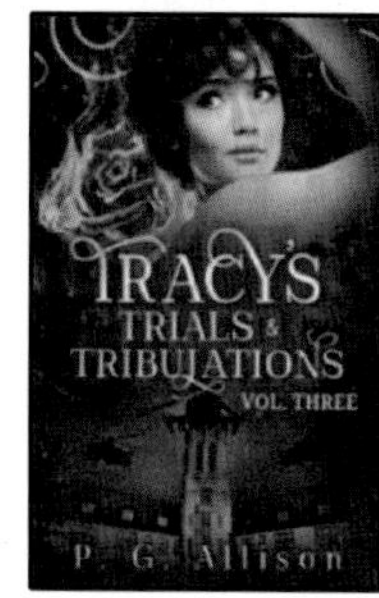

By the late 1990s, after several thousand women had graduated and served on active duty, additional accounts of their passage through the cadet years would seem passe. Some authors wrote about the challenges and lives of company grade officers and memoirs of advancement through the ranks of corporate America. There certainly is room for more fiction in this sub-genre.

Queen of Battle

WP Author, WP Female, Drug War

John W. Cooley Xlibris Corporation (1999)

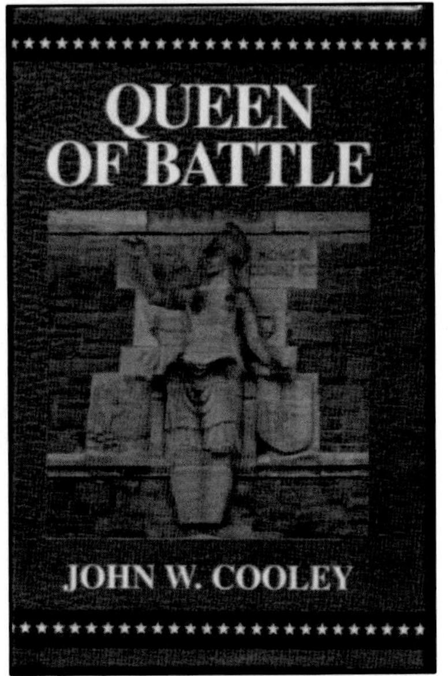

Graduating as valedictorian of her West Point class, Kate McKeane's first decisive action is to untangle the political intricacies of the Pentagon concerning women in the military. The opening of the infantry branch to women becomes her private crusade; a challenge that unfolds from the sawdust pits of Fort Benning's paratrooper school and snake-infested swamps of Ranger training to the drug cartels of steamy Colombian jungles. As leader of Operation Athena, McKeane walks a tightrope of self -doubt, courage, and persistence, as she confronts both the vicious drug lords and guerrilla warfare of the America's rightwing politicians.

McKeane's drive fuels her ambition to penetrate the Army's glass ceiling and to ultimately propel women to the historical relevance of MacArthur, Eisenhower and the like. The synergy of McKeane's roles as military daughter, guilt-ridden sister, and passionate lover powerfully reiterates that real diamonds do cut glass. [DJ]

John W. Cooley (1943–2009), lawyer and former US Magistrate judge, is a 1965 graduate of West Point and a decorated Vietnam War veteran. During the Second Tet Offensive in 1967-68, he served as a battery commander for a 175mm artillery unit. In the mid-1970s, as women first became eligible to attend the Academy, he was active in encouraging and recruiting young women to join the ranks of the Long Gray Line. [7-09]

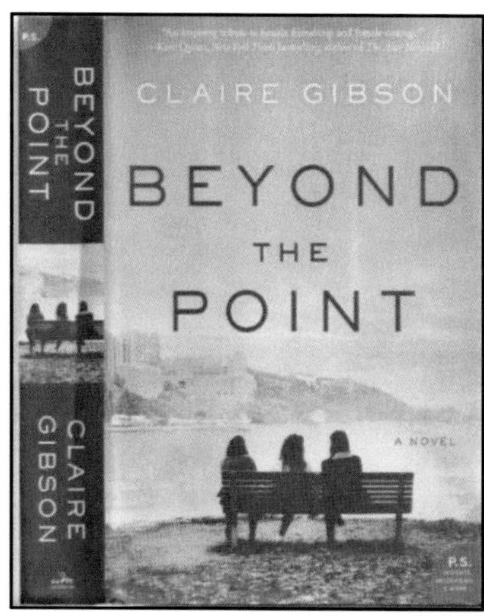

Beyond the Point: A Novel

WP Female, Global War on Terror

Claire Gibson William Morrow (2019)

DUTY, HONOR, COUNTRY

Every cadet who passes through West Point's stone gates vows to live by these words. On the eve of 9/11, as Dani, Hannah, and Avery face the years ahead, they realize they'll only survive if they do it together. With athletic talent and a brilliant mind, Dani navigates West Point's predominantly male environment with wit and confidence, breaking racial stereotypes and embracing new friends.

Hannah lets faith and family honor guide her. When she meets her soul mate at West Point, the future looks perfect, just as planned.

Wild child Avery doesn't mind breaking a few rules (and hearts) along the way. But she can't outpace her self-doubt, and the harder she tries, the further it leads her down a treacherous path.

After graduation, the world -- of business, of love, and of war -- awaits Dani, Hannah, and Avery beyond the gates of West Point. But as they're pulled in different directions, will their hard-forged bond prevail or shatter? [DJ]

Claire Gibson was raised at the U.S. Military Academy at West Point. She grew up captivated by cadets and the beautiful Hudson River Valley. Her compelling stories of women's experiences have been featured in the *Washington Post*, *The Christian Science Monitor*, and other publications. [7-10]

Chapter 8

Army Life & Army Wives

The 19th Century

At the conclusion of the Civil War, General William T. Sherman encouraged officers' wives to record their experiences, as a "useful occupation" so that others may understand what the Army was undertaking in the West.

"Though dozens of Army officers' wives followed their husbands to large and small posts on the Great Plains, only a few left letters, journals, or memoirs. Some of the officers' wives published books about their experiences with the hope of adding to their income, or to secure a proud history of their husband's service. Others wrote memoirs for their families, or scholars discovered their diaries years later and published them."

- Army Officer Wives of the Great Plains, http://plainshumanities.unl.edu

"With acknowledgments to Lieutenant General Sherman, whose suggestions at Fort Kearny, in the spring of 1866, were adopted, in preserving a daily record of the events of a peculiarly eventful journey and whose vigorous policy [promises] the final settlement of the Indian troubles and the quick completion of the Union Pacific Railroad...This narrative is respectfully dedicated."

- Margaret Carrington *Absaraka: Home of the Crows,* 1868

"In the cavalcade of men's western memoirs, books written by frontier women have too often gone unheralded and almost unnoticed. Yet women were among the keenest observers of the nineteenth-century West and its inhabitants, as seen nowhere better than in Frances Roe's vivid account of life with the western Army."

- *Army Letters from an Officer's Wife,* Introduction

We start with the 19th century "memoirs" of West Pointer wives on the Great Plains. These are not fictional accounts, but perhaps better for the detailed portrayal of Army life. "Fictional accounts" would emerge at the end of the century with the writings of West Point graduate Captain Charles King.

Army Letters from an Officer's Wife

Army Life, Memoir

Frances M. A. Roe University of Nebraska Press (1981)

In the summer of 1871, Frances Marie Antoinette Mack married Fayette Washington Roe, fresh out of West Point, and left the East behind to join his infantry regiment at Fort Lyon, Colorado, where her sprightly account of frontier life begins. As a western army wife, Frances Roe found herself in the shadow of the Rockies -- Lt. Roe was stationed at Piegan Agency, Montana Territory, as well as in the Cheyenne country of Colorado and Indian Territory -- and her book is filled with the beauty of the wilderness. She records the problems of camp and garrison life with servants, sand, and shortages, and the pleasures of parties and new friends, of hunting, fishing, and camping trips, and of long romps with her dog Hal. One chapter reports a fine summer's outing to twelve-year-old Yellowstone National Park in 1884. [BC]

AB-Sa-Ra-Ka or Wyoming Opened

Army Life, Army Wife, Indian War

Margaret Irvin Carrington Lippincott 1870

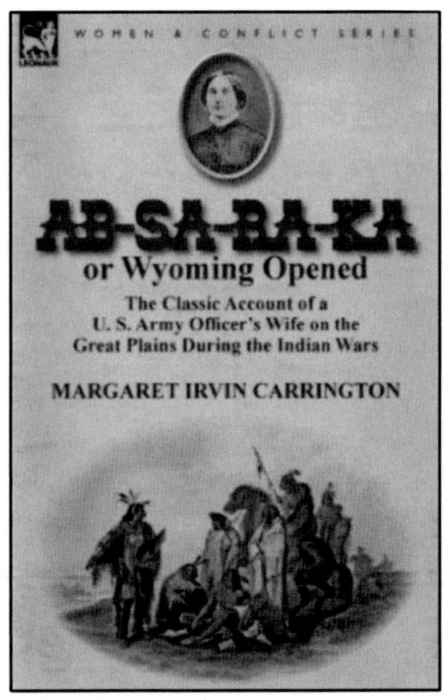

WOMEN & CONFLICT SERIES
AB-SA-RA-KA
or Wyoming Opened
The Classic Account of a
U. S. Army Officer's Wife on the
Great Plains During the Indian Wars
MARGARET IRVIN CARRINGTON

This is an account of army life on the western frontier, by the wife of Colonel Henry B. Carrington the post-commander of Fort Phil Kearney during 'Red Cloud's War' of 1866-68. It was substantially enhanced by Colonel Carrington himself after his wife's death in 1870. Colonel Carrington was a central personality in the events described in Margaret Carrington's book because, with her two children, she accompanied her husband as he built the fort and commanded the soldiers who would defend this dangerous outpost in Wyoming. She shared his experiences of the ensuing conflict and, as the fort was all but under siege by Plains Indian tribes and following the infamous Fetterman Massacre. [BC]

Margaret Irvin (Sullivant) Carrington (1831–1870) was the first wife of Col. Henry Beebe Carrington. She authored the book *Absaraka: Home of the Crows* which was published in 1868 based upon her first-hand experiences of the time spent at Ft. Phil Kearny. The book presented here is a later revision substantially updated and expanded by her husband. [8-01]

Cavalry Life in Tent & Field

Memoir, Army Life

Mrs. Orsemus Boyd J. Selwin Tait & Sons (1894)

Immediately after graduation from West Point in 1867, Orsemus B. Boyd married Frances Anne Mullen, a woman who would prove his equal in stamina and courage for eighteen years of army life in the West. She accompanied him on bruising and treacherous journeys across the Sierra Nevada and Mojave Desert to live in some of the most remote outposts the army saw fit to garrison… Her home in Nevada was a two-room tent with a barley sack carpet. The better part of social lire in Fort Clark was the exchange of grievances.

Intensely proud of her husband, Mrs. Boyd endured much for his sake: severe heat and cold, drudgery, a poor and monotonous diet, frustration, disappointment, malaria, and filth. By the time she reached Texas she had become so accustomed to making much out of little that she could prepare custards and other dainties in a tent stove. Her depictions of army life, of the landscapes of the Southwest, and of rough western travel are exceptional, but no less so is her portrait of herself as the steadfastly loyal wife of an unjustly dishonored officer. Her rage and bitterness at their treatment by the army were gradually tempered by her affection and respect for other army wives, her own sense of duty, and her deep love for the sky, land, and rivers of the Southwest. [BC]

Frances Mullen Boyd (1848–1926). Her husband, Orsemus Boyd, asked for a western post because of his unhappy years at West Point. Lacking close association with other officers, he spent fourteen years as a lieutenant. He was promoted to captain shortly before his death from illness while on a campaign in New Mexico. During their eighteen years of marriage, Fannie gave birth to a daughter and two sons. Though they spent months apart while she tended to her children in New York, Fannie loved the West and Army life. She rendered an exceptional portrayal of life on Army posts in the western states during and following the Civil War. The life may have had its fond memories, though they were swamped by recurring tragedy and daily drudgery and discomfort. [8-02]

The best-known chronicler of Army life on the western plains was Elizabeth "Libby" Custer who accompanied her husband, Brevet Major General George Armstrong Custer (with General Sheridan's permission), in both his Civil War campaigns and against the Indians until his death. She wrote three popular books about his campaigns.

Tenting on the Plains or General Custer in Kansas and Texas

Indian Wars, Army Wife, Army Life, Memoir

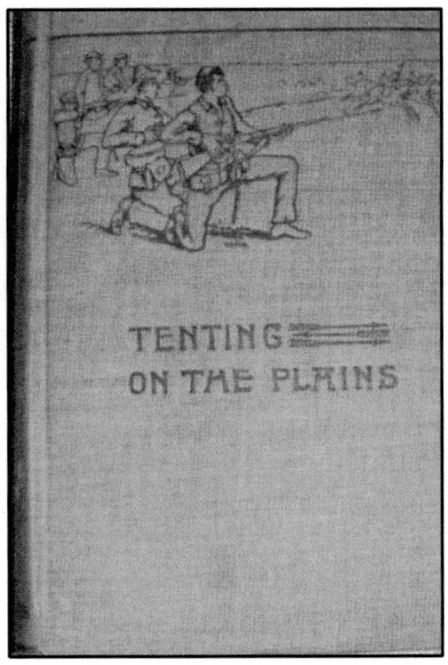

Elizabeth Bacon Custer Harper & Brothers (1897)

Elizabeth Custer was a prolific letter writer. These letters as well as the diaries she kept formed the basis in later years for three volumes of reminiscences of those Army camp experiences. *Tenting on the Plains*, first published in 1887, deals with the years immediately following her marriage in 1864. It ends in 1867. Her comments and observations throughout this period provide a valuable insight to a fascinating aspect of our history. During these years, General Custer was stationed in Texas and later in Kansas. Mrs. Custer writes of this period from the woman's point of view and with energy, humor and insight. Her reputation as a writer and lecturer was firmly established following the publication of her first book, *Boots and Saddles,* in 1885. That volume dealt with their life in Dakota when the regiment was most actively involved in campaigning against the Indians. The success of this volume and her need to supplement the meager Army pension led her to write *Tenting On The Plains*. It is an absorbing account and provides us with an invaluable, first hand source of information not only on the role of Army wives but how life was lived on isolated frontier posts 100 years ago. [DJ 1973 Edition, Corner House Publisher]

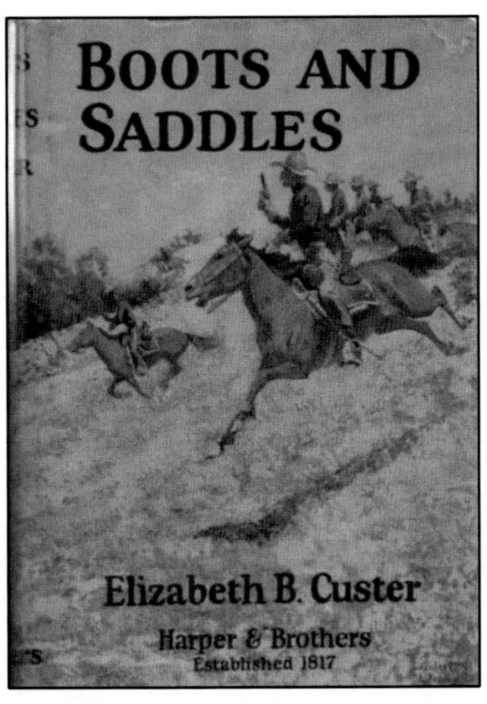

Boots and Saddles: Life in Dakota with General Custer

Memoir, Army Life, Indian Wars, Army Wife

Elizabeth Bacon Custer Harper & Bros. (1885)

The widow of General Custer tells the story of life in a frontier garrison, in the midst of Indian perils and alarms, far from the outposts of civilization. It is a simple but dramatic account, filled with the details of life in a cavalry post, with General Custer as the central figure.

A real contribution to the annals of America, of vital interest in the study of our westward expansion, this story has been delighting succeeding generations of readers for over fifty years and has sold hundreds of thousands of copies. This new edition, entirely reset in larger type and in a larger size, has been issued in answer to the continuous publishing demand. [DJ]

Following the Guidon

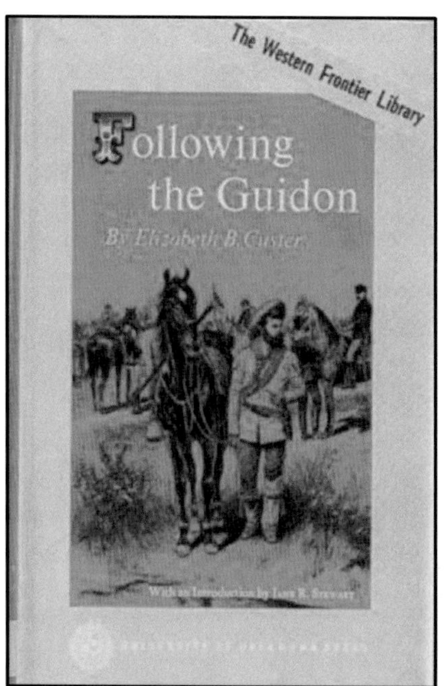

Indian Wars, Army Life, Memoir

Elizabeth Bacon Custer Harper & Bros. (1890)

Here is the story of the Garryowen regiment of one hundred years ago, told by the only woman who always accompanied it, Elizabeth Bacon Custer, the unabashed hero-worshiper of her husband, General George Armstrong Custer, whom history knows best as the man whose Seventh Cavalry was later defeated in battle at the Little Big Horn. "Libbie" Custer's volume, rich in the personalities and details of Western frontier army life, was first published in 1890 and has long been unavailable. Little-known details of the Battle of the Washita are disclosed, captured Indian chiefs are described, and the Seventh Cavalry troopers gain an added luster as they are followed from the Washita to winter quarters in Fort Leavenworth, Kansas. [DJ]

Elizabeth Bacon Custer (1842–1933) was married to Brevet Major General George Armstrong Custer. She spent most of their marriage in relatively close proximity to him despite his numerous military campaigns as cavalry officer.

After his death, she became an outspoken advocate for her husband's legacy through her popular books and lectures. As a result of her endless campaigning on his behalf, Custer's iconic portrayal as the gallant fallen hero amid the glory of 'Custer's Last Stand' remains a canon of American history for almost a century and a half after his death. Elizabeth Custer is buried in the West Point cemetery next to her husband. [8-03]

The Lady of Arlington: A Novel Based on the Life of Mrs. Robert E. Lee

Army Life, Army Wife

Harrnett T. Kane Doubleday & Company (1953)

Years later Mary recalled their time at West Point as the least clouded of their lives. She felt a dignity, a sense of quiet achievement in Robert's position. Best of all, she and her husband saw each other more often than they had in years. Though these were days of hard work for both of them, they were always within calling distance at least.

Mary liked the placid academy grounds, sweeping back: from the Hudson, the solid structures that looked as if they had been standing for centuries, the forested edges of the fields, the tramp of cadets. There was a sense of long tradition about the place.

As the Superintendent's wife, Mary had responsibilities on her own. Arrangements for housing and entertainment of visiting officials, Army leaders, and their wives were left to her, and often they had to be made at an hour's notice. When she told Robert, "I'm in harness as much as you," she meant it. She added, "I'm enjoying it, too," and she meant that as well.

The official residence proved to be a big stone house with a garden and stables. The younger children loved it; the older girls, Mary observed, did not fail to appreciate their new status as the superintendent's daughters. In young Mary, the independent one, she saw an even greater poise; command might be a better word. "My drum major," Robert nicknamed her. [EB]

Harnett T. Kane (1911–1984) authored 26 other books of fiction and nonfiction. Mr. Kane specialized in books about the South. *Louisiana Hayride*, which exposed political corruption, was published in 1941. Among his other works were *The Bayous of Louisiana, Spies for the Blue and the Gray, The Gallant Mrs. Stonewall, Queen New Orleans* and *The Romantic South*. He was a frequent contributor of travel articles and book reviews to *The New York Times*, and also wrote for *Reader's Digest, National Geographic* and *Saturday Review*. [8-04]

An Army Doctor's Wife on the Frontier: Letters from Alaska & the Far West 1874-1878

Western, Indian Wars, Army Life, Medical

Emily McCorkle Fitzgerald and Abe Laufe, Editor
Univ. Pittsburgh (1962)

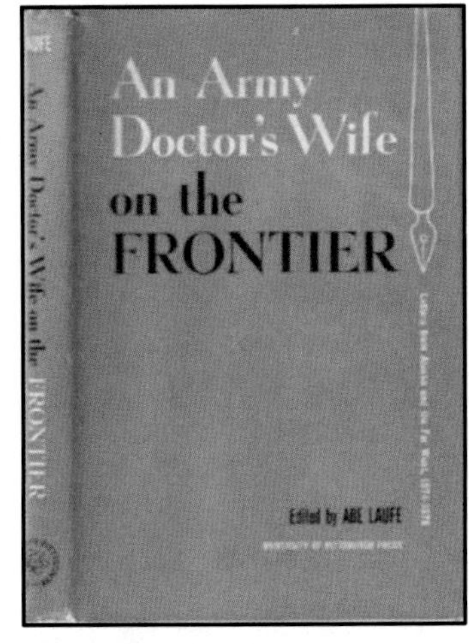

These letters, written by a young woman who followed her husband in the nineteenth century to Alaska and the Far West have preserved in a very human way an interesting period in American history. They are at once informative about living conditions on America's frontiers and a moving account of human endurance and love.

Two years after Dr. Jenkins Fitzgerald, an assistant surgeon at the United States Military Academy, married Miss Emily McCorkle, he received orders to proceed to Sitka, Alaska. Emily accompanied her husband, making the trip by water down the Atlantic coast from New York, across the Isthmus of Panama by rail, up the Pacific coast by ship to Portland, Oregon, and finally by steamer through the hazardous passage to Sitka. During the trip and the next four years, she wrote regularly to her mother in Columbia, Pennsylvania.

One of the first white women to live in Alaska less than a decade after the United States purchased it from Russia, Emily suffered desolation during the monotonous Arctic winters. Then the Fitzgeralds were transferred to Fort Lapwai in present-day Idaho, where they faced the ordeal of an Indian uprising. Emily's description of these months shows the horror and bitterness of Indian warfare on the frontier.

That story includes firsthand information about methods of travel, the hardships of life in the northern frontier, and a woman's viewpoint of existence in a western fort. But perhaps the letters of Emily Fitzgerald are most valuable for what their account of day-to-day life shows of the spirit behind the settlement of America's frontiers. [FP]

Emily McCorkle Fitzgerald (1850–1912) first came to Sitka in 1874 when her husband, Dr. Jenkins A. Fitzgerald - who she affectionately referred to simply as "Doctor"- was stationed there as a military surgeon. Emily documented her experiences in Sitka in the letters she wrote to her family in Pennsylvania. Emily's family saved those letters, passed them down through generations, and finally donated them to the Sitka Historical Society & Museum in 1980. [8-05]

Abe Laufe (1906–1984) was a Professor of English at the University of Pittsburgh, retiring in 1971. He served in the US Army during World War II. Laufe published short pieces in popular magazines, like *Women's Day* and *Ladies Home Companion*. He enjoyed a long career as a popular lecturer and author on musical and American theater. [8-06]

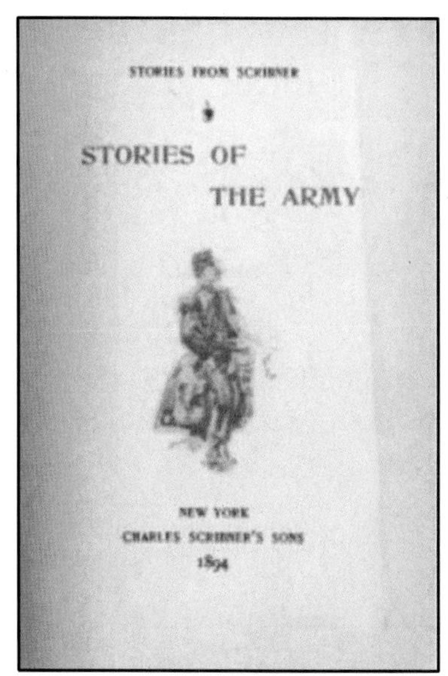

STORIES OF

THE ARMY

NEW YORK

CHARLES SCRIBNER'S SONS

1894

Stories of the Army: "Memories"

Anthology, Army Life

Brander Mathews — Charles Scribner's Sons (1894)

When Christmas broke over the fort in the far Northwest where Lieutenant Robert Douglas, U.S.A., was stationed, the wind was blowing gently from the southeast. There had been a light snowfall during the night, and as the sun arose there was a faint suggestion of warmth in the beams that glistened across the crystalline flakes. It seemed as though the cold had loosened its grip for a while.

All through the morning the weather was mild for the season and for the place, and by noon there was even a vague hint of a possible thaw. The mail-rider who brought the weekly bag of letters and newspapers had trotted his bronco into the quadrangle little before one o'clock, exactly on time. No railroad and no telegraph line linked Fort Roosevelt with the rest of the world, and only once in seven days did the soldiers who were stationed on the outpost of civilization get news from its headquarters.

Time was when the troopers quartered there had fought the Indians of the border; but the rotting stockade had been torn down long since, and Fort Roosevelt was now a fort in name only. Its narrow, low buildings, made of logs, shacked sometimes, and sometimes squared and more regularly joined, still sheltered brave men, but they no longer needed to do battle with redskins; they had to confront a white enemy only, and they found cold winter a fiercer foe and more unrelenting than the Sioux. Its assault was harder to withstand, for, although the Indian is now armed with the repeating rifle his armory is not exhaustless -- and nature's is. Outside of the government reservation there was no house within fifty miles, save the tumble-down cabin of a Missouri squatter four or five furlongs away at the bend of the river. No friendly smoke curling hospitably upward comforted the eye that might interrogate the horizon. [EB]

James Brander Matthews (1852–1929) was an American writer and educator. He never needed to work for a living (given his family fortune) and turned to a literary career, publishing in the 1880s and 1890s short stories, novels, plays, books about drama, biographies of actors, and three books of sketches of city life. He was a professor of literature at Columbia and thereafter held the Chair of Dramatic Literature until his retirement in 1924. [8-07]

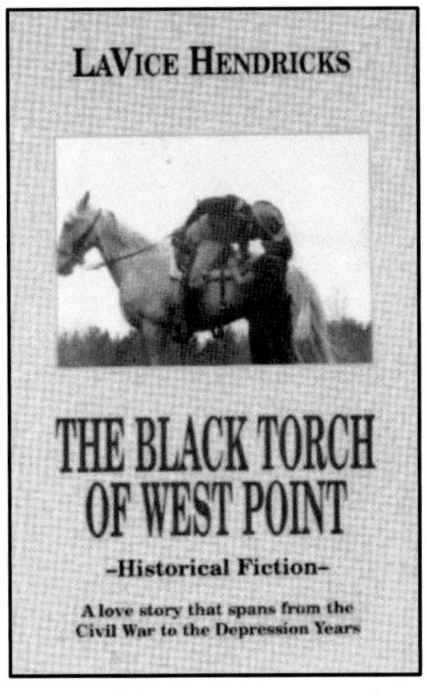

The Black Torch of West Point: A Love Story

Black Cadet, Army Life

LaVice Hendricks LaVice & Company (2001)

The playwright/author had been looking for a dynamic story about a black American -- a story with a reasonable number of facts -- but could use a stroke of fiction. He found it in Henry Flipper. After completing 17 stage plays and over 20 years of theatre, "The Black Torch of West Point" was presented in Thomasville, Georgia, in 1978, as a musical stage production. Hendricks portrayed Henry Flipper. Flipper was the first man of color to graduate from West Point Military Academy in 1877.

Twenty-three years later, LaVice Hendricks decided to write the book. A passionate and emotion driven story about a boy who came out of slavery to achieve What many thought unachievable by a former slave...Henry Flipper led an adventurous life that spanned from the Civil War, during the days of racial bigotry, to the Depression Years.

This love story will keep your heart beating with excitement with each page yet bringing tears to your eyes to a fallen and almost unknown black hero. [BC]

Detroit native **LaVice Hendricks** studied acting after a stint in the US Navy, but soon turned to his primary passion: writing plays and screenplays. In 1969, he began his own theater company based at Detroit's Bethel A.M.E. Church. Four years later he moved on to larger productions, culminating in his first musical, "Two Sisters from Bagdad." [8-08]

The Army Wife

Army Life, Western, WP Author

Charles King Tennyson, Neely (1895)

Randy Merriam, a West Point graduate stationed in the East has lived a bachelorhood of partying and gambling leaving him with significant debts. He wishes to marry Fanny Hayward who is very fond of him. Alas, Randy is fonder of living well. She rejects Randy.

Randy is despondent and vows to improve himself. He accepts a post in remote Ft. Sedgwick in the Arizona territory. There he redeems himself with good performance and meets Florence (Floy) Tremaine daughter of a major.

They are married (not without some reservations from the father of the bride) and plan a wedding trip to California.

Meanwhile, Fanny, the tease, plans a trip West with her husband, intending to stop by Ft. Sedgwick to visit her sister-in-law (married to Captain Grafton) and interrupt Randy's wedding. She learns by telegrams that she is 48 hours too late but manages to encounter the Merriams on the train leaving Ft. Sedgwick for the coast. . .

When Fanny's husband is murdered in San Francisco, she, now a widow, determines to visit Ft. Sedgwick and torment Randy and Floy Merriam. Jealous fits ensue along with calls to duty pursing outlaws and Indians. [EB]

A Garrison Tangle

WP Author, Army Life, Western

Charles King F. Tennyson, Neely (1896)

The setting of this novel is Fort Russell near Cheyenne, WY in the year 1878. The fort had been established in 1867 to protect workers for the Union Pacific Railroad. It was named after a Civil War general killed at the Battle of Opequon. The story centers around a West Point Lieutenant Maynard and several officers and their wives. The latter promote more drama than the restless Comanche with whom the two troops of cavalry are assigned to monitor. There is rivalry among the officers' wives; romance unrequited between Maynard and young Nathalie Baird from the East who is caring for the battalion commanders' ailing wife; and a mysterious stranger who torments Nathalie. The stranger "Boston" later wounds Lieutenant Maynard who is rounding up AWOL troopers in Cheyenne. Most of Russell's soldiers are called north to deal with an Indian uprising, leaving Maynard behind recovering with the ministrations of his sister Grace who has come West. She stirs the drama plot by trying to poison the relationship between her brother and Nathalie. Then there is a fire and theft of much of the wives' silver cutlery and jewelry. A real tangle! [EB]

A Soldier's Trial: A Story of the Canteen Crusade

WP Author, Army Life, Philippines

Charles King The Hobart Co. (1905)

The war with Spain was at an end, and so were the hopes and aspirations of many a warrior. For several reasons Colonel Ray of the --th Kentucky was a disappointed man. One of the best soldiers doing duty with the volunteers, he had had some of the worst luck. Through long years of service in the regular cavalry he had borne the reputation of being a most energetic and valuable officer. The Civil War was fairly ended when he stepped from the Point into his first commission. Over thirty years had he done valiant and faithful duty yet was he only just wearing the gold leaves as junior major of his regiment, when the long-expected happened in the spring of '98. He did not receive the command of troops in Cuba or the Philippines that he felt he deserved.

He had long been most happily married. His wife was charming, admired, and beloved. His children were all a father's heart could wish. Health and competence had always been theirs. They had, indeed, for years known the joys of moderate wealth, for Mrs. Ray had brought her husband something besides beauty and grace, physical and spiritual. Mrs. Ray's property was mainly in real estate, some of which became gradually unproductive. The family wealth dwindled as did that of their relations - including a niece, Priscilla Sanford.

Sandy Ray, their eldest son, commissioned like his father in the cavalry, was no longer to be provided for. Maidie Ray, their daughter, had married the man of her choice, a well-to-do young New Yorker. So, the Colonel asks his wife:

"Why not have 'Cilla come to us?" —and thereby hangs very much the rest of this tale.

Affairs at Fort Minneconjou once more became alive, for Miss 'Cilla was a woman with a mission, actually several. Several plots unfold to create a "soap opera" on the Plains.

Son Sandy Ray having been posted in the Philippines sends a note home that he is "engaged" to a young woman Inez Farrell, the daughter of a well-to-do businessman. This stunned his parents, but more shocking was following Sandy's departure from the Philippines, Inez became enamored of the widowed Major Dwight a long-time friend of the Rays and married him in Japan enroute home to Minneconjou.

Cousin 'Cilla, a devout Presbyterian and busybody, is shocked that the post has a Canteen where soldiers may imbibe wine and beer when off duty. Canteens had been established on Army posts to discourage soldiers from wandering into town, drinking whisky, and engaging in regular brawls. 'Cilla mounts a campaign to abolish the Canteen and "save" the soldiers. This causes great angst among the officers who dread the consequences.

Inez had a maid-servant who is adept at spreading rumors about others while zealously trying to protect her mistress' reputation, not easily done when Inez is observed taking long carriage rides on the plains for possible private meetings.

There is a mysterious, Private Blenke, a man of exceptional talents, who appears throughout the book at the nexus of every crisis. And the natives are restless. Renegade Sioux on the nearby reservation are angered by the treatment they are receiving from the Indian Agent. [EB]

Charles King (1844–1932) was the son of Civil War general Rufus King, grandson of Columbia University president Charles King, and great grandson of Rufus King, a signer of the U.S. Constitution. He graduated from West Point in 1866 and served in the army during the Indian Wars under George Crook. He was wounded in the arm and head during the Battle of Sunset Pass forcing his retirement from the regular army as a captain in 1879. He then served in the Wisconsin National Guard from 1882 until 1897. He was appointed Brig. Gen. of volunteers and sailed to the Philippines during the Spanish-American War. The fighting with Spain was over by the time he arrived. [8-09]

King wrote over 60 books and novels with subjects ranging from West Point, the Civil War, battling the Plains Indians, garrison life and the Philippine campaign. A few of his other novels can be found in the chapters "Civil War" and "Manifest Destiny."

Betty at Fort Blizzard

Western, Romance, Army Life

Molly Elliot Seawell J.B. Lippincott & Co. (1916)

This is a sequel to the author's earlier work - Betty's Virginia Christmas – which is described in the "West Point Romances" chapter. Young Lt. John Fortescue courted Betty Beverly and married her at the end of that book.

Some twenty years later, Fortescue is now a colonel and post commander at Fort Blizzard, a new cavalry post in the far Northwest circa 1910. He and Betty now have a son at West Point, a daughter Anita, who at 17, is a coquette like her mother and the apple of her father's eye. There is also a young son, a "late arrival," of two years with the moniker "After-Clap."

While there are no great military challenges at this remote snow bound fort in the far Northwest, there is drama. It revolves around Anita's attraction, amid her father's discomfort, to a Lt. Broussard, West Point graduate. He is the most accomplished of cavalry officers, and from a family of some financial means. Lt. Broussard falls for Anita and a courtship begins with horseback rides, holiday parties, and post dances. But the course of true love does not run true. Broussard receives orders posting him to the Philippines, but before departing he is seen in the company of the wife of a Private Lawrence. Broussard apparently has some relationship with Lawrence, but why is he so familiar with the fellow's wife?

Broussard leaves for the Philippines with Anita having her doubts but still passionately longing for him. Soon thereafter Private Lawrence is involved in a scuffle with a Staff Sergeant and deserts the post to avoid punishment. Mrs. Lawrence falls into a deep depression gaining the sympathy of the Colonel and Beverly Fortescue. For some reason, Lt. Broussard is supporting Mrs. Lawrence financially so she can remain in her quarters at the fort...with Colonel's knowledge and consent!

Eventually Broussard returns from overseas to recuperate from a terrible case of jungle fever. The story winds up with Lawrence returning to accept his punishment; Mrs. Lawrence recovering her vigor; and Anita and Broussard reconciling. Even Colonel Fortescue is pleased. [EB]

Molly Elliot Seawell (1860–1916) was a late 19th century American columnist and writer. Seawell made many trips to Europe. These travels expanded her literary subjects to include the sea, England, France, and Central Europe. Her literary production included forty books of fiction, collected short fiction, non-fiction, essays, and numerous political columns from Washington for New York dailies. Two of Ms. Seawell's novels *Thru Thick and Thin: A Soldier Story and a Sailor Story* and *Betty's Virginia Christmas* can be found in other chapters of this book. [8-10]

A Season of Change: Chronicles of Faith

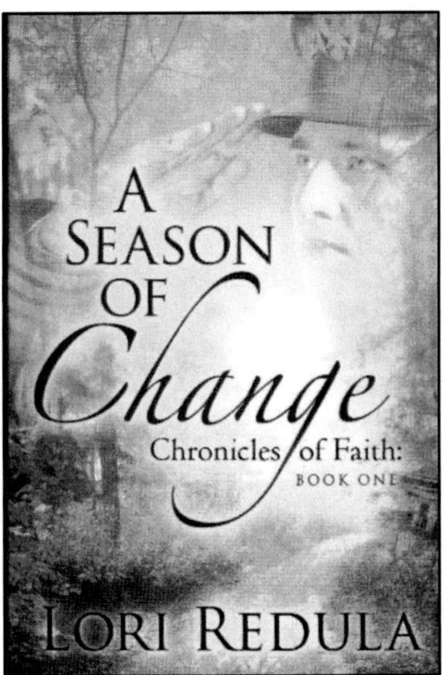

Army Life, Faith, Civil War

Lori Redula Xulon Press (2007)

When Kathleen Ramsey's eldest son is unexpectedly assigned to Fort Moultrie following his graduation from West Point, she is forced to relive the painful memories of the day she fled her childhood home in Charleston, South Carolina over twenty years ago. And as if that weren't painful enough, the young man then informs her that he wants to meet the grandparents he has never known! Would Kathleen deny his request, choosing to cling to the fears and resentments of her past? Or would she recognize the sovereign hand of her loving Heavenly Father faithfully guiding her son's every step?

Set against the backdrop of the Civil War. A Season of Change is the first book in the Chronicles of Faith series. [BC]

Lori Redula wrote a sequel *Season of Hope*. No other biographical information was available.

To Love and to Honor (The Dalton Saga #1)

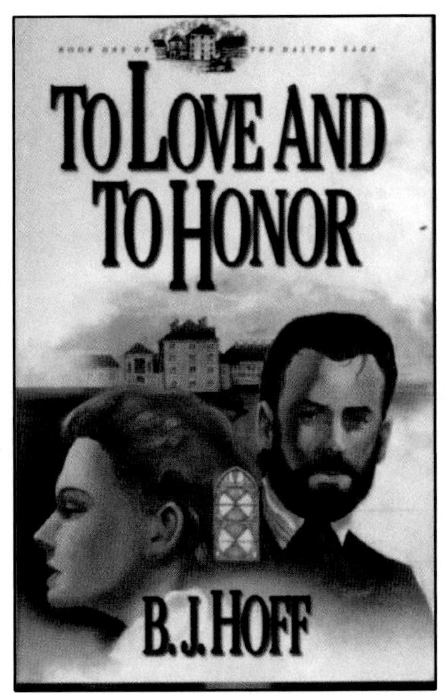

Army Life, Faith

B. J. Hoff Chariot Victor Publishing (1993)

Against the colorful backdrop of West Point in 1842, the saga of a giant of a man and his innocent ward begins to unfold. Caught up in his own private battle against bigotry and injustice, West Point Chaplain Jess Dalton is suddenly confronted by a different kind of conflict.

His guardianship of the young Irish immigrant, Kerry O'Neill, thrusts him into struggle of forbidden love that threatens to tear him apart from within. Bewildered by the longing of his heart, the betrayal of friends and his desire to know God's plan, Jess Dalton must find the balance between love and honor. [BC]

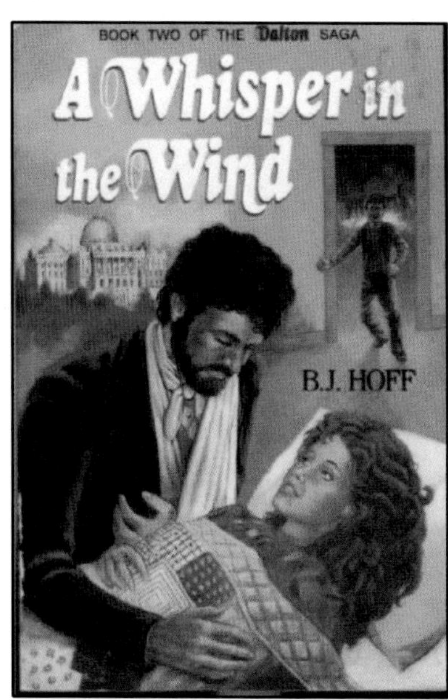

BOOK TWO OF THE Dalton SAGA
A Whisper in the Wind
B.J. HOFF

A Whisper in the Wind (The Dalton Saga #2)

Army Life, Faith

B. J. Hoff Abbey Press (1987)

In the sequel to *To Love and to Honor*, B. J. Hoff continues the love story of the controversial northern clergyman, Jess Dalton, and his young wife, Kerry. The former West Point chaplain kindles the flame of freedom from his new pulpit in the nation's capital at a time of increasing conflict between native-born Americans and Irish immigrants. While Jess defends the rights of the enslaved, his Irish bride, rejected by Washington society, fights her own battle for equality. [BC]

B.J. Hoff (1940-) is the author of several historical fiction series. Her five-volume Emerald Ballad series was the first major work of fiction to bring the Irish immigration experience to the Christian Booksellers marketplace, and the work that first brought B.J. an international reading audience. [8-11]

The 20th Century

With the end of World War I and the frontier finally settled, the Army was reduced in size and many remote outposts closed. However, garrison life continued for the Army wife with its low pay, tedium, and regular relocations.

The Army Wife

Who said, "Variety is the spice of Life?"
No doubt 'twas first said by an Army wife.
Poor girl doesn't know just where she's at-
Her home is wherever he parks his hat.
She moves happily into new sets of quarters,
During which she bears their sons and daughters.
She packs up to move to the plains of Nebraska
Then orders are changed, and they go to Alaska.
Her house is a hut with no room for expansion,

It may be a tent or even a mansion.
She uncrates the furniture in snows or rains.

And lays the linoleum between labor pains.
She wrangles saw horses and makes all the beds,
Hangs curtains of target cloth last used for spreads.
And during each move—now isn't it strange?
The brats catch the mumps, the measles or mange!

She hardly gets settled when she dresses up pretty,
To go to a party and be charming and witty.
She must know Contract Rules, Mah Jongg, and Chess,
And whether a straight or a flush is the guess.
All subjects she knows on which to discourse,
She must swim, ski and golf, and ride any old horse.
She knows songs and traditions of the Kaydet Corps,
And fast learns the details "How he won the war!"
She dances with Lieutenants who are always so glamorous-
And Waltzes with Colonels who usually are amorous.
She drinks all concoctions; gin, whiskey and beer—
But, of course, does so moderately, or she'll wreck his career!

He insists on economy and questions the check stubs,
She entertains plenty, both early and late,
Any number of guests, from eighty to eight.
The first of each month there is plenty of cash,
She orders good steak but the last week it's hash!
She juggles the budget for his tropical worsted,
Though the seams on her own best outfit have bursted.
Then, she gets the uniform payments arranged—
When the blouse is no good regulations have changed!
One year she has servants and lives like a lady,
But the next—does her own work and has a new baby.
That there'll be a bank balance she has no assurance-
It all goes for likker or some damned insurance!

At the age to retire he is still hale and hearty,
Fit as a fiddle and the life of the party;
While she is old, haggard, cranky and nervous-
Really a wreck after his "Thirty years' service."
But, then, when all is said and done
She still thinks that Army life is fun!
She has loved every minute, and why not? Good Grief
She'd have been bored with a doctor, or merchant, or chief.
But there's one fine medal—some Army men wear it–
It's their Wives who should have it—the Legion of Merit!

Mrs. R. D. Smith. *The Pointer Magazine*, April 18, 1952

Parade Ground

Army Life

Jaquelin (Janet) Deitrick Century Life Press (1930)

The author's debut novel, described by a contemporary reviewer as "a grim and depressing story of the childhood and early married life of Janet Custis, born of Army parents, [whose] life is in perpetual revolt against the gossiping, bridge-playing, hypocritical society in army posts." In rebellion against this way of life, "she learns to drink, marries a 2nd Lt. to escape from home, studies dress designing in New York to escape from army wifehood, runs away from the sordidness of Greenwich Village, and fails again to adjust herself to life in a military station." [EB]

Tomorrow the Accolade

Army Life

Jaquelin (Janet) Deitrick Doubleday, Doran & Co. (1937)

Thirty per cent of West Point's cadets are "Army children"—boys born and raised on Army posts. Bill Deane was one of these, about to graduate, but he didn't feel as an Army boy should about the glory of the commission, he had struggled for during four years. He accepted "the accolade," however, because of Judy MacGee. Judy, a colonel's daughter, couldn't be happy out of the Army; Bill, a colonel's son, would never be happy in it.

The story of Bill and Judy's marriage is a moving, deeply-human one. Steady hard luck and the mediocrity of low rank made Army life increasingly irksome to Bill, but he loved Judy too much to let her down. Never for a moment did Judy's fierce loyalty allow him to forget that she was an Army daughter who wanted her husband and her children to hold to the Army traditions.

Matters between them were heading inevitably towards estrangement when Duke Meredith, a former classmate of Bill's, discharged from the Academy for dishonor, appeared at the Post and began to force his attentions on Judy. The emotions that flared then brought them all close to tragedy, and Bill to court martial for attempted murder. [DJ]

Marion Rolfe Johnson Deitrick (1903–unknown) employed the pseudonym Jacquelin Deitrick. From the *Wilmington Morning News* in Wilmington, Delaware on November 6, 1930:

> "Even the army seems to be a woman's game now. Born of army parents at Fort Strong, Boston Harbor, demure Jaquelin Deitrick picked the army to write about in her first novel, *Parade Ground.* Slim, brunette, and young, she covered the Tum-Arica boundary dispute between Peru and Chile for the *Panama American*, dodged a few bullets and came back to New York to freelance."

As an Army brat she wrote about life on Army posts – and the books are not very cheerful, but that was the lot for those who did not care to spend their life in the Army family. Her other book in this collection *Johnny Mouse of Corregidor* can be found in the "Army Mascots" chapter.

Here are two novels about several West Point couples as their marriages wend their way through World War II, the Korean War, and Viet Nam.

The Officers' Wives

Army Life, Korea, Viet Nam

Thomas J. Fleming Doubleday (1981)

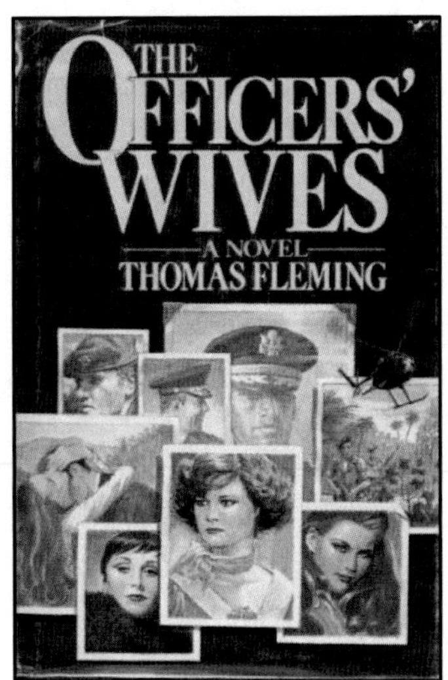

This is a book about Americans trying to live personal lives, to cling to touchstones of faith and hope in the grip of the blind, blundering history of the last 25 years. It is about marriage, the illusions and hopes that people bring to it, the struggle to maintain and renew commitment. On June 5, 1950, graduation day at West Point, Joanna Welsh of Cincinnati, poet and idealist, walks beneath the arch of shining sabers, the bride of Peter MacArthur Burke, one of the stars of Army's perennially victorious football team. Within minutes she is followed by Amy Kemble, the cool, tough-minded Philadelphia heiress, who has married George Rosser, a somewhat bland but clever Californian. Next comes red-haired Honor Prescott of Charlottesville, Virginia, giddily in love with Adam Thayer of Maine, who hides his brilliance - and his reckless idealism - behind a stream of jokes and comic impersonations.

Even as the new second lieutenants and their wives drank champagne, tanks and artillery were being positioned on an obscure Asian peninsula named Korea. War explodes before their honeymoons are over - and history becomes a dark presence in their lives. For Joanna it is the beginning of a spiritual journey that strips away her simplistic Catholic faith and teaches her harsh lessons about life's brutality & love's limitations. For Amy, war whether in Korea or Vietnam -- merely complicates her efforts to make George a general -- until she discovers that courage is at the heart of the kind of love she needs and wants. Honor must grapple with a marriage that often teeters on oblivion, as Adam's experience in the Army -- above all his opposition to the war in Vietnam -- turns him into a savage cynic.

Ranging from occupied Germany and Japan of the 1950s to the steamy chaos of Saigon and Bangkok in the 1960s, this is a global drama told by a gifted novelist and historian. [DJ]

Thomas Fleming (1927–2017) was a novelist and historian. He served in the Navy on board the USS Topeka and graduated from Fordham University. After brief stints as a journalist and magazine editor, he began his writing career in 1960. He wrote 23 novels and 25 books on American history. He was a frequent guest on C-Span, PBS, A&E, and the History Channel. [8-12]

Handsome Women

Army Life, Army Wife

Judith Henry Wall Viking (1990)

For two sisters born into a military family, nothing seemed more romantic than a West Point wedding beneath crossed sabers. . . followed, of course, by a husband's steady rise through the ranks to become a general.

Louise: Serious, ladylike, she takes lessons in small talk from her self-confident older sister. She knows that Franklin Cravens, the most promising cadet in his class, wants a wife who will make him proud, and when he asks for her hand, Louise wants nothing more than to win her husband's admiration. Yet, as Louise will learn, wifely duty may come at a great price—the price of one's heart.

Marynell: The charismatic flirt, she can hardly believe that little Louise has snared the best catch at the Point. Humiliated by a man who forces himself on her, she's certain that no man will ever tempt her again. But when sensitive Captain Jeffrey Washburn, a widower, asks her to marry him and be a mother to his son, Marynell accepts - though Jeffrey's military ambitions cannot match her own.

From war-torn Corregidor to peacetime Germany, from Fort Sill to Washington, D.C., the two sisters learn what it truly means to be married to the military. As they grow from girls to women, wives to mothers, they learn that life beneath the crossed sabers can truly be a double-edged sword. [DJ]

Judy Henry Wall (1938–2020) was born an "Army Brat" in Evansville, Indiana. Judy's early childhood was spent in Japan where her father served in the high command of the occupying Allied Forces. She never forgot the kindness of the Japanese people she met. Like so many avid readers, Ms. Wall aspired to write the great American novel. Her talents quickly developed and later works such as *Love and Duty*, *Handsome Women* and *Blood Sisters* were masterworks of women's fiction that brought her worldwide publication and critical acclaim. [8-13]

We conclude this chapter with two 20th-21st century memoirs by officers' wives recounting the challenges of their "Army careers."

Together: Annals of an Army Wife

WW2, General Officer, Memoir, Army Life

Katherine Tupper Marshall People's Book Club (1947)

What are the thoughts, emotions and adventures of a man and woman who travel side by side - always together - along the winding road that leads from obscurity to the heights of fame?

In 1930 the Author married a Lieutenant Colonel who was destined to become one of the greatest military leaders in history and a statesman whose full stature cannot even yet be measured.

How did he gain this position? How did he discipline his body and mind to perform the most exacting military task of all times? And what part did she play? What were the dominant characteristics of the people she met -the great and near great? What amusing mistakes did she make? And above all, what were the human qualities, the moods, likes and dislikes, the real character of the man about whose life so little is known that he seems almost a legendary figure.

With delightful friendliness, humor and charm, Katherine Tupper Marshall, wife of our war-time Chief of Staff and Secretary of State, answers these and countless other absorbing questions. Into an unforgettable tapestry she weaves world shaping events and everyday incidents of the home wherein humor contrasts with deep emotions. [DJ]

Katherine Boyce Marshall (née Tupper 1882 – 1978) was an actress, writer, and wife of soldier, and statesman George C. Marshall. [8-14]

I Love a Man in Uniform: A Memoir of Love, War and Other Battles

Army Life, GWOT, Memoir

Lily Burana Weinstein Books (2009)

In this brave, eloquent, and often funny memoir, critically acclaimed author Lily Burana writes about love, war, and the realities of military marriage with an honesty few writers would dare.

A former exotic dancer who once had a penchant for anarchist politics and purple hair dye, Lily's rebellious past never would have suggested a marriage into the military. But then she met Mike, a military intelligence officer, and fell hopelessly in love, resulting in a most unorthodox romance -- poignant, passionate, and utterly unpredictable.

After Lily and Mike said "I do" in a brief, pre-deployment City Hall ceremony, Mike left for Operation Iraqi Freedom, and Lily was left in a strange town to endure his absence alone, with no support system and little knowledge of the vast and confusing military world into which she had married.

Upon Mike's return from the war, the couple moved to historic West Point, where Lily found that life on base had its own challenges. As the war continued and the past intruded unexpectedly into the present, Lily and Mike found themselves plunged into the nightmare of PTSD. Struggling to cope in a community where admitting weakness is the ultimate taboo and "suck it up" is the suggested response to emotional pain, Lily suffered from depression so severe, it almost ended her marriage. With the help of a revolutionary therapeutic technique, the couple made their way out of the darkness and back to each other. Through it all, Lily wrangled with her preconceptions about the military and found her place within the uniquely supportive sisterhood of military wives.

From harrowing emotion to the dishy details of life on base, Lily Burana bares her heart and soul as a modern military spouse. *I Love a Man in Uniform* is a profoundly moving story of how a woman can locate, and heal, her true self as a dedicated Army wife, free spirit, and freedom-loving American. [DJ]

Lily Burana started writing while still a teenager. Burana married an Army officer in 2002. In 2008, she began "Operation Bombshell," a burlesque class for wives of deployed soldiers. As a journalist, Burana frequently writes about media, pop culture, religion, and spirituality. She has written for over 50 publications. [DJ]

Chapter 9

Soldiers of Fortune, Paladins, Miscreants & Rogues

The image of West Point as visualized by their motto "Duty, Honor, Country" is of disciplined cadets, crisply attired, absorbed in studies and athletics, and as young officers marching to the defense of our nation. That is certainly true for the great majority of cadets and graduates. But not always. There are ample accounts of those who have taken a different path. After all, opportunities abound beyond the strictures of a military career, especially between the Civil War and World War II when the Army was poorly paid, advancement slow, and the postings often undesirable, especially for families. As the song "Benny Havens" goes:

> Come, fill your glasses, fellows, and stand up in a row,
> To singing sentimentally we're going for to go;
> In the army there's sobriety, promoting's very slow,
> So we'll sing our reminiscences of Benny Havens, OH!

Most who departed the army used their West Point education and military training honorably with distinction in civilian endeavors or in other lands…but not all as you shall see.

Soldiers of Fortune

In the 19th century some graduates, finding their services "under-appreciated" by the Army, resigned to employ their military skills abroad.

Captain Landon: A Story of Modern Rome

WP Author, Adventure Abroad

Richard Henry Savage Rand McNally (1899)

The story opens with the arrival in Rome of Captain Sydney Landon, West Pointer, age 27, recently resigned officer of the storied Gray Horse troop – no explanation offered – after earning a Medal of Honor in the Indian wars on the western plains. He has obtained the position of Vice Consul General for the U.S. in Rome. Landon becomes the defacto General Consul because Consul Arthur Melville much prefers artistic pursuits and leaves the office to Landon. Lawson immediately applies his considerable management skills to improve the functioning of the office and root out a corrupt local employee. However, the Army is not done with Landon. With the President's approval a pair of his former commanders are visiting Rome to persuade Landon to return to the Army.

Thriving in his new office and surroundings, Landon favors the company of the youthful Mrs. Gertrude Melville and her guest for the summer, nineteen year old Agnes Hawthorn. The latter is an orphan and heiress to an enormous Philadelphia fortune. Landon realizes that he could never hope to win Agnes given the disparities in their station. Trouble is afoot, however, in the person of Rawdon Clark, a western mining magnate wintering in Rome, who hopes to secure Ms. Hawthorn's hand in marriage thereby furthering his ambitions in Philadelphia society and commerce. Agnes has no interest in Clark, but is attracted to Sydney Landon.

Landon is escorting Mrs. Melville and Ms. Hawthorn to the sites late one evening when they are attacked by thugs. Landon shoots one of the attackers to drive them away. To avoid all scandal for the ladies, the fracas is kept under wraps. Landon comes down with a serious case of Rome's swamp fever and is laid low for months. Meanwhile, Rawdon Clark mounts a campaign to drive Landon from Rome (and Agnes' affections). He spreads the rumor that Landon left the Army after some disgraceful behavior and is unsuitable for the position he had taken in Rome. Moreover lies and innuendos are spread about the circumstances surrounding the shooting incident. It looks exceedingly gloomy for Landon and his supporters when he refuses to reveal why he left the Army. Instead. he resigns his post and leaves Rome to serve in the Egyptian army in Sudan. . . .

Fortune soon begins to shine on Captain Landon following his heroism in Egypt. [EB]

Richard Henry Savage (1846–1903) was an American military officer and author who wrote more than 40 books of adventure and mystery, based loosely on his own experiences. Savage traveled to many exotic lands but in 1890 he was struck with jungle fever in Honduras. While recuperating in New York state he wrote his first book: My Official Wife. This very successful action-and-adventure story was followed by more, at the rate of about three per year, written for the general public rather than for literary critics. He is buried in the cemetery at West Point. [9-01]

Captain Macklin

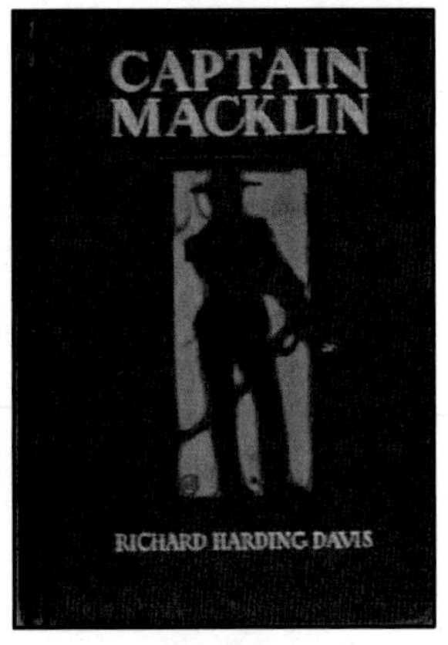

Adventure Abroad, Romance, WP Ex

Richard Harding Davis Charles Scribner's Sons (1902)

Macklin is a quixotic young man from several generations of soldiers who gets kicked out of West Point for dallying with women during unauthorized hours. Determined to be a soldier somewhere he consults the newspapers, discovers that a revolution is going on in Honduras, and forthwith sets out to offer his sword to the insurgents and seek personal redemption.

Upon his return to the states, young Macklin has to decide whether to settle down or continue with a life of adventure. Lots of satire in this story and some of the points are hilarious. [EB]

Richard Harding Davis (1864–1916) was a romantic novelest, playwright and the foremost American journalist at the end of the 19th century. He was the first American correspondent to cover the Spanish-American War, the Second Boer War, and the First World War. His writings greatly boosted the political career of Theodore Roosevelt. [9-02]

A Soldier of the Legion: A Romance of Algiers & the Desert

Adventure Abroad

C.N. & A.M. Williamson A. L. Burt (1914)

Between the Civil War and World War I more than a few West Point graduates employed their military skills as soldiers of fortune for foreign governments. Max Doran, scion of a well-to-do family in New York having graduated fourth in his class at West Point, is stationed at Ft. Ellsworth Kansas, when a telegram calls him home to his dying mother. Events ensue which cause him to resign his commission and travel to France. He meets a young woman, who is the daughter of a Colonel in the French Foreign Legion. Max decides to join up . . . adventure and romance ensue. [EB]

British authors **Charles Norris (C.N.) Williamson** (1859–1920) **and his wife Alice** (1858–1933) collaborated on many novels and eventually films before the Great War. She did most of the writing apparently. They used West Point as a background in two of their works: *A Soldier of the Legion* described here and *Lady Betty Across the Water* in another chapter of this book. [9-03]

Crofton's Fire

Adventure Abroad, Indian Wars, Boer War, Cuba

Keith Coplin Putnam (2004)

In 1876, a green lieutenant named Crofton barely escapes Little Big Horn—where before his startled eyes, Custer is killed by his own enraged men—only to find that his own adventures have just begun. Over the next three years, curiosity, fate, and the schemes of others will take Crofton halfway around the world, from a "whore's war" in Kansas to a rebellion in Cuba to the horrors of the Zulu war in East Africa. Along the way, he will encounter such figures as Grant, Sherman, and Hayes; get shot; find love; endure betrayal—and somehow, through the crucible of blood and fire, arrive at something that might be called wisdom. [DJ]

Keith Coplin (1942–) received undergraduate degrees from the University of Texas and his PhD. From Kansas University. He taught at Colby Community College in Colby, KS. Though this is his only novel, he has contributed numerous stories and poems to literary and popular magazines. *Crofton's Fire* certainly complements the Fenwick Travers novels which are also included in this chapter.

The next three works are not novels, though they may read like one. Each is a memoir of an actual West Pointer who served in foreign lands in the 19th and 20th centuries.

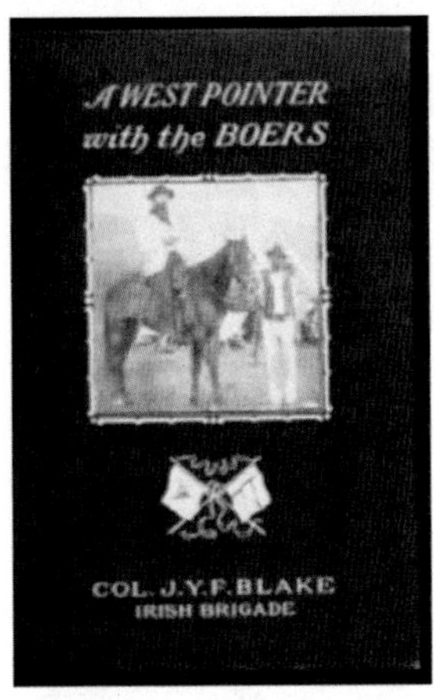

A West Pointer with the Boers

Boer War, Memoir

John Y. Blake Angel Guardian Press (1905)

Freed of family obligations following his divorce, Blake became a soldier of fortune exploring Africa, eventually serving under the governors of South Africa. He joined the Boer forces as commander of the Irish Brigade fighting against the British until he was seriously wounded. He returned to New York City and advocated for Irish independence until his untimely death from gas asphyxiation in January 1907. [EB]

John Y. F. "Beau" Blake (1856–1907) graduated from West Point in 1880 then served in Arizona with the 6th U.S. Cavalry leading scouts under Generals Wilcox, Crook, and Miles against the Apache. The nickname "Beau" apparently derived from his charming ways with the ladies. In 1889 his wife of four years, pregnant with their second child, persuaded Beau to resign his commission and return to her hometown of Grand Rapids, Michigan. She promptly divorced him. Blake is buried in the cemetery at West Point, NY. [9-04]

West Pointer in the Land of the Mikado

Adventure Abroad, Faith, Memoir

Laura Garst H. Revell (1913)

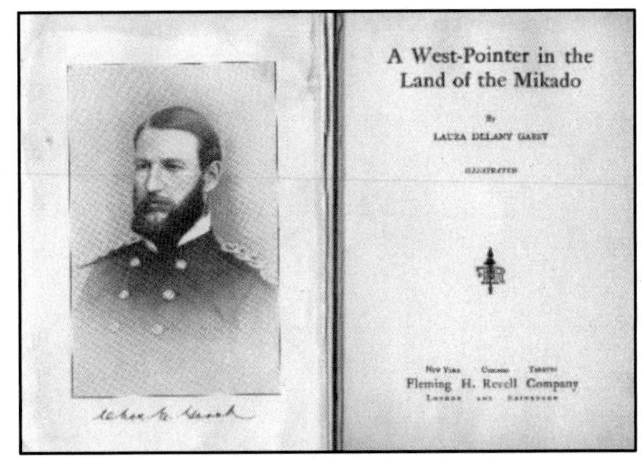

From the book's forward:

"When, in 1893, we returned to Japan for a second term of service, Mr.[Charles] Garst expressed the wish that together we might write a book especially for young people, which would, he hoped, increase their interest in the Japanese. His desire has inspired me to undertake the task, feeling keenly my insuficiency without his assistance, but sure that he speaks through these pages. True, he would have said little about himself. I feel, however, that his passion for his work was so intense that this further gift of a more intimate acquaintance with his life purposes and accomplishments would he have gladly laid on the altar. I want to thank friends who have helped and encouraged me to persevere in the trying work, in spite of strenuous field duties and pressing home cares, and to acknowledge my debt to sources of information which I have freely consulted."

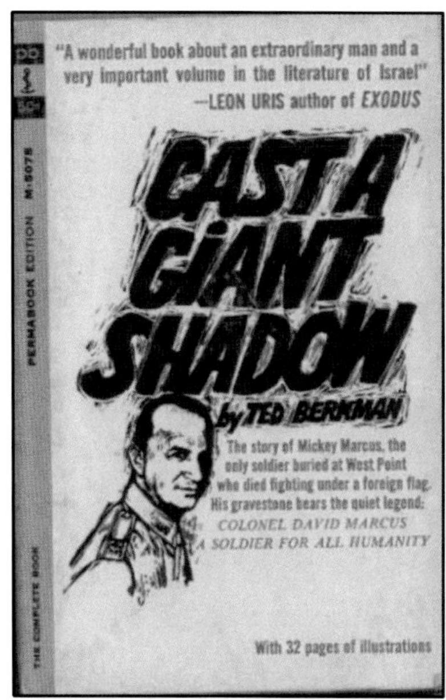

Cast a Giant Shadow

Adventure Abroad, Judaism

Ted Berkman Doubleday (1962)

Whether he was defending his rights in a tenement scuffle, boxing at West Point, racket busting in New York City, parachuting into Normandy, or advising presidents—Mickey Marcus never ducked a fight, especially where freedom was involved.

So, when the Israelis, outnumbered sixty to one and lacking food, fuel, tanks, planes, and even rifles, sought his help, he came, brought off a miracle - and then was killed by a tragic quirk of fate, only a few hours before the cease-fire. Marcus is interred in the West Point Cemetery under a headstone donated by the State of Israel. [9-05] [EB]

Ted Berkman (1914–2006), an American author, screenwriter and journalist, attended Cornell University, graduating in 1933, and Columbia University.. During World War II, he served as an intelligence officer for the US Army. After the war, Berkman became a foreign correspondent giving the first report of the explosion of the King David Hotel in Jerusalem in 1946. He is best known for writing the screenplay for *Bedtime for Bonzo* starring Ronald Reagan. [9-05]

The Paladins

The term "paladin" arose from twelve fictional knights of legend from King Arthur's Round Table or the members of Charlemagne's court in the 8th century. They were depicted as heroic characters through the later middle ages and into the European courts of the 19th century. Modern depictions of paladins are often an individual knight-errant holy warrior or justice seeker.

It would not stretch the imagination to see a West Pointer disciplined in duty, honor, and integrity taking up the cause of an oppressed individual or group. They would fall in the line of Superman and Batman protrayed in the comic books and movies of the late 20th century. Two fictional West Pointers came to television and literary prominence as "paladins."

The first actually took the named Paladin in the book, comic books, and television series *Have Gun Will Travel*. The second, named Jack Reacher, was the protagonist in a series of novels written by Lee Child, a British author. Reacher never returned to West Point in the novels, but regularly referred to his youth as an Army brat and experince as a major in the military police.

Have Gun Will Travel

Western, Crime, Paladin

Noel Loomis Dell Publishing (1960)

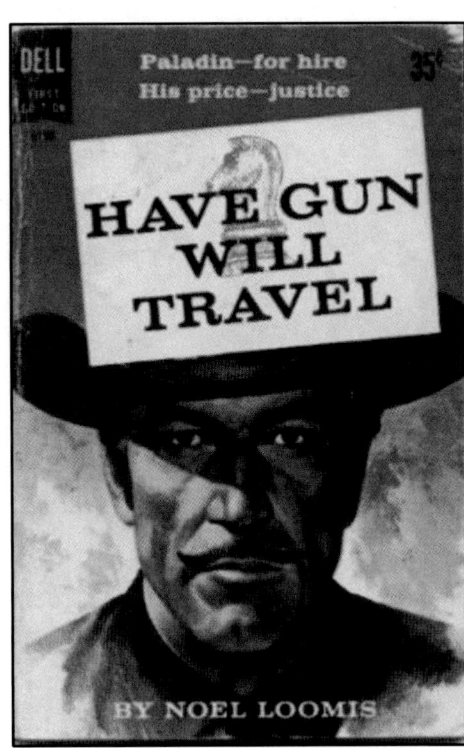

This book is a by-product of the television drama series that aired on CBS from 1958 to 1963 starring Richard Boone as the hero Paladin.

"Paladin is a graduate of the United States Military Academy at West Point and a veteran of the American Civil War, in which he served as a Union cavalry officer. Paladin prefers to settle the difficulties clients bring his way without violence, but this rarely happens. When forced, he excels in fisticuffs. Under his real name, which is never revealed, he was a dueling champion of some renown.

His permanent place of residence is the Hotel Carlton in San Francisco, where he lives the life of a successful businessman and bon vivant, wearing elegant custom-made suits, consuming fine wine, playing the piano, and attending the opera and other cultural events. He is an expert chess player, poker player, and swordsman. He is skilled in Chinese martial arts and is seen in several episodes receiving instruction and training with a Kung Fu master in San Francisco. He is highly educated, able to quote classic literature, philosophy, and case law, and speaks several languages. He is also president of the San Francisco Stock Exchange Club.

When out working, Paladin changes into all-black Western-style clothing. His primary weapon is a custom-made, first-generation .45 caliber Colt Single Action Army Cavalry Model revolver with a rifled barrel, carried in a black leather holster (with a platinum chess knight symbol facing the rear), hanging from a black leather gun belt. He also carries a lever action Marlin rifle strapped to his saddle, and a Remington derringer concealed under his belt." [9-06]

Noel Miller Loomis (1905–1969), was an editor, printer, newspaperman, teacher and writer of western, mystery and science-fiction in the mid-20th century. [9-07]

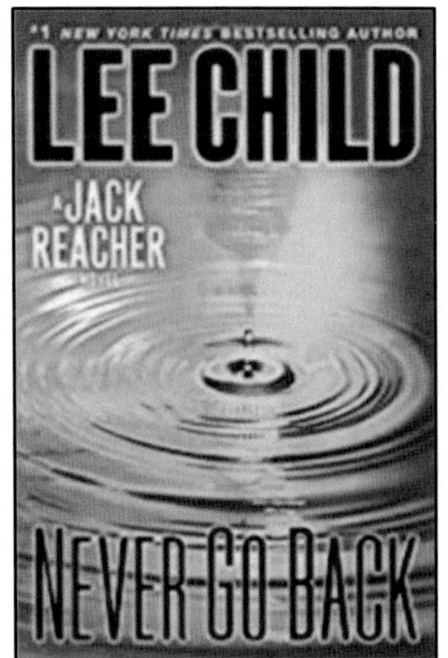

Never Go Back: A Jack Reacher Novel

Crime, Intrigue, Paladin

Lee Child Delacorte Press (2013)

Army brat, West Point graduate, and former military cop Jack Reacher makes it all the way from snowbound South Dakota to his destination in northeastern Virginia, near Washington, D.C.: the headquarters of his old unit, the 110th MP. The old stone building is the closest thing to a home he ever had.

Reacher is there to meet—in person—the new commanding officer, Major Susan Turner, so far just a warm, intriguing voice on the phone.

But it isn't Turner behind the CO's desk. And Reacher is hit with two pieces of shocking news, one with serious criminal consequences, and one too personal to even think about. When threatened, you can run or fight.

Reacher fights, aiming to find Turner and clear his name, barely a step ahead of the army, and the FBI, and the D.C. Metro police, and four unidentified thugs. Combining an intricate puzzle of a plot and an exciting chase for truth and justice, Lee Child puts Reacher through his paces—and makes him question who he is, what he's done, and the very future of his untethered life on the open road. [DJ]

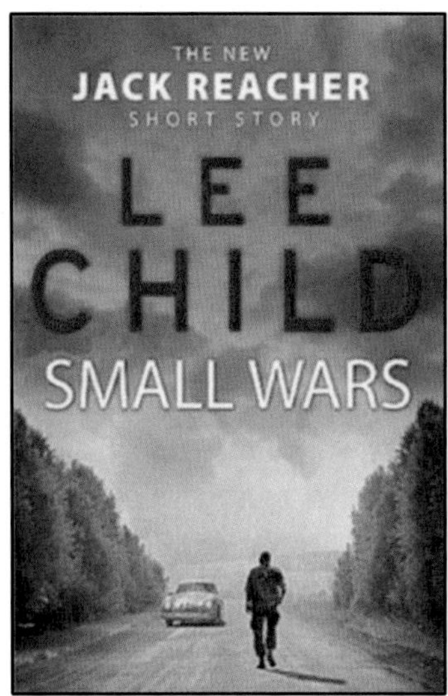

"Small Wars"

Crime, Mystery, Paladin

Lee Child Random House Publishing Group (2017)

"Small Wars" is a short story written by Lee Child and appears in the anthology *No Middle Name*, which is in this collection.

The telex is brief and to the point: One active-duty personnel found shot to death ten miles north of Fort Smith. Circumstances unknown. Found in a silver Porsche along an isolated forest road in Georgia, the victim was shot twice in the chest and once in the head. A professional hit. Clean. The crime scene suggests an ambush. Military police officer Jack Reacher is given the case. He calls his older brother, Colonel Joe Reacher, at the Pentagon for intel and taps Sergeant Frances Neagley to help him answer the big question: Who would kill a brilliant officer on the fast-track to greatness? For Jack Reacher, the answer hits home. [9-08]

The Midnight Line: A Jack Reacher Novel

Crime

Lee Child Delacorte Press (2017)

Army brat, West Point graduate, and modern-day paladin - Jack Reacher rides the bus north from Milwaukee. At a comfort stop in Wisconsin dairy country he takes a stroll. Among the cheap junk in a pawn shop window, he notices a West Point class ring for sale. It's tiny. A woman cadet's ring. Why would she pawn it? Reacher knows what Serena Sanderson must have gone through to get it. He fights through a biker gang and a South Dakota gangster, following the trail of the ring to the emptiness of Wyoming, in search of Major Sanderson. [DJ]

Born **Jim Grant** in Coventry England in 1954. **Lee Child** entered Law School in Sheffield in 1954. Upon graduation, he turned instead to commercial television as a script and commercial writer in Manchester. Finding himself unemployed in 1995 at 40 years of age, Child decided to try his hand at writing fiction. He then pennned his first Reacher novel, *Killing Floor*. As of 2021, there have been 27 Reacher novels. He moved to New York in 1998. [9-09]

Miscreants

In any human organization there are those whose behavior is undisciplined…at least from the organization's perspective. West Point and the Army are no exception. Much of the behavior is mere mischief, but some is self-serving and detrimental to the organization's objectives.

Fenwick Travers is the archetypical "wild child" of Army officers whose career is depicted with great humor and irony. These are certainly "entertainments," and not at all shocking.

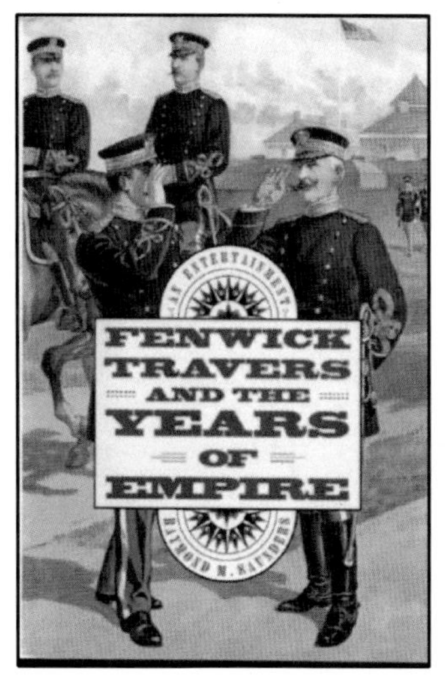

Fenwick Travers and the Years of Empire: An Entertainment

WP Author, Rogue, Cuba

Raymond M. Saunders   Berkley Pub Group (1993)

Fenwick Travers is a rollicking, good-natured, and thoroughly unmilitary brawler who finds himself in the army as the result of pure happenstance. Above all else, he wants to establish himself comfortably in the world without undue exertion. Unexpectedly, he excels in his new career. While campaigning in Cuba during the Spanish-American War, Travers acquires a completely gratuitous reputation for valor in combat while hobnobbing with Teddy Roosevelt and Black Jack Pershing. After the war, he remains in Havana to conduct a cozy gunrunning operation.

After things begin to sour in Cuba, our hero is off to China to help put down the Boxer Rebellion. He battles howling fanatics, becomes aware of unlimited opportunities for looting, and like Tom Sawyer and Huck Finn before him is soon off on a treasure hunt. Travers eventually returns to New York as a national hero, feted and honored by the nation's political and military leadership. This first-class rogues romp through turn-of-the-century American history will leave you in stitches, while bringing to life a rich and exciting time in our nation's past. [DJ]

Fenwick Travers and the Forbidden Kingdom: An Entertainment

WP Author, Rogue, Philippines

Raymond Saunders   Lyford Books (1994)

Although Fenwick Travers is a cheating, drunken, sycophantic libertine; a charlatan; an adulterous, cowardly, gluttonous blackguard; a bounder; a dastardly, caddish, philandering mountebank; a poltroon; a besotted, lecherous, scheming toady; a roué; a sybaritic rapscallion; and a rakehell, he remains a thoroughly lovable fellow, an enduring character upon whom the completely undeserved mantle of "all-American hero" manages to rest easily.

In Fenwick Travers and the Years of Empire, we followed Fenny from Indian-fighting in Arizona to West Point, on to San Juan Hill, and finally to Peking for the Boxer Rebellion. Now Lieutenant Travers is off to the Philippines, newly acquired from Spain in the recent war. While there he happens on a treasure map that leads him on a series of adventures which sorely tests his ingenuity as he searches for the treasure, all the while attempting to avoid any danger to himself. The results are predictably hilarious as Fenny finds his honor sorely tried but manages not to let it interfere overmuch with his riotous enjoyment of all that life has to offer. [DJ]

Fenwick Travers and the Panama Canal: An Entertainment

WP Author, Rogue, Panama

Raymond Saunders Presidio Press (1995)

Fenwick Travers, the delightful rapscallion who always manages to become a hero while running away from trouble, is at it again.

The story begins when Fenwick, just back from the Philippines and happily living a life of ease and dissipation, suffers some gambling losses and gets mixed up in an Army procurement swindle. In need of a change of air, he is off to Panama to plant the seeds of rebellion against Colombia, which is blocking construction of the Panama Canal, the pet project of Penny's presidential sponsor, Teddy Roosevelt. Getting the peaceful Panamanians to rebel without overtly involving the United States is a ticklish business requiring a devious agent provocateur. Who better than our Fenwick?

But fomenting a rebellion is not as easy as it's cracked up to be. Before he knows it, Fenwick is involved with a beautiful widow, makes an enemy of the local strongman, gets captured by Indians, and must escape through some of the fiercest wilderness in the world. And things go downhill from there. [DJ]

Raymond Saunders, Class of 1974, wrote three books about this miscreant West Point officer serving in Cuba, the Philippines, the Panama Canal in the early 20th century. The second book in this series is included in the chapter "In the Far East." [9-10]

Rogues

There are "bad apples" in many a barrel, even among West Pointers, that need to be culled out. Here are a few good stories, all entertaining reads, and each quite different. Concluding this chapter is an account of a West Point graduate, who was tried for murder in 1909. It is not uplifting, not fictional, but does belong in this section of rogues from West Point.

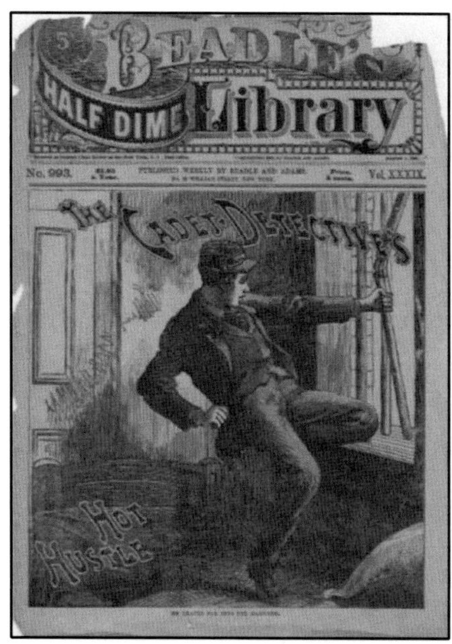

"The Cadet Detective's Hot Hustle" or *"West Point Rogues"*

Cadet, Crime, Pulp Fiction

Howard Boynton Beadle's Half Dime Library (Aug. 1896)

General Earl, then commanding officer at the West Point Military Academy, rushed out of his private office bareheaded, and started for the railroad station, situated about a quarter of a mile from the Government buildings, on a dead run. Reaching it, he dashed inside and aroused the drowsy telegraph operator.

"Here, Jackson!" he shouted, handing a slip of paper through the window; "wire this down as soon as God will let you!"

The operator took the message, read it carefully, and the next moment it was on its way. Here it is:

To HENRY R. PARSONS, Chief Secret Service Bureau, New York City.
Send me at once the best man on the force under twenty years of age.
Janus D. EARL, Commanding Officer M. A.

"Bring the reply to the message direct to me," ordered the general, "if any is returned." Then the officer turned and ran back toward the main building of the Academy. He had scarcely disappeared over the hill before a young man in a sergeant's uniform took his place at the window of the telegraph office. [EB]

From 1882 to 1900 the dime novel featuring a clever detective or sleuth proliferated. **Howard Boynton** (probably a pseudo name) produced many of these stories in the 1890s including his one shown above. They were ultimately supplanted by the pulp fiction story magazines at the turn of the century.

Only the Losers Win

Cold War, Rogue

Glenn M. Barns Fawcett Gold Medal (1968)

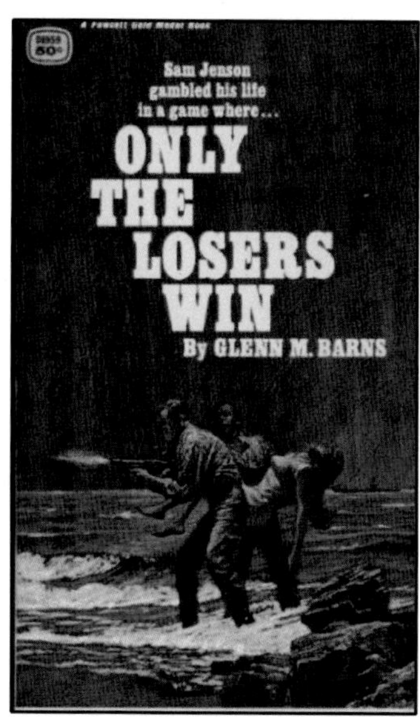

"No one was quite what he seemed....

MARKO, an Albanian killer, talked like a British pansy...
JACK, a career officer from West Point, acted like a Black Nationalist elevator operator....
SAM, a captain with a grudge against the Army, masqueraded as a private with a grudge against the Army....
JANET WING, a delicate and lovely Chinese girl, seemed thoroughly American, but attended anti-war demonstrations....
SMITTY, a light-skinned Negro, disguised himself as one of the hated whites....
Each played a part in a desperate game of deception." [EB]

From an online reviewer: Not much could be found about **Glenn M. Barns** other than he produced a nice collection of works that seemed to have slipped beneath the pop culture radar.

Masquerade In Blue (1956)
Deadly Summer (1957)
Murder Walks the Stairs (1959) is a British edition.
Murder Is a Gamble (1953)
Only The Losers Win (1968) [9-11]

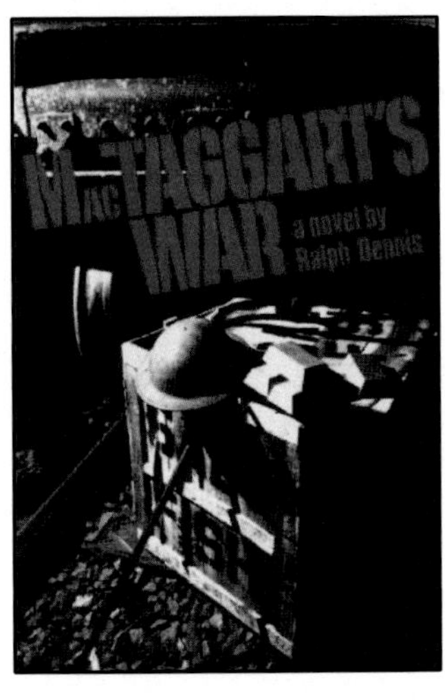

MacTaggart's War

WW2, Rogue, Crime, Canada

Ralph Dennis Holt, Rinehart, and Winston (1979)

June 1940. France is about to fall to the German invaders. England prepares for what seems to be the hopeless defense against the expected invasion across the Channel. The cruiser, His Majesty's Ship Emerald, sets sail for Canada, her task to deliver more than $500 million in gold bullion and securities to the safety of North America. In Fort Sam Belwin, North Carolina, two men watch their lives rot away in the peacetime American Army: Captain Johnny Whitman, who left the coal mines to become a football star at Duke, the "golden boy" gone to seed and saddled with a nagging ex-showgirl wife; and Major Tom Renssler, West Point 1930, born to wealth, but now plagued with gambling debts and the knowledge that his military career, once so promising, is about to come to a sudden end.

Even a small portion of that English gold will go a long way toward restoring some of the glitter to their shabby lives. A former drinking friend of Major Renssler's, a British major on a military mission to the States, arrives from London and unwittingly sets a scheme to steal the gold, which is as audacious as it is brilliant, in motion.

Whitman and Renssler lead six former enlisted men—a retired gunnery sergeant dying of tuberculosis, a weapons expert who has become a strongarm man for the Mob, an expert in explosives, a mechanic, and two roughneck railroaders to Canada where at Wingate Station, an isolated Canadian National Railway Depot, their lust for money intersects with a train hearing the fortune in English gold bullion and securities.

And on this train is Duncan MacTaggart, a dour Scotsman assigned by the Bank of England to see that the British gold and securities are safely transported to the underground vaults in Canada. Nothing has mattered as much to MacTaggart since his service in the Great War. And nothing in that slaughter has prepared him for his war at Wingate Station. [DJ]

Ralph Dennis (1931–1988) was an American author of crime fiction, best known for his Hardman series of detective novels, all in paperback. His only novel in hardback was *MacTaggert's War*. It was the last book published in his lifetime. [9-12]

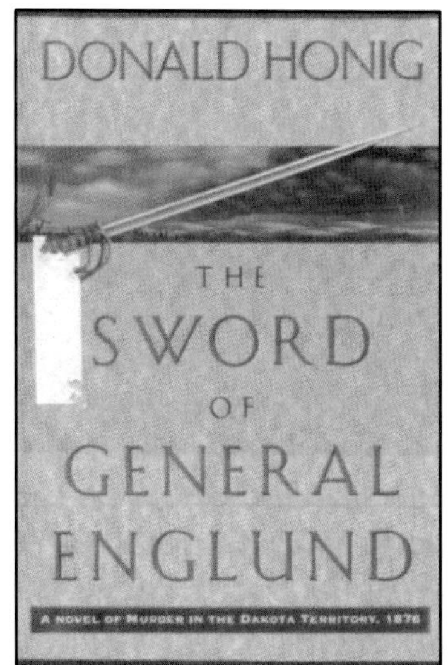

Sword of General Englund: A Novel of Murder in the Dakota Territory, 1876

General Officer, Western, Crime, Mystery

Donald Honig Scribner (1996)

In 1876, at Fort Larkin, a small military outpost fifty miles from nowhere in the Dakota Territory, General Alfred England, alone in his office in the middle of the night, is stabbed to death. Civil War hero, eccentric, religious fanatic, and brilliant fighting soldier, he was both feared and respected by his men. And hated, perhaps, by one.

The preliminary investigation rules out an intruder, and none of the noncoms or enlisted men had the opportunity to commit the crime. All signs point instead to one of the general's senior staff officers as the killer. The military cannot condone the assassination of one of its own. This is a murder that demands attention from the highest authorities, even from President Ulysses S. Grant. Captain Thomas Maynard arrives from Washington to unmask the murderer, with orders that carry the authority of the President himself. But Maynard has secrets of his own, and his judgment may be affected by his growing fondness for the deceased general's lovely daughter.

Englund, a larger-than-life hero who, according to legend, once inflamed the passions of his men by hurling his sword up into the air, where it was struck by a blinding flash of lightning, had been brusque and arrogant; his men had followed him into battle with a fidelity that was not so much loyal and devoted as dominated and bewitched.

Now, with the help of Sergeant Billy Barrie, a man who usually says little but knows just about everything that goes on in the fort, Maynard must penetrate and discover the real General Englund. His investigation leads him to seven suspects: the command's five senior officers, each of whom had a motive for killing the general; the seductive young wife of one of the officers; and a mysterious army scout who disappeared on the night of the murder and is rumored to be somewhere in the surrounding Black Hills.

Through a process of sly cat-and-mouse interrogations, Maynard begins a dogged assault on the truth. The answer, when he finds it, is not what the military wants to hear. [DJ]

The Ghost of Major Pryor: A Novel of Murder in the Montana Territory, 1870

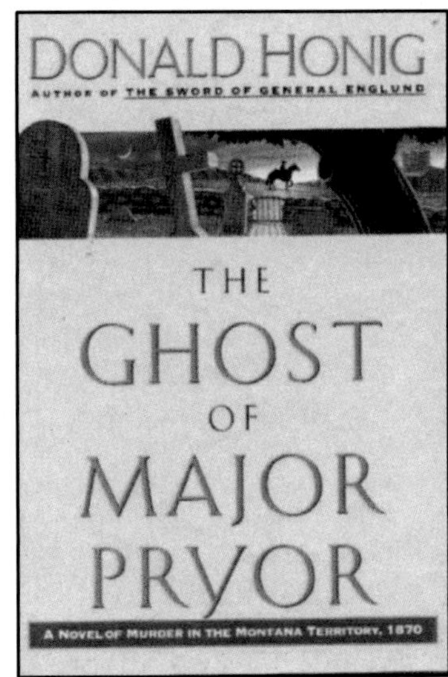

Western, Rogue, Mystery, Crime

Donald Honig Scribner (1997)

Donald Honig's post-Civil War mystery, *The Sword of General England*, received extraordinary acclaim from the critics. Now he returns with Captain Thomas M. Maynard's second investigation. Barley Newton is cold sober the day he walks down the dusty street in the gold-mining town of Baddock in the Montana Territory. The year is 1870, and Barley knows he couldn't have seen what he just saw: The man who passes him on the street is Major Andrew Pryor. But this is impossible! Pryor was Barley's commander in one of the bloodiest of all Civil War battles. And Pryor was killed in battle in 1864, more than five years ago. His body was found and buried.

So why is Barley so sure it's Pryor he sees in the remote town of Baddock? And, stranger still, why is Barley Newton found dead soon after the mysterious encounter?

Back in Washington, officials at the War Department want some answers. It is almost unheard of for an officer to desert his troops. If Pryor, a West Point man, is indeed still alive, he must be apprehended and punished for the traitor he is. But Pryor has clearly taken a new name and identity and may be difficult to locate now that Barley Newton is dead. Captain Thomas Maynard, traveling incognito, is sent west to investigate. Before Barley died, he made it clear that Pryor was prominent in the town—perhaps the banker, the lawyer, the doctor, the businessman—someone with much to lose if his identity were revealed. And Maynard, too, has much to lose, perhaps even his life, if Pryor discovers that Maynard is on his trail.

In a tale of greed, murder, and aching love, Maynard must deal with his growing attraction to Theo, a beautiful, enigmatic prostitute, even as he plays a deadly cat-and-mouse game against Pryor, with survival as the prize. [DJ]

Donald Honig is a prolific author primarily of non-fiction books and stories on baseball and other sports. His forays into crime fiction described here involve West Pointers engaged in criminal activity on post-Civil War army posts. The clever Captain Maynard is dispatched from Washington to investigate. [9-13]

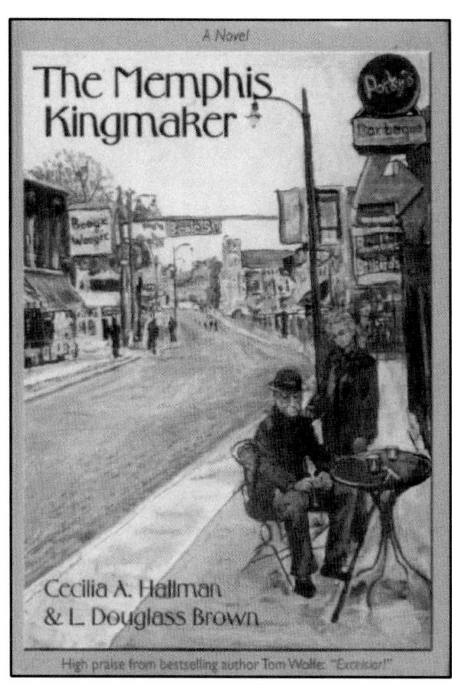

The Memphis Kingmaker

Rogue, Crime, Intrigue, Tennessee

Cecilia A. Hallman & L. Douglass Brown
IRG Press (2006)

Cadet John Henry Thompson, Class of 1946, was a not-too-tall, thin young man when he entered West Point. He had never been this far from home, much less in a very foreign land. Yankee territory, just up the Hudson River from that metropolis of New York City at The United States Military Academy, West Point, just 'The Point' to him and the other cadets.

To John, the Hudson River Valley was not unlike the Tennessee Valley near back home, rolling hills and lots of fresh water. But there were stately mansions there, a definite sense of being out of his world. Sure, there were old plantation homes back home, but none like these. It seemed that everyone lived this way up there, definitely upscale, 'landed gentry' he would call them.

He didn't have to worry. He would rarely see the outside of the gates that were the confines of The Point for his stay. Summers were spent doing extra work and earning money, most of which he sent home to his parents to help out during his absence. John had met businessmen from New York City while at The Peabody Hotel in Memphis and had dreamed of one day seeing their world for himself. He knew that he would. It was never an impossible dream.

The Memphis Kingmaker is a rags-to-riches story of a Tennessee man, John Henry Thompson, and his Georgia-born companion, Ophelia Hartwell. Beale Street, Memphis, the nightlife of Miami, and the Atlanta social scene are among the locales that take the reader on a journey of politics, treachery and international intrigue. [DJ]

Cecilia A. Hallman completed her university studies in South Carolina, at the University of Oxford and Tulane University. When not traveling and writing, she lives in Aiken, South Carolina. **L. Douglass Brown**, PhD, is a published author who lives in the American South. He holds an advanced diploma in history from the University of Oxford in England. [9-14]

Custer's Gold

Custer, Indian Wars, Crime, Western

M. John Lubetkin Bookstand Publishing (2014)

When George Armstrong Custer sets out to guard Northern Pacific Railroad engineers in the Yellowstone Valley from Sitting Bull, he is looking forward to a reunion with his West Point friend and Confederate foe, Tom Rosser. Little does he know that Rosser has discovered the location of stolen gold, nor that the man who stole the gold a decade earlier is shadowing them, intent on recovering it for himself at any cost. Bristling with action, *Custer's Gold* is a work of historic fiction...taking the reader from bar room brawls to bordellos, from robber barons to hard fought Indian battles, all with the violence, realism and irony that typified this dynamic period of American growth. [DJ]

John Lubetkin has studied the expansion westward by gold seekers and railroads into the Dakotas, Wyoming, and Yellowstone River Valley in the 1870s. He has written several books on those topics. [9-15]

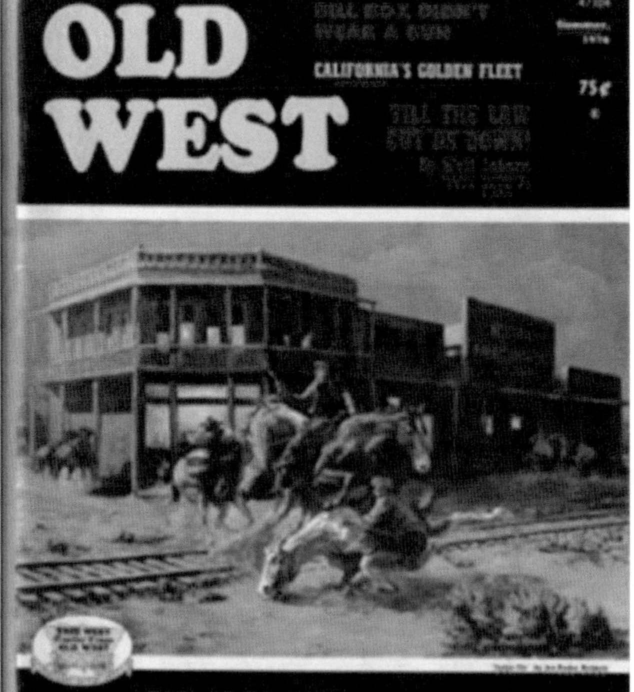

"The Killer from West Point"

Crime

Larry Warren

Old West Magazine (Summer 1976)

This is a bizarre tale from the beginning of the 20th century. Edward Martin of New York City graduated from West Point in 1898 and served honorably in the ensuing Cuban campaign. Returning to NYC he was engaged to the daughter of a prominent family, but soon broke it off to the consternation of all. He became a lay-about, began drinking heavily, and gambling. Martin was caught embezzling Army funds and forced to resign. It just became worse. Drinking and gambling left him indebted, so he persuaded his father to give him one last chance by funding a medical education in Portland, Oregon for a new start…with a new wife. The long downhill slide into moral degradation continued. Eventually, a pawnbroker he frequented was found shot dead. Martin was the prime suspect. True story. [EB]

Chapter 10

Mystery, Crime & Intrigue

We honor the heritage of a one-time West Point cadet with this chapter of the collection. Many of the works are obscure while others are popular bestsellers.

Edgar Allan Poe, ex-West Pointer (dropout 1834) is best known for his poetry and short stories, particularly his tales of mystery and the macabre. He is widely regarded as a central figure of Romanticism in American literature and considered the inventor of the detective fiction genre.

Ever since Edgar Allan Poe first penned *Murders in Rue Morgue*, mystery and crime stories have been among the most read of American literature. Poe's early detective fiction tales featuring C. Auguste Dupin, laid the groundwork for future detectives in literature. Sir Arthur Conan Doyle said, "Each of Poe's detective stories is a root from which a whole literature has developed. . .Where was the detective story until Poe breathed the breath of life into it?" [10-01]

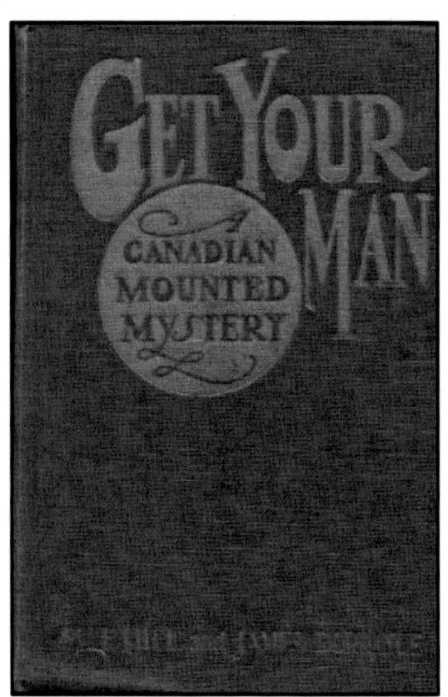

Get Your Man: A Canadian Mounted Mystery

WP Ex, Western, Crime, Canada

Ethel & James Dorrance A. L. Burt (1921)

The time was the early fall of 1908. Marcus Moor's summons home had been a telegram, delivered as he was forming his company of plebes on the parade ground of the United States Military Academy at West Point. After a snipping of official red tape, he was allowed at once to return to Seattle and the changed conditions of his life.

Scarcely could he recognize the vigorous, kindly, responsive parent whom, through boyhood years, he had worshiped as a sort of latter-clay god, in that which lay in state, awaiting an only son's farewell. They had buried him, rather, this sphinx-like reminder of him—with dust-to-dust solemnity. Afterward, Marcus had been dealt the second blow. [EB]

James French Dorrance (1879–1961) sold news stories to other local area papers and short fiction to the popular pulp fiction magazines. James married **Ethel Arnold Smith** in 1906. Together, from 1914 to 1930, they wrote and published over 40 works, from short stories appearing in magazines like *All-Story Weekly*, *Ranch Romances* and *Top-Notch Magazine* to full-length novels. [10-02]

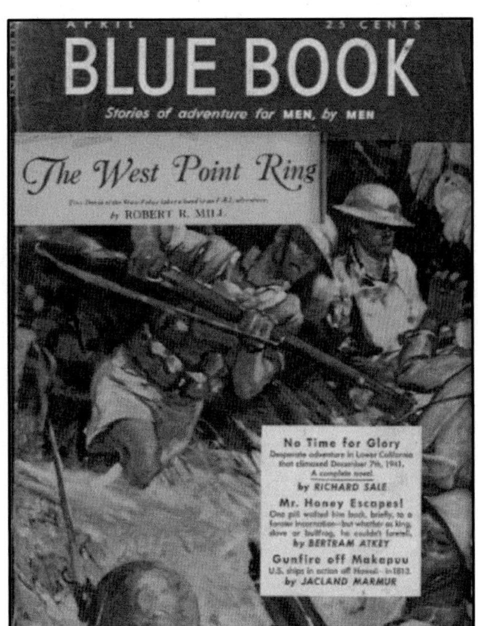

"The West Point Ring"

Crime, New York, WW2, Pulp Fiction

Robert R. Mill Blue Book Magazine (April 1942)

State Police respond to a shooting in upstate New York. The dying man, thrown out of an automobile by a speeding car, has a West Point ring on a chain around his neck. With his dying words, the victim murmurs words about a nefarious scheme to steal technology from a nearby plant working on an innovative bomb sight. The ring convinces the police detective, "Tiny" David, that his statement had a basis of truth and pursues the case. [EB]

Robert R Mill (1895–1942) was a reporter for many newspapers, including the *Syracuse Herald Tribune*. He covered a lot of crime investigations with the New York State Police and the Federal Bureau of Investigation. Between 1933 and 1942, he published nearly 75 stories in *Blue Book*, an average of eight per year. [10-03]

Dress Gray

Cadet, Crime

Lucian K. Truscott IV Doubleday (1978)

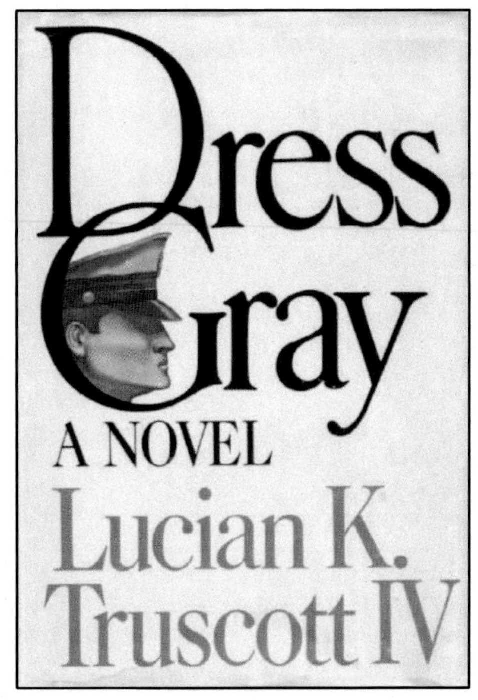

Ry Slaight was walking punishment tours on Central Area when he heard the news. "They found a body floating up in Lake Popolopen this morning," a voice said. "Drowned," the cadet spoke from the corner of his mouth, eyes straight to the front. "Been dead a couple of days. Grim scene, they say."

This is a novel about the soft underbelly of the Long Gray Line—West Point's men and its boys—and what happens in the delicate process when knowledge of power is passed between them. Never before has the academy and its secret strength, power in the absence of money, been portrayed in such human terms. In *Dress Gray*, West Point lives up to its image: as a way of life, not as a college. That its purpose is to teach a way of death is well illustrated in this story of the grisly murder of a cadet. [DJ]

Full Dress Gray

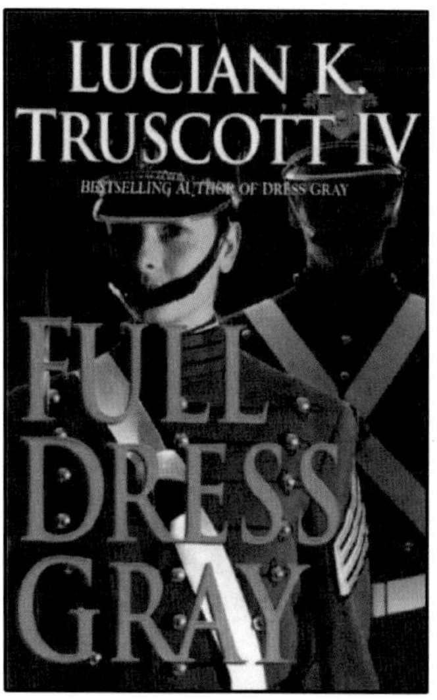

WP Author, WP Female, Mystery, Intrigue

Lucian K. Truscott IV William Morrow (1998)

In Lucian Truscott's earlier novel *Dress Gray*, Ry Slaight was an inquisitive, rebellious cadet who nearly brought West Point to its knees when he exposed and solved the murder of a gay cadet in 1969. Now, nearly three decades later, Slaight has been promoted to lieutenant general and appointed Superintendent of the Military Academy. This time he is dealing with the complexities of women at West Point and fighting to save the Academy's honor and integrity, in a modern military thriller packed with the secrets behind today's headlines.

When a female cadet dies during parade, an autopsy establishes that she had sex with multiple partners the night before. Was she the victim of a gang rape or was she a willing participant in an orgy? "Don't ask. Don't tell."

As Superintendent, Slaight has his hands full: adultery among the senior faculty, sexual harassment, an off-post beating involving cadets, and suspicions that West Point's Honor Code has been compromised. The Commandant of Cadets, convinced that West Point is a den of loose morals and military feminism, aligns himself with a scheming conservative congressman who is trying to close down the Academy. Suddenly, Slaight finds himself on the receiving end of the kind of assault he launched against West Point as a cadet.

With his own daughter caught up in the web of intrigue and conspiracy surrounding the death of her female classmate, Slaight's loyalties are tested, and his will is stretched to the limit. But where once he challenged the Academy, now he is the only one who can save it, as *Full Dress Gray* marches inexorably toward a shocking and dramatic conclusion. [DJ]

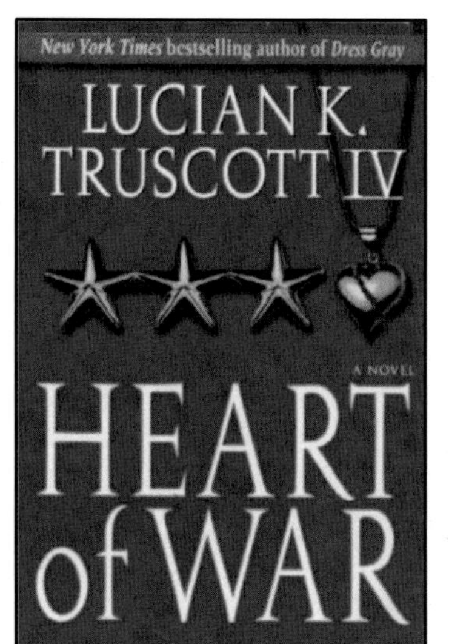

Heart of War

WP Author, Crime, Mystery, Intrigue

Lucian K. Truscott IV Dutton Adult (1997)

The brutal murder of Lieutenant Sheila Worthy has sent shock waves of fear throughout Fort Benning, Georgia, and the task of finding her killer has fallen to Major Kara Guidry. As the top lawyer in the judge advocate general's office, Kara has to tread lightly, for news of the death of Lieutenant Sheila Worthy has spread from the base to the most powerful corridors in Washington.

Breathing down Kara Guidry's neck for a fast solution is General William Beckwith, Fort Benning's commanding officer and the man many say could be the army's new chief of staff. As the tension between them builds, Kara learns that nothing is sacred and no one is free from suspicion. And the secrets she uncovers could forever alter the lives of the men and women of Fort Benning, hers included. [DJ]

Lucian King Truscott IV (born April 1947) graduated from West Point in 1969. He is the son and grandson of West Pointers. His first novel, *Dress Gray*, appeared thirteen weeks on The New York Times hardcover bestseller list. He followed up with five more novels, three of which are included in this collection. 10-04

Does the *Heart of War* plot sound familiar? Perhaps you will recall *The General's Daughter,* by Nelson DeMille, published five years earlier which was later made into a movie starring John Travolta.

The General's Daughter

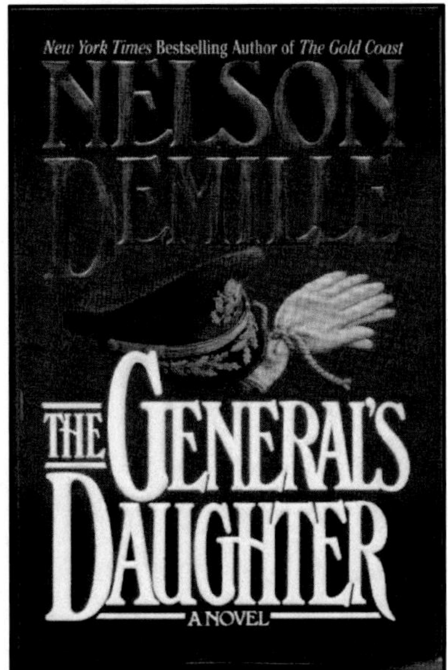

General Officer, Mystery, Crime

Nelson DeMille Warner Books (1992)

Paul Brenner is a member of the Army's elite undercover investigative unit, with the authority to arrest any military person anywhere in the world. He has always wondered just how far he could push his power. He is about to find out.

Captain Ann Campbell is the daughter of General "Fighting Joe" Campbell. She is a West Point graduate, beautiful, bright, and the pride of Fort Hadley. Her raped and murdered body is found on the firing range, naked and spread-eagled, her hands and feet bound with tent rope—but there is no sign of a struggle. All of Brenner's instincts tell him to avoid the case. Yet Brenner's natural curiosity is aroused. He takes the case. As if that decision wasn't reckless enough, he finds himself teamed with rape specialist Cynthia Sunhill, a woman with whom Brenner once had a tempestuous, ultimately doomed affair and with whom the temperamental sparks still flare.

Together, they will discover the truth about the brass above them: that beneath the neatly pressed uniforms, the military codes of honor, pride, and order hide a corruption as rank as Ann Campbell's own astonishing secret life. Paul and Cynthia learn that any number of people were sexually, emotionally, and dangerously involved with the Army's "golden girl," and any one of them could have wanted her dead. [DJ]

Nelson DeMille (1943–) is a former U.S. Army lieutenant who served in Vietnam. The author of 18 action/suspense novels, many of which have become New York Times bestsellers, he is best known for his John Corey series, which includes the following books *Plum Island*, *The Lion's Game*, *Night Fall*, and *Wild Fire*. *The General's Daughter* was a major motion picture starring John Travolta as investigator Paul Brenner. 10-05

Legacy

Mystery, Intrigue

James A. Michener Random House (1987)

In the year of his eightieth birthday, and the two-hundredth anniversary of our Constitution, James A. Michener contributes a short novel of great impact.

Major Norman Starr, West Pointer, attached to the National Security Council is told that he will shortly be called before a congressional committee. Through a tense, reflective weekend, the officer talks over the situation with his wife and a street-wise Washington lawyer—and begins to think back to the long line of Americans from whom he is descended.

One was a Supreme Court justice, another figured importantly in the unofficial nightly debates about drafting a new document to unify

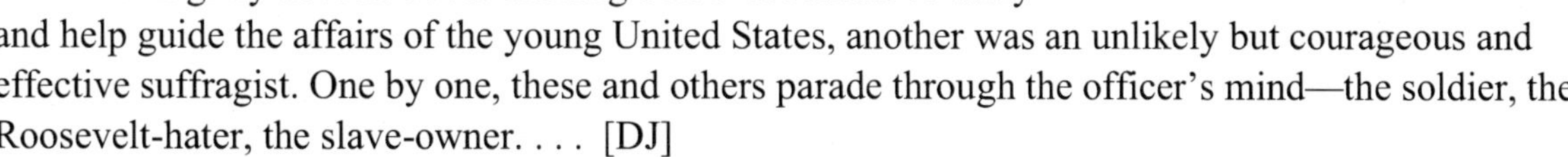

and help guide the affairs of the young United States, another was an unlikely but courageous and effective suffragist. One by one, these and others parade through the officer's mind—the soldier, the Roosevelt-hater, the slave-owner. . . . [DJ]

James Albert Michener (1907–1997) wrote more than 40 books, most of which were long, fictional family sagas covering the lives of many generations in particular geographic locales and incorporating detailed history. He was known for the meticulous research that went into his books. Michener's books include *Hawaii; Centennial; The Source; Chesapeake; Caravans; Alaska; Texas; Poland*; and *The Bridges at Toko-ri.* [10-06]

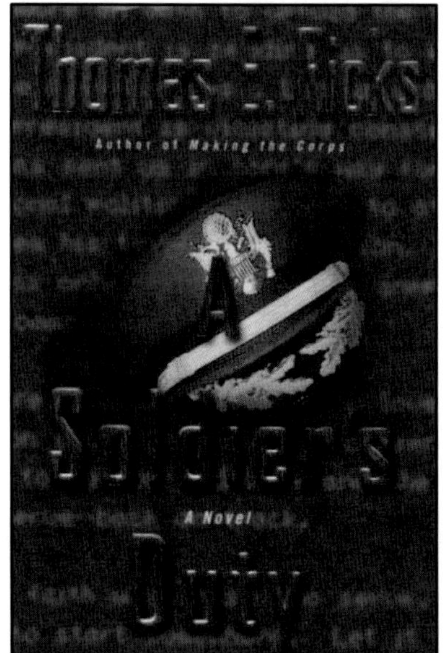

A Soldier's Duty: A Novel

Mystery, Intrigue, Global War on Terror

Thomas E. Ricks Random House (2001)

Majors Sherman and Lewis are the best the Army has, young combat officers who have aced every posting and now find themselves tapped for career-making positions as aides to two of the Pentagon's most senior generals. But the Pentagon is a cauldron of naked ambition and factional squabbling in the best of times, and these are not the best of times. A president whom the officer class widely loathes sits in the White House, and dissent is growing more vocal. Some officers are openly asking; If you believe the president is betraying his country, where does your responsibility lie? What do you do if your duty to your superiors seems at odds with your duty to your subordinates?

Shortly after the two majors arrive for duty, the White House involves the military in a police action in central Asia that some are calling a quagmire in the making. In protest, an anonymous group of military officers calling itself the Sons of Liberty begins to make itself heard, first through e-mails, then through symbolic acts. But as the fighting grows bloodier and more futile, the group's acts become more serious, and its efforts to avoid a mounting investigation become more violent. As the Pentagon teeters on the brink of all-out war with itself, Majors Sherman and Lewis, unsure of where their duty lies, struggle to avoid becoming casualties in a conflict that is growing deadlier by the day. [DJ]

Thomas Edwin "Tom" Ricks (1955–) is an American journalist and author who specializes in the military and national security issues. He is a two-time winner of the Pulitzer Prize for National Reporting as part of teams from the *Wall Street Journal* and *Washington Post*. He has reported on military activities in Somalia, Haiti, Korea, Bosnia, Kosovo, Macedonia, Kuwait, Turkey, Afghanistan, and Iraq. [10-07]

Four Blind Mice

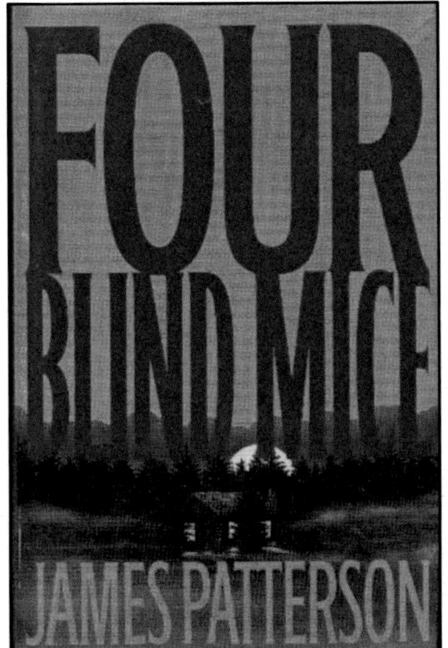

Crime, Mystery

James Patterson Little, Brown (2002)

Detective Alex Cross is on his way to resign from the Washington, D.C., Police Force when his partner shows up at his door with a case he can't refuse. One of John Sampson's oldest friends, from their days together in Vietnam, has been arrested for murder. Worse yet, he is subject to the iron hand of the United States Army. The evidence against him is strong enough to send him to the gas chamber.

Sampson is certain his friend has been framed, and Alex's investigation turns up evidence overlooked -- or concealed -- by the military authorities. Drawing on their years of street training and an almost telepathic mutual trust, Cross and Sampson go deep behind military lines to confront the most ruthless -- and deadliest -- killers they have ever encountered. Behind these three highly skilled killing machines there appears to be an even more threatening controller. Discovering the identity of this lethal genius will prove to be Cross' most terrifying challenge ever. [DJ]

While the book is not about a West Pointer per se, the detectives do travel to West Point in pursuing the solution. [EB]

James Brendan Patterson (1947–) is an American author and philanthropist. Among his works are the *Alex Cross*, *Michael Bennett*, *Women's Murder Club*, *Maximum Ride* series, as well as many stand-alone thrillers, non-fiction, and romance novels. His books have sold more than 300 million copies, and he was the first person to sell 1 million e-books. Patterson has donated millions of dollars in grants and scholarships with the purpose of encouraging Americans of all ages to read more books. [10-08]

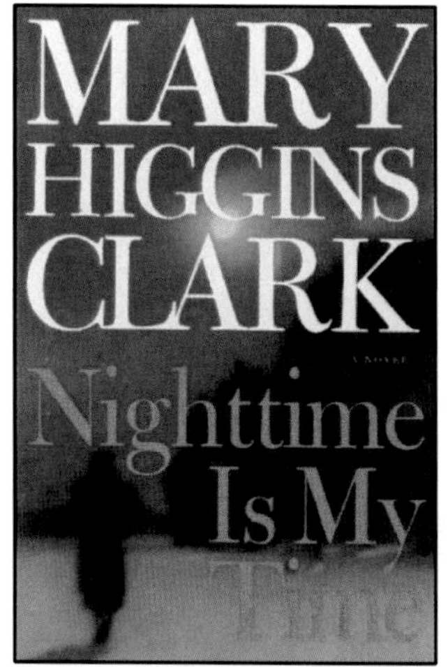

Nighttime Is My Time

Crime, Mystery, Hudson Highlands

Mary Higgins Clark Simon & Schuster (2004)

Jean Sheridan, a college dean and prominent historian, sets out to her hometown in Cornwall-on-Hudson, New York, to attend the twenty-year reunion of alumni of Stonecroft Academy, where she is to be honored along with six other members of her class. There is, however, something uneasy in the air: one woman in the group about to be feted, Alison Kendall, a beautiful, high-powered Hollywood agent, died just a few days before, drowned in her pool during an early-morning swim, the fifth woman in the class whose life has come to a sudden, mysterious end. Also adding to Jean's sense of unease is a taunting, anonymous fax she has just received, referring to her daughter, Lily, a child she had given up for adoption twenty years ago, the offspring of a romance between her and a West Point cadet killed in an accident a week before graduation. She had always kept the child's existence a secret. So, who has found out? And why the implied threat now?

Struggling to conceal her fears, Jean arrives at the hotel where the reunion is being held. One by one she sees the other honorees, including Laura Wilcox, the class beauty, whose dazzling exterior belies the fact that her television career is sinking, and the four men who, like Jean, had spent four bitterly unhappy years at Stonecroft....

At the award dinner, Jean is introduced to Sam Deagan, a detective obsessed for years by the unsolved murder of a young woman in Cornwall, who may also hold the key to the identity of the Stonecroft killer and the source of the anonymous threat to her child. She does not suspect that among the distinguished people she is meeting is The Owl, a murderer nearing the countdown on his mission of vengeance against the Stonecroft women who had mocked and humiliated him, with Jean his final intended victim. [BC]

Mary Theresa Eleanor Higgins Clark (1927–2020) was an American author of suspense novels. Each of her 51 books was a bestseller in the United States and various European countries. Higgins Clark began writing at an early age. Her suspense novels have sold more than 100 million copies in the United States alone. [10-09]

The Line

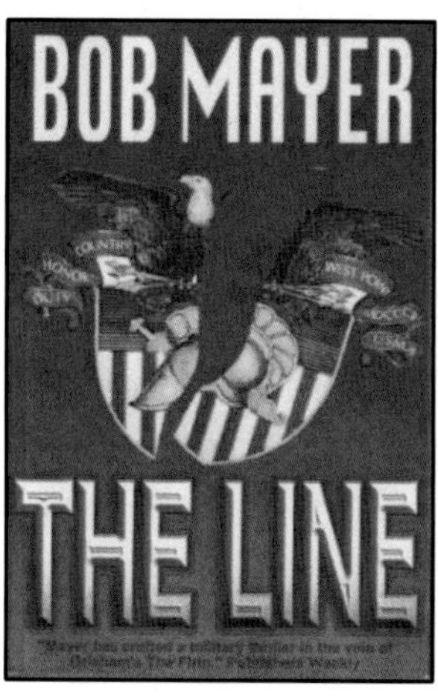

Intrigue, Rogue, WP Author

Bob Mayer St. Martins (1996)

Bob McGuire is the 'nom de plume' for Bob Mayer, a prolific writer, who republished this book in 2020 under his real name Bob Mayer.

From the book cover:

For more than half a century, a secret organization of Army officers known as The Line has been covertly manipulating U.S. policy. Now in a political climate rife with dissent and unrest, The Line has ordered a pivotal top-secret operation that will let the world know who is really in charge.

But The Line didn't count on Boomer Watson—a member of the elite Special Operations Delta Force—who honors the chain of command with a vengeance. Together with his West Point compatriot, Major Benita Trace, Boomer sets out to protect his Commander-in-Chief. As the clock ticks down to the final firefight, one man and one woman cross The Line and can't look back. [BC]

The Jefferson Allegiance

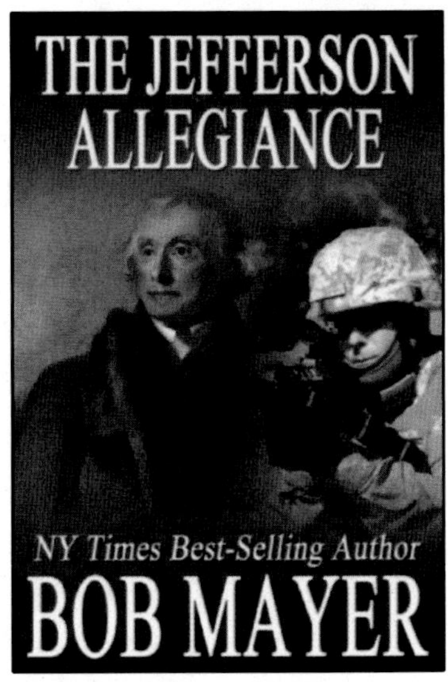

Mystery, Crime, Intrigue, WP Author

Bob Mayer Cool Gus Publishing (2013)

As Thomas Jefferson lies dying, he gives his part of his Jefferson Cipher to Edgar Allan Poe, with instructions to take the disks to West Point. In Massachusetts, John Adams entrusts his part of the Cipher to Colonel Thayer, the superintendent of the Military Academy. As Thayer rides away, Adams utters his final words: "Thomas Jefferson survives." In the present, Green Beret Paul Ducharme has been recalled from Afghanistan after the 'accidental' death of his best friend, the son of one of the Philosophers. While Ducharme is visiting his friend's gravesite in Arlington, an old man is executed by a member from the Society of Cincinnati known as the Surgeon, who is seeking to gather all the pieces of the Cipher. In a nearby restaurant, former CIA and now Curator at Monticello, Evie Tolliver, waits anxiously for her mentor to arrive, but he's killed by the same assassin at the Zero Milestone. His heart and the Philosopher's head are displayed as a grisly message on top of the stone, echoing Jefferson's famous head-heart letter.

Ducharme and Tolliver, the unknowing heirs to become the next generation of caretakers of the Jefferson Allegiance, team up and must battle the Surgeon to assemble the Cipher and find the Jefferson Allegiance, a document that has kept the balance of power in the United States for over two centuries. The story is a race back through history and the founding of the country. [BC]

Robert John "Bob" Mayer (1959–) graduated from West Point in 1981 then served in the infantry with the 1st Cavalry Division. He joined Special Forces and commanded a Green Beret A-Team from 1984 to 1988. Mayer's prolific writing encompasses both his military experience and his fascination for history, legends and mythology. To date, he has published over 65 titles. Another of Mayer's works in the collection is *Duty, Honor, Country: West Point to Shiloh: A Novel of West Point and The Civil War* in the "Civil War" chapter. [10-10]

The mysterious disappearance of Cadet Richard Cox in 1950 is not fictional, but it is stranger than fiction.

The following two documents provide plenty of clues. Draw your own conclusions.

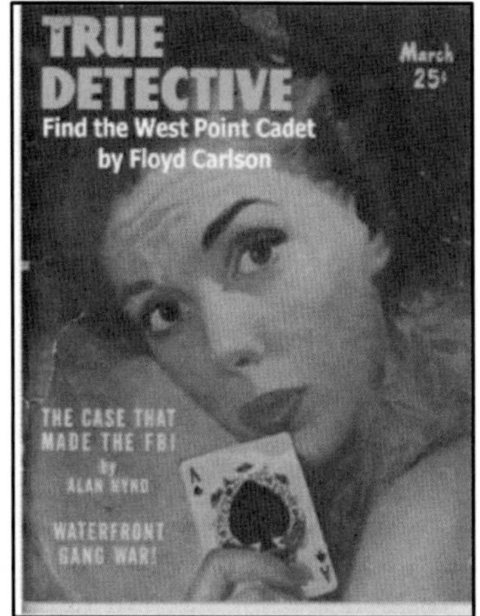

"Find the West Point Cadet"

Cadet, Mystery Intrigue

Floyd Carlson True Detective Magazine (March 1951)

Cadet Richard Cox walked out of his barracks on January 25, 1950 at 6 pm to meet a fellow named "George" at the Hotel Thayer. He was not observed at the Thayer and was never seen again. Read the book *Oblivion* published in 1996 for a lengthy analysis and a likely solution. [EB]

Oblivion: Mystery of West Point Cadet Cox

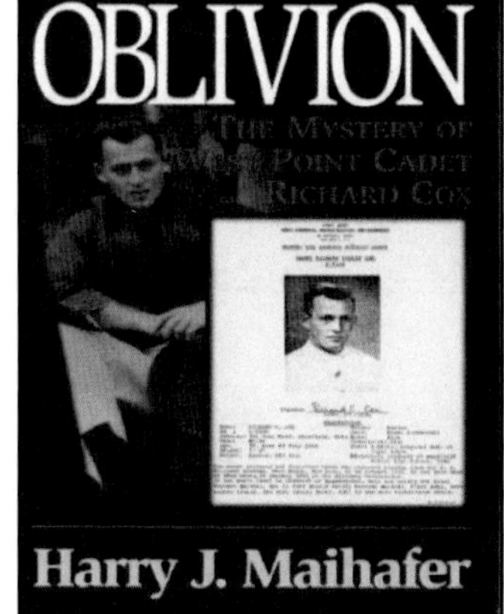

Cadet, Mystery, WP Author

Harry J. Maihafer Brassey's (1996)

On Saturday, January 14, 1950, at 6:18 P.M., Cadet Richard Cox left his room at the U.S. Military Academy at West Point to go to dinner with an unidentified visitor. The man was supposedly someone Cox had known when they served in an intelligence unit in Germany. Cox never returned.

A disappearance rivaling in mystery that of Judge Crater, Jimmy Hoffa, or Amelia Earhart, the strange case of Richard Cox became one of the country's most baffling unsolved cases. Newspapers and magazines gave it headlines and made it a national story. Military and civilian investigators spoke to thousands of witnesses and pursued hundreds of leads, both in the United States and overseas. Embarrassed by the FBI's failure to find Cox, J. Edgar Hoover assigned dozens of agents to the case. Countless citizens contacted the authorities about alleged Cox sightings. Over time, several plausible theories were advanced, including one holding that Cox had been abducted by Soviet agents as a result of his intelligence work. Another was that Cox was enmeshed in a sexual relationship with the visitor. Despite a massive manhunt, he was not found. In 1957, Richard Cox was declared legally dead, and the files were closed. It was as if he had vanished off the face of the earth.

Then in 1985, thirty-five years after Cox's disappearance, a retired history teacher named Marshall Jacobs decided to pursue the mystery as a research project. Through the Freedom of Information Act, he obtained voluminous once-secret files from the Army and FBI. Jacobs plunged into a labyrinthine search—and what began as a hobby became an obsession. He traveled the country interviewing witnesses from the Florida Keys to the Pacific Northwest. What he discovered were tales of murder, intrigue, and cover-up. It took more than seven years, but Jacobs eventually found the one witness who enabled him to bring the case to closure.In *Oblivion*, Harry J. Maihafer tells the enthralling story of Jacobs' search for Richard Cox. Its startling climax is one that readers will long remember. [DJ]

Harry James Maihafer (1924–2002) volunteered for the Army Air Corps in 1943. While at the San Antonio Aviation Cadet Center, he received his appointment to West Point. The Korean War started while he was in Officer Basic at Fort Knox. As an infantry platoon leader in Korea, he was wounded by a rifle bullet through his left thigh. His combat awards in Korea included the Silver Star, the Bronze Star with "V" for valor, an Army Commendation Medal, the Combat Infantry Badge, Purple Heart, and the Korean Service Medal. He retired as a Colonel in 1969 and began a career in banking, while pursuing love of writing. His book *From the Hudson to the Yalu* related the firsthand combat experiences of his classmates - the Class of 1949. [10-11]

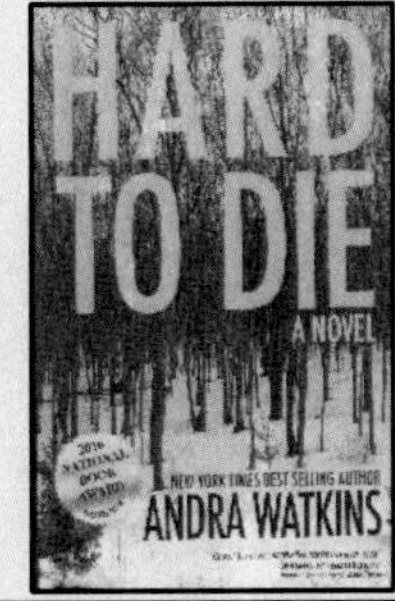

For those who can't get enough of the Richard Cox conundrum, the novel *Hard to Die* (2016) by Amanda Watkins features Richard Cox as a principal character. It can be found in the chapter "Paranormal, Supernatural & Futuristic."

Breaking Ranks

Crime, WP Author

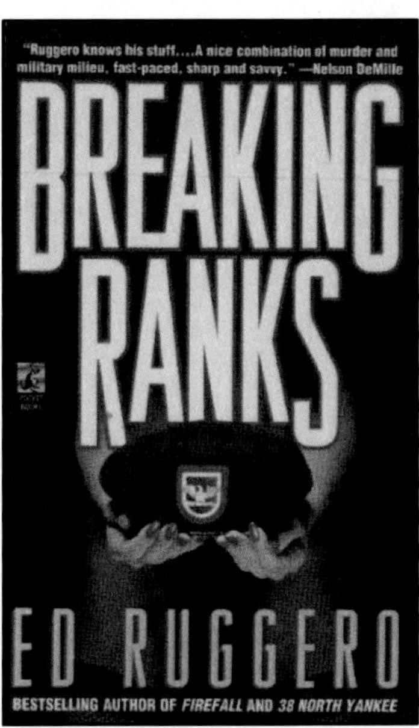

Ed Ruggero Pocket Books (1995)

The report out of Fort Bragg is succinct: 2nd Lt. Michael Hauck, 82nd Airborne, cut short a drunken visit to a strip club with a bullet to his brain. But Hauck's high-ranking uncle doesn't buy the official line. He asks Major Mark Isen to conduct an informal investigation. Immediately, the paratroopers of the 82nd - "America's Guard of Honor" - close ranks, greeting Isen with both stone-cold silence and outright hostility. They fear what Isen is beginning to sense: that this investigation may threaten the reputation of the 82nd, a reputation embodied by the Army's golden boy, Lt. Col. Harlan Veir.

Hailed in the media as the new breed of warrior, Veir is known to others as the "Dark Prince," a symbol of unbridled military power. Navigating a minefield of deadly conspiratorial forces, Isen engages in a fierce, lonely battle with the wounded 82nd Airborne, its arrogant icon...and the dark side of military pride. [DJ]

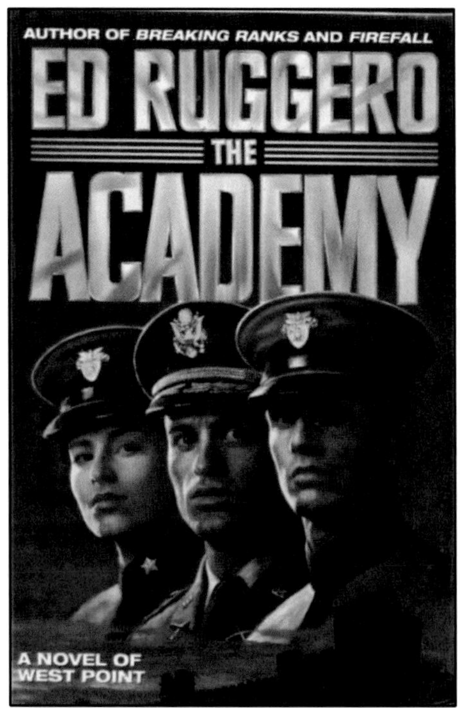

The Academy: A Novel of West Point

Mystery Intrigue, Cadet, WP Author

Ed Ruggero Atria Press (1997)

A bitter wind is blowing from Washington across West Point, and Major Tom Gates—a muddy-boots soldier ill at ease in a spit-and-polish world—is about to face a battle more brutal than any he has ever known. It began with an all-too-human mistake -- Gates had too much to drink and pushed a cadet too far -- and it will explode into a political firestorm that could leave careers, lives, and West Point itself, in ruins.

Senator Lamar Bruckner has his eye on the White House, but his target is West Point. He flagrantly condemns the Academy as a waste of taxpayer money, a military ivory tower -- and Gates' momentary lapse in judgment is the first charge in a smear campaign that could propel Bruckner to the presidency. Caught in the middle of Bruckner's manhunt is Wayne Holder, a fourth-year cadet, whose golden surfer looks and reputation as a ladies' man are far from the pristine image of the Long Gray Line. But for Holder to join that line, he faces a private conflict between honor and desire—upon which the ultimate fate of the Academy rests. Now, enemy lines are drawn in a war of political motives and personal emotion that touches many lives. . . .

Kathleen Gates, Tom's wife, is as calculating as her husband is bullheaded, and she will use any weapon to protect him. Bruckner's aide, Claude Braintree, has come to West Point to further the senator's career—and will exploit the Academy to do it. Alex Trainor, a cadet from the heartland, is trapped in a personal crisis that shatters his conservative ideals. And Brigadier General David Simon dreams of taking control of the Point to re-create it in his own image. [DJ]

Ed Ruggero (1956–) is a former infantry officer, student, practitioner, and teacher of leadership turned author of historical fiction, mystery and thriller novels. Upon graduation from West Point (1980), he was commissioned in the Army and spent several years in the infantry before he returned to West Point teaching writing and literature. After leaving the military Ruggero became a trainer, public speaker and author on leadership and life. [10-12]

Ruggero wrote four novels in the Mark Isen series covering the officer's career from 2nd lieutenant and through the rank of major. See the chapters "In the Far East" and the "Cold War & Global War on Terrorism." Two of his other novels are in the "World Wars" and "Army Medical Service Corps" chapters.

What would a chapter on mysteries about West Pointers be without stories featuring the master himself? These two imaginative novels with Edgar Allan Poe as a central figure were published in 2006.

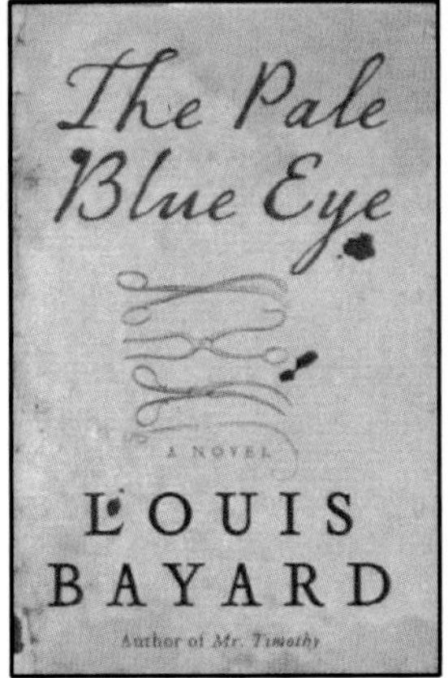

The Pale Blue Eye: A Novel

Cadet, WP Ex, Mystery

Louis Bayard Harper (2006)

At West Point Academy in 1830, the calm of an October evening is shattered by the discovery of a young cadet's body swinging from a rope just off the parade grounds. An apparent suicide is not unheard of in a harsh regimen like West Point's, but the next morning, an even greater horror comes to light. Someone has stolen into the room where the body lay and removed the heart.

At a loss for answers and desperate to avoid any negative publicity, the Academy calls on the services of a local civilian, Augustus Landor, a former police detective who acquired some renown during his years in New York City before retiring to the Hudson Highlands for his health. Now a widower, and restless in his seclusion, Landor agrees to take on the case. As he questions the dead man's acquaintances, he finds an eager assistant in a moody, intriguing young cadet with a penchant for drink, two volumes of poetry to his name, and a murky past that changes from telling to telling. The cadet's name? Edgar Allan Poe.

Impressed with Poe's astute powers of observation, Landor is convinced that the poet may prove useful—if he can stay sober long enough to put his keen reasoning skills to the task. Working in close contact, the two men -- separated by years but alike in intelligence -- develop a surprisingly deep rapport as their investigation takes them into a hidden world. [DJ]

Louis Bayard (born 1963) is an American author. His historical mysteries include *The Pale Blue Eye*, *Mr. Timothy*, *The Black Tower*, *The School of Night*, and *Roosevelt's Beast*, which have been translated into 11 languages. A Princeton graduate, he teaches fiction writing at George Washington University. [10-13] Netflix produced a movie based on the *The Pale Blue Eye* in 2022.

Grim Legion: Edgar Allan Poe at West Point

Cadet, WP Ex, Mystery

Jack Alcott Bewildering Press (2006)

It is a little-known fact that Edgar Allan Poe was expelled from the U.S. Military Academy at West Point in 1831, after only six months as a cadet. To this day, the reasons for the 21-year-old poet's court martial remain murky at best. *Grim Legion* liberally borrows from Poe's own life and works to fill in where the historical record leaves off. This novel of suspense starts with a murder, and then another.... Young Poe is soon plunged into the world of horror, mystery, and intrigue that is his destiny. [BC]

Jack Alcott is an editor at the *Journal News* in White Plains, New York. Aside from ten years in Berkeley and San Francisco, he has lived in and around the Hudson Valley for most of his life. [10-14]

In the Name of Honor

Crime, Intrigue

Richard North Patterson Henry Holt and Co. (2010)

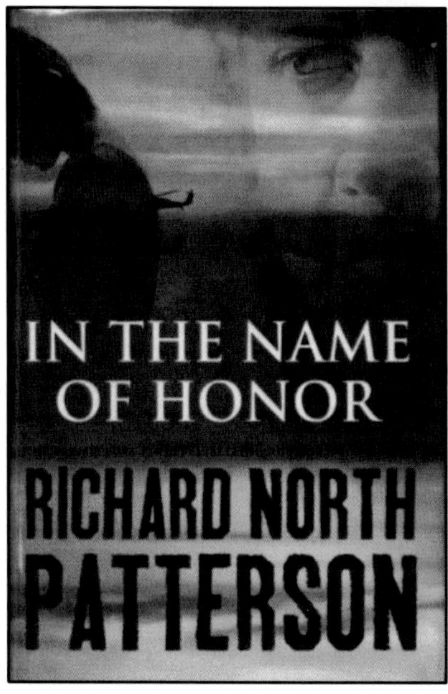

Home from Iraq, a lieutenant kills his commanding officer -- was it self-defense or premeditated murder?

The McCarrans and the Gallaghers, two military families, have been close for decades, ever since Anthony McCarran -- one of the army's most distinguished generals—became best friends with Jack Gallagher, a fellow West Pointer who was later killed in Vietnam. Now a new generation of soldiers faces combat, and Lieutenant Brian McCarran, the general's son, has returned from a harrowing tour in Iraq.

Traumatized by wartime experiences he will not reveal, Brian depends on his lifelong friendship with Kate Gallagher, Jack's daughter, who is married to Brian's commanding officer in Iraq, Captain Joe D'Abruzzo. But since coming home, D'Abruzzo also seems changed by the experiences he and Brian shared--he's become secretive and remote.

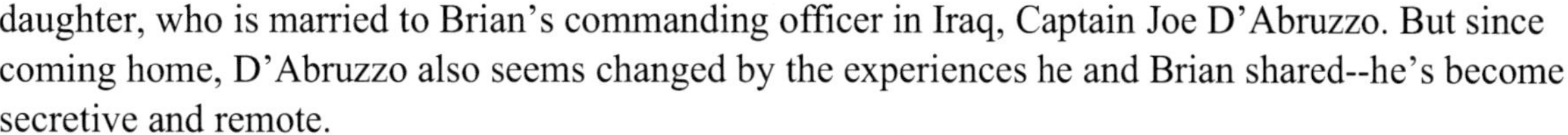

Tragedy strikes when Brian shoots and kills D'Abruzzo on their army post in Virginia. Brian pleads self-defense, claiming that D'Abruzzo, a black-belt martial artist, came to his quarters, accused him of interfering with his marriage, and attacked him. Kate supports Brian and says that her husband had become violent and abusive. But Brian and Kate have secrets of their own, and now Captain Paul Terry, one of the army's most accomplished young lawyers, will defend Brian in a high-profile court-martial. Terry's co-counsel is Meg McCarran, Brian's sister, a brilliant and beautiful attorney who insists on leaving her practice in San Francisco to help save her brother. Before the case is over, Terry will become deeply entwined with Meg and the McCarrans—and learn that families, like war, can break the sturdiest of souls. [DJ]

Richard North Patterson (born in 1947) graduated in 1968 from Ohio Wesleyan University and in 1971 from the Case Western Reserve University School of Law. He has served as an Assistant Attorney General for the State of Ohio; a trial attorney for the Securities & Exchange Commission in Washington, D.C.; and was the SEC's liaison to the Watergate Special Prosecutor. More recently, Patterson was a partner in the San Francisco office of McCutchen, Doyle, Brown & Enersen before retiring from practice in 1993. He has published over 20 novels. [10-15]

John Vermillion, Class of 1970, has independently published a series of novels featuring Simon Pack, a retired Marine general, called back into service to resolve a crisis of leadership at West Point.

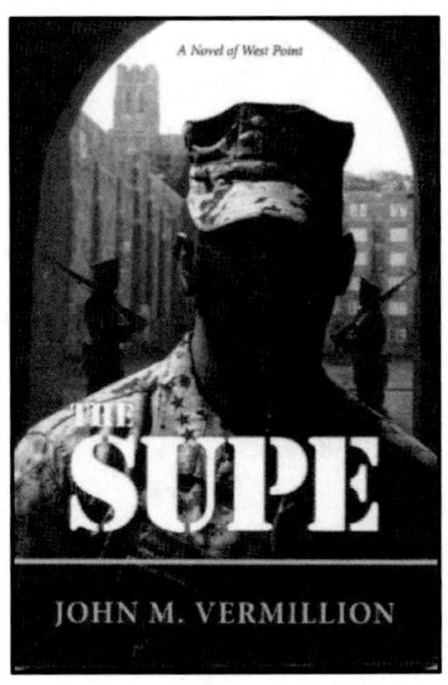

The Supe: A Novel of West Point

WP Author, Mystery, Intrigue

John M. Vermillion CreateSpace Publishing (2015)

General Harris Green is in a race against time...and against Keith Rozan, President of the United States --a man who has secret plans to change the character and mission of the US Military Academy.

General Green knows he cannot sit by while the president tampers with the entire future of America's defense system. In a situation this serious, he is in desperate need of a powerful ally who can help him stand up to Washington to preserve the future of the Academy and, by extension, the military. That ally is Marine General Simon Pack.

The only problem? General Pack has gone missing. Having resigned in protest at the rise of careerism among senior military leaders, he's now wandering the country with no forwarding address.

Will General Green be able to find General Pack in time to install him as superintendent of the Academy? Or will President Rozan's horrifying plan prevail? [BC]

Don't Call Me General

WP Author, Mystery, Intrigue

John M. Vermillion CreateSpace Publishing (2016)

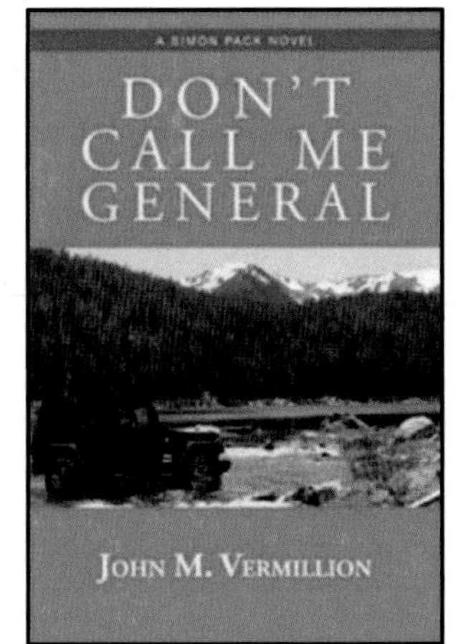

With only two weeks from retirement as Superintendent of the US Military Academy at West Point, Marine Lieutenant General Simon Pack is looking forward to some time in his secluded Montana cabin with his devoted dog Chesty. The arrival of a threatening note comes as a surprise. Signed only "EKW," the letter demands Pack keep a low profile after retirement or suffer some dark consequence. Pack gives the letter some thought, but the only change he makes in his plans is to add his personal weapons to his packing.

After delivering a passionate graduation address at West Point that ruffles the feathers of the politically correct, Pack receives a second missive from EKW, this one declaring the Marine is "on a path of destruction." The discovery of a GPS tracking device on his jeep confirms that the mysterious EKW is a potential threat. With America under attack from without and within, many look to pragmatic, patriotic men like Pack for solutions. Others see only a threat to their own political and economic control. Powerful, frightened men are dangerous, but so is Simon Pack. If his country needs him, he'll make whatever sacrifice is necessary. [BC]

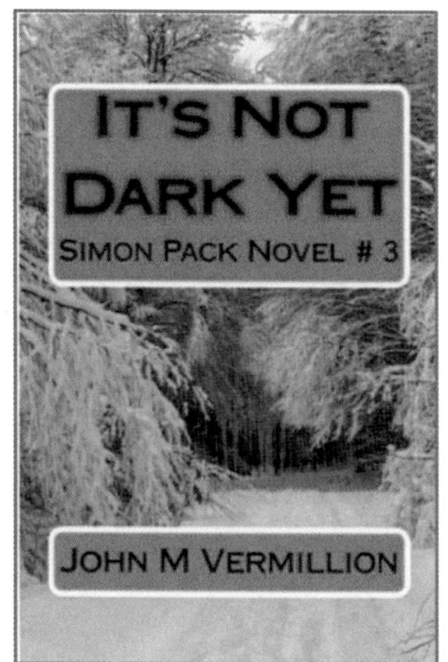

It's Not Dark Yet: Simon Pack #3

Author, Mystery, Intrigue

John M Vermillion CreateSpace Publishing (2017)

In the waning days of his Governorship, Simon Pack learns he did not leave the Upper Yaak Valley of Montana in sound health. The area is teeming with criminal enterprises and countercultural elements. Not wanting to dump problems he believes he's responsible for onto the new Governor, Pack burrows into the unique Upper Yaak to identify and root out those complicated troubles. A crooked Sheriff pins a murder on Pack, and his release from charges involves a colossal legal confrontation. After his release from confinement, Pack returns to the cauldron of the Yaak, this time to be taken hostage inside a compound of anti-government radicals. Pack's final act involves tracking down a man and woman bent on perpetrating terrorist attacks in the four corners of America. Main characters from the previous Pack novels are still here, but they are joined by a host of quirky new ones, including a lazy minister; a brilliant, exotic Asian lady and her evil boyfriend; Pack's love interest, Keeley Eliopoulous; a crooked game warden who colludes with a County Sheriff; Tetu's fiance, Swan Threemoons; an honest Forest Ranger, Ranklin Shiningfish; and a 90-year-old man who in many ways is pivotal to solving the problems Pack faces. [BC]

Evil in Disguise: Simon Pack #4

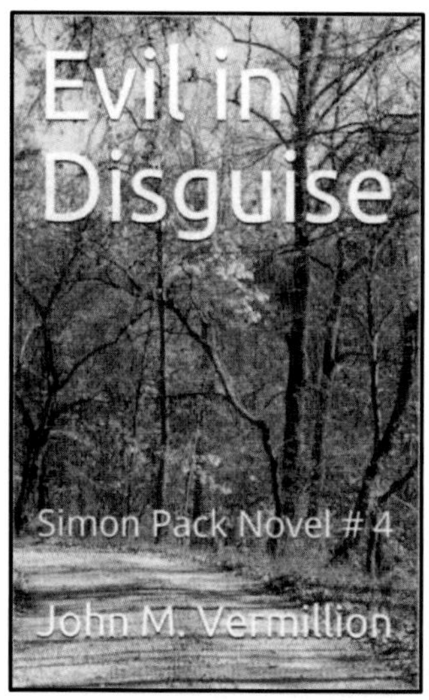

WP Author, Mystery, Intrigue

John M. Vermillion Independently published (2018)

A horrid train wreck sets in motion a miserable chain of events for Simon Pack, Former Marine General and Governor of Montana. After dealing with the awful effects of the accident, Pack plumbs the depths of personal despair. Upon regaining his taste for life, he's visited by a man from his past. The man who abducts Pack eventually is exposed as a former Super soldier and rogue agent who has murdered scores, including Americans, overseas. Now targets in America, including Pack, are fueling his vengeance-induced killing rampage. Pack needs to stop this Bad Man, Blaise Paschal. The action moves from Virginia to Louisiana to Montana.

John M. Vermillion (1948–), Class of 1970, served in the US Army as a career infantry officer, Airborne and Ranger qualified, retiring in 1995. The author believes the main cause of America's present, pervasive problems is a dearth of leadership throughout society, and that if the leadership vacuum created our problems, filling the vacuum can solve them. *The Supe* shows the vast positive influence one genuine leader like Simon Pack can trigger. [BC]

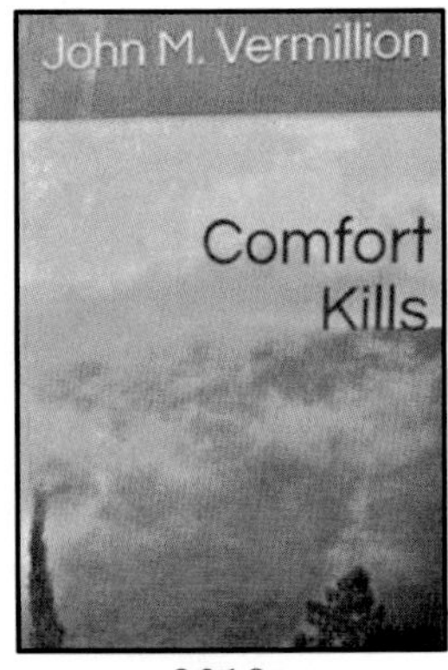

2018

2019

2019

2020

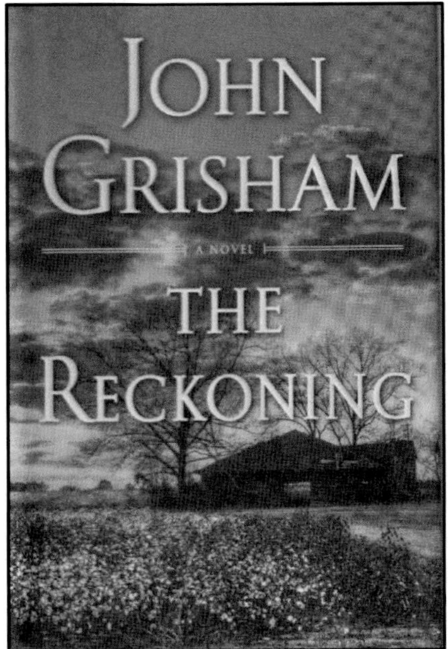

The Reckoning: A Novel

Crime, Philippines, Mississippi

John Grisham Doubleday (2019)

October I946, Clanton, Mississippi

Pete Banning was Clanton, Mississippi's favorite son, a West Point graduate, decorated World War II hero, the patriarch of a prominent family, a farmer, father, neighbor, and a faithful member of the Methodist church. Then one cool October morning he rose early, drove into town, walked into the church, and calmly shot and killed his pastor and friend, the Reverend Dexter Bell. As if the murder wasn't shocking enough, it was even more baffling that Peter's only statement about it to the sheriff, to his lawyers, to the judge, to the jury, and to his family was: "I have nothing to say." He was not afraid of death and was willing to take his motive to the grave.

In a major novel unlike anything he has written before, John Grisham takes us on an incredible journey, from the Jim Crow South to the jungles of the Philippines during World War II; from an insane asylum filled with secrets to the Clanton courtroom where Pete's defense attorney tries desperately to save him. [DJ]

John Ray Grisham Jr (1955–) is an American novelist, attorney, politician, and activist, best known for his popular legal thrillers. His books have been translated into 42 languages and published worldwide. Grisham graduated from Mississippi State University and received a J.D. degree from the University of Mississippi School of Law in 1981. He practiced criminal law for about a decade and served in the Mississippi House of Representatives from January 1984 to September 1990. His books have sold 300 million copies and he has written 28 consecutive number one bestsellers. [10-16]

Absent without Leave

Mystery, Intrigue, WP Author

Duane Gundrum   Create Space Publishing (2013)

Twenty years ago, Military Police Investigator Derek Thompson disappeared while investigating a shadowy criminal conspiracy operating out of San Francisco. After vanishing, he was declared absent without leave, and eventually a deserter....

Never to be heard from again....

Today, his son Mark Thompson, a Criminal Investigation Division agent stationed at Presidio of San Francisco, always believed his father disappeared during the Vietnam War. During a routine investigation, he begins to uncover information about his father and that ancient investigation, revealing a very powerful and dangerous organization that will do anything, and everything, to keep its secrets sealed and hidden.

Mark's investigation involves a ruthless CIA operative tasked with keeping secrets buried, a Texas family with ties to national government, and an FBI agent and his nemesis who have adopted the personalities of Sherlock Holmes and Professor Moriarty in their timeless battle with one another. [DJ]

Duane Gundrum, West Point ex '87, has another novel, *Deadly Deceptions,* in the collection. See the chapter, "In the Far East."

Brian Haig, West Point Class of 1975, authored a series of political/intrigue novels featuring an irreverent JAG attorney Sean Drummond as the central character in most of his works.

The Secret Sanction

Intrigue, Kosovo, WP Author

Brian Haig   Warner Books (2001)

You can't put one over on Major Sean Drummond, a maverick lawyer with a sharp tongue and brilliant legal mind. A combat veteran with a secret past, he knows that the elite team of Green Berets he's investigating for war crimes in Kosovo are lying. What he doesn't know is that their lies are a minefield of deception, where the truth is set to explode. [BC]

Mortal Allies

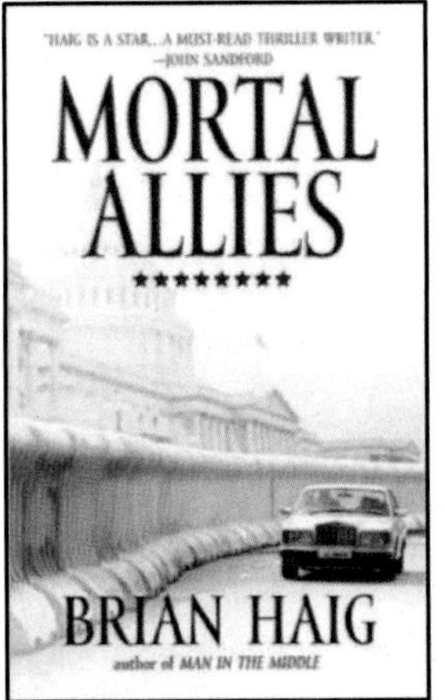

Intrigue, Korea, WP Author

Brian Haig Warner Books (2001)

JAG lawyer Sean Drummond has gotten himself in way over his head -- with a case that challenges his deepest fears and a co-counselor who challenges just about everything else. Assigned to South Korea as an advocate for a gay officer accused of brutally killing the son of a South Korean war hero, Drummond is teamed up with an old law-school nemesis. Katherine Carson is a curvy, liberal, William Kunstler-like attorney with a reputation for manipulating the media on behalf of her mostly gay clients. Drummond is as distraught to be working with a woman who knows how to push all his buttons as he is to be defending this client. However, it's just this lack of political correctness that makes him the one man the CIA can trust with its disturbing secrets, and Drummond quickly learns that what appears to be an open-and-shut case is really just the top layer of a deep conspiracy. [DJ]

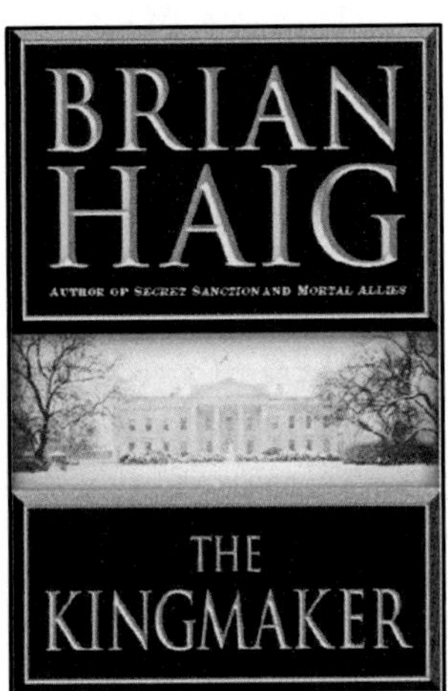

The Kingmaker

Intrigue, Politics, WP Author

Brian Haig Warner Books (2003)

Sean Drummond returns to defend the biggest traitor America has ever known.

Sean is called upon to defend Brigadier General William T. Morrison against a messy list of charges that amounts to the worst case of treason in U.S. history. Up against the fiercest prosecutor in the Army, Drummond may be in way over his head. Oddsmakers give Sean zero chance of saving his client from a death sentence. Yet Morrison and his CIA executive wife, Mary, won't consider anyone else for the job, and Drummond can't say no to Mary, his old flame.

Drummond is going to need a lot more than the confidence of those counting on him. To aid him he recruits a Russian-speaking co-counsel with body piercings and a skintight black leather outfit. Katrina Mazorski is the antithesis of a buttoned-down lawyer, but Drummond soon learns how indispensable she is as they penetrate the layers of secrets and cover-ups to find the man who is the kingmaker — the force behind decades of Russian leaders. [BC]

Private Sector

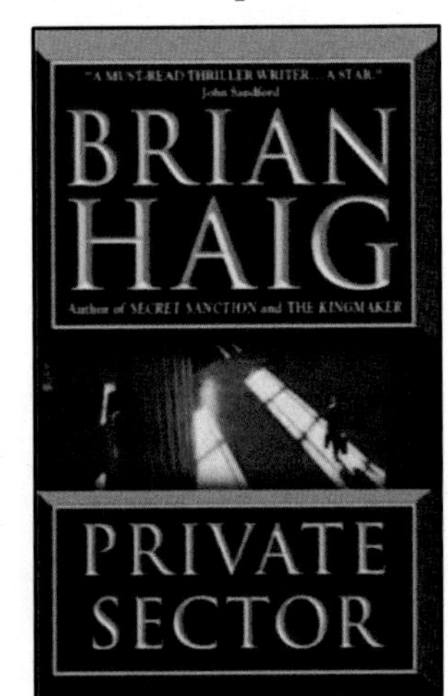

Intrigue, Politics, WP Author

Brian Haig Warner Books (2003)

Army lawyer Sean Drummond is loaned out to a law firm whose #1 client may have ties to a vicious serial killer and a massive international crime ring.

Wherever Sean Drummond goes, it seems that the JAG officer leaves a trail of political fallout in his wake. So, when his superiors get an opportunity to loan him to a prestigious law firm, they jump on it, hoping he'll soak up the nuances of civilian lawyering. But almost immediately, dark clouds appear when Sean's predecessor in the loan-out program is murdered. Then Sean begins to sense something amiss with the firm's biggest client, a telecom behemoth with large defense contracts.

Now, he must survive in D.C.'s buttoned-down lawyer culture long enough to stop the killer, and long enough to discover why his firm and its top client are willing to kill anyone who gets in their way. [DJ]

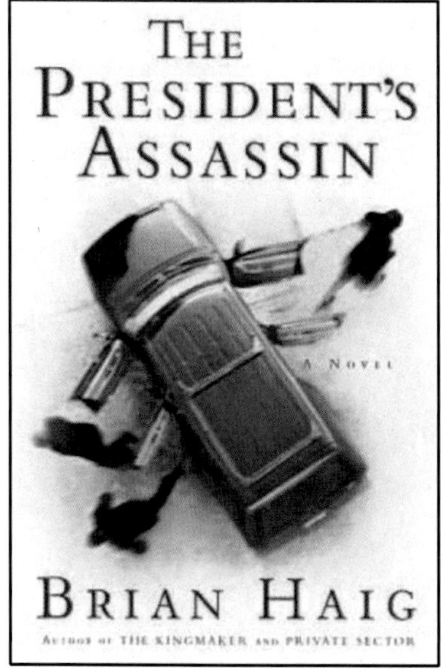

The President's Assassin

Intrigue, Politics, WP Author

Brian Haig Grand Central Publishing (2005)

In 48 hours, the U.S. President will be HISTORY.....

It looked like a mass execution: six people, systematically shot and killed in a private Washington Mansion. One of the targets happened to be the White House Chief of Staff. But that wasn't the reason Sean Drummond was called in on the case. Newly enlisted in a CIA cell called the Office of Special Projects, the former Army lawyer was informed that the murders were just a warning. The Killer had left a note: "You can't stop us. There will be others, and the President will be history in the next two days."

The clock is ticking. The hunt begins for the ultimate killer-for-hire - a brilliant, cold-hearted professional with an insider's knowledge of Washington. For Sean Drummond, it is the greatest challenge of his career, a terrifying can-and-mouse game with unthinkable consequences. If he fails, the world will never be the same, and one calculating killer will collect the $100 million bounty on the President's head. [DJ]

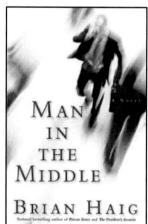

The Man in the Middle

Intrigue, Politics, WP Author

Brian Haig Grand Central Publishing (2007)

The question Congress wants answered is: Who cooked up the evidence that led our nation to war on phony premises? Specifically, the Iraqi nuclear progress that turned out not to exist. The stockpiles of chemical weapons that have never been found. The terrorist connections that haven't materialized... Clifford Daniels knew where the truth is buried.

For newly promoted Army lieutenant colonel Sean Drummond, his latest assignment starts off simply enough: find out if the death of one of D.C.'s most influential defense officials was murder or suicide. Most investigators would call it a cut-and-dried case, but nothing is ever that simple.

Teamed with Brian Tran, the attractive Army Military Police officer investigating the case, Drummond is about to embark on a journey that takes him from the labyrinthine channels of American intelligence to the killing rooms of Iraq. None of it will be more difficult than navigating the shadowy minds and motivations of his enemies and so-called colleagues. [DJ]

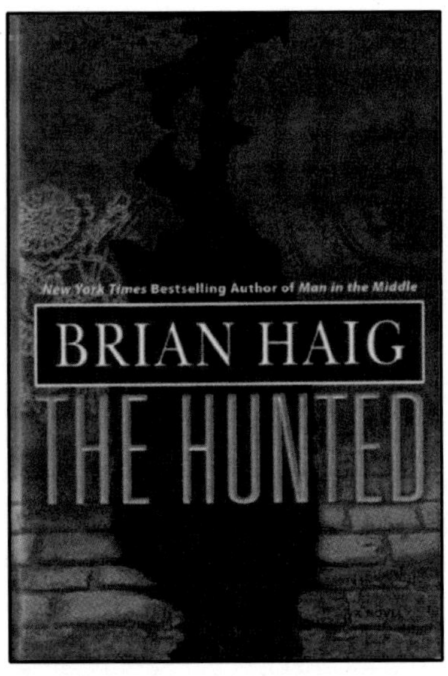

The Hunted

Intrigue, Russia, WP Author

Brian Haig Grand Central Pub (2010)

It's 1991, the Soviet Union has just collapsed, and a new democratic government is beginning to emerge. Alex Konevitch, who was thrown out of Moscow University in 1987 for indulging his entrepreneurial spirit, is now worth $300 million and is a major financial supporter of the new government. In a country where greed and corruption run rampant and wealth is stolen, not earned, he is on track to become both Russia's wealthiest man — and a huge target.

Then top executives in his company start getting brutally murdered one by one, and Alex makes a critical mistake: He hires the former deputy director of the KGB to handle his corporate security. Kidnapped, beaten, and forced to relinquish his business and his fortune by those hired to protect him, Alex manages to escape to the United States with his wife, only to be accused by his own government of stealing millions from his business.

With a contract out on his life and the FBI hot on his trail, Alex is the number one most-wanted fugitive in Russia. He is a man on the run with no country to call home. And he must elude the bounty on his head and prove his innocence . . .if he is ever to build a new life for himself and his family. [DJ]

Capital Game

Intrigue, Politics, WP Author

Brian Haig Grand Central Publishing (2010)

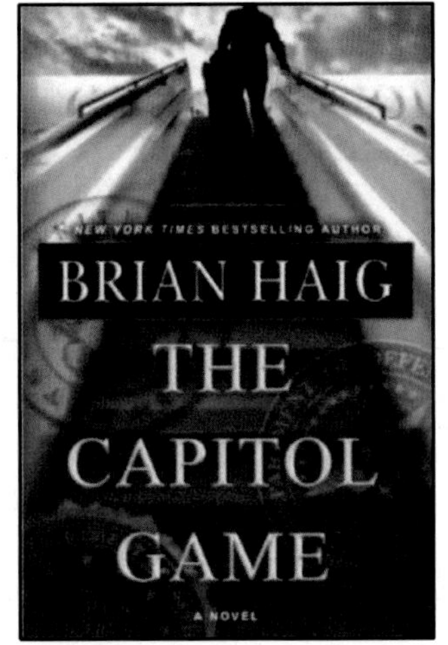

It was the deal of the decade, if not the century. A small, insignificant company on the edge of bankruptcy had discovered an alchemist's dream; a miraculous polymer, that when coated on any vehicle, was the equivalent of 30 inches of steel. With bloody conflicts surging in Iraq and Afghanistan, the polymer promises to save thousands of lives and change the course of both wars.

Jack Wiley, a successful Wall Street banker, believes he has a found a dream come true when he mysteriously learns of this miraculous polymer. His plan: enlist the help of the Capitol Group, one of the country's largest and most powerful corporations in a quick, bloodless takeover of the small company that developed the polymer. It seems like a partnership made in heaven...until the Pentagon's investigative service begins nosing around, and the deal turns into a nightmare. Now, Jack's back is up against the wall and he and the Capitol Group find themselves embroiled in the greatest scandal the government and corporate America have ever seen... [DJ]

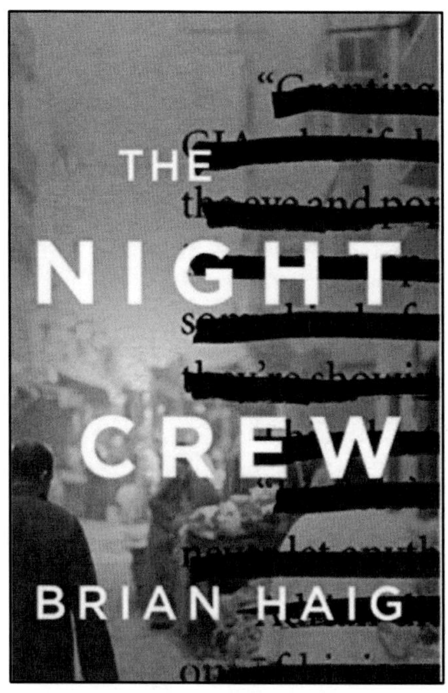

The Night Crew

Intrigue, Politics, WP Author

Brian Haig Thomas & Mercer (2015)

Lieutenant Colonel Sean Drummond, a cocky US Army lawyer who's not afraid to be blunt, finds himself up to his neck in a case he didn't ask to take.

Five US soldiers, tasked with guarding Iraqi prisoners, stand accused of committing depraved atrocities against their charges. Drummond is assigned to defend one of them: a hardscrabble young woman who is either incredibly naive or deceptively evil…and whose incriminating photos made the case an international scandal.

Drummond and his co-counsel, the fiercely antiwar Katherine Carlson, have a complicated and combative history, but they can't afford to get distracted now. They must determine what drove five young patriots to fall so far to the dark side of human nature. As Drummond uncovers evidence that his client has been used as a pawn in a secret strategy involving torture, he realizes that he is caught up in a conspiracy that reaches the highest levels of government. Breaking down the US military's formidable stonewalling could destabilize the government and put his life at risk—but Drummond's not the type to back away from a good fight. [BC]

Brian Haig (1953–) graduated from West Point in 1975 and was commissioned an infantry lieutenant. He served in Fort Carson, Colorado, and the Lebanon peacekeeping operation before obtaining a master's degree from Harvard. He spent three years as the Special Assistant to the Commander-in-Chief of the United Nations Command in Seoul. Haig concluded his military career as the special assistant to the Chairman of the Joint Chiefs of Staff. He retired from active duty as a lieutenant colonel in 1997 then served as a corporate executive before becoming a full-time author.

His father, Alexander Haig also graduated from West Point, rose to the rank of General, and served as Secretary of State under Ronald Reagan. [10-17]

The Knights Templar

The Knights Templar was a Christian military order, the Order of the Poor Fellow Soldiers of Christ and of the Temple of Solomon, that existed from the 12th to 14th centuries to provide warriors in the Crusades. These men were famous in the high and late Middle Ages, but the Order was disbanded very suddenly by King Philip IV of France, who took action against the Templars in order to avoid repaying his own financial debts. He accused them of heresy, ordered the arrest of all Templars within his realm, put the Order under trial and many of them burned at the stake. The dramatic and rapid end of the Order led to many stories and legends developing about them over the centuries…. In modern works, the Templars generally are portrayed as villains, misguided zealots, representatives of an evil secret society, or as the keepers of a long-lost treasure. Several modern organizations also claim heritage from the medieval Templars, as a way of enhancing their own image or mystique. [10-18]

Relating to this collection, the most prominent is the **"Templar"** series by Paul Christopher published between 2009–2015. The protagonist in each is John "Doc" Holiday, a retired Army Ranger and West Point professor.

The Sword of the Templars

Intrigue, Crime, Masonic

Paul Christopher Berkley (2009)

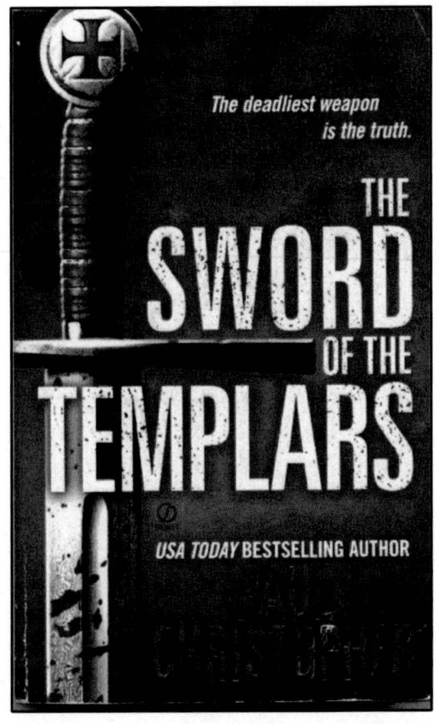

After a lifetime on the front lines, Army Ranger John Holliday has resigned himself to ending his career teaching at West Point. But when his uncle passes away, Holliday discovers a mysterious medieval sword—wrapped in Adolf Hitler's personal battle standard. Then someone burns down his uncle's house in an attempt to retrieve the sword, and Holliday realizes that he's being drawn into a war that has been fought for centuries.

Accompanied by his adventurous niece Peggy, Holliday must delve into the past and piece together the puzzle that was his uncle's life and his involvement with the enigmatic warriors known as the Knights Templar. But this search for answers soon becomes a race against ruthless, cunning opponents willing to die for their cause. . .and to kill Holliday for daring to uncover their past. And it proceeds through eight subsequent novels. [BC]

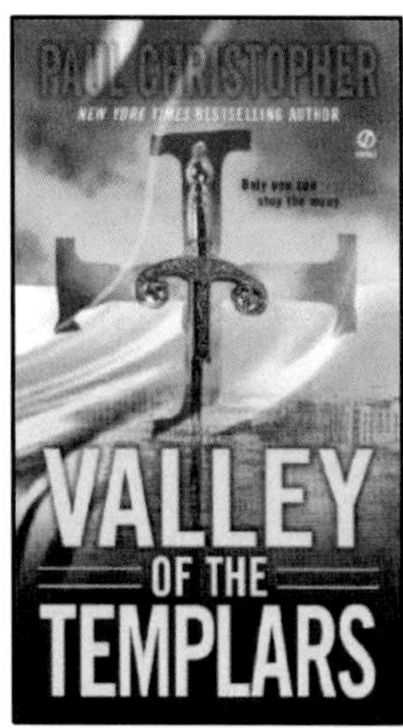

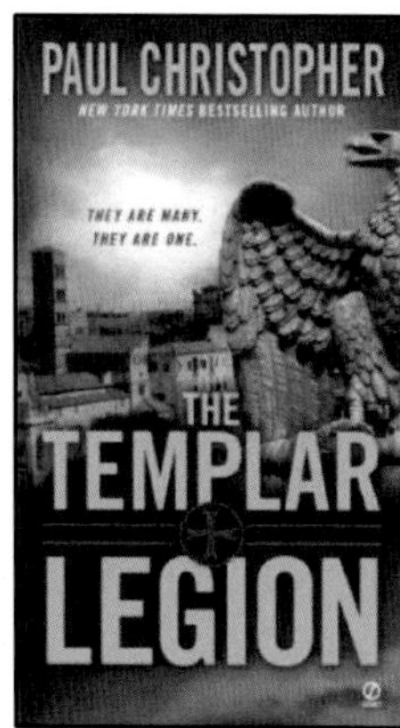

Paul Christopher is a pseudonym used by Canadian, Christopher Hyde (1949–). He has worked as a researcher, editor, and TV interviewer specializing in stories of technology, intelligence, and the environment. He also uses the pseudonym A. J. Holt. He has written over 30 novels under his various pseudonyms including seven in the "Templar" series. [10-19]

7 Knights

Crime, Intrigue, Masonic

Brian Cox Tate Publishing (2011)

Recent West Point graduate Walt Tyler has nearly everything in life: respect as a successful quarterback, the affection of an attractive doctor, and a well laid-out military career. But Walt is plunged into the fight of his life when terrorists begin killing off the hidden network of Templar Knights, led by seven vital figures. Walt's grandfather, newly elected U.S. President Preston Tyler, one of the seven, holds the key to protecting the knights. He reveals to Walt the clandestine establishment intended to protect Christians during the last days. Having existed since the inception of the Knights Templar, the cryptic order of the Seven Knights has remained veiled for centuries. Brought up through history under the blanket of the Ancient Free and Accepted Masons, the Seven Knights maintain an exclusive membership of only seven men, powerful individuals including politicians, military leaders, corporate geniuses, and financiers from around the globe.

The sudden attack on the knights can only mean one thing: the antichrist is coming. Walt and Preston's desperate escape leads them along a modern underground railroad through the long-established safe havens of the Biltmore and the Hermitage as they attempt to discover by whom their death is being sought and how their centuries-old secret has leaked. Can Walt and Preston stop the terrorists before all Seven Knights are murdered? [BC]

Brian Cox is an active Freemason and a Past Master of his local Masonic lodge as well as a member of several Masonic bodies: York Rite (Knights Templar), Scottish Rite (32nd degree), and a Noble of the Shrine. [BC]

Jason Kasper has authored two series of novels about combatting international crime lords and terrorists. They are ***American Mercenary*** and ***Shadow Strike***.

The *American Mercenary* series' principal character, David Rivers, is an Army Ranger— a combat veteran of the wars in Afghanistan and Iraq. He has almost completed his final year at West Point when his world is turned upside down by a sudden discharge from military service. David is struggling with his own demons while striving to exterminate a criminal warlord. There is not much subtlety in the six novels, just plenty of intrigue, betrayal, and hard-core action. Books in the *Shadow Strike* series can be found in the "Global War on Terror" chapter.

Greatest Enemy

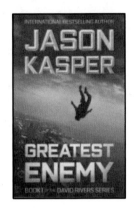

Crime, Intrigue, WP Author

Jason Kasper Regiment Publishing (2016)

Angry and confused, David soon hits rock bottom.

And that's when they appear. Three mysterious men. Men who know David's dark secret–they know that he has murdered someone in cold blood. And they want him to do it again. David is soon plunged into the covert underworld of ex-special operators for hire, where victory is defined by profit, and the rates are set by the highest bidder. But as the stakes continue to rise, he learns that his new employer is more ruthless than anyone he's faced in combat—and he just might be David's greatest enemy. [BC]

Offer of Revenge

Crime, Intrigue, WP Author

Jason Kasper Regiment Publishing (2017)

David Rivers, the sole survivor of a mercenary team betrayed by its employer, is living in exile and haunted by the loss of friends he failed to save. When a mysterious ally brings an offer of revenge, David accepts without question. But in order to kill his greatest enemy, David must first join the same secretive and lethal organization that slaughtered the only family he had.

To prove his allegiance, he enters a life-or-death battle against a savage force of enemy fighters in the badlands of Somalia. The closer he gets to his target the more David realizes that the betrayal of his team was not as random as he believed. Someone inside the organization seems to know David's true purpose, and that could mean only one thing: David might not have been the sole survivor after all. [BC]

Dark Redemption

Crime, Intrigue, WP Author

Jason Kasper Regiment Publishing (2018)

David Rivers has returned from a brutal combat mission in Somalia with only one thing on his mind: revenge. After killing his teammates' betrayer, he's set his sights on the ultimate prize, assassinating the faceless mastermind who orchestrated their deaths from afar. And for the first time, that prize is within reach.

In a feat accomplished by few, David has managed to secure an elusive meeting with the Handler-- but nothing in his murderous past could possibly have prepared him for what happens when he finally meets his greatest enemy face-to-face.

Before he can kill the Handler, David must first serve him once more. This time, the task is new: not to kill a target, but to defend one. As David negotiates a labyrinth of twisted loyalties in the violent slums of Rio de Janeiro, he realizes that the betrayal of his former teammates was just the beginning.

But as a whirlwind of lethal confrontations in Rio brings David and the Handler together for the final time, he realizes that the consequences of his tireless search for vengeance might just be worse than death. [BC]

Other books in the ***American Mercenary Thriller*** series are shown below.

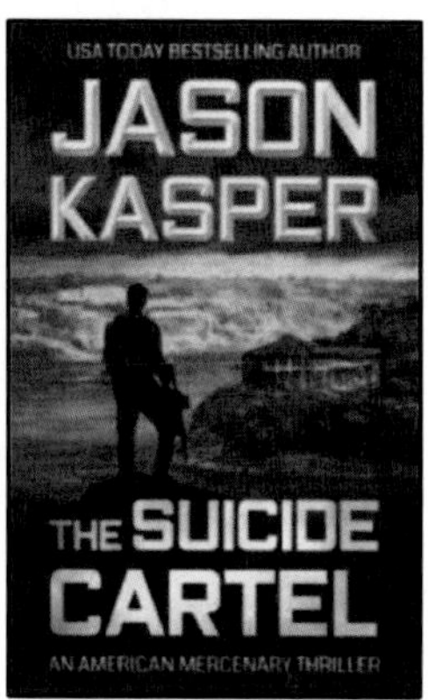

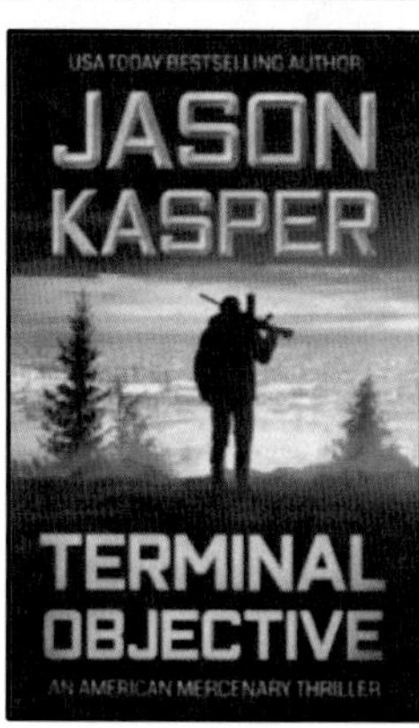

Jason Kasper has also authored *The Spider Heist* series depicting the capers of a group of master thieves.

The Spider Heist

Intrigue, Crime, WP Author

Jason Kasper Severn River Publishing (2019)

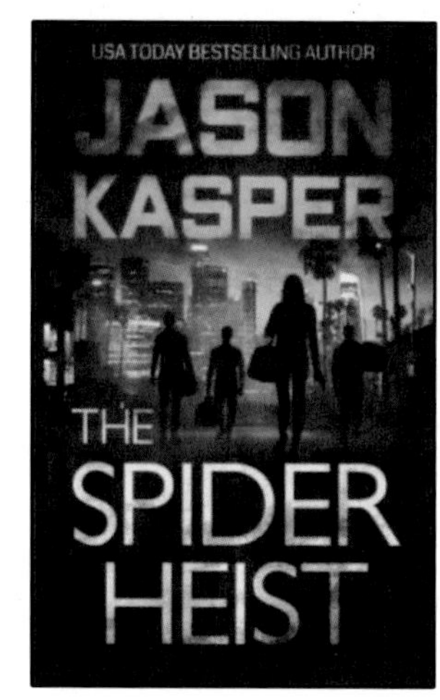

After being used as a scapegoat by a corrupt former boss, Blair Morgan is unceremoniously fired from the FBI. Now, with her reputation, pride, and years of service stripped away, Blair just wants to start over.

But when a chance date turns into a mysterious job offer, her past comes crashing back to haunt her. In a flash, Blair becomes entangled in a high stakes bank heist. Her status as a former FBI-agent-turned-hostage transforms her into an instant media sensation. And the unwanted attention makes her a target for ruthless killers that will stop at nothing to silence her.

Caught in the crosshairs, Blair must confront her past before she loses her freedom—or her life. But there is something strange about this team of bank robbers. They aren't who they seem. And as a deadly SWAT raid closes in, Blair discovers that she may not be either... [DJ]

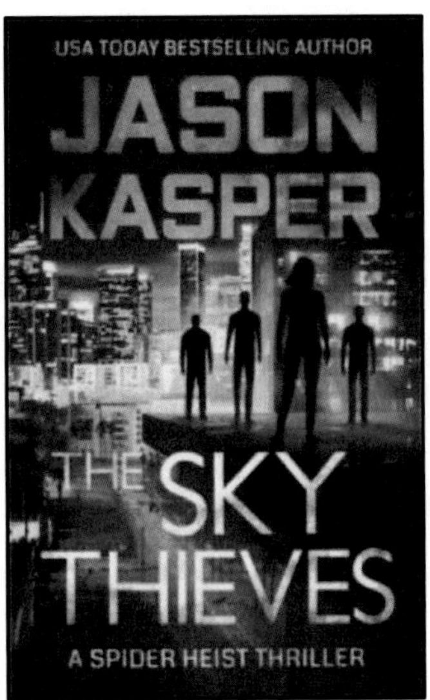

The Sky Thieves

Intrigue, Crime, WP Author

Jason Kasper Severn River Publishing (2020)

Blair Morgan has embraced her second career—as an elite thief. Her heist crew has set their sights on their latest target: the Sierra Diamond, an 872-carat stone worth $27.3 million. It will be encased in a new vault known as the Sky Safe, a revolutionary strong room built into the side of a Los Angeles high rise.

The FBI says the Sky Safe is impenetrable. Naturally, Blair and her crew think otherwise…and if they succeed, it will be the greatest heist ever pulled. But Blair's corrupt former boss at the FBI has other plans. He knows Blair will be coming for the diamond and intends to catch her in the act…along with her entire team. [BC]

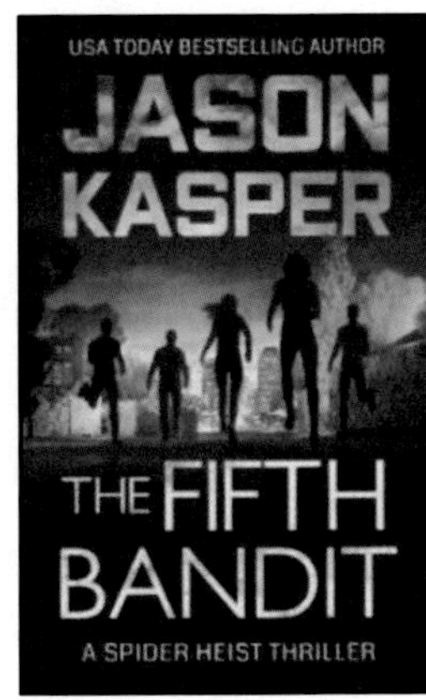

Jason Kasper enlisted in the US Army in June 2001. His first assignment was as a Ranger private, where he conducted operations in Afghanistan and Iraq before attending West Point. Jason then served as an Airborne Infantry and Special Forces officer, deploying multiple times to Afghanistan and Africa. During his off-duty time he began running marathons and ultramarathons, skydiving, BASE jumping, and writing fiction. Upon returning from his final deployment in 2016, Jason began his second career as an author. [10-20]

Chapter 11
Army Aviation

ARMY Aviation had its inception soon after the Wright brothers first flight in 1903. In 1905, the Wright brothers built and flew their third flyer. It was the world's first practical powered flyer, capable of performing banking maneuvers, circling, and flying figures of eight…

On May 1908, **Thomas E. Selfridge, Class of 1903,** became the first US military officer to pilot a modern aircraft when at Hammondsport, NY, he flew solo traveling 100 feet on his first attempt and 200 feet on his second. Later in the month, he made several flights culminating in a flight of fifty seconds covering a distance of 800 yards. Although not fully trained as a pilot, Selfridge was nevertheless the first U.S. military officer to fly any airplane unaccompanied.

In December 1907, Wilbur Wright appeared at a hearing before the U.S. Army Ordnance Board and stated that he could furnish a heavier-than-air flying machine for the price of $25,000…. Signal Corps Specification Number 486 was issued to provide the U.S. Army with its first heavier-than-air aircraft–the first military aircraft in the world. This aircraft was transported to Fort Meyer, Virginia, where it made its first demonstration flight at the parade grounds on September 3, 1908.

On September 17, 1908, Selfridge was the first person to die in a crash of a powered airplane while a passenger with Orville Wright at Ft Myers. Selfridge is buried in Arlington National Cemetery. There is a cenotaph in the West Point cemetery commemorating his life and contribution to Army aviation.

Source: the U.S. Army Aviation Museum website

Born for Flight Series

These novels are about the early years of aviation. The Harrison family is committed in the effort to achieving first flight. John Harrison is obsessed with the engineering and mechanics of flying higher, faster, longer, but his wife, Maggie, and son, David, have reservations. The first novel sets the stage for young David's important involvement in the flying game in later volumes. David meets Thomas Selfridge and is inspired to attend West Point and become an Army aviator. David does become "The Fledgling" pilot in the second volume. Because the military is at the forefront of aviation, David elects to enter West Point and ultimately World War I in the final two volumes.

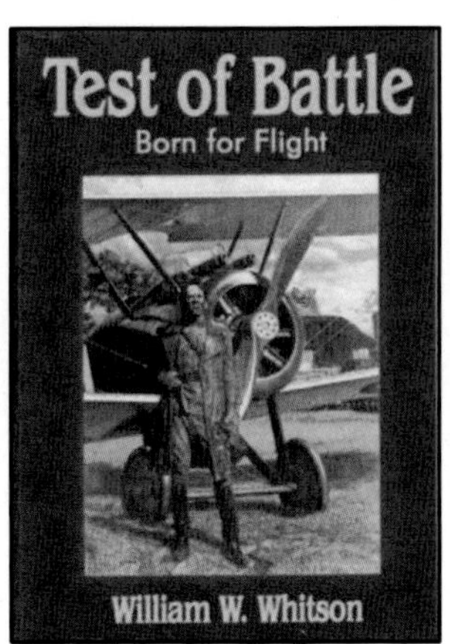

The Books in the Series (and years covered)

Book I: ***Something Glorious*** (1894 – 1905)
Book II: ***The Fledgling*** (1905 – 1912)
Book III: ***Apprentice Warrior*** (1912 – 1916)
Book IV: ***Test of Battle*** (1916 – 1917)

Apprentice Warrior: Born for Flight

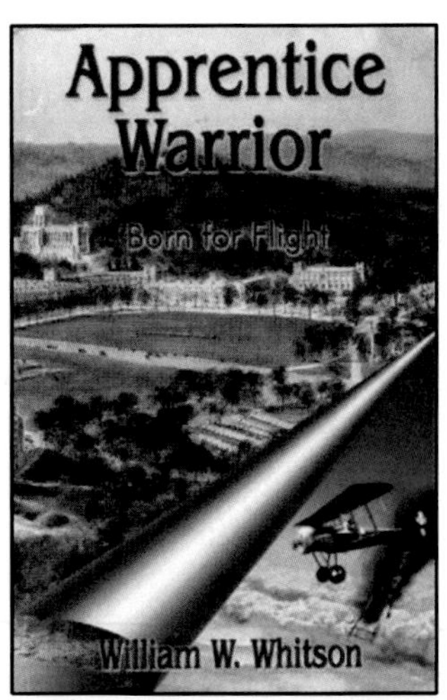

Aviation, WWI, WP Author

William W. Whitson Cogent Publishing (2003)

This is the third novel in the Born-For-Flight series about the historic development of the airplane during the period from 1894 to 1916. *Something Glorious* and *The Fledgling* were the first two novels of the series.

It is a fictional process by which a West Point Cadet's illusion about the glory of war begin to fade before he graduates with the Class of 1916. As war clouds loon in Europe, David Harrison enters the United Sates Military Academy at West Point in the summer of 1912. The major thread of the story traces his effort to make sense out of his passion for flight, his extraordinary intuition, the ideals of West Point, and a prospective career in the Army. The second theme is the development of the airplane for combat. During the summer of 1915, one year before graduation, the two themes become entangled. Major Billy Mitchell sends David to London to discover what military air power is all about. [BC]

Test of Battle: Born for Flight

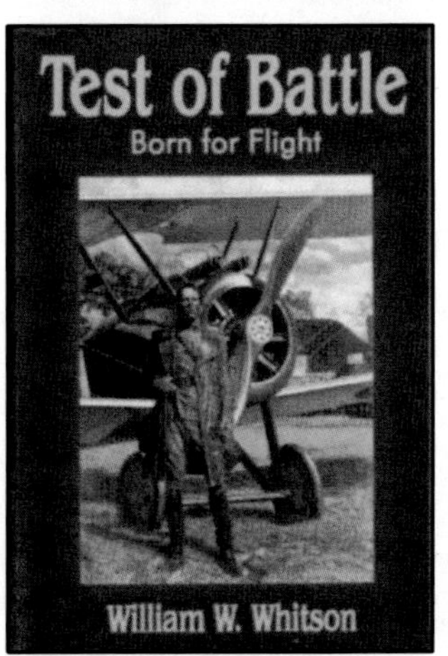

Aviation, WWI, WP Author

William W. Whitson Cogent Publishing (2006)

From the author of *Apprentice Warrior* comes a story of the odds a special breed of men faced when air battle first came of age: wings and engines that fell apart without warning; guns that jammed; toxic fumes, nausea, noise, vibration, g-forces, frostbite, windburn, fear, insomnia and chronic exhaustion.

In this story David Harrison surmounts these odds to meet the two great tests of battle: leaving home to search for his warrior self and his struggle to return home after he finds it. The tempo starts with a deceptively bucolic romance in the summer of 1916. It picks up speed on its way through flight training to gut-wrenching air combat over the Somme and a final twist at the end of the year. The story's seamless mix of fictional imagination and historical authenticity, reinforced by maps and photographs, never fails to entertain. As a timeless inner conflict haunts our journey through the mind of a novice American pilot, suspense grips our attention. [BC]

William W. Whitson (1926–2018), Class of 1948, having enjoyed his career as an army officer, West Point professor, historian, and China scholar turned to his lifelong interests: writing about the early development of aviation and the scientific study of human consciousness. [11-01]

World War I and After

In the late 1920s as the military expanded the development of modern war planes, there was great need to augment the personnel to fly and care for the aircraft. Henry Arnold, a Colonel in the Air Corps wanted to encourage more young men to pursue flying careers, so he authored the Bill Bruce series of six books for youth.

Bill Bruce and the Pioneer Aviators

Aviation, WP Author

Henry (Hap) Arnold A. L. Burt Company (1928)

The exciting adventures of two boys on Governor's Island, NY with escaped prisoners, meeting Wilbur Wright, perilous balloon and airplane flights, and Bill Bruce's prize-winning glider. [DJ]

Bill Bruce the Flying Cadet

WP Author, Aviation, WW1

Henry (Hap) Arnold A. L. Burt Company (1928)

A complete account of the life at the flying schools held during World War I. The vivid story of a flying cadet and his various duties up to the time he was commissioned. [DJ]

Bill Bruce Becomes and Ace

Aviation, WW1, WP Author

Henry (Hap) Arnold A. L. Burt Company (1928)

After graduating from the flying schools, Bill Bruce showed his courage by joining an air squadron in France. Flying and fighting above the lines, he proved his mastery of the air by downing five enemy airplanes. [DJ]

Bill Bruce On Border Patrol

WP Author, Aviation, Western

Henry (Hap) Arnold A. L. Burt Company (1928)

This is a story of a young air officer and his various encounters with rum, dope, and human smugglers while on duty with the border patrol on the Mexican Border. [DJ]

Bill Bruce on Forest Patrol

Aviation, WP Author

Henry (Hap) Arnold A. L. Burt Company (1928)

Flying with the famous Forest Patrol in the Northwest, the young air pilot has many hazardous experiences, spotting fires in that heavily timbered region and assisting in their control and prevention. [DJ]

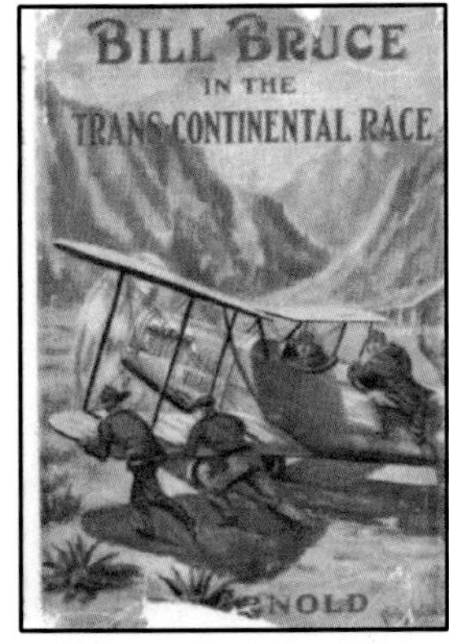

Bill Bruce in The Trans-Continental Race

WP Author, Aviation

Major Henry (Air Corps) Arnold A. L. Burt Company (1928)

Competing with the best fliers in the world, Bill Bruce went out to win -- and did win in an unusual manner, the First Transcontinental Airplane Race held in 1919. [DJ]

Henry H. "Hap" Arnold (1886–1950) Class of 1907, was an aviation pioneer, first flying with the Wright brothers. He was instrumental in building the Army Air Force in World War I and for the Second World War. He became a five-star general and head of the Army Air Forces in the Second World War. [11-02]

Wings Over West Point

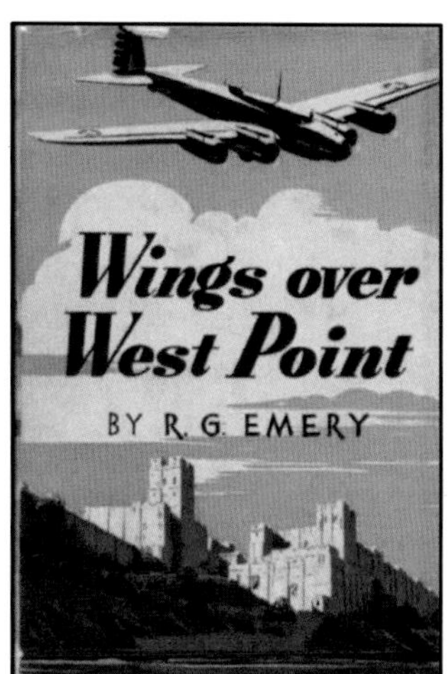

Cadet, Aviation, WP Author

R. G. Emery Macrae Smith Company (1940)

In spite of his confidence in his own ability -- or perhaps because of it -- Don Moore, who is not only an outstanding athlete, a good student and a skilled pilot, manages to antagonize most of the upperclassmen at West Point with whom he comes in contact. He is constantly getting into trouble, although his motives are beyond question. Misfortune dogs him on the football field, and his solicitude for a friend nearly results in his dismissal from the Academy. His roommates, who really understand him, manages to win back his place on the team, the esteem of his classmates and the respect of all who know him.[DJ]

To interest young men in the Academy **R. Guy Emery** (1909–1965), Class of 1930, wrote several books about West Point athletics and other mystery novels. See the chapters "Army Sports" and "Other Books by West Point Authors." [11-03]

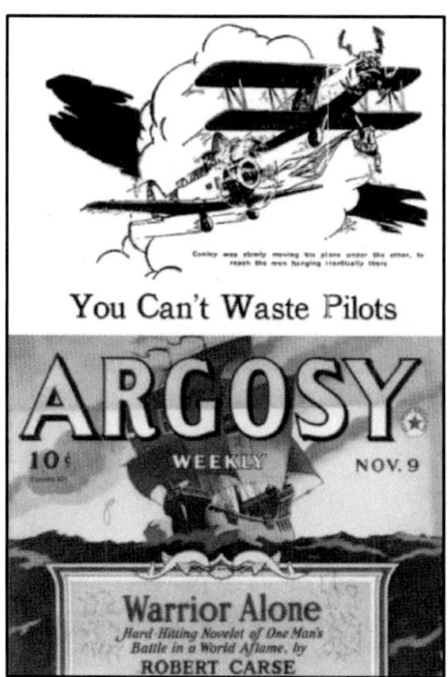

"You Can't Waste Pilots"

Aviation, WW2, Pulp Fiction

Louis C. Goldsmith Argosy Magazine (November 9, 1940)

"But pilots are expendable, cadet. Maybe you'll learn what that means when you're up in the sky playing hide-and-seek with disaster."

Ed Stuart tried to catch up with Jacobs and Frank Conley as they walked together from hangar line to the solo-flight stage. His good-looking face was a moist red, but not from his running.

"That was a fast one you pulled, Conley," he growled. "You're getting pretty smart since Johns patted you on the back for your stunt flying."

Frank Conley turned to meet the cadet's anger. Ed was getting set to start a fight. He'd known Ed so many years, fought with him so much, that he could read the signs.

"I don't get you Ed," he said mildly. There was a placating smile on his round, homely face to meet the other's scowl." [EB]

"Fools Fly High"

Aviation, Pulp Fiction

Louis C. Goldsmith Argosy Magazine (Dec 7, 1940)

"See that plane way up there, brother? Well, this is the story of men who risked their lives and souls to put it there. Here are the epic days when the flying fools of '18 were kings of American skies, and whose who dreamed of safety in the air were branded cowards.

The weight of the Florida heat lifted slightly as they climbed. Capt'n Dan Moore, sitting in the front cockpit of the Curtis trainer, could guess their altitude pretty closely from that alone...Eleven hundred feet. The climb already slowing. This OX Jenny would not go much higher than 4000 feet in such air.

He watched idly the small movements of the joy stick. In the rear cockpit, behind him, Captain Nagel was flying the plane with the dual controls. Much as Moore disliked Alvin Nagel there were two things he would credit him with: flying skill and courage.

He glanced up at the center-section reserve tank, just above his head. There were seven gallons of gasoline in it. When they crashed it would burst and pour down on him. There was little chance of it not catching fire...." [EB]

IN MEMORY OF
LOUIS C GOLDSMITH
MAJ US ARMY AIR CORPS
JUN 17 1898 SEP 30 1943
CHARLOTTE FRANCES
HIS WIFE
JUN 24 1906 MAR 18 1989

Louis Goldsmith (1898–1943) was an early barn storming soldier-of-fortune. He flew in conflicts in Mexico, World War I and China and later became a test pilot for Boeing before joining the Army Air Corps in 1941. He had dozens of short stories and novelettes – mostly aviation oriented – published in *Argosy* magazine between 1927 and 1943. Major Goldsmith perished in the crash of a Lockheed Loadstar in Scotland in September 1943.[11-04]

World War II

Flying military aircraft was fraught with danger. During World War II, more West Pointers perished serving in the Army Air Corps than in any other branch of the Army. Training flights were especially dangeous.

"KEEP 'EM FLYING"
IS OUR BATTLE CRY!
DO YOUR PART
FOR
DUTY - HONOR - COUNTRY

The Red Randall Series

Red Randall was in Hawaii on that fateful morning of December 7, 1941, when the Japanese struck their treacherous blow. The son of an Army Air Force Colonel, Red was determined to be an Army pilot himself and was to enter West Point the following summer. But, when war came, he was thrown into a series of exciting events that permitted him to serve his country much sooner than he had hoped.

Red Randall at Pearl Harbor

Aviation, WW2, WP Candidate

Robert Sidney Bowen Grosset & Dunlap (1944)

On December 7th, 1941, on Oahu, Red encounters a secret agent of Japan, putting his courage and ingenuity to the supreme test. How Red, and his flying pal, Jimmy Joyce, outwitted the diabolical Kato Harada and foiled the planned Japanese invasion, makes a rapid-fire story that will keep the reader breathlessly interested from beginning to end. [DJ]

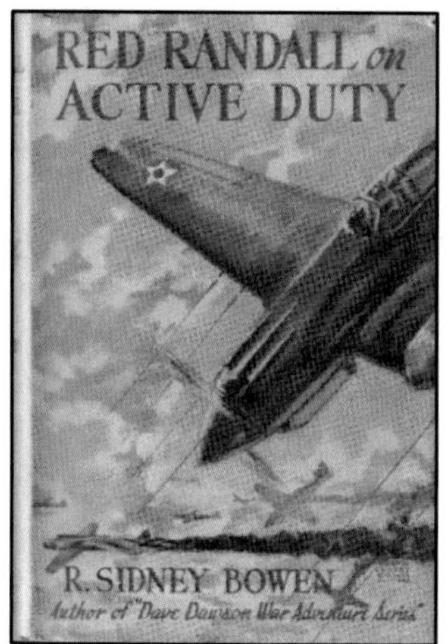

Red Randall on Active Duty

Aviation, WW2

Robert Sidney Bowen Grosset & Dunlap (1944)

Red Randall and Jimmy Joyce, lieutenants in the Army Air Corps, found things pretty dull at the Darwin base, after their electrifying adventures at Pearl Harbor. But when they volunteered for a dangerous and vital mission which took them to the hotbed of the Pacific -- the Philippines—the boys got the action they craved. From the time Red and Jimmy left Australia until they accomplished their secret mission, the fearless young airmen found themselves in one perilous situation after another: among them a crash landing on a Japanese-infested island; prisoners of the Japs; and a spectacular escape in a Mitsubishi fighter plane. [DJ]

Red Randall Over Tokyo

Aviation, WW2

Robert Sydney Bowen Grosset & Dunlap (1944)

Red Randall and Jimmy Joyce, heroes of Pearl Harbor, are detailed on a perilous secret mission . . . to contact a United States Intelligence Agent in Japan who possesses information vital to the American forces in the Pacific.

The fearless young airmen fly and fight their way from Australia to the coast of China where they are to meet General Chan, a Chinese guerrilla leader, who is to help them reach their destination. Led into a trap by a clever Japanese trick, Red and Jimmy are taken prisoners. Their rescue by General

Chan's guerrillas, their flight to Japan in a captured enemy plane, and their mad dash over a Tokyo blazing from Yank bombs, make a rip-roaring tale of aerial combat and breathless adventure that will thrill all readers, particularly those already familiar with the daring exploits of these intrepid young fliers. [DJ]

Red Randall at Midway

Aviation, WW2

Robert Sidney Bowen Grosset & Dunlap (1944)

An urgent summons for Red Randall and Jimmy Joyce to report to Air Forces Headquarters in Melbourne, an exciting secret flight over the Pacific, climaxed by their being temporarily attached to the U.S. carrier Falcon is only the beginning of a story full of the gripping adventure of dogfights, bombings and sea battles into which the two sensational air heroes of Pearl Harbor and Tokyo carry their war wings with miracles of daring and accomplishment.

How they hunt out a Jap task force steaming toward Midway behind a protective weather front and pull off a daring single-handed raid; how their courage and ingenuity saves them from death at the hands of a Jap naval officer; and how their amazing escape with enemy plans turns the tide at the battle of Midway make intensely exciting reading. [DJ]

Red Randall on New Guinea

Aviation, WW2

Robert Sidney Bowen Grosset & Dunlap (1944)

Readers who were thrilled with the breath-taking exploits of Red Randall over Tokyo and in the Battle of Midway will find in this new story a further record of his indomitable fighting spirit and spectacular flying skill.

How Red and his flying pal, Jimmy Joyce, are shot down over New Guinea and captured by headhunters, how they make their way down a jungle river through Jap-infested territory to reach an outpost held by the renowned 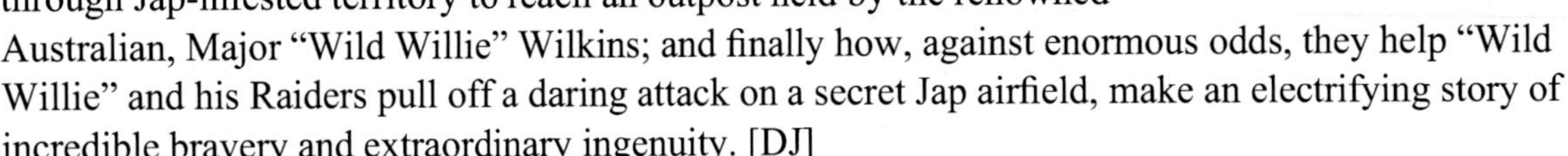 Australian, Major "Wild Willie" Wilkins; and finally how, against enormous odds, they help "Wild Willie" and his Raiders pull off a daring attack on a secret Jap airfield, make an electrifying story of incredible bravery and extraordinary ingenuity. [DJ]

Red Randall in the Aleutians

Aviation, WW2

Robert Sidney Bowen Grosset & Dunlap (1945)

When Red Randall volunteers for special duty in the Aleutians he wants action -- and he's not disappointed! Here in the Aleutians where visibility is zero, where williwaws rage, and where jagged mountain peaks are blanketed in fog, Red and his flying pal, Jimmy Joyce, have some of the most harrowing experiences of their careers for not only are the Japs their dangerous enemies, but the elements, too, are a constant challenge to their flying skill and courage.

How they hunt out a Jap task force moving stealthily through the fog toward Dutch Harbor, and how they rescue the crew of a Catalina flying boat stranded on one of the fogbound islands, make a thrilling story charged with high-voltage suspense and swift tense action. [DJ]

Red Randall in Burma

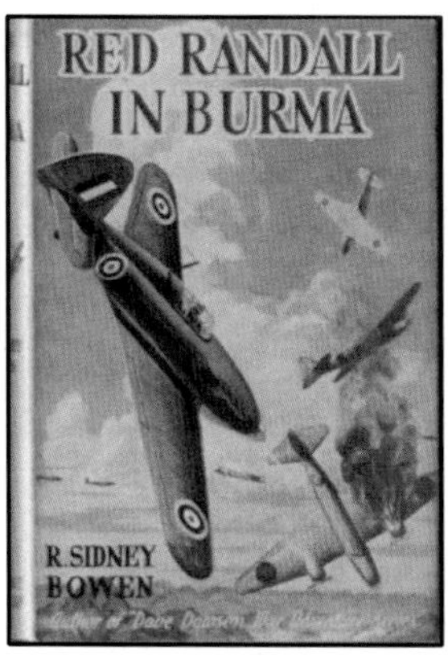

Aviation, WW2

Robert Sidney Bowen Grosset & Dunlap (1945)

Red Randall and Jimmy Joyce are enroute to Calcutta to join the Twelfth Air Force when Jap dive bombers swoop down out of the sky and send Transport 58 to the bottom of the Indian Ocean. Adrift on a life raft, the two Yank air aces cling to the hope that they will be rescued. They are "rescued" . . . by a Jap submarine.

In their dank little cell aboard the submarine, they find another airman — an R.A.F. officer—more dead than alive. The story of his escape from Burma in a Jap plane, and of the plight of Allied men trapped there behind the enemy's lines, fires Red and Jimmy with a grim determination to finish the work he had set out to do. How, through a strange twist of fate, Red and Jimmy escape and carry to a daring finish the R.A.F. officer's uncompleted mission makes a high-powered story of flying and adventure in World War II. [DJ]

Robert Sidney Bowen, Jr. (1900–1977) was a World War I aviator, newspaper journalist, magazine editor and author born in Boston, Massachusetts. Being too young to serve in the American armed forces, he joined the British RAF in 1918 and saw some combat. He is best known for his boys' series books written during World War II, the Dave Dawson War Adventure Series and the Red Randall Series.
11-05

Whisper Flight: A Special Glider Mission in Burma

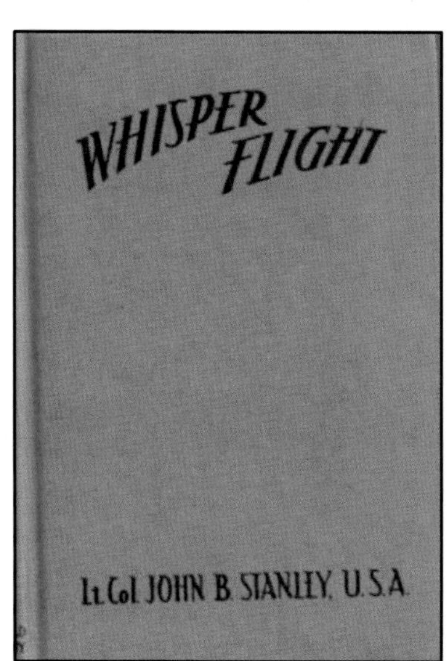

WW2, Aviation, WP Author

John B. Stanley Dodd, Mead & Company (1945)

While working on restoration and construction of airfields in Italy in 1943, Lt. Bob Hilton is abruptly ordered to leave his unit and report to a British unit fighting the Japanese in Burma. There were plans to construct airfields in central Burma to supply paratroopers and fighting behind Japanese lines.

"Where do we fit in, sir?" Bob asked the question with some diffidence.

"I was just coming to that." The general smiled. "Let's sit down again and I'll get on with it."

Without exception, when they once more seated themselves around his desk, the three officers leaned forward eagerly to hear the next words of General Craigie. "Until about a week ago, the staff was satisfied that our plans were complete. Every key man had been assigned a job; and each had his responsibilities. Then we discovered that there was a special task for which we had made no provision. We needed experts and needed them quickly. So, we sent cables asking for help. The result is that you men are here. You were carefully selected both because of your records and your specialties. [EB]

After West Point, **John B. Stanley** (1910–1999) Class of 1934 served in the infantry at various posts around the country and Central America. With the outbreak of World War II, Colonel Stanley was assigned to the War Department in Washington until early 1945, when he was sent to the European Theatre of Operations. His short stories were published in Boys' Life and anthologies. He wrote other books including *Cadet Derry, West Pointer* which is included in the "Cadet Experience" chapter of this book.

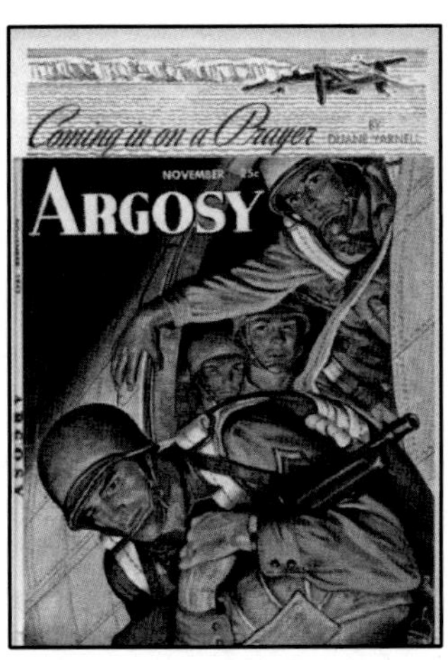

"Coming in on a Prayer"

Aviation, Pulp Fiction, WW2

Duane Yarnell Argosy Magazine (November 10, 1943)

"There comes a time when even the best soldier must choose between himself and a pal....

A burst from an F-W 20-mm A-cannon ripped into the belly of the big Fortress just as she unloosed her bombs over the German airfield. Up front, Captain Joe Naylor swore and fought the controls. The Fortress shuddered as Joe Naylor pushed her nose into the clouds. Joe always felt responsible for the ten lives in his hands, but today he had an additional responsibility. Today, Eddie Bates was Joe's tail gunner...

They were still fifty miles from the channel when the clouds gave out. The sky was suddenly a clear blue. The rest of the squadron had disappeared. "Pilot to crew." Joe spoke with a soft Texas drawl into the interphone, "Keep your eyes peeled for F-W's."

"Here they come! Six o'clock!" Eddie Bates' voice came through the interphone, from the tail turret. The fear in Eddie's voice made Joe Naylor feel a little sad. . . . [EB]

Duane Yarnell (1914? – 1994) was an outstanding athlete in high school and college. Yarnell was a prolific contributor to the sports pulps from 1935 to 1950, along with a few stories in the Western and detective pulps. After that he published only a handful of stories in mystery digests and men's magazines before vanishing from the fiction business. [11-06]

"**The Women Airforce Service Pilots (WASP) was a civilian women pilots' organization,** whose members were United States federal civil service employees. Members of WASP became trained pilots who tested aircraft, ferried aircraft, and trained other pilots. Over 1,100 women learned to fly "the Army way," but never received military status. When the program ended on December 20, 1944, the women returned to their previous lives and the file on them was sealed. In 1977, President Jimmy Carter signed a law giving the WASP retroactive veteran status. On March 10, 2010, 66 years after the program was disbanded, President Barack Obama awarded the WASP the Congressional Gold Medal for their service." [11-07]

The Flight Girls

Aviation, WW2

Noelle Salazar MIRA Books (2019)

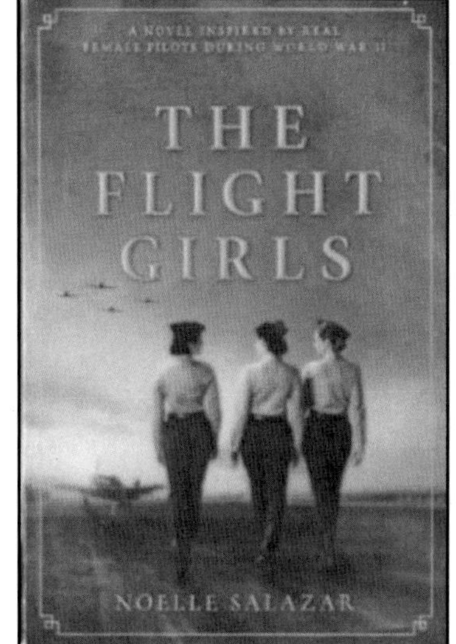

1941. Audrey Coltrane has always wanted to fly. It's why she implored her father to teach her at the little airfield back home in Texas. It's why she signed up to train military pilots in Hawaii when the war in Europe began. And it's why she insists she is not interested in any dream-derailing romantic involvements, even with the disarming Lieutenant James Hart, who fast becomes a friend as treasured as the women she flies with. Then one fateful day, she gets caught in the air over Pearl Harbor just as the bombs begin to fall, and suddenly, nowhere feels safe.

To make everything she's lost count for something, Audrey joins the Women's Airforce Service Pilots program. The bonds she forms with her fellow pilots reignite a spark of hope in the face of war, and —

especially when James goes missing in action — give Audrey the strength to cross the front lines and fight for everything she holds dear.

Shining a light on a little-known piece of history, *The Flight Girls* is a sweeping portrayal of women's fearlessness in the face of adversity, and the power of friendship to make us soar. [DJ]

Noelle Salazar, a native of the Pacific Northwest, has been a Navy recruit, a medical assistant, an NFL cheerleader and always a storyteller. When she's not writing, she can be found dodging raindrops and daydreaming about her next book. *The Flight Girls* is her first novel. [11-08]

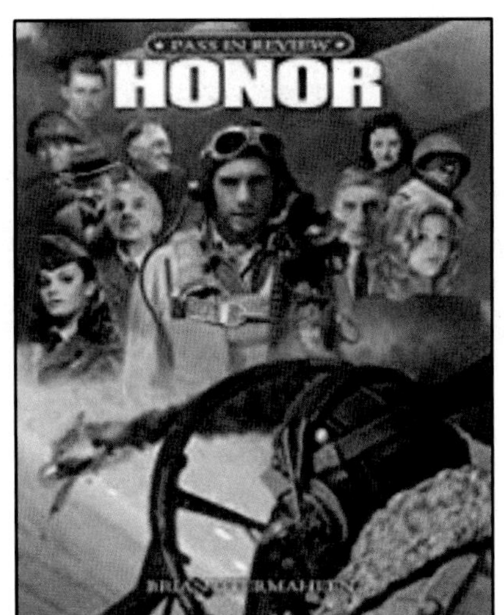

HONOR: Pass in Review Series

Aviation, World War II, WP Author

Brian Utermahlen CreateSpace Publishing (2012)

This is the second book of the *Pass in Review Trilogy* – a saga of the Nolan family spanning the 20th Century. It is reminiscent of Herman Wouk's grand saga *The Winds of War*. The first book *Pass in Review - Duty* related Dave Nolan's passage through West Point, his heroics as an infantry company and battalion commander in key battles of World War I and Army life as a field grade officer during the years before World War II.

This story takes place during the World War II years as Dave's son Mitch becomes the central military figure as a pilot-in-training and then a fighter pilot (P-38's) in Europe. Family and friends introduced in the first book continue their roles often central to the story as in the original. Both Dave and son Mitch interact with many of the great leaders of the era: Eisenhower, Churchill, Roosevelt, and Marshall. [BC]

The Vietnam War

By the 1960s Army aviation was primarily helicopters and spotter planes. The following novel takes you into the cockpit of the workhorse Huey helicopter to fly with Brad Nolan on combat assaults into hot Landing Zones, medical evacuations, and night fire support missions. *Pass in Review – COUNTRY* is the sequel to *Pass in Review: HONOR* described above.

COUNTRY: Pass in Review Series

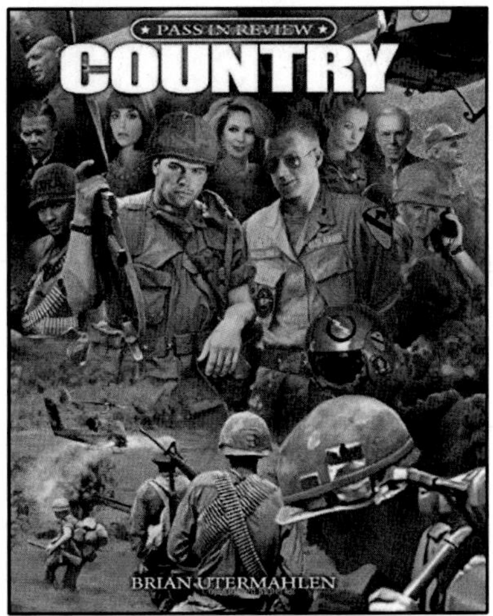

WP Author, Vietnam

Brian Utermahlen CreateSpace Independent (2014)

From Amazon:

Two brothers - one a helicopter pilot, the other an infantry soldier - and a gutsy, dedicated nurse bring to life the real story of Vietnam that the news media, protestors, politicians, and the public never saw or understood.

COUNTRY takes you into the cockpit of the workhorse Huey helicopter to fly with Brad Nolan on combat assaults into hot Landing Zones, medical evacuations, and night fire support missions.

COUNTRY puts you on combat patrol with Glenn Nolan, on an American firebase being overrun and in the middle of firefights with North Vietnamese regulars in the jungles of Vietnam and Cambodia.

And COUNTRY also puts you inside the trauma-laden operating rooms of American Surgical hospitals with Jenny Kolarik and her nurses as they fight for the life of every wounded soldier.

Pass in Review - COUNTRY is the third and final book of a three generational saga about the Nolans, a twentieth century military family. This is the story of a family, a nation, an Army and the institution of West Point struggling with challenges to the concept of Duty-Honor-Country during the Vietnam era. [BC]

Brian Utermahlen, Class of 1968, was an infantry combat veteran and helicopter pilot with the 1st Air Cavalry Division in Vietnam. Following six years on active duty, he returned to civilian life as a manager for the DuPont Co. He flew helicopters for 12 years in the Delaware National Guard. [BC]

The Majors

Aviation, Vietnam

W.E.B. Griffin G. P. Putnam (1983)

Dien Bien Phu. Saigon. Hanoi. In 1954, they were only exotic names from a French campaign halfway around the world. But now American fighting men--proven on the bloody beaches of Normandy and in the minefields of Korea--are summoned to help beat back the guerilla forces of Ho Chi Minh. To some, the "secret" war in Indochina was the depth of folly. To others, like the Majors, it pointed to the heights of glory... [BC]

This novel sees the officers we met previously in this series (Lowell, MacMillan, Felder, Bellmon) pushing for a rotary-wing (helicopter) force with Ft. Rucker, Alabama as its headquarters. [EB]

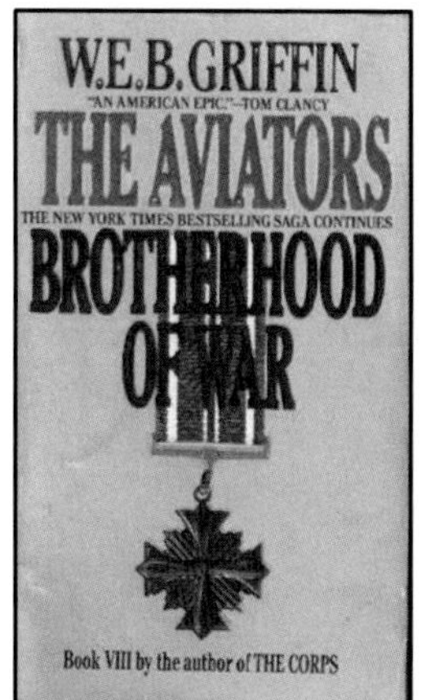

The Aviators

Vietnam, Aviation

W.E.B. Griffin G. P. Putnam (1988)

1964. The Vietnam War has begun to escalate, its new style of battle demanding new weapons and tactics and men who can use them.

Overnight, it seems, the U. S. Army must scramble to create its first-ever Air Assault Division, a force critical to its chances of success, but the obstacles facing it are staggering—untrained men, mysteriously failing aircraft, vicious inter-service rivalries. As the hostilities increase, the warriors and the women who love them are swept into the struggle, their personal and professional lives twisting and intertwining as they race against time—and the fortunes of war... [BC]

"The eighth volume of Griffin's "Brotherhood of War" series is a detailed and absorbing view of military life and military men that readers will find fascinating. Protagonist Johnny Oliver is a born soldier who distinguishes himself as a helicopter pilot in Vietnam and is promoted to aide-de-camp to the commanding officer of Fort Rucker. In his new post, he finds himself directly involved with the development of the Army's first Air Assault Division a new force crucial to meet the challenge of guerrilla warfare in Vietnam. This is the story of Johnny's year of work and crisis, the making and breaking of rules, the development of friendships, and the awakening of love." [11-09]

William Edmund Butterworth III (1929–2019), better known by his pen name **W. E. B. Griffin**, was an American writer of military and detective fiction. See the "West Point Legacies" chapter for a more complete bio and other novels in this series.

Beyond the Wars

The Lotus Redemption

Aviation, Vietnam, Romance, WP Author

W. Darrell Gertsch iUniverse, Inc. (2007)

After Frank Gerard graduates from the United States Military Academy at West Point, he's commissioned in the U.S. Air Force and becomes a B-52 pilot. For many months of his eight years in service, he flies bombing missions during the Vietnam War from his bases in Guam and Thailand. Years later, he is an internationally renowned energy consultant, but he wants more than anything to return to Southeast Asia and revisit the landmarks of his past.

One of Frank's colleagues introduces him long distance to Le Chi, a woman from North Vietnam whose own family was involved in the decades of resistance and war with the French, the Japanese, and the Americans. She agrees to set an itinerary and accompany Frank to visit some of the most horrendous battle sites in Vietnam.

Leaving his wife and children behind, Frank begins a fantastic three-week odyssey with Le Chi. Together, they develop an understanding of each other's perspectives on the many years of war in Vietnam. But when a powerful bond emerges between them, Frank encounters difficult contradictions between exotic romance and his own traditional values. [BC]

W. Darrell Gertsch was commissioned in the U.S. Air Force upon graduation from West Point in 1971. He earned his doctoral degree from the University of Washington then enjoyed a successful business career, also serving on the staffs at Los Alamos Laboratory, Georgia Tech, and the University of Oklahoma. [11-10]

Hurricane Alley

Aviation, Drug War, WP Author

Richard H. Dickinson Berkley Publishing Group (1990)

They are America's most daring peacetime flyers - the brave men who defy nature's fury, flying through vast hurricane walls collecting vital meteorological data. When John Ludlow of the Weather Reconnaissance Squadron falls in love with Michelle Parkes, a high-class hooker who wants to go straight, drug smugglers hatch a plot to use the relationship as a means to employ the Squadron's planes for their own purposes. [BC]

Richard H. Dickinson (1951–) West Point 1973, was commissioned into the U.S. Airforce, spending 12 years as a hurricane hunter and air traffic controller. He has written several military thrillers which appear elsewhere in this book. See "In the Far East" and the "Cold War & Global War on Terrorism" chapters. [11-11]

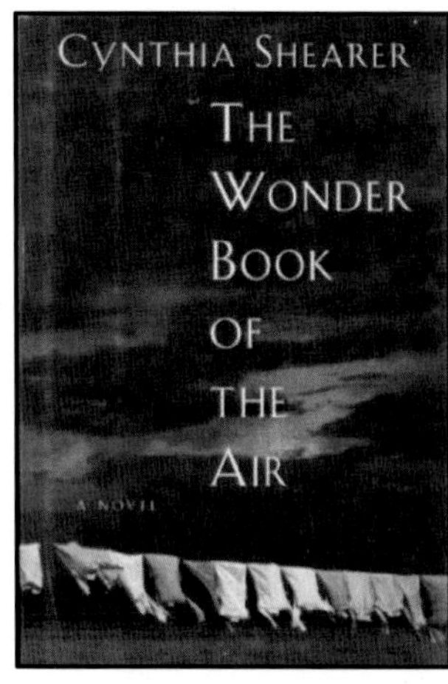

The Wonder Book of Air: A Novel

Aviation, Cold War

Cynthia Shearer   Pantheon (1996)

The Wonder Book of the Air leads us through the lives of three generations in a Southern family.

At the center is Harrison Durrance, West Point graduate, who learns early that the nature of love is both transaction and transgression. As a young man he comes into his own during World War II, where he falls for the magic of flight and thrives on the danger of battle. He has become a man of undeniable magnetism, brash and vigorously optimistic. But when the war is over, and he is back on the ground—in cold-war America—Harrison loses his bearings and catapults out of orbit. As his notions of the world begin to fail him and the people he claims to love fail to understand him, he sabotages his career, drinks to excess, and drives his family into emotional bedlam. [DJ]

Cynthia Shearer (1955–) was born in Chicopee, Massachusetts, the daughter of a West Point-trained Air Force officer. Her father, Irvine Harrison Shearer, was an alcoholic, so her parents divorced when she was three. Shearer describes herself as a loner who "worked at not fitting in." She has pursued a career as an author and teaching writing at the college level. [11-12]

Chapter 12

Army Medical Service Corps

The Army Medical Service Corp, critical as it is to the well-being of our warriors and their families, is scarcely mentioned in fiction. Works relating directly to West Pointers are almost non-existent. One reason may be that less than two percent of graduates branch to the medical service. That's hardly a large enough cohort to generate a shelf of novels.

There are numerous memoirs from nurses and doctors who served from the Civil War through the World Wars, Korea, Vietnam, and Iraq. Well worth reading to gain perspective on their essential contributions to sustaining our Army in wartime, but this chapter focuses on fictional accounts. Since there are few direct references to West Pointers, I decided to relax the criteria and include a range of fiction about Army medical personnel.

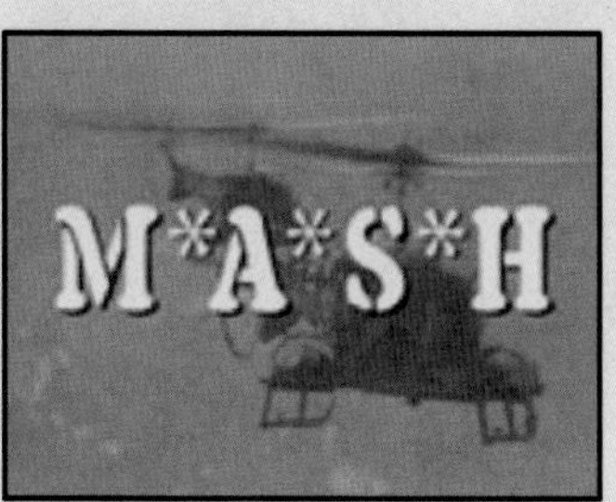

Of course, there were two popular Army medical series on network TV: **MASH** (1972–1983) and **China Beach** (1988–1991), the former being more comedic featuring surgeons in the Korean War, while the latter more dramatic about nursing in Vietnam. Both are available on DVD.

Nursing

"Nurses Are Needed Now," the posters proclaimed. "Join the Army Nurse Corps." And so they did. Over 59,000 American women signed up to serve their country in the war effort. Some joined expecting to experience the romance and adventure of war in faraway places while working to save lives. Many more quickly learned war's harsh realities -- and that their own lives could also be in danger. The Army nurses of World War II served in the United States and abroad, in dense jungles, war-torn villages, and on barren ice fields. Many encountered hardships: bombings, crude living conditions, inadequate food. They also experienced the frustration of receiving lesser pay and privileges than their male counterparts as they worked, sometimes around the clock, to treat the wounded while confronting air raids, the threat of invasion, and capture by the enemy. Nonetheless, in addition to their devotion to saving lives, some of the most important things the nurses brought to their units were courage and cheer. From holiday parties in makeshift hospitals to fudge making and softball games amid the grueling conditions of war, these angels of mercy brought light -- and life -- to the American forces of World War II.

From the Introduction to *Army Nurses of World War II* by Betsy Kuhn
Aladdin Paperbacks, 1999.

In support of this plea to American youth, Helen Wells devoted four novels in her Cherry Ames nursing series to encourage young women to join the Army Nurse Corps.

Cherry Ames, Army Nurse

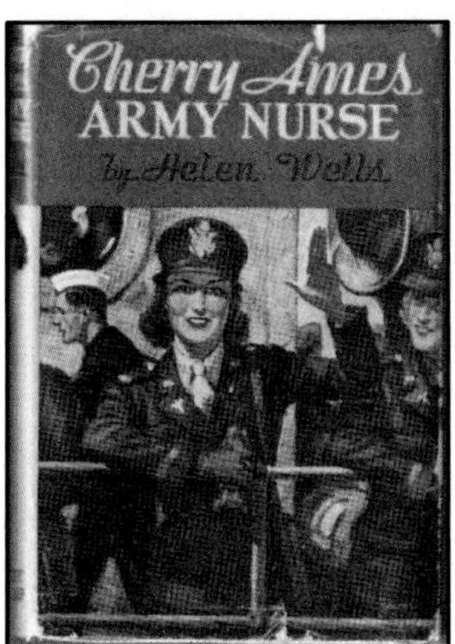

Medical, WW2, Youth

Helen Wells Grosset & Dunlap (1944)

Here is a fascinating, inspiring picture of the Army Nurse Corps, and a thrilling story about a brave, lovable girl. Cherry Ames responds with unhesitating loyalty to the Army's call for nurses. With her pals, Ann, Gwen and Vivian, young Dr. Lex Upham, who is romantically interested in the pretty young nurse, and her old friend Dr. Fortune, Cherry goes to a large Army post. Here she submits to the military discipline and training which are required of every Army Nurse. How she capably manages a ward of mischievous young soldiers; tries to reform Bunce, her irrepressible assistant; and, with her fellow nurses, carries on a lively feud with "Lovey," the tough sergeant, who regards all women in the Army as intruders, nuisances, and nitwits, is only the beginning of her Army adventures.

Sailing under sealed orders, Cherry finds herself in an exotic foreign port. She stumbles into a fantastic house and into a mystery which has far-reaching results. How Cherry recognizes and meets a strange danger — and how a great medical victory is achieved through her courage, alertness and initiative — make absorbing and exciting reading. [DJ]

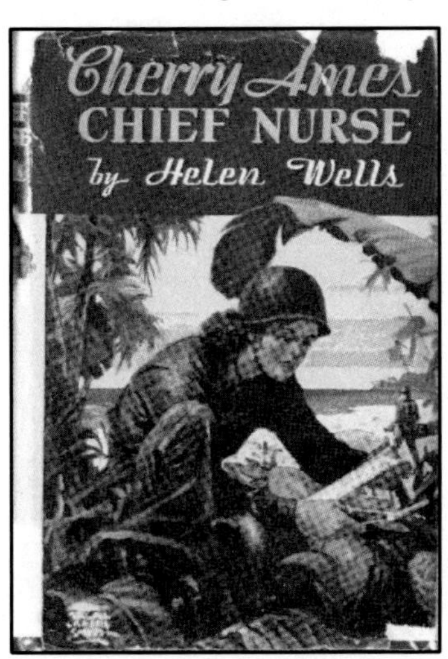

Cherry Ames, Chief Nurse

Medical, WW2, Youth

Helen Wells Grosset & Dunlap (1944)

When Cherry Ames boards the bomber which is to take her to the South Pacific to deliver Dr. Fortune's new serum for tropical fever to his research colleagues at Port Janeway, she knows that a new assignment awaits her. She expects a promotion to First Lieutenant, but never dreams that the added distinction of Chief Nurse is to be hers. Incurably adventurous and brave as she is, Cherry is proud but apprehensive when she finds herself in charge of Spencer Hospital's unit of Army Nurses.

Working under the most difficult conditions to set up an evacuation hospital in the jungle, under constant threat of enemy attack, Cherry and her nurses find their lot one of hard, grueling toil that requires all of their resourcefulness and courage.

To add to Cherry's problems, the Commanding Officer feels that she is too young and pretty for such a great responsibility. But when her brother Charles arrives at the secret air base on Island 14 in an Army transport plane, bringing with him a strangely wounded flier, she is confronted with an even more complicated problem to solve: to get the silent flier to speak again, and to trace the mysterious enemy weapon that injured him. What happens when she uncovers the truth, and a desperate emergency arises, make an unforgettable story of a heroic girl at the battlefront. [DJ]

Cherry Ames, Flight Nurse

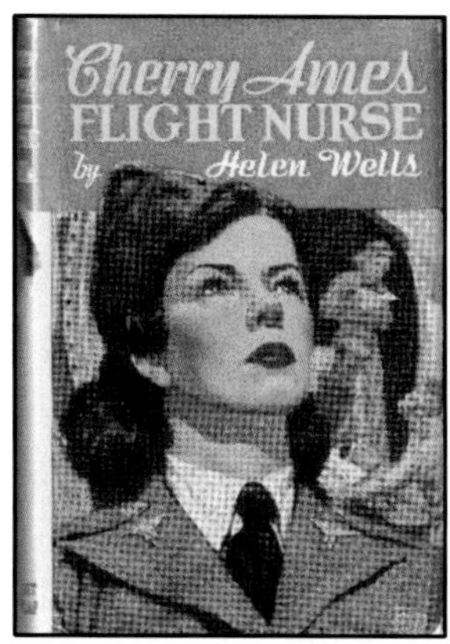

Medical, WW2, Youth

Helen Wells Grosset & Dunlap (1945)

This is the fifth book in the Cherry Ames nursing series published during World War II to encourage young women to enter nursing. After returning from the war zone in the South Pacific, Cherry and her friends are accepted as Army Air Force flight nurses. Upon graduation they are sent to England, where they evacuate wounded soldiers from European battlefields, sometimes under fire themselves. The story has a mystery about a guy that could be a spy or he could just be a loving father, which Cherry puzzles over. She gets a taste of aerial combat while flying wounded soldiers from the Continent back to hospitals in England. [DJ]

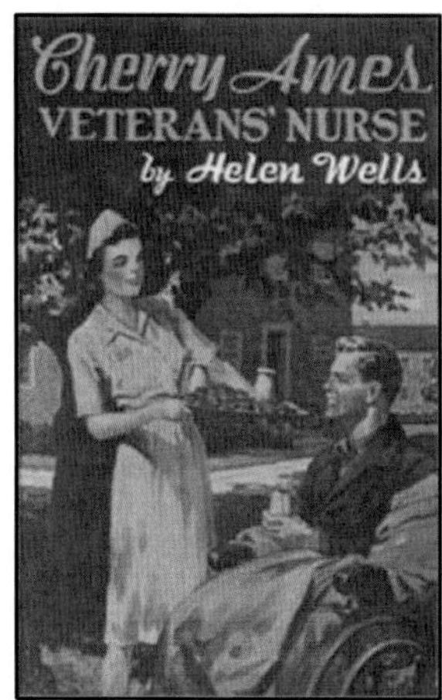

Cherry Ames, Veterans' Nurse

Medical, WW2, Youth

Helen Wells Grosset & Dunlap (1946)

The war is over, and Cherry is sent home. Her new assignment is working in a veteran's hospital, where she finds her biggest challenge in raising the spirits of men who have lost arms, legs, or other body parts. Will they be welcomed back to their families and able to work again?

Jim Travers, the woodworker who has lost a leg and was the sole support of his elderly mother, isn't convinced. But he finds he is of critical assistance to Cherry as she tracks the mysterious thief who has robbed the Veteran's Center of a medicine that can help a small boy recover from a deadly disease. [DJ]

Helen Weinstock (1910–1986) was a social worker turned full-time young adult writer. Writing as **Helen Wells,** she authored twenty-seven Cherry Ames, Nurse books and sixteen Vicki Barr, Flight Stewardess books. In 1934 she graduated from New York University where she'd been the first female editor of the literary quarterly. During World War II, she served as a volunteer with the State Department's Office of the Coordinator of Inter-American Affairs, escorting Latin American visitors. [12-01]

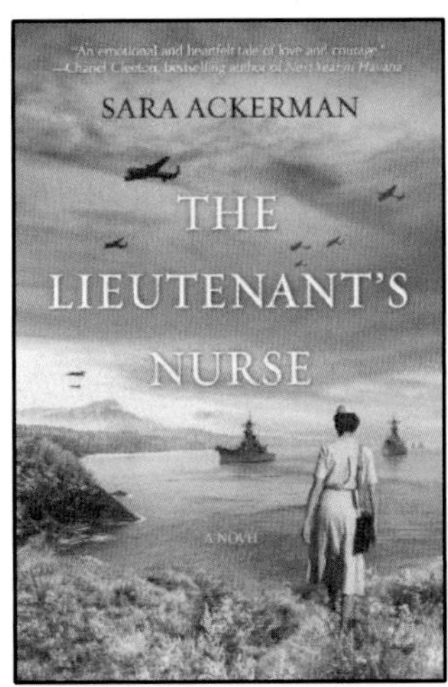

The Lieutenant's Nurse

Medical, WW2, Romance

Sara Ackerman Mira Books (2019)

It is November 1941:

She's never even seen the ocean before, but Eva Cassidy has her reasons for making the crossing to Hawaii, and they run a lot deeper than escaping a harsh Michigan winter. Newly enlisted as an Army Corps nurse, Eva is stunned by the splendor she experiences aboard the steamship SS Lurline; even more so by Lt. Clark Spencer, a man she is drawn to but who clearly has secrets of his own. But Eva's past—and the future she's trying to create—means that she's not free to follow her heart. Clark is a navy intelligence officer, and he warns her that the United States won't be able to hold off joining the war for long, but nothing can prepare them for the surprise attack that will change the world they know.

In the wake of the bombing of Pearl Harbor, Eva and her fellow nurses band together for the immense duty of keeping the American wounded alive. And the danger that finds Eva threatens everything she holds dear. Amid the chaos and heartbreak, Eva will have to decide whom to trust and how far she will go to protect those she loves. Set in the vibrant tropical surroundings of the Pacific, *The Lieutenant's Nurse* is an evocative, emotional WWII story of love, friendship and the resilient spirit of the heroic nurses of Pearl Harbor. [BC]

Sara Ackerman was born and raised in Hawaii. She studied journalism and later earned graduate degrees in psychology and Chinese medicine. To date she has written four novels about World War II in Hawaii. [12-02]

The Girls of Pearl Harbor

Medical, WW2

Soraya M. Lane Lake Union Publishing (2019)

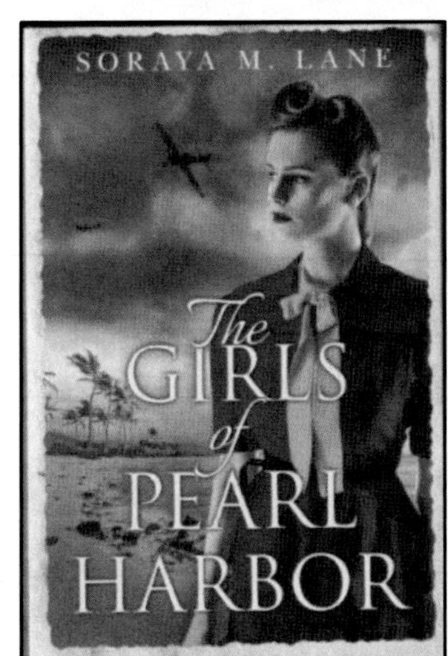

This is a tale of four brave young nurses whose lives change forever in the wake of the 1941 attack on Pearl Harbor.

When Grace, April, and Poppy join the US Army Nurse Corps, they see it as little more than an adventure, one made all the better by their first station: Pearl Harbor, Hawaii. Joined at the hip, idealistic Grace, exuberant Poppy, and brave but haunted April frolic in the sun, attending parties, flirting with the handsome soldiers, and becoming fast friends with seasoned nurse Eva. Like the Hawaiian sun, their future seems warm and bright—until the infamous morning of December 7th.

Within just a few horrifying hours, their sparkling hopes turn to black rubble and ash. Now embroiled in a war they never could have imagined; they must decide what truly matters to them and face grief as they never have before. Death may await them but so do hope and purpose. In the midst of the carnage, can they find happiness and learn to fight not just for their country's honor but for themselves? [BC]

Soraya Lane lives with her family on a small farm in New Zealand, surrounded by animals and with an office overlooking a field where their horses graze. Soraya's historical women's fiction novels are released under the name Soraya M. Lane. [12-03]

West Point Nurse

Romance, Medical, Cadet

Virginia B. McDonnell R.N. McFadden (1965)

ONE LAST DANCE . . .

"You have it all wrong," Cadet Bob Thompson told Nurse Sandy as they danced at the West Point hop. "I have no intention of leaving the Army—ever!"

"But ever since you were a little boy, your father has hoped you would practice medicine with him," Sandy protested.

The last dance was over! Had she turned Bob against her? Would she ever see him again? She knew she was in love with the headstrong cadet, the son of the man she had promised to marry. [BC]

Virginia B. McDonnell (1917–1998) was a graduate of the Samaritan Hospital School of Nursing and attended Russell Sage College, both in Troy, N.Y. She was a medical journalist and author of many books of both fiction and non-fiction that included nurses as characters. Playing no favorites, she also wrote stories about an *Annapolis Nurse* and an *Aerospace Nurse*. McDonnell and her husband were avid skiers so many of her books featured details of skiing as well as nursing. [12-04]

Doctors

While there is not a large body of fiction on Army nursing, there are even fewer fictional accounts of West Point physicians. Because so few doctors graduate from West Point, the "West Pointer" criteria for inclusion has been relaxed for this section. The first entry here involves two officers – one Yankee, one Rebel – and a civilian doctor in the Civil War. The second entry – actually a memoir – might be more appropriate in the "Army Life & Army Wives" chapter, but it is about a West Point physician and his family in the 19th century. The chapter concludes with five very different medical novels: World War II, Korea, a drama, a satire, and a "whodunit."

"River Risin'"

Medical, Civil War, Pulp Fiction

Richard Sale Argosy Weekly (October 21, 1939)

The veterinarian's formula for peace included a Confederate flag, a Union jacket, a newborn black child, and a seasoning of thunder.

THAT terrible spring the cannon in northern Virginia pounded and pounded. Down in Junesburg you could hear the voice of the fire, and the shudder of the tortured earth at the repercussion. And in April, when the rains came, they could not tell the thunder from the cannon. The heavens crashed and the earth crashed. The rain poured down across the clay of Virginia; the earth was so fed with water and blood, it was hard to say which there was more of. It was a battle—a steady, grim, relentless battle; and the men in tired gray were slowly falling back. By day they came through Junesberg, heading for Richmond, the casualties looking sad, numb and ghastly. Dr. Juniper knew there was a great battle going on. It had been going on for some time, and there was every likelihood that it would continue.

When he told his story, in the years that followed, Dr. Juniper never quite understood how it had happened in such an atmosphere of hate, such a miasma of death. It was a small miracle. Two weeks later the war ended. [EB]

Richard Sale (1911–1993) was an American screenwriter, pulp fiction author, and film director. He wrote 40 screenplays, numerous pulp fiction stories, and directed 14 films. Another of his stories appears in "The Civil War" chapter of this book. [12-05]

Blame the Dead

WW2, Crime, WP Author

Ed Ruggero Forge Publishing (2020)

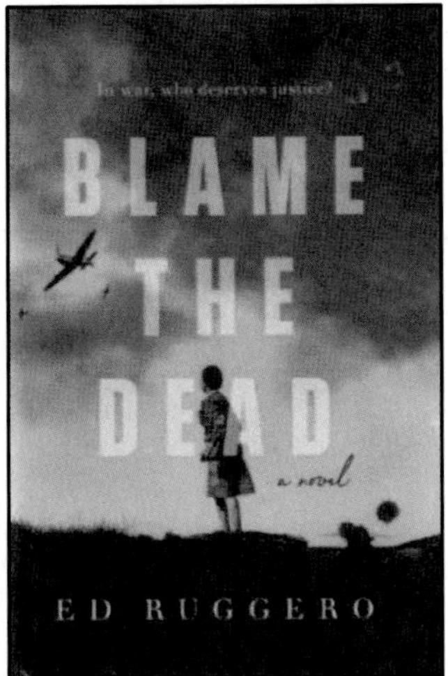

Sicily, 1945. Eddie Harkins, former Philadelphia beat cop turned military police lieutenant, reluctantly finds himself at the scene of a murder at the U.S. Army's 11th Field Hospital. There the nurses contend with heat, dirt, shorthanded staff, the threat of German counterattack, an ever present flood of horribly wounded Gls, and the threat of assault by one of their own - at least until someone shoots Dr. Meyers Stephenson in the head.

With help from nurse Kathleen Donnelly, once a childhood friend and now perhaps something more, it soon becomes clear to Harkins that the unit is rotten to its core. As the battle lines push forward, Harkins is running out of time to find the killer before he can strike again. [DJ]

Ed Ruggero, West Point class of 1980, has several works in this catalog including *Comes the War,* a sequel to this novel, in "The World Wars" chapter.

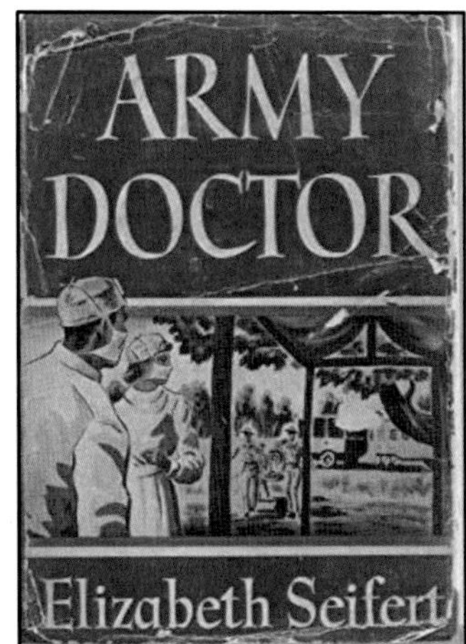

Army Doctor

Medical, WW2

Elizabeth Seifert Grosset & Dunlap (1942)

From NY Times Review of Books, March 8, 1942

"Paul Saunders is a young man of 29 snatched by the draft from a promising career as a surgeon and plumped into the Medical Corps at a raw new Army camp where he feels very much a square peg altogether disinclined to try to fit into the round Army niche. Except for his unusual gift as a surgeon, Paul Saunders's case has the appeal of being a fairly common one. He hates war, he dislikes regimentation, and Army red tape and antiquated regulations make him furious with his new life. He has radical ideas about how the world should be run and talks a great deal about them. He feels that being a good doctor is far more important than being a good officer.

The author's problem is to iron out the kinks in young Saunders. On the negative side there is his commanding officer, an elderly major whose medical and military knowledge bare the outdated stamp of the First World War. For a helpful influence there is a friendly captain who understands Saunders's discontent but tries to make him see that discipline is necessary for the salvation of the country.

As for romance, Captain Gregg's wife is a blonde siren full of "subversive ideas" who takes a flattering fancy to young Saunders. Her rival is pretty, young Kitty, the major's daughter, who likes Saunders but flies into red-headed rages at his callow ideas and unsoldierly conduct. The young doctor is sympathetically pictured as a talented but brash type who needs only proper guidance to develop into a soundly patriotic citizen.

Army Doctor gives a realistic picture of the issue confronting new citizen soldiers, men and officers. The dangers of camp boredom, town temptations, disease, and radical agitation are discussed as they arise in this particular camp." [DJ]

Elizabeth Seifert (1897–1983) wrote more than 80 novels. She had wanted to study medicine but was thwarted by poor health and family disapproval. She did manage to study physiology and anatomy and after graduating from Washington University, she became a clinical secretary in a hospital. A self-described "wife, housewife, and mother who writes," Seifert began a new career at age forty when *Young Doctor Galahad* won the 1938 Dodd, Mead-Redbook Magazine $10,000 prize for a first novel. Almost all Seifert's novels are medical romances. [12-06]

Surgeon U.S.A.

Medical, WW2

Frank D. Slaughter Doubleday (1966)

In his hands the doctor held a small reel of tape from a recording machine. It contained all the evidence necessary to smash the career of the wounded man lying a few doors away on the hospital ship. Nobody had ever guessed the truth about Hal Reardon, the Congressman from Florida. Hal Reardon hardly knew it himself. And yet, here it was, the truth—and a man's fate as well-right between the doctor's hands. Should he use it? Should he destroy it? Was Congressman Reardon a force for good or evil? These were difficult questions for a young surgeon to ask, quite unlike any he had ever faced before. And yet, the answers to them were to become as important to the career of Dr. Bruce Graham as any decision he would make in the operating room.

This is the story of a war behind World War II, a very private war between two public people. The conflict, as old as time, opposes the man of principle to the man who has none. War holds surprises for all men. Bruce Graham's greatest surprise, when he volunteered for active duty with the Army, was to find himself in a battle against corruption more killing, in its way, than the bullets he would later encounter at the front lines. Entanglement with a handsome, unscrupulous politician, with a Congressional Committee, where his loyalty is impugned, and with two beautiful women, were only some of his troubles. Entanglement with his conscience was constant, until, in a great victorious surge, his conscience goaded him into inevitable, unavoidable action. [DJ]

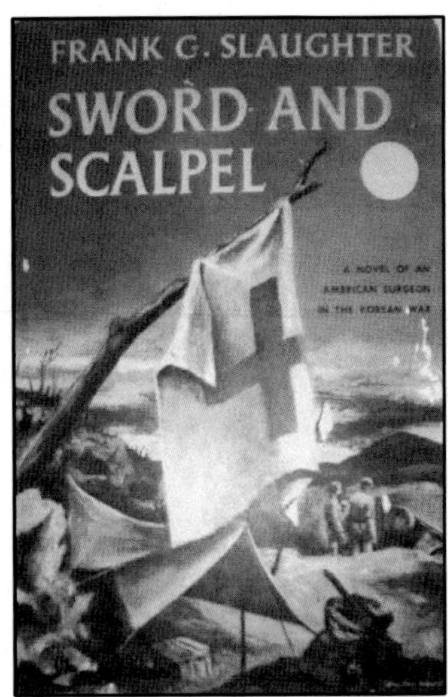

Sword and Scalpel

Medical, Korea

Frank G. Slaughter Doubleday & Co. (19570

SWORD AND SCALPEL is the story of Dr. Paul Scott, a Johns Hopkins-trained surgeon who is taken prisoner by the North Koreans when they overrun his frontline MASH unit at the outset of the Korean War. Dr. Scott is imprisoned in Pyongyang along with his commanding officer Colonel Jasper Hardin, Kay Storey a famous entertainer known as "The Girl Next Door," and the unit chaplain, affectionately known as Father Tim. While imprisoned, the Americans are subjected to torture, sensory deprivation, brainwashing, starvation, and all forms of physical and mental abuse. The frail Father Tim becomes deathly ill and Kay Storey is threatened with ongoing sexual abuse. In order to spare his friends from death, Dr. Scott chooses to sign a spurious war crimes confession. After they are repatriated, Colonel Hardin has Dr. Scott court-martialed. The news report said:

> *Tomorrow, in San Francisco's Presidio Captain Paul Scot! of the Army Medical Corps fresh from two years in a Chinese prisoner-of-war camp, faces court-martial for treason . . .* [DJ]

Frank G. Slaughter (1908 – 2001), pseudonym C.V. Terry, was an American novelist and physician whose books sold more than 60 million copies. His novels drew on his own experience as a doctor and his interest in history and the Bible. Through his novels, he often introduced readers to new findings in medical research and new medical technologies. He began writing fiction in 1935 while a physician at Riverside Hospital in Jacksonville, Florida. [12-07]

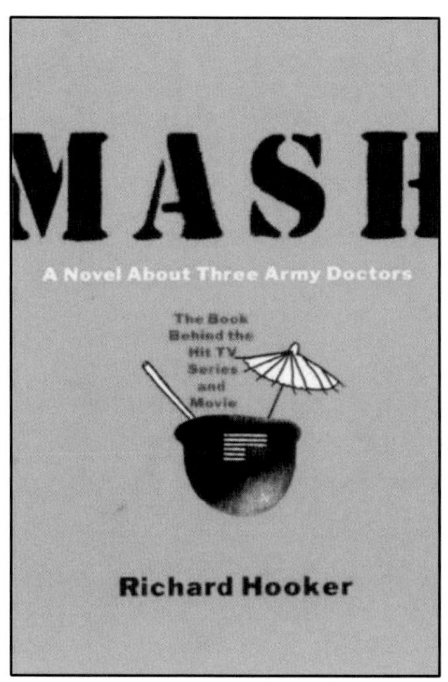

*M*A*S*H*

Medical, Korea

Richard Hooker William Morrow & Company (1968)

The heroes of M*A*S*H, Captains Hawkeye Pierce, Duke Forrest and Trapper John McIntyre, have two things in common: they are the best surgeons in the Far East Command, and they are certified lunatics. Their certification as hell-raising nuts is made by the army bureaucracy, which the three heroes turn into bedlam, by those doctors and chaplains who show more talent for witchery than surgery or godliness and by Major Hot-Lips Houlihan, the pompous Chief Nurse at the 4077th Mobile Army Surgical Hospital (M*A*S*H).

At M*A*S*H the boys in a playful fashion terrorize Shaking Sammy, the forgetful Protestant chaplain who writes all-is-well letters to the families of mortally wounded G.I.'s. And they send a stoned, bearded Trapper John aloft, where he hangs from a helicopter posing as Jesus, while they sell genuine photos of the Savior to the boggle-eyed troops below.

Underlying the ribald, irreverent humor is a serious theme—how men of war survive the waste of war and how in the midst of destruction they strive to maintain their humanity. The pseudonymous Richard Hooker tells a wildly funny story that never loses sight of the dedication and purpose of three very human doctors and the wounded G.I.'s who are brought to them. [DJ]

H. Richard Hornberger (1924–1997) was an American writer and surgeon, born in Trenton, New Jersey, who wrote under the pseudonym Richard Hooker. A graduate of Cornell Medical School he became a physician for the U.S. Army during the Korean War. He used his experience at the 8055th Mobile Army Surgical Hospital as background for this work. [12-06]

This book is the basis of a popular movie and a long running television series. While there is no specific West Point connection, it is about Army doctors working with wounded soldiers during the Korean War. [12-08]

West Point's Sentinel Event

Mystery, Medical

Jules M. Seletz   Denlingers Publishing (2002)

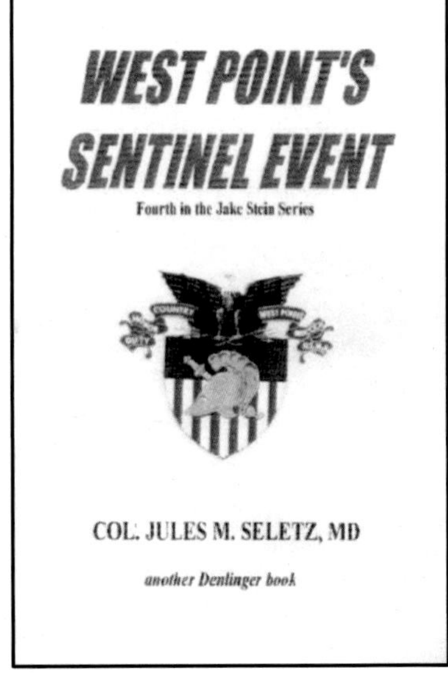

West Point's Sentinel Event is the fourth in a series of mystery/ medical thrillers that deal with untoward incidents, mishaps and catastrophic outcomes known as sentinel events that in reality turn out to be nefarious deeds perpetrated by people from different walks of life. The first of the Jake Stein Series, *Sentinel Event*, introduced Jacob M. Stein, MD, a resident of New Hampshire, who is a physician surveyor for the Joint Commission on Accreditation of Healthcare Organizations.

... Now, in the fourth of the series, while Jake is at West Point—the United States Military Academy (USMA) in New York State—he is once again challenged, this time to determine the cause of a senior cadet's unanticipated and inexplicable death in an Intensive Care Unit of a large Medical Center close to the USMA.

Jake combines forces with Josh Taylor, a local agent for ClD—Criminal Investigation Division—linked with a Company of Military Police under the Provost Marshal's command. As Jake comes close to uncovering the who, the how and the why of the cadet's death, his life is threatened. When about to be killed, Jake uses his wits to manage a miraculous and unbelievable escape.

After he eludes certain death, Jake, with his wife, Rhoda, enjoys a pleasant evening with the senior leadership of the Corps of Cadets whom Jake has befriended during his investigation. Jake and Rhoda leave the cadets to return to their hotel room, but they never make it there.

To the delight of the Superintendent and Commandant of USMA, and the bewilderment of a United States Senator visiting West Point on a fact-finding mission, the Corps of Cadets volunteer to undertake an extraordinary, unprecedented rescue mission that includes the apprehension of the criminals. [BC]

Jules M. Seletz (1930–2012) graduated from the Virginia Military Institute in 1953 and the Chicago Medical School in 1958. He enjoyed a 41-year military career in the United States Army, rising to the rank of colonel after serving as a second lieutenant in the field artillery during the Korean conflict. After retiring from the Army in 1994 while stationed at West Point, Dr. Seletz served for the next seven years as a physician surveyor for JCAHO, the Joint Commission on Accreditation of Healthcare Organizations. [12-09]

Chapter 13
The Revolution, War of 1812 & Sylvanus Thayer

The Revolutionary War

A military post at West Point was originally established in 1775 to occupy the strategic high ground overlooking the Hudson River fifty miles north of New York City. It played a critical role in the defense of the colonies during the Revolutionary War (1775–1783).

After the Continental army was disbanded in 1783, West Point served as an artillery training school. The military academy was founded at West Point in 1802 under the administration of President Thomas Jefferson. He was convinced by others that the fledgling United States of America should establish a formal school to educate engineers and artillerists. These vital military skills could not be quickly mastered by an army entirely composed of civilian volunteers.

The Academy's early years were characterized by leadership and academic disarray. Still, a few of its early graduates distinguished themselves in the War of 1812 and the exploration of these lands of the Louisiana Purchase and beyond.

Initially this chapter describes novels that cover the Revolutionary War, particularly the events surrounding the betrayal by Benedict Arnold. The second part of this chapter covers the War of 1812. The chapter concludes with several works about the tenure of Sylvanus Thayer as Superintendent at the Academy.

The Perilous Night

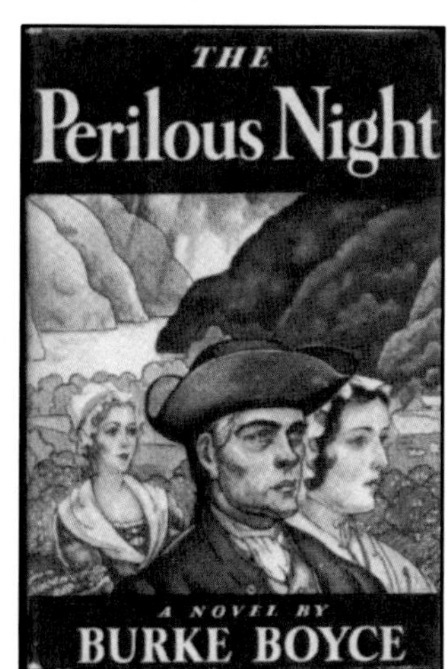

Revolution, Hudson Highlands

Burke Boyce The Viking Press (1942)

Burke Boyce lives today in the fat farming region just back of the Hudson River's Highlands. Just across the valley was West Point.

Living in country so saturated with history, Mr. Boyce began to wonder what the well-to-do farmers who preceded him on his acres did when the storm of freedom enveloped them—how they continued to care for their fields, how they responded to the alarms and rumors that sped up the river from New York and down the river from Lake Champlain. He consulted the records, still to be found in the district, explored the rolling countryside, collected household effects of the period, imagined his neighbors in the colonial setting, and the story, his first novel, began to take form.

On both sides of his family Mr. Boyce counts ancestors who took part in the Revolution—but one branch was for Washington and the other for King George. So he comes naturally by his sympathetic interest in the conflict of convictions that grew deeper and more irreconcilable as the war increased in fury. That struggle of conscience provides one of the dramatic threads of this story.

The other thread is formed of the personal lives Mr. Boyce has created. To the rumbling thunder of revolution, these people worked out their personal ambitions, knew the lure of wealth and the power of sudden love. The Americans in The Perilous Night, and particularly the father, sons, and daughters of one family, fight their private battles along with the more famous battles that have come down to us in the history books. [DJ]

Burke Boyce (1901–1969) graduated from Harvard 1922. He captained the fencing team his senior year and participated in the 1924 Olympics. Burke later became a professor of English at Harvard. He wrote several historical novels and numerous short stories and poems for *The New Yorker* magazine. [13-01]

Treason at the Point

Revolution, Hudson Highlands

J.C. Nolan Julian Messner (1944)

Thunder in the highlands; horses' hooves clanging on the cobblestones; strange men moving warily through the night carrying strange cargo; the tramp, tramp of weary feet as General Washington's troops make their way to West Point—and underneath a current of restlessness, a foreboding of evil, a nervous tension that none can explain. It is the year 1780. Benedict Arnold has been appointed commandant at West Point and his family comes to live at the Robinson House, center of military activity in the Hudson River Valley country.

This is the story of Jed Drake, a courier for General Washington; his sister Emmiline, who works as serving maid in the Arnold household, and their young brother Kirby, who wishes he were older so that he too could fight in the war. Through no desire of their own, the Drakes become involved in a series of swift-moving, mysterious events that lead to the exposure of Benedict Arnold and his attempted betrayal of West Point, and the capture of Major John André, British spy.

Most of the action takes place in the Hudson River Valley country and at the Robinson House, Arnold's official residence at West Point. Molly Pitcher, George Washington, Alexander Hamilton, Lafayette and many other famous characters from history are woven into this story of Arnold's treachery. [DJ]

Jean Covert Nolan (1896–1974) was a native of Evansville, Indiana and graduated from Indiana University. Initially working as a local news reporter, she wrote over forty-five children's books including biographies, essays, and historical non-fiction. In 1968, Ms. Nolan was added to the Indiana University Writers' Conference Hall of Fame. [13-02]

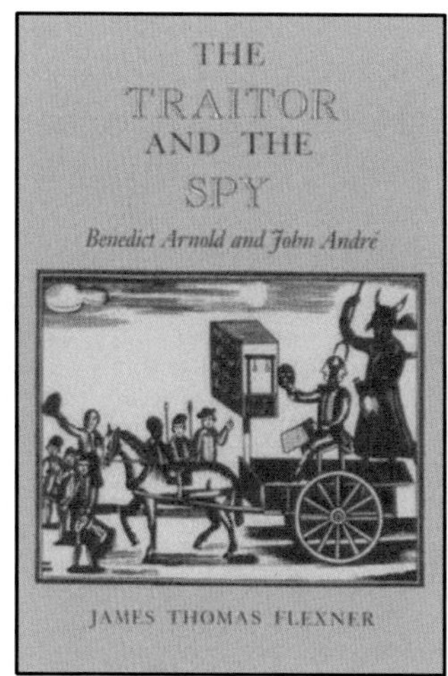

The Traitor and the Spy: Benedict Arnold and John André

Revolution

James Flexner Harcourt, Brace (1953)

The lives of Benedict Arnold, Peggy Shippen, and John André are of peculiar significance for our time. Their story, in which the elements of heroism and greed, loyalty and ambition, passion and frivolity, are combined, culminated in the classic treason of American history.

Mr. Flexner has presented the facts of these three lives in a graphic and powerful style. Shorn of obscuring legend, the conspirators emerge from his pages as from life, colorful and real. We are shown the tragic figure of Arnold, the greatest combat general of the Revolution, impelled by his darker nature to betray the cause he had so courageously served. His lovely wife Peggy emerges as a key figure in the communications between the traitor and the spy; in her tempestuous girlhood she had carried on lively flirtations with the British officers-including Andre—quartered in Philadelphia. And Andre himself, the sensitive young man, is revealed in later life as an officer so ruthless he urged that captured American soldiers be tried for treason and hanged; when taken himself, he died so bravely he was mourned on two continents. [DJ]

James Thomas Flexner (1908–2003) was a prolific and graceful writer of 26 books on subjects from American art to steamboats to medicine, who achieved his greatest fame for his four-volume biography of Washington, winning both the National Book Award and a special Pulitzer citation for the final volume. 13-03

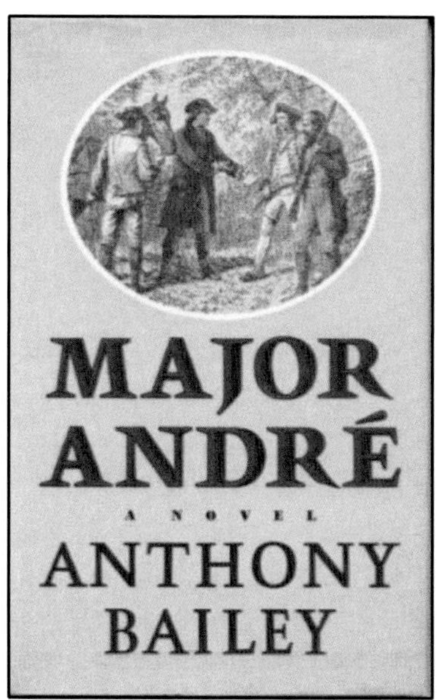

Major André

Revolution

Anthony Bailey Farrar, Straus & Giroux (1987)

A day in the last week of September 1780: a young English officer sits in a room of a small stone house in the village of Tappan, New York, where the Continental Army under General Washington is encamped. The young man is reflecting on the events of the last few days. His name is John André, and he is the acting Adjutant-General of the British Army in New York. His captors, to whom he talks amicably now and then, have until recently believed that he was a merchant named John Anderson. Is he or is he not a spy? Should he or should he not be hanged?

The conspiracy in which General Benedict Arnold planned to surrender West Point to the British is regarded not only as a crucial moment in the Revolutionary War but as a maneuver that—had it gone the other Way—could well have changed the course of the war, and subsequent history. Anthony Bailey looks at this episode from the point of view of a leading participant, the charming and talented professional military man, amateur actor, and poet who abruptly finds himself in highly charged and then tragic circumstances, and who is compelled in the end by his code of conduct to rise above his own shortcomings. An individual, rather than a historical figure, is movingly and dramatically evoked. [DJ]

Anthony Bailey (1933–2020) was a British art historian and author of 23 books. In 1955, he emigrated to New York City and became a staff writer at *The New Yorker* magazine for over 30 years. [13-04]

Dark Eagle: A Novel of Benedict Arnold and the American Revolution

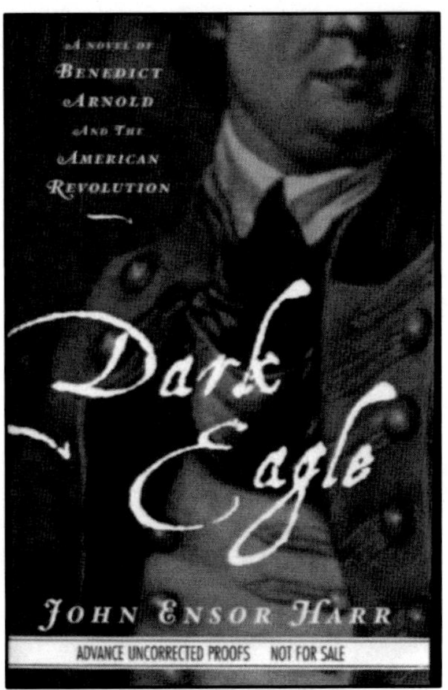

Revolution

John Ensor Harr Viking Adult (1999)

The Indians called him "Dark Eagle" out of respect for both his military genius and his ruthlessness. His men worshiped him as a hero—the legendary general of the Continental army who led them against formidable British forces. But as he neared the pinnacle of success, things began to go wrong, drawing Benedict Arnold inexorably toward the greatest crime of the age, one that would forever make his name synonymous with the word "traitor." Dark Eagle encompasses the action on both sides of the Revolutionary War from 1775 to 1780. John Ensor Harr traces Arnold's spectacular rise—outwitting the British at Valcour Bay; the relief of Fort Stanwix; and a stunning victory at Saratoga, the turning point of the war. He also traces Arnold's decline—a wound that nearly cost his life; harassment by the radical government of Pennsylvania; his sense of betrayal by Congress and his Commander-in-Chief, George Washington, and finally the treasonous triangle with his new wife, Peggy Shippen, the beautiful daughter of a prominent Philadelphia family, and Major John André, the Englishman she loved.

From the glory of Arnold's early days on the battlefield to the wrath he incurred as he attempted to deliver West Point and three thousand American troops into the hand of the British, Dark Eagle is the extraordinary story of one of the most complex, tragic heroes in history. [DJ]

Jonathan Ensor Harr (1926–2004) was an American writer and historian. Dr. Harr earned his doctorate in political science and public administration at the University of California at Berkeley; his master's degree at The University of Chicago; and his bachelor's degree at Beloit (Wisconsin) College. From 1983 to 1993, Dr. Harr was vice president of ABC television for special projects. [13-05]

The Exquisite Siren: The Romance of Peggy Shippen and Major John André

Revolution, Romance

E. Irvine Haines Lippincott (1938)

The most glamorous story in the annals of American history is that of the lovely Peggy Shippen, arch-conspirator of the Revolution, of her love for the gallant young Major John André, and of the part she played in the treason of West Point. This novel, which is based on a new and authentic interpretation of the events leading up to that treason, is one of great dramatic intensity. Young, beautiful, ambitious, Peggy Shippen was inevitably drawn into the web of intrigue, of plots and counterplots woven by Major john André, the man she loved, and by Colonel Aaron Burr, his adversary.

Benedict Arnold, Peggy's husband, is revealed as a selfish, unscrupulous scoundrel to whom gold was the only god. Major André appears, not as the hated spy of orthodox history, but as a brave and talented young man, who placed honor above everything else, and for it sacrificed love, happiness, even his life. [DJ]

E. Irvine Haines (1877–1959) was an editor of newspapers and magazines and an author of feature articles, stories, a play, and a novel. He specialized in the history of colonial times and the American Revolution and was a member of the American Scenic, Historic and Preservation Society. [13-06]

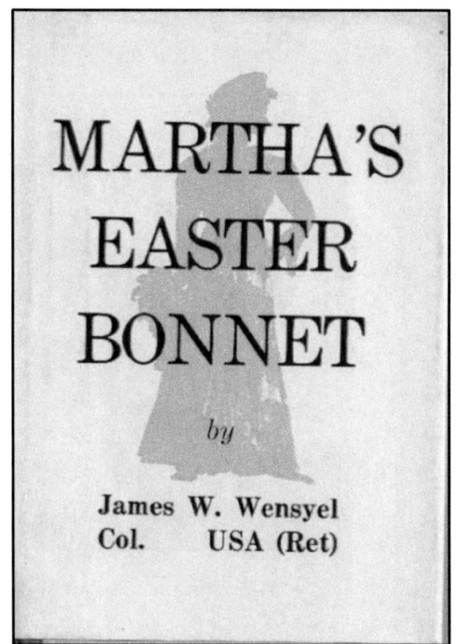

Martha's Easter Bonnet

WP Author, Revolution, Hudson Highlands, Army Life

James Wensyel, Col. Ret. Spear Printing Company, Inc (1977)

Easter, April 20, 1783, marked the first complete day of a general cease fire between British and American forces in America's eight-year War of Independence.

A weary commander, General George Washington, welcomed the end of the fighting but saw it bringing new concern to his still ragged, hungry, unpaid army now in its final winter quarters at New Windsor, near West Point, New York.

That morning he visited the army to measure again its temper should long the overdue promises by Congress not materialize. Martha Washington sensed his deep concern and, like his soldiers and the mountain people near their camp, found a way to assure him that all would yet be well with the infant nation.

The things General Washington determined from his army and from his lady that day are of significance to Americans nearing the Bicentennial of that Easter morning. [DJ]

James Wensyel, West Point Class of 1952, has written several historical novels. See "The Civil War" chapter for his bio and descriptions of two of his books.[13-07]

The imagery of West Point has been an attractive setting for writers to entertain the youth of this country. The Revolutionary War and events in the Hudson River Valley were the setting of several novels intended for youth which were published in the early 20th century.

The Story of West Point

Revolution, Cadet, Pulp Fiction

Author not stated True Comics (1942)

During the Revolutionary War, Alexander Hamilton called on General George Washington:

"These are General Knox's plans for a military school"

"I've long hoped for such a plan" responded Washington.

He approved the plans, but due to the war, it was decided that West Point should be a fort rather than a military school. April 1778–the fort was so vital that a great iron chain was stretched across the Hudson River from West Point to Constitution Island. Meantime in Philadelphia a school for future officers was established. After the Revolution the "cadets" were marched from Philadelphia to West Point. So, in 1794 a school was established to teach artillery and engineering. March 16, 1802–Congress passed the act which really established West Point. President Jefferson signed the papers. [EB]

Tomahawk: The Frontiersman of West Point

Revolution, Youth, Pulp Fiction

Frances Edward Herron DC Action Comics (July 1956)

The military post on the Hudson River was the key to American victory or defeat. At all costs, it had to remain in colonial hands! But a cunning British scheme was launched to capture the under-manned garrison. The security of the fortress fell squarely upon the shoulders of [the frontiersman] Tomahawk, young Dan Hunter and the Frontiersmen of West Point.

Shortly after the outbreak of the Revolutionary War, grim news reaches General Washington at his temporary headquarters in White Plains, New York.

"General, Sir...our agents in the city report the Redcoats are mounting a land and naval force against the Point"

"The British have us over a barrel, General! If we do not withdraw to protect West Point, it will mean evacuating this entire territory!"

General Washington: "True, major...but what if we rallied our forces here in West Chester and formed a blockade? We could hold West Point safely without giving up our positions."

And Washington's strategy proves effective. . . but now a new unforeseen danger threatens the small garrison guarding West Point . . . Skinner's colonists loyal to the British cause, harass the strategic military post behind Washington's lines.

It's time for Tomahawk and his Frontiersmen. . . [EB]

Frances "Ed" Herron (1917–1966) was a comic book writer and editor, active on the time periods known as the Golden Age and Silver Age of Comics. He worked for Marvel Comics' predecessor "Timely Comics" on the title *Captain America*, where he created the character, Red Skull. Later on, he worked on various other titles including *Superman*, *Batman*, *Detective Comics*, *Tomahawk*, *Our Army at War*, *Star Spangled War Stories,* and many more. [13-08]

Dare Boys: After Benedict Arnold

Revolution, Youth, Hudson Highlands

Stephen A. Cox A. L. Chatterton (1910)

From the opening chapter:

> "In the aftermath of Benedict Arnold's betrayal at West Point, Washington's staff pondered: How was Arnold to be captured, for he had sailed down river to New York City on the British ship "Vulture." It was certain no ordinary scheme would suffice:
>
> "There were a few moments of silence, and then one of the officers said, slowly and thoughtfully: "I have one other name to offer, your excellency. The only possible objection to the person I have in mind is his youth. But he has done a great deal of dangerous work for you, during the past year, and I believe that he has had sufficient experience so that he would be able to accomplish the task you wish undertaken and do the work in an exceedingly acceptable and satisfactory manner."
>
> The commander-in-chief looked at the speaker with an interested air and said: "Tell me this person's name."
>
> "It is -- Dick Dare."
>
> General Washington gave a start, and uttered a low exclamation, while his face lighted up. "The very one for the task," he ejaculated. "Why did I not think of him, myself, I wonder."

Stephen Angus Cox (1863–1944) lived much of his life in Humboldt Kansas. In the early 1900s he accepted a position as editor for the Frank Tousey Publishing Company, White Plains, New York. Later he returned to Humboldt and continued his literary pursuits. He wrote thirteen *Dare Boy* books chronicling the boys' exploits at every key event in the Revolutionary War. [13-09]

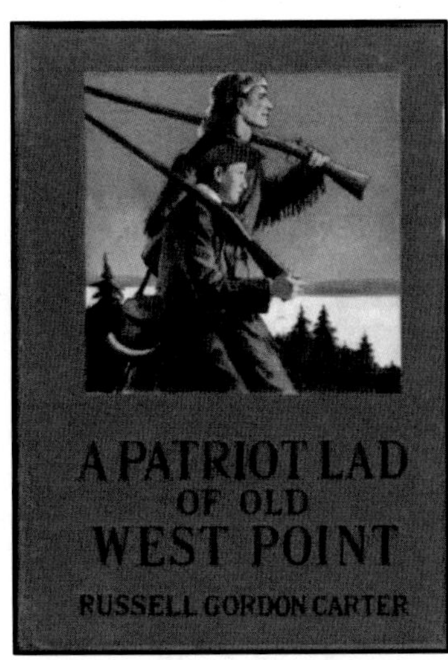

A Patriot Lad at Old West Point

Revolution, Hudson Highlands, Youth

Russel Gordon Carter Penn Publishing (1936)

Youthful George Dale and Jacob Blooker meet at a shop in Haverstraw, NY and navigate the river by rowboat between Haverstraw and West Point, observing the British movements along Hudson and the Highlands. They greatly aid the cause by catching a British spy and facilitating General Anthony Wayne's victory at Stony Point. [EB]

Russell Gordon Carter (1892–1957) became a freelance writer and novelist after serving in World War I. He published thirty books and numerous short stories, many with military and animal themes. [13-10]

A Spy in Old West Point

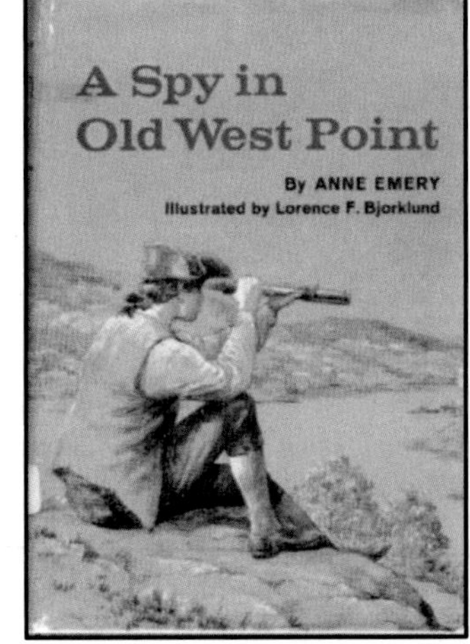

Youth, Revolution, Hudson Highlands

Anne Emery Rand McNally Co. (1965)

In this, the fourth of her "Spy" books, the author has chosen a historical episode from the Revolutionary War. It involves a real spy—Major André. The fictional hero, Jock Fraser, is given an important part in his apprehension.

The only fictional characters involved in this exciting story are Jock, his gunsmith father, their family, and a few friends. Jock has come to know Major André and to like him. Readers will sympathize with Jock's dilemma: if he helps Major André escape, he will collect enough money to fulfill his own ambitions and free his father from debt; but to help André, Jock will have to violate what he knows to be his patriotic duty. *A Spy in Old West Point* is, first of all, an engrossing story. It is also an excellent way of absorbing information about an important episode in American history, and of learning many fascinating facts about guns and gun making. [DJ]

Anne McGuigan Emery (1907–1987) attended Northwestern University, and then taught school in Evanston, IL for many years. In 1941, Emery began writing short stories then went on to write 30 romance novels and seven historical novels for children, of which this is one. [13-11]

The Corduroy Road

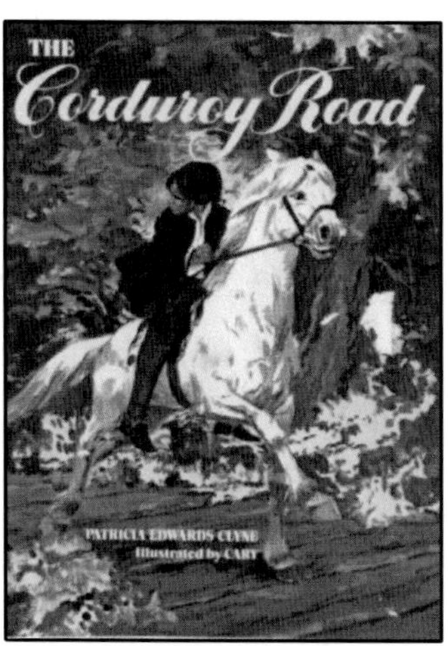

Youth, Revolution, Hudson Highlands

Patricia Edwards Clyne Dodd, Mead & Co. (1973)

The Corduroy Road was only a dim dream in young Tib's mind that hot July day in 1779, but before long it became a reality--a means of escape from his Tory uncle and the end of a long and dangerous adventure in the cause of patriotism.

Since the realization that his uncle's loyalties were with the British, Tib knew he had to run away from the farmhouse near Stony Point in upstate New York. But what was it his father had meant about the Corduroy Road, just before he died?

Tib's flight was hastened by his discovery of an American lieutenant hiding in the barn—he couldn't just leave him there. And so began the hazardous trip to West Point with the ill lieutenant through territory swarming with Redcoats, finding out about the American victory in the Battle of Stony Point and, at last, the chance to carry the news about General Anthony Wayne to Morristown and reach safety over the secret Corduroy Road. [DJ]

Patricia Edwards Clyne (1935–), American writer, editor, received her degree from Hunter College in 1959. She worked as an editorial assistant for various magazines and book publications, 1959–1975 and as contributing editor to *Hudson Valley* magazine, 1990–2000. She is an active member of Palisades Interstate Parks League of Naturalists. [13-12]

Links to Liberty: Defending the Great Chain at West Point

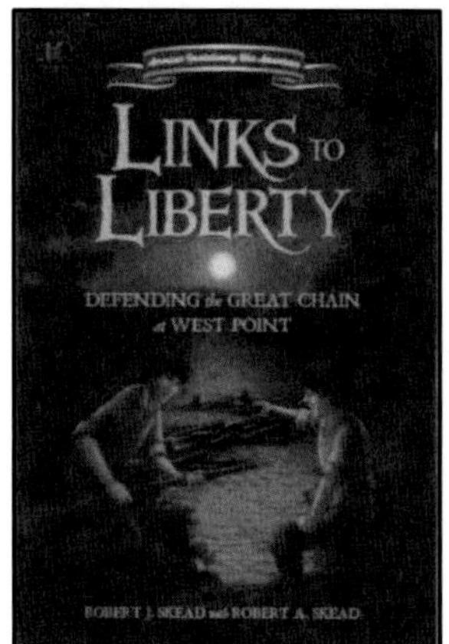

Revolution, Youth, Hudson Highlands

Robert J. Skead & Robert A. Skead Permuted Press (2019)

The year: 1779
The war: the American Revolution
The secret weapon: twin boys and a Great Chain at West Point

In this third book in the American Revolutionary War Adventures series, John and Ambrose Clark are hot on the trail of the spy who gave away the secret of their father's mission, which ultimately led to him being shot by Redcoats. But when there is an attack of America's new strategic defense on the Hudson River - the Great Chain at West Point - the twins must protect it.

They soon discover things aren't always as they seem, and their friends have deadly connections. Discover how the boys' faith in Providence and each other help the cause for Liberty! [BC]

Robert Skead is the author of several popular books for children. For the American Revolutionary War Adventures series, Robert partnered with his father to develop the stories. The father-son writing team are members of Sons of the American Revolution. Their ancestor, Lamberton Clark, one of the main characters in the stories, fought in the Revolutionary War as a member of the Connecticut Militia and the Continental Army. [BC]

The Linger-nots and the Valley Feud or *The Great West Point Chain*

Youth, Mystery, Hudson Highlands

Agnes Miller Cupples & Leon (1923)

The Linger-Nots thought they had done well enough, when, in the first volume of this series entitled *The Linger-Nots and the Mystery House*, they cleared up the mystery, but a club of nine lively girls, who enjoy reducing the troubles around them, are not likely to do much in that line without getting into exciting experiences. The following story tells what happened when the club had its summer outing in the Ramapo mountains. When the quarrels of great-grandfathers are passed on to the innocent ones, who had no part in the original feud, there is room for misery and tragedy. The Linger-Nots happened to come into just such a feud, and the way they took the misery and tragedy out of it makes interesting and instructive reading. [DJ]

Agnes Miller wrote five stories from 1923 to 1931 about this group of girls – The Linger-Nots – and their talent for resolving long standing mysteries. This is the second volume in the series.

Mystery of the Haunted Pool

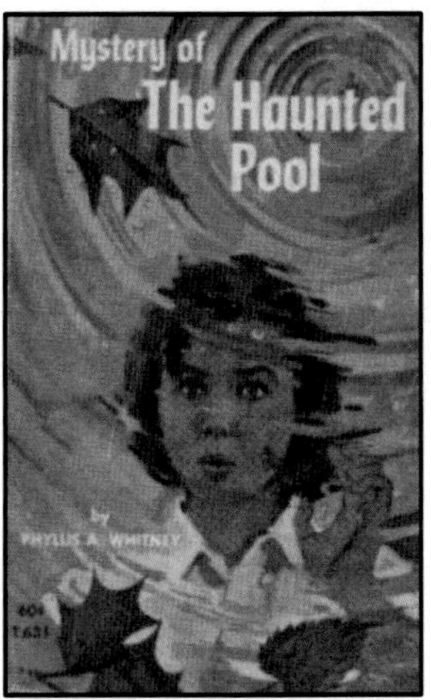

Mystery, Hudson Highlands, Youth

Phyllis A. Whitney Scholastic (1970)

This is a youth mystery that takes place in Fort Montgomery between Bear Mountain and West Point. When a strange face that appears—then disappears at the bottom of a pool near an old sea captain's mansion, Susan Price and her brother, Adam, unravel the clues to a century-old mystery. [BC]

Phyllis A. Whitney (1903–2008) was an American mystery writer of more than 70 novels. Born in Japan to American parents in 1903, she spent her early years in Asia. A rarity for her genre, she wrote mysteries for both the juvenile and the adult markets, many of which feature exotic settings. Yes, she survived 105 years, the longest-lived author in this collection. [13-13]

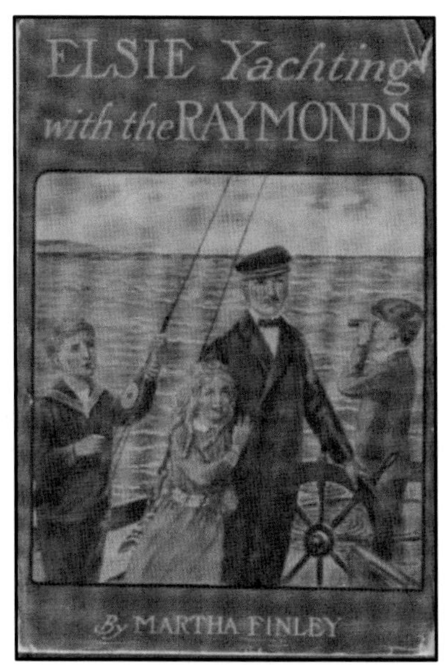

Elsie Yachting with the Raymonds

Youth, Hudson Highlands

Martha Finley Cumberland House (2000)

Originally published in 1890 as Book 16 of the Elsie Dinsmore series:
On their way to join the rest of the family on the coast of Rhode Island, Max, Lucy, and Captain Raymond tour West Point, Saratoga, and other points of interest. While at West Point, they meet Elsie's cousin, Donald Keith, who joins them on their eastward trek. As their summer stay at the beach concludes, the captain invests in a yacht for the family to enjoy. The Dolphin carries the Dinsmores, Travillas, Lelands, and Raymonds up and down the East Coast as they witness naval exercises and explore Boston, Bunker Hill and other Revolutionary War sites. The final stop on their sojourn by water brings them to Annapolis, Maryland, where Max, like his father before him, enrolls at the Naval Academy.[EB]

Elsie on the Hudson

Youth, Hudson Highlands, Revolutionary War

Martha Finley Routledge Press, London (1928)

Elsie Dinsmore returns to the Hudson for a cruise on the Raymond's yacht, Dolphin. About a quarter of the book concerns a storyline with the Dinsmore and Raymond family connections. Most of the book is a recounting of characters and events of the Revolutionary War, including the activites around West Point and Fort Montgomery. [EB]

Martha Finley (1828–1909) was a teacher and author of numerous works, the most well-known being the **Elsie Dinsmore series** which was published over a span of 38 years. The 28-book series went on to be the most popular and longest running girl's series of the 19th century, with the first volume selling nearly 300,000 copies in its first decade, going on to sell more than 5 million copies in the 20th century. They are still in print, updated for 21st century sensibilities. [13-14]

War of 1812

June 1812 – February 1815

America's Second War of Independence in 1812 was also its first war fought as an independent nation. America again fought the British Empire in what would later be called the "War of 1812" under President James Madison over violation of its economic freedom and territorial integrity. Battles occurred along the Great Lakes, The Atlantic Coast, and the southern states. West Point graduates saw their first action as they led soldiers and sailors in combat. Lieutenant George Ronan (USMA 1811) was the first West Point graduate killed in action falling near Fort Chicago, Illinois on August 15, 1812.

The American Navy, although vastly outnumbered and outgunned, won many major battles and established itself as a respected fighting force. Francis Scott Key, a Maryland lawyer, wrote the "Star Spangled Banner" while a prisoner of war aboard a British POW ship in Baltimore Harbor. The US lost 2,260 Americans killed in action with 4,505 wounded. Six West Point graduates were killed in action.

Inscription on a memorial stone on the West Point golf course.

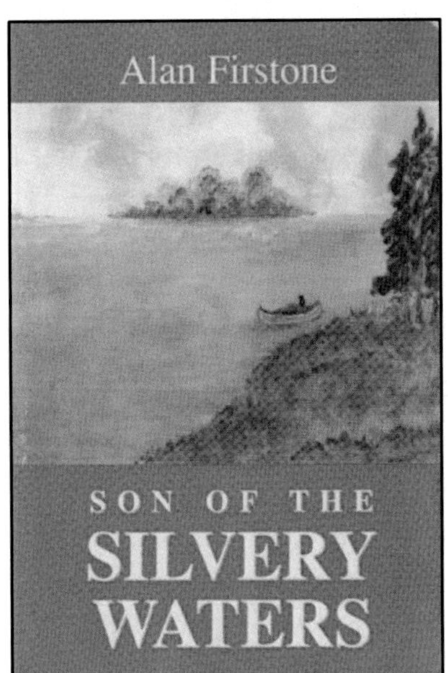

Son of the Silvery Waters

WP Author, War of 1812, Lake Ontario, NY State

Alan Firstone (aka Chris Arney) Rutledge Books (2001)

From the book cover:

"Evocative in its depiction of Native American culture, attuned to the rhythms of rural life, rich in period detail, *Son of the Silvery Waters* captures the excitement and rapid change of life in Antebellum America. This historical novel about a Cayuga Indian growing up along the shores of Lake Ontario unfolds against an expansive tapestry as Soso and his friends are drawn into the War of 1812, the world of Hudson River steamships and canal building projects, and the Underground Railroad."

-- Elizabeth Samet, Professor, USMA [BC]

"This charming novel begins as a late eighteen century Iroquois coming of age tale. It evolves into a magnificent epic which puts the reader into a 19th century depiction of the wildly beautiful Iroquois territory. Soso is an engaging hero, a Cayuga Indian whose early memories are of a time when the silvery waters belonged to his people. He is a boy who must become a man by straddling conflicting cultures in the wild frontier of upstate New York. As he ages, he must face the increasing complexities of a new country with its expanding population and settlement, war with the British, and the insidious racism and prejudice…"

-- Amanda Parsons, anthropologist with National Geographic [BC]

Alan Firstone is a pen name used by **Chris Arney**, a West Point graduate and retired professor of mathematics at West Point. His other novel, *Goatnapping Gladiators of West Point* is in the "Army Sports" chapter.

Elizabeth Samet's book, *A Soldier's Heart: Reading Literature Through Peace and War at West Point* is included in the collection. It can be found in the chapter, "Other Books by West Point Authors."

West Point Gray

War of 1812, Comic Book

H. Bedford Jones Adventure Magazine (July 1937)

A story regarding the long-term impact on West Point from the Battle of Chippewa, July 5, 1814:

"Farmer by name and farmer by nature," said Lukes, not hiding his sneer. "You're belly-achin' like a weaning calf when you'd ought to be proud of wearing the uniform of your country."

"Uniform, hell!" exploded Zack Farmer. "Look at it! Gray instead o' blue and you call it a uniform?"

"You'll never make a sojer, that's sure."

"I didn't 'list for this kind o' sojering." Tow-headed, with mild blue eyes in a round face, Farmer glowered. "What is it anyhow? Support arms, load in twelve motions, stick in your belly, fasten that collar, charge with the bayonet—arrgh! We been here four months at one blasted thing after another, over and over again. I didn't enlist for chilblained feet and a headache from a tarbucket hat." . . . .

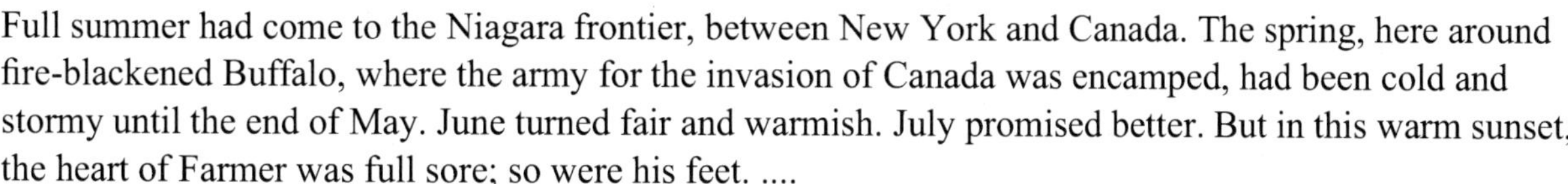

Full summer had come to the Niagara frontier, between New York and Canada. The spring, here around fire-blackened Buffalo, where the army for the invasion of Canada was encamped, had been cold and stormy until the end of May. June turned fair and warmish. July promised better. But in this warm sunset, the heart of Farmer was full sore; so were his feet. ....

Farmer grunted, "If I'd known there wasn't any blue cloth left for this new army, and we had to be trussed in Quaker gray from Philadelphy, I sure wouldn't have 'listed. But the rest of you got to wear it too."

"Oh, us old hands have our blues tucked away to go home in," said Lukes. He regarded his own sober gray uniform with a grimace. "Gen'ral Scott's idee is that the rank and file have got to be uniformed alike. He's hell for looks — allows sojers fight better when they're smart dressed and smart drilled."

"I'm sick o' being drilled like militia on a common," Farmer growled. "All this bayonet exercise—yah! I don't see much sojer glory in being butchered like venison. Nor use in it, neither. Did you ever work close quarters with the bayonet?"

"Many's the time, many's the time," and Lukes wagged his head as he bragged. "Cold steel don't scare me. All you do is stick the other feller first."

Henry James O'Brien Bedford-Jones (1887–1949) was a Canadian-American historical, adventure fantasy, science fiction, crime and Western writer who became a naturalized United States citizen in 1908. He wrote nearly 200 novels, 400 novelettes, and 800 short stories, earning the nickname "King of the Pulps." His works appeared in most of the popular pulp magazines. [13-15]

In memory of the Battle of Chippewa and in honor of the troops engaged there, the uniform of the cadet corps of the United States Military Academy is gray.

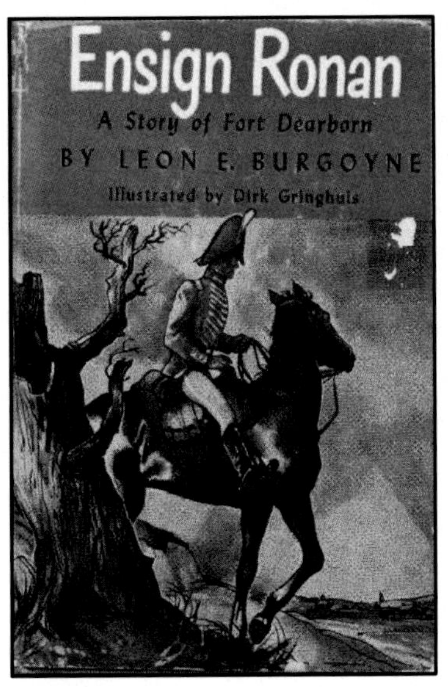

Ensign Ronan: A Story of Fort Dearborn

War of 1812

Leon Burgoyne   John C. Winston Co. (1955)

Early in the spring of 1811 a young officer named George Ronan left the Military Academy at West Point and headed for duty at a small fort in the troubled Northwest Territory. Traveling through the uneasy wilderness of the raw frontier, he subsequently arrived at Fort Dearborn to share in the fortunes and misfortunes of the small garrison of the Fourth Infantry stationed at that place.

It was while doing research on the massacre of Fort Dearborn that the author uncovered the name of Ensign Ronan. History briefly records the young officer as "somewhat stubborn and headstrong, but an extremely brave young man." The ensign immediately captured the author's fancy, and thus it was that George Ronan became the central figure of this story. ("Ensign" was an Army rank in the period of this story.)

Ensign Ronan is a work of fiction, but most of the characters were real persons. The names of the officers and men were taken from the last muster roll of the garrison. The names John Kinzie, Antoine Ouilmette, John LaLime, Black Partridge, Sauganash, Topenebe, and many others can be found in accounts of the massacre. A great many of the events depicted in the story actually occurred, but, wishing no quarrel with historians or possible descendants of the characters, the author requests that *Ensign Ronan* be read as fiction and not fact. [DJ]

Leon Burgoyne (1916–2008), a native of Michigan, graduated from Western Michigan College and served four years with the Navy in the South Pacific during World War II. He was a high school basketball coach who published two novels for youth on that sport: *Jack Davis, Forward* and *State Champs.* [13-16]

Attack at Fort Lookout

WP Author, War of 1812

Russell Reeder Duell, Sloan, Pearce (1976)

This book recounts the adventures of a young officer at a frontier outpost in the Old Northwest just before the War of 1812. Fresh from West Point, Lieutenant Andrew Raeburn knew that Army life on the frontier was going to be different, but he didn't know just how different. He certainly wasn't prepared for the pistol-shot reception his commanding officer gave him, and despite that officer's reputation as a rough-and-ready Indian fighter Andrew had his doubts about him. His doubts increased when Private Swanflick, through no doing of his own, was thrown in the hole and Snap Lewis was given the even more severe dose of "Barrel-head justice."

Life at the little fort some fifty miles beyond the small settlement of Detroit was indeed different. It was rugged, challenging, and full of action. Rumors of Indians on the warpath came in more frequently, soldiers deserted, and the raw winter began to descend on the still unfinished fort.

But disaster threatened him when, faced with a mutiny, Andrew struck a soldier and was arrested and court-martialed. Reaching its climax with the Indian attack on lonely little Fort Lookout, this story is authentic in every detail. It presents a brilliantly clear and very fast-moving picture of what life was really like for the defenders of the frontier in the old Michigan territory. [DJ]

Russell "Red" Reeder (1902–1998) graduated from West Point in 1926. He authored many books of military non-fiction and fiction including the popular "Clint Lane" series about cadet life. A more extensive discussion of his life and works can be found in the chapter "The Cadet Series of Books."

Sylvanus Thayer

In 1817, President James Monroe ordered Colonel Thayer of West Point to become superintendent of the Military Academy following the resignation of Captain Alden Partridge. He served in that role until 1833, when differences with President Andrew Jackson caused him to resign and renew his Army engineering career. Under his stewardship, the Academy became the nation's first college of engineering.

One of Thayer's reforms was to establish a standard four-year curriculum with the cadets organized into four classes. Starting with the Class of 1823, the date each year when the graduating class was commissioned, and the entering class was sworn in, was July 1st. The graduation date has since moved up to June 15th, beginning with the class of 1861.

Thayer's monumental contributions earned him the title Father of the Military Academy. The following book is not a novel, but a biography of an extraordinary man. He deserves this space in any historical perspective of the military academy. [13-17]

Sylvanus Thayer of West Point

Thayer

George Fielding Eliot Julian Messner (1959)

Although the Military Academy at West Point was founded by Congress fifteen years before Sylvanus Thayer became its Superintendent, it was not until he took command that any real claim could be made for it as a school for the military training of officers…

At sixteen Sylvanus was teaching school and studying hard to achieve the goal he had set for himself -- a college education. He worked his way through Dartmouth College and then accepted an appointment to West Point, by this time determined to become an engineer.

As a second lieutenant, he helped in the construction of coastal defenses and was an instructor of mathematics at the Military Academy until the outbreak of the War of 1812. Under fire from the British and Indians, he was aghast at the shameful blundering of our forces and realized the tragic cause -- we had neglected to train officers in peacetime. West Point, with its lax, outmoded standards, must be completely reformed. Young as he was, Sylvanus Thayer hoped to bring about that reform.

Under government orders, he went to Europe to study foreign methods, tactics, and military schools; to collect books and instruments for West Point. Upon his. return to America, President James Monroe appointed him Superintendent of West Point… Slowly, steadily, he developed the strict discipline, the code of honor and high educational standards that made West Point the mightiest military school in the world, and justly earned him the title of Father of the Military Academy.

…Almost all of the principles, policies and methods of chief importance established by him have endured for more than 125 years to remain the vital substance of West Point today. They have made West Point the model that is followed faithfully in whole or in part by all of the military schools and colleges of the country. [DJ]

George Fielding Eliot (1894 -1971) was a second lieutenant in the Australian army in World War I and experienced combat at Gallipoli and in the trenches in Belgium. After the war he emigrated to Canada and joined the Royal Canadian Mounted Police. He later served as a major in the U.S. Military Intelligence Reserve. Fielding authored over a dozen books on military and political matters in the 1930s through the 1960s, wrote news columns on military affairs, and was a military commentator for CBS News during World War II. [13-18]

Eggnog Riot: The Christmas Mutiny at West Point

Cadet, Scandal

James B. Agnew Presidio Press (1979)

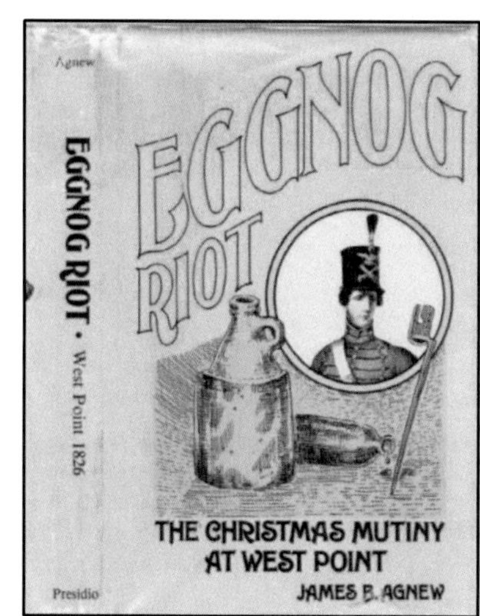

"The flat-bottomed skiff glided out of the winter darkness and bumped its prow against the shadowed wooden pilings at the Academy dock. In the board were three figures -- one rowing and two seated on the thwarts at the bow and stern of the small craft. At the boat's approach, a figure on the dock turned toward the shore and walked away a few yards as if purposefully to avoid witnessing the craft's arrival.

The three helped each other onto the dock. Burnley clutched a cloth sack from which occasionally sounded the "clunk" of crockery jugs bumping together. The soldier, his back still turned away from the cadets, stood immobile as if he were oblivious to the incident transpiring behind him.

"Well gentlemen" said Center, "not a bad evening's work. We have among us two gallons -- and a row over and back not that difficult, despite the chill." He hefted the bag he had retrieved from Burnley and declared, "Boys, there will be a good Christmas at West Point this year, if our cargo is any measure. Sylvanus Thayer be hanged!" [DJ]

Col. James B. Agnew (1930–1980) was a 1952 graduate of The Citadel. His military assignments included command of an artillery battalion in Vietnam, teaching history at West Point and directing the Army's Military History Research Collection (later the Military History Institute) at Carlisle Barracks, Pennsylvania from August 1974 to August 1977. He authored many articles published in military journals. [13-19]

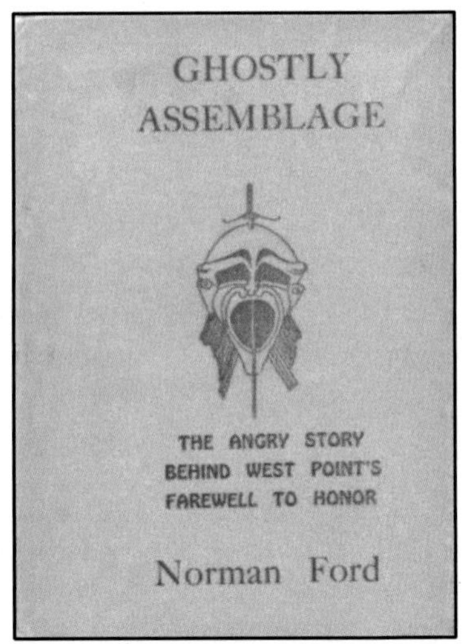

Ghostly Assemblage: The Angry Story Behind West Point's Farewell to Honor

WP Author, Scandal, Cemetery, Paranormal

Norman R. Ford St. Johnsbury Vermont (1954)

This is a unique story (actually a play) written by a West Pointer. The ghosts of West Pointers past and present assemble on the Plain when Sylvanus Thayer convenes an assembly to pass judgment on the 90 cadets discharged during the 1951 seating scandal. Alumni, faculty, and cadet representatives express their convictions, then following eminent "moralists" take the stage to pronounce their surprising (and conflicting) judgements: Socrates, Schopenhauer, Shakespeare, and Napoleon. [EB]

From the introduction:

> "This book is written in anger - an anger laced with surprising flashes of malevolent humor - but nevertheless a real and devastating anger which strains at the words and flares out repeatedly against two objectives: first, the negligence and the near-criminal guilt of those in authority at West Point who by their unbelievable weakness in permitting the game of football to encroach upon their obligation as teachers and counselors of the Cadets at the Military Academy brought about the Cheating Scandal of 1951; second, the smugness and narrow mindedness of all, authorities, officers, graduates, and cadets alike, who have heaped contumely upon the Ninety Cadets and then closed their minds in hypocritical and puritanical bigotry. With the publication of this book, three years of their cunningly contrived silence are ended, and their secret becomes known. In these pages there is proof positive that the Ninety Cadets were not alone in bidding farewell to Honor in 1951."

Thayer of West Point

WP Author, Thayer

Norman R. Ford Thayer Book Press (1953)

Taken from the book's opening chapter:

"West Point was dying. In 1871 in a spacious room of a white house in Braintree, Massachusetts, an old man lay on a wide bed surrounded by a few friends and those of his relatives who felt able to brace what they fancied was the bitterness of the principal actor in the little pageant. He had never married, so there was no wife to sit by his bedside. Instead, his niece took that place. It was quite early in the morning, about two o'clock of a day in September. A mildly scented wind, laden with a reminiscence of summer and the promise of sharp, ruthless days to come, winged its way past the window which had been opened at the old General's order. While the watchers in the room stood or sat with their cloaks and coats about their shoulders against the seeking drafts, their thoughts, and the thoughts of Sylvanus Thayer lying on the bed turned steadfastly and irrevocably to West Point. For West Point was dying."

"Everyone was saying that. Every cadet at the Military Academy, every instructor there, hundreds of officers in the Army...they were all saying the same thing. How else could you feel about a man who had symbolized the place for over half a century? What else was there to say when the man who had changed the Military Academy from an insignificant and shoddily operated boys' school to a world-famous institution where American's finest officers were trained was finally leaving his rightful place of honor? Was it only yesterday that a young boy had hurried through the snowy paths of the Dartmouth campus, his mind filled with conflicting desires, his steps bent toward a romantic spot on the Hudson River? Could it have been sixty-five years ago that this same lad held before himself a vision of learning from Napoleon those things about military science which were absorbing many hours of his time? And was West Point new to break its long term of existence because the man within whose physical being was the full spirit of the Military Academy was new to leave those Hudson scenes forever?" . . .

"He wanted mightily to tell them his secret, yet he need have had no fear. That secret had been imparted by a thousand acts throughout his life. Seven hundred men had come under the influence of those acts and they had gone on to impart the secret to others who would know how to make good use of it. They would go on forever telling the secret to others living it out in their lives and building great men and forts with it. Sylvanus Thayer had no need to shout those words from his deathbed for already they were being clamored to Americans in a never-ending chain which would serve to ring the country 'round with its iron loops." . . .

"He returned to the West Point he had never quite lost. He stands today in stone, austere, dignified as in life, at one corner of the green Plain where he loved to pause so often. There he looks straight across the Parade Ground toward the Great Chain whose links he touched with reverence. When the Corps is at Parade he gazes inflexibly down the straight lines, and where we see an end, he sees none, for he sees the Chain of Iron which loops upon itself and has no termination short of the eternity he dreamed and exemplified so well."

Norman Ford, Class of 1926, has other books in the collection. *Black, Gray, and Gold* along with his biography is in the chapter "Army Sports." Also in this collection is this pre-publication 1st edition manuscript #122 of 500.

Thayer's Return: Early History of West Point in Verse

Poetry, Thayer, Paranormal

H J. Koch Lulu Publishing Services (2019)

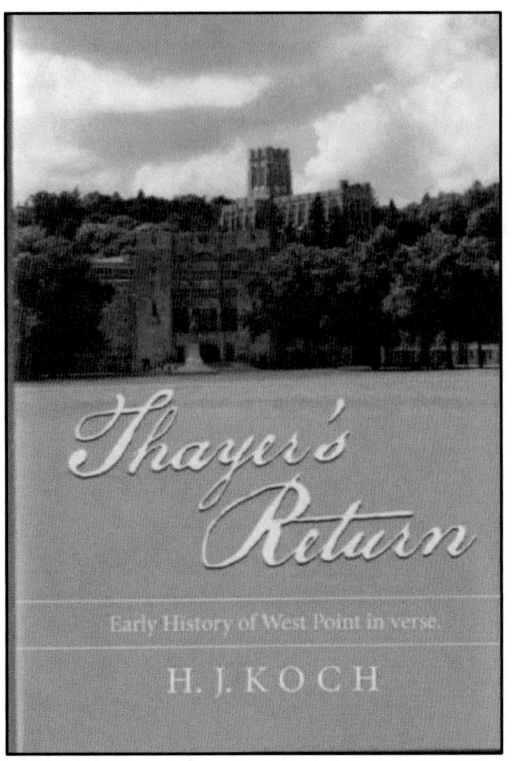

A compilation of historical verse divided into four parts provides a unique perspective on the early history of West Point. The Father of West Point, Sylvanus Thayer, has returned from the mist of history in the form of a ghost to seek an update on the Academy from a cadet. As the two men converse over a number of nights, they lyrically explore the history of West Point's founding in 1802 until World War One. [DJ]

"Thayer am I!" the apparition said,
And with his finger to the window led.
"From yon plain this academy was grown.
Its father am I! I, its seed had sown.
What year is this, and with whom do I speak?
Answer! And discard that count'nance so meek!

"Cadet McKinley at your service, sir.
Ready answers have I and will confer.
Two centuries at this citadel has run.
A new millennium is just begun,"
The youth well with great vigor made reply.
Sternly asking and peering to the sky,

"Pray, Muse, your just assistance I invoke."
With humble countenance, the cadet spoke,
"Give me remembrance and clear vision so
The Long Gray Line I may relate and show.
Much has transpired since the days of yore.
Many a battle fought on distant shore." . . .

H. J. Koch describes himself as a passionate poet whose spouse and three children graduated from West Point. [BC]

Chapter 14

Manifest Destiny

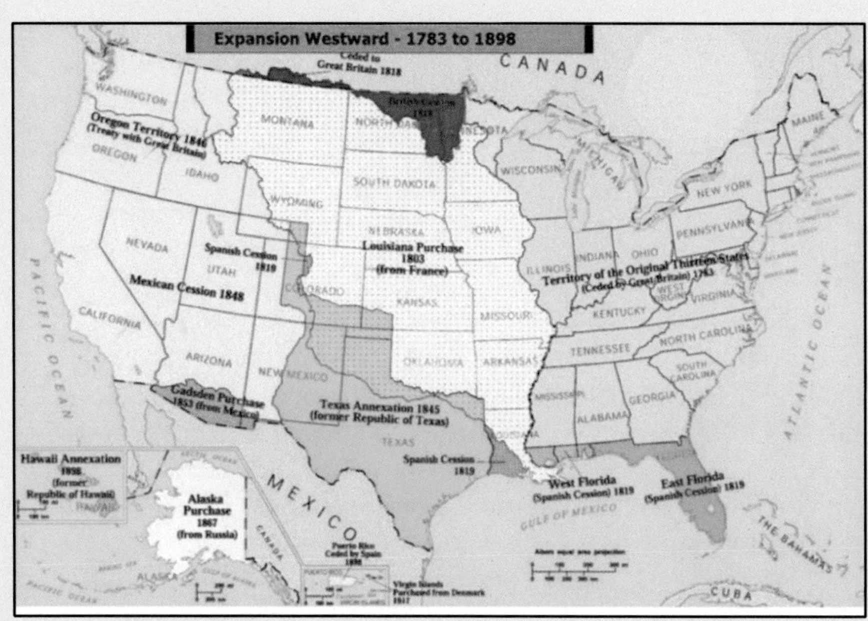

The concept of Manifest Destiny emerged in the 1840s. It posited that the United States is destined—and blessed by God—to expand its dominion and spread democracy and capitalism across the entire North American continent. The expansion was accomplished in several stages from 1803 to 1867, though the term was first coined in 1855. Acquisition was one thing, settling the territory quite another, as these novels and stories will attest.

"American Progress" is an allegorical representation of the modernization of the new West by John Gast (1872). Columbia, a personification of the United States, is shown leading civilization westward with the American settlers. She is shown bringing light from east to west, stringing telegraph wire, holding a book and highlighting different stages of economic activity and evolving forms of transportation.

This philosophy was used to justify the forced removal of Native Americans and other groups from their homes. The rapid expansion of the United States intensified the issue of slavery as new states were added to the Union, leading to the outbreak of the Civil War.

Indian Wars

1835–1890

Beginning with the first established British colony at Jamestown in 1607, a continuous tension existed between European Colonists (eventually Americans) and the Native American Indians for nearly 300 years. This tension frequently erupted into armed conflicts ranging from minor skirmishes to massacres, to wars as the continued American westward expansion pushed Native American populations westward. Although the earliest of the Indian Wars occurred in 1622 against the Powhatans in Virginia, the first 28 Presidents from George Washington to Woodrow Wilson in 1918 all faced varying levels of these conflicts, the brunt of which included the Second Seminole War from 1835–1842 (the longest costliest war waged against Native Americans) and the Black Hills War from 1876–1877 (leading to the death of LTC George A. Cluster; (USMA 1861) at the Battle of the Little Big Horn in 1876). Numerous West Pointers saw action throughout the Indian Wars while 21 graduates received the Medal of Honor.

- Text from a memorial marker on a tee box at the West Point golf course. Photo of Crazy Horse monument by author

The United States Army and its West Point graduates played a central role in "winning the west." From the introduction to *Yesterday's Reveille* by Robert Vaughan:

> "Though they never fielded forces of more than 15,000 men, the army surveyed railroad lines, guarded construction crews, defended trails west, provided protection for settlers, miners, ranchers, and farmers, and engaged the Indians in over 250 battles, not counting small skirmishes of platoon size or less. They were nearly always outnumbered, and often the Indians were better armed due to the greed of white traders. The Indians were better horsemen, fought as a way of life, knew their home territory, and could move as silently as the dust. But in the end, the West was opened, and peace was won by the United States Army."

The books and stories in this chapter are grouped by their association with one of these "stages" of expansion, though some of the book plots cover more than one stage.

Florida, Louisiana, Arkansas

The West Point Cadet or *The Young Officer's Bride*

Cadet, Manifest Destiny

Harry Hazel U.S. Publishing Co. (1845)

The story opens in Boston with recently graduated cadet Eugene Merrill attending a soiree in which he encountered a childhood playmate, the lovely Effie Stanwood. Effie was escorted to the dance by George Sumpter, a law clerk, who has the blessing of Effie's father to court her. In fact, Sumpter and Mr. Stanwood have a scheme by which Effie would marry Sumpter, and in a complex arrangement Stanwood would retain title to properties willed to Effie by her deceased mother. However, Effie cannot abide with George Sumpter, and refuses to marry him. She is smitten by Lt. Merrill, and they pledge their love to each other. Alas, Lt. Merrill, an artillerist, is on graduation leave before reporting to his regiment in Harpers and then heading to engage the Seminoles in Florida.

The spurned Sumpter undertakes several schemes to bring dishonor to Merrill and remove him as a competitor for Effie's hand – to no avail. With Merrill out of reach in Florida, Sumpter arranges through his father's influence in the War Department to obtain a commission and be assigned to Merrill's regiment near Tampa Bay. He attempts more efforts to eliminate Lt. Merrill aided by a ne'er-do-well friend, Ned Dawson, who enlists in the army to assist Sumpter…for monetary considerations.

In battling the Seminoles near Ouithlacoochee, Lt. Sumpter's unit abandons a key position endangering the regiment. However, Lt. Merrill demonstrates great courage in moving artillery to save the day. The former is disgraced while the latter lauded in the eyes by the troops and officers. Sumpter then arranged through Dawson to drug Merrill's coffee the night he is to command the sentries. Sumpter had previously sent an anonymous note to the commandant saying one of his guard officers often slept during his duties. Hardly the case, but Eugene Merrill falls into deep sleep after being drugged and is discovered by the commandant and a patrol. Eugene is arrested and court-martialed. He claims no defense, not understanding how this could have happened. The general wished to set an example and sentenced Merrill to be shot. The execution is on hold pending an appeal to Washington, which will take several months. Everyone expects that the sentence will be pardoned given Merrill's otherwise sterling record.

Meanwhile, Lt. Sumpter resigns his commission and returns to Boston to woo Effie. She refuses him, still, especially after learning his nefarious dealing with her father, who turns out to be an uncle who raised her from childhood.

In Tampa, as the anticipated pardon does not arrive the execution date is set, to the great disappointment of the entire post…and the day arrives. Who will step forward to prevent this miscarriage of justice? [EB]

Harry Hazel is a pen name employed by **Justin Jones** (1814–1899) who authored more than forty adventurous dime novels. Born in 1814 in Brunswick, Maine, he was trained as a printer working on several publications in the 1830s and 1840s. In 1844, Jones began to use the name Harry Hazel for a series of short fictional works (all of approximately 100 pages). He was at the emergence of the wildly popular dime novel era. [14-01]

The Long Hunters

Manifest Destiny, Florida

Jason Manning Signet (2002)

In 1814, the fledgling U.S. Army is nothing more than a ragtag collection of veterans and boys, bound by blood, duty, and more than a little luck. The army's commander in chief Andrew Jackson, has turned his attention from the waning British threat to a conflict closer to home: "Old Hickory" hopes to capture and kill the Creek Indians responsible for murdering American "long hunters" on their home soil.

Lieutenant Timothy Barlow has just graduated from West Point, full of ideals but with no experience. In Indian country, this combination may prove fatal. Barlow is mandated to pillage peaceful Indian camps along the Tallapoosa. But when his conscience gets the better of him -- and his troops take matters into their own hands -- Barlow has to find a way to obey orders, follow his heart, and survive what history will call the First Seminole War. [BC]

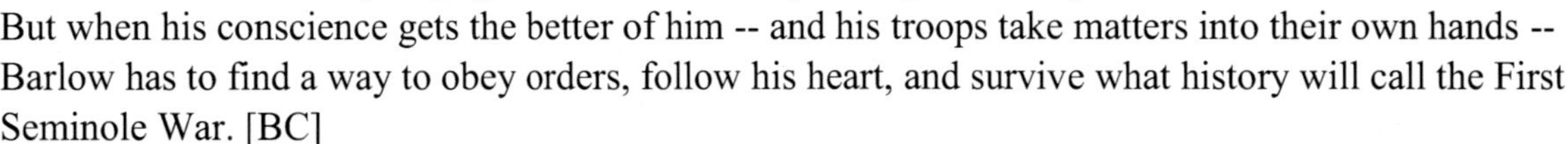

Jason Manning is a Texan. He started writing short stories when he was twelve. He is currently writing his 58th novel. As a historian, Manning has taught at Stephen F. Austin State University, Southern Illinois University, and Montgomery College in Texas. His website, The Eighties Club is regarded as an excellent resource on the history and pop culture of the 1980s.[14-02]

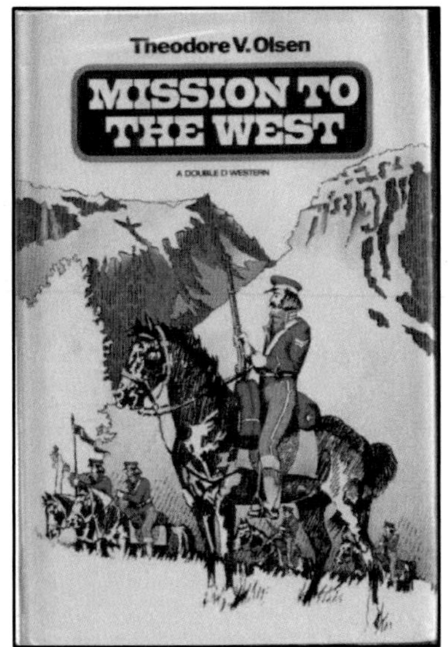

Mission to the West

Manifest Destiny, Arkansas, Oklahoma

Theodore V. Olsen Doubleday (1973)

The establishment of the 1st Regiment of the U. S. Dragoons in 1833 marked the birth of the United States Cavalry and set the stage for the conquest of the frontier. It seemed the perfect unit for Lieutenant Stennis Fry, fresh out of West Point and looking for a dash of adventure. Indeed, when the Dragoons set out on their first mission, an expedition to the Far West to impress the proud plains Indians with a show of mounted might, Fry had only the grandest hopes of success.

But the harsh realities of the trail soon displaced those heady dreams of triumph as first a disastrous outbreak of cholera and then a growing scarcity of food and water took their terrible toll. Danger from marauding renegades as well as the constant threat of violence among civilian members of the party added to the problems, and the presence of a white woman and two Indian girls on the expedition made the situation truly explosive. Torn between his duty as an officer to see the mission through at all costs and his more human concern for the appalling hardships it imposed, Fry found himself caught in the middle as he tried to keep peace in the unruly ranks. But as this gripping tale moves through the actual events on which it is based, Fry and all those left alive are forced to ask themselves whether their mission is really worth the price. [DJ]

Theodore Victor Olsen (1932–1993) born in Rhinelander, Wisconsin, was an American author of western novels and short stories. His wife was fellow western fiction author Beverly Butler. [14-03]

Seneca Patriots: The White Indian Series

Manifest Destiny, Arkansas, Texas

Donald Clayton Porter Bantam Books (1991)

THE THREAT—General James Wilkinson is a notorious scoundrel—treasonous and corrupt. Yet as an American commander on the Southwest frontier, he wields power with a deadly grip. That is, until he falls under the lascivious thrall of the witch Melisande of New Orleans. Through her manipulations, Wilkinson plots to exterminate once and for all Renno, the White Indian.

THE LEGACY—Meanwhile, young Little Hawk has been selected for President Jefferson's prestigious new military academy at West Point. There, despite excelling in every field, he struggles in the terrible grip of prejudice. In the Southland, the young Mingo warrior White Blanket, a fervent follower of Tecumseh, joins a new Indian Union to fight the white man as the tumultuous young United States tests its newfound strength by annexing the Louisiana Territory and waging a faraway war with the Barbary pirates. [BC]

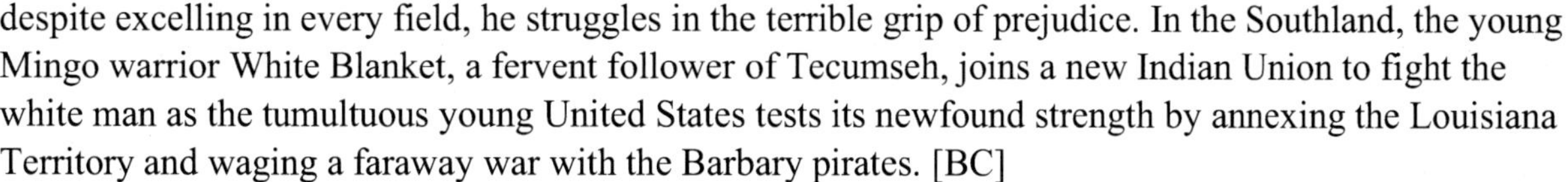

Noel Bertram Gerson (1913–1988) was an American author who wrote 325 books. Beginning in 1979, Gerson initiated a series called *The White Indian* using the pen name of Donald Clayton Porter. The book shown above is 22nd in the series and takes place in the early 19th century. [14-04]

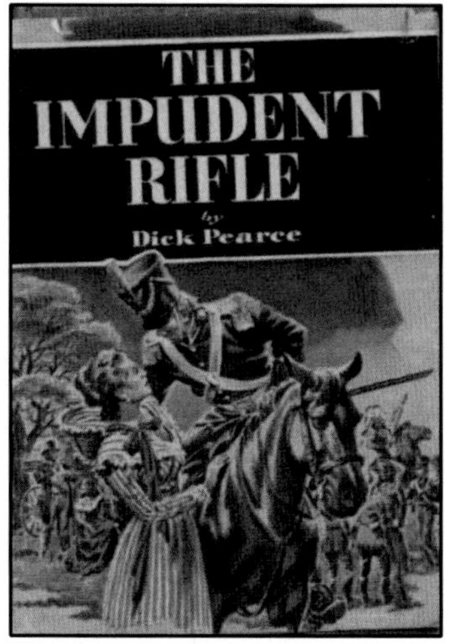

The Impudent Rifle

Manifest Destiny, Arkansas, Oklahoma

Dick Pearce J.B. Lippincott (1951)

This story of frontier Army life in the American Southwest has plenty of action, moves rapidly, and has its full share of romance. Lieutenant Philip Royall, a young West Pointer who volunteers for duty beyond the Mississippi, is not only one of the finest marksmen seen in recent fiction, but one of the most reckless and attractive heroes.

Service in the Army under a tyrannical commanding officer at Fort Gibson, troubles with a corrupt frontier politician, and a battle with the Comanches provide plenty of opportunity to test the courage and character of the handsome Easterner. So does the love of two women: a wild and passionate half-Indian girl, and the shy, lovely daughter of the Indian Commissioner.

There is a tough, hard-bitten private whose murderous assault on Royall is one of the most shocking and brutal fights. Finally, out of murder and tragedy, and out of a battle that never should have been fought, Royall finds himself. [DJ]

Texas, Mexico, and Kansas

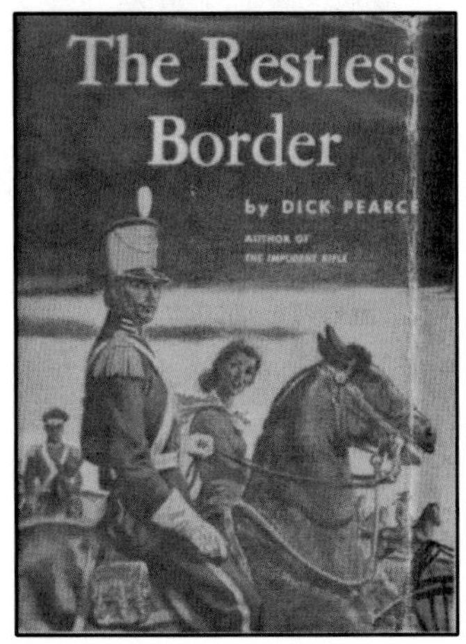

The Restless Border

Manifest Destiny, Texas

Dick Pearce Sears Readers Club (1952)

When Captain Alexander Prince of the U.S. Army was sent to the United States-Texas border, soon after Texas freed itself from Mexico, he had secret orders to give the new Republic all possible help, without straining neutrality too far. Prince found himself in the austerity of the border outpost, Fort Catron, on the Red River.

The Restless Border is an exciting tale of intrigue and Indian warfare as Prince endeavors to prevent the Comanches from harassing Texas, on one hand, and to discourage the Mexicans, under Santa Ana, on the other. In addition to helping the Texans, he meets (and falls in love with) the attractive Mary Millard, who is searching for her son kidnapped by the Comanches. He has to pit every ounce of skill against the wily French trader, Henri Beauchamp, who is headed for Santa Fe at the wrong season of the year, and Red Hair, the villainous Comanche chief who is out to thwart the plans of both Prince and the Texans. And in the background is the dominating figure of Sam Houston, that redoubtable hero who devoted his life to the cause. [DJ]

Born in Springer, Oklahoma, **Dick Pearce** has had a lifelong interest in Indians and the early frontier days. After graduating from the University of Oklahoma, Dick Pearce started work for the Oklahoma City Times, but moved to San Francisco in 1937 to work for the San Francisco newspapers. He published short stories and serials in *Cosmopolitan*, *Colliers*, *The Saturday Evening Post* and other magazines, and authored several other novels. [DJ]

Fort Starke/First Command

Manifest Destiny, Kansas

Will Cook Leisure Books (1994)

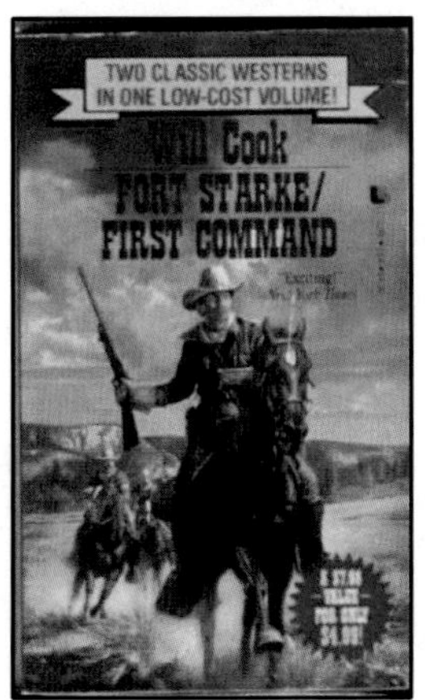

Fresh out of West Point, Lieutenant Jefferson Travis counted on doing everything by the book to keep out of trouble. Unfortunately, Kansas was grim and indifferent to the problems of buffalo hunters, settlers, and Indians alike. Driven by harsh necessity, every man would cheat, steal, or murder if he thought he could get away with it. In that pitiless territory, Travis would need more than rules to survive -- he'd need the guts, courage, and strength no book could ever teach him. [BC]

William Everett Cook (1922–1964) was a writer of western and adventure novels and stories. During his brief life Cook was a soldier, commercial aviator, deep-sea diver, logger, peace officer, and writer. His pseudonyms include Wayne Everett, James Keene, Frank Peace, and William Richards.[14-06]

Mexican-American War

April 1946 – February 1848

The United States went to war with Mexico in 1846 under President James K. Polk after Mexico refused to recognize America's annexation of Texas and the Rio Grande River as the US-Mexican border.

General Zachary Taylor, 12th US President, and General Winfield Scott led the major wings of the American Army during the invasion of Mexico. Taylor won key battles at Monterrey and Buena Vista while Scott successfully conducted a complex amphibious landing at Veracruz and won a string of impressive battles ending with the capture of Mexico City on September 14, 1847 (while fighting outnumbered, poorly supplied, and deep within enemy territory). Scott was so impressed by the performance of West Point graduates he noted in his "Fixed Opinion" that the officers were invaluable to the rapid and decisive nature of the US victory.

Although a military success leading to the incorporation of California, New Mexico, Arizona, and Utah, the war inflamed tensions over the expansion of slavery in these newly acquired territories that would be a major cause of the Civil War. Many of the junior officers in the Mexican-American War later went on to lead both Union and Confederate forces in the Civil War. The US lost 1,507 killed in combat while 13,200 died of disease. Another 4,152 soldiers were wounded. Forty-eight West Point graduates were killed in action.

- Text from a memorial stone on the West Point golf course. Painting of Battle to Resaca de Palma by Karl Nebel, published by D. Appleton & Company, 1851.

Gone for Soldiers

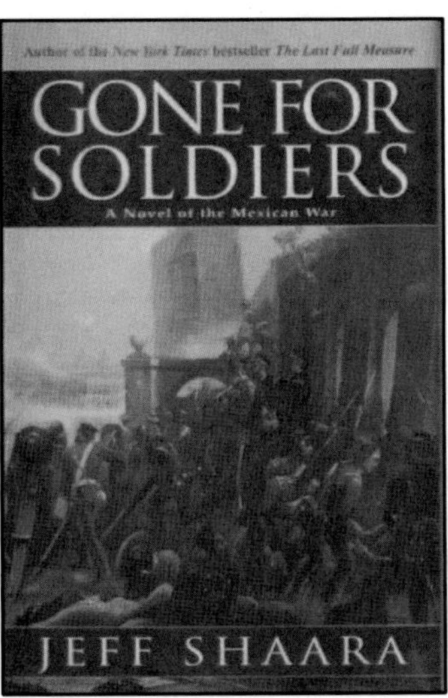

Manifest Destiny Mexican War, General Officer

Jeff Shaara Ballantine Books (2000)

In *Gone for Soldiers*, Jeff Shaara carries us back thirteen years before the Civil War's when that later conflict's most familiar names are fighting for another cause, junior officers marching under the same flag in an unfamiliar land, experiencing combat for the first time in the Mexican-American War. In March 1847, the U.S. Navy delivers eight thousand soldiers on the beaches of Vera Cruz. They are led by the army's commanding general, Winfield Scott, a heroic veteran of the War of 1812, short tempered, vain, and nostalgic for the glories of his youth. At his right hand is Robert E. Lee, a forty-year-old engineer, a dignified, serious man who has never seen combat.

Scott leads his troops against the imperious Mexican dictator, General Antonio Lopez de Santa Anna. Obsessed with glory and his place in history, Santa Anna arrogantly underestimates the will and the heart of Scott and his army. As the Americans fight their way inland, both sides understand that the inevitable final conflict will come at the gates and fortified walls of the ancient capital, Mexico City.

Cut off from communication and their only supply line, the Americans learn about their enemy and themselves, as young men witness for the first time the horror of war. While Scott must weigh his own place in history, fighting what many consider a bully's war, Lee the engineer becomes Lee the hero, the one man in Scott's command whose extraordinary destiny as a soldier is clear. The author illuminates the dark psychology of soldiers and their commanders trapped behind enemy lines bringing to life the haunted personalities and magnificent backdrop, the familiar characters, the stunning triumphs, and soul-crushing defeats of a fascinating, long-forgotten war. [DJ]

Jeff Shaara has written several series of books on the generalship in the Civil War, the Revolution, and World War II. His works and bio are further described in the chapters on "The Civil War" and "The World Wars."

Blood on the Plains

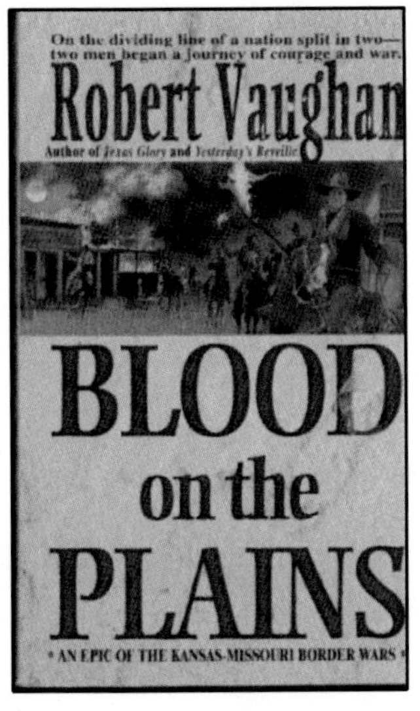

Manifest Destiny, Kansas, Civil War

Robert Vaughan St Martin's Press (1997)

The men swarmed out of the night, brandishing swords of bloody righteousness. When they were done, innocent lives were shed, and a nation was one step closer to war.

Between one man's mad dream and another's outlaw raiders, a nation was exploding. And two West Point cadets, sent by the President himself on a secret mission to the burning Kansas-Missouri border, would be swept into the maelstrom -- friends turned enemies across a thundering landscape of savagery, courage, and war. [BC]

Yesterday's Reveille

Manifest Destiny, Indian Wars, Kansas, Dakotas

Robert Vaughan St. Martin's Press (1996)

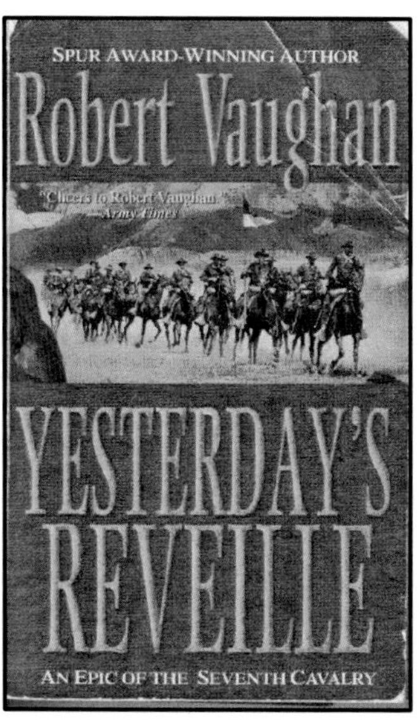

They were soldiers young and brave in a war that would change America forever. Some came from the gray cliffs of West Point, some from the bloody caldron of the Civil War. By train and steamship, they traveled West to fight an enemy battling for a way of life. They were the men of the U.S. Seventh Cavalry, whose name would echo in history.

Joe Murchison was a young officer who learned that no amount of training could prepare him for life and death on the frontier. Rising through the officer ranks, he fought toe-to-toe with an enemy who sometimes was not what he seemed. And above him loomed the dashing figure of George Custer, the man who would lead Joe and the Seventh Cavalry to glory and tragedy. [BC]

Robert Vaughan authored more than 250 published works including *The Valkyrie Mandate*, which was nominated for a Pulitzer Prize, and *Andersonville*, which was made into the popular TNT television mini-series. His subject matter embraced westerns, romances, historical fiction, and adventures. Vaughan is a retired Army Warrant Officer (CW-3) with three tours in Vietnam where he was a helicopter pilot and a maintenance and supply officer. [14-05]

Blood Across Kansas

Pulp Fiction, Western, Indian Wars

Lt. John T. Hopper Argosy Magazine (1933)

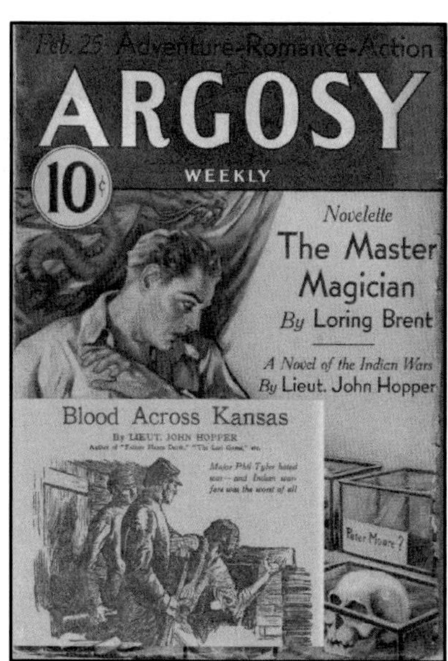

"Major Phil Tyler hated war -- and Indian warfare was the worst of all…"

CHAPTER I. NEW BATTLEFIELDS.

THE secretary to the governor of the State of Kansas smashed his heavy fist down upon the table. "Gentlemen," he cried vehemently, "there's blood all across Kansas! Even in the trying days when our fair state was known as ' bleeding Kansas,' there was no such shedding of the blood of innocent victims! The Indians are on the war path. All summer and fall they have been murdering and pillaging. And the Cheyenne are the worst of the lot . . .

"Gentlemen," he leaned forward earnestly, " it must stop! Can't you see our poor citizens—your fellow men— stricken down beside the plow, their homesteads burned? Ranches destroyed—the screams of mothers and the wailing of little children."

Silas Williams paused to regain his breath. He was a “stump” orator, and whenever he spoke on political matters, whether his listeners were one or a hundred, he was apt to speechify, making full use of the melodramatic, sentimental appeal that permeated the stage of the day.

The Army officers stared in astonishment and horror.

P. H. Sheridan, commanding general of the Military Division of the Missouri, sat at the head of the long table of unpainted boards. As the day was warm, he had thrown open his heavy coat of midnight blue broadcloth. Whenever he moved, the gold-plated buttons glinted in the late afternoon sunlight that poured through a small window beside him. The window was small because glass, like everything else in this barren country, was hard to obtain. His black felt hat, encircled by a cord of gold, and possessed of a wide brim, lay on the table beside his elbow. Behind him was his aide, leaning against the log wall.

Sheridan’s physical appearance gave the impression of bigness and solidity. His thick, powerful fingers thoughtfully caressed his long, dark mustache while his eyes glowed somberly upon the boyish face of General George Armstrong Custer, commanding the Seventh Cavalry. Custer sat farther along the table, at one side, wearing his usual plains uniform, the blouse of which was a double-breasted jacket of doeskin, fringed across the shoulders and sides and around the upper arms.

His fair hair hung to his shoulders.

Custer sat across from the speaker, Silas Williams. The governor’s secretary was dressed in the most advanced fashion of the day. His tight coat was checked with tiny brown and gray squares. Above his full, brown beard, which did not go quite low enough to hide his high collar and cravat, his piercing eyes were hot and angry as they turned from one general to the other.

At the foot of the table sat Major Phil Tyler, present at the conference because he happened to be on Custer’s staff and had accompanied the general the ninety miles to Fort Hays from Bluff Creek. Bluff Creek was near Fort Dodge, on the Arkansas River, where the Seventh Cavalry, Custer’s command, was encamped after a summer’s unsuccessful chase of marauding Indians. Unlike Custer, Major Tyler was clad in the usual regulation blue uniform. His folded hands on the table were encased with gray gauntlets.

It was evident that Tyler was the youngest man in the room, several years younger than Custer, who himself was a major general at the almost unheard of age of twenty-nine. The army was full of young generals, colonels, and majors, brevet ranks of the Civil War. With the vast shrinkage of that service after Appomattox Court House, generals had found themselves commanding regiments, colonels headed battalions, and majors looked after' mere companies, with brevet captains as their lieutenants. Unusual for a day when practically all men wore a beard, or at least a generous mustache, Major Tyler was clean-shaven. His dark hair was carefully parted above his lean face, in which his eyes, contrasting with the tan of his skin, were like a pair of sapphires, hard, clear, and deep blue.

Tyler had not been long with the Seventh Cavalry, having been recently transferred from a station in the East. joining the regiment at Bluff Creek, he had seen little of Indians save the regiment’s own scouts. He had listened intently to Mr. Williams’s theatrical speech of a moment before. Although his eyes had remained hard and cold, Tyler had been afraid that his face had betrayed the sickish feeling in his breast. He had glanced furtively at Custer, Sheridan, and the aide, but apparently, they had noticed nothing wrong with him.

As he leveled his gaze once more upon Williams’s flushed, arrogant, and not too intelligent face, Tyler thought bitterly that it was just such politicians as he who caused the wars and the bloodshed. War! Tyler shivered inside his uniform. Even now, three years after the peace of Appomattox, he sometimes awakened at night in a bath of perspiration, his ears ringing with the awful cries of the dying on the fields of Antietam, Gettysburg, and in the burning forests of the Wilderness. As long as he lived, the cries of those men and the sight of their blood would live with him.

It was a rotten thing, young Major Tyler reflected bitterly, to haul a kid out of West Point and thrust him so soon into the roaring inferno of arms, bayonets, and blood. Four years of it had ruined his life. Major Tyler knew that beyond doubt. Since then, he had looked upon the world with a hard, cold, blue eye, which hid the weariness and the burned-out embers of feeling inside him.

He had been an innocent, callow youth when he had picked soldiering for a profession and gone to West Point. How ignorant he had been of war's frightful suffering and terror! Then he had seen only the uniforms and the flags and had heard only the martial music. After the war, thoroughly disillusioned, quite changed even to himself, and tired of life, he had nevertheless kept on in the army. It was a living, and there would be no more wars. In his efforts to become human again, to be like the rest of the men who had gone to the war and returned, seeming ly unaffected, he had tried many things. He had buried himself in work, with the result that his leisure hours were only more horrible. He had tried to..."[EB]

"The Long Knives Ride"

Manifest Destiny, Texas, Pulp Fiction

William Foster-Harris Argosy Magazine (June 1938)

"For a year before this hurried mobilization for a winter Indian campaign the regiment had been split up in one and two troop stations all over south Texas. Cordis' outfit, K Troop, had drawn a particularly isolated border post. And then, to set the stage for trouble, it had also rated a new troop commander, First Lieutenant Carl Dealey and a new sergeant, Stiegel. Dealey, fresh from staff duty in the East, was one of those unfortunate failures of the Military Academy, a graduate who had absorbed all the hardness of the code the Point teaches, but none of its compensating impartiality and good sportsmanship. He would, perhaps, have made a good Prussian officer, of the cast-iron Junker type. And in Stiegel, who had actually served in the Prussian ranks before emigrating to America, he had found a drillmaster of the same merciless mold...

Over the prairie thundered the naked redskins -- and amid the tumult of the wild war-cries five white fugitives had to decide a question of loyalty and sacrifice.

The Quahada attack was so well masked, so murderously fast sprung, that even the shivering Tonkawa scout was caught flat-footed. He was dead before he could lift a death wail. Riding beside the lurching army wagon, Sergeant Stiegel, in command, had just time for one frantic command…

The whole, brushy hillside ahead and to the right was alive with screaming, charging, red warriors. On foot, that was the amazing part. Comanches attacking dismounted, separated from their horses. Good generalship on the part of the red commander, whoever he was. With any luck at all, he'd bag this whole detachment of hated blue troopers, in the next minute or so. And then . . .

The very air itself seemed to be one vast, hideous explosion now. Winchesters, Spencer cavalry carbines, revolvers were pounding deep rhythm. Back at the creek bank, Corporal Gregg was trying to form a rallying point. In complete rout, all the troopers still alive were spurring desperately toward him. Twenty paces ahead Cordis could see big Sod Ryan and Joe Teel, the other two deserters, running like scared deer. Sprinting, he and Hunter with their convulsive burden had reached the cut bank. Stiegel had not even had time to draw his revolver before death had reached him. Cordis ripped the heavy weapon free from its holster, as he let the non-com's legs drop. "Get that key," he screamed at Hunter. . . .He found the key, clicked himself free, and pounced for Stiegel's slung carbine. . . .

All of a sudden it was no longer a rout. There were six troopers against the bank, working carbines and revolvers with furious speed. Six left out of thirteen who had formed the detachment just a moment before. Yet now a resistance was organized. Automatically, shoulder to shoulder, the blue remnant was meeting the onslaught. And no attack lacking iron discipline could have roared right over those flaming muzzles. Immediately the whole cohesion of the charge was gone. It stopped cold, milled an instant, then burst howling back. Mounted and afoot, somehow miraculously carrying even their own dead and wounded, the Comanches were gone like flying smoke.

But now the prisoners were free and armed!" [EB]

William Foster-Harris was a popular writer who also has taught the principles of writing to hundreds of students in the University of Oklahoma professional writing courses. His most well-known work is *The Look of the Old West – a Fully Illustrated Guide.* 14-07

"Texas Joins the Army"

Manifest Destiny, Crime, Texas, Pulp Fiction

Lt. John T. Hopper   Argosy Magazine (May 1929)

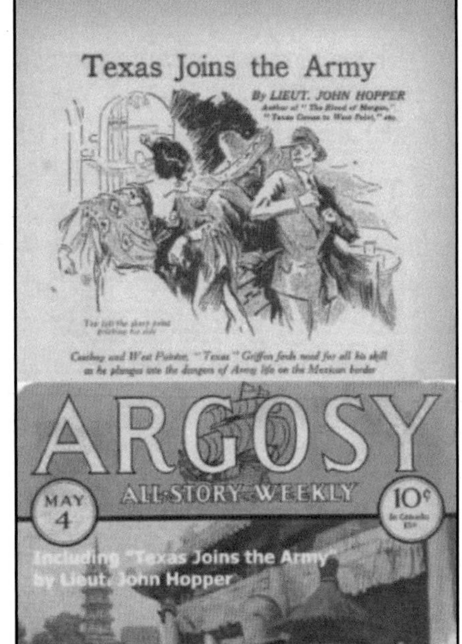

Cowboy and West Pointer, "Texas" Griffen finds need for all his skill as he plunges into the dangers of Army life on the Mexican border:

Cross the level desert, the train headed toward the border, rattling through the hot Texas night. This was no deluxe, cross-continent special. The passenger cars, both day coaches, had known better and younger days.

The second car carried an assortment of passengers - a heavy-set, red-faced soldier was snoring audibly. Opposite him sat two Mexicans. In the center of the car, on the same side with the Mexicans, was a party of four. Wealthy ranch owners, evidently with their wives. A lone passenger sat in the rear of the car. He was a young man of about twenty-four years of age....

An altercation ensued when the train was boarded by Mexican bandits.... Griffen lost some valuables but was unharmed, not the case with others. Later Griffen was deposited at the gates of Fort Smith Texas. Gone were the Broadway clothes of the evening before. In their stead was the uniform of Uncle Sam.

Tex surveyed the small, weather-beaten building, over the door of which was nailed a sign: Headquarters Fort Smith, Texas Ninety-Seventh Cavalry.

He was joining the army. Taking in a full breath, he squared his shoulders and marched in to report to the commanding officer of the Ninety-Seventh Cavalry. Tex's spurs clicked together as he saluted. "Sir, Lieutenant Griffen reports for duty." [EB]

John Hopper (1903–1970) graduated from West Point in 1927 but resigned his commission in 1930 and took up writing for pulp fiction magazines. There are eighteen of Hopper's stories in this collection distributed through several chapters. See the "Army Sports" chapter for more on Hopper.

Skirmish

Manifest Destiny, Texas

Bert Cloos Avalon Books (1957)

When Andrew McCabe graduated from West Point in 1870, a brand-new second lieutenant in the United States Cavalry, he had one burning drive--to be the best officer he could for as long as he lived. The army was all the career he wanted. His first mistake -- everybody called it a mistake -- was to marry Nancy Fowler, of the St. Louis Fowlers, an influential Family who had given Nancy more luxury in her nineteen years than McCabe could give her in a lifetime.

But McCabe didn't care what anybody thought. And Nancy thought it was a "glorious" adventure. So off McCabe went to his first assignment at Fort Natchi, a motley collection of old adobes and huts that was a Fort in name only. What McCabe thought was to be the first step toward a wonderful career turned out to be the first step in a struggle that was to wreck McCabe's career and almost destroy him as a man.

For McCabe's first commanding officer turned out to be Captain "Mad" Milton, a man who thrived on hatred and vengeance; a man who feared nothing alive. From the first moment they met, Captain Milton was after McCabe, and when Milton's son, Benny, framed McCabe and disappeared, "Mad" Milton brought McCabe before a general court on charges of neglect of duty, drunkenness, and disobeying orders. Although McCabe was cleared because of lack of evidence, the trial followed him from outpost to outpost, robbing him of promotion and heaping upon him scorn and humiliation.

Andrew McCabe lived only for the day when he could get revenge on Captain Milton and Benny, now turned renegade. And after five long years, he did. Brought face to face with the man who had wrecked his life, he got vengeance. But not the kind he had planned. [DJ]

Bert Cloos authored a handful of western novels. Otherwise, little is known about him, except that he lived in California.

The Dakotas, Wyoming, Colorado, Montana

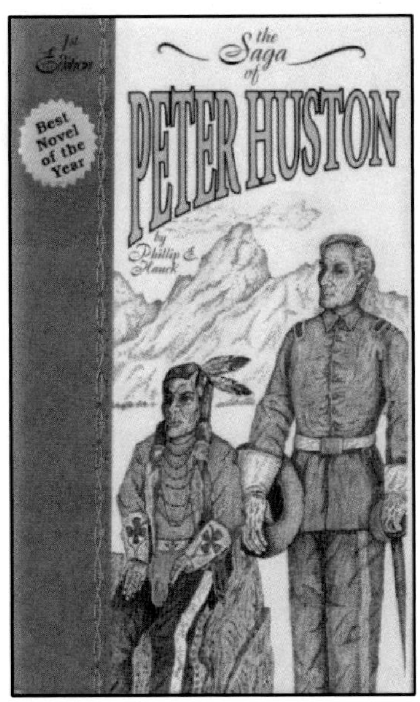

The Saga of Peter Huston

Manifest Destiny, Wyoming, Colorado

Phillip Hauck Dab Publishing (1998)

This moving, fictionalized history tells the story of Peter Huston. Searching for the American dream, the Huston family head west. While Peter and the Cherokee Indian scout are away from the wagon train, the settlers are massacred. Revenge fills Peter's heart.

The Indian prompts his commanding officer to enlist the boy in the army. He works his way up the command chain and graduates from West Point a topographical engineer.

A Sioux war party sends Peter to the hospital where a brassy, young journalist, Elizabeth Turner, demands the story. Amused and infatuated, he wants her for his bride. She shuns his advances. Traveling with a historical party to the Yellowstone Basin, Elizabeth is abducted by the Blackfeet tribe. Peter's skin crawls. Is he skilled enough to save her from a fate worse than death? [DJ]

Phillip Hauck (1920–2007) grew up in Pocatello, Idaho, adjacent to the Fort Hall Indian Reservation. In WWII, his engineer company was one of the first that stormed Omaha Beach. The war ended for him at the Battle of the Bulge. He is the recipient of three battle stars and the Bronze Star medal. Working for Markhams Advertising, he covered the states of Idaho, Utah, Wyoming, Nebraska, and Colorado. His personal knowledge is reflected in this story. [DJ]

The Novels of Charles King

Charles King, Class of 1866, authored more novels than any graduate of West Point. The subjects of his 60 novels ranged from West Point cadets to the Civil War, battling the Plains Indians, garrison life, and the Philippine campaign. A few of his novels are described below and others can be found in the chapters "Civil War" and "Army Life & Army Wives."

King's novels of the Army on the Western frontier share common plot lines and character types: a good officer, a bad officer, a young West Point lieutenant new to the regiment, a commanding officer's attractive daughter, a spinster aunt or companion that stirs up controversy, local civilian merchants, cowboys or ranchers exciting war with native Americans for profit; with a dash of romance thrown in. Of course, the names change, and the army posts are different.

Warrior Gap: A Story of the Sioux Outbreak of '68

Manifest Destiny, Wyoming, WP Author

Charles King F. Tennyson Neely (1898)

Warrior Gap is a post that the Army is attempting to establish along the upper Platte River to protect settlers accompanying the construction of the Union Pacific railroad through Wyoming and beyond. Unfortunately, the site chosen was on one of the Indians' most prized hunting grounds, and they were not going to accept it without a fight. The Army is warned by the Folsom family, long-time settlers and traders with the tribes, to no avail

"Old John Folsom, he whom the Indians loved and trusted, grew anxious and went from post to post with words of warning on his tongue.

"Gentlemen," he said to the commissioners who came to treat with the Sioux whose hunting grounds adjoined the line of the railway. It is all very well to have peace with these people here. It is wise to cultivate the friendship of such chiefs as Spotted Tail and Old-Man-Afraid-of-His-Horses but there are irreconcilables beyond them, far more numerous and powerful, who are planning, preaching war this minute. Watch Red Cloud, Red Dog, Little Big Man. Double, treble your garrisons at the posts along the Big Horn; get your women and children out of them, or else abandon the forts entirely. I know those warriors well. They outnumber you twenty to one. Reinforce your garrisons without delay or get out of that country, one of the two. Draw everything south of the Platte while yet there is time."

But the authorities in Washington said the Indians were peaceable, and all that was needed was a new post and another little garrison at Warrior Gap, in the eastward foothills of the range. Eight hundred thousand dollars would build it, "provided the labor of the troops was utilized," and still leave a good margin for the contractors and "the Bureau." Escorting the quartermaster and engineer officer and an aide-de-camp on preliminary survey was the assignment of "C" Troop of the cavalry, Captain Brooks commanding. They had been sent on the march from the North Platte at Frayne to the headwaters of the Powder River in the Hills, and with it went its new first lieutenant, West Point graduate, Marshall Dean. [EB]

Fort Frayne

Manifest Destiny, Wyoming, WP Author

Charles King The Hobart Company (1901)

This is one of Charles King's dozens of stories of life at a post-Civil War on the Plains. The plots don't vary greatly, though the individuals and locale certainly do. Fort Frayne is a fictitious post on the Platte River in the Wyoming territory, but the depiction of Army life as the 12th Cavalry stationed at Frayne struggles to maintain the equilibrium between settlers, miners, and Indian tribes is most real. Colonel Farrar, a distinguished leader is the commandant, while his wife is beloved by all on the post. They have two sons. The first, Royale, attended West Point, but was forced out for his egregious behavior only to become a wastrel and ne'er-do-well, a challenge to the family trying to keep him from jail or worse. The second son, Will, graduates from the academy and returns West to assume his 2nd lieutenant duties. A lovely daughter, Ellis, adores her younger brother and garners the favor of a couple of officers in the command. The renegade Sioux are raiding off their reservation, so the troop is sent to gather them back. As in most of King's novels, there is a spinster sister or companion of a high-ranking officer who engages in questionable activity and elevates the drama on the post. [EB]

To the Front

Manifest Destiny, Dakotas, WP Author

Charles King Harper & Bros (1908)

A sequel to *Cadet Days* by Charles King.

"It was graduation day at West Point, and there had been a remarkable scene at the morning ceremonies. In the presence of the Board of Visitors, the full-uniformed officers of the academic and military staff, the august professors and their many assistants, scores of daintily dressed women, and dozens of sober-garbed civilians, the assembled Corps of Cadets, in their gray and white, had risen as one man and cheered to the echo of a soldierly young fellow, their "first captain," as he received his diploma and then turned to rejoin them. It was an unusual incident. Every man preceding had been applauded, some of them vehemently. Every man after him received his meed of greeting and congratulations, but the portion accorded Cadet Captain 'Geordie Graham, exceeded all others."

Soon after, Geordie headed West to engage in policing unrest among the settlers, coping with villainous outlaws, and pursuing renegade Sioux and Sitting Bull. He displays exceptional leadership because of his prior experience as an "Army brat" augmented by his development at West Point. Back East, they received the "first news of the bitter midwinter battle that ended the days of Big Foot and so many of his band, that cost us the lives of so many gallant officers and men, among the icy flats and snow-patched ravines along the Wounded Knee." Not exactly the currently held version of the massacre at Wounded Knee, but Geordie endeavors to avoid harming women and children….

The telegram read: "Severe action. Graham wounded; left thigh. Serious but doing well. Our losses heavy." A recuperating Graham was escorted back East and welcomed at West Point as a great hero. [EB]

Charles King (1844–1932) was the son of Civil War General Rufus King, grandson of Columbia University president Charles King, and great grandson of Rufus King, a signer of the U.S. Constitution. He graduated from West Point in 1866 and served in the Army during the Indian Wars under George Crook. He was wounded in the arm and head during the Battle of Sunset Pass forcing his retirement from the regular army as a captain in 1879. He then served in the Wisconsin National Guard from 1882 until 1897, becoming Adjutant General in 1895. [14-08]

“The Lieutenant’s Horse”

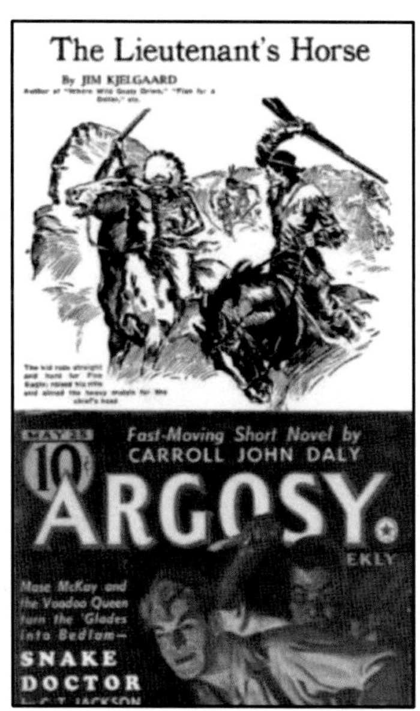

Manifest Destiny, Wyoming, Pulp Fiction

Jim Kjelgaard Argosy Magazine (May 25, 1940)

“More about that magnificently left-handed youngster whose chief weapon in fightin’ Injuns is an outstanding talent for doing things the wrong way.”

Ben Egan’s eyes were fixed between the bobbing ears of his horse. He couldn’t see anything else unless he looked up at the stars because he and Lieutenant Searles had left the army post at ten o’clock at night. An hour out of the post Ben halted his horse and listened. He still did not believe in his incredibly good luck and would not until he was three or four hours farther away. The round-faced, adventure-struck kid, who had attached himself to Ben and apparently never would be shaken off, had not been in the post when Ben left it.

But this place was Indian country. Ben had an amazing talent for doing things wrong; only incredible luck had so far kept his hair on his head.... [EB]

Jim Kjelgaard (1910–1959) was an American writer. His books were primarily about dogs and wild animals, often with animal protagonists and told from the animal’s point of view. Kjelgaard also wrote short fiction for several magazines, including *The Saturday Evening Post*, *Argosy*, and *Adventure*. His other work in this catalog and biography can be found under “Mascots & Other Army Animals.” [14-09]

“Warrior Breed”

Manifest Destiny, Pulp Fiction, Wyoming

William R. Cox Argosy Magazine (April, 1943)

Lieutenant James Ferrell, known to his old classmates at West Point as “Beautiful Jamesy,” stood in the dust and watched the Sioux come in for their rations. The silent, stolid line seemed nondescript in the extreme. The squaws were thick-bodied, ugly. The men wore hybrid hand-me-downs, wrapped themselves in blankets against the heat of the sun, although Jamesy could scarcely endure the regulation tunic which threatened to smother him in this Western clime, with heat waves rising from the endless plain which stretched to an infinitely distant horizon.

When the Indian Agent’s office opened, the line shuffled forward. It was 1880 and President Garfield had newly come to office in Washington. Captain Harry Grayce of the harsh voice and impeccable New England ancestry said, “Look at them! Ugly, worthless, treacherous. Next month, if they gain horses and arms, they will be slaughtering the ranchers, running off livestock. They would rather steal than earn. The noble redman! Pahh!"

Captain Grayce was elegant. He had become inured to heat, Jamesy supposed wistfully. The blue uniform fitted the slim-waisted man like a glove; his hat tilted rakishly; all his accoutrements were part of him. Grayce was thirty-ish and had been in the West for seven years. Major Classen was even more experienced. He had been a subaltern at Gettysburg. His lean, hawk's face was restless, his eyes pale from scanning far horizons, but there was tolerance in him. Jamesy liked Classen. The major was human. He told Jamesy, "The Plains Indian was the second noblest of them all—after the Confederacy Tribes. Until we took away his buffalo, he was self-sufficient. Warlike—but noble enough. You've spent too much time chasing them." [EB]

William Robert Cox (1901–1988) was a prolific writer of short stories primarily for the pulp and paperback markets. He wrote under at least six pseudonyms. A one-time president of the Western Writers of America, he was said to have averaged 600,000 published words a year for 14 years during the era of the pulp magazines. He wrote television scripts for shows such as *GE Theater*, *Bonanza*, *Outer Limits*, *The Virginian* and others. [14-10]

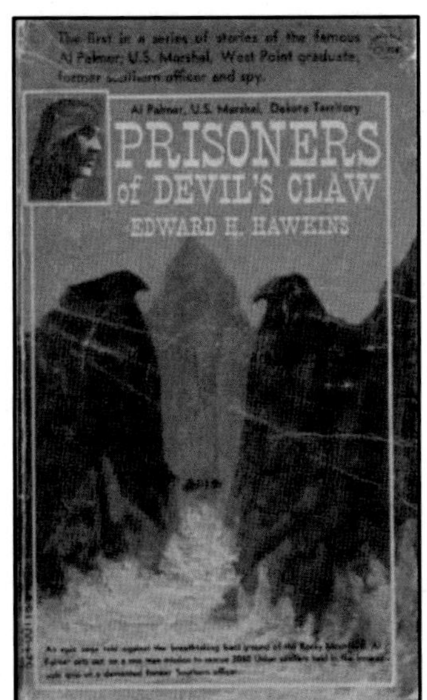

Prisoners of Devil's Claw

Manifest Destiny, Civil War, Colorado

Edward H. Hawkins Apollo Press (1971)

The first in a series of the famous Al Palmer, U.S. Marshall, West Point graduate, former southern officer, and spy.

U.S. Marshal Al Palmer had been summoned from the Dakota Territory to Washington, D.C., in the early Spring of 1869 and sat listening to Assistant Secretary of War Jonas Lamphere unwind a gruesome tale which was shortly to become his next assignment.

Deep in the Rocky Mountains of the little-known Colorado Territory, Major Larson, a former Confederate Army officer, secretly holds over 2000 Union soldiers in slavery. For more than four years Larson has been mining silver with Northern soldiers taken captive during the Civil War. In an inescapable box canyon slave mine, Larson is sending silver to the South for reconstruction. Larson's natural fortress is revealed in history to be Devil's Claw, a canyon named by the Indians and virtually impossible to escape from or attack.

In 1869, few white men knew anything of the new and savagely beautiful Colorado Territory. Al Palmer was one of the few. He was rough, cunning, and ruggedly handsome. Palmer was a loner and save for the small glint of his badge, he looked every bit the part of a white man turned Indian. [BC]

No biographical information was found for this author.

Trumpets of Company K

Indian Wars, Dakotas, WP Author

William Chamberlain Ballantine Books (1954)

In Fort Duncan the news was grim. Lieutenant Hardin's patrol had come in with two men dead and the lieutenant captured. All summer the Dakota Territory had seethed with rumors of a new plot in Washington against the Indian lands, and how the Sioux had broken out of the reservation to pillage the frontier.

Captain Garland had his orders: Take Company K into the fields against the hostiles and break the uprising. Bring back the son of Senator Mark Hardin -- if he was still alive. On a raw October morning in 1878, Captain Garland led Company K through the main gate of Fort Duncan...sixty-two men against the savage Sioux. [BC]

Forced March to Loon Creek

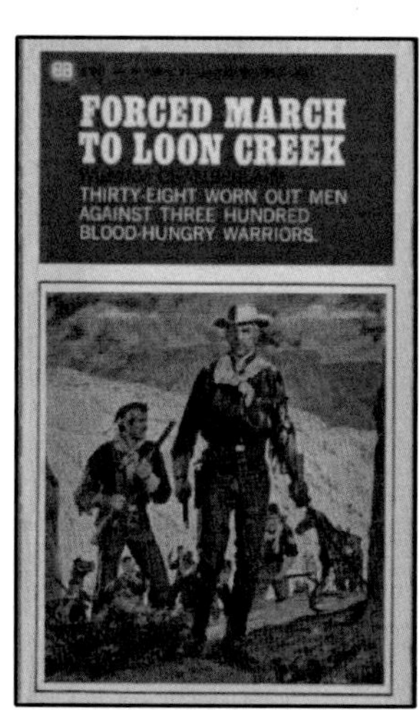

Manifest Destiny, WP Author

William Chamberlain Ballantine Books (1964)

WYOMING TERRITORY 1872

And Fort McKeogh was virtually deserted, the entire regiment sent off to fight at Powder River, when Colonel Bexar got the dispatch that Hat, a notorious Indian war chief, had broken out of the reservation and was heading up to Galena on Loon Creek for a rendezvous with the Teton Indians.

There were just thirty-eight men who could be mustered to stop the war-dance at Loon Creek — the lame, the halt, the drunks — and they would have to be led by an ex-Confederate Captain nobody trusted. . . . [BC]

Edwin William Chamberlain (1903–1966), Class of 1927, started selling his short stories and novels to various magazines while still on active duty. His bio and other stories are in the "General Officers" and "The World Wars" chapters.

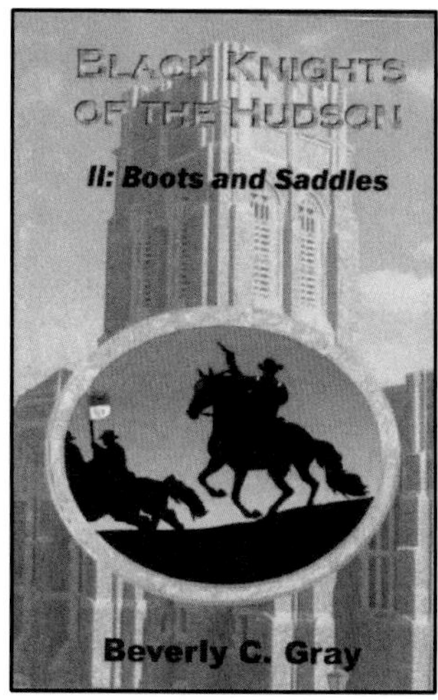

Boots and Saddles: Black Knights of the Hudson, Book II

Manifest Destiny, Indian Wars

Beverly C. Gray Self-published (2012)

BOOTS AND SADDLES is the second book in this sweeping family saga of the MacKendricks, who live by West Point's motto - Duty, Honor, Country. With the Civil War over, James seeks a return to the cheerful fatalism of the professional soldier and is even willing to serve in the hated Cavalry. Timothy, cooling his heels in a Staff position, has his hands full with his willful wife who has yet to learn that a good Army wife does not hesitate to follow her husband even to dismal outposts in the Western territories. She pays a heavy price for her obstinacy and independence in the glittering social whirl of post-Civil War New York. Gwyneth O'Donnell, a young Army brat at an Arizona post, has learned the role of a true Army wife at her mother's knee and is prepared to throw herself into a passionate love for a professional soldier; in a way that Timothy's wife cannot match. In Arizona and the turmoil of the Plains, James and Timothy face Apache, Cheyenne, and Sioux in the great Indian wars of the post-Civil War era; as they come to terms with a military policy that in one breath wants to protect Indian treaty lands and, in the next, seeks to conquer them in the name of Manifest Destiny. [BC]

Beverly Gray has written a six-book series, *Black Knights of the Hudson*, about the West Point journey of the MacKendrick family from the Civil War to World War I. See the "West Point Legacies" chapter for more on the series. [EB]

Undoubtedly the hardest-to-find book in this collection is the 1878 original printing of *The Cadet Button* by Frederick Whittaker. Fortunately, reprints (like this one) are readily available on the major book sites.

The Cadet Button

Manifest Destiny, Romance, Army Life

Frederick Whittaker — Sheldon Co. (1878)

From the book dedication and forward:

> To the Cadet Corps of The U. S. Military Academy at West Point - Prodigal alike of their Buttons and their Blood, I dedicate this story!
>
> The first thing men will say when they take up this book, is: "Why was it written? Have you not too many books now? You must tell what is new if you want us to listen."
>
> . . .
>
> The men and women in this book are types of army life, no better nor worse than they really are. If you say that my Indians are not true Indians, that such never lived, I say that the man from whom Mac Diarmid is drawn died in New York not ten years ago, and that the others in my story are alive to-day. I have tried to show them truly, with all their faults and good points.
>
> If this tale rouse any to speak out against the wrongs daily done to those who once held all our land, it will have done all I hope for it. It is right that the men who have broken the fetters of the slave should save the Indian from those who cheat him under the mask of law, and then kill him for fighting against the thieves who have robbed him. May that time soon come for the fair fame of our land! [14-12]

The story begins with June week at West Point where two cousins, Juliet Brinton and Nettie Dashwood, collect a cadet button from 2nd year cadets as mementos. Cadet Frank Armstrong, who suffered a punishment tour for a missing button at inspection, is smitten by the older Juliet and seeks to court her while being a good friend to younger Nettie. Juliet is coquettish, and has her eye on a dark, handsome cadet Mac Diarmid. Two years later at graduation, Frank is a 2nd lieutenant, while his friend Mac Diarmid has been dismissed for excessive demerits, the final ones being fostered by a faculty member who is a relative of the Brintons. He vows revenge and has the means to do it, being the heir to the Hudson Bay Fur company….and his mother was a Sioux. He plays an ominous role throughout the novel.

The story moves from the Brinton house on the Hudson to Fort Marengo on the Northern Plains overseen by General St. Aure, his brother Colonel Jim Aure, and wife Isabel. Frank Armstrong and the 12th Cavalry soon arrive on re-assignment. The elder Brintons have journeyed to the fort for a buffalo hunting party bringing along Juliet, Nettie, and their formidable Aunt Lacy. Romance is in the air with several officers attempting to woo the Brinton cousins. Armstrong and a company of cavalry leave on a month long trek to scout out the Sioux. Mac Diarmid appears in a Sioux village plotting to stir up an uprising. Armstrong is separated, missing and presumed lost. The Brinton cousins are devastated, but particularly Nettie who, it is revealed, carries the cadet button on a chain around her neck.

The tale returns to the Hudson Valley with all present, including Frank Armstrong. Surprising events unfold, and the cadet button makes a third and final appearance. [EB]

George Armstrong Custer and the Seventh Cavalry stand center stage in the panorama of Manifest Destiny. They epitomized the inherent conflict between the Native Americans being forced off their lands and the growing American population surging west to create ranches, homes, and businesses. The struggle and bloodshed began decades before 1876 as the Army established posts West of the Mississippi and Missouri Rivers. It lasted for two decades after the debacle at the Little Big Horn.
The number of books and articles written about Custer is staggering, and many are fiction or at least speculative to a large degree. That is certainly true of accounts of the Last Stand at the Little Big Horn, since none of the cavalry survived, and just one horse - Comanche. To include so many accounts would overwhelm this chapter and the entire collection. So here are a few notable novels.

A Popular Life of Gen'l Geo. A. Custer

Manifest Destiny, General Officer

Frederick Whittaker Sheldon Co. (1878)

"In the election year of 1876 the Battle of the Little Big Horn was horrifyingly fresh to opinion makers, who divided along political lines in assigning blame. The late General George A. Custer, who had been a Democrat with aspirations to high office, was more pilloried than praised by President Grant and influential editors of Republican newspapers. Coming to the defense of Custer was Frederick Whittaker, who less than six months after the disaster published this first biography of him. *A*

Complete Life was the beginning of a legend, and Whittaker did more than anyone else except Libby Custer to make the flamboyant Boy General a permanent resident of the national consciousness. Quite aside from its contribution to the public image of Custer, this important book placed him and his associates against a concrete background of onrushing events. Drawing on newspaper reports and the general's own words, Whittaker captures the excitement of the era. [It begins with] a boy's life in Ohio, his escapades as a cadet at West Point, his courtship of Judge Bacon's saucy daughter, and his exceptional service as a cavalryman in the Civil War which are described in vivid detail. From the first Battle of Bull Run through Gettysburg and the Virginia campaign he is seen in action, conspicuously defying death and winning promotion. After 1985 the story deals with Custer's fighting in the West, ending his last stand at the Little Big Horn in June 1876." [14-11]

Frederick Whittaker (1838–1889) was born in England, came to America as a youngster, and enlisted in the Union cavalry in 1861. He fought with distinction, was wounded in The Wilderness campaign, and attained the rank of 2nd lieutenant by the wars end. He retired to Mt. Vernon, NY, married, became a teacher, but quickly turned to a writing career, publishing in many widely circulated magazines. Whittaker developed a large readership as a pulp fiction writer in *Beadles* dime weeklies, producing more than 80 novels over a period of fifteen years. His tales were set on the colonial frontier, in the Wild West and in Napoleonic Europe; his characters were always brave and dashing figures. His most famous work was *A Popular Life of Gen. George A. Custer*. He died in 1889 from a gunshot wound to the head while falling down the stairs at his home. [14-12]

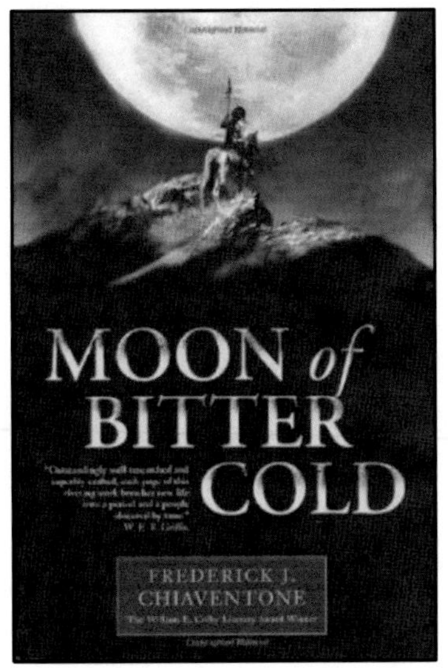

Moon of Bitter Cold

Manifest Destiny, Wyoming

Frederick J. Chiaventone   Forge Publishing (2002)

Set in 1866, with the Civil War finally at an end, General Henry Carrington is assigned to lead troops and their families into the Wyoming Territory in an effort to open new areas for settlers to homestead. At the same time, the Indians are becoming more and more agitated by what they see as the ever-encroaching white man. In an effort to drive them out permanently, Red Cloud, a Lakota Sioux war leader, succeeds in uniting the Sioux, Cheyenne, Arapaho, and Crow into a massive strike force to do just that.

Chiaventone very effectively gives his readers both points of view and a much deeper understanding of what eventually culminated into the only war the Western Indians ever won against the encroaching settlers. Tragically, General Carrington spent most of the rest of his life defending his reputation. Although the Army's official investigation fully exonerated him, the findings were filed away in obscurity by the government and the military to avoid having to admit their own culpability in what became known as the "Fetterman Massacre". [EB]

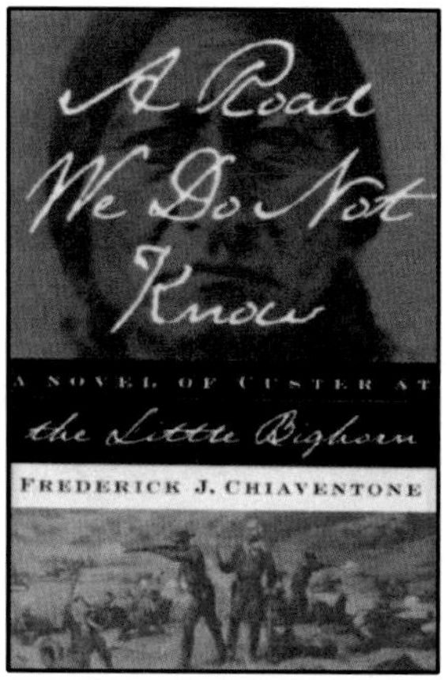

A Road We Do Not Know: A Novel of Custer at the Little Bighorn

Custer, Manifest Destiny, Montana

Frederick J. Chiaventone Simon & Schuster (1996)

In A Road We Do Not Know, Chiaventone's deeply felt and vividly written first novel, the Little Big Horn battle and its participants are presented with the narrative power that derives from profound understanding and extraordinary research. Also, Chiaventone is the first writer to give equal emphasis to the Seventh Cavalry and their Sioux opponents. Combining the intensity of truth and historical fact with the dramatic range of fiction, this memorable novel takes us, along with Custer, Sitting Bull, Reno, Crazy Horse, Benteen, Gall, and the many other fighters, on both sides. [DJ]

Frederick J. Chiaventone (1951–) is an award winning author writing about Native Americans and the Western frontier. His first novel, *A Road We Do Not Know*, was recently chosen by the Little Big Horn Association as the best novel ever written about the battle and is the winner of the William E. Colby Award. 14-13

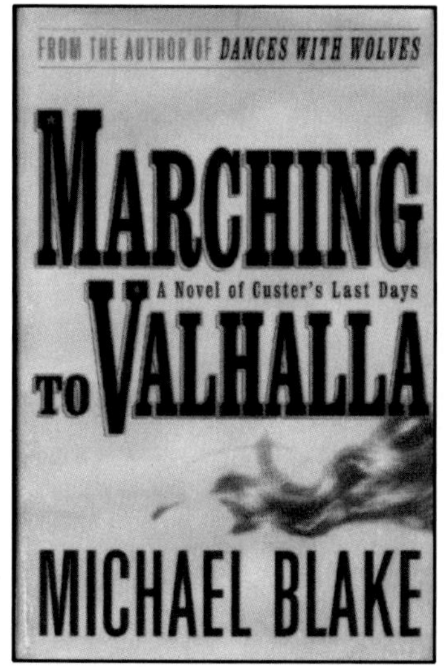

Marching to Valhalla: A Novel of Custer's Last Days

Custer, Manifest Destiny

Michael Blake Villard (1996)

By the author of *Dancing with Wolves*, in *Marching to Valhalla*, Blake turns his storyteller's eye on George Armstrong Custer, West Pointer, youngest Union general of the Civil War, horseman, passionate lover, explorer, ardent husband, and, most famously, Indian hunter. In Blake's pages, Custer emerges as a dashing, driven soldier, suspicious of his friends, respectful of his enemies, and ever unable to feel quite alive in the civilian World.

Composed in the form of Custer's journal, *Marching to Valhalla* is an impeccable merging of fact and fiction, a powerful evocation of our bloody past, and a tribute to the endurance of a human heart facing adversity and disaster. [DJ]

Michael Lennox Blake (1945–2015) was best known for the film adaptation of his novel *Dances with Wolves*, for which he won an Academy Award for Best Adapted Screenplay. He authored six other novels and as many screen plays. 14-14

For a different take on the events of June 25, 1876, John Hough's novel features a young reporter from Ohio invited by Custer to accompany the command. The reporter manages to survive the massacre, which leads to a remarkable concluding chapter. For the Custer purists, it's just a story!

Little Bighorn: A Novel

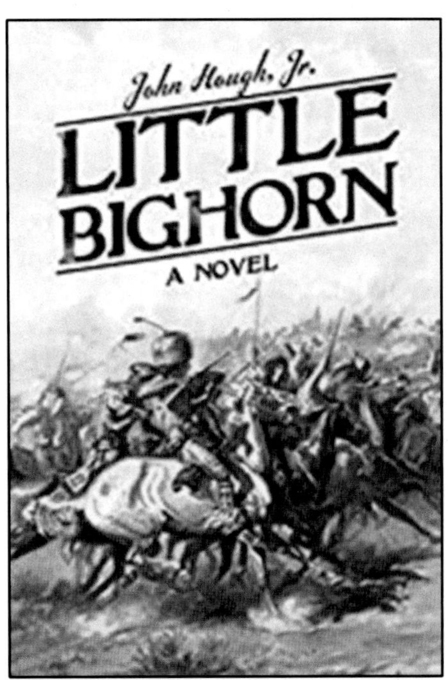

Manifest Destiny, Romance, Custer, Montana

John Hough, Jr. Arcade (2014)

As favor to the beautiful actress Mary Deschenes, Lt. Colonel George Armstrong Custer hires her eighteen-year-old son Allen Winslow as an aide for his 1876 campaign against the Sioux and Cheyenne. Traveling west against his will, Allen finds himself on a train in the company of Addie Grace Lord, sixteen, sister of one of Custer's regimental surgeons. The two fall in love. They arrive at Fort Lincoln in time to meet all the major players in the famous events before they unfold.

In a few days, Addie Grace watches Allen and her brother ride out with Custer's Seventh Cavalry. Through letters, Allen conveys to Addie the details of the epic westward adventure until, weeks later in Montana, the Seventh brings its quarry to bay beside the river called the Little Bighorn. [DJ]

John Hough, Jr. (1946–) grew up in Falmouth, Massachusetts and now lives on Martha's Vineyard. He is a graduate of Haverford College, a former VISTA volunteer, and assistant to James Reston at the Washington Bureau of *The New York Times*. Hough is the author of five previous novels, including *Seen the Glory: A Novel of the Battle of Gettysburg*, winner 2010 W. Y. Boyd Award, and three works of nonfiction. [14-15]

Comanche and His Captain

Animal, Youth, Manifest Destiny, Custer

A. M. Anderson Harper and Row (1965)

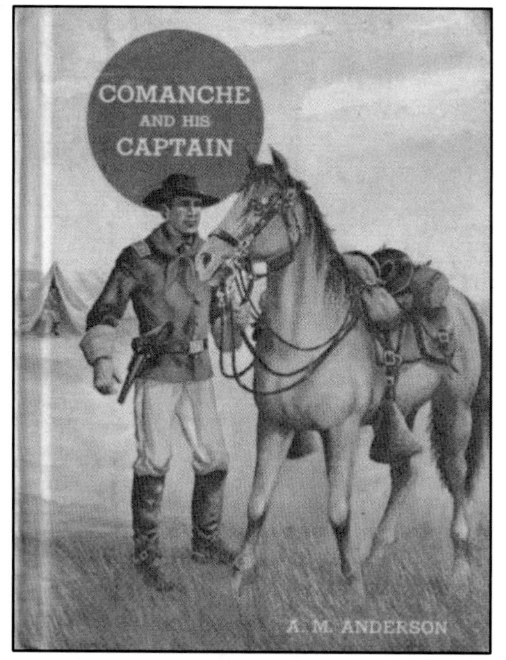

"This is a true story of an army horse and his young captain. It is also a story of the riding, fighting horse soldiers of the Seventh United States Cavalry.

Here are their forts and camps in the Old West. Here are the warpath trails they followed to the valley of the Little Big Horn. Here in the valley Custer's Last Stand was made against the Sioux.

Many years have come and gone since the battle. The soldiers in blue, the Sioux with their war paint and feathers—all are gone.

Even the United States Cavalry of horse soldiers is no more. Brave and strong they were, these men of the old cavalry. Brave and strong was the little horse they loved - Comanche of the Fighting Seventh…" [FP]

Comanche was the lone cavalry survivor on Last Stand Hill. Badly wounded, he was walked 120 miles back to the Missouri River and transported by steamboat to Fort Riley, Kansas. Comanche served as an honored member of the Seventh Cavalry until his death in 1891. The soldiers had him mounted and gave him to the Natural History Museum at Kansas University in Lawrence where he can be seen to this day. [EB]

Anita Melva Anderson (1906–?) authored a dozen books of historical fiction for youth in the 1950s for the "American Adventure Series." [14-16]

Easy Company

***Easy Company* is a series of thirty-one books featuring two West Point officers on the Wyoming frontier** in the decade following the Battle of the Little Big Horn. Outpost #9 (fictitious) hosts the Easy company of mounted infantry.

From the book forward – the cast of characters.

MATT KINCAID . . .West Point, class of 1869. A Connecticut Yankee turned Indian fighter. He's Regular Army, handsome, frontier tough—and Easy Company's second-in-command…and an attraction for the women they encounter.

WARNER CONWAY . . . Captain of the Post. He's a virile Virginian, West Pointer, a Civil War hero, a born leader. . . and putty in his sexy wife's hands.

FLORA CONWAY. . .The Captain's Lady. She's an Army wife through and through . . . and a stunning beauty with a soft woman's ways.

SERGEANT BEN COHEN . . .The tough, brawny top kick. He'd taken many a wisecracking recruit to "fist city" behind the barracks, but to those ready to soldier, he was as fair as they came.

WINDY MANDALIAN . . . Easy's buckskin-clad chief scout. Doesn't say much. But you couldn't have a better man beside you in a firefight with hostiles.

The plots go beyond conflicts with the Sioux, Comanche, Arapaho, and Utes. Trouble also arises from cattlemen, outlaws, surveyors, gamblers, confidence men, miners, merchants, tourists, blizzards, Indian agents, shady ladies, and the railroad.

The cover work is remarkable. Each book of 200 pages is an easy read. All 31 books are in the collection.

Prevailing wind

OUTPOST NINE

Wyoming Territory

KEY

- **A.** Parade and flagstaff
- **B.** Officers' quarters ("officers' country")
- **C.** Enlisted men's quarters: barracks, day room, and mess
- **D.** Kitchen, quartermaster supplies, ordnance shop, guardhouse
- **E.** Suttler's store and other shops, tack room, and smithy
- **F.** Stables
- **G.** Quarters for dependents and guests; communal kitchen
- **H.** Paddock
- **I.** Road and telegraph line to regimental headquarters
- **J.** Indian camp occupied by transient "friendlies"

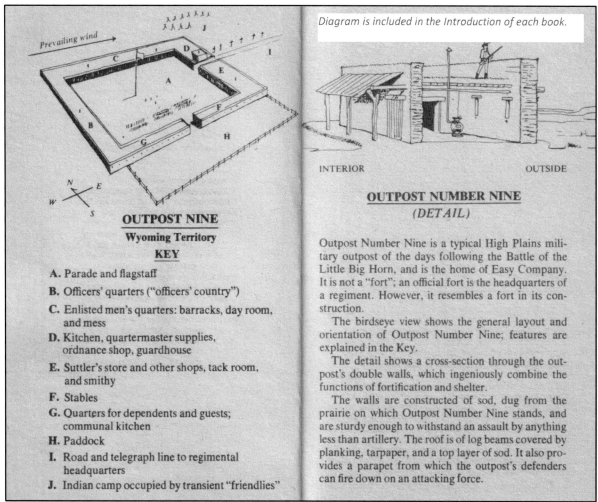

Diagram is included in the Introduction of each book.

INTERIOR OUTSIDE

OUTPOST NUMBER NINE

(DETAIL)

Outpost Number Nine is a typical High Plains military outpost of the days following the Battle of the Little Big Horn, and is the home of Easy Company. It is not a "fort"; an official fort is the headquarters of a regiment. However, it resembles a fort in its construction.

The birdseye view shows the general layout and orientation of Outpost Number Nine; features are explained in the Key.

The detail shows a cross-section through the outpost's double walls, which ingeniously combine the functions of fortification and shelter.

The walls are constructed of sod, dug from the prairie on which Outpost Number Nine stands, and are sturdy enough to withstand an assault by anything less than artillery. The roof is of log beams covered by planking, tarpaper, and a top layer of sod. It also provides a parapet from which the outpost's defenders can fire down on an attacking force.

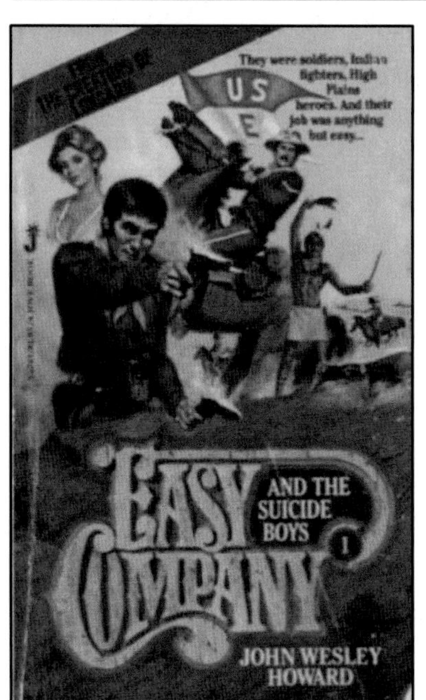

Easy Company and the Suicide Boys (#1 of 31)

Manifest Destiny, Wyoming

John Wesley Howard Jove Publications (1981)

The West was Never Wilder!

Especially for the men of Easy Company. Their job was to police the High Plains tribes, keep the peace...and stay alive. No one ever said it would be easy. Now a band of blood-lusting Cheyenne "suicide boys" are using Outpost Nine for target practice. A lost wagon train is in trouble, and scouts are picked off for scalps. When the death toll rises, it's up to Lt. Matt Kincaid to stop the bloodshed—without igniting a full-scale uprising. With a nit-picking Army Inspector cramping the Company's style, and raw, unruly recruits to forge into fighting machines, Kincaid tries to end the killing, and finds himself knife-to-knife with the Cheyenne leader, a firebrand named 'American Tears.'

Easy Company – Rough-Riding Adventure on the High Plains! [BC]

John Wesley Howard was a pseudonym employed by a half dozen writers who collaborated on the 31 books in the *Easy Company* series. Each had authored numerous western stories and novels of their own. They included: James Wyckoff, Paul Lederer, James Reasoner, Kenneth Bjorgum, and Lou Cameron. [14-17]

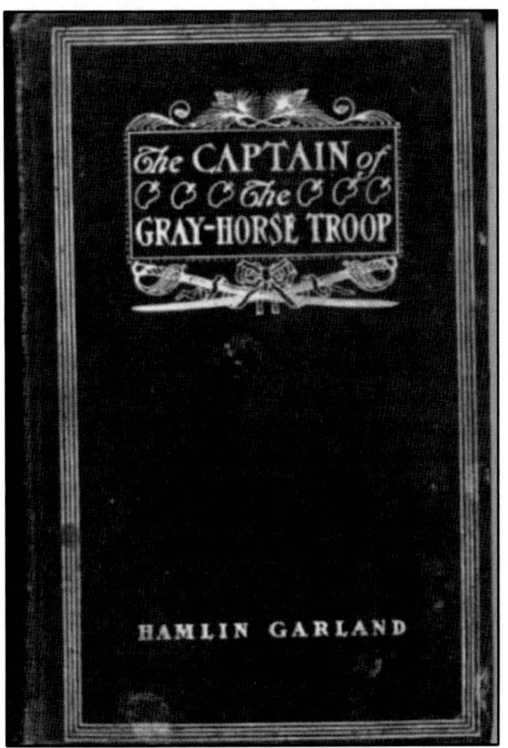

The Captain of the Gray-Horse Troop

Manifest Destiny, Dakotas

Hamlin Garland Curtis Publishing (1902)

The Indian Wars are over. The plains that rang with war cries and gunshots are silent. But now a new war is about to start. Deadlier, bloodier, and even more cruel. . . Captain George Curtis of the U.S. Cavalry has been sent to take over the Indian Agency at Pine Ridge. His job is to make and maintain a fragile peace between cattlemen and the Indians. What Curtis doesn't know is that he has secret enemies in Washington who want him to fail. After ousting a prejudiced government agent, George earns both the allegiance of the Indians and the hostility of neighboring cattlemen, who hope to appropriate the reservation through political corruption. George also falls in love with Elsie, the daughter of ex-Senator Brisbaine, a sworn enemy of the tribe. When the murder of a white rancher by an Indian incites an attack on the reservation, George marches his Gray Horse Troops into town to quell the violence. He then captures the perpetrator and assures the ranchers that the incident was isolated. Although they demand revenge on the entire tribe, George maintains the peace, and wins Elsie's love. [EB]

Hannibal Hamlin Garland (1860–1940) was an American novelist, poet, essayist, and short story writer. He is best known for his fiction involving hard-working Midwestern farmers. A prolific writer, Garland continued to publish novels, short fiction, and essays well into the 20th century. *Captain of the Gray Horse Troop* was the basis for a 1917 silent Western film directed by William Wolbert. [14-18]

The Southwest and Far West

The Young Scout: Story of a WP Lieutenant

Manifest Destiny, Arizona

Edward S. Ellis A. L. Burt (1897)

With pluck, good fortune, and (great mathematical aptitude), James Decker earns a position as a plebe at West Point, and graduates near the top of his class. He could have chosen a coveted billet in the engineers or artillery, but he is determined to go join the cavalry. He is assigned to Fort Reno in Arizona. Full of ambition and hope, he bade his friends good-by and made the long journey to that section, his spirits unaffected by the flaming weather and the desolate appearance of the half civilized region through which he was compelled to pass, a portion by stage and much by horseback.

Lieutenant Decker wrote to his old classmate, who had a pleasant berth at Washington:

"... If it was not that the atmosphere is dry, no one could stand it. Human beings would be driven out as from Sahara, but no one knows what he can undergo until he makes the experiment. Trouble is certain to come with the Apache and I am as confident as ever that if I can bring my scalp out of the flurry I shall win promotion, which you know is the dream of all of us."

"Having located the brave young lieutenant in his new quarters, with his dreams of glory, some attention must now be given to others with whose fortunes he became closely identified before he had spent a year at Fort Reno in Arizona."

In the ensuing adventures against the Apache and Geronimo Decker meets Captain Maurice Freeman, a Confederate veteran, who is a local rancher and family man. They are accompanied by two talented White Mountain Apache scouts Mendez and Cemuri in a deadly "cat and mouse" game against raiding bands of Apache who then retreat to mountain hideaways. The central plot involves the pursuit of a renegade band that has taken Freeman's son hostage.

"By taking the direct trail of the raiders and following it into the mountains every rod of advance would become known to the Apache. They would form their ambush, empty many a saddle and scatter the survivors in dismay. It was for just such a campaign that the hostiles planned and which they believed was to be attempted against them…The intelligent officers and soldiers of the Southwest learned fast, and speedily became adepts in the subtlety of Apache warfare. They learned how to ambuscade their dusky foes as well as to avoid the traps set for them, and the fight was often that of cunning against cunning rather than bravery against bravery." [EB]

Edward Sylvester Ellis (1840-1916) was a teacher, school administrator, journalist, and the author of hundreds of books and magazine articles under his own name and by a number of pen names. [14-19]

Thru Thick and Thin: A Soldier Story and a Sailor Story

WP Candidate, Cadet, Manifest Destiny, Arizona

Molly Elliot Seawell D. Lothrop Company (1893)

Jack Randolph and Tony Scaife are boyhood friends growing up in the Tidewater region of Virginia in the 1880s. Jacks lives on his grandfather's run-down plantation. The elder Randolph was a West Pointer, veteran of the Seminole and Mexican Wars, and former Confederate cavalry officer. Tony lives nearby in a humble cottage with his widowed mother. Jack is urged by his grandfather to study hard and attend West Point. Tony has little education but is an expert boatman and oyster man. Jack's haughty visiting cousin, Edgar Mount, dislikes Tony and wrongly accuses Tony of a theft to cover his own misdeed. Tony flees in his boat to become a crew member of a commercial fishing ship. He is presumed drowned in a wreck off Cape Hatteras.

Jack and Edgar both receive appointments to West Point where they have an uneasy friendship and rivalry while cadets, but graduate and are posted as cavalry officers in the West.

As the story progresses, Tony, Jack, and Edgar eventually meet up at a remote Southwestern fort confronting the Apache. Their old rivalries continue and come to a head in a pitched battle against the Apache. [EB]

Molly Elliot Seawell (1860–1916) was a late 19th century American columnist and writer. Seawell made many trips to Europe. These travels expanded her literary subjects to include the sea, England, France, and Central Europe. Her literary production included forty books of fiction, collected short fiction, non-fiction, essays, and numerous political columns from Washington for New York dailies. Two of Ms. Seawell's other novels, *Betty's Virginia Christmas* and *Betty at Fort Blizzard* can be found in other chapters of this catalog. [14-20]

An Apache Princess: A Tale of the Indian Frontier

Manifest Destiny, Arizona, WP Author

Charles King with Frederick Remington, Illustrator
Grosset & Dunlap (1905)

The novel takes place at Camp Sandy in the southwest: Arizona – New Mexico territories.

"The incidents and mysteries of this story of what happened to a slender young Lieutenant of cavalry, who combined fine soldierly qualities with repose at manner and a taste for entomology will keep the reader trying to read ahead of himself, as it were, in his eagerness to find out what is really, going to happen. The reader will read to the end, however. The Apache Princess of the title cherishes a passion for the bug-hunting young Lieutenant, [from an earlier encounter, which is revealed much later] and uses a long knife with bloody effect on two private soldiers [who threaten him]. The bug-hunting Lieutenant lies under suspicion of lax morals, in the mind, at least, of a maiden lady at Scotch descent [this sister of another officer]. However, the officer's daughter - the maiden lady's youthful niece - falls in love with the Lieutenant and he with her. Then there is the French maid of a Major's wife, who seems conceived in the spirit of melodrama. . . . However, the maid is villainous, and at the end appears guilty of bigamy, theft, and arson. There is an Indian uprising, galloping of troopers hither and thither, a last stand of a scouting party amid the rocks, with a rescue at the dramatic moment. A party goes out on scout, another party goes out to rescue the first, and a third to rescue the second, and so on.

General King has relieved the hurly-burly at wild alarums by saying a good deal about the petty jealousies and gossips of the ladies at the army post, which is the center of action. This part of the tale at least bears a relation to familiar actualities which the average civilian will have no difficulty in appreciating. For the rest, as has been said, the story inspires the overmastering desire to read ahead at a mad gallop -- taking pages sometimes as a hunter does fences -- and if possible, catch the flying thread of events. That, after all, is not an uncomplimentary thing to say about a story of adventure." [EB]

Medal of Honor: A Study of Peace & War

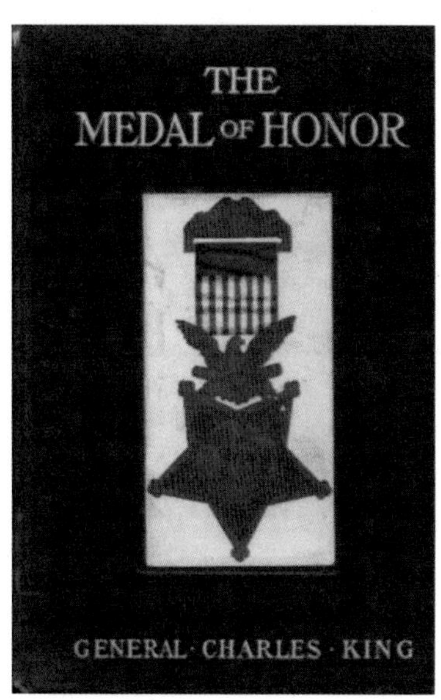

WP Author, Manifest Destiny, Arizona

Charles King Clafin Company (1905)

PROLOGUE: AT THE POINT

"It was nearly time for parade. The drum major in his tall lynx-skin shako was already marshaling the band in the hollow north of Trophy Point, preparatory to the march over to camp. The sun had sunk behind the westward heights but was still glinting from cornice and window among the scattered summer homesteads across the Hudson and taking a last peep through the rift of Washington's Valley. Even the snowy tents of the battalion, pitched at the eastward verge of the "cavalry plain," were deep in shadow, though the whispering crests of the leafy square that hemmed the little white city, as well as the dense cluster in the heart of old Fort Clinton, were all agleam in the golden light. . . ."

FROM A *NEW YORK TIMES* BOOK REVIEW:

"In this newest story of his, Gen. King has put his army officer hero through a good many various paces. First you have him at West Point as an instructor and devoted attendant upon a pretty girl. Next, he is torn away from that delightful scene and sent out to fight Indians in Arizona to make a gallant rescue but becomes badly wounded. He is then (OR finally, he is) cruelly wronged in the report of his commanding officer, a political Major of the vintage of the early sixties, who appears to be a scoundrel and a poltroon of the uttermost.

The young officer is then assigned as instructor in military drill to one of those colleges aided by the Federal Government— upon the understanding that a school of the soldier is to be maintained. The authorities of the college "thinking the drill is a nuisance" and neglect it. The young officer thinks the contract with the Government should be kept and insists upon the drill. There is a dreadful time of it between the polite college president, a conscientious drillmaster, and shirking students.

Besides, the beautiful girl of the West Point episode is at the same college teaching French, and for mysterious reasons will have nothing to do with her old admirer. And it presently appears that the rascally commanding officer of the Arizona post has his finger in the pie -- he and saloon-keeping boss in the neighboring town who has vast political influence and a young cur of a son at college. This hopeful, of course, will not drill.

Things get very complicated. The young officer has a tiff with the college president. He gets assaulted by thugs; murder is done; the young officer is accused of it; and clapped into jail. Mysterious lights are seen at night, the "Adjutant's call" is tapped upon the windowpane, notes are found beneath the window of the pretty French teacher, a fire in started in a gin mill, and there's an unexplained wounded man rescued from the cellar.

Of course, everything clears up; the drill becomes the saving feature of the college; and the drill master the most popular of the instructors. Then there is another Indian war and more gallant fighting for the young officer, and— at last — exactly what should happen at the end in all romances of love and war and teaching." [14-21]

In Spite of Foes or *Ten Years' Trial*

WP Author, Manifest Destiny, Philippines

Charles King J. B. Lippincott & Co (1901)

Eric Langdon graduated near the top of his West Point class, celebrated as an officer with exceptional leadership capabilities. However, he entered a marriage with a woman who did not care for Army life, returned to Washington, and ran up huge bills in his name. She passed away after three years, but left Langdon indebted and disgraced.

While with his regiment in Kansas, Langdon encountered Captain Felix Nathan who had married into wealth and achieved his commission by political influence. Nathan lent money to Langdon and others on onerous terms. However, Nathan was terrified of facing combat, so arranged to shift to the artillery with its fancier uniforms and "Germanic" demeanor. This would begin an enmity that caused Eric to be separated for indebtedness despite the great respect he had earned among the troops and several senior officers.

Eric fell into despair, eventually found desperate and homeless on the streets of Chicago. He was found by several of his soldiers from Fort Sheridan who arranged for his nursing to recovery, which enabled him to apply for an engineering job in Nebraska where rival railways, the Big Horn and the Seattle, were vying to complete their roads to the West Cost. He also joined the local militia to maintain his military skills. Soon he had drilled them to a level of excellence which garnered them great honors in the state, and the enmity of Nathan's supporters at the Seattle Road. Langdon became a local hero after he led the militia to quell a strike by railroad workers that kept the militia from moving west to cope with a Sioux uprising. Still, political rivalry kept Langdon from earning his promotion to the Colonelcy of the state militia. Langdon had been studying law in the evenings and passed the bar exam.

About 1990, Langdon relocated his law practice to Washington state where "better prospects" were sure to emerge. Langdon resumed his involvement in the state militia and soon rose in rank. By that time the

Spanish American war necessitated the mobilization of the West Coast militias for fighting in the Philippines. Langdon and Nathan are heading battalions in the same battle for Manila. One emerges as a hero and receives a general's star. The other is exposed as a coward, despite his contrary tales to the media. Justice is served by dint of honor, duty and focus on the missions. [EB]

Charles King wrote over 60 novels. See his biography earlier in this chapter.

"Bugles are for Soldiers"

Manifest Destiny, Arizona Pulp Fiction

Charles M. Warren
Argosy Magazine (April 13, 20, 27, May 4, 11, 1943)

This is a novel in five parts appearing over five weeks in 1943. Here are the heroes, riding to war: The kind of war that lays on the blade of an Apache tomahawk, and never got into the books at West Point.

Foreword:

"Almost every story has a hero; and this one is certainly no exception. But in a larger sense we are concerned here with the intimate personal stories of more than a dozen men who learned (some of them too late) what the fighting was about. The Civil War is over; the Union endures. But the body of the Nation continues to writhe, tortured and flayed by the savagery still in Indian Territory.

And as soldiers march out from Fort Wingate, their scalps tighten in painful anticipation of the knife whose wielder lurks behind every covert. There are heroes among these men; and some who you would call villains or fools or cowards. But in the tangled threads of their separate lives, you will find why these classifications don't always fit as neatly as they should. And how the things that happen to them square with the things that happen in them. And so we give you Company B."

"Bugles Are for Soldiers" was republished in a book length version which was retitled *Valley of the Shadow*. [EB]

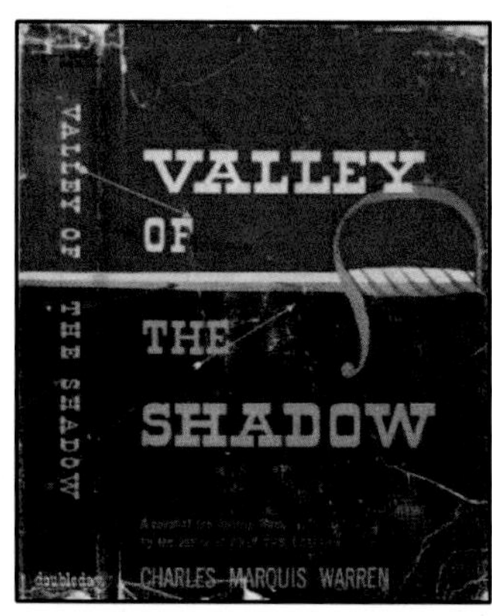

Valley of the Shadow

Manifest Destiny, Indian Wars, Arizona

Charles M. Warren Doubleday & Co. (1948)

"Lieutenant John Reardon, US. Army cavalry officer, graduated from West Point honor man, ranking first in everything. . . There hadn't been a cadet who would not have exchanged places with Reardon and the future they'd predicted for him. That had been in '64.

Four years later, straggling back to the post after another disastrous encounter with the Apache, the survivors of Lieutenant Reardon's column either hated or feared him, each for his own reason. Only Steve Vance, the fourteen-year-old bugler, and the scout Jerry Kitchen, retained their confidence in Reardon. Riding with them as an observer was First Lieutenant St. John, who had been sent out to take over Reardon's command.

As for Reardon, each step carried him closer to the post and to dishonor. In his four years in this desolate land, he had fought with every device he had known — and many he had learned from his Apache enemy, Deesohay —but all had failed. In addition to military disgrace John Reardon faced the loss of Angela Owen, the girl he loved, who could not forgive him because he had not ridden out at once against the Indians who had murdered her parents.

The column bivouacked at the Owen ranch for the night, and when Kitchen reported "signs," Reardon knew that Deesohay was nearby. At dawn they engaged the Apaches in what seemed a decisive victory until they sighted Deesohay's main force - every tribe in the vicinity. As B Company galloped back to the Owen ranch to prepare a siege, Reardon knew that military defeat and disgrace were nothing compared with what would happen if they surrendered to the Indians." [DJ]

Only the Valiant

Manifest Destiny, Indian Wars, Arizona

Charles M. Warren Bantam Books (1950)

Captain Richard Lance (Peck), a West Point graduate, arrives at Fort Invincible, a fortification set up in the New Mexico Territory, soon after a band of Apache assaulted the fort and captures their leader, Tucsos. Lance is ordered to assign an officer to command an escort to take Tucsos to a larger post. Lance decides to lead the patrol himself, but at the last minute, he is told to stay at the fort in case of an Apache attack, and is ordered to assign another popular officer, Lieutenant Holloway, to lead the small group of men escorting Tucsos. The Apache ambush the group, kill Lieutenant Holloway and free Tucsos. The men at the fort blame Captain Lance, unaware of the orders he received, believing that his decision to assign Lieutenant Holloway to the dangerous mission was for a personal reason, as both officers were vying for the affection of the same woman, Cathy Eversham. Lance's standing with the soldiers at the fort only gets worse when he assembles a group of misfit cavalrymen to hold off the rampaging Indians at the ruins of Fort Invincible, which is considered a suicide mission. [BC]

Only the Valiant is a 1951 Western film directed by Gordon Douglas and starring Gregory Peck, Barbara Payton, and Ward Bond. It was based on the novel by Charles Marquis Warren. [14-22]

Charles Marquis Warren (1912–1990) was an American motion picture and television writer, producer, and director who specialized in Westerns. Among his notable career achievements were his involvement in creating the television series *Rawhide* and his work in adapting the radio series *Gunsmoke* for television. In his early career he wrote stories for the pulp fiction magazines. His screenplay *Beyond Glory* can be found in chapter 21. [14-23]

Black Apache

Manifest Destiny, Arizona

Clay Fisher Bantam Books (1976)

He was a legend with a blood price on his head both north and south of the border; a renegade, black West Point man now living among the hostile bronco Apache, waging a war of vengeance against two governments. But when a courageous Mestizo priest with a desperate dream needed a man of strength to fulfill his vision, there was only one warrior fierce enough to turn to. It was the one they called the Black Apache. [BC]

Henry Wilson Allen (1912–1991) was an American author and screenwriter. In 1937 he began working as a contract screenwriter for the Metro-Goldwyn-Mayer cartoon studio, later working for Walter Lantz Productions on several *Woody Woodpecker* cartoons. He used several different pseudonyms for his own works starting in 1950. His 50+ novels of the American West were published under the pen names Will Henry and Clay Fisher. [14-24]

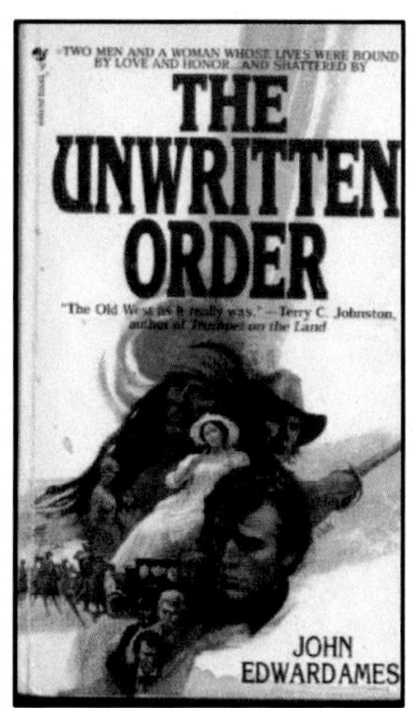

The Unwritten Order

Manifest Destiny, Arizona

John Edward Ames Bantam Books (1995)

As the American frontier was pushed farther west, the Indian conflict ignited into an all-out war of extermination. The bright young cadets of West Point were issued an order never acknowledged by the army—and never set down on paper: A soldier was honor-bound to die even in a hopeless battle...and to kill a woman before seeing her captured.

Hungry for the glory of war, Seth Carlson and Corey Bryce are two young officers who volunteer to fight Indians in the Arizona territory. But soon the order will force one of them to make a terrible decision...a decision that will change the lives of both forever.

From the hallowed lecture halls of West Point to a barren, sun baked Apache reservation, from the Indians who fight for their land and an honorable death to the newspapermen who create and destroy heroes to suit the whims of politicians and businessmen, The Unwritten Order is a searing novel of the American frontier. [BC]

John Edward Ames (1949–) is an American educator and writer of novels and short stories educated at Eastern Michigan University. Ames began his career writing for pulp magazines while teaching at Eastern Michigan before penning horror novels and stories. In 1995, Ames' historical novel *The Unwritten Order* was a finalist for a Western Writers of America Spur Award. [14-25]

"Satan Sounds Boots and Saddles"

Manifest Destiny, Pulp Fiction, Arizona

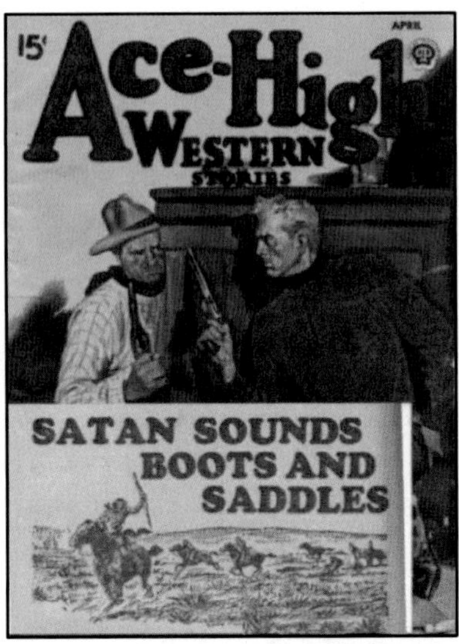

Roy Vandergroot Ace High Western Stories (April 1946)

"The detail rode at a slow walk. Lieutenant James Darrel Flynn sleeved the sweat out of his eyes and cursed under his breath. The sun stood brassy above them. The desert cast back that heat as from an open oven. The black rocks appeared to spew it, and greasewood and cacti looked fried to a crisp. The landscape shimmered, and the air above it danced till a man's senses swam looking at it.

Inside Flynn's brain, two words kept hammering with the irritating repetition of the clock-clock of a mount's loose shoe: good luck . . . good luck . . . good luck. Old-time troopers, Lieutenant Flynn knew, would whisper of his cowardice in the desolate years to come. So, for a West Point hero shavetail, there was only one thing left to do: choose between Apache torture and an unmarked, lonely grave!" [EB]

Roy Vandergroot had over 60 western stories published in a dozen pulp fiction magazines between 1945 and 1950. [14-26]

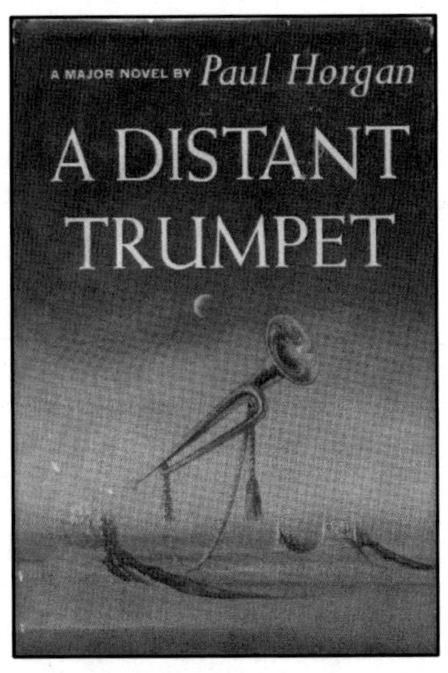

A Distant Trumpet

Western, Indian Wars

Paul Horgan Farrar, Straus & Company (1951)

The War and the West are its two background themes. Though the main story occurs in the 188O's it has its beginnings in, and is affected by forces arising out of, the Civil War; and the chief scene of action is an Army outpost on the Indian frontier in the southwest United States.

When Matthew Carlton Hazard receives his commission from West Point in June 1880, he fulfils an ambition dating from his childhood encounter with President Lincoln. His first assignment to duty comes at a moment when his engagement to Laura Greenleaf faces the formidable opposition of her mother; the fact that this assignment is to Fort Delivery, Territory of Arizona, does not further his cause. Yet it is through his devotion to duty as much as his devotion to Laura that he wins her as his bride.

At Fort Delivery, Matthew and Laura learn a great deal about themselves and the fellow-officers and their wives—Colonel Hiram and Jessica Prescott, First Lieutenant Theodore and Kitty Mainwaring, Captain Cedric and Maud Gray—but principally they learn that Fort Delivery brings out in full relief whatever character one's previous history has formed, whether back East, elsewhere in the Army, abroad, or (as in one case) beyond the Indian frontier. They learn too that one cannot know in advance whether men like

Trumpeter Rainey. Sergeant Blickner, Indian scout Joe Dummy, Private Cranshaw, and Private Clanahan will turn out to be heroes, deserters, or just soldiers.

A Distant Trumpet is rich in dramatic action and brilliant characterizations. Memorable among the latter are Major General Alexander Upton Quait, Laura's "Uncle Alex," an inventive, resourceful, Latin-quoting eccentric whose actions -- including an "inspection" of Fort Delivery which drives Colonel Prescott and his officers nearly to distraction -- are unpredictable but militarily effective; and White Horn, the Indian they call Joe Dummy, whose origins and rearing as an Apache of the Chiricahua nation make him one of the most fascinating figures in the novel. The mark of a master storyteller is visible in such episodes—to cite only three as the strange desert fate of Sergeant Reimmers, Hiram Prescott's wartime courtship of Jessica, and Matthew's momentous mission to Chief Rainbow Son which comes as the book's climax. [DJ]

Paul Horgan (1903–1995) was an American writer of historical fiction and non-fiction who mainly wrote about the Southwestern United States. He was the recipient of two Pulitzer Prizes for History. [14-27]

Tombstone Stage

Manifest Destiny, Rogue, Arizona

William Hopson Berkley Books (1948)

HE PLAYED A LONE HAND

Jim Cort had thrown away an inheritance and a West Point career because of what had happened that night six years ago. Now he was a suspected smuggler and badman, with a reputation feared along the toughest stretch of the Arizona border.

The last six years of his life came to a thundering climax the day he came upon a band of crazed Apache raiding the Tombstone stage . . . [BC]

William Lee Hopson (1907–1975) was primarily a Western author. He was sometimes published under the name William L. Hopson and used a pseudonym, John Sims, for at least four Western novels. In World War II Hopson served with the Marines weapons instructor. After the war he wrote crime novels and Western stories for pulp magazines between 1938 and 1958. Hopson's publishers wanted nine books a year, but Hopson got it down to six and was happy if it was four or five annually. [14-28]

Guns of Arizona

Manifest Destiny, Arizona

Charles N. Heckelmann Doubleday (1949)

TREACHERY PULLS THE TRIGGER

Cavalry Lieutenants Bob Dallas and Frank Holland had hated each other since their West Point days. Now, at Camp Breadon in southern Arizona, that hatred flamed more fiercely than ever—a living, palpable thing threatening to consume them. Even when the renegade Apache, led by the scalp-hungry Naquino, went on the warpath, and every man in the outnumbered Fourth Cavalry was pressed into desperate action, the bitter feud did not end.

And then an act of treachery brought it to a point of no return. The Apache were storming the gates, the traitor within had to be unmasked... and one man had to die! [BC]

Charles Newman Heckelmann (1913–2005) graduated from University of Notre Dame and was a pulp fiction writer who authored twenty western novels between 1944 and 1982. He was president of the Western Writers of America in 1964-65. [14-29]

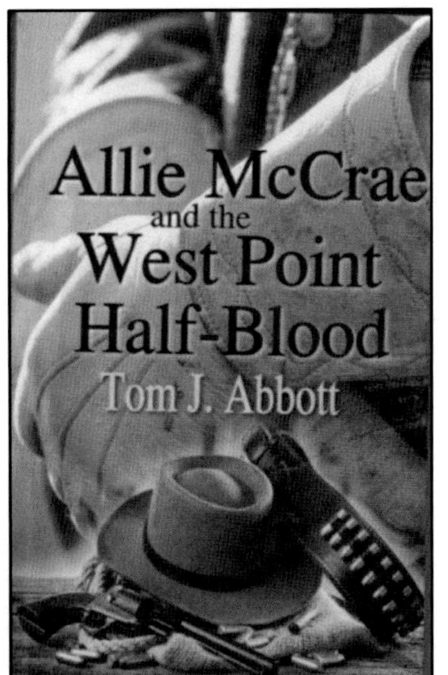

Allie McCrae and the West Point Half-Blood

Manifest Destiny, Arizona

Tom J. Abbott Roots and Branches (2016)

Allie McCrae is broken-hearted at the death of his parents and wife during the Irish Potato Famine. Armed with his father's gold watch and little money, he boards a cholera-laden ship for America, in search of his dream. The unexpected occurs his first day in New York when he is robbed--not the dream he had in mind.

Allie joins the U.S. Army, which takes him West. He rescues and marries a Choctaw woman. Their son, Mark, graduates from West Point and is sent to Fort Hellsgate in Arizona Territory, where his father is stationed. Mark is white, Indian, and now a soldier, who feels split loyalties.

To further complicate the situation, Mark finds himself attracted to Amanda, the niece of the commandant. Gold thieves, crooked Indian agents and Draco, murderous renegade follower of Chief Victorio, add to the drama as it races to a startling conclusion. [BC]

No biographical information is available on this author.

The following is the first of five novels in Tom Willard's "Black Sabre Chronicles." others may be viewed in "The West Point Legacies" chapter.

Buffalo Soldiers: Black Sabre Chronicles #1

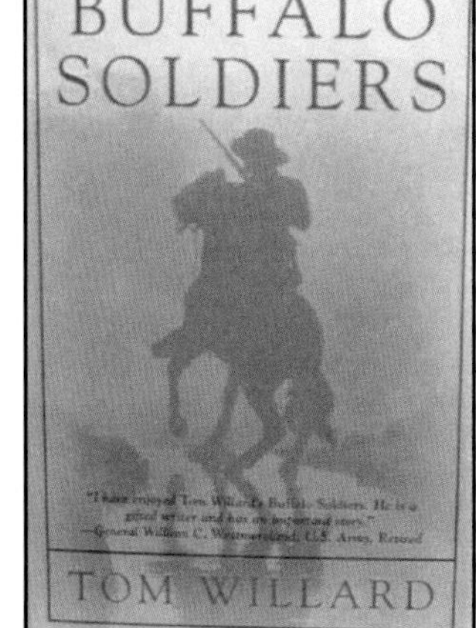

Manifest Destiny, Legacy

Tom Willard Forge (1996)

From the Civil War to Desert Storm, there stretches an unbroken line of dedicated and distinguished service by African-Americans in the United States military. The Black Sabre Chronicles, a compelling new series, is a tribute to the bravery, honor, and sacrifice of these black American fighting men.

Buffalo Soldiers is the story of Sergeant Major Augustus Sharps of the l0th Cavalry, one of the six African-American regiments authorized by Congress in July 1866. He and other former slaves had proven that they could fight valiantly for their freedom, but in the West they were to fight for the freedom and security of white settlers who often despised them. The Cheyenne thought the hair of this new kind of soldier resembled buffalo hides and so the men of the 9th and 10th Cavalry became known as "buffalo soldiers."

Serving with General Custer, and scouts like "Buffalo Bill" Cody and "Wild Bill" Hickok, these exemplary soldiers endured lower pay and fewer privileges than their white counterparts, in addition to the other hardships of the frontier. The perseverance and devotion to duty of these troopers carried them through the bloody battles with the Mescalero Apache and the capture of Geronimo—and even to the charge up San Juan Hill in Cuba with Colonel Theodore Roosevelt and his Rough Riders. These men, and other volunteers with the Rough Riders, were the first African - Americans to serve on foreign soil. [DJ]

Here is the third of six novels in Beverly Gray's *Black Knights of the Hudson* series. The others may be viewed in "The West Point Legacies" chapter.

Changing of the Guard: Black Knights of the Hudson III

Legacy, Manifest Destiny, Cuba

Beverly C. Gray Self-published (2013)

CHANGING OF THE GUARD is the third book in this sweeping family saga of the MacKendricks; who live by West Point's motto - Duty, Honor, Country. With the Indian Wars tapering down, the attention of the young nation turns to flexing its muscles. The MacKendrick offspring are involved thoroughly with the changes facing their country and their vivid family. Randolph follows his father to West Point but finds the Academy much changed from its early days. Instead of producing the brilliant engineers, soldiers, and statesmen of previous decades, West Point has become an iron-bound institution that seems content to churn out little tin soldiers. Philip, a maverick like his mother, has little interest in pursuing a military career but turns to a path that will take him to the depths of a collapsing coal mine and the heights of San Juan. Young Jackson Lee and Fitzjames yearn to follow in the footsteps of their fathers and yield to the call of the bugle when it sounds for Cuba long before they are old enough to even enter West Point. In *CHANGING OF THE GUARD*, the MacKendricks eagerly embrace destiny as their country spreads its arms beyond the continental shelves. From the political games of Washington to the jungles of Cuba with 'Fighting' Joe Wheeler and Theodore Roosevelt, the MacKendrick men and women turn their faces to the wind and endure tragedy and triumph with all flags flying. [BC]

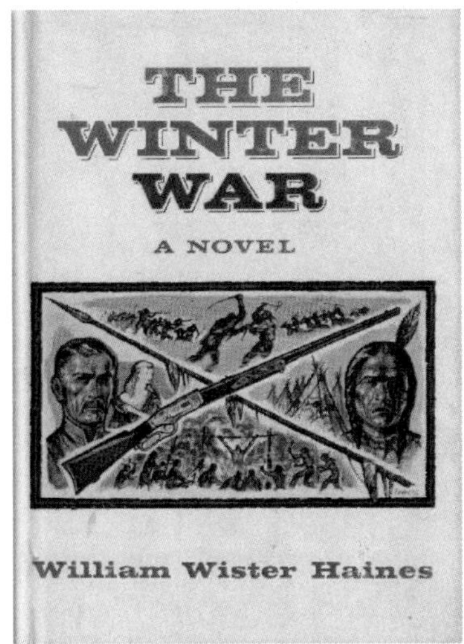

The Winter War

Manifest Destiny

William W. Haines   Little, Brown & Co. (1961)

In this novel William Wister Haines answers the question, "But what did happen after Custer. . . ?" This exciting story follows the Indian fighting in the Montana Territory in the fateful summer and winter of I876. The Indian chiefs Crazy Horse, Sitting Bull and Lightning's Friend for the first and only time had formed a great federation of Sioux, Cheyenne and lesser tribes, and in four months they had dealt General Crook two humiliating defeats, eluded pursuit, and massacred Custer. To revenge the failure of forty regiments, the Administration dispatched to Montana General Nelson Miles and his 5th Regiment, U. S. Infantry. It is their exploits and courage which give this book its vitality...

Believing the Indians vulnerable only when hunting or hibernating, Colonel Selkirk has staked his reputation on a plan for a winter campaign which would destroy forever the Indians' recuperative power. General Miles backs him, and Washington finally gives them the chance to put their plan into operation with their small force of one regiment and some improvised cavalry. Their force is outnumbered six to one by the Indians and their danger is compounded by Grafton, the Indian trader, and by Lita Littleton, who spent her girlhood as an Indian captive, and who has a foot in either camp. She is attracted to Colonel Selkirk, but her loyalties are divided. Though she serves as a go-between, no one is ever sure how far she can be trusted.

Full of the drama of a long and hard-fought campaign through the worst winter in Montana history. [DJ]

William Wister Haines (1908 – 1989) was an American author, screenwriter, and playwright. His most notable work, *Command Decision*, was published as a novel, play, and screenplay following World War II. [14-30]

Chapter 15

The Civil War

America's bloodiest war began after eleven southern states seceded following the 1860 election of President Abraham Lincoln. Jefferson Davis (USMA 1828) was elected President of the Confederacy. Initially a war to restore the Union, Lincoln's war aims evolved to include, most importantly, the abolition of slavery.

Early Confederate victories at 1st and 2nd Bull Run, in the Peninsula and Shenandoah Valley Campaigns, Fredericksburg, and Chancellorsville, proved that the war would not end quickly. The Union eventually mobilized its resources and gained key victories at Shiloh, Antietam, Vicksburg, Gettysburg, the Wilderness, and Atlanta. Ultimately, the North overwhelmed and outlasted the Confederacy and restored the Union.

West Point graduates led the way for both sides — of the 60 major Civil War battles, 55 had West Point graduates leading both armies with the remainder having a West Point graduate leading on one side. Among these leaders were Union Generals Ulysses S. Grant (USMA 1843 and 18th US President), William T. Sherman (USMA 1840), and George B. McClellan (USMA 1846); and Confederate Generals Robert E. Lee (USMA 1829), and Thomas J. "Stonewall" Jackson (USMA 1846).

The Union lost 364,511 soldiers killed with 281,881 wounded, while the Confederacy lost 258,000 soldiers killed with 137,000 wounded. Sixty West Point graduates died fighting for the Union and 45 graduates died for the Confederacy. Twenty-two West Point graduates and two former cadets received the Medal of Honor.

From a memorial stone on the West Point golf course.

It is not surprising that there is a large body of historical fiction on West Pointers and the Civil War given the enormity of that event in our history and the dominance of West Point officers in the military leadership of both the Northern and Southern armies.

Authors employ different techniques to present the characters and events in the form of "documentary fiction" as seen in this chapter. They adhere to events of the era striving to be historically accurate but apply fictional artistry to breathe drama and passion into the novel. [15-01]

This chapter divides the works into three sections:

- The first section involves **fictional characters** in **real events** during the Civil War. There may be interaction with real people, often general officers.
- There is a short second section (one author) who chose to portray **real and fictional characters** in largely **fictional events** of the war.
- Books in the third section feature **actual events** of the war, and **real characters (typically senior army officers)**. The fiction derives from the author's attribution of thoughts, emotion, and speech attributed to the characters and how their strengths and foibles contributed to conflict resolution.

Fictional Characters Set Against Real Events

Shadow of the Flags: Black Knights of the Hudson I

Cadet, Civil War

Beverly C. Gray CreateSpace Publishing (2012)

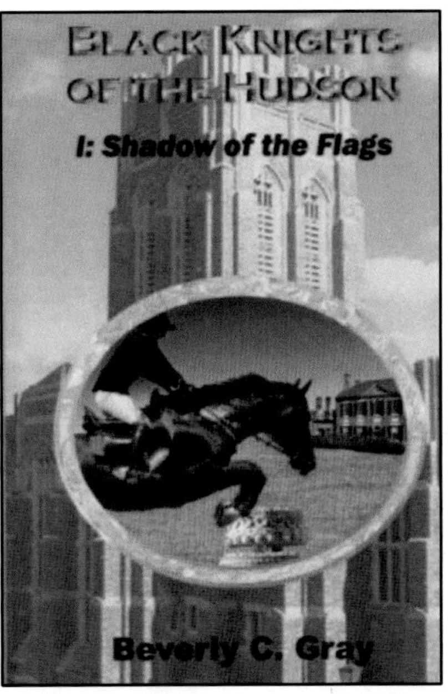

Black Knights Of The Hudson is an historical fiction series that traces a fictional U.S. Army family from the Civil War through World War II.

Shadow Of The Flags is the first book in this sweeping family saga of the MacKendricks; who live by West Point's motto — Duty, Honor, Country. James MacKendrick and his younger brother, Timothy, are graduates of West Point but have been raised in a proud Virginia family. When Civil War rips their country apart, each must make the heartbreaking decision as to whether to stay loyal to the United States or join the tide of other Southern-bred Army officers who choose to follow their home states out of the Union. [BC]

Beverly C. Gray is the daughter of a career U.S. Army officer. Her six books in this series are all included in this catalog across several chapters. For an overview of the series and their placement the reader should refer to "The West Point Legacies" chapter.

His Sombre Rivals

Hudson Highlands, Romance, Civil War

Edward Payson Roe Dodd, Mead & Company (1883)

From a review on Amazon.com:

"This novel is a romance that embraces the Civil War, reflecting the author's services as a chaplain to Union forces in Virginia. The protagonist Alford Graham, who is capable of deep emotion beneath his analytical exterior, falls in love with Grace. But unknown to himself, Grace has already given her heart to his best friend, Warren Hilland. Then the Civil War disrupts their lives.

The author's balanced view of the North vs. the South was his actual contemporary view of the Civil War. He doesn't unfairly portray either side. Some honorable characters are Southern, though the protagonists are mostly Northern. There are several extended descriptions of battles fought with horses and muskets, but this book is by no means violent. One thing I found unexpectedly relevant for today was the conversations between characters who are aghast that large numbers of people are being swayed by the extreme speech and distorted views of politicians and newspapers who purposefully mislead and divide." [15-02]

An Original Belle

New York, Civil War, Romance

Edward Payson Roe Dodd, Mead & Co (1885)

From a review by Teri-K on Goodreads, April 1, 2016:

"Beautiful and popular 20 year old Marion lives in New York during the Civil War, which hasn't touched her life at all. Her father does some type of work for the government, but she has no idea what. Her mother is an empty headed, pleasure loving woman who enjoys hosting her daughter's friends and pays no attention to anything serious, including her husband. Marion is on her way to becoming as vapid as her mother when she overhears a conversation that shocks her. Vowing to change her behavior she appeals to her father for help. After several long sermons, he encourages to change her life and use her personal appeal to encourage those around her to better themselves, also. This means several of her suitors end up going off to war, while another finds himself on a different path. Including first-person accounts of Gettysburg and other battles, the reader wonders who will survive the war and win Marion's now virtuous hand."

"This is a very old-fashioned book, but since I sometimes enjoy the sermonizing, strong patriotism and noble ideals such books promote, I found it fun. It surprised me to find Southerners treated with respect, rather than castigated as the source of all evil, as I expected of a book written by a Northerner so soon after the war. Also, set primarily in New York, there was a lot of interesting detail about the failures of the Northern Army, their poor leadership, resistance to the fighting among those who want peace, draft riots, etc. It's an aspect I've rarely seen in novels." [15-03]

Edward Payson Roe (1838–1888) was a minister and a horticulturist, residing after the Civil War in Highland Falls and Cornwall, NY. He authored more than a dozen novels which were quite popular in the 1880s. Their strong moral and religious purpose, did much to break down a Puritan prejudice in America against works of fiction. One of his most consistent criticisms was that his work resembled sermons. [15-04]

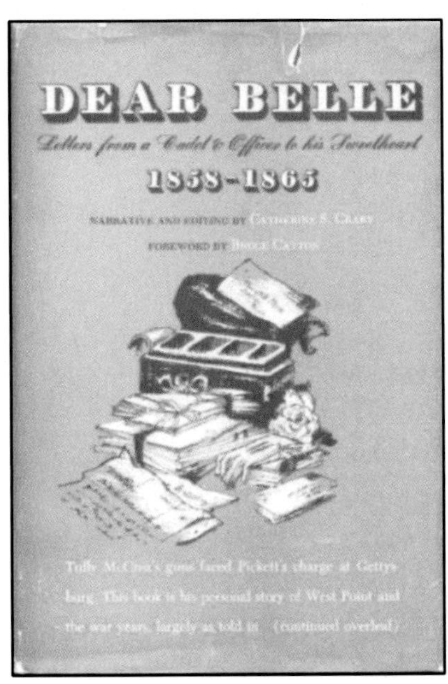

Dear Belle: Letters from a Cadet and Officer to his Sweetheart

Romance, Memoir, Civil War, Cadet

Catherine Crary — Wesleyan University (1965)

The spring of 1861 was a bad time for everybody in the United States. Nobody really knew what was happening, although the blindest could see that whatever was going on was likely to be shattering, and the average man was torn between patriotic emotion and the desire to look for a storm cellar. But the bewilderment probably was most complete on the parade ground at West Point. The cadets at the United States Military Academy were dedicated young men, trained to take guidance from on high and living by unquestioning obedience, and suddenly they found that there was no guidance to be had anywhere. The people who ordinarily gave them orders did not know what to say to them. All in all, it was hard to live through, and the most revealing account of it that this writer knows about is to be found in the letters of Tully McCrea, whose experiences in that difficult spring somehow epitomize the terrible problem that the outbreak of the Civil War brought to the entire country. . . .

Tully McCrea was a gallant soldier too, and there obviously was a very good fellow indeed wrapped up in the casings of a restless West Point cadet and a disillusioned lieutenant of artillery. Reading his letters, one begins to see the value of the work done by the Military Academy, exemplified in McCrea's own career. He never became famous, but he did become one of the solid, reliable, dedicated young offieers without whom the war could not have been won, and the devotion to duty that was instilled into him in his cadet days was a substantial asset to his country. These letters of his not only make us acquainted with an interesting and admirable man; they bring a better understanding of a remarkable institution as well. [DJ]

Catherine Crary (1909–1974) was an American academic & historian of the American Revolution. She earned her degrees at Mt. Holyoke College and Radcliffe. [15-05]

Henry in the War

Civil War, WP Author

General Oliver O. Howard Lee & Shepard Company (1886)

PREFACE (to a later printing)

The war with Spain, just finished, called out over 200,000 more volunteers. As Henry has lived through both the civil strife and this later foreign struggle, he is now a veteran indeed, and a fair representative of our citizen volunteers. My young friends who are acquainted with "Donald" and had glimpses in *Donald's School-Days* of the younger of the two boys will, I trust, welcome a continuance of Henry's noticeable career. My promise in my first volume, to carry Henry through the Civil War and give a recital of actual campaigns and battles, I have carefully borne in mind. In this new effort I have striven to present only the truth of history in all matters of importance, while cherishing a great hope of adding something to the attractions and inducements which make boys become manly, upright men. [FP]

Oliver O. Howard (1830–1909) needs no introduction to West Pointers. He was a major general and corps commander in the Civil War, losing an arm in 1862 and earning the Medal of Honor. Following the war, he was commissioner of the Freedmen's Bureau where he played a major role in the Reconstruction era, charged with integrating freedmen (former slaves) into American society. He served as a university president from 1869–1874, which was later named Howard University in his honor. He later led expeditions to Arizona and the Far Northwest to secure a treaty with Cochise and pacify with the Nez Perce tribe. He was Superintendent of West Point in 1881–1882. Howard wrote two novels for youth. *Donald's School Days* is the other one in this collection. [15-06]

Captain Charles King was the most prolific novelist of all West Point graduates. The subjects ranged from the Civil War to West Point cadets, to "wining the West" following the Civil War. Here are a few of his novels about the Civil War.

Between the Lines: A Story of the War

Civil War, WP Author

Charles King B. W. Dodge & Co (1888)

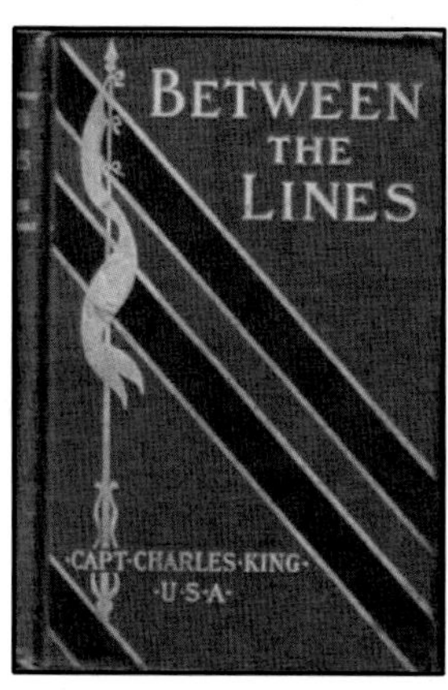

The setting of this novel centers on the Armistead family plantation a few miles west of the Manassas Battlefield. It begins in August 1862 with military activities on around the Second Battle of Manassas and concludes in the aftermath of Gettysburg. There is vivid description of the cavalry maneuvers during Second Manassas and the cavalry action at Gettysburg.

Elderly Judge Armistead has a son Henry, a Confederate cavalry officer and a daughter Lucy who is at home along with a handful of loyal servants. Henry

Armistead's best friend in college (West Point not mentioned) is Frank Kearny, now an officer in the Union cavalry. Both are bold officers having achieved reputation for daring while engaged in the "cat and mouse" skirmishing with their respective troops in and around the villages that were between the armies of McDowell and Lee.

Kearny, carrying dispatches between General Bufford and McDowell, is skirting between the lines when he is chased by a Confederate patrol and ultimately falling under his wounded horse and injuring himself badly. Henry Armistead's patrol captures Kearny and, not wanting him to face prison in Richmond where he would surely die, arranges for some local servants to transport Kearny by wagon to the Armistead home, along with letters pleading for his father and sister to nurse Kearny and preserve him from Confederate patrols. This is where the conflict in the novel begins. Over the months of recuperation, the Union Army looks for Kearny, among rumors of desertion, while Lucy Armistead and Frank Kearny come to love one another. She hides him from Confederate patrols and eventually turns him over to a Union patrol, not revealing how Kearny came to be there to preserve the Armistead reputation among the Virginia neighbors.

Henry is captured in disguise trying to visit his family and faces a court martial and hanging as a spy. Kearny faces his own disciplinary issues, including a possible murder charge, while trying to track down those officers who accused him wrongly of desertion. Meanwhile Mosby's Confederate irregulars are marauding Union camps and supplies between the Rappahannock and Potomac Rivers causing great turmoil and futility chased by the poorly led Union cavalry. Lots of moving parts in this story. [EB]

Norman Holt: A Story of the Army of the Cumberland

Civil War, WP Author

Charles King G.W. Dillingham Co. (1901)

"Straight for the scattering ranks he headed."

Then came the thing that kept the division in talk for a month! Out from the rear of the Kentucky right wing sprang a tall, slender lieutenant; his new uniform dripping wet, his sash, belt, and sword spick-span and gleaming, his dark eyes flashing, and his cheeks aflame. A word to the major, as he pointed to the disintegrating blue battalion beyond them, a nod from that appreciative fellow-Kentuckian, and the junior had sprung into the vacated saddle, and away sped a startled, astonished, excited steed under the hand of a practiced horseman. Straight for the scattering, stooping, half "rattled" ranks he darted, heading them as a skillful cowboy heads stampeding cattle. In an instant he was among them, his new blade flashing even through the rain, his voice ringing out about the clash and clamor of battle. Vehemently he drove his horse into the very faces of the foremost, and a sudden cheer went up at sight of him, for those on the right were the Emmets themselves, and he in saddle was the lad they loved. [EB]

A Broken Sword: A Tale of the Civil War

Civil War, WP Author

Charles King The Hobart Co (1905)

The first half of *Broken Sword* is set in NYC in 1861. The story focuses on the division of the sympathies, North and South, among the city's well-to-do. The wealthy Rutherfords support the North but are anguished by the death of their older son in a duel over honor with Union Major Holt before the war. Lurking around seeking the favor of young Lucy Rutherford is Major Wallis, a politically connected infantry officer of the 7th NY Regiment, aka the "Silver Spoons." He has many southerners in this coterie of friends including his brother, a Confederate officer. His allegiance to the Union cause is often questioned. Wallis is an impeccably comported, excellent officer, but with an arrogant attitude and glib tongue for explaining away questions about his loyalties. The conflicts and questions expand as the war reaches into 1864–65. [EB]

A War-Time Wooing

Civil War, Romance, WP Author

Charles King Harper & Bros. (1900)

July 1862, Washington D.C.

"Bessie Warren was still so young—so much a child in her father's fond eyes—still his sweet-faced, sunny-haired baby Bess. He could hardly realize she was eighteen even when with blushing cheeks she came to show him the photograph of a manly, gallant-looking young soldier in the uniform of a lieutenant of infantry. Strange as the story may seem today, there was at the time nothing very surprising about its most salient feature—she and her hero had never met. With other girls she had joined a "Soldiers' Aid Society;" had wrought with devoted though misguided diligence in the manufacture of "Havelocks" that were bearers of much sentiment but no especial benefit to the recipients at the front; and like many of her companions she had slipped her name and address into one of these soon-discarded cap covers...

As luck would have it, their package of "Havelocks" fell to the lot of the 7th Massachusetts Infantry, and a courteous letter from the adjutant told of its distribution. Bessie Warren was secretary of the society, and the secretary was instructed to write to the adjutant and say how grateful they were to find their efforts so kindly appreciated and hoped the adjutant would answer. He did, and sent, moreover, a photographic group of several officers taken at regimental headquarters. Each figure was numbered, and on the back the name of each officer with Mr. Paul Revere Abbot being the most handsome, the ladies judged. One of the young ladies reciprocated by returning a photo of themselves to the adjutant of the regiment. Central figure in this group was Bessie Warren, unquestionably the loveliest girl among them all, and one day there came to her a single photograph, a still handsomer picture of Mr. Paul Revere Abbot, and a letter in hand somewhat stiff and cramped, in which the writer apologized for the appearance of the scrawl, explained that his hand had been injured while practicing fencing with a comrade, but that having seen her picture in the group he could not but congratulate himself on having received a "Havelock" from hands so fair, could not resist the impulse to write and personally thank her, and then to inquire if she was a sister of Guthrie Warren, whom he had known and looked up to at Harvard as a "soph" looks up to a senior; and he enclosed his picture, which would perhaps recall him to Guthrie's mind."

Guthrie dies a hero's death at Seven Pines in the Peninsula Campaign. The letter writing continued between Bessie and Abbot until word came to the Warrens that Abbott was gravely wounded at Antietam. The Warrens rushed to Frederick Maryland to see if they could tend to Abbott. There they learned that Abbot denied writing those letters at all!

There is skullduggery afoot involving a rival in Abbot's regiment for two women: Bessie Warren and Genevieve Winthrop in Boston, his intended in an arranged marriage of the Abbott and Winthrop mothers. Mystery, drama, and shocking revelations. The story concludes on the battlefields at Fredericksburg in December 1862. [EB]

The General's Double: A Story of the Army of the Potomac

Civil War, WP Author

Charles King J. B. Lippincott company (1898)

This book is a great depiction of army operations in Maryland following the battle of Antietam, especially Stuart's raid into Pennsylvania and the Union cavalry trying to entrap him north of the Potomac. Who was the double and why did he exist? All is revealed at the end, but there is plenty of drama in the Union officer ranks before we learn the details.

The story takes place along the Potomac River in the Maryland countryside between Harpers Ferry and Frederick. It opens with a series of family letters written after the Battle of Bull Run concerning the death of Union soldier Jack Lowndes. Then there is no further mention of him for many pages. Most of the narrative takes place around Heatherwood, a family estate on heights with commanding views of the surrounding Maryland countryside and even over the river into Virginia. The Heatherwood women (who also have a home in Baltimore), are Confederate sympathizers, under Union protection because of their exceptional nursing efforts for wounded Union troops following the battles at Manassas and Balls Bluff.

There are strange comings and goings around Heatherwood, which arouses the interest of Union cavalry Major Foulweather. He is in search of Captain Floyd Fairfax, Confederate cavalry, whom he believes is visiting Heatherwood to spy. Foiling his intrusions is a Colonel (later General) Clark of the New Hampshire Volunteers who is charged with the protection of Heatherwood.

Eventually, Captain Fairfax is apprehended out of uniform at Heatherwood, charged as a spy, but escapes his imprisonment, with some mysterious assistance. He is later recaptured in 1865 and taken to Baltimore, where Secretary of War Stanton wants him hanged. That doesn't happen, thanks to the General's Double. [EB]

Charles King (1844–1933) was a Union drummer boy in the Civil War, and for conspicuous battlefield bravery was appointed to West Point by Lincoln. As a cavalry officer on the frontier, he was the first army officer on the scene after the massacre of Custer and his men at Little Bighorn. Forced to retire from the cavalry because of a severe shoulder wound received in 1877, he took up writing. Why? "Circumstances, chiefly. I wasn't long in finding out that keeping a family on retired captain's pay is a beggar's business. I had to go to work, so I took to writing." He later obtained an appointment as a General of volunteers to lead American forces in the Philippines during the Spanish-American War. [15-07]

Civil War Dragoon

Civil War, Romance

W. C. Fordyce, Jr. Exposition Press (1965)

This novel explores a facet of the Civil War neglected in literature—the predicament of the professional army officer forced to decide whether he shall fight for the North or for the South. First Lieutenant Gordon McLean was such a man. Born in the South, he was a career officer trained at West Point who shortly before the outbreak of the war commanded E Company of the Second Dragoons at Fort Laramie on the frontier. Because his men esteemed him, they felt concern about his prospective decision.

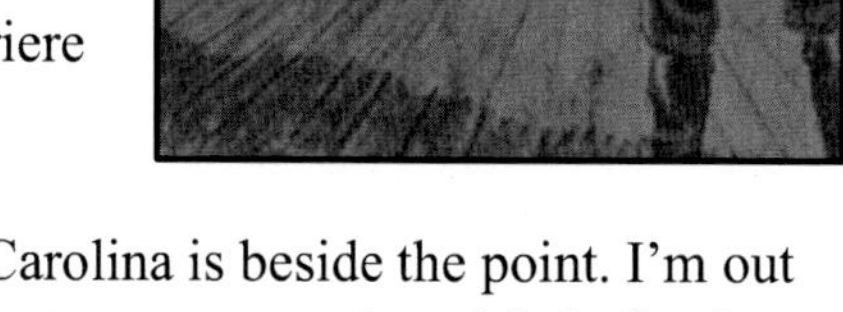

One of them, Sergeant O'Reilly, blurted out, "Will you be staying in the Old Army, sir, or resigning like Major Hayward, Lieutenant L'Empriere and the others?" The lieutenant felt a dryness in his throat. "I Wish I could say that I was sure, Sergeant. My state, North Carolina, hasn't secceded yet, but probably will. What I might do if I were in North Carolina is beside the point. I'm out here. I've done a lot of thinking about it. If there's a war I hope I'll be true to my oath and fight for the United States, not the Cotton States."

How Gordon McLean made his choice, how he handled the seductive dark-haired Southern agent Kate Evans amid the intrigues and maneuvers for control of the key city, St. Louis, and how he rode into battle on his chosen side make this account fascinating for both the general reader and the Civil War specialist. [DJ]

Few biographical details on **W. C. Fordyce** could be located. However, it appears that he was a St. Louis attorney and descendent of Daniel Marsh Frost, a 19th century Missourian who graduated fourth in the West Point, Class of 1844 then served with gallantry in the Mexican War. However, in the Civil War Frost's performance as a Confederate general officer was only adequate.

Frost's daughter, Harriet, married into the Fordyce family. It was she who left the family mansion and a considerable bequest to the St. Louis University and the family papers to the Missouri Historical Society. [15-08]

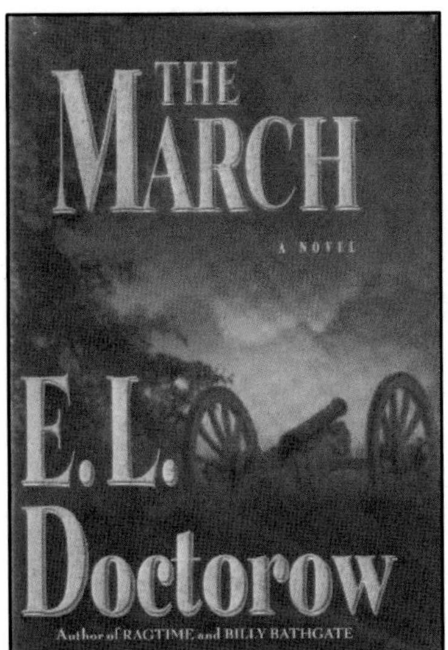

The March

Civil War, General Officer

E. L. Doctorow Random House (2005)

In I864, after Union General William Tecumseh Sherman burned Atlanta, he marched his sixty thousand troops east through Georgia to the sea, and then up into the Carolinas. The army fought off Confederate forces and lived off the land, pillaging the Southern plantations, taking cattle and crops for their own, demolishing cities, and accumulating a borne—along population of freed blacks and white refugees until all that remained was the dangerous transient life of the uprooted, the dispossessed, and the triumphant. Only a master novelist could so powerfully and compassionately render the lives of those who marched. The author has given us a magisterial work with an enormous cast of unforgettable characters—white and black, men, women, and children; unionists and rebels, generals and privates; freed slaves and slave owners. At the center are General Sherman himself, a beautiful freed slave girl named Pearl, a Union regimental surgeon, Colonel Sartorius; Emily Thompson, the dispossessed daughter of a Southern judge: and Arly and Will, two misfit soldiers. [DJ]

Edgar Lawrence Doctorow (1931 – 2015) was an American novelist, editor, and professor, best known for his works of historical fiction. He wrote twelve novels, three volumes of short fiction and a stage drama. They included the award-winning novels *Ragtime, Billy Bathgate*, and *The March*. These, like many of his other works, placed fictional characters in recognizable historical contexts, with known historical figures, and often used different narrative styles. His stories were recognized for their originality and versatility, and Doctorow was praised for his audacity and imagination. [15-09]

Sons of Glory #1

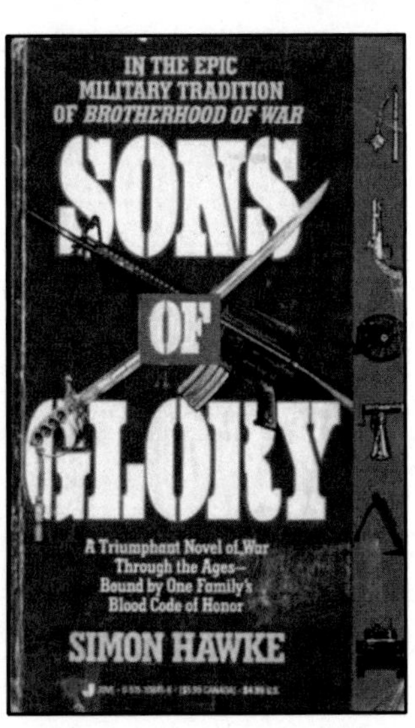

Civil War, Global War on Terror

Simon Hawke Jove (1992)

Bound by blood and honor, they have fought the greatest battles of all time—and survived. A glorious family of fighting men and women, the Gallios are descendants of a legendary general, sworn to a timeless tradition of strength and courage. Their military heritage is their pride. They live and die by the words:

"For the greater good, the greatest glory"

201 B.C. - Gladiator Hanno the slave survived the bloodstained arenas to ancient Rome, bestowing the Gallio family ring—and a code of honor—to his son.

1859 A.D. - West Point. Major A. W. Gallio, the Academy's master swordsman has passed the family tradition to his three children at West Point in 1859. The rumors of a devastating war between the states causes him grave conceren because members of the Gallio family might be fighting on both sides, North and South. The bulk of this novel portrays their experience in the armies fighting in northern Virginia.

1985 A.D. - Tony Gallio carried this sacred tradition to the battlefields of Vietnam, Cambodia, Nicaragua. But his covert mission for the CIA in Afghanistan could end the Gallio bloodline once and for all. [BC]

Simon Hawke (1951–) is an American author mainly of science fiction and fantasy novels. He was born Nicholas Valentin Yermakov, but began writing as Simon Hawke in 1984 and later changed his legal name to Hawke. He has also written near-future adventure novels under the pen name J. D. Masters and a series of humorous mystery novels. [15-10]

The Devil Gun

Civil War, Texas

J.T. Edson Corgi Books (1979)

The Ager Coffee-Mill Gun was the first successful automatic-fire weapon, the deadliest innovation to warfare since the discovery of gunpowder.

One of these guns was in the hands of a pair of fanatical Union supporters and the use to which they intended to put it turned Lieutenant Jackson Marsden, West Point honor cadet, into a deserter from his regiment and a traitor to the Union cause. It also caused Captain Dusty Fog of the Texas Light Cavalry to be sent from his command with orders to capture the gun at all costs.

Two young men, one in Confederate grey, the other wearing Union blue, rode three hundred miles with danger and death lurking every inch of the way. At last Dusty Fog stood with his two Army Colts pitted against the fanatics and their Devil Gun . . . with the lives of every man, woman and child in Texas forfeit if he should fail! [BC]

John Thomas Edson (1928–2014) was an English author of 137 Westerns, Civil War dramas, escapism adventure, and police-procedural novels. He lived near Melton Mowbray, Leicestershire from the 1950s onwards, and retired from writTing due to ill-health in 2005. [15-11]

The Soldier and The Rebel

Civil War

Patricia Potter Silhouette (1999)

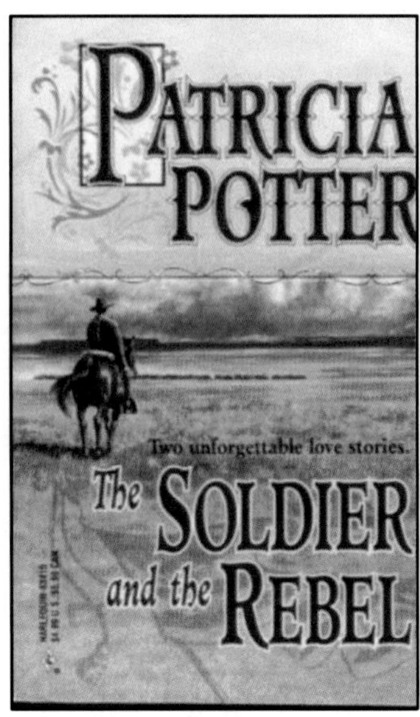

Dear Reader: *The Soldier and the Rebel*, first published years earlier as *Between the Thunder*, is a book very dear to me. It is the book...that sparked my writing career, my first novel.

Until I started writing the book, I considered myself a journalist, trained to report only the facts. I had learned the evils of an adjective, the horrors of adverbs. Fiction? Never.

And yet a germ of an idea would not go away. I had read a snippet of history--the tale of a Rebel general ordered to cross New Mexico and raid the Colorado gold fields for much-needed funds for the Confederacy. The Union colonel sent to stop him was his brother-in-law and a classmate at West Point. True story.

My mind rushed ahead with "what ifs." That general became Rebel Captain Sean Mallory. The Union colonel became Bennett Morgan, an officer sent to stop and hang, rebel raiders. Throw into the mix: Captain Mallory's sister who was the raiders' doctor. Season the stew with men's bitter parting years earlier. [BF]

Patricia Potter (1940–) worked as a reporter before turning to writing romance fiction in 1988. She has authored over forty novels of historical and contemporary romance. She headed the Georgia Romance Writers Association from 1988 to 1990 and served as President of the Romance Writers of America in 2004. [15-12]

Miss Mary's Honor Guard

Civil War, Romance, WP Author

Donald C. Bowman Wheatmark (2010)

A Confederate cavalry officer valiantly rescues his sweetheart, Mary, when she is snared by the Union Army and charged with espionage. She must then flee across the South through a gauntlet of danger. While she navigates her way to safety, the officer strikes deep into Union territory with Morgan's cavalry. When the unit is trapped, he must evade capture working as a spy behind Union lines until he can make his way back to her...if she has survived.

The Union Army, out for blood, hunts him as he puts his life on the line to find her again. This exciting and emotional story, set amid the violence and destruction of the Civil War, is about the special quality that makes fearsome soldiers and indestructible families. Enduring great tragedy, they learn to persevere and protect the things that really matter, soldiering on when hope has no reason beyond one driving force: love. [BC]

Donald Bowman (1935–) graduated from West Point in 1957 and retired as a Lt. Colonel in 1977. He reports that at West Point he was a mule rider and enjoyed "considerably more fun than I was supposed to have had." He became a public accountant in 1992. His book was motivated by stories told him about his great grandfather's rides with John Hunt Morgan in Kentucky. [15-13]

The Uncommon Soldier

Civil War, Judaism

Robert D. Abrahams　　　Farrar, Straus, & Cudahy (1959)

Alfred Mordecai was a brilliant young officer in the United States Army when the crisis which led to the Civil War began. Son of a famous school master in North Carolina, Alfred had graduated with honors from West Point and became a professor there. He was an American military observer in the Crimean War, and after the outbreak of the War of 1848, at great personal danger, he investigated a scandal in Mexico on behalf of the United States War Department. These achievements and others had gained him the reputation of one of the most promising officers in the United States Army.

Having married a Philadelphia girl, whose sympathies were with the North, and having become father of a son who was a cadet at West Point at the outbreak of the Civil War, Major Mordecai, like so many other Americans of his day, was torn between loyalties to the state of his birth and to his own family and to his wife's family and his own children and their friends. How he faced the dilemma created by the outbreak of the war is the theme of this true story of an American Jewish hero. [DJ]

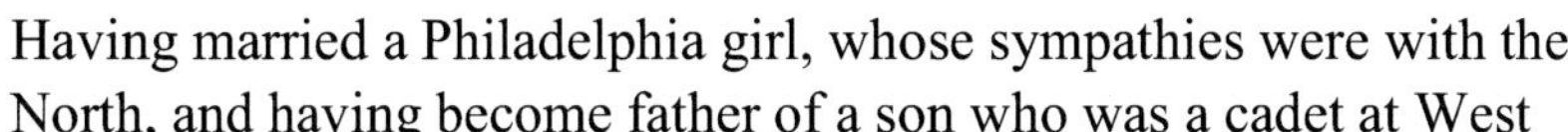

Robert D. Abrahams (1905–1998) was active in the law profession in Philadelphia while he published poetry and authored juvenile fiction. Abrahams balanced his many interests with a healthy sense of obligation to his community and to his Jewish heritage. [15-14]

The popular pulp fiction magazines from 1890 to 1950 were a favored venue for West Point stories. And the Civil War was no exception. Because these were mostly "short" stories, the authors created characters and settings from the initial page. For this reason, the stories were less documentary fiction, but more likely historical mysteries and thrillers.

"Captain Redspurs"

Civil War, Pulp Fiction

F. V. W. Mason   Argosy Magazine (October 1933)

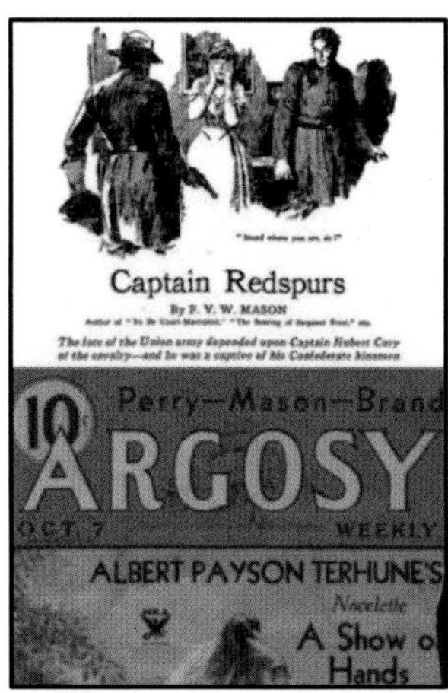

Captain Hubert Cary, Union cavalryman, was doing scout work with a small band of his horsemen in the vicinity of Harper's Ferry, Virginia, when he came across a band of guerrillas, dressed as Yankees, looting a farm. Before Cary learned the true identity of the marauders they escaped. Cary saw, to his horror, that they had killed a boy and tortured an old man.

Captain Cary freed a girl who had imprisoned herself in the farmhouse and she promptly gave the alarm to the Confederates. Cary was captured and was about to be hanged when he was saved by the timely arrival of his cousin Craig who, like the other Southern Careys, spelled his last name with an "e."

Craig explained Hubert's true role to his captors, telling them that guerrillas had done the pillaging. So, Captain Hubert Cary, Northern cavalryman, was taken to Philomont, VA, home of the Southern Careys, as a prisoner of Captain Craig Carey, Rebel cavalryman.

There he met the girl he had rescued, Lenore Duveen, and fell in love with her, although he learned that Craig was also in love with her.

When a Yankee patrol attacked Philomont, Hubert escaped by seizing Lenore Duveen and using her as a shield until he got to his horse. He realized that this would make the Careys and the Duveen girl hate him, but he had learned a military secret of vast importance and would stop at nothing to get back to his headquarters and report. [EB]

Francis Van Wyck Mason (1901–1978) was an American historian and novelist. He had a long and prolific career as a writer spanning 50 years including 78 published novels. He started with pulp fiction adventure stories in 1928 and continued until he authored his more serious historical fiction after 1938. [15-15]

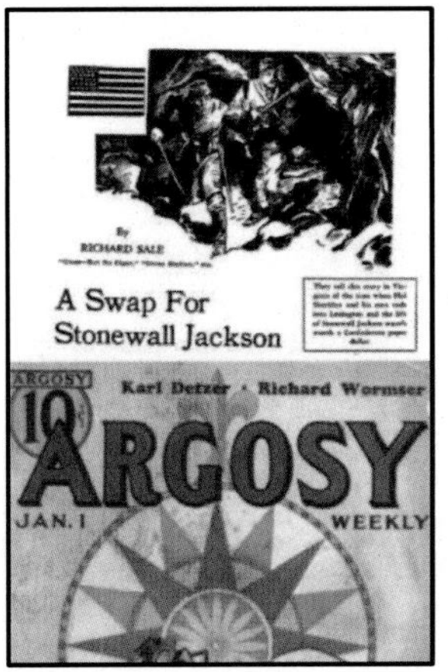

"A Swap for Stonewall"

Civil War, Pulp Fiction

Richard Sale   Argosy Magazine (January 1938)

An old man's recollection of a Civil War event:

Like Mr. Longfellow used to say when he wrote that poem about the midnight ride of Paul Revere: "Hardly a man is now alive who remembers that famous day and year. . . ." Only I'm not talking about Paul Revere. I'm talking about Johnny Ragoo of Lexington, Virginia, and what he did on that April morning in 1863. And what I mean by quoting Mr. Longfellow is that hardly a man is now alive who can tell that story about Johnny Ragoo and the Yankees in

Lexington. I guess that Jeeta Dixie and me are about the only ones left who know the whole thing, because Dr. Caldwell and Stonewall Jackson and General Lee are all dead. And as for Jeeta Dixie, I reckon his memory don' work so good for him now because he must be 'most seventy million years old and things get confused in his mind.

. . . Nowadays it seems to be the fashion to debunk everything you've been taking for granted in your history books. Like Paul Revere, for instance. Nowadays it's said he never made the midnight ride at all. A friend of his did, and Paul got caught by the British before he had a chance to do any good. And another thing you hear is that George Washington was not the first president of the United States. And that it was really Edward Stanton's fault that Mr. Booth shot Mr. Lincoln . . .

The poem about Phil Sheridan. I guess everyone knows it. The one about him riding from Winchester twenty miles away to turn the rout of his army into a victory. Maybe I am a Johnny Reb, but I always sort of looked up to General Sheridan in that poem. That is, until I remember Johnny Ragoo. And then I can't help laughing at General Sheridan.

Because Johnny Ragoo was only fourteen years old, mind you, defeated the whole blanking army of General Sheridan all by himself and what's more he did it in three days and without firing a shot. . . . [EB]

"The Rebels are Coming!"

Civil War, Pulp Fiction

Richard Sale Argosy Magazine (May 1939)

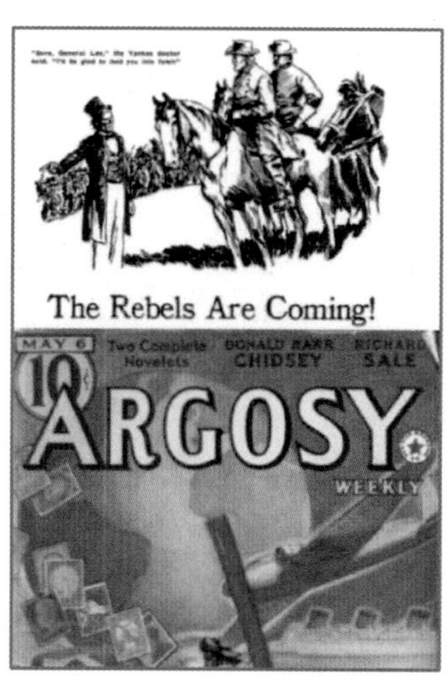

The history of a small, forgotten corner of the Civil War—where a Yankee doctor gave General Lee and a hundred thousand Rebels a lesson in home-made strategy…

The news reached Portaupeck at nine a.m. that morning when old Tom Cobbler, who drove the shay with the mail in from Spring Hill across near Cashtown, came thundering into town, driving his two mares at a more than reckless gait, his iron red wheels clattering noisily upon the cobbles in the square.

"They're coming" Tom Cobbler yelled as he passed town folk. "They're comin' down from Heidlerburg way, the whole pack and passel of 'em! They blowed Spring Hill off'n the map and they're on their way here! General Lee and his rascals! And Longstreet from Chambersburg. The Rebels are comin' and comin' fast!"

For a while the panic was intense, but people soon realized that there was little they could do to stop the advance, and that the best thing to do was to sit back and let the soldiers through and that probably no one would get hurt that way. But it did seem a shame to be eaten out of house and home by the Confederate Army. It did seem as though President Lincoln could have been more vigilant about the whole thing.

It was the end of June, and when Dr. Joseph J. Jines awakened the heat had already started to grow, and he found himself sweating. Out the window, he could see a cloud of dust approaching on the pike, and presently, he made out the horses and knew it was Tom Cobbler's shay.

"Morning, Tom," Dr. Jines said. "Did you bring me my paper from Spring Hill?"

"Bring you nothin'" Tom Cobbler panted. He came in and shut the door and leaned against it as though he were holding it closed against an enemy. "The Rebels are coming!"

Dr. Jines frowned. "What's the matter with you, Tom? Your liver bothering you? You look kind of peaked and pale."

"The Rebels are comin', Doc! The Rebels are coming! They're marching up and down Pennsylvania! They've razed Spring Hill."

"Oh, shucks," Dr. Jines said, "Is that why you didn't get my paper?" [EB]

"The Judas Tree"

Civil War, Pulp Fiction

Richard Sale Argosy Magazine (May 13,1939)

There are many strange sights in Virginia, strange, moving, and wonderful. There are the baroque Cyclops Towers, formations of rock rising raggedly into the sky like something out of the Mesozoic Era; and near New Market, the gorgeous caverns underground, without end, honeycombing themselves deep into the red clay beneath Virginia; and the blue grottos, near Harrisonburg, where Confederate soldiers successfully hid themselves from General Hunter when he raided the Shenandoah Valley, the grave of Stonewall Jackson in Lexington, Harper's Ferry, Appomattox, the Wilderness....

But the strangest of all sights is a tree on the northern outskirts of a small town near Richmond, named Truman Gap. Truman Gap, today, merely exists, but at one point during the War between the States, it was so important that the South might have won because of it...

When you approach Truman's Gap, coming down from Washington, you spot the tree instantly. It is a shaggy monster, twisted and grotesque, intertwined like the agony tree in Gethsemane. It is still remarkably healthy, and it hangs over the roadway so that you pass beneath its very branches. They are long and thick and not too high, those first ones.

You are impressed with this before ever you read the identification sign. There is something ominous about that tree, it can be felt. It was built for death. Nothing soft or pretty about it. Monstrous, grim, and hard. The marker says simply:

> *THE JUDAS TREE*
> *General Robert E. Lee Visited this Spot in July,1865,*
> to Erase Virginia's Shame and Sorrow...

Well, there you are. There's a story behind it, and the sign, instead of helping you out, only whets your appetite. [EB]

Richard Sale (1911–1993) was an American screenwriter, pulp fiction author, and film director. He wrote 40 screenplays, numerous pulp fiction stories, and directed 14 films. Most notable was the TV western series, *Yancy Derringer* (1958–1959), which he produced with his wife, Mary Loos. [15-16]

Real and Fictional Characters Set Against Fictional Events

In this next series, the author takes a very non-standard technique, but not the only one of its kind encountered in this book collection. The novels are far more fiction than history, but they are very much about West Pointers.

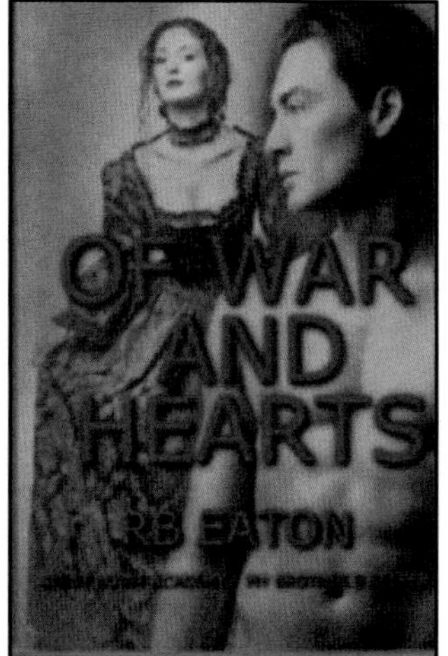

Of War and Hearts: West Point Academy

Cadet, Civil War, Romance

Rosemary B. Eaton Self-published (2015)

How better to start a war than pit the parents of the nation's highest ranking Politicians, Military, and Business leaders in a desperate battle to protect their children? As the West Point legacy parents from both the North and South find themselves transformed once more into the world of spies and intrigue, follow the cadets of West Point Military Academy as they grow up in the days before the Civil War. Join a young George Custer and see how all those demerits were earned. Follow Miles, Conner, Rory, and David Fraser as the brothers find themselves pitted against each other and their fathers to protect the loves of their lives. Can Doc Crawford and his spy ring stop the South from starting a war or will they all be caught up in this deadly game of poison, attempted murder, and sabotage? [BC]

Of War and Hearts: Licking Valley

Cadet, Civil War, Romance

Rosemary B. Eaton Self-published (2015)

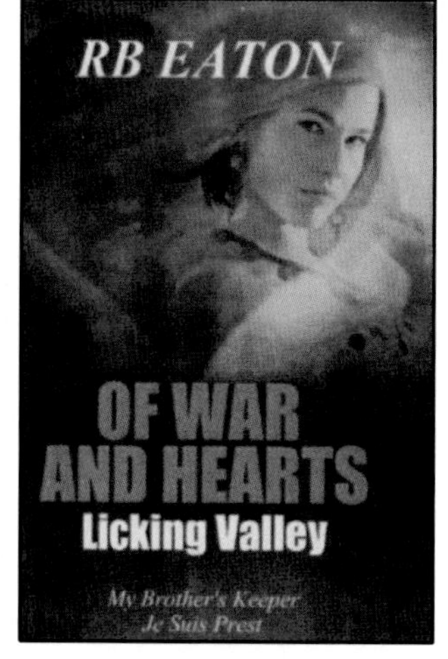

Book two of the series, *Of War and Hearts,* continues the saga started in West Point Academy as the cadets leave West Point headed to Licking Valley with Aeronaut Thaddeus Lowe to test the practicality of ascending in a hydrogen balloon for spying their enemy's position. Follow the continuing romance of Rory and Isobel and his brother Miles and Sarah as they leave campus and head West toward Kentucky.

Find out more about what happens to Sam Pollard and his sister Sybil and the dirty picture taken of Isobel's date, Jason Hunter, at the Charity Ball of 1859. Don't forget about the Women's Club Meeting notice that Rory gave to J.E.B. Stuart's mother Elizabeth. What exactly did Eliza Jane scribble on the back and who knows about it now? Did Leontine make a splendid selection of land to rent in Licking Valley for experimenting on the Enterprise or did she fall into a trap of the man who knows enough to blackmail every important family in the North and South? Everything was fair in love and war as both the North and South escalate their fire at each other's children, relations, business associates, and lovers. Before this Spring is over both parents and children will understand exactly how far they will or will not go to follow orders, make a profit, and protect the ones they consider their families whether by blood or bond of the heart. [BC]

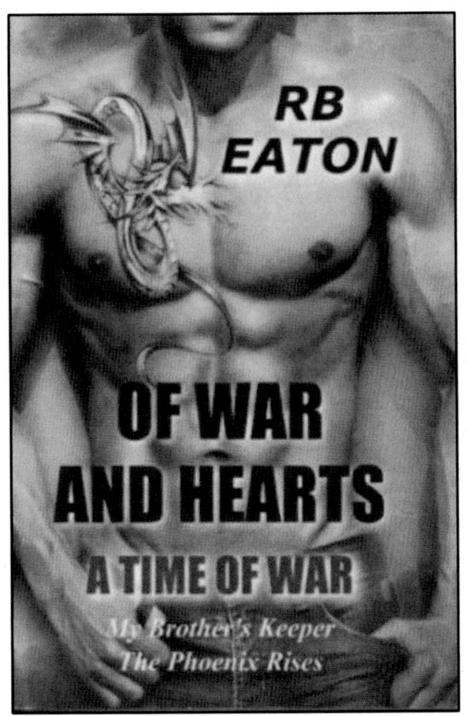

Of War and Hearts: A Time of War

Cadet, Civil War, Romance

Rosemary B. Eaton Self-published (2015)

A Time of War, the third book in *Of War and Hearts* concludes the story of the cadets as they graduate or enlist early as the Civil War starts. The story takes us into the First Battle of Bull Run and that damned Balls Bluff as Sybil finds herself behind enemy lines. Hydrogen balloons take to the sky, Hermon Haupt takes over logistics of transporting troops and supplies by railroad. Northern Generals come and go in record fashion. George Custer meets William Sherman.

Find out what happens to the plans for the C.S.S. Arkansas. Does Sybella finally find out what the Russians wanted? Who is "She Who Cries Weather" and how did Albert Pike muster Cherokees who both favored the North and South into the Confederate Army? Who is Long Hair Clan? Who is really a phoenix and who is really a griffin and what do you get if they have children? Our spies and soldiers do what they can to inform or misinform as best suits their goals. As the stakes get higher, the pain deeper, the weather stranger, and the explanations less truthful, desperation, love, faith, and family take on whole new meanings as the phoenix rises in a time of war. [BC]

Rosemary B. Eaton is a retired IT Manager that has found a passion for writing fictional humorous romances that explore the relationships between lovers, family, friends, and arch enemies. She enjoys writing about bits of history that seem too good to be true….Her trilogy, *Of War and Hearts* tells the story of cadets from West Point, Virginia Military Institute, and the Citadel in the years 1860–1863 as the country heads to the war and creates a fertile ground for graft that would make millionaires or bankrupt businesses as they vied for contracts of either the North or South. [15-17]

Real People and Real Events

Now let us shift the focus to scenes, dialogue, and plot created by the author to fit real events. The following books provide a "fictional gloss" to the characters and humanize them while coping with the horrific events of the Civil War.

The Killer Angels: The Classic Novel of the Civil War

Civil War, General Officer

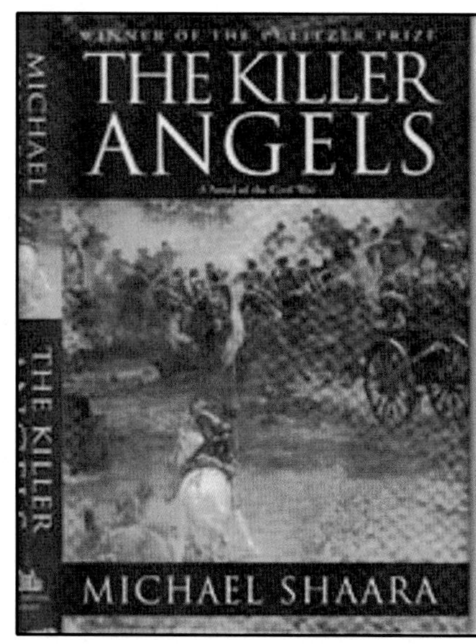

Michael Shaara Ballantine Books (1996)

July 1863, The Confederate Army of Northern Virginia is invading the North. General Robert E. Lee has made this daring and massive move with seventy thousand men in a determined effort to draw out the Union Army of the Potomac and mortally wound it. His right hand is General James Longstreet, a brooding man who is loyal to Lee but stubbornly argues against his plan. Opposing them is an unknown factor: General George Meade, who has taken command of the Army only two days before what will be perhaps the crucial battle of the Civil War.

In the four most bloody and courageous days of our nation's history, the armies fight for two conflicting dreams. One dreams of freedom, the other of a way of life. More than rifles and bullets are carried into battle. The soldiers carry memories. Promises. Love. And more than men fall on those Pennsylvania fields. Bright futures, untested innocence, and pristine beauty are also the casualties of war. *The Killer Angels* is unique, sweeping, unforgettable–a dramatic re-creation of the battleground for American destiny. [DJ]

Michael Shaara (1928–1988) grew up wanting to become a writer. In the early 1950s, Michael published a number of award-winning science-fiction short stories in the most popular pulp magazines of the day. He later began writing straight fiction, and published more than 70 short stories in such magazines as *Playboy*, *Redbook*, *Cosmopolitan*, *The Saturday Evening Post*. He moved to Florida in the mid-1950s to teach English, literature and creative writing at Florida State University.

Reflecting on an extraordinary experience with his family visiting the battlefield at Gettysburg, Michael became obsessed with telling the story of that momentous event through the eyes of the main characters themselves, something that had never been done. To Michael's disappointment, *The Killer Angels* was rejected by the first fifteen publishers who saw the manuscript. It was a shock to both Michael and the literary community when the announcement was made that *The Killer Angels* had been awarded the 1975 Pulitzer Prize for Fiction.

After a prolonged decline in his health, Michael died in May 1988. Five years later, the film *Gettysburg* was released, propelling *The Killer Angels* to number one on the New York Times Bestseller list (19 years after its initial publication!). [15-18]

Michael Shaara's son, Jeff, picked up the fallen banner in the late '90s by writing a prequel and sequel to *The Killer Angels*.

Gods and Generals

Civil War, General Officer

Jeff Shaara Ballantine Books (1998)

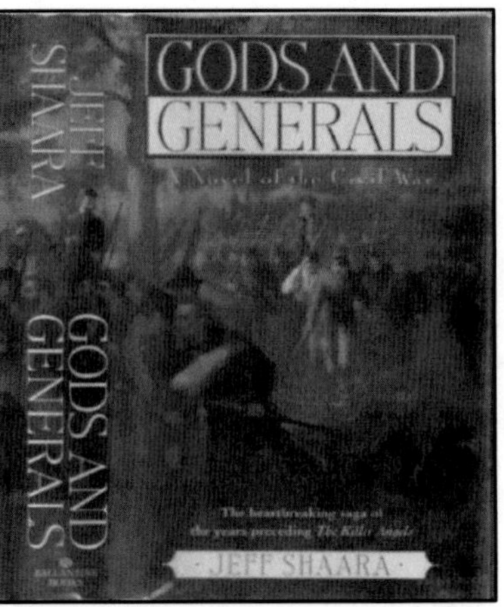

The Killer Angels, Michael Shaara's classic Civil War novel about the men who led the fight at the Battle of Gettysburg, was a major literary event, winning the Pulitzer Prize, becoming a bestseller, and selling more than two million copies. Now, in *Gods and Generals*, Jeff Shaara carries forward his father's vision in an epic story that traces the lives, passions, and careers of these great military leaders from the first gathering clouds of the Civil War.

Here is Thomas "Stonewall" Jackson, a hopelessly by-the-book military instructor and devout Christian. His fierce exterior hides a compassionate soul that few - students and soldiers alike - will never see, and he becomes the greatest commander of the Civil War. We follow Winfield Scott Hancock, a Captain of Quartermasters who is assigned command of a brigade of infantry, quickly establishing himself as one of the finest leaders in the Union army. Then there is Joshua Chamberlain, who gives up his promising academic career to volunteer for service in the new army, only to become one of the most heroic soldiers in American history. And here too is a brilliant portrait of the complex, aristocratic Robert E. Lee, who is faced with the agonizing decision of resigning from a distinguished thirty-year army career in order to defend his home, not believing until too late that a civil war would never truly come to pass.

As the war gathers momentum, Stonewall Jackson wins his reputation by a series of stinging victories over ineptly led Union forces. Lee, finally given command of the Confederate forces, recognizes that this strange devout, and dangerous man is his greatest weapon. For a time, it truly seems as if God is on their side and that Lee will lead his army to final victory against overwhelming odds. Nowhere is this plainer than at the Battle of Fredericksburg, where, for the first time, all four men meet on the same field and experience the exhilaration and raw horror of battle from four very different points of view.

But it is in the next great fight, the Battle of Chancellorsville, that Lee's brilliant strategy, and Jackson's supreme achievement, are over-shadowed when Jackson is mortally wounded by his own men. This loss is the true turning point of the war. Lee now realizes that against the ever growing numbers of Union forces, he can only win by a direct threat to Washington. So the battle-hardened armies of the Confederacy begin their fateful invasion of the North, toward an obscure crossroads in Pennsylvania called Gettysburg. [DJ]

The Last Full Measure

Civil War, General Officer

Jeff Shaara Ballantine Books (1998)

As *The Last Full Measure* opens, Gettysburg is past and the war advances to its third brutal year. On the Union side, the gulf between the politicians in Washington and the generals in the field yawns ever wider. Never has the cumbersome Union Army so desperately needed a decisive, hard-nosed leader. It is at this critical moment that Lincoln places Ulysses S. Grant in command and turns the tide of the war.

For Robert E. Lee, Gettysburg was an unspeakable disaster- compounded by the shattering loss of the fiery Stonewall Jackson two months before. Lee knows better than anyone that the South cannot survive a war of attrition. But with the total devotion of his generals—Longstreet, Hill, Stuart—and his unswerving faith in God, Lee is determined to fight to the bitter end.

Here too is Joshua Chamberlain, the college professor who emerged as the Union hero at Gettysburg—will rise to become one of the greatest figures of the Civil War.

Battle by staggering battle, Shaara dramatizes the escalating confrontation between Lee and Grant—complicated, heroic, deeply troubled men. From the costly Battle of the Wilderness to the agonizing siege of Petersburg to Lee's epoch-making surrender at Appomattox, Shaara portrays the riveting conclusion of the Civil War through the minds and hearts of the individuals who gave their last full measure. [DJ]

A dozen years later, Jeff Shaara again took up his pen to produce a companion set of volumes (a tetrology) focusing on armies and leaders of the Civil War west of the Appalachain mountains.

A Blaze of Glory: A Novel of the Battle of Shiloh

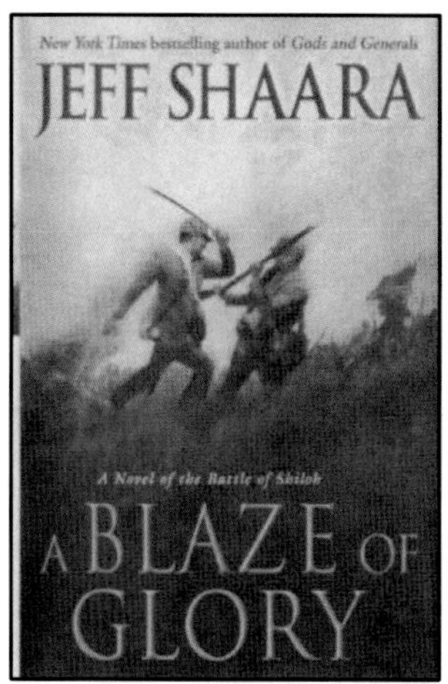

Civil War, General Officer

Jeff Shaara Ballantine Books (2012)

In the first novel of a spellbinding new trilogy, author Jeff Shaara returns to the Civil War terrain he knows best. *A Blaze of Glory* takes us to the action-packed Western Theater for a vivid re-creation of one of the war's bloodiest and most iconic engagements—the Battle of Shiloh. It's the spring of 1862. The Confederate Army in the West teeters on the brink of collapse following the catastrophic loss of Fort Donelson. Commanding general Albert Sidney Johnston is forced to pull up stakes, abandon the critical city of Nashville, and rally his troops in defense of the Memphis and Charleston Railroad. Hot on Johnston's trail are two of the Union's best generals: the relentless Ulysses Grant, fresh off his career-making victory at Fort Donelson, and Don Carlos Buell. If their combined forces can crush Johnston's army and capture the railroad, the war in the West likely will be over. There's one problem: Johnston knows of the Union plans, and is poised to launch an audacious surprise attack on Grants encampment—a small settlement in southwestern Tennessee anchored by a humble church named Shiloh.

With stunning you-are-there perspective Shaara takes us inside the maelstrom of Shiloh as no novelist has before. Drawing on meticulous research, he dramatizes the actions and decisions of the commanders on both sides: Johnson, Grant, Sherman, Beauregard, and the illustrious Colonel Nathan Bedford Forrest. Here too are the thoughts and voices of the junior officers, conscripts, and enlisted men who gave their all for the cause, among them Confederate cavalry, lieutenant James Seeley and Private Fritz "Dutchie" Bauer of the 16th Wisconsin Regiment—brave participants in a pitched, back-and-forth battle whose casualty count would far surpass anything the American public had yet seen in this war. By the end of the first day of fighting, as Grant's bedraggled forces regroup for what could be their last stand, two major events—both totally unexpected—will turn the tide of the battle and perhaps the war itself. [DJ]

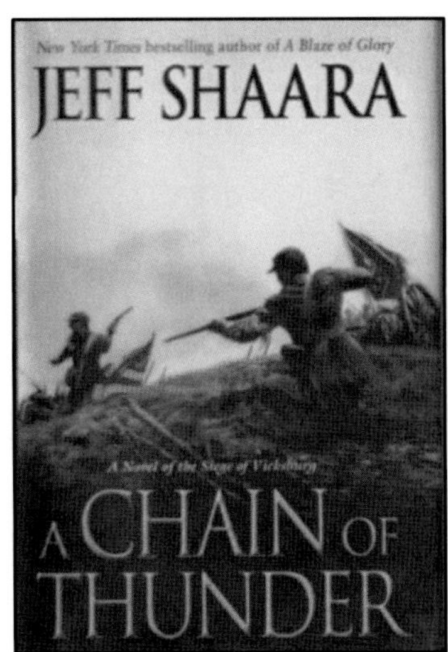

A Chain of Thunder: A Novel of the Siege of Vicksburg

Civil War, General Officer

Jeff Shaara Ballantine Books (2013)

Continuing the series that began with *A Blaze of Glory*, author]eff Shaara returns to chronicle another decisive chapter in America's long and bloody Civil War. In *A Chain of Thunder*, the action shifts to the fortress city of Vicksburg, Mississippi. There, in the vaunted "Gibraltar of the Confederacy" a siege for the ages will cement the reputation of one Union general—-and all but seal the fate of the rebel cause. In May 1863, after months of hard and bitter combat, Union troops under the command of Major General Ulysses S. Grant at long last successfully cross the Mississippi River. They force the remnants of Confederate lieutenant general John C. Pemberton's army to retreat to Vicksburg, burning the bridges over the Big Black River in its path. But after sustaining heavy casualties in two failed assaults against the rebels, Union soldiers are losing confidence and morale is low. Grant reluctantly decides to lay siege to the city, trapping soldiers and civilians alike inside an iron ring of Federal entrenchments. Six weeks later, the starving and destitute Southerners finally surrender, yielding command of the Mississippi River to the Union forces on July 4 - Independence Day - and marking a crucial turning point in the Civil War. Drawing on comprehensive research and his own intimate knowledge of the Vicksburg campaign, Jeff Shaara once again weaves brilliant fiction out of the ragged cloth of historical fact. From the command tents where generals plot strategy to the ruined mansions where beleaguered citizens huddle for safety, this is a panoramic portrait of men and women whose lives are forever altered by the siege. On one side stand the emerging legend Grant, his irascible second ,William T. Sherman, and the youthful "grunt" Private Fritz Bauer; on the other, the Confederate commanders Pemberton and Joseph Johnston, as well as nineteen-year-old Lucy Spence, a civilian doing her best to survive in the besieged city. By giving voice to their experiences at Vicksburg, *A Chain of Thunder* vividly evokes a battle whose outcome still reverberates more than 150 years after the cannons fell silent. [DJ]

The Smoke at Dawn : A Novel of the Civil War

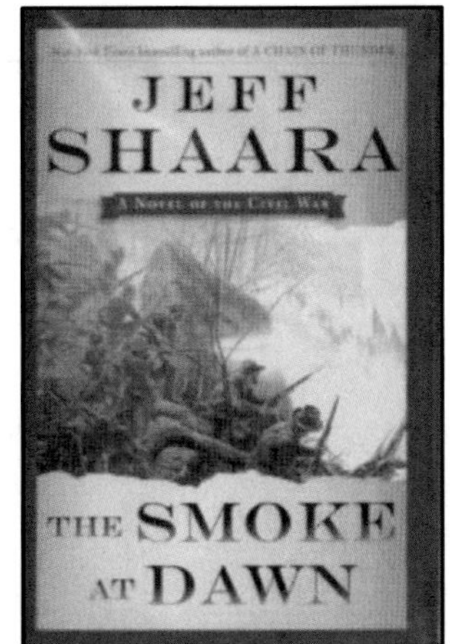

Civil War, General Officer

Jeff Shaara Ballantine Books (2014)

In The Smoke at Dawn, the last great push of the Army of the Cumberland sets the stage for a decisive confrontation at Chattanooga that could determine the outcome of the war, Summer 1863. The Federal triumph at Vicksburg has secured complete control of the Mississippi River from the Confederacy, cementing the reputation of Ulysses S. Grant. Farther east, the Federal army under the command of William Rosecrans captures the crucial rail hub at Chattanooga. But Rosecrans is careless, and while chasing the Confederates, the Federal forces are routed in north Georgia at Chickamauga Creek. Retreating in a panic back to Chattanooga, Rosecrans is pursued by the Confederate forces under General Braxton Bragg. Penned up, with their supply lines severed, the Federal army seems doomed to the same kind of defeat that plagued the Confederates at Vicksburg. But a disgusted Abraham Lincoln has seen enough of

General Rosecrans. Ulysses Grant is elevated to command of the entire theater of the war, and immediately replaces Rosecrans with General George Thomas.

Grant gathers an enormous force, including armies commanded by Joseph Hooker and Grant's friend William T. Sherman. Grant's mission is clear: break the Confederate siege and destroy Bragg's army. Meanwhile, Bragg wages war as much with his own subordinates as he does with the Federals, creating dissension and disharmony in the Southern ranks, erasing the Confederate army's superiority at exactly the wrong time. Blending evocative historical detail with searing depictions of battle, Ieff Shaara immerses readers in the world of commanders and common soldiers, civilians and statesmen. From the Union side come the voices of Generals Grant, William Tecumseh Sherman, and George Thomas—the vaunted "Rock of Chickamauga" —as well as the young private Fritz "Dutchie" Bauer. From the Rebel ranks come Generals Bragg, Patrick Cleburne, and James Longstreet, as well as the legendary cavalry commander Nathan Bedford Forest. *The Smoke at Dawn* vividly re-creates the war in the West, when the fate of a divided nation truly hangs in the balance. [DJ]

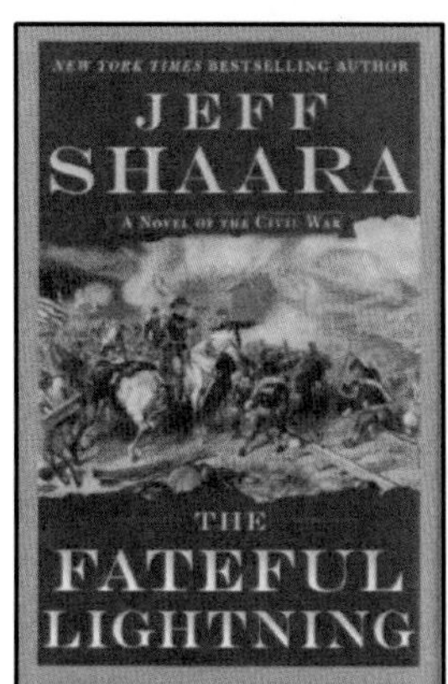

The Fateful Lightning: A Novel of the Civil War

Civil War, General Officer

Jeff Shaara Ballantine Books (2015)

This is the final installment in the Civil War series that began with *A Blaze of Glory* and continued in *A Chain of Thunder* and *The Smoke at Dawn*. November 1864: As the Civil War rolls into its fourth bloody year, the tide has turned decidedly in favor of the Union. A grateful Abraham Lincoln responds to Ulysses S. Grant's successes by bringing the general east, promoting Grant to command the entire Union war effort, while William Tecumseh Sherman now directs the Federal forces that occupy all of Tennessee. In a massive surge southward, Sherman conquers the city of Atlanta, sweeping aside the Confederate army under the inept leadership of General John Bell Hood. Pushing through northern Georgia, Sherman's legendary "March to the Sea" shoves away any Rebel presence, and by Christmas 1864 the city of Savannah falls into the hands of "Uncle Billy." Now there is but one direction for Sherman to go. In his way stands the last great hope for the Southern cause, General Joseph E. Johnston.

In the concluding novel of his epic Civil War tetralogy, Jeff Shaara tells the dramatic story of the final eight months of battle from multiple perspectives: the commanders in their tents making plans for total victory, as well as the ordinary foot soldiers and cavalrymen who carried out their orders until the last alarum sounded. Through Sherman's eyes, we gain insight into the mind of the general who vowed to "make Georgia howl" until it surrendered. In Johnston, we see a man agonizing over the limits of his army's power, and accepting the burden of leading the last desperate effort to ensure the survival of the Confederacy. The Civil War did not end quietly. It climaxed in a storm of fury that lay waste to everything in its path. *The Fateful Lightning* brings to life those final brutal, bloody months of fighting with you-are-there immediacy, grounded in the meticulous research that readers have come to expect from Jeff Shaara. [DJ]

Michael's son, **Jeff Shaara** (1952–), has followed his father's footsteps writing historical fiction and documenting American wars and their most historically relevant characters. In total, Jeff has written fifteen *New York Times* bestselling novels. [15-19]

Continuing with the Civil War west of the Appalachians, another prominent American author uses a technique employed by the Shaara's to highlight the thinking, emotions, hopes, doubts and fears of the generals leading North and South.

Bright Starry Banner: A Novel of the Civil War

Civil War, General Officer

Alden R. Carter Soho Press (2004)

On the eve of battle, while the bands of both armies play "Home Sweet Home," eighty-thousand men join in singing. At dawn, they will set about killing each other. Five days after Christmas, 1862, in the damp and cold outside Murfreesboro, Tennessee, the men of General William S. Rosecrans's Army of the Cumberland face the Confederate soldiers of General Braxton Bragg's Army of Tennessee. Other eminent West Pointers are featured: Sheridan, Thomas, Hardee, and Wheeler.

The Battle of Stones River will last three days. The savage fighting, across the fields and woods of Tennessee, will awaken the best in some men—courage, self-sacrifice, and honor; the worst in others—cruelty, cowardice, depravity. This is the story of those hours and the men who went forth. [DJ]

Alden R. Carter (1947–) is an American writer primarily known for his young adult novels, stories, and non-fiction. Aside from his young adult work Carter has published several works of adult non-fiction, and given over six hundred presentations to schools and conferences. [15-20]

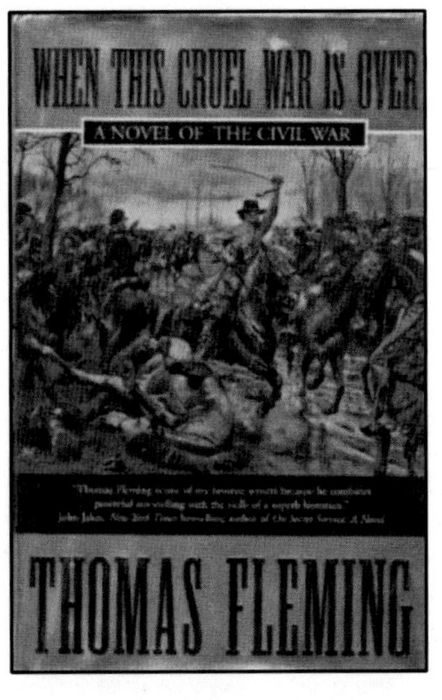

When This Cruel War Is Over: A Novel of the Civil War

Civil War

Thomas J. Fleming Forge Books (2001)

This is the story of two generations of Americans struggling to make sense of a national catastrophe, to rescue love in a country whose future is shot through with darkness. The time is the summer of 1864, the third year of the bloody Civil War that has already killed a half million Americans. The place is Indiana and Kentucky, divided by the Ohio River, but united in a growing Fury at the federal government's ruthless censorship and intolerance of dissent. It is the story of Americans, once loyal to the Union, paid back with spies and forced enlistments while the Emancipation Proclamation forces the region to rethink its customs and prejudices.

Janet Todd is a courier and evangelist for the Sons of Liberty, a revolutionary conspiracy that intends to unite the American heartland into a western Confederacy—and stop the war. Major Paul Stapleton was badly wounded in the battles of Antietam and Gettysburg. He commands a troop of black cavalrymen who hunt Union deserters. The pride and love he felt for the Union when he took his oath at West Point is weakening as the war drags on. The number of deserters increases while the number of volunteers dwindles. Stapleton's heart and mind turn toward Janet Todd. It is a love closely observed by Henry Gentry, Lincoln's boyhood friend and a clandestine Union intelligence officer in the Heartland.

The book is a landmark novel about the guerrilla war sponsored by the South and waged by disgruntled Northerners at the height of America's bloodiest war. It is a story that climaxes on both sides of the night-shrouded Ohio when Paul and Janet must make life-defining, love-driven choices that will leave the reader stunned and tearful. [DJ]

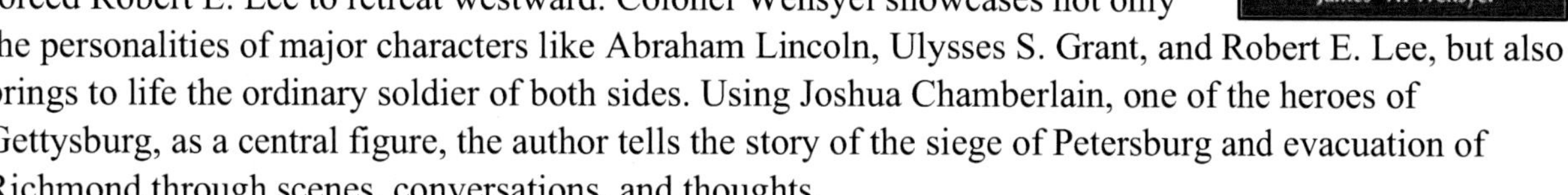

Thomas Fleming (1927–2017) was a prominent American novelist and historian. His other book in the collection, *Officer's Wives*, can be found in the chapter, "Army Life & Army Wives."

Petersburg: Out of the Trenches

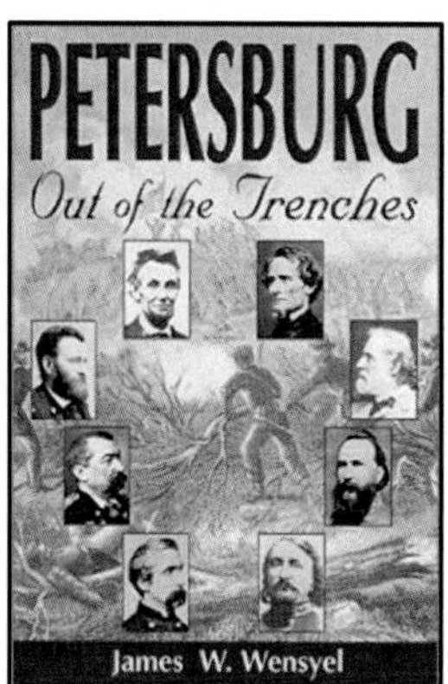

Civil War, WP Author, General Officer

James Wensyel, Lt. Col. Ret. Burd Street Press (1998)

When John B. Gordon's Confederate assault at Fort Stedman fails and Union cavalry and infantry under Philip Sheridan sweep away Lee's right flank at Five Forks, Lee's only remaining option is a fighting retreat to join Joseph E. Johnston's army in North Carolina.

Petersburg traces the individuals who took part in that desperate fighting which forced Robert E. Lee to retreat westward. Colonel Wensyel showcases not only the personalities of major characters like Abraham Lincoln, Ulysses S. Grant, and Robert E. Lee, but also brings to life the ordinary soldier of both sides. Using Joshua Chamberlain, one of the heroes of Gettysburg, as a central figure, the author tells the story of the siege of Petersburg and evacuation of Richmond through scenes, conversations, and thoughts.

Though written as historical fiction, the background and events are accurately researched and portrayed. This book vividly recreates the people and events of the last few weeks of the war. [DJ]

Appomattox: The Passing of the Armies

WP Author, Civil War, General Officer

James Wensyel, Lt. Col. Ret. White Mane Books (2000)

On March 31, 1865, Union General Philip H. Sheridan turns the right flank of Confederate General Robert E. Lee's Army of Northern Virginia at Five Forks, Virginia. Hours later Union General in Chief Ulysses S. Grant orders an all-out assault across the Confederate front. By evening, Lee's line is shattered, and his army has begun a retreat to the west, abandoning Richmond and Petersburg in a desperate attempt to link with Confederate General Joseph E. Johnston's army in North Carolina. Richmond and Petersburg are burning, and Confederate President Jefferson Davis is moving his government to the relative safety of Danville, Virginia. Appomattox is the story of the retreat of Lee's army, the constant skirmishing which accompanies that retreat, and Lee's surrender to Grant on April 9, 1865.

Appomattox is told through conversations and scenes involving individuals on each side. Including narrative, it is accurate in its portrayal of the events leading to the end of our Civil War and its portrayal of the individuals and the armies caught up in the Appomattox Campaign. [DJ]

James Wensyel (1930–2015) graduated from West Point in 1952. He saw combat with the infantry in Korea and during three tours of duty in Vietnam, retiring as a Lt. Colonel. He resided in Carlisle, Pennsylvania, and volunteered as a Gettysburg battlefield guide. Another of his books, *Martha's Easter Bonnet* can be found in the chapter on the Revolutionary War. [15-21]

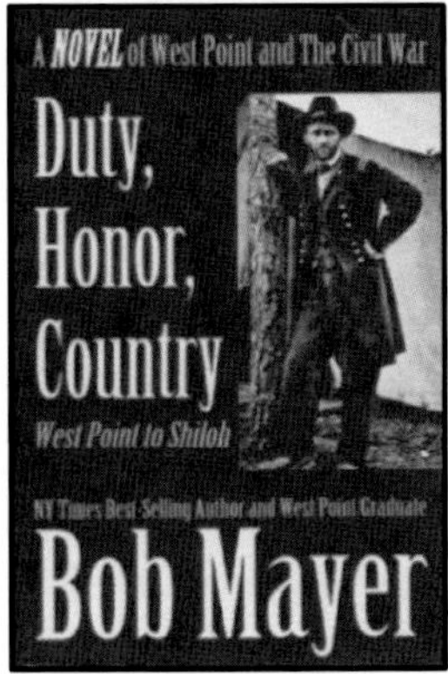

Duty, Honor, Country - West Point to Shiloh: A Novel of West Point and the Civil War

Mexican War, Civil War, WP Author

Bob Mayer Cool Gus Publishing (2013)

Two West Point cadets are caught up in the historical events of the most significant era in United States history when the nation was torn apart by a Civil War. Lucius Rumble and Elijah Cord encounter war, political intrigue, personal tragedies and more while encountering historical figures such as Ulysses S. Grant, Robert E. Lee, William Tecumseh Sherman, Abraham Lincoln, Kit Carson and more.

The story begins at West Point in 1840 when Rumble and Cord clash over tavern owner Benny Haven's daughter. The decision they make that day reverberates with them as the story ranges from West Point; to a plantation in Natchez, the richest city in the United States where cotton was king; to the only mutiny in the United States Navy; to St. Louis where Kit Carson is preparing to depart on a famous expedition to the west with Fremont that would eventually bring California into the Union; to Mexico, where the United States Army suffered its highest casualty rate to this day and brought most of the western United States into the Union; to the founding of the Naval Academy; to John Brown's hanging; to the firing on Fort Sumter; through First Bull Run; the first battle of ironclads, the Monitor and Virginia; and culminating in the epic battle of Shiloh, where the United States had more casualties in one battle than in all previous wars combined and the face of warfare changed forever.
The key to this series is a simple fact I had to memorize as a plebe at West Point: Who commanded the major battles of the Civil War? — There were 60 important battles of the War. In 55 of them, graduates commanded on both sides. [DJ]

Robert "Bob" Mayer (1959–) is a *New York Times*-bestselling author and the CEO of Cool Gus Publishing. He is a West Point graduate, Class of 1981, and former Green Beret. Mayer has authored over 60 novels in multiple genres, selling more than 4 million books. Two of his other novels, *The Jefferson Allegiance* and *The Line* are also included in this book collection. [15-22]

Chapter 16

The World Wars

World War I

Europe became embroiled in a global war that consumed the continent from July 28, 1914 to November 11, 1918. For the first three years America attempted neutrality as the Triple Entente (Britain, France, and Russia) battled the Central Powers (Germany, the Austro-Hungarian Empire, and the Ottoman Empire) to a bitter stalemate - particularly on the Western Front. When Germany resorted to unrestricted submarine warfare in 1917, America was compelled to declare war on Germany and entered the conflict under President Woodrow Wilson on April 6, 1917.

The American Expeditionary Force (AEF), led by General of the Armies John "Blackjack" Pershing (USMA 1886), arrived in France in May1917, and saw its first action in October 1917. By May 1918, the full weight of fresh US troops helped turn the tide of the war as the AEF was instrumental in halting the 1918 German Offensives at Chateau-Thierry and Belleau Wood; and then going on the offensive at Saint-Mihiel and the Meuse-Argonne. An uncertain post-war settlement at Versailles in 1919 set the stage leading to World War II.

America's time in the war was relatively short, but the price was high as the US lost 116,516 killed in action and 204,002 wounded in thirteen months of combat. Thirty-two West Point graduates were killed in action and one West Point graduate received the Medal of Honor.

- From a memorial stone on the West Point golf course.
- Picture by James M. Flagg from Smithsonian poster collection

The Boy Scouts' Victory

WP Ex, WWI

George Durston The Saalfield Co. (1921)

A Greek boy, who is in West Point at the time all Europe is becoming involved in World War I is summoned home to Greece because of the serious illness of his father, Count Zaidos. Before he can reach his father's side, however, he is pressed into service, starting army life as a stoker on a transport ship. When a submarine torpedo shatters the vessel, Zaidos leaps into the sea. Keeping himself afloat, he witnesses a most thrilling sea fight involving four great battleships and a huge Zeppelin.

When the battle is over, the boy is picked up by a Red Cross ship. He receives a leg injury which incapacitates him for active soldier duty, but as soon as the leg mends, he throws himself wholeheartedly into Red Cross duty on the front. His early Boy Scout training makes him a cheerful, quick, and skillful first-aider. [DJ]

Colonel George Durston was a fictional author created by the Saalfield Publishing Company. Writers for "The Boy Scouts'" series included Frederick Dey, J.W. Duffield, William A. Wolf, and Georgia Roberts Durston. [16-01]

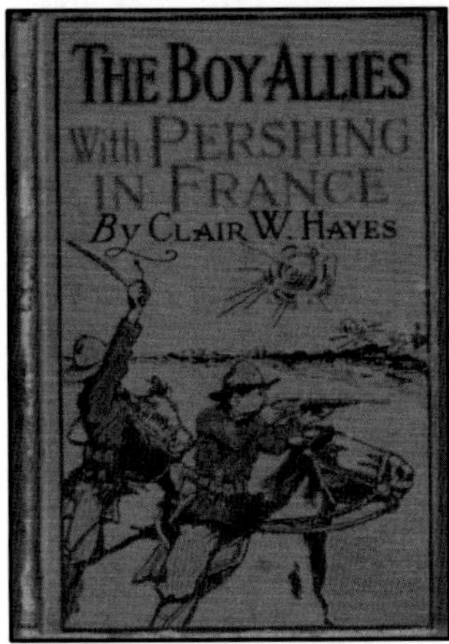

The Boy Allies with Pershing in France

WWI, Youth

Clair W. Hayes A.L. Burt Co. (1919)

"Hal Paine and Chester Crawford, in spite of the fact that the United States had not declared war on Germany until April of 1917, already had seen virtually four years of fighting in Europe.

They had been in Berlin when the European conflagration broke out and had been with the Allied armies almost from the first. The lads had seen active service with the Belgian, British, French, Italian and Russian armies and, through their courage and bravery, had won captaincies in the British Army.

When the United States entered the war, Hal and Chester were among the officers sent back to America to help train the young men in the various officers' training camps. When they returned again to the fighting front with the first contingent of American troops to join the Allies, it was as first lieutenants, U.S.A.

After surviving fierce battles, Hal and Chester were behind their lines delivering important messages to their general staff:

> Eight o'clock Thursday morning found Hal and Chester, in a large army automobile, returning from the quarters of General Lawrence. . . . As they rode along, Hal, turning a sharp curve, applied the emergency brakes and brought the car to a stop only a few feet from a second machine, which appeared to be stalled in the middle of the road.
>
> There were only two figures in the second automobile, and as Hal looked quickly at the man in the tonneau he jumped to the ground and came to attention. Chester, with a quick look at one of the occupants of the car, did likewise.
>
> Both lads had recognized General Pershing.
>
> General Pershing said, "And it is good fortune that brings you here now. My own car has run out of 'gas,' due to the carelessness of my driver. I have sent him for another car, but now that you are here, I shall change…"
>
> "You will drive me to General Lawrence's quarters," said General Pershing, "I must see General Lawrence and be back at my own headquarters by noon."
>
> General Pershing leaned forward in the car and gazed at the two lads closely. "Surely I know you two officers," he said. "Your faces are very familiar."
>
> "Yes, sir," said Hal. "We had the pleasure of going to Berlin for you, sir."
> General Pershing clapped his hands. "I know you now," he said. "Colonel, these are the young officers who went to Berlin and brought back the list of German spies in America."
> "Am I right?" he asked of Hal.

"Yes, sir."

"Now, sir," said General Pershing, "you will make all haste toward my headquarters."

Hal and Chester became the General's drivers but soon embroiled themselves in combat, even being captured by the Germans. [EB]

Clair Wallace Hayes (1887–?) was a journalist and the author of early twentieth century novels and stories about the First World War. He also wrote under the pseudonym Ensign Robert L. Drake. [16-02]

War Clouds in the East: *Black Knights of the Hudson V*

WWI

Beverly C. Gray Self-published (2013)

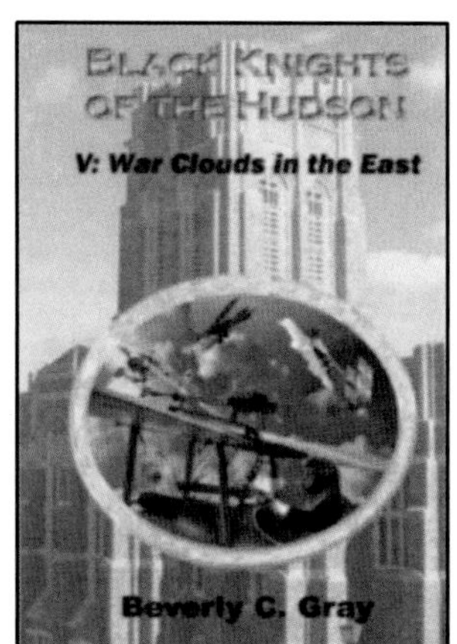

War Clouds in the East is the fifth book in this sweeping family saga of the MacKendricks; who live by West Point's motto – Duty, Honor, Country. With the war in Europe almost a year old, the MacKendricks are already involved in spite of their own country's neutrality.

Fitzjames, who comprehends the significance of a growing mechanized world and the dawn of air power, has forsaken his beloved Cavalry as it becomes increasingly obsolete. Seduced by the promise of a new challenge, he turns his talents to the shadowy world of intelligence. Oliver, newest member of West Point's Long Gray Line, must decide whether to honor a promise made to a classmate whose parents died on the Lusitania or fulfill his commitment to the Academy. Philip turns his own substantial skills to the European conflict and dons the uniform of a war correspondent for the second time in his life.

The MacKendrick women are no longer content to sit at home waiting patiently for their men to return from the front. Instead, they find their own places as nurses and journalists as the war in Europe turns into the heartbreaking stalemate of trench warfare. In *War Clouds in the East*, the MacKendricks find ways to serve in a conflict to which their own President Wilson keeps a stern, isolationist face as he attempts to broker a peace between the battling European nations. The MacKendrick patriarch is baffled as to why so many of his boys are at risk since the United States has not even entered the war. He discovers that even he will be in the thick of world events when he is called out of retirement to active duty. [BC]

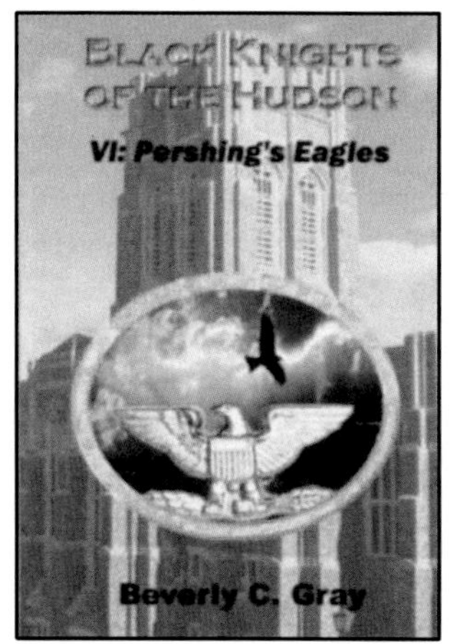

Pershing's Eagles: Black Knights of the Hudson VI

WWI

Beverly C. Gray Self-published (2013)

This is the sixth book in this sweeping family saga of the MacKeridricks who live by West Point's motto – Duty, Honor, Country. The war in Europe is over three years old and the MacKendricks stand ready to serve when their country throws its youthful might to the support of the Allies. At odds with his own senior generals and out of step with his West Point classmates, Fitzjames struggles to find a path back to his own army from the murky shadows of British intelligence. Oliver continues his storied career with the RFC; in spite of German air supremacy and the short-survival rate for Allied pilots. Jackson Lee, favored by subordinate and superior alike, is one of the first to accompany the American Expeditionary Force to France. While Philip and John follow the events in the uniforms of war correspondents, Chloe serves in her own fashion as a VAD in a London hospital. Elsa holds the fort at the country house in Gloucestershire where she tries to provide a tranquil base for the rest of the family. In Washington, Timothy has been recalled to active service. Adria, worried that he too will hear the sweet call of the bugles even at his age tries to make sense of a war that has pulled sons, grandchildren, and husband into its greedy maw; a war not even fought on U.S. soil but in far-off Europe.

In *Pershing's Eagles*, the MacKendricks participate in the first great war of the Twentieth Century. Swept up in the struggle along the Western Front, each of them must find a way to master a new kind of warfare waged with armies of staggering numbers and terrible innovations of weaponry. [BC]

Beverly C. Gray has authored six books in the series ***Black Knights of the Hudson***. They can be viewed in "The West Point Legacies" chapter.

The Sable Doughboys: Black Sabre Chronicles #2

WWI

Tom Willard Forge (1997)

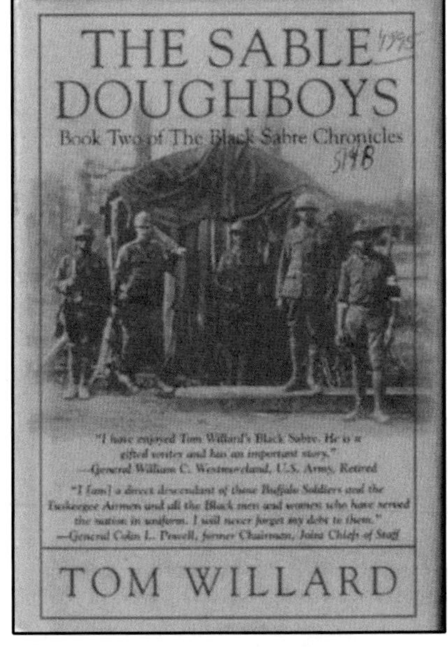

A nickname for the African-American soldiers of World War I, The Sable Doughboys chronicles the Sharps family through the war. Adrian and David Sharps, the sons of Sergeant Major Augustus and Selona Sharps, have become officer candidates in the first Negro officer training program at Fort Des Moines, Iowa, with the 17th Provisional Training Regiment. During training they are faced with violence and brutal attacks from white racists.

The novel also follows Adrian and David Sharps, and their families, to Virginia, where they join the 93rd Division, and to France, where they experience more racial discrimination, endure the horrors of trench warfare, and face death in the battle of the Meuse-Argonne. [DJ]

This is the second of **Tom Willard's** five novels about the Sharps family's service to this nation. The third novel in the series appears under "World War II"; the fourth "In the Far East" [Vietnam], and the fifth in "The Cold War & Global War on Terrorism."

Henry "Hap" Arnold - later General of the Armies in World War II - authored a series of six books in the 1920s to encourage young men to consider Army aviation. This is the third book. The others can be found in the chapter "Army Aviation," along with the author's bio.

Bill Bruce Becomes an Ace

Aviation, WWI, WP Author

Henry (Hap) Arnold A. L. Burt (1928)

After graduating from the flying schools, Bill Bruce showed his courage by joining an air squadron in France. Flying and fighting above the lines, he proved his mastery of the air by downing five enemy airplanes. [DJ]

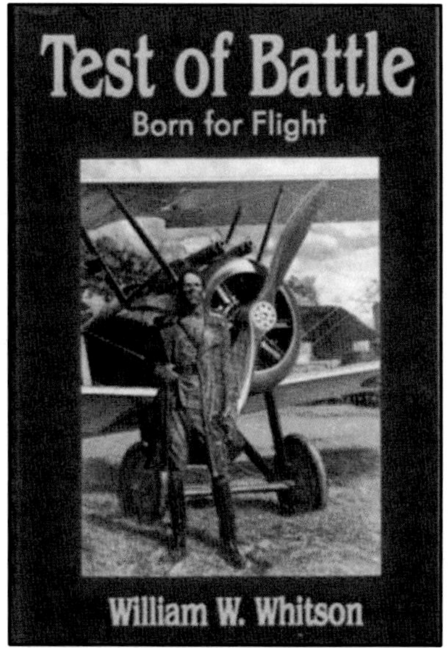

Test of Battle: Born for Flight

Aviation, WWI, WP Author

William Whitson Cogent Publishing (2006)

From the author of *Apprentice Warrior* comes a story of the odds a special breed of men faced when air battle first came of age: wings and engines that fell apart without warning; guns that jammed; toxic fumes, nausea, noise, vibration, g-forces, frostbite, windburn, fear, insomnia and chronic exhaustion.

In this story David Harrison surmounts these odds to meet the two great tests of battle: leaving home to search for his warrior self and his struggle to return home after he finds it. The tempo starts with a deceptively bucolic romance in the summer of 1916. It picks up speed on its way through flight training to gut-wrenching air combat over the Somme and a final twist at the end of the year. The story's seamless mix of fictional imagination and historical authenticity, reinforced by maps and photographs, never fails to entertain. As a timeless inner conflict haunts our journey through the mind of a novice American pilot, suspense grips our attention. [BC]

William W. Whitson (1926–2018), Class of 1948, has written about the early development of aviation and the scientific study of human consciousness. [16-03]

The other books in the *Born for Flight* series can be found in the "Army Aviation" chapter.

DUTY: Pass in Review Series

WWI, Cadet, WP Author, Philippines

Brian Utermahlen CreateSpace Independent Pub. (2011)

From Amazon:

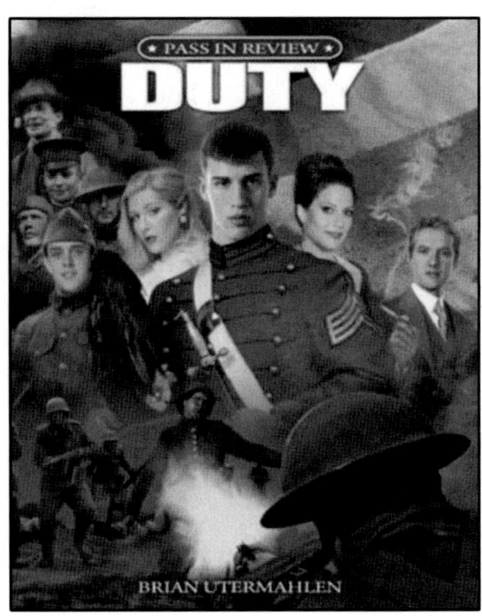

> *Pass in Review* is a trilogy about men and women totally involved in their rewarding but difficult relationship of military service to country. This is a saga of a 20th Century military family…three generations and their contemporaries – some famous, some not, but all of them intensely American.
>
> It is the story of Dave Nolan – part man, part legend – who leaves a small river town in Pennsylvania to chase his destiny in the Army as a professional soldier. To him the Army is more than just a career, it is the essence of who he is – his very life. From the Plain of West Point, high above the Hudson, to the trenches of WWI France and the wearying decades between the two world wars of the 20th century, he devotes himself wholly and tirelessly to his country and the Army, even when they do not reciprocate.
>
> And woven throughout this saga is the historically accurate story of Dwight Eisenhower, Omar Bradley, George Patton, Douglas MacArthur, and others who graduated from West Point and interact with the fictional Nolan, all of whom forged the victories on battlefields around the world, across a century. They along with Nolan, his friends, family and others – like the legendary “Wild Bill” Donovan, Dave Nolan’s mentor in war and during the peace – make and mold their Army, their country, their Alma Mater and their world.

This series of books is reminiscent of Herman Wouk’s *Winds of War* and *War & Remembrance* about the experience of Victor “Pug” Henry and his family during World War II. [EB]

World War II

The Second World War (1939–1945) involved the majority of the world’s nations—including all of the great powers—in two opposing military alliances, the Allies and the Axis. It resulted in 50 to 70 million fatalities, making it the deadliest conflict in all of human history. By 1941, Axis Germany had conquered or controlled the European continent.

Aligning with the Axis of Germany and Italy, Japan set upon dominating East Asia and Indochina. In December 1941, the Japanese attacked the United States and Great Britain at Pearl Harbor, the Philippines, Indochina, and Malaysia, quickly conquering much of the western Pacific.

The Axis advance was stopped in 1942 after Japan lost a series of naval battles to the U.S. Navy, while in Europe Axis forces were defeated in North Africa and, decisively, at Stalingrad in the winter of 1943. In June 1944, the U.S forces and western Allies invaded France, while the Soviet Union regained all of its territorial losses and set upon Germany. The war in Europe ended with the capture of Berlin by Soviet troops and the subsequent German unconditional surrender in May 1945.

During 1944 and 1945 the United States routed the Japanese Navy, capturing key Pacific archipelagoes and the Philippines. Faced with the invasion of the Japanese home islands and the prospects of a staggering loss of life, President Truman approved the dropping of atomic bombs on Hiroshima and Nagasaki in August 1945. Japan promptly surrendered and the war ended with the surrender ceremony in Tokyo Bay on September 2, 1945.

The United States suffered just over 405,000 deaths, 487 of them West Point graduates. The largest number of West Pointers perished in the Army Air Force. Flying and flight training were exceptionally perilous. Nine USMA graduates and one former cadet were awarded the Medal of Honor.

Source: Memorial Stone on the West Point golf course

The relatively few fictional books included here about this huge conflict is deceiving. Many entries that might be included here can be found instead in other chapters: "Army Aviation," "Army Medical Service Corps," and "General Officers."

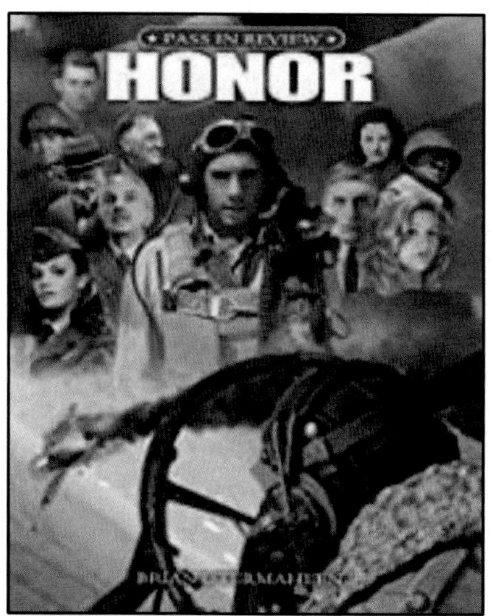

HONOR: Pass in Review Series

Aviation, WW II, WP Author

Brian Utermahlen CreateSpace Independent Publishing (2012)

This is the second book of the *Pass in Review Trilogy* – a saga of the Nolan family spanning the 20th Century. It is reminiscent of Herman Wouk's grand saga *The Winds of War*. The first book *Pass in Review - Duty* related Dave Nolan's passage through West Point, his heroics as an infantry company and battalion commander in key battles of World War I, and Army life as a field grade officer during the years before World War II.

This second book takes place during the World War II years as Dave's son Mitch becomes the central military figure as a pilot-in-training and then a fighter pilot (P-38's) in Europe. Family and friends introduced in the first book continue their roles often central to the story as in the original. Both Dave and son Mitch interact with many of the great leaders of the era: Eisenhower, Churchill, Roosevelt, and Marshall. [BC]

Brian Utermahlen (1946–) Class of 1968, has authored a trilogy about the Nolan family, beginning with World War I and concluding in Vietnam. The trilogy can be viewed in "The West Point Legacies" chapter.

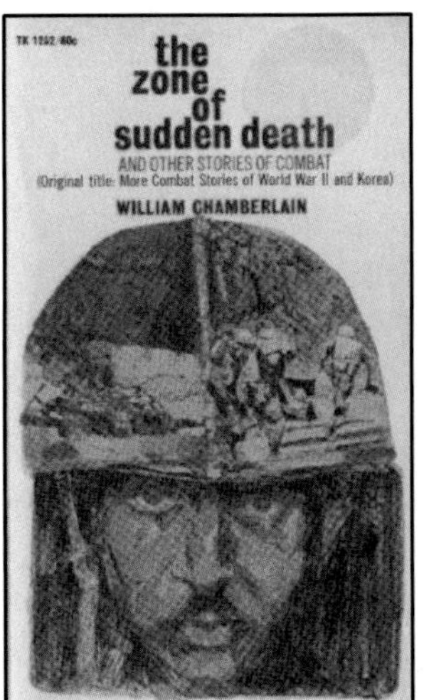

The Zone of Sudden Death

WW2, Korea

William Chamberlain Scholastic Book Svcs (1969)

"You're going into the DMZ—tonight!"

"There's a special reason, Lieutenant: Colonel Wright has just crashed up there somewhere in a copter. Hurt-maybe dead. We've got to get him out before the Chinese find him and start another incident. Take as many men as you need-but get him out!"

Lieutenant Pete Flagler goes, even though he knows it probably means a one-way ticket to a Chinese prison camp!

Eight thrilling stories of tough fighting men in World War II and in Korea. [BC]

Matt Quarterhill, Rifleman

WW2, Philippines, WP Author

William Chamberlain John Day & Co (1965)

Matt Quarterhill, a rifleman in the second squad, second platoon of Charlie Company need not have been involved in bloody combat with the Japanese at Leyte in World War II. He was an "army brat," with an appointment to West Point that would have kept him out of action for the rest of the war. But he would have none of that. Instead, he had volunteered for combat duty in the toughest fighting in the Pacific, and he got what he asked for.

Just being there, however, was enough. Matt had to uphold the traditions of a military family, to prove himself, under fire. Even more important, had to prove himself to Turk Hamid, the battle-hardened first sergeant of Charlie company, and to pokey Walt Sweeny, whom he was determined to make into a good soldier in spite of his tendencies to be a tag-along. [DJ]

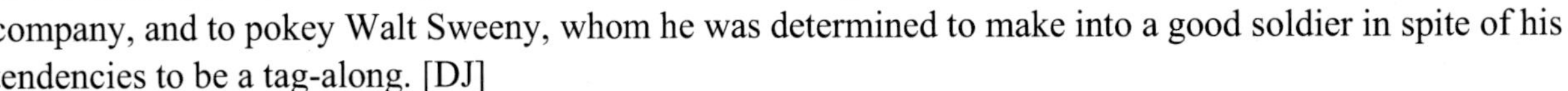

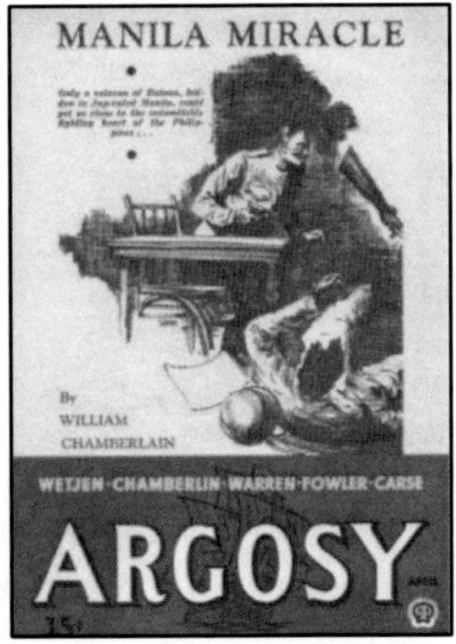

"Miracle in Manila"

WW2, Philippines, Pulp Fiction, WP Author

William Chamberlain Argosy Magazine (April 4, 1943)

"Only a veteran of Bataan, hidden in Jap-ruled Manila, could get so close to the indomitable fighting heart of the Philippines. . . .

His wounds had been healed for a month now and, as his strength began to come back, the restlessness took possession of Joel McQuain. It was bad this night as he sat in the little walled patio behind the house which fronted on the Calle Mabini.

There were thunderheads in the west and the dark had come down early; it lay in velvety shadows heavy with the dying heat and the smell of growing things and the hint of the coming rain. Carlota's monkey chattered and rattled his chain in an angle of the wall as a heavy vehicle rumbled by in the street outside, backfiring noisily as it went. That would be the scout car of the Jap patrol, McQuain knew. The patrol passed along the Calle Mabini only occasionally now that Corregidor had fallen. Manila, outwardly at least, was a conquered city.

McQuain rolled a cigarette from the coarse, sweet-smelling Philippine tobacco and smiled tightly as he listened to the sound of the patrol die away into the night. It wasn't every man who could smoke in a garden while his hunters passed him by—not fifty feet away—on the other side of a brick wall. The fancy pleased him a little but goaded his restlessness. Now that the time had finally come for him to go, impatience gripped him.

He lay back in the rattan chair and allowed his thoughts to drift back across the months since Christmas Eve of 1941. They were a confused pattern high-lighted with the splash of bombs and the scream of the wind around the wings of his plane and dark figures running in black silhouettes against the fires. . . ." [EB]

Edwin William Chamberlain (1903–1966), Class of 1927, worked on the U.S. Military Academy's literary magazine as a cadet and started selling his short stories and novels to various magazines while still on active duty. His book Combat General is described in the "General Officers" chapter. He also has two books in the "Manifest Destiny" chapter. [16-04]

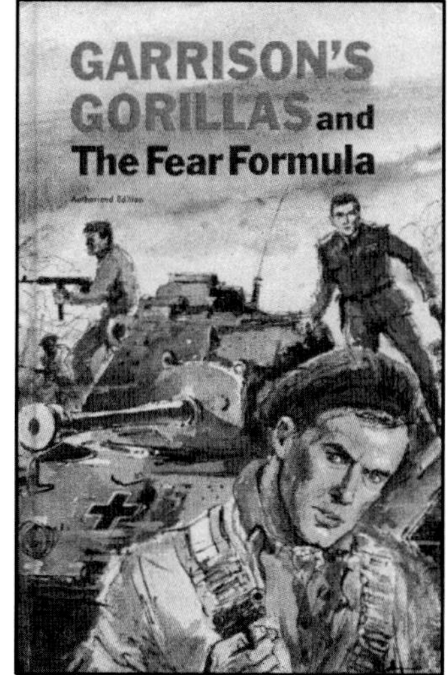

Garrison's Gorillas and The Fear Formula

WW2

Jack Pearl Whitman Publishing (1968)

Here are the adventures of a group of convicts recruited into the U.S. Army by the offer of a post-war parole. Commanded by West Point graduate, Lt. Garrison, the "Gorillas" function as commandos behind Nazi lines. Based on a TV series (a total of 26 hour-long episodes) inspired by the 1967 film *The Dirty Dozen*.[EB]

Jack Pearl (real name Jacques Bain Pearl, 1923–1992) was a prolific author of movie and television novelizations. After obtaining his Masters' from Columbia University, Pearl served three years in the U.S. Army as an MP during World War II. After the war, Pearl began a short career as an engineer, but soon became a full-time writer. His works include many crime/gangster/combat stories, but also the novelization of the movies *Our Man Flint*, the *Yellow Rolls Royce*, and the musical, *Funny Girl.* [16-05]

The Lieutenants: Brotherhood of War

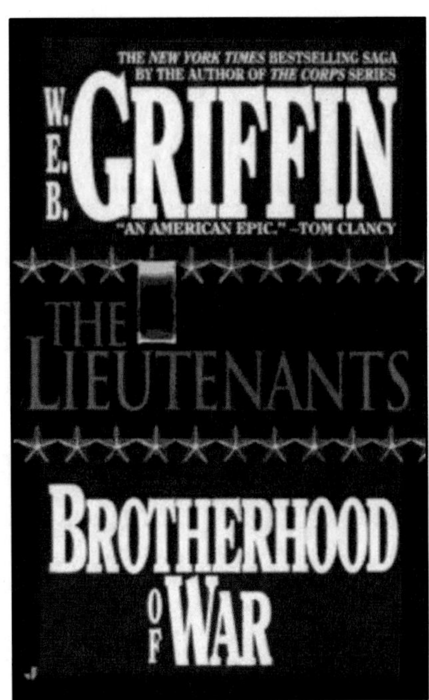

WW2

W.E.B. Griffin G. P. Putnam (1982)

"*Brotherhood of War* -- This series which made W. E. B. Griffin a national bestseller, is a saga of the lives of the men of the U.S. Army, and the women who love them. Nearly twenty years and nine novels later, it's still going strong: stories filled with crackling authenticity, rich characters, real heroes, and a special flair for the military heart and mind.

The Lieutenants They were the young ones, the bright ones, the ones with the dreams. From the Nazi-prowled wastes of North Africa to the bloody corridors of Europe, they answered the call gladly. War: it was their duty, their job, their life. They marched off as boys, and they came back—those who made it—as soldiers and professionals forged in the heat of battle." [DJ]

This novel is the first of the series. The other novels are presented in several chapters of this catalog, but they can be viewed along with the author biography in "The West Point Legacies" chapter. [EB]

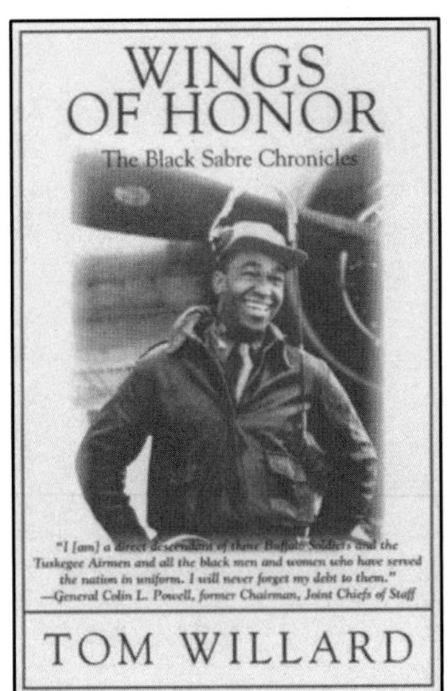

Wings of Honor: Black Sabre Chronicles #3

WW2, Aviation

Tom Willard Forge (1999)

"Adrian Samuel Sharps was born literally to a military life. His grandfather, Augustus, served as a Sergeant Major in the "Buffalo Soldier" campaigns against Indians in the Southwest. His father, Adrian, fought in Cuba in 1898 and in the trenches of the Western Front in France during the First World War.

The Sharps family, respected Arizona ranchers, have high hopes for young Samuel — a college education, taking over the Sabre Ranch, and raising a family there. But America's wars have haunted the family for seventy years, claiming some of its members, and Samuel, too, hears the call. After the bombing of Pearl Harbor, Samuel takes down the battled sabre his father and grandfather carried into war and makes his way to Tuskegee, Alabama, where, for the first time in history, black men are being trained as combat pilots.

Samuel Sharps bears many burdens, not only the bigotry that dogs the steps of all "colored" people in the South and in the army, but also his family's illustrious history, symbolized by the sabre he carries.

In *Wings of Honor*, Tom Willard tells the story, both poignant and exciting, of this third generation fighting man and the obstacles he overcomes to become a member of the all Negro 99th Pursuit squadron—the "Red-Tail Angels"—flying P-40 Warhawks and P51 Mustangs over North Africa, Sicily, and France in the Second World War." [BC]

Tom Willard, (1934–) penned five novels about the Sharps family's service to this nation. This is the third in the series. See the "West Point Legacies" chapter for the other books in the series. [16-06]

The Rising Tide: A Novel of World War II

WW2, General Officer

Jeff Shaara Ballantine Books (2007)

This is the first book in a trilogy about the military conflict that defined the twentieth century. Utilizing the voices of the conflict's most heroic figures, some immortal and some unknown, Jeff Shaara tells the story of America's pivotal role in World War II: fighting to hold back the Japanese conquest of the Pacific while standing side-by-side with her British ally, the last hope for turning the tide of the war against Germany. As British and American forces strike into the soft underbelly of Hitler's Fortress Europa, the new weapons of war come clearly into focus. In North Africa, tank battles unfold in a tapestry of dust and fire unlike any the world has ever seen. In Sicily, the Allies attack their enemy with a barely tested weapon: the paratrooper. As battles rage along the coasts of the Mediterranean, the momentum of the war begins to shift, setting the stage for the Battle of Normandy. [DJ]

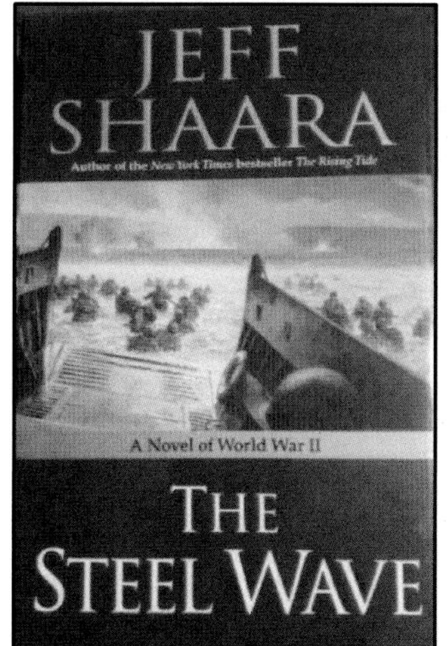

The Steel Wave: A Novel of World War II

WW2, General Officer

Jeff Shaara Ballantine Books (2008)

The Steel Wave is the second volume of a trilogy begun with *The Rising Tide*, that tells the story of the Second World War in Europe. As Jeff has done so many times before, this story is told through the points of view of some of history's most colorful and dynamic characters. *The Steel Wave* focuses primarily on the Normandy campaign, what we more commonly know as "D-Day," the Allies' invasion of France...

Readers of *The Rising Tide* will again see the story through the eyes of General Dwight Eisenhower, who once again commands a diverse army that must find its single purpose in the destruction of Hitler's European fortress. His primary subordinates, Omar Bradley and Bernard Montgomery must prove that this unique blend of Allied armies can successfully confront the might of Adolf Hitler's forces, who have already conquered Western Europe.

From *The Rising Tide* another voice returns, German commander Erwin Rommel, who has been assigned to fortify the French coastline, to prepare for the invasion he knows is inevitable. Eisenhower and Rommel know each other well, and both men know they must bring all their skills to bear on a fight crucial to both sides. But Rommel's challenge lies not just with the enemy to his front, but the ever-present conflicts in the German High Command, made worse by the increasing insanity of Adolf Hitler. If Rommel's Atlantic Wall holds, the Germans could win the war. If the Allies can secure their beachheads and drive the Germans back, they will open the door for a massive thrust by Eisenhower's most controversial and colorful general, George Patton, who waits in England, anxious for his opportunity to secure the destiny he believes he deserves.

Also returning from Shaara's previous saga is Sergeant Jesse Adams, a no-nonsense veteran of the 82nd Airborne, one of fourteen thousand paratroopers who must lead the way by dropping straight into the teeth of the German positions. The chaotic and desperate struggle is a story rarely told, the allied paratroopers enduring more than a month of continuous combat against some of the finest soldiers in Rommel's army.

As the invasion force surges toward the beaches of Normandy, Shaara carries us into the mind of Private Tom Thorne of the 29th Infantry Division, who faces the horrifying prospects of fighting his way ashore on a stretch of coast more heavily defended than the Allied commanders anticipate – Omaha Beach.

From G.I. to general, this story carries the reader through the war's most crucial juncture, the invasion that altered the flow of the war, and ultimately, changed history. [DJ]

No Less Than Victory: A Novel of World War II

WW2, General Officer

Jeff Shaara Ballantine Books (2010)

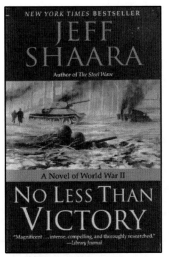

After the success at Normandy, the Allied commanders are confident that the War in Europe will soon be over. But in December 1944, in the Ardennes Forest, the Germans launch a ruthless counteroffensive that begins the Battle of the Bulge—the last gasp by Hitler's forces and some of the most brutal fighting of the war. The Fuhrer will spare nothing—not even German lives—to preserve his twisted vision of a "Thousand Year Reich," but stout American resistance defeats the German thrust, and by spring 1945 the German army faces total collapse. With Russian troops closing in on Berlin, Hitler commits suicide. As the Americans sweep through the German countryside, they encounter the worst of Hitlers crimes, the concentration camps, and young GIs find themselves absorbing firsthand the horrors of the Holocaust.

No Less Than Victory is a riveting account presented through the eyes of Eisenhower, Patton, and the soldiers who struggled face-to-face with their enemy, as well as from the vantage point of Germany's old soldier, Gerd von Rundstedt, and Hitler's golden boy, Albert Speer. Jeff Shaara carries the reader on a journey that defines the spirit of the soldier and the horror of a madman's dreams. [DJ]

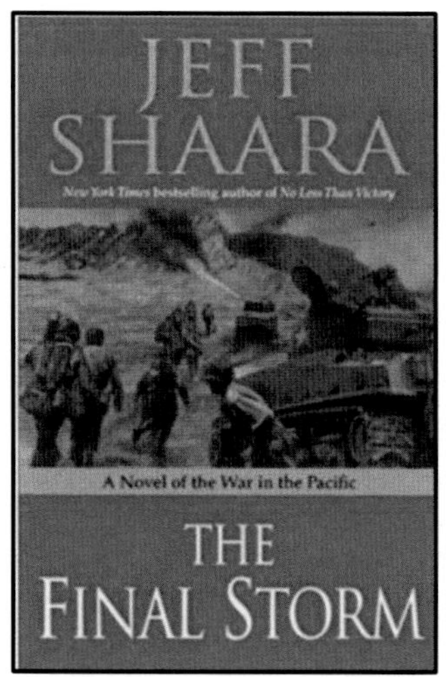

The Final Storm: A Novel of War in the Pacific

WW2, General Officer

Jeff Shaara Ballantine Books (2011)

The Final Storm completes Jeff Shaara's four-volume World War Two series, moving past the end of the war in Europe, to the horrific fighting still to come in the Pacific.

The Final Storm begins with preparations for the last great fight, Okinawa, an island country only 350 miles from Japan. On April 1, 1945, Marine and Army divisions invade the island in an amphibious landing reminiscent of the Allied landing at Normandy. But instead of bloody chaos on the beaches, the Americans are astounded to find no opposition at all. In a brilliant strategic move, Japanese commanding General Mitsuru Ushijima prevents what he knows will be the obliteration of his forces from overwhelming American naval and aerial assaults and keeps the bulk of his army hidden in a vast network of underground bunkers and caves, waiting for the ideal moment to strike at the invaders. And strike they do. The Americans are led by Army General Simon Bolivar Buckner Jr., whose father was a noted Confederate commander in the Civil War. Buckner and his planners anticipate victory on Okinawa within 30 days. The reality is a stunning and horrible surprise.

After a vicious 3-month fight, victory does finally come, and with American eyes now focused on Japan itself, the last great event to end the war erupts in a way that few have anticipated, the most well-kept secret in military history. In early August 1945, Colonel Paul Tibbets commands the B-29 bomber "Enola Gay," unleashing the atomic bomb on the Japanese city of Hiroshima. Days later, a second bomb is exploded over the city of Nagasaki. Japan has already been subjected to a brutal American assault from the air by massive incendiary bombings, the strategy put forth by the colorful General Curtis LeMay. LeMay's bombers have nearly obliterated the city of Tokyo, but the Japanese have shown no inclination to stop the war, and in fact, Japanese commanders seem eager for the Americans to invade, by preparing virtually the entire Japanese populace to confront the invaders any way they can, what could result in the greatest slaughter of military and civilian forces in all history. But the Japanese Emperor Hirohito tempers his military's lust for the great final showdown and reeling from the reality of this new display of American atomic firepower, Hirohito orders the final surrender.

The Final Storm tells these stories through the eyes of the leadership on both sides, American Admiral Chester Nimitz and President Harry Truman, as well as the resolute and efficient General Ushijima. But the story follows others as well, notably Marine Private Clay Adams, who struggles through the horrors on the 3-month fight on Okinawa. Adams comes to this story having been introduced by his brother, Sgt. Jesse Adams of the 82nd Airborne Division, who was a primary voice in the first two volumes of the European series. Here too is Paul Tibbets, who must prepare his flight crews for their most crucial mission, the details of which none of them can know, a mission whose outcome not even the bombs' creators can predict. On the ground in Hiroshima, an aging physician, Dr. Okiro Hamishita, already dispirited by the endless war and empty promises of his government, now will bear witness to the most astounding and horrifying weapon ever unleashed on this planet. [DJ]

Jeff Shaara (1952–) writes historical fiction documenting American wars and their most historically relevant characters. He has written fifteen New York Times bestselling novels. See Chapter 15, "The Civil War" to view a large number of his novels. [16-07]

Hitler Invades England

WW2, WP Author

George Crall Create Space Independent Publishing (2011)

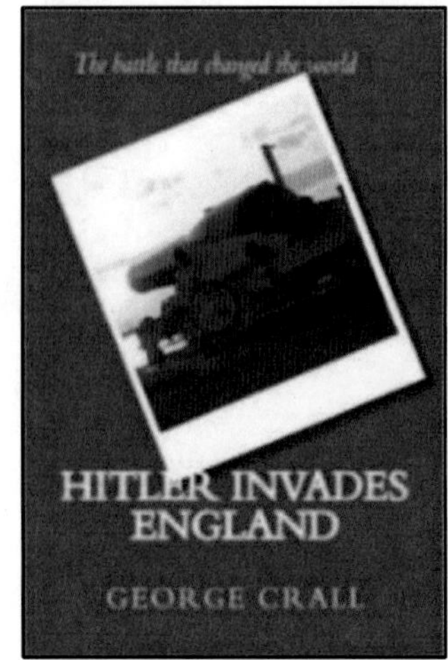

Hitler Invades England is a historical novel starting before World War II. It describes England's failure to prepare for war, Germany's preparations for war, the invasion of the Low Counties and France, the Battle of Britain, the invasion of England, the successes and final defeat of Hitler's navy, and how Germany's invasion of England ultimately succeeded. Invasion actions take place at strategic beaches, ports, cities and airfields throughout England. The book finishes with the final occupation of the entire country. The author researched actual historical events and modified them to show how it would have been possible for Germany to invade England, and to eliminate it as a threat to the existence of the Reich. Characters in the book include: Stauffenberg, Hitler, Goering, Speer, Rommel, von Rundstedt, Kesselring, Raeder, Doenitz, Neville Chamberlin, Winston Churchill, and other British and German soldiers, sailors, airmen and civilians. The book contains battles at sea, on land, and in the air over Britain. Battles, captures, escapes, treachery and murder are included in the action. [DJ]

George Crall (1923–?) He served in WW2 before attending West Point, graduating in 1949 and commissioned in the Marine Corps retiring years later from the reserve as a Colonel. He then entered the construction business later managing major industrial projects throughout Africa and the Middle East. Another of his works is included in the chapter "The Cold War & Global War on Terrorism." [DJ]

Blame the Dead

WW2, Crime, WP Author

Ed Ruggero Forge Publishing (2020)

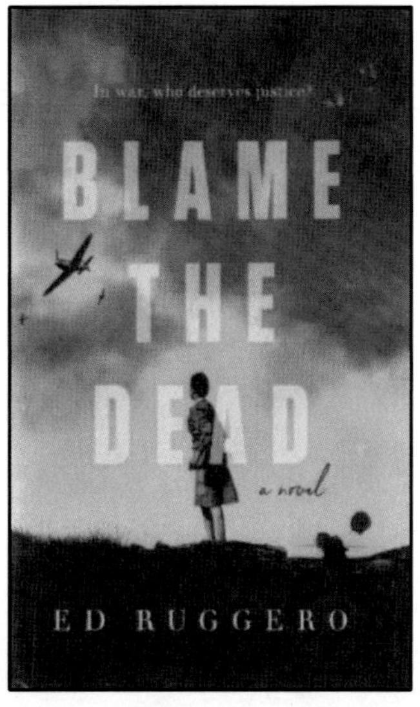

Sicily, 1945. Eddie Harkins; former Philadelphia beat cop turned military police lieutenant, reluctantly finds himself at the scene of a murder at the U.S. Army's 11th Field Hospital; There the nurses contend with heat, dirt, shorthanded staff, the threat of German counterattack, an ever present flood of horribly wounded Gls, and the threat of assault by one of their own - at least until someone shoots Dr. Meyers Stephenson in the head.

With help from nurse Kathleen Donnelly, once a childhood friend and now perhaps something more, it soon becomes clear to Harkins that the unit is rotten to its core. As the battle lines push forward, Harkins is running out of time to find the killer before he can strike again. [DJ]

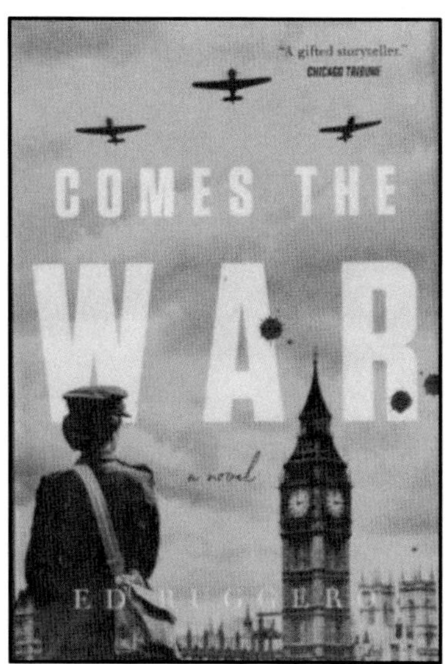

Comes the War

WW2, Crime, WP Author

Ed Ruggero Forge Publishing (2021)

April 1944, the fifty-fifth month of the war in Europe. Lieutenant Eddie Harkins investigates the murder of an American OSS analyst as the entire island of Britain buzzes with the coiled energy of a million men poised to leap the English Channel to France.

Soon a suspect is arrested and Harkins is ordered to stop digging. Suspicious, he continues his investigation with the help of his resourceful British driver, Private Pamela Powell, only to find himself trapped in a web of Soviet secrets. As bombs fall, Harkins must solve the murder and reveal the spies before it is too late. [DJ]

Ed Ruggero, West Point class of 1980, is a former infantry officer and teacher of leadership turned author of historical fiction, mystery, and thriller novels. Ruggero wrote four novels in the Mark Isen series covering the officer's career. See the chapters "In the Far East," "The Cold War & Global War on Terrorism," and "Mystery, Crime & Intrigue." [DJ]

Chapter 17

General Officers

From the end of the Civil War until the latter half of the 20th century, most soldiers with a rank of General were graduates of West Point. The notable exception was George C. Marshall during World War II. Generals are distinguished by the symbol of stars on their collars, epaulets, and the flags that proceed with them.

Perhaps the mystique of "generals" was expressed succinctly by Michael Shaara in *The Killer Angels* which appears in this book's chapter on the Civil War.

> "There's nothing so much like a god on earth as a General on a battlefield."

Many biographies and historical fiction have been written about the Army's generals. The historical fiction found in this chapter falls into three categories:

- Accounts of real generals in fictional circumstances
- Accounts of fictional generals in real situations
- Real generals and real conflicts but told in a primarily fictional context

Real Generals in Fictional Circumstances

In all their broad and essential features, the events herein portrayed are taken literally out of the life of one of our fellow countrymen. In the non-essentials, particularly in matters of sentiment, the writer has intentionally and from motives which, it is hoped, all will understand, broken entirely away from the historical basis and drawn on the resources of the imagination.

Thus, while the romantic incidents found within these pages are purely a creation of fancy, still all will admit that they might be easily duplicated in the life-story of many a person living today.

On the other hand, it is in the events herein portrayed having their foundation in historical fact which are likely to tax the credulity of the reader. In brief, it all shows the verity of the trite saying that "truth is stranger than fiction."

- Thomas Gold Frost, from the introduction of *The Man of Destiny*

The Man of Destiny

Civil War, Mexican War

Thomas Gold Frost Grammercy Press (1909)

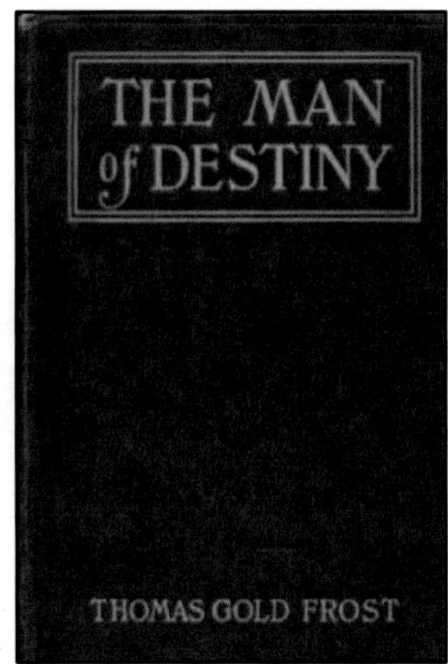

From the final chapter of this novel about U.S. Grant:

On an afternoon in the late summer of 1865, a man still in the vigor of midlife, drove a handsome Kentucky thoroughbred along a traveled Ohio roadway, which leads inland from the river which bears that name. To the few farmers who gazed at him as he passed them rapidly by, there was something about him which seemed familiar. Unaccompanied, he drove rapidly on until he came to a farmhouse much run down, but evidently occupied by some tenant who had drifted thither in recent years. Hitching his horse, he stopped for a moment to gaze long and earnestly at the old farmhouse ... he now strode rapidly in the direction of the farmhouse. Once arrived there, he was greeted by a strapping young farmer—the master of the home. He held in one hand that of his little son of seven, while in the other he grasped an oil lump. He gave a start of awesome recognition at his visitor's countenance.

The latter now spoke. "Would it be demanding too much of you, sir, if I asked permission to visit the attic room overhead? I used to sleep there as a boy," he said by way of explanation.

The young farmer quickly granted the desired permission, and still leading his little son by the hand, he escorted him up the steep staircase.

The visitor cast one look of absorbed interest at the humble quarters, which he had known as a boy. Then, turning to the little lad whose eyes had followed his every movement, he stroked his hair and put in his chubby hand a shining piece of gold. "That is for luck, my little man. Someday, when you get older, you will sleep here, where I used to sleep years ago, when your father was no larger than you. And when that day comes, I don't want you to forget the 'other boy' who used to sleep here then."

And now, with a word of thanks to the young farmer, he pressed out into the darkness.

"Papa, who was that man, who gave me this penny?" said the little lad, as the door closed behind the late visitor. "That, my child, was the next President of the United States." [EB]

Thomas Gold Frost, Jr. (1866–1948) was a native of Galesburg, IL, the son of an eminent lawyer. He himself graduated from Columbia Law School in 1888. He entered the practice of law in Minneapolis and was quite successful, later writing several books on the law. *Man of Destiny* was his only work of fiction.

17-01

Captain Grant: A Novel

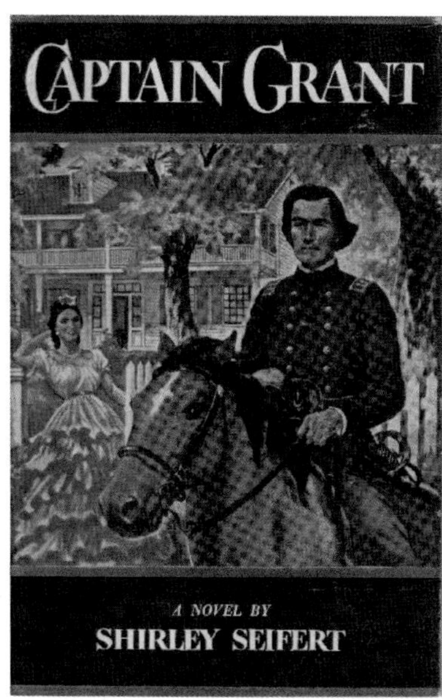

Mexican War, General Officer

Shirley Seifert J.B. Lippincott Company (1946)

This is the story of the younger and lesser known years of Ulysses Grant, beginning with his entrance at West Point and ending in the summer of 1861, when he took command of a regiment of Illinois volunteers, with the rank of Colonel. These years were filled with the very essence of drama, and with a romance which gives a special glow and charm to the story of a man caught up by destiny and elevated to the heights.

His courtship was typical of Ulysses Grant's life. He won all his victories by refusing to recognize obstacles as insurmountable—and many stood between him and Julia Dent, a Southern girl in the best Southern tradition. Her fiery father and all her relatives had marked her for a distinguished marriage. But she fell in love with the young officer from Jefferson Barracks, her brother's classmate from West Point, and that was that. She was small, dark and vivacious; her spirit, loyalty and courage matched that of her husband. She never dipped her colors, whatever the struggle.

And the years of the young lovers together were compounded of many struggles, which destiny seemed to create for the special purpose of beating and hardening Ulysses Grant into shape for the great conflict ahead. Julia Dent shared them all and emerges at the end as one of the most lovable wives a man ever had to spur him on to the end which lay in the unknown future. Surely it is a great romance, gaining in its excitement because it is true. [DJ]

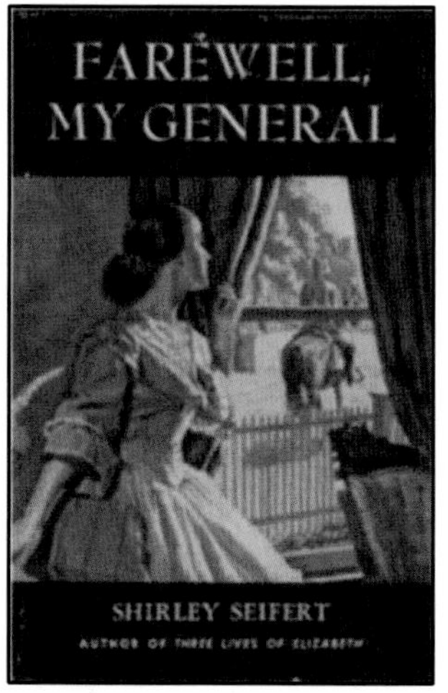

Farewell, My General

General Officer, Romance, Army Life

Shirley Seifert J.B. Lippincott (1954)

Army wives, then as now - -

A leading interest for me in this story and a challenge to me as an author is the fact that the heroine is an Army wife of the 1850's and 1860's. In this day when half the women of the world seem to have tasted that experience, it seems pertinent to fashion a story around an outstanding example from the past. Flora Cooke, Mrs. E. B. Stuart, was born at Jefferson Barracks near St. Louis. She spent most of her girlhood, except for intervals away at school, in various army posts—Fort Gibson, Indian Territory; Jefferson Barracks, Missouri; Carlisle Barracks, Pennsylvania; and Fort Leavenworth, Kansas.

It was at Fort Leavenworth that she met young Lieutenant Stuart, a second lieutenant, newly commissioned to the United States Cavalry by Jefferson Davis, Secretary of War under Franklin Pierce. They were married a short time later at Fort Riley, Kansas. The early years of their married life were passed at the two Kansas forts—except for two important visits to Virginia. The story is the story of any young officer of that day on the western frontier, and his wife's adventures those of any adoring young woman making the best of army quarters and army subsistence, shaking in her boots when her husband was out fighting Indians, helping him to hold his own in the tense struggle for promotion and recognition.

Then in 1861 to Virginia with her young husband, her heart torn by separations, her father remaining with the Union Army, her husband and brother going with Virginia. A very different life now for this army wife, in a land strange to her, though her own. No stout garrison walls about her. Sometimes she is close enough to the desperate fighting to see the flashing of gunfire, to hear its horrid echoes. Sometimes she is so removed that all she knows is from news dispatches and rumor. Bright days and dark days and periods of plain terror, and how her army discipline brings her through everything—I think that is her story. And through her devotion, I hope to have also achieved a true picture of James Ewell Brown Stuart, the lover, the husband, the man, as well as the great soldier. It is a love story throughout, one of history's best. That's how I tried to tell it. [DJ]

Shirley Seifert (1888–1971), a graduate of Washington University in St. Louis, was an historical novelist. Her novel, *The Wayfarers*, was nominated for a Pulitzer Prize. Among her other works were *Land of Tomorrow*, *River Out of Eden*, and *Never No More*. Several of her books were about major historical figures: Ulysses S. Grant, Jefferson Davis, and George Rogers Clark. [17-02]

The Victim: A Romance of the Real Jefferson Davis

Civil War, General Officer

Thomas Dixon — Grosset & Dunlap (1914)

Jefferson Davis was a West Point graduate, Mexican War officer, Secretary of War, and then President of the Confederacy.

"Although there is a prologue about Davis in his youth, most of the book is set during and immediately after the Civil War. For most of the novel, Davis is an important bit player who has an occasional walk-on or is talked about by others. The real plot of the novel involves a love triangle between a loyal (to the Confederacy) Southern girl, a Northern spy masquerading as a foreign diplomat and a Southern young man in love with the girl. There is intrigue, handwringing, and assorted conflicts." [17-03]

Thomas Frederick Dixon Jr. (1864–1946) was an American white supremacist, Baptist minister, politician, lawyer, lecturer, novelist, playwright, and filmmaker. [17-04]

My Dearest Cecelia: A Novel of the Southern Belle Who Stole General Sherman's Heart

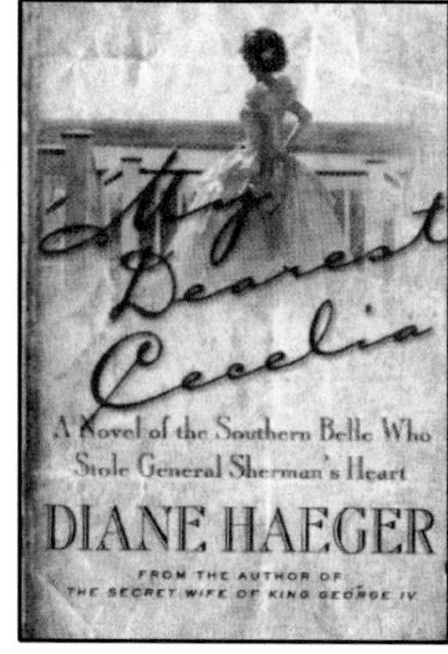

Civil War, Romance, General Officer

Diane Haeger St. Martin's Griffin (2004)

My Dearest Cecelia,

You said once that you would pity the man who would ever become my enemy. Do you recall my reply? Although many years have passed, my answer is the same now as then. I would ever love and protect you. That I have done. Forgive all else. I am only a soldier.

William T. Sherman

As she enters the commencement ball at WEST POINT MILITARY ACADEMY on a spring evening in 1837 in her pink gown with white silk roses and ropes of pearls, Cecelia Stovall looks -- and feels -- like the perfect, innocent Southern belle. Little does she know that at that dance she will meet the man who will change her life -- and the lives of all her fellow Southerners -- forever. Cecelia falls instantly in love with the dashing young Northern cadet, William Tecumseh Sherman, and they embark on a fiery, secret rendezvous despite their broad cultural differences and the expectation that they will marry others.

Their love remains poignantly kindled through the worst obstacles and years of separation and longing. And when the long-threatened Civil War starts, Cecelia and William take their places of prominence on opposite sides of their country's deepest and fiercest challenge, as William becomes the very same General Sherman who was feared and hated throughout the South. Legend has it that Sherman's love for Cecelia was the reason he spared her hometown of Augusta during his infamous march to the sea, in which his troops cut a swath through nearly every other town in Georgia and burned Atlanta to the ground. [DJ]

Diane Haeger holds a BA in English Literature from UCLA and an MA in Clinical Psychology from Pepperdine. She has travelled extensively through the United States and Europe to research and develop background for her thirteen books of historical fiction. [17-05]

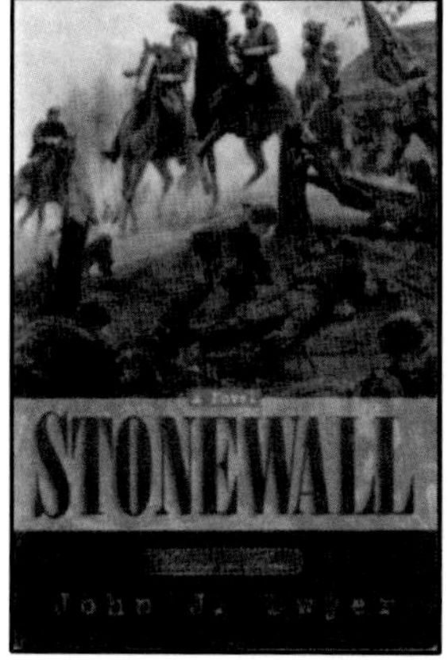

Stonewall

General, Civil War

John J. Dwyer Broadman & Holder (1998)

Stonewall is a powerful work of historical fiction that reveals many little-known facts about this extraordinary soldier as it vividly dramatizes the romantic, brutal, and glorious life of one of the Civil War's greatest heroes. This penetrating look at the man behind the myth follows Stonewall on his spiritual pilgrimage to becoming a devoted husband, a faithful Christian, and one of the greatest tacticians in military history. Blending historical fact with literary flair, John Dwyer weaves a … heart-stirring tale of one courageous man who gave his life for the Southern homeland he cherished and the Heavenly Father he revered. *Stonewall* also tells about Jackson's mysterious and stormy relationship with Margaret Junkin Preston, who history knows as the "poetess of the Confederacy [BC]

John J. Dwyer was born in Dallas, Texas, but was reared in Oklahoma. He graduated from Oklahoma University in 1978 with a degree in journalism. He worked as a sports announcer and publisher of the *Dallas-Fort Worth Heritage* newspaper for ten years. Dwyer has written several histories as well as historic fiction novels. His most prominent work is the *Oklahomans* which was published in 2016. [17-06]

Fictional Generals in Real Situations

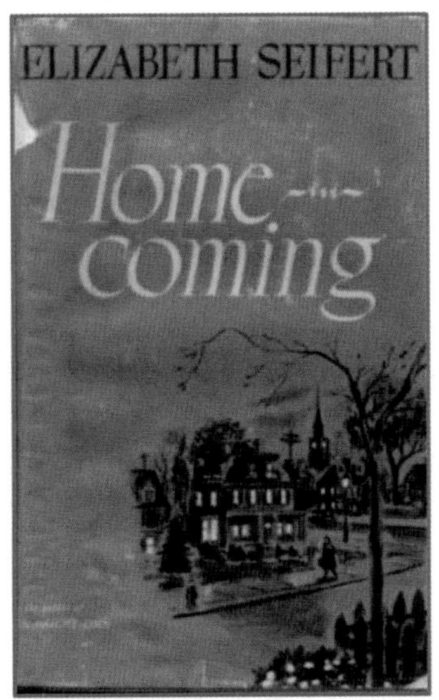

Homecoming

General Officer, WW2

Elizabeth Seifert Dodd, Mead & Co. (1950)

From the Prologue:

"I'll have to be careful what I say," thinks the General, facing the semicircle of reporters who have been brought on from as far as New York. He doesn't know their names -- one never knows the names of these pleasant, alert people—they are eyes, quick pencils, a woman's hat or two -- men and women who are friendly enough, and yet avid for the word, the unconsciously revealed fact that will give them a story beyond the stereotyped information of the routine interview. So-- a man must be careful what story he reveals.

A hundred years from now some author -- a schoolteacher on vacation, perhaps -- a spinster, surely—let's see—fiftyish and earnest; she'll take her briefcase, her lunch and vacuum bottle to some library--that of a Historical Society, or some Foundation collection letters and newspapers—she'll change her shoes and put on a smock over her clean shirtwaist, and she'll thumb through all the papers of the World War II era.... The General's gray eyes smile ever so slightly, and a little fondly, as his mind builds up this earnest seeker after facts. In any case, she'll come upon the accounts these newspaper chaps are about to write. These personal interviews -- how little she knows! What is personal or intimate about a single man facing fifteen or sixteen smart-as-paint reporters, and telling them just what he and the War Department want them to know?" [EB]

Elizabeth Seifert (1897–1983), a graduate of Washington University in St. Louis, authored 80 novels, mostly about the medical profession and nursing. Her other work in this collection, *Army Doctor*, is included in the chapter "Army Medical Service Corps." Elizabeth should not be confused with Shirley Seifert, a contemporary author, and also a graduate of Washington University, whose novels also appear in this chapter. [17-07]

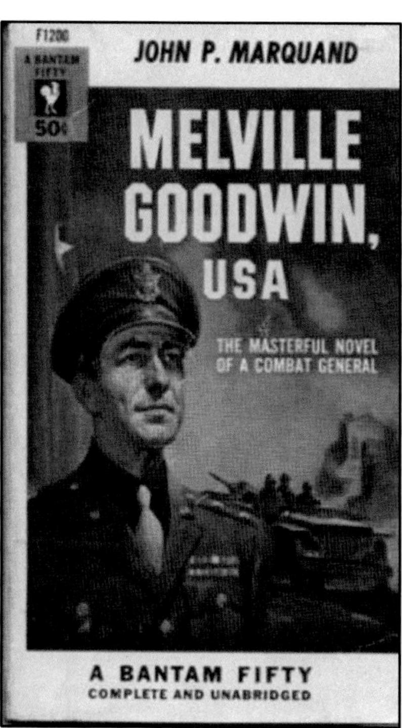

Melville Goodwin, USA

General Officer, Intrigue, WW2

John P. Marquand Bantam Books (1951)

Melville Goodwin, Major General in the U. S. Army, and second only to Goodwin in importance is the narrator of this compelling story, Sidney Skelton, a radio commentator whose rise to fame has made him quite as much a national figure as the General.

Melville Goodwin was a specialist in combat who become a general through the ambition of his wife Muriel. General Goodwin had led tanks through the turmoil of war with only the usual press attention. But when he pushed aside the tommy gun of a Russian sentry in Berlin, he become the focal point of publicity and of the attentions of Dottie Peale. Muriel did not know Dottie, and the General soon found himself in fields of action for which he had not been trained. John Marquand has brought a great sympathetic understanding to this highly trained leader in war who had become isolated from the sophisticated world outside the army. Dottie was noticeably attractive in any society and in the freedom of wartime Paris she represented for Mel Goodwin a break in the monotony of high-echelon routine. That taste of excitement was not forgotten amidst his much publicized return to New York and Muriel's ambitious planning. Dottie understood Mel's need and was heedlessly eager to satisfy it. And Muriel knew that her husband was a general who could only belong to her by remaining a general.

The conflict between these two women and the General's struggle with himself as he searches for a normal lite despite his lifetime special training make the most dramatic novel Mr. Marquand has written. The characters spring from the tensions at our own times and the scenes are those most prominent in the minds of this generation. The activities of the Pentagon, the excitement at New York, the liberties of Paris, the crisis of battle, the life in foreign stations and the quiet at small-town New England are all part of the General's career and responsibility. [BC]

John Phillips Marquand (1893–1960) was an American writer of novels and short stories. Originally best known for his *Mr. Moto* spy stories, he achieved popular success for his satirical novels, winning a Pulitzer Prize for *The Late George Apley* in 1938. [17-08]

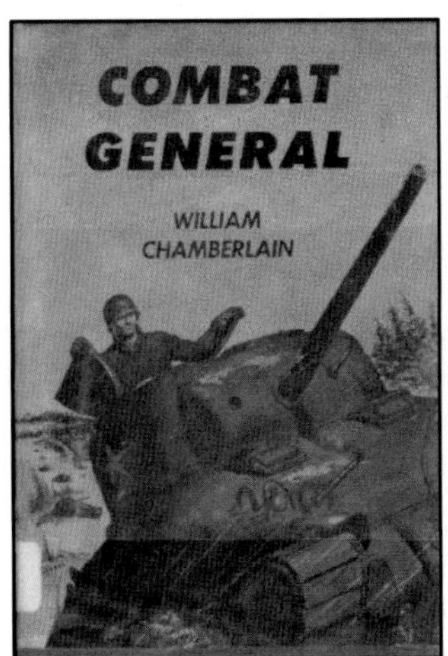

Combat General

General Officer, WW2, WP Author

William Chamberlain John Day & Co (1963)

Until he arrived in Belgium to take command of Hammerhead Division against an impending German tank breakthrough, Brigadier General Miles Boone had been forced to sit out World War II at a desk in Washington. In fact, he had grown almost accustomed to being referred to as a "Pentagon general." But he never liked the term, and he knew that once he came under fire he would prove his worth as a commander.

When the assault came Boone had the best assistant a combat general could ask—Sergeant Lute Heard, his driver and orderly, who had worn the Army's cloth for more years than either of them liked to admit. Before it was all over, both had seen more fighting that they wanted to see again. In this story of front-line action between American and German armored units, a detailed knowledge of men at War and their machines is the keynote -- a sure knowledge acquired personally by the author in several combat theaters around the world. [DJ]

Edwin William Chamberlain (1903–1966) was born in the Salmon River country of central Idaho. After graduating from West Point, he served through the grades in the artillery, infantry, and Air Corps, being retired with the rank of brigadier general in 1946. After retirement, Chamberlain published numerous pieces in *The Saturday Evening Post* and other magazines. His best-known story was probably "Imitation General," which MGM made into a 1958 film starring Glenn Ford. His book *Matt Quartermain, Rifleman* and story "Manila Miracle" also appear in this collection. [17-09]

The General: A Novel

WW2, Korea, Intrigue, General Officer

Stephen Longstreet Putnam (1974)

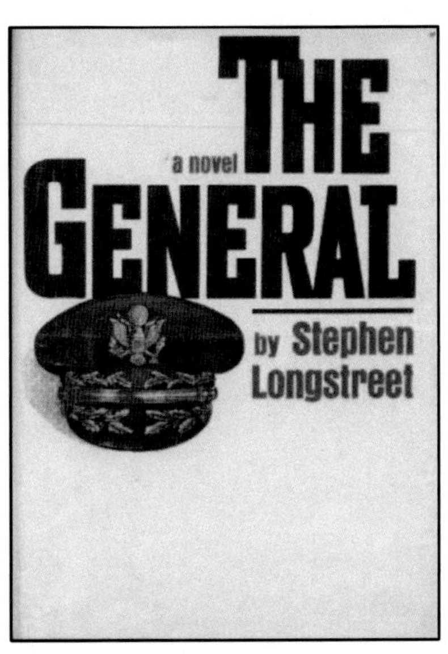

A touch of "Bull" Halsey, a trace of Patton, a bit of Ike and MacArthur, but indisputably a unique, complex individual, four-star General Simon (Bolivar) Copperwood at sixty-eight stands on the brink of honorable retirement or the supreme glory—the bestowal of a fifth star, making him one of the tiny elites of history, a General of the Armies, the five-star general he has longed to be.

Through flashbacks, we see Simon as a boy in Montana during the pre-World War I period. Family circumstances lead to his obtaining a West Point appointment, and after two years he is off to France, in the AEF under General Pershing in the legendary Rainbow Division. He distinguishes himself in service, as not only a "good soldier" but one now tempered with actual combat experience.

After the war he marries the first of his three wives, flapper Ada Roch, a marriage which ends in divorce and his promotion to major in command of a unit in Peking. But the path to Army success is not always straight, and Simon experiences a fall from grace during his tour in Asia when he charms and marries a Senator's wife and is "exiled" to command of a supply dump and fails to make colonel. Sarah dies in an accident. Simon is stricken with grief and turns to alcohol. But the soldier in him prevails and by perseverance he builds up his reputation as he warns of the power of Hitler and performs brilliantly to become a one-star general.

Back in Virginia after the war, Simon marries the third of his wives, a delicate young poetess named Margerie. Called into action in Korea, he is awarded his second star, and doing duty in Vietnam he receives his third and fourth. The third marriage ends in Margerie's suicide. Lonely after the death of his last wife and many friends, Simon waits for the climax of his career. He has lived and loved with an intensity matched only by his desire for the fifth star. The story has now come full circle. The choice of the fifth star is the President's, and for one terrible day of national homage, Copperwood's fate hangs in the balance. [DJ]

Stephen Longstreet (1907–2002) was an artist, musician and author of fiction and non-fiction. Among his books are the *Pedlock* series, *Chicago*, *Man of Montmartre*, *Lion at Morning*, and *The Wilder Shore*. As a friend of some of America's great generals, Mr. Longstreet wrote extensively about military life (*The Canvas Falcons*, *Gettysburg*) and created films for the War Department. [17-10]

A Fistful of Ego

General Officer, Intrigue

B. H. Topol Critics Choice Paperbacks (1987)

Once boyhood friends, the President and the General had risen to the pinnacle of their chosen professions. They began a rivalry that would span from the hallways of West Point to the steaming jungles of Viet Nam.

But now, with the world on the brink of nuclear holocaust, the Secretary of Defense discloses an incredible piece of news to the General - the President will not retaliate to a Soviet first nuclear strike.

Determined to expose the President, the General embarks on a perilously fragile plan that could well throw the super-powers into a war that nobody wanted. You'll never stop turning the pages until you reach the most unbelievable climax you have ever read. [BC]

There is no biographical information about this author. This appears to be his only book.

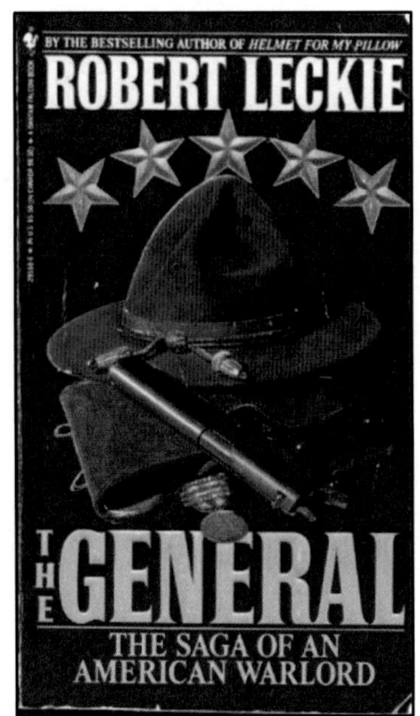

The General: The Saga of an American Warlord

General Officer, WW2, Korea, Intrigue

Robert Leckie Bantam (1991)

Mark Duggan was a man born to lead. As a second lieutenant during the Spanish American War, his heroic exploits made him a military legend. His bravery in the bloody trenches of World War I made him a national hero. And when war broke out again for the U.S. in 1941, General Mark Duggan was the natural choice to lead the offensive against the Japanese in the Pacific. There the general would turn a shattering defeat in the Philippines into one of the most dramatic victories in military history. But it was during the bitter standoff on the Korean peninsula that Duggan would face his greatest struggle: a bitter fight to the finish against an American president fearful of triggering World War III.

The General is the unforgettable portrait of a man whose public arrogance enraged presidents, whose private passions scandalized his family, but whose unyielding courage under fire was indispensable in a world at war. [BC]

Robert Leckie (1920–2001) was author of books on military history, sports, fiction, autobiographies, and children's books. As a young man, he served with the 1st Marine Division during World War II as a machine gunner and a scout in the Pacific Theater. [17-11]

Real Generals and Real Conflicts in a Fictional Context

Duty, Honor, Country - West Point to Shiloh: A Novel of West Point and the Civil War

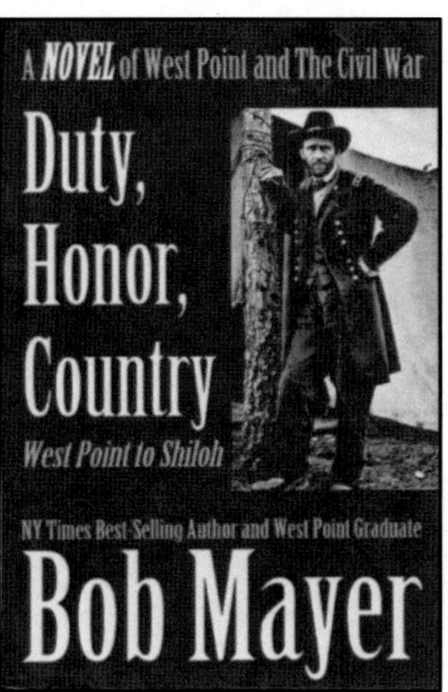

Mexican War, Civil War, WP Author

Bob Mayer Cool Gus Publishing (2013)

Two West Point cadets are caught up in the historical events of the most significant era in United States history when the nation was torn apart by a Civil War. Lucius Rumble and Elijah Cord encounter war, political intrigue, personal tragedies and more while encountering historical figures such as Ulysses S. Grant, Robert E. Lee, William Tecumseh Sherman, Abraham Lincoln, Kit Carson and more. [DJ]

Robert "Bob" Mayer (1959–) is a *New York Times* best-selling author and the CEO of Cool Gus Publishing. He is a West Point graduate, Class of 1981, and former Green Beret. Mayer has authored over 60 novels in multiple genres, selling more than 4 million books. Two of his other books are included in this collection. [17-12]

"Douglas MacArthur: Battlefield General"

WP Candidate, Pulp Fiction

Frances E. Crandall Treasure Chest Comics (1967)

This is a series of comic book stories about the life of Douglas MacArthur.

#8: MacArthur's life as an Army brat and his struggle for admission to West Point in 1898 is depicted.

#9: This comic depicts MacArthur's experience at West Point and his baptism in fire during the Philippine Insurrection.

#10: In this comic, MacArthur's career is covered from the Philippines through WWI to the onset of WWII.

#11: This portrays MacArthur's career in World War II, the occupation of Japan, the Korean War, and his retirement years. [EB]

Frances E. Crandall was a staff writer for *Treasure Chest Comics,* a Catholic-oriented comic book series created by Dayton, Ohio publisher George A. Pflaum. Its inspirational stories of sports and folk heroes, saints, school kids, Catholic living, history, and science were distributed to parochial schools from 1946 to 1972. Many prominent illustrators including the renowned comic Reed L. Crandall were engaged. There does not appear to be a relationship to the author of these comics. [17-13]

The masters at portraying real generals and real conflicts in a fictional context are Michael Shaara (1928–1988), and son Jeff Shaara (1952–), in their many best-selling novels about the Civil War, Mexican War and World Wars. It all began with the elder Shaara's novel *The Killer Angels* which was immortalized in the film version *Gettysburg*.

In each novel, well-known generals interact with their peers while fictitious junior officers and soldiers engage in the dreadful activities of warfare…and you are there! The books' details are presented in other chapters of this catalog, but the covers are displayed here.

The Civil War in the East

This novel covers the **Second Battle of Bull Run**, Fredericksburg, and Chancellorsville featuring Robert E. Lee, Stonewall Jackson, Winfield Scott Hancock, and Joshua Chamberlain.

The **Gettysburg** campaign features Robert E. Lee, James Longstreet, JEB Stuart, George Meade, John Reynolds, Winfield Scott Hancock, and Joshua Chamberlain.

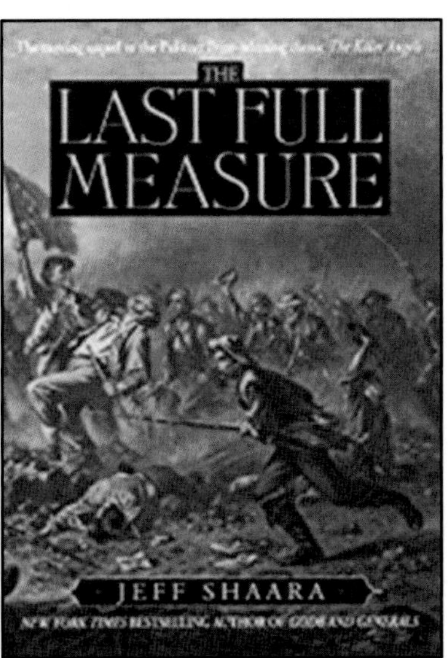

The last battle in the east from the **Wilderness to Appomattax** includes Robert E. Lee, James Longstreet, A.P. Hill, Jeb Stuart, Ulysses S. Grant, Winfield Scott Hancock, and Joshua Chamberlain.

The Civil War in the West

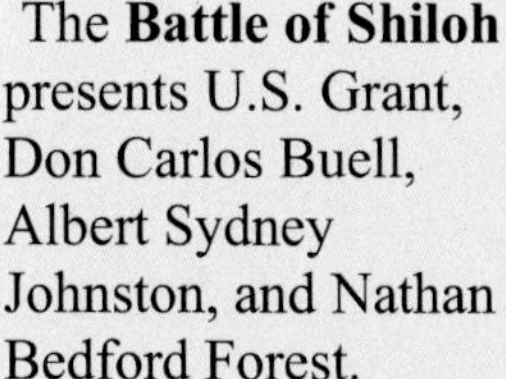

The **Battle of Shiloh** presents U.S. Grant, Don Carlos Buell, Albert Sydney Johnston, and Nathan Bedford Forest.

The **Siege of Vicksburg** featuring U.S. Grant, William T. Sherman, Albert Sydney Johnston, and John Pemberton.

The **Battles of Chickamauga and Chattanooga** with William Rosecrans, U.S. Grant, George Thomas, William T. Sherman, Braxton Bragg, and Nathan Bedford Forest

The Battle of Atlanta, March to the Sea and the final months of the war featuring William T. Sherman, Oliver O. Howard, Judson Kilpatrick, John Bell Hood, Joseph E. Johnston, and Joseph Wheeler.

Alden Carter is another prominent American author who highlights the thinking, emotions, hopes, doubts and fears of the generals leading the North and South in recounting the **Battle of Stones River**, December 1862. General William S. Rosecrans's Army of the Cumberland faces the Confederate soldiers of General Braxton Bragg's Army of Tennessee. Other eminent West Pointers are featured: Sheridan, Thomas, Hardee, Wheeler. See the "Civil War" chapter for more details.

Chapter 18

In the Far East

The presence of the United States Army in the Far East began in 1898 with the Spanish-American War. It continues to this day through several wars and occupations. The Philippines, Korea, and Vietnam experiences are included in this chapter.

The Philippines

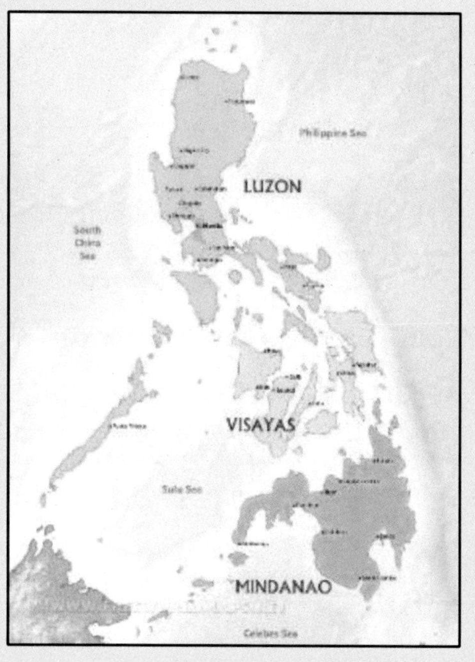

The Spanish-American War

April 1898 – December 1898

Citing mistreatment of Cubans by the Spanish and following the mysterious bombing of the USS Maine in Havana Harbor, Cuba, the United States went to war with Spain under President McKinley. Fighting took place in both the Caribbean and the Philippines in the Pacific. In the Caribbean, the US won battles at Santiago, San Juan Hill, Kettle Hill, and El Canay. In the Philippines, the US fleet defeated the Spanish fleet in Manila Bay and later took Manila while aided by Filipino rebels. In defeating the Spanish, the US became a global empire gaining sovereignty over Cuba and acquiring the Philippines, Puerto Rico, and Guam from Spain.

The US lost 2,446 Americans killed in action with 1,662 wounded. Sixteen West Point graduates were killed in action. Among them was Dennis M. Michie (USMA 1892), Army football's first head coach and founder of the Army-Navy football game, who was killed in action in Santiago, Cuba. Four West Point graduates received the Medal of Honor.

- Text from dedication plaque on the West Point golf course
- Map Source: Freeworldmaps.net

The Philippine Insurrection

February 1999 – May 1902

Following America's victory in the Spanish-American War, Spain ceded control of the Philippines to the United States. Filipino leader Emilio Aguinaldo, resistance leader against the Spanish, refused to accept this control and declared independence under a separate Philippine Republic. After initial engagements with US forces at Manila and Malolos, Aguinaldo disbanded his army and led a guerrilla war for the next two years. American forces fought Filipino rebels in brutal campaigns on Luzon, the Visayan Islands, Mindanao, and Sulu until Aguinaldo's capture on March 23, 1901, when he was forced to swear allegiance to the United States and issued a proclamation calling for peace. The guerrilla war lasted another year until most of the Filipino generals surrendered. Nearly 4,200 US soldiers were killed and 3,000 wounded – among those killed in action were 22 West Point graduates. Nine West Point graduates received the Medal of Honor.

- Text from dedication plaque on the West Point golf course

Most of the West Point related fiction shown here is based on the Army's engagement in the insurrection that followed the ouster of the Spanish in 1898.

Found in the Philippines: The Story of a Woman's Letters

California, Philippines, WP Author

Charles King The Hobart Co (1901)

The initial chapters of this novel take place in California where volunteer regiments from the Western states await transport to Manila. Admiral Dewey's fleet has conquered the Spanish navy and deposed the Spanish colonial government. The Army must now subdue an insurrection of Filipinos led by Aguinaldo. The brigade by General Drayton is encamped in tents on the cold, damp heights of the Presidio, while many officers' wives and families are comfortably housed in San Francisco waiting to wish their soldiers farewell.

The Prime family has traveled from the East in search of a wayward son who reportedly fled to join the Army. Accompanying them is a lovely niece, Amy Lawrence, who has attracted the eye of the handsome, respected, and thoroughly honorable Colonel Armstrong. Armstrong plays a role in preserving sensibilities among the many characters.

Two sisters, the Whites, Margaret (aka "Wichy"), and Nita play a prominent role in the intrigue that ensues. The elder sister , Margaret, married to Major Frank, an aide to a general already in the Philippines. She has a very gay time flirting with officers and as hostess of the ladies' social circle.

Wichy has tastes that the major could ill afford, so earlier she engineered the marriage of her sister to a Colonel Frost, from a well-to-do family. Nita is reluctant to marry but is convinced by Margaret that their financial well-being (hers mainly) requires the union. The Colonel wants assurances from Margaret that Nita was not otherwise "encumbered," which Margaret offers, but there are issues.

Alas, there are love letters from Nita to another officer she had met at West Point a few years earlier. Margaret must acquire and destroy the letters to save the marriage and her own financial well-being.

Who has the love letters and where is he? Apparently, the packet was delivered by courier to General Drayton's tent in the Presidio, but mysteriously disappeared before they were read.

Of course, there are other characters that complicate the primary plot as the scenes shift by steamer from San Francisco to Honolulu to Manila and return to Honolulu. Mrs. Margaret Frank somehow manages to accompany the troops and keep the intrigue alive. [EB]

Charles King is a West Point graduate and author of 60 novels. His books and biographical information appear in the chapters "Manifest Destiny," "The Civil War" and the "Cadet Experience."

"The Bucko"

Philippines, Pulp Fiction, WP author

Ernest R. Dupuy Argosy Magazine (1912)

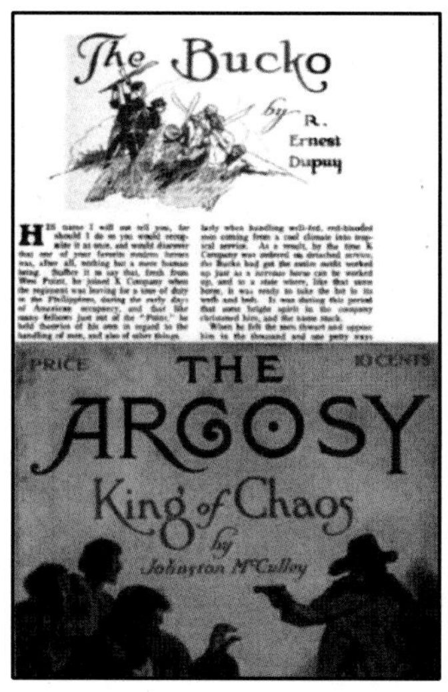

"His name I will not tell you, for should I do so you would recognize it at once and would discover that one of your favorite modern heroes was, after all, nothing but a mere human being. Suffice it to say that, fresh from West Point, he joined K Company when the regiment was leaving for a tour of duty in the Philippines, during the early days of American occupancy, and that like many fellows just out of the "Point," he held theories of his own in regard to the handling of men, and also of other things.

This exaggerated ego, which is perhaps pardonable in the boys who, from the pick of the country, have just finished four years of hard work in the finest school in the world, is usually thoroughly taken out of "shavetail" second lieutenants after they have been in their outfits for a little while, but in "The Bucko's" case there had not been time for the curing process before K Company was shipped away to a lonely corner of Mindanao to scatter a band of marauders who had been raising Cain in that part of the island.

This was unfortunate, for Ferguson, the captain, and Williams, the first lieutenant, both went down with malarial fever when the regiment struck the islands, and the Bucko, left alone, started in at once to practice his theories. One of these was that a tight rein must be held on the enlisted man.

Now, to hold a tight rein is only proper but there is a difference between a tight rein and a pressure on the curb, particularly when handling well-fed, red-blooded men coming from a cool climate into tropical service. As a result, by the time K Company was ordered on detached service, the Bucko had gotten the entire outfit worked up just as a nervous horse can be worked up, and to a state where, like that same horse, it was ready to take the bit in its teeth and bolt. It was during this period that some bright spirit within the company christened him "Bucko," and the name stuck." [EB]

Richard Ernest Dupuy (1887–1975) was a United States Army officer and military historian. Dupuy was a reporter with the *New York Herald* before his National Guard artillery unit was called up to serve in World War I. He transferred to the regular army after the war, serving in a number of public relations roles. During World War II, he was a director of news and public relations under General Eisenhower. Dupuy retired from the Army after the war and became a prolific military historian. He wrote several books on the history of West Point. [18-01]

"A Soldier's First Duty"

Romance, Philippines, Pulp Fiction

George M.A. Cain   Argosy Magazine (Nov. 1921)

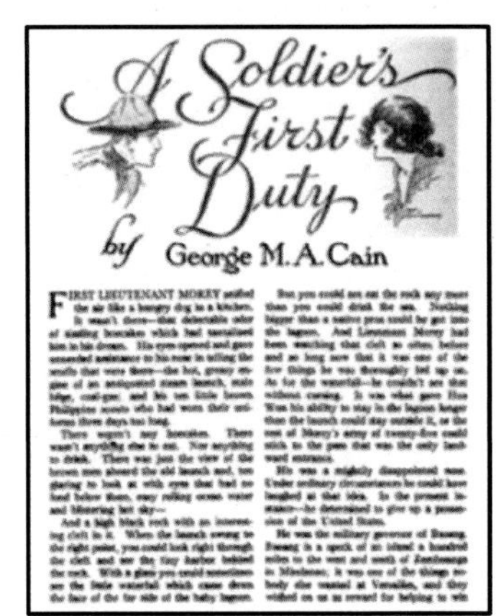

First Lieutenant Morey was the military governor of Basang. Basang is a speck of an island a hundred miles to the west and south of Zamboanga in Mindanao; it was one of the places nobody else wanted at Versailles, and they wished on the US as reward for helping to win the war. The navy had it for a while then wished it on the army. The army wished it down to the Philippine scouts.

Morey had met a girl named Irene, at a college prom. Her father had just been appointed revenue collector somewhere in the Philippines. From that time on, Morey could not be happy until he got to the Philippines to see her again. Meanwhile, her father died, and she and her mother had become too acclimated to want to return to the States.

Morey had carried his second lieutenancy into the command of the scouts. When the Major got Basang handed to him to bring order out of the chaos Hua Wua made of Basang—he handed Morey a promotion to first lieutenancy and the dignified job of a military governor. It all sounded so good to Irene and Mrs. Brennan and to Morey that they celebrated it with a wedding almost on the spot. Then Morey had two weeks of honeymoon and preparation for the assumption of his new and important post. [EB]

George M. A. Cain may have been the pseudo name for **George Caryl Sims** (1902–1966), better known by his pen names Paul Cain and Peter Ruric, an American pulp fiction author and screenwriter. [18-02]

Williams on Service

Philippines, WP Author

Hugh S. Johnson   Hearn Dept Stores (1934)

This book is a sequel to *Williams at West Point*, written years earlier by Hugh Johnson. The protagonist Bob Williams proceeds from West Point to the Island of Luzon and plunges at once into the guerilla warfare of the steaming jungles of the Philippines. He finds himself in the dangerous guardianship of the greatest treasure in the Islands. In trying to fight off a powerful attempt to loot it, he is enmeshed in a conspiracy which threatens to ruin him but from which he escapes through the gallantry and loyalty of his comrade. Through the scenes skulk or bluster some of the most romantic figures in the half-legendary "Days of the Empire"- in Luzon -- the gigantic negro deserter and outlaw who, for a time, terrorized the Island --the cool, designing, sinister figure of a well-known ex-cadet whose treason more than once threatened American troops--the evil plotting of that pretended priest who tried to be a new Mahdi and, as the Black Pope, to seize all power -- and the silent little people who hide in the gloom of the tropical forests--head-hunters and blowpipe men, whose tiny poisoned darts were more deadly than bullets. [DJ]

Hugh Samuel Johnson (1882–1942) was a U.S. Army officer (West Point 1903), businessman, speech writer, government official and newspaper columnist. He is best known as a member of the Brain Trust of Franklin D. Roosevelt from 1932–34. He wrote numerous speeches for FDR and helped plan the New Deal. Appointed head of the National Recovery Administration (NRA) in 1933, he was highly energetic in his "blue eagle" campaign to reorganize American business to reduce competition and raise wages and prices. *Time Magazine* declared him "Man of the Year" in 1933 bypassing Roosevelt. The NRA was terminated by a 1935 ruling of the Supreme Court, and Johnson left the administration after a little more than a year. [18-03]

"Feud's End"

Cadet, WP Ex, Western, Philippines, Pulp Fiction

Meigs Frost Blue Book Magazine (July 1939)

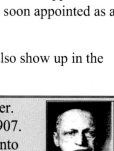

Plebe Cadet Peter Grayle and Yearling John Harkford come from South Carolina families that have had bitter bloody feuds since before the Civil War. However, this is now 1901 at the U.S. Military Academy and they have revived the feud. They determine to "settle" the matter with pre-dawn fisticuffs at Battery Knox. Both are severely hurt, ending up in the infirmary. The brawl leads to their dishonorable discharge from the academy.

Grayle wishes to become an army officer in the family tradition and determines to gain a commission through the ranks. He enlists and with the aid of his congressman is assigned to a Texas regiment that is forming up to leave for the Philippines. Grayle's brief sojourn at West Point has him shine over the country recruits and he is soon appointed as a company sergeant.

He soon ships out for the Philippines to deal with the insurrection. And who should also show up in the Philippines, but John Harkford. The feud is not yet resolved. [EB]

Meigs O. Frost (1882–1950) was a newspaper reporter, a writer, and a soldier. After graduating from Harvard, he took a job with *The New York Times* in 1907. He subsequently served in the Marines in Mexico and Central America and into World War I, and then returned to reporting. He retired from service as a Lt. Colonel. His works include four novels and 600 short stories. [18-04]

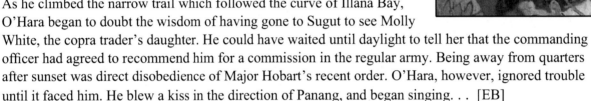

"One Step from Hell"

Philippines, Pulp Fiction, WP Author

E. Hoffman Price Argosy Magazine (August 5, 1939)

In the Philippines an order is an order—even when it doesn't make sense. So, O'Hara has to risk a neck to save a man from death in order that he can be killed according to the rules.

It was perhaps three in the morning when Lieutenant O'Hara of the 47th Philippine Scouts left Sugut to make the dangerous six-mile hike back to barracks. Though decently drunk, he walked straight. He was inches taller than the average native, but O'Hara carried himself well, as most short men do.

As he climbed the narrow trail which followed the curve of Illana Bay, O'Hara began to doubt the wisdom of having gone to Sugut to see Molly White, the copra trader's daughter. He could have waited until daylight to tell her that the commanding officer had agreed to recommend him for a commission in the regular army. Being away from quarters after sunset was direct disobedience of Major Hobart's recent order. O'Hara, however, ignored trouble until it faced him. He blew a kiss in the direction of Panang, and began singing. . . [EB]

Edgar Hoffmann Price (1898–1988) was an American writer of popular fiction for the pulp magazine marketplace. Aspiring to be a career soldier, Price served in the American Expeditionary Force in World War I, and with the American military in Mexico and the Philippines subsequently graduating from West Point in 1923. He was a champion fencer and boxer, and an amateur Orientalist. He resigned his Army commission in 1924 to pursue a career in writing. Price worked in a range of popular genres—including science fiction, horror, crime, and fantasy—but he was best known for adventure stories with Oriental settings and atmosphere. [18-05]

Fenwick Travers and the Forbidden Kingdom: An Entertainment

WP Author, Rogue, Philippines

Raymond Saunders Lyford Books (1994)

This is the second book in a trilogy about Fenwick Travers - a dastardly, caddish, philandering mountebank; a poltroon; a besotted, lecherous, scheming toady; a roué; a sybaritic rapscallion; but a rakehell who remains a thoroughly lovable fellow. Now Lieutenant Travers is off to the Philippines, newly acquired from Spain in the recent war. While there he happens on a treasure map that leads him on a series of adventures which sorely tests his ingenuity as he searches for the treasure, all the while attempting to avoid any danger to himself. The results are predictably hilarious as Fenny finds his honor sorely tried but manages not to let it interfere overmuch with his riotous enjoyment of all that life has to offer.

The other two books in the series and author's bio are included in the chapter "Soldiers of Fortune, Paladins, Miscreants & Rogues." [DJ]

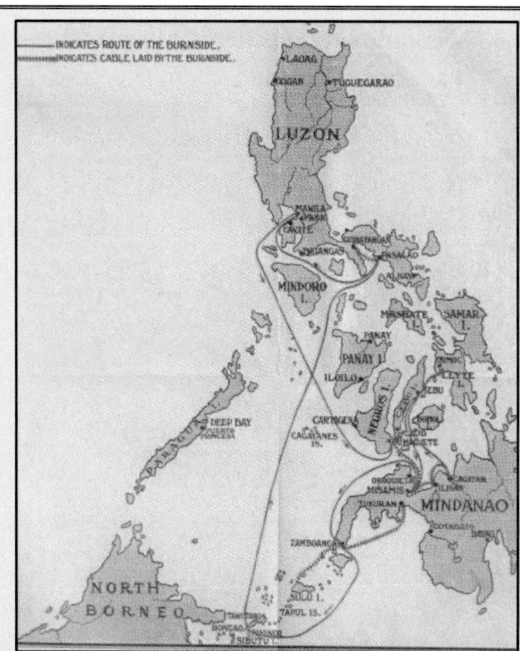

This section on the Philippines concludes with a delightful memoir by a West Pointer's wife on a journey through the Archipelago during the Insurrection. From the book's forward:

Lt. Col. Edgar Russel co-authored the Signal Corps manual on laying underseas cable while leading an expedition through the Philippine Archipelago from December 21, 1900 to April 7, 1901.

Florence Kimball Russel accompanied her husband and penned a memoir of her travels on that ship through several months of cable-laying aboard a converted Spanish freighter renamed the Burnside. This fascinating story describes the trials and tribulations of cable laying and the ship and shore life of the two officers' wives and one child. Shore visits were frequent and the natives not always friendly. It is an engaging tale of a special Army assignment. [EB]

A Woman's Journey Through the Philippines

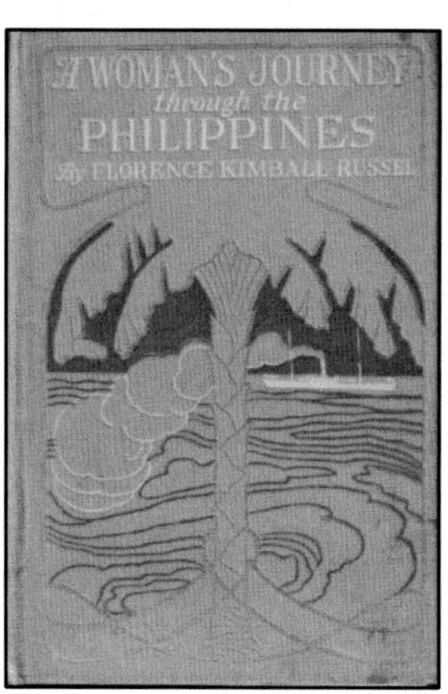

Philippines, Army Life

Florence Kimball Russel L.C. Page & Co. (1907)

From the 1902 Signal Corps Technical Manual:

> "...The war of 1898 necessitated on the part of the Signal Corps extensive cable operations in the Caribbean Sea and in the Philippine Archipelago, while later they have been extended to Alaskan waters. Under such conditions it was impracticable to either lay such cables by contract or to operate them by civilian force. In consequence, it devolved upon the Chief Signal Officer of the Army, Gen. A. W. Greely, to organize a system under which the installation, operation, and maintenance of long submarine cables should be efficiently performed by the officers and men of the Signal Corps of the Army."

From the wife's memoir:

> "It was a busy trip, everyone on the ship being occupied, with the exception of the women who spend most of their time under the cool blue awning of the quarterdeck, where many a letter was

written, and many a book read aloud and discussed, though more often we accomplished little, preferring to lie back on our long steamer chairs and watch the wooded islands with cloud shadows on the shaggy breasts drift slowly by and fade into the purple distance." [EB]

Florence Russel kept a detailed diary accompanied by dozens of photos of the islands and the inhabitants she encountered. She also wrote three novels about West Point which along with her bio may be found in the chapter "The Cadet Series of Books." The map shown above was included in the book which has been reprinted and popular over a century later.

Korea

The "Land of the Morning Calm" has been anything but that for the United States Army since 1950.

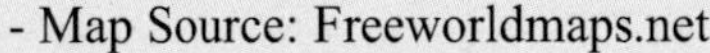

- Map Source: Freeworldmaps.net

The Korean War

June 1950 – July 1953

The Korean War was the Cold War's first major armed conflict after Communist North Korea crossed the 38th parallel and invaded South Korea in an attempt to unify the peninsula. The United States under President Harry S. Truman, with the support of the United Nations, formed a coalition to save South Korea. With US and South Korean forces driven to a small perimeter around Pusan, General Douglas MacArthur (USMA 1903) led a daring and decisive amphibious invasion at Inchon in September 1950 to aid the forces around Pusan.

The US/UN forces eventually drove North Korean forces back across the 38th parallel and continued north to the Yalu Rivers as the war aim changed from liberating South Korea to uniting all of Korea. In the wake of nuclear threats, China entered the war in October 1950 to protect its borders and defend North Korea. Chinese forces pushed US/UN forces back across the 38th parallel. After re-establishing the border in June 1951, the remainder of the war saw bitter fighting (Bloody Ridge and Heartbreak Ridge – 1951; the Battle of Triangle Hill – 1952; and the Battle of Pork Chop Hill – 1953) that yielded little exchange of territory. For the next two years, protracted negotiations reached a July 1953 armistice that re-established the border in roughly the same pre-war location and is still in effect today.

Officially, the war has not yet ended. The US lost 36,572 killed in action and 103,284 wounded – among those were 167 West Point graduates killed in action. Two West point graduates received the Medal of Honor.

- Text from dedication plaque on the West Point golf course

Thirty-Eight North Yankee

WP Author, Korea

Ed Ruggero Atria (1990)

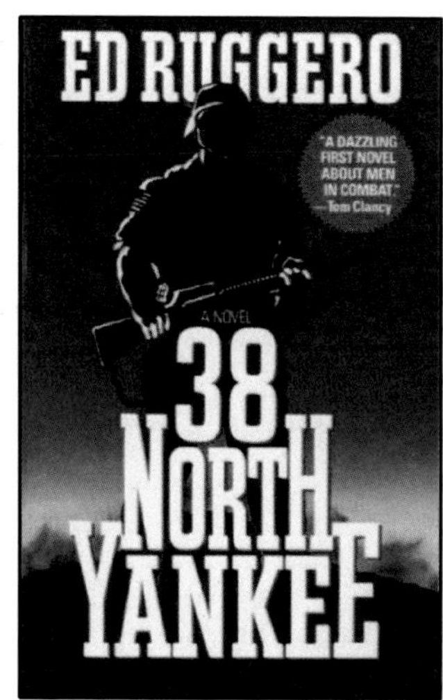

38 NORTH YANKEE is a tale of what it is like to be an untried, unproven fighting man in a war the U.S. has been trying to prevent for nearly forty years. In one savage thrust the North Korean People's Army has crossed the 38th parallel and invaded South Korea, viciously ambushing a routine American convoy. The shock waves reach across the globe to the glimmering beaches of Oahu, Hawaii, where U.S. Army Captain Mark Isen is a twenty-seven-year-old second-generation professional soldier and the commander of C Company, part of a light infantry division. Like most of his peers, Isen has never seen combat.

While the President addresses the nation, and the anti-war activists organize, the Army's lightest, most mobile units are rushed to Korea. Charlie Company—three rifle platoons, a thirteen-man anti-armor section and a six-man mortar section—reaches Korea weeks ahead of the Army's heavy forces. In a matter of days, Isen's men are at war.

While the North Koreans move on Seoul, South Korea's capital, desperately trying to score a quick knockout blow before the U.S. can marshal its full military might, C Company follows sometimes baffling orders, engaging the North Koreans wherever they can. From a daring extrication of a joy-riding divisional chief of staff trapped in a Korean village to dangerous counterattacks against advancing NKPA units, Isen's men learn how to fight in the brutal confusion of combat, armed with high-tech weapons that don't always perform the way they did in training. Exhausted, numbed, and low on ammunition, C Company is airlifted north of Seoul, where the NKPA is running out of time. Isen's orders: help stop them from retreating over the Demilitarized Zone before the U.S. reinforcements arrive.

Reaching a thundering climax with a heroic stand against a desperate enemy force, *38 NORTH YANKEE* is a story of men facing the ultimate challenge -- a striking portrayal of courage, commitment, and, in the hell of war, humanity. [DJ]

Ed Ruggero (1956–) graduated from West Point in 1980, served as an infantry officer, and was teaching English at West Point when he wrote this, his first novel. He has other novels in this collection. See the chapter "Mystery, Crime & Intrigue," "The World Wars," and "Army Medical Service Corps." [18-06]

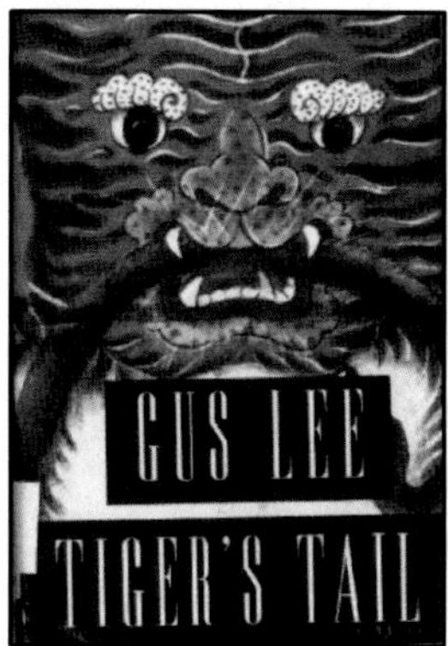

Tiger's Tail

WP Author, Korea, Mystery, Crime

Gus Lee Knopf (1996)

January 14, 1974. US. military prosecutor Jackson Kan is bound for Korea on a civilian passport—the better to make his way in—country, deep and dark, on the riskiest business imaginable. His destination is Camp Casey, a frigid and decrepit outpost on the brink of the DMZ, within spitting distance of North

Korea's Inmingun: the fourth largest, and definitely the angriest, army in the world.

As for Jackson Kan, he's not angry yet, but there's plenty troubling him. A moment of brutal truth in the Vietnamese jungle seven years before still robs him of all peace, battering his heart with sorrow and guilt. The closest thing to relief he's experienced in those seven years, his relationship with a green-eyed woman named Cara Milano, hangs by a thread back in San Francisco. And the man he's charged with finding, an American investigator missing for an eternity of six days, is none other than James Thurber Buford—his best friend, the father of his godson, the steadfast witness to his gin-soaked combat fatigue.

Now Kan must match wits with Camp Casey's formidable staff judge advocate, the bizarre Colonel Frederick LeBlanc—a white-haired, Bible-thumping patrician whose corruption seems to know no bounds, and may very well extend to murder. For nine years, for reasons unknown even to the Pentagon, LeBlanc—known locally as the Wizard—has remained out on the border, cultivating an inbred colony of minions and staring down the communists he abhors. Against such an adversary Kan's assets are few: two fellow lawyers who get on each other's nerves; a Korean driver with a death wish; a gargantuan sergeant major festering in an underground prison; and a gorgeous and compassionate kidae, ritual assistant to a mountain dwelling sorceress.

Then Kan discovers a dire secret that stretches the odds of finding Buford and getting his team out alive. But Jackson Kan is the number-one son, precious steward of his clan line and no stranger to danger. And at last, he may have picked the right fight. [DJ]

Augustus Samuel Mein-Sun "Gus" Lee (1946–) was born in San Francisco, the subject of his childhood memoir/novel *China Boy* (1991), about growing up as a broken, poverty-stricken immigrant. He attended West Point, then served as Army drill sergeant before completing his undergraduate and law degrees from UC Davis. [18-07]

His novel "Honor and Duty" is included in the "The Cadet Experience" chapter. "China Boy" is in the chapter "Other Books by West Point Authors."

The *Armored Corps* series was published under the pseudo name Peter Callahan. Initially, my son Eric Blomstedt, who commanded an Abrams tank platoon "White 1" at Camp Casey shortly before these books were published, thought that Callahan might have been the previous company commander in another battalion. We believed that to be the case for a decade until I had to produce this bio and checked the author's credits. Not so! It seems that a lengthy list of technical advisors who served in Korea and armor units coached Peter Telep on "getting it right." For an individual who never served in the Army or in Korea, the *Armored Corp* series is a remarkably realistic depiction of mobile combat on the Korean peninsula.

Armored Corps

Korea

Peter Callahan Jove (2005)

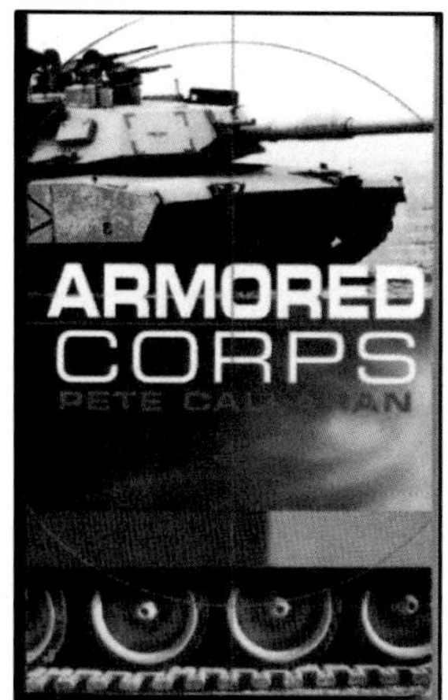

THUNDER APPROACHING

West Point graduate Lt. Jack Hansen is stationed near the 38th Parallel in South Korea with the 1st Tank Battalion. They haven't seen action yet, but there's plenty of tension. The non-stop grueling training combined with the heated competition between Hansen's oddball crew and the other tankers—has the entire 72nd armor division ready to go at each other's throats. But nothing puts a stop to internecine warfare like international warfare...On Christmas Day, all dissent within the ranks is forgotten. The power-mad dictator of North Korea has just launched a surprise attack. And Hansen and his battalion of untested warriors must charge into battle to halt the invasion with the only weapon they need—the heavy metal hell bringer known as the M1 A1 Abrams. [BC]

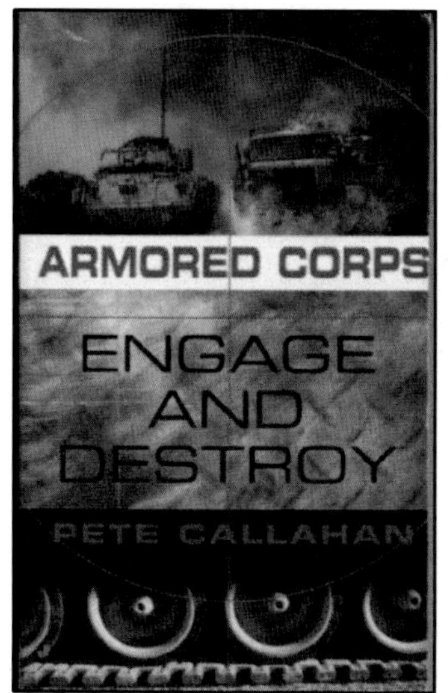

Engage and Destroy: Armored Corps:

Korea

Pete Callahan Jove (2005)

URBAN WARFARE

War is raging as North Korean forces continue their campaign to overthrow their countrymen to the south and unite the Korean Peninsula under the iron hand of their "beloved leader." So far, forces under Lt. Jack Hansen of the American 1st Tank Battalion have helped hold off the invaders in the mountain forests.

But their battlefield is about to change. Tongduch'on has come under attack, and Hansen and his platoon find themselves caught in a brutal street-by-street battle for the city. With Communist infiltrators fueling the people's anti-American sentiments, the line between friend and foe is blurred—and Hansen must drive his tankers on a razor-thin line between fighting the enemy and all-out slaughter... [BC]

Attack by Fire : Armored Corps

Korea

Peter Callahan Jove (2006)

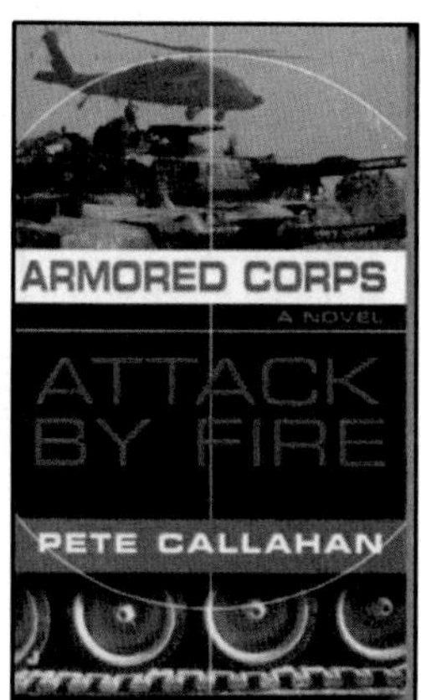

ROAD TO RUMBLE

As both sides take losses and make gains, the war for the Korean peninsula still rages. Now, tank commander Lt. Jack Hansen and Charlie Company are finally doing what they've been waiting to do—go on the offensive. They're part of a big push to take the fight to the North Koreans on their own ground. But the strain of constant battle is beginning to take its toll on both Hansen and his men—and it gets much worse when they're ordered to lead a strike force into the icy heart of North Korea.

To reach their objective, they must fight their way through a communist stronghold that will test each man's skills to the limit, and push them all to the breaking point... [BC]

The *Armored Corps* series was published under the pseudo name **Pete Callahan.**

Peter Telep (1965–) is an American author, screenwriter, and educator. He has written over 50 books – primarily science fiction – and scripts for multiple television shows. "Immediately after the 9/11 terror attacks, my editors strongly urged me to write realistic military fiction, and for years after that I focused on those stories." [18-08]

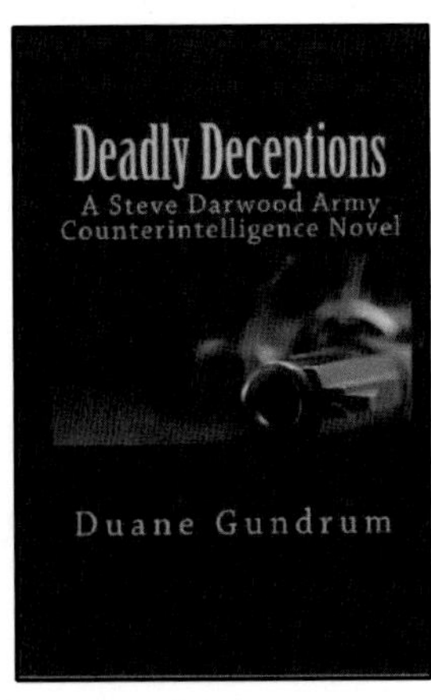

Deadly Deceptions: A Steve Darwood Army Counterintelligence Novel

Korea, Intrigue, WP Author

Duane Gundrum Self-published (2013)

The year is 1987 and the Cold War is still raging strong. Steve Darwood is a US Army counterintelligence agent in South Korea, working in Tongduchon, a small city close to the North Korean border and the demilitarized zone, when he stumbles upon a black-marketing operation that is blackmailing soldiers for various types of information. Investigating further, he uncovers a network of criminals who appear to be linked to numerous military personnel.

As Darwood continues to investigate, he begins to come against resistance from his own chain of command. Soon, Darwood finds himself alone, working against many of his own people, relying on his extensive network of sources, connections, and allies. Slowly, he begins to realize that the network might go even higher, pushing him into a situation where he must challenge his own people, who hold the reins of his job, his livelihood and even his life. Several members of the Counter Intelligence community are murdered to discourage Darwood's investigation. This is serious stuff. [BC]

Duane Gundrum is the author of mystery/suspense novels, science fiction and fantasy, and humor/satire. He attended West Point (ex 1987) and served in the US Army for several years in counterintelligence. After the Army, he became an investigator, a website designer, and then a programmer for a software gaming company, and, of course, a writer. Gundrum has two other mystery novels in this collection: *Absent without Leave* and *Innocent Until Proven Guilty.* The former is described in "Chapter 10 Mystery Crime & Intrigue." [18-09]

Morning Calm

Korea, WP Author

Jason M. Morwick Nortia Press (2011)

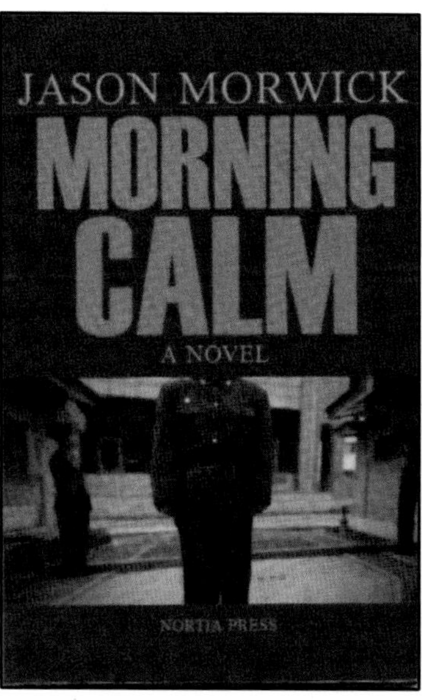

For an American soldier stationed between the two Koreas nothing is what it seems.

Soju hangovers, prostitution, bar brawls, riots, training accidents and the monotony of garrison life describe the environment of 1990s Korea for First Lieutenant Greg Thomlin. While Thomlin balances bouts with women and alcohol, threats from North Korea are ever-present. North Korean infiltrators battle with South Korean police as Thomlin and his cohort become desensitized to the world around them. Thomlin's life is disrupted when he is assigned to investigate a missing automated network control device -- a loss that is a cardinal sin for unit commanders, and a potential windfall for enemy spies.

For the soldiers who served in an era between wars, Korea was a surreal experience -- a land filled with temptations while the threat of war constantly loomed in the background. [DJ]

Jason Morwick (1972–) graduate of the United States Military Academy in 1994, then served as an infantry officer in Korea. He is a co-author of several non-fiction books directed at business leadership and published articles in a variety of business journals. [18-10]

The Captains

Korea

W.E.B. Griffin G. P. Putnam (1982)

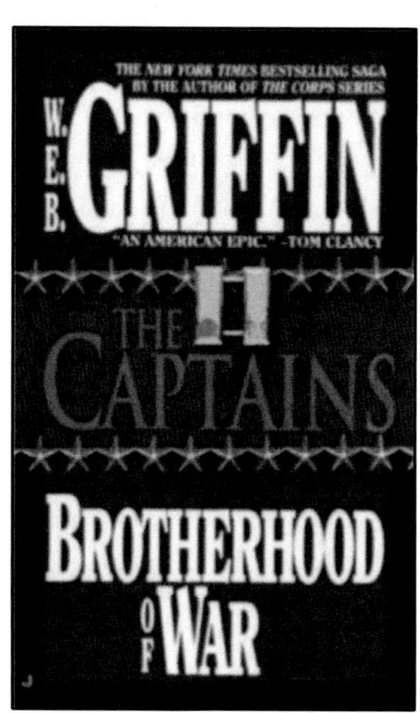

It was more than an incident. It was a deadly assault across the 38th parallel. It was the Korean War.

In the fear and the frenzy of battle, those who had served with heroism before were called again by America to man the trenches and sandbag bunkers.

From Pusan to the Yalu, they drove forward with commands too new and tanks too old, brothers in war, bonded together in battle as they had never been in peace... [BC]

From a book review on Amazon:

> "With the Korean War starting, our protagonists start finding their way toward it. We see the sudden and devastating North Korean invasion, the enclave at Pusan, the breakout from there along with

the Inchon Landing, the tide changing once more as China invades, and the war's settling into a stalemate.

The path is most difficult for Mac MacMillan. The Medal of Honor he won in World War II proves an obstruction as the brass quail at the public relations impact should he get killed. Although he distinguishes himself in the war's opening hours, evacuating troops (and a colonel's mistress) in a daring flight, the highest orders are given to keep him away from the fighting. He doesn't want to spend the war as a White House aide passing out hors d'oeuvres. A skilled operator – at heart still a master sergeant although he's now an officer – MacMillan learns to fly a helicopter in addition to a light airplane and maneuvers first to get sent overseas, then to stay there and finally to work with a top secret coastal base infiltrating agents behind North Korean lines, conflicting with his orders to stay away from the front.

Craig Lowell, called up from the National Guard as a tank commander, formulates a classically daring cavalry maneuver during the breakout from the Pusan perimeter. He leads a column of tanks deep into enemy territory, locating and destroying enemy gunnery positions, wreaking havoc, and disrupting its communications, and he continues to distinguish himself during the retreat after the massive Chinese invasion. His men worship him and call him "the Duke" as he violates numerous Army regulations on their behalf. He is then relegated to staff work, and higher-ups keep being divided between those appalled at the notion of a 24-year-old tradition-defying major who is neither a West Pointer nor a college graduate, and those who work most closely with him and realize how good he is.

Sandy Felter, deeply ensconced in the spook world as a military officer assigned to the new CIA, ends up commanding the spy base MacMillan works at.

Phil Parker, despite distinguishing himself in the field, finds himself up on charges before a court-martial. Trying to stop a panicking unit from fleeing during before the surprise North Korean onslaught, he shoots a lieutenant. When Lowell learns of it, he wants to do everything possible to help Parker avoid a seemingly certain murder conviction. What happens derails both of their careers. Neither can look forward to a career in armor, but they discover something: a brand-new combat role for Army Air, one that hasn't really been created, offers a way up for those not wanted elsewhere."

18-11

W. E. B. Griffin, the pen name of **William Edmund Butterworth III** (1929–2019), was an American writer of military and detective fiction with 59 novels in seven series published. See "The West Point Legacies" chapter for a more complete bio and other novels in this series.

Vietnam War

July 1959 – April 1973

America's second major armed conflict of the Cold War was the Vietnam War as the US replaced the French in support of the Republic of Vietnam (South Vietnam). Initial US support included financial aid and military advisors to support South Vietnam's fight against Communist insurgents and prevent the "domino theory" of successive nations falling to Communism.

This commitment gradually escalated over the next two decades peaking in 1968 with about 540,000 troops under President Lyndon Johnson. Fighting both conventionally and unconventionally against the North Vietnamese Army and Vietcong insurgents, America employed a range of options that included aerial bombing campaigns, "search and destroy" operations; and counter-insurgency operations to achieve "pacification."

Conventional operations dominated from 1965–1973 and were first led by General William Westmoreland (USMA1936) and then General Creighton Abrams (USMA 1936). Despite overwhelming tactical success on the battlefield, factors such as political limitations, changing objectives, and waning support from the American public after the 1968 Tet Offensive caused America to re-evaluate its commitment. Pursuing a strategy of "Vietnamization" under President Richard Nixon, the US gradually withdrew its combat forces by 1973.

The US lost 58,200 Americans killed in action with 303,644 wounded - among those were 273 West Point graduates killed in action. Six West Point graduates, one former Cadet, and one professor received the Medal of Honor.

- Text from dedication plaque on the West Point golf course
- Map Source: Freeworldmaps.net

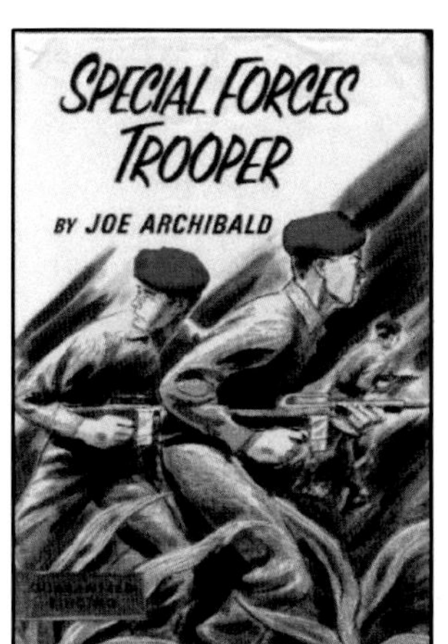

Special Forces Trooper

Vietnam

Joe Archibald David McKay Company (1967)

Corporal Stanley Rusat aspires to be a Weapons Leader among the Green Berets, but he has two individual problems: will he get into the real action, and will an old grudge against rigid authority haunt him?

Stanley and the others with him plunge into the specialized training. A patrol moves in where there may be an ambush; they work on another ambush called the Hammer and Anvil. The trainees practice scaling and rappelling, crossing chasms. In the survival area they learn to recognize and prepare strange foods and to live off the country. The weird devices of the Vietcong to trap, maim, and kill engage them. They study spoken Vietnamese. They work on Morse code and the many tricks of radio communication. At times Stanley and his buddies feel they'll never be able to master it all, especially when they try each other's specialties.

For those who do last, there is a full-scale operation. Trainees who pass this test are certain to be sent to Vietnam. Corporal Rusat finds, as he had hoped, that pride in full measure goes with the Green Beret—and that he still has that grudge. It shows up during the Pineland Operation with the arrival of the stiff lieutenant, and they are to serve together in Vietnam, right where teamwork is essential. Patrols, skirmishes, alarms, increasing knowledge of the South Vietnamese they are helping, and of the Vietcong with whom they are struggling weld the men. When the big attack comes, they acquit themselves as a perfectly trained team, Corporal Rusat sees that he himself has been imposing authority all along—as is done wherever men must bring others through to efficiency. He takes another look at being a Green Beret. [DJ]

Joe Archibald (1898–1986) is best remembered today for the numerous juvenile sports fiction books he wrote, especially his baseball titles. See the chapter "Army Sports" for his West Point football book and biographical information.

One Very Hot Day

Vietnam

David Halberstam Houghton, Mifflin (1968)

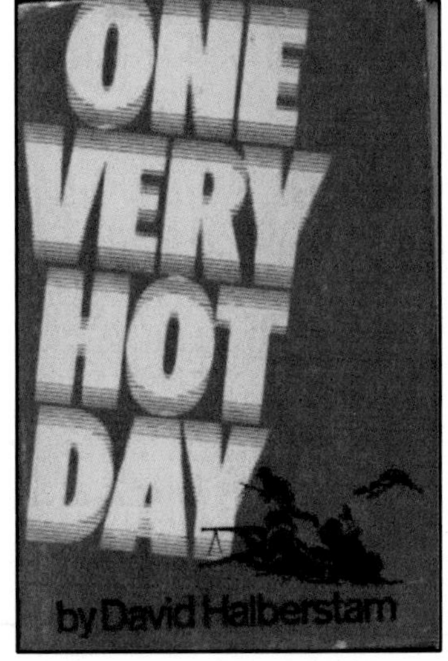

This is a novel about the war, the smaller and very different war we were once fighting out in Vietnam. It is about one day and some men and the ambush they fear past the canal at Ap Thanh Thoi. It is the novel you will think of when you see pictures of the war or read the paper or watch the news on television. It is by a man whose reporting from Vietnam won the Pulitzer Prize in 1964.

Some of the characters are Americans, as different from each other as from the Vietnamese troops they lead. There is Captain Beaupre, a veteran on his way down, too old for this new war, overweight, tired, frightened, with many enemies besides the Viet Cong. The most terrible enemy of all is the sun, burning his thirst, the thirst itself a killer; another is fear. Fear, for instance, of the helicopters, the choppers meaning action, and making Beaupre choose the long walk by the canal as his part of the three-pronged operation.

Anderson, Beaupre's lieutenant, is the opposite. A new-style West Pointer, serious and ambitious, he not only likes the Vietnamese but has bothered to learn their language and to interest himself in their culture. He wants to be friends, to make the United States respected -- with minimal results. The daily letters Anderson receives from his pretty wife irritate Captain Beaupre whose only female contacts result from Saturday night forays in the brothels of Saigon.

Then there is Big William, a captain, a giant Negro, liberating and fully liberated in the nightclubs of Saigon, a grand operator. And there are the Vietnamese troops, with their young officer, Thuong, proud, able, completely fatalistic, uneasy with the Americans.

The action takes place in one long hot day against the larger background of this particular war, the decadence of Saigon and the boredom of the base camp, an abandoned seminary, with its dull food and Doris Day movies. Its focus is the actual story of the attack mission, of the terrible pressure and tension of fighting an enemy one never sees, hearing a language one doesn't understand, enduring the blazing sky, the mendacity of the villagers, and the jungle growth as menacing as the constant threat of ambush. [DJ]

David Halberstam (1934–2007) was an American writer, journalist, and historian, known for his work on the Vietnam War, politics, history, the Civil Rights Movement, business, media, American culture, and later, sports journalism. [18-12]

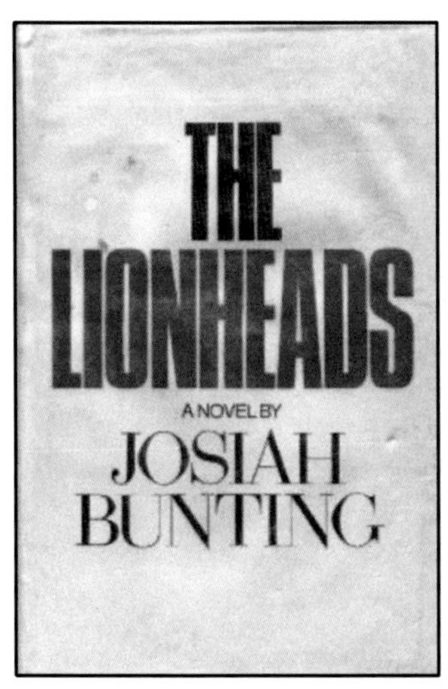

The Lionheads

Vietnam, Intrigue

Josiah Bunting George Braziller (1972)

"This book is a novel, not a history," Major Bunting writes, and it seems necessary to stress this point for at times his story reads like a fascinating report of precisely what goes on in the chain of command from division headquarters down to the "real sharp individual" in combat, the low man on the totem pole..

Major Bunting, who is presently teaching English history at West Point, writes: "What I observed during my own tour of duty provides some of the background for the story: the geography, the organization of military units, the 'hardware,' some of the tactics. But no 'Twelfth Infantry Division'—the 'Lionheads' of the title—fought as part of the American army. Similarly, the directives, operations orders, the formal battle analyses, the combat 'after action' reports, the appendices and map - are all fictional."

If the primary concern of the troopers was to survive and come home, that of the career officers was usually success in the military system - "getting their tickets punched." The members of this cadre, the young officers and sergeants excepted, suffer relatively few casualties. It is a condition of war: those who least comprehend the purposes of organized fighting to which the state commits them those least attracted to military service, suffer most, most often the supreme price.

Implicit in the story of *The Lionheads* is a modern commentary on this continuing condition. The three principal characters are George Simpson Lemming, the general commanding the division, George Robertson, a colonel commanding one of Lemming's brigades, and Paul Compella, a private soldier. Each does his job according to his lights, though the lights of one can spell darkness for the others.

The action takes place in the spring of 1968, when Robertson's Riverine brigade is dispatched in search of body counts. The General, whose enormous competence is surpassed only by his ambition, orders the attack but refuses the necessary helicopter support; he survives and is promoted. The Colonel, a brave man and a good soldier, yet a hindrance to the fulfillment of the General's ambition, must carry out the order he knows is faulty; he, too, survives and is ruined. The trooper dies. The one who dies is the youngest by twenty years. He comprehends least what he is fighting for. [DJ]

Josiah Bunting III (1939–) is an American educator. He has been a military officer, college president, and an author and speaker on education and Western culture. Bunting attended Virginia Military Institute and was later a Rhodes scholar. He served in the Army from 1966 to 1972. He was stationed at Fort Bragg, Vietnam, and West Point, where he was assistant professor of history and social sciences. *The Lionheads* is based on his experiences as an officer of the 9th Infantry Division in Vietnam in 1968. [18-13]

The Berets

Vietnam

W.E.B. Griffin G. P. Putnam (1985)

They were the chosen ones—and the ones who chose to be the best. Never before had the United States given so select a group of fighting men such punishing preparation.

Now they were heading for their ultimate test of skill and nerve and sacrifice, in a war unlike any they or their country had ever fought before, in a land that most of America still knew nothing about—Vietnam... The Army's organizational battle over the Green Berets – whether they'll be a new and independent fighting force, or a subordinate part of Airborne, and whether they'll keep wearing those funny hats – continues. [BC]

From a book review on Amazon:

> "Lowell's nephew Geoffrey Craig, a draftee, faces court-martial after punching out a bullying drill sergeant. Lowell faces the ticklish task of whether to use his influence to help Craig or whether that will backfire, and even if successful teach the boy the wrong lesson.
>
> New characters include Karl-Heinz Wagner and his sister Ursula. Wagner is a former East German soldier who has escaped, with his sister, by crashing a truck through the Berlin Wall. He joins Special Forces but he and his sister teeter on the brink of poverty as he tries to support her on a private's salary.
>
> Felter develops the same relationship with Kennedy that he had with Eisenhower. Griffin really captures Kennedy's wit, charm, and appreciation for fighting men.
>
> Parker accompanies to Vietnam a secret shipment of armed Army small planes – secret not from the enemy, but from the Air Force as the Army struggles under its restriction to leave air combat to the Air Force, which does little to support ground troops. Parker's wife, an Army doctor, struggles with his going to war once more.
>
> Lowell is too talented a paper-shuffler for the Army to give him a field command, and chafes under the restriction. The brass exile Lowell for a month to keep him away from Defense Secretary Robert MacNamara, whom the brass fears is close to accepting Lowell's recommendations to expand Army aviation. Lowell's latest flame is an attractive Army psychiatrist." [18-14]

The Chopper 1 Series consists of fifteen action stories about Air Cavalry operations in Vietnam. The unit is led by Corporal (later Sgt) Brody and Lt. Vance, a recent West Point graduate.

Blood Trails

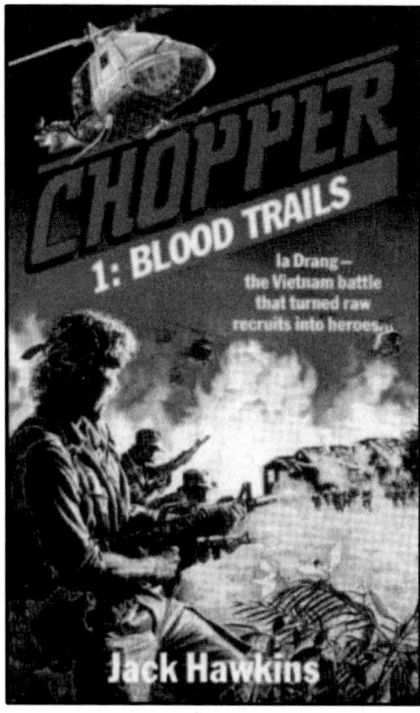

Vietnam

Jack Hawkins Sphere (1988)

THE MEN OF THE FIRST AIR CAV...

They were the cowboys of the sky - the US helicopter gunship soldiers who believed in what they fought for and laid their lives on the line.

Corporal Treat Brody: Handsome, cocky, jack-of-all-trades. Specialty: anti-tank guns. Sideline: women.

Lieutenant Jake Vance: First in his class at West Point: yet to be tested in the heat of battle. Will he keep his cool?

THE BATTLE OF IA DRANG

Jets scream down, unloading napalm. Tanks roll up the hillsides belching smoke and flame. When it's over, the Americans will have won one of the most decisive victories of the Vietnam War — or the ground will be stained by their...BLOOD TRAILS. [BC]

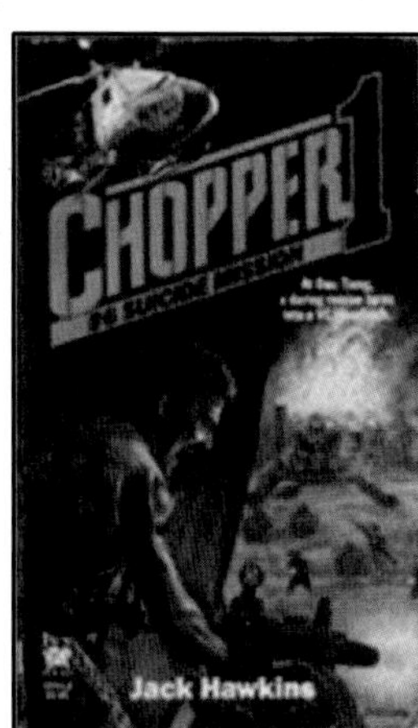

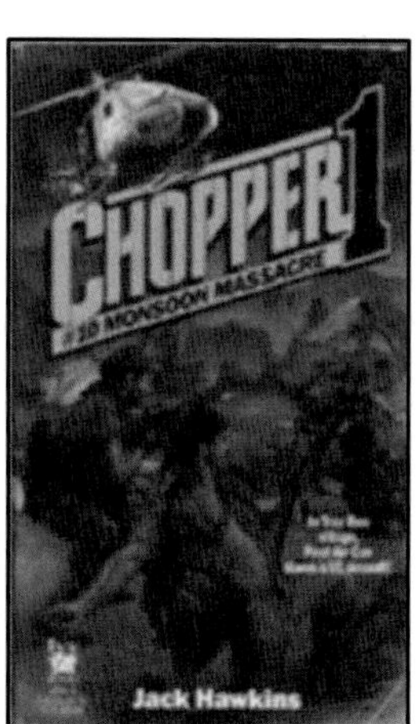

Jack Hawkins in a pseudo name employed by **Nicholas Cain** in authoring the Chopper 1 series. Cain first volunteered for the Vietnam War, in 1972 serving as a military policeman. He then served with the 281st MPs in Thailand as well as the 110th MPs in South Korea. In 1975, Cain left with an honorable discharge and the rank of sergeant. Between 1982 and 1989 he authored over 40 action novels in several series about the Vietnam War and aftermath. He stopped writing in 1990 and became a private investigator. [18-15]

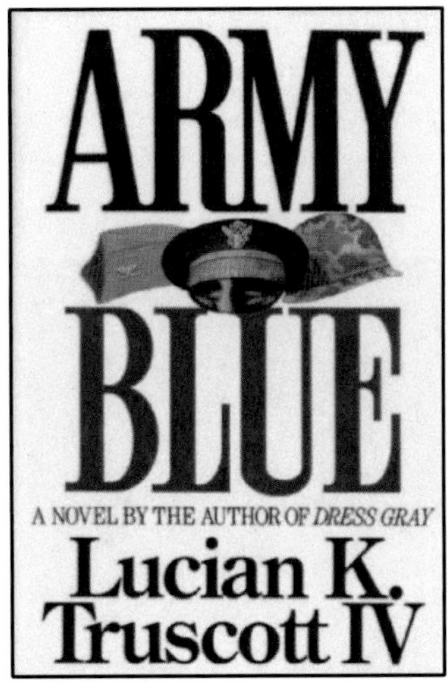

Army Blue

Vietnam, Intrigue, WP Author

Lucian K. Truscott Crown (1989)

It is 1969, the height of the Vietnam War, and Lieutenant Matthew Nelson Blue, IV is being held in a military prison in Saigon. He is charged with cowardice and desertion in the face of the enemy, a capital offense. But the Lieutenant is being framed by his superiors; he knows about a scandal so severe that the public outcry could bring the war to a halt. Racing halfway across the world to the Lieutenant's aid are his father, a Colonel who served in Korea, and his grandfather; a retired General, a hero of World War II, and a confidant of presidents. The Colonel and the General have been estranged for years, but now they must join together to confront both Lieutenant Blue's court-martial and the Byzantine web of politics and self-interest that is Vietnam. It is a war unlike any either has fought.

Army Blue takes you into the foxhole, the officers' quarters, the office of the Secretary of Defense, and a military courtroom. It tells the real story of Vietnam -- how the war was fought, and why it was so difficult to end. Army Blue probes the intense bonds that unite—and divide a Southern military family as it follows the Blues through the battles of two world wars and the battles within the Pentagon over policy and politics. As war threatens to split the family irreparably, the scandal that Lieutenant Blue has uncovered threatens to bring down the whole military establishment in Vietnam. Lieutenant Blue's court-martial forms the riveting and shocking conclusion to Army Blue. [DJ]

Lucian King Truscott IV (born April 1947) graduated from West Point in 1969. This is his second novel of four in this collection. See the chapters on "Mystery, Crime & Intrigue" and "The Cadet Experience" for his other novels.

The Stone Ponies: The Black Sabre Chronicles #4

Vietnam

Tom Willard Forge (2000)

Black Sabre Chronicles, telling the story of the Sharps family of military men and women from the Buffalo Soldier era of the Indian Wars to the present day, continues in *The Stone Ponies*, the fourth book in the series.

Franklin LeBaron Sharps is a young paratrooper sent to Vietnam in 1965 with the celebrated l0lst Airborne Division - the "Screaming Eagles." The great-grandson of Sergeant Major Augustus Sharps and son of Brigadier General Samuel Sharps, a former member of the Tuskegee Airmen of World War ll. Franklin fights aware on two fronts. He is bent on avenging the death of his brother by the Vietcong, and back home he fights against reconciling with the father who deserted his family.

Based on the author's own experiences as a paratrooper in Vietnam. The Stone Ponies takes a brutally graphic look at the war in its early years when the United States was divided over its conduct and its military heroes were suffering both abroad and at home. [DJ]

Tom Willard, born into a military family, quit high school to join the army and served as a paratrooper and combat medic in Vietnam. He was wounded in action and decorated with the Bronze Star with "V" device for valor, and the Purple Heart, among other medals. [18-16]

The other four books in this series can be viewed in "The West Point Legacies" chapter.

Flames of War

Vietnam

George C. Christensen Vantage Press (1976)

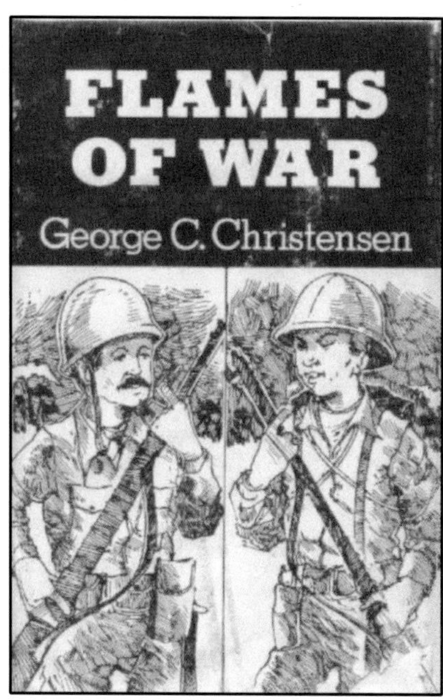

Dan Bryant, a West Point graduate, is a young officer who believes that he is fighting to save a small country from being overrun by totalitarian forces. Lieutenant Nguyen Cau Thieu of the People's Army of Liberation is also a dedicated soldier who believes that he is fighting to save his country from foreign invaders who seek to set up a puppet government and exploit his birthright.

...the two men play a tragic and deadly game of hide-and-seek across the Delta. They never meet, but each is very much aware of the other. Their struggle ranges across the length and depth of the jungle. climaxing in a bloody battle aftermath which follows one of the well-known "punitive" raids by the Vietnamese forces.

Flames of War is a fast-moving, suspenseful story of men at war; it is also a portrayal, sometimes brutal—but always fascinating of how young idealists can be turned into cold-blooded killers. Now that we have reached a point in history that we can be objective about the Vietnam War, it is important that we understand it, and the fact that the true victim of war is always the innocent bystander. [DJ]

George C. Christensen (1929–?) grew up in North Dakota - "just another small-town kid." In 1951, he enlisted in the U.S. Army and served in Korea and, later, in Europe. In 1965, Mr. Christensen spent two years in Vietnam working with the different combat units in the Mekong Delta. Although never in actual combat, the close support missions he did take part in gave him the opportunity to see some of the bloody and broken results of the struggles that took place in the wet jungles over there. He retired from the Army in 1971. [DJ]

The Silent Men

Vietnam, WP Author

Richard H. Dickinson Rugged Land Press (2002)

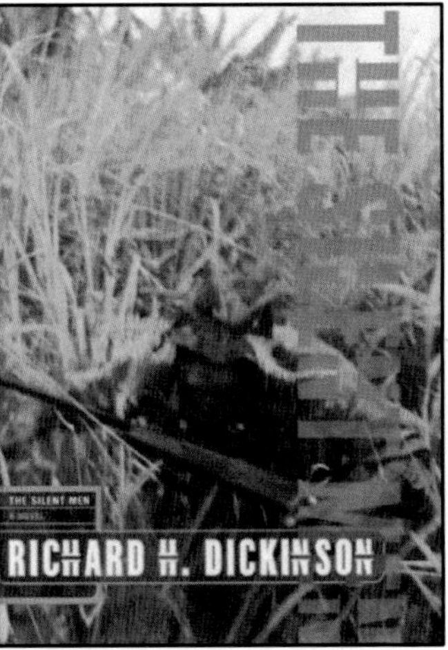

Jackson Monroe is the finest American sniper in Vietnam's treacherous Mekong Delta. The Viet Cong call him "Black Ghost." Dispatched for a classified "illegal" mission on the Cambodia border, Monroe succeeds beyond expectation, only to be abandoned behind enemy lines and left for dead by his superior officers. Suddenly, the hunter becomes the hunted when Monroe discovers that a VC assassin--an expert marksman like himself--is intent on eliminating the legendary Black Ghost before he compromises the North Vietnamese Army's carefully planned Tet Offensive. With superb writing, brilliantly realized characters, and nonstop action, The Silent Men introduces readers to a new hero in the first of a series of thrilling adventures. [DJ]

Richard H. Dickinson (1951–) was commissioned from West Point into the U.S. Airforce, spending twelve years as a hurricane hunter and air traffic controller. [DJ] He has written several military thrillers which appear elsewhere in this catalog, but Jackson Monroe only appears in one of them….as a General officer!

COUNTRY: Pass in Review Series

Vietnam, Aviation, Medical, WP Author

Brian Utermahlen CreateSpace Publishing (2014)

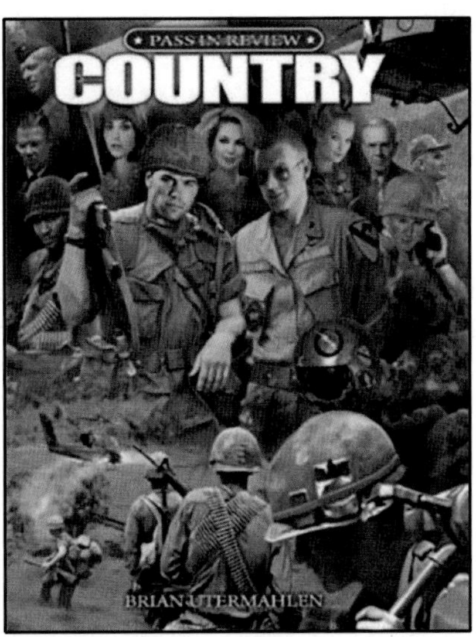

A review from Amazon.com:

"Pass in Review – COUNTRY" is the third and final book of a three generational saga about the Nolans, a twentieth century military family.

Two brothers - one a helicopter pilot, the other an infantry soldier - and a gutsy, dedicated nurse bring to life the real story of Vietnam that the news media, protestors, politicians and the public never saw or understood.

COUNTRY takes you into the cockpit of the workhorse Huey helicopter to fly with Brad Nolan on combat assaults into hot Landing Zones, medical evacuations and night fire support missions.

COUNTRY puts you on combat patrol with Glenn Nolan, on an American firebase being overrun and in the middle of firefights with North Vietnamese regulars in the jungles of Vietnam and Cambodia.

And COUNTRY also puts you inside the trauma-laden operating rooms of American Surgical hospitals with Jenny Kolarik and her nurses as they fight for the life of every wounded soldier.

This is the story of a family, a nation, an Army and the institution of West Point struggling with challenges to the concept of Duty-Honor-Country during the Vietnam era.

Throughout this series, the fictional Nolan family interacts with actual historical characters including Douglas MacArthur, Dwight Eisenhower, Charles Lindbergh, FDR, Winston Churchill, JFK, Lyndon Johnson, and many others.

The final book of this trilogy brings to conclusion this saga and finally reconciles many of the personal and professional issues of family and service to country begun in the very first chapter of DUTY. Yet questions still linger about the future of the family, the country, and the Academy. [BC]

The first and second volumes in this series—*Duty* and *Honor*—are described in "The World Wars" chapter of this catalog and also in "The West Point Legacies" chapter.

Operation White Star

Vietnam, WP Author

Richard Sutton Daring Publications (1990)

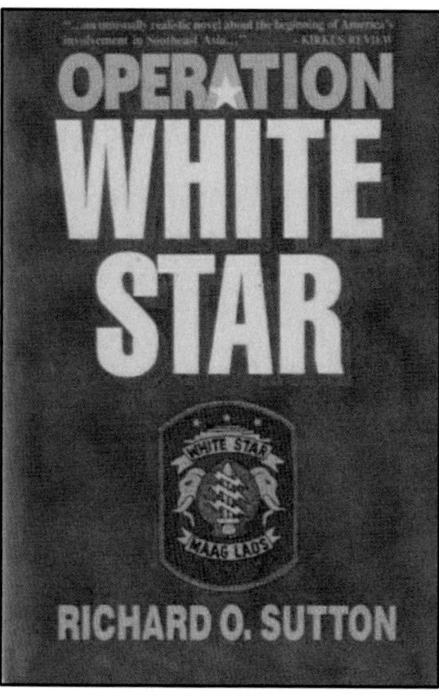

Here are the true-to-life adventures of a young U.S. Army Lieutenant fresh out of West Point who answered the call for seventeen volunteers to join the "Sneaky Petes" (soon to be known as "Green Berets") and found himself a member of a top-secret advisor team sent to Laos in the early '60s. Operation White Star details the initiation of Second Lieutenant Ed Meadows into the U.S. Army Special Forces unit at Fort Bragg, NC. The unit was comprised of tough, combat hardened sergeants who kept assuring Ed and his cohorts, "There ain't no TO&E slots for DASLs in this unit!" *

Through the eyes of LT Meadows, the reader experiences the escapades of Special Forces life. . . the training, the harassment, and the one-upmanship between brothers-in-arms. LT Meadows is one of the first junior officers to be assigned to Laos in the early 1960s as part of a top-secret mission to "assist and advise" the Forces Armées Royale (FAR).

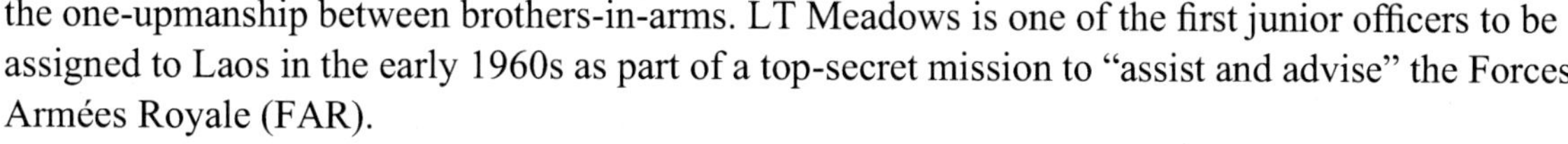

Not content to be idle, LT Meadows initiates some of the first American combat engagements in SE Asia since WWII. Eventually a planned ambush to interdict communist forces on the Ho Chi Minh Trail goes haywire. LT Meadows and one of his sergeants are separated from their unit and relentlessly pursued for five days by 25 crack NVA scouts.

The adventures shared in this book are presented with the self-deprecating humor of someone who has been there and totally understands the military community, the language and the people. [DJ]

* Table of Organization & Equipment; Dumb-Ass Second Lieutenants

Richard Sutton graduated from West Point in 1960. He attended Ranger School, Airborne School and Artillery Officers Basic Course. As a 2LT, Sutton was assigned to the 7th Special Forces at Ft. Bragg, NC and completed the Special Forces Officers Course. He was then sent to Laos where he participated in Operation White Star. When shipped back to the U.S., he attended medical school. In 1970, he returned to Vietnam as a surgeon in the 5th Special Forces Group at Bien Hoa. Sutton resumed active duty at Fort Stewart, GA continuing his orthopedic practice. [DJ]

The Pathfinder

Vietnam, Crime

E. James DuBois Christian Faith Publishing (2017)

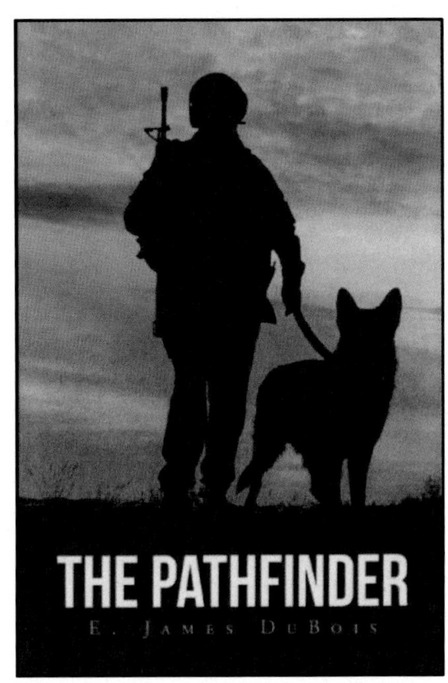

The *Pathfinder* is a novel in which West Point graduate Lincoln Davis comes to realize that Vietnamese orphaned girls were not being captured by enemy forces as assumed; rather, they were being forced into an international human trafficking scheme. With the assistance of a friend and fellow West Pointer, Lincoln Davis arranges for two Vietnamese sisters to testify against those who took the girls into captivity under the cover of war.

In the *Pathfinder* Lincoln Davis becomes a soldier at war with the known enemy in the jungles of Vietnam. The battles of an infantry unit in Vietnam present a variety of life-threatening challenges. However, the battle of the unknown enemy in a human trafficking scheme reveals that war comes in a variety of settings. Bringing the "bad guys" into court and providing a loving family for young, displaced heroes doesn't guarantee that the battle is over in the end. [BC]

E. James DuBois is a graduate of Philadelphia Biblical University (Cairn University) and the California Graduate School of Theology. He has served as a pastor, teacher, school administrator, state prison chaplain, and coordinator of chaplaincy services and retired from the New Jersey Department of Corrections as an assistant divisional director. Jim DuBois is a decorated Vietnam War veteran. [BC]

Chapter 19

The West Point Legacies

Merriam-Webster defines legacy as "something transmitted by or received from an ancestor or predecessor or from the past." As with many institutions of higher learning a significant percentage of West Point cadets are the children or grandchildren of former cadets. This is not so much a matter of favoritism, but of environment and upbringing being instrumental in the youth's intention to become an Army officer.

This chapter stretches the concept of "legacy." Several writers have produced exceptional novels about family members who attended West Point or fought America's wars through multiple generations, or they trace their family members and the Army experience over several decades. Here are those "legacies." The books of several series appear here, although the individual novels are presented in chapters that match their plots.

Photos taken by Edward Blomstedt – West Point Cemetery

Black Knights of the Hudson

This series traces a fictional U.S. Army family, the MacKendricks from the Civil War through World War I. It begins with two brothers attending West Point on the eve of Fort Sumpter.

Self-published (2012–2013)

The Books in the Series	**Chapter in this Catalog**
Book I: ***Shadow of the Flags*** (1860 – 1868)	The Civil War
Book II: ***Boots and Saddles*** (1868 – 1883)	Manifest Destiny
Book III: ***Changing of the Guard*** (I885 – 1898)	Manifest Destiny
Book IV: ***Long Gray Line*** (1901 – 1915)	The Cadet Experience
Book V: ***War Clouds in the East*** (1915 – 1917)	The World Wars (WWI)
Book VI: ***Pershing's Eagles*** (1917 – 1919)	The World Wars (WWI)

Beverly C. Gray is the daughter of a career U.S. Army officer. She has been a technical writer/editor for almost thirty years but has never outgrown her passion for history and historical research. Writing historical fiction satisfies her yen to learn more about the past and enables her to live in different eras via her characters. [BC]

Pass in Review

This trilogy is about men and women absorbed in their rewarding but difficult relationship with military service for our country. It is the saga of a 20th Century military family – three generations and their contemporaries – some famous, some not, but all of them intensely American.

Throughout this series, the fictional Nolan family interacts with actual historical characters including Douglas MacArthur, Dwight Eisenhower, Charles Lindbergh, FDR, Winston Churchill, George C. Marshall, JFK, Lyndon Johnson, and others.

CreateSpace Independent Publishing (2012–2013)

The Books in the Series	**Chapter in this Catalog**
Book I: ***DUTY*** (1905 – 1919)	The World Wars (WWI)
Book II: ***HONOR*** (1920 – 1948)	The World Wars (WWII), Army Aviation
Book III: ***COUNTRY*** (1955 – 1969)	In the Far East (Vietnam), Army Aviation

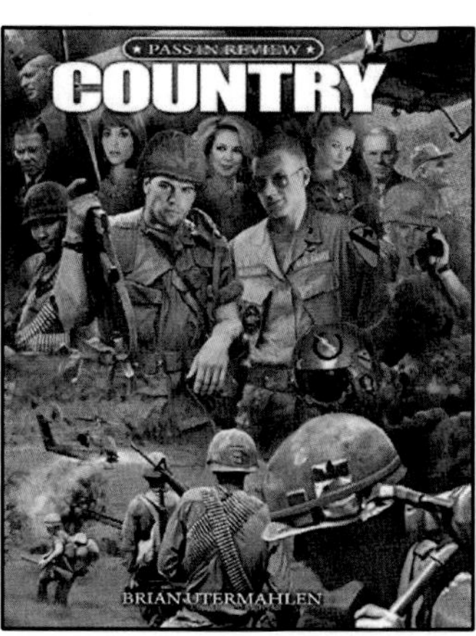

Brian Utermahlen (1946–) Class of 1968, was an infantry combat veteran and helicopter pilot with the 1st Air Cavalry Division in Vietnam. Following six years on active duty, he returned to civilian life as a manager for the DuPont Co. He flew helicopters for 12 years in the Delaware National Guard. [BC]

The Black Sabre Chronicles

The Sharps family of military men and women have a long history of service to the Army from the Buffalo Soldier era of the 19th century though World War I, World War II, Vietnam, and the Gulf War of the early 21st century.

Forge Press (1997–2003)

The Books in the Series		Chapter in this Catalog
Book I:	***Buffalo Soldiers***	Manifest Destiny
Book II:	***The Sable Doughboys***	World Wars (WWI)
Book III:	***Wings of Honor***	World Wars (WWII), Army Aviation
Book IV:	***The Stone Ponies***	In the Far East (Vietnam)
Book V:	***Sword of Valor***	Cold War & Global War on Terrorism, Army Aviation

Tom Willard (1934–) was born into a military family, quit high school to join the army and served as a paratrooper and combat medic in Vietnam. He was wounded in action and decorated with the Bronze Star with "V" device for valor, and the Purple Heart, among other medals. He is a University of North Dakota graduate who has lived in Europe, the Middle East, and Africa. [19-01]

The Brotherhood of War

This series of novels written between 1991 and 2002 is about the United States Army from the Second World War through the Vietnam War. The saga is focused on the careers of four U.S. Army officers who became lieutenants in the closing stages of World War II and progress through the ranks during the subsequent conflicts. The series is notable for the amount of attention it *does not* devote to combat. Between conflicts, it follows the main characters through their peacetime service as the army evolves in the 1940s, 1950s and 1960s, particularly in the development of Army Aviation and the Special Forces. Published by G. P. Putnam's Sons. [19-02]

The Lieutenants (1982)
Chapter: The World Wars

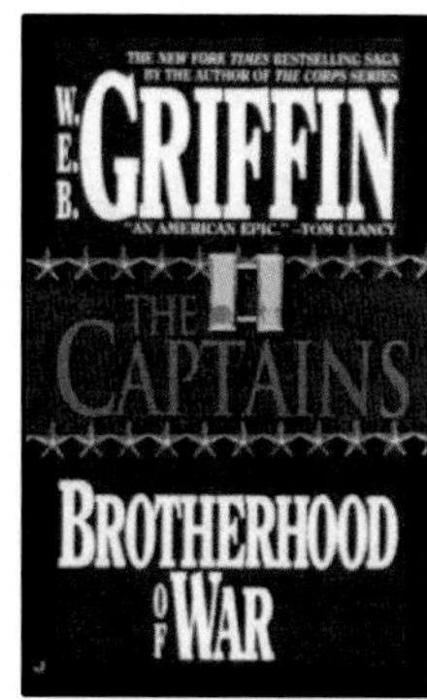

The Captains (1982)
Chapter: In the Far East

The Majors (1983)
Chapter: In the Far East

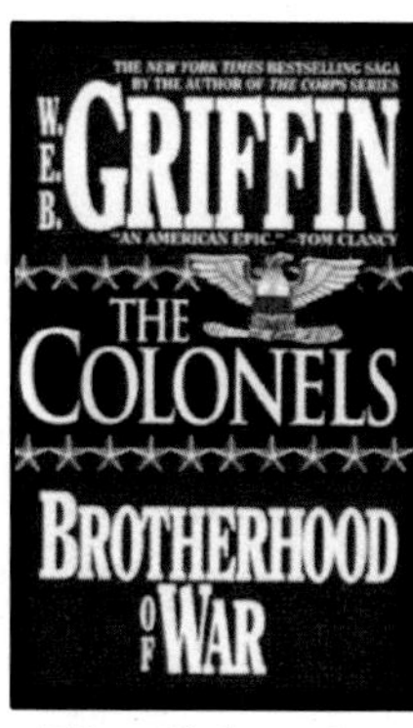

The Colonels (1983)
Chapter: The Cold War

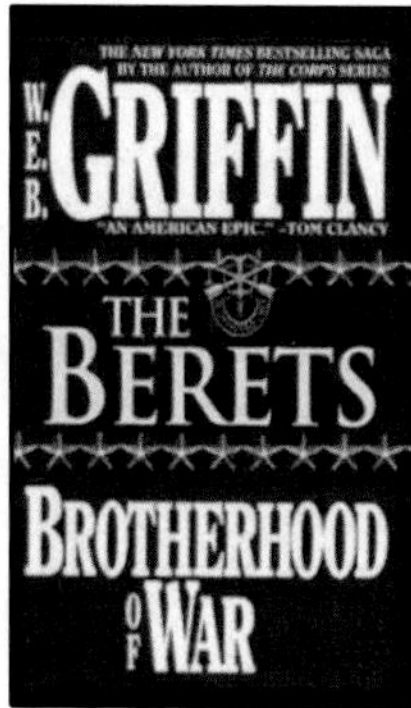

The Berets (1985)
Chapter: In the Far East

The Generals (1986)

The New Breed (1987)

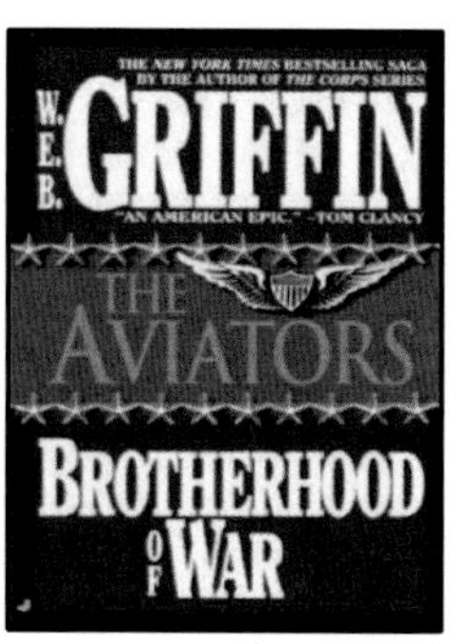

The Aviators (1988)
Chapter: Army Aviation

Special Ops (2001)
Chapter: The Cold War & Global War on Terror

William Edmund Butterworth III (1929–2019), better known by his pen name **W. E. B. Griffin**, was an American writer of military and detective fiction with 59 novels in seven series published under that name. Twenty-one of those books were co-written with his son, William E. Butterworth IV. He also authored another 190 books under various pseudo names. Butterworth entered the U.S. Army in 1946, was assigned to the Army of Occupation in Germany in Military Intelligence, and later recalled in 1951 to active duty in the Korean War. [19-03]

Here are two novels in which West Pointers and their wives serve through multiple wars and the intervening years. Not a parent and child legacy, but still legacies of service that are well worth reading. Both are included in the "Army Life & Army Wives" chapter.

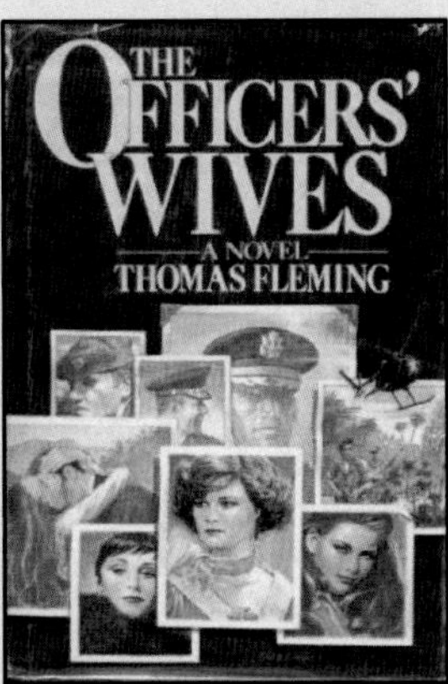

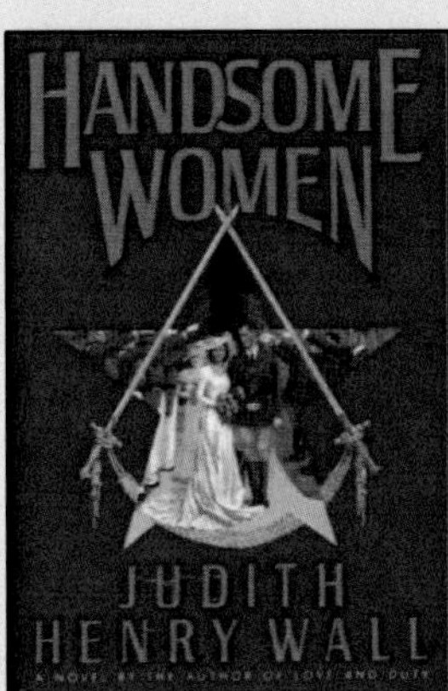

The Long Gray Line

Finally, here is one of the great stories of West Point and West Pointers. It is non-fiction; a memoir told by a third person about the Class of 1966 from R-Day through graduation, the Vietnam War and the decades that followed. It reads like a novel, focusing on the experiences and relationships of three cadets – Tom Carhart, Jack Wheeler, and George Crocker – through war and peace.

After leaving the service, Tom Carhart authored several non-fiction books about the Vietnam War, while Jack Wheeler championed the building to the Vietnam Memorial on the Washington Mall. George Crocker rose through the ranks to become a Lt. General before retiring in 1999.

The book was re-printed in 2019 as a 30th anniversary edition.

The Long Gray Line

Cadet, Vietnam

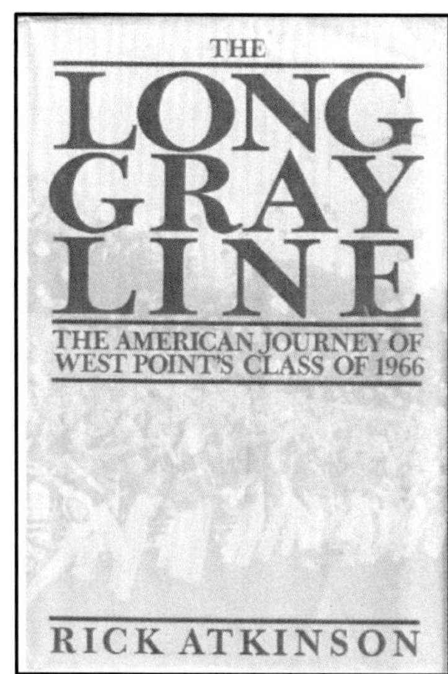

Rick Atkinson Houghton, Mifflin (1989)

Theirs was the dream of all young men: to become heroes. Inspired by John F. Kennedy's call to serve the nation, the West Point class of 1966 first gathered above the Hudson River on a glorious afternoon in July 1962. But as the cadets swore their oath of allegiance, they could not begin to imagine the dark journey that lay ahead. *The Long Gray Line* is the true story of that journey, an epic tale about an extraordinary generation of military officers and the women they loved.

This spellbinding narrative brings to life a rich cast of characters, including Douglas MacArthur, William Westmoreland, and a score of other memorable figures. Yet the story is told primarily through the lives of three classmates. Jack Wheeler, whose intelligence is surpassed only by his idealism, comes from a long line of soldiers, but gradually he discovers that he lacks any real appetite for the bloody art of war. Brash and impetuous Tom Carhart aspires to wear a general's stars, yet he is haunted by bad luck and his stubborn refusal to compromise his principles. George Crocker, born to lead troops through the dark of night, becomes ever more proficient as a warrior, and his story is the story of the Army over the past quarter century.

Rick Atkinson tracks the men of '66 through their high-spirited cadet years and into the fires of Vietnam, where dozens of them died and hundreds more grew disillusioned. During the hard peace that followed, they resigned from the Army in record numbers, only to find that civilian life offered no easy answers either. West Point — an institution of mythic proportions — remained a powerful influence in their lives, even as the academy itself weathered a period of profound change.

The tragic war, a shameful cheating scandal, the divisive questioning of the ideals upon which the academy had stood for nearly two centuries — all shook West Point to its foundation, forcing soldiers and civilians alike to reconsider the role of the military in a democratic society. Brilliantly conceived, eloquently written, *The Long Gray Line* tells a deeply affecting story that spans twenty-five turbulent years. The West Point class of 1966 straddled a fault line in American history, and Rick Atkinson's masterly book speaks for a generation about innocence, patriotism, and the price we pay for our dreams. [DJ]

Lawrence Rush "Rick" Atkinson IV (1952–) is an American author. After working as a newspaper reporter, editor, and foreign correspondent for *The Washington Post*, Atkinson turned to writing military history. His seven books include narrative accounts of five different American wars. He has won Pulitzer Prizes in history and journalism. [19-04]

Chapter 20

The Cold War & Global War on Terrorism

The Cold War

September 1945 – December 1991

The Cold War was an ideological, political, economic, and military conflict that developed after World War II when the Grand Alliance of the United States and Soviet Union, a "marriage of convenience" to defeat Germany, dissolved over irreconcilable differences. Tensions within the alliance developed during the war itself as both the US and the Soviet Union sought to shape a post-war world that favored their respective systems.

As a result, the stage was set that placed the world in two opposing camps–the US and its allies on one side, and the Soviet Union and its communist allies on the other. Fearful of an uncertain future, both nations competed for nearly half of a century to expand their ideologies through spheres of influence, alliances, economic supremacy, and military strength. A vast arms race featuring nuclear weapons played a central role in nearly every aspect of that competition, and the fear of a US-Soviet nuclear confrontation always underscored international tensions.

Although never directly engaging each other in war, both sides supported numerous regional and proxy wars in Korea, Vietnam, Central America, and elsewhere as the Cold War influenced and shaped political and military leaders spanning nine presidential administrations. By 1989, the Soviet Union collapsed economically and then completely dissolved by liberating the oppressed people of Eastern Europe and the former Soviet Union in its wake.

Text source - a memorial stone on the West Point golf course/
Photo elements - https://wallpaperaccess.com/nuclear-explosion

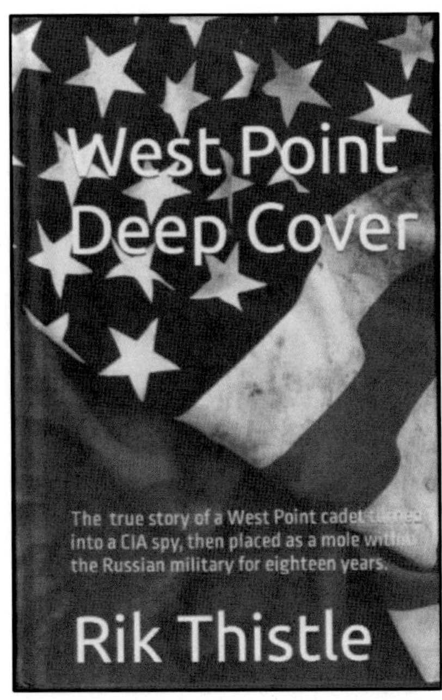

West Point Deep Cover

Cold War, Russia

Rik Thistle Red Barn Publishers (2022)

West Point Deep Cover is a historical spy thriller based on the true story of Mark Durden who, at the age of eighteen, joins the Unite States Army to escape a difficult home situation. Through a series of international happenstances, he wins an appointment to the Military Academy at West Point. He is recruited by the CIA as a deep cover spy within the USSR military. There he becomes Demitri Kamenev who, in less than eighteen years, advances to be the youngest Lieutenant Colonel in the Russian GRU with access to its most important nuclear secrets. During his meteoric rise within the military, he makes an enemy of a KGB officer whose life mission is to expose Mark as a spy. This Cold War novel is set in the 1960s - 1970s where the penalty for spying for the CIA is a quick death. [DJ]

Rik Thistle has written six novels, three of them based on bio-terrorism. He lives in San Diego, CA. [DJ]

Conclave

Cold War, Vatican, Poland, WP Author

Tom Davis Create Space Independent Publishing (2016)

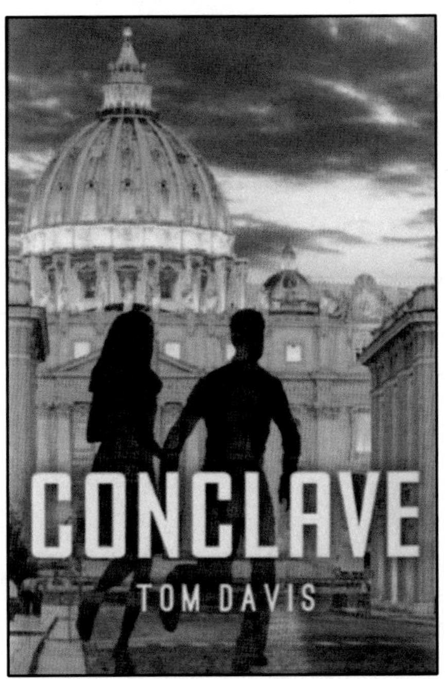

As the Cold War looms over Europe in 1978, Pope John Paul I dies after barely a month in office. Half a world away, Major Carter Caldwell, a junior member of the National Security Council, views the election of the next pope as a chance to diminish Moscow's clout in Eastern Europe. He persuades higher-ups that America should push for a non-Italian pope. There are just two hitches:

Someone must convince the cardinals at the conclave to choose the first non-Italian pope in five centuries.

And the Soviets are determined to keep an Italian on the papal throne.

Dispatched to Rome, Carter lands in the midst of a deadly struggle between CIA and KGB agents. Thrilling gunfights, exhilarating chases, sinister assassinations, and more await him as he takes a stand against the Soviets. [DJ]

Empty Quiver

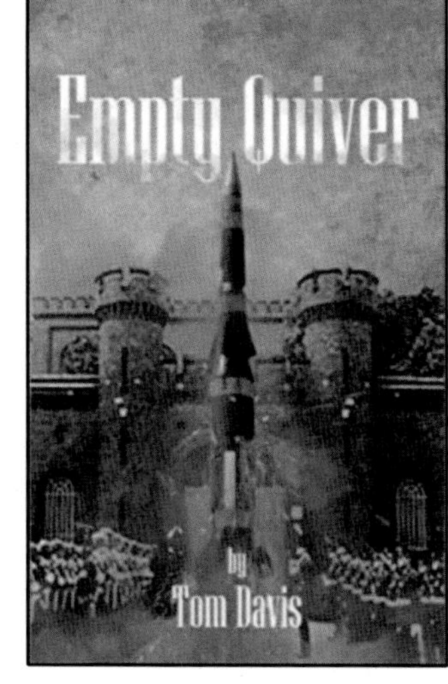

Cold War, Germany, WP Author

Tom Davis Independently Published (2022)

As the Soviet Union deploys its new SS-20 missile, the US decides to counter by stationing its new Pershing II missile in West Germany. But many Germans are opposed to having the new weapons on their soil, a resistance the Soviet KGB decides to exploit, no matter who they must team with to halt the US deployment.

In Washington, NSC staffer Carter Cardwell is sent to find out what forces are at work and what the KGB is up to. He brings with him CIA Analyst Katherine O'Connor, an expert on the Soviet Union with whom he has a personal relationship. Meanwhile, the KGB decides upon a very risky and complicated approach to broaden German opposition against the arrival of the new Pershings. The KGB chief responsible for Western Europe, Dimitry Zhukov, takes personal charge of the Soviet effort.

Carter, Katherine, and Zhukov have confronted each other before, but now find they must work together before a nuclear confrontation spins out of control as both sides discover they have to confront dark forces from the past in order to create the conditions for a more peaceful future. Will they succeed? Or will nuclear terrorists upset the nuclear balance? [DJ]

Tom Davis is a retired army officer and corporate executive. After graduating from West Point, he had numerous assignments and experiences in the army including commanding an artillery battalion in Operation Desert Storm, serving as an Assistant Professor of Social Sciences at West Point teaching International Relations, Political Science, Economics, and Middle Eastern Affairs. He served a brief tour in the Department of State as part of the Palestinian Autonomy negotiating team, where he heard a story that inspired *Conclave.* [20-01]

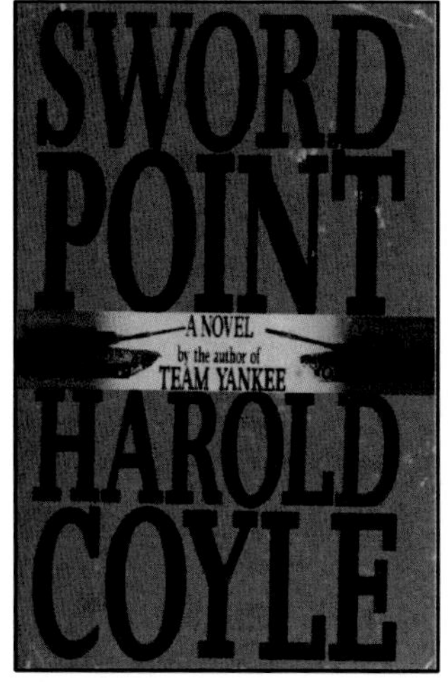

Sword Point

Cold War, Iran

Harold Coyle Simon & Schuster (1991)

Sword Point begins with an army at peace. as ordinary men and women—soldiers—go about their daily lives. unaware that thousands of miles away. the war they have been preparing for is about to begin. Sword Point begins the Soviet Union is on the eve of invading [ran to secure its borders against the spread of Moslem fundamentalism and to seize the Strait of Hormuz together with the free world's oil supply...

What makes Sword Point special is the human element: each character in Coyle's huge cast is unforgettable and sharply etched. from the young

American lieutenant thrust into combat for the first time to a Soviet officer who is repelled by the cold inhumanity of his KGB superior. The author takes us from the White House and the Kremlin to the battlefield. as the life of each character is changed—or brutally ended—by the rapidly escalating war. The stakes are raised with the Iranians reportedly on the verge of assembling a nuclear device. . . [DJ]

Trial by Fire

Cold War, Mexico, Armor

Harold Coyle Simon & Schuster (1992)

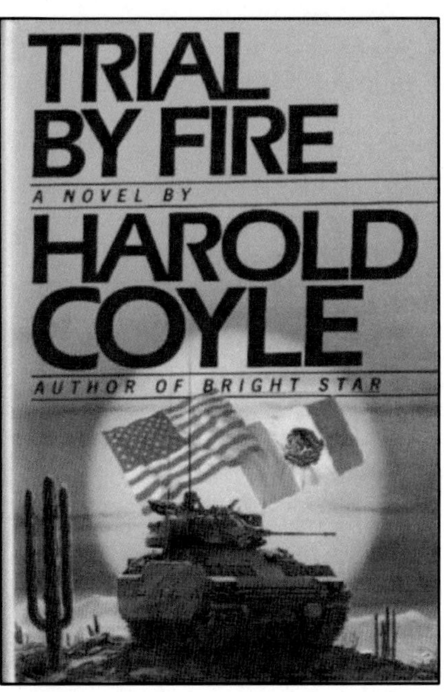

The United States is caught by surprise as a Mexican revolution suddenly destabilizes the most-2000-mile-long undefended border between the two countries. Diplomatic negotiations begin, but a series of savage cross-border attacks on American civilians forces the United States to mobilize its armed forces, invade Mexico and establish a security Zone. While the controversial invasion is debated, the United States Army must win quickly what could become a long, bloody war.

In Trial by Fire, Harold Coyle's memorable characters, from men and women soldiers to congressmen and correspondents, have achieved a new depth and realism, and such continuing characters from Sword Point and Bright Star as Scott Dixon, Harold Cerro, and Jan Fields, are more compelling than ever.

- Lt. Col. Scott Dixon, winner of the Medal of Honor, is troubled by the difficulties and justice of the invasion but committed to victory....

- Lt. Nancy Kozak has a double burden because she is one of the first female combat officers and is facing battle for the first time....

- Colonel Alfredo Guajardo, Defense Minister, and commander of the Mexican forces, knows that only through an exhausting war of attrition can he hope to defeat the United States....

- Jan Fields, gutsy, beautiful, and involved with Scott Dixon, is sending back to the United States explosive TV news stories about the Mexican government and armies....

- Hector Alaman, El Duefio, a legendary criminal overlord, is driven from his fortress by the revolution, while his mercenaries trigger a counterrevolutionary war....

- Congressman Ed Lewis is a smart, clear-eyed combat veteran who knows the United States shouldn't go blindly into battle, and who risks his life in Mexico to uncover the truth....

As these characters are caught in the swirl of revolution, bloody fighting, paralyzing controversy, and stark political realities, the United States and Mexico move deeper into mortal struggle. [DJ]

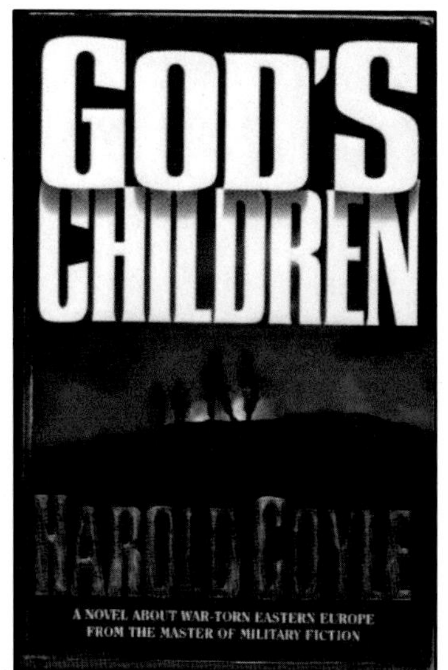

God's Children

Cold War, Balkans

Harold Coyle Forge Books (2000)

Peacekeeping is not child's play. *God's Children* is the story of the 3rd Platoon, C Company, 2nd Battalion of the 13th Infantry, and two young officers who attempt to keep a peace that is falling apart before their very eyes. Fresh from West Point, Second Lieutenant Gerald Reider finds himself thrust into the middle of this growing crisis. As a new platoon leader, he is eager to take on the challenges of command, but his superiors are not as confident.

Faced with an uncertain situation on the ground, the battalion commander sends a seasoned officer along with Reider during his first patrol. For First Lieutenant Nathan Dixon, the assignment to accompany the 3rd Platoon during a routine patrol is a welcome break from a staff assignment that he finds stifling and mundane. But Reider's first patrol quickly becomes anything but routine as ethnic tensions, so long held in check by the peacekeepers, break into open conflict. Caught in the middle, isolated from their parent unit, and assailed by both warring parties, the 3rd Platoon finds itself in a struggle for survival against overwhelming odds. [DJ]

Harold William "H.W." Coyle (1952–) is an American writer and author of historical and speculative fiction and of war novels. He graduated from the Virginia Military Institute in 1974, spent 14 years on active duty with the US Army, and is a veteran of the Persian Gulf War. [20-02]

The Common Defense

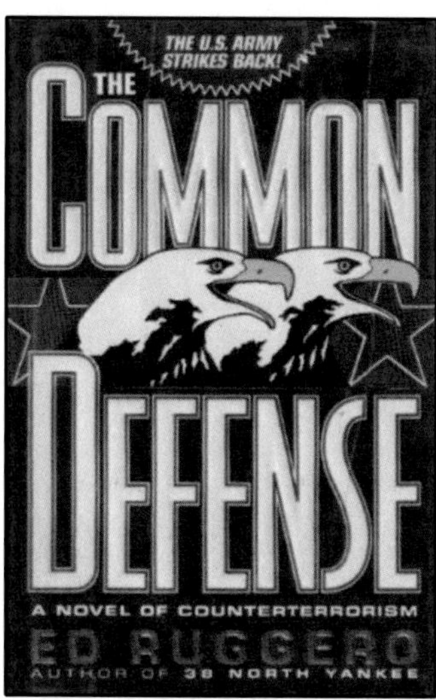

Cold War, Mexico, WP Author

Ed Ruggero Pocket Books (1992)

With the role of the U.S. Armed Forces rapidly changing, American servicemen and women are being called upon to fight a whole new kind of war. Captain Mark Isen is one of those men. The distinguished war hero of 38 North Yankee and the son of a Vietnam veteran, Isen arrives in Mexico on a mission to advise Mexican troops at war with heavily armed drug smugglers. There, amidst the dusty hills and mesas, he realizes that intervention is causing more problems than it's solving: the Mexicans resent the deployment of American military forces in their country.

Determined to get the job done, Isen helps build the fighting spirit of his Mexican troops. Then one conflict near a drug-ferrying airstrip lands him in the middle of a political firestorm. The Army brass leaves Isen twisting in the wind—until events halfway around the world change the nation's priorities.

A fastidious and calculating German terrorist has begun his own war against America. Heinrich Wolf captured the attention of the Joint Chiefs of Staff and the President with a deadly bomb set off on a U.S.

base in Germany. Financed by the Soviet Union but spinning quickly out of control, Wolf aims to force the U.S. Navy's withdrawal from the Mediterranean and to weaken the will of the President. He and his small organization of terrorists are stockpiling a deadly arsenal of explosives and nerve gas in Mexico, to be used ultimately against the United States. When he strikes within American borders, it is clear to the world that Heinrich Wolf is succeeding at his mission.

Delta Force, the U.S. Army's elite counterterrorist unit, is sent to Mexico by the White House to stop Wolf. There, they request the assistance of Captain Mark Isen; the team needs his special knowledge of the territory and the people. Wolf will carry out his ultimate strike in less than forty-eight hours—a precisely-timed attack on an innocent crowd of millions. Working with Delta Force Special Operations Major Ray Spano and a rule-breaking NCO named Worden, Isen is trying desperately to stop him. While the White House Situation Room prepares for the worst, Delta Force follows the quickening maneuvers of Wolf's network in Mexico, hunting for the man who'd soon launch the chemical weapons. [DJ]

Ed Ruggero (1956–) graduated from West Point in 1980, served as an infantry officer, and was teaching English at West Point when he wrote this, his first novel. See chapters "Mystery, Crime & Intrigue," "The World Wars," and "Army Medical Service Corps" for other novels in this collection. [20-03]

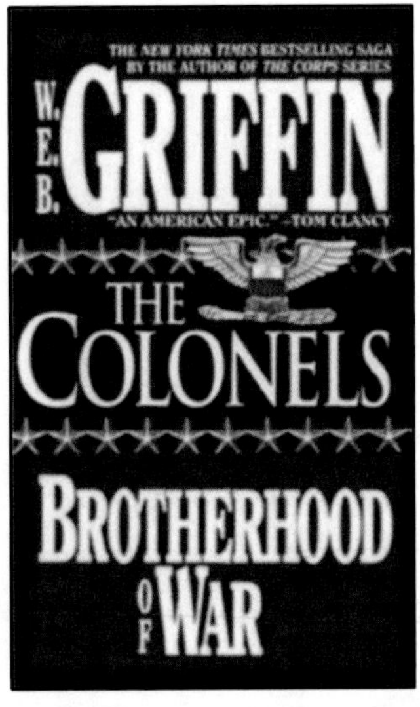

The Colonels

Cold War, Cuba, Green Berets

W.E.B. Griffin G. P. Putnam (1983)

They were the professionals, the men who had been toughened by combat in the mine-laden fields of Europe, in Korea, in Greece, in Indochina. Now, in the twilight of a dying decade, they must return to the United States to forge a new type of American soldier—one to be tested on the beaches of Cuba and in a new war yet to come... [BC]

"It mostly takes place in the aftermath of the Christmas 1958 events at the end of [its prequel] *The Majors*...A full third of it is run-up to a New Year's Eve party a week later, bringing many principal characters together, and affecting the career of one.

Our characters fret their failure, so far, to get promoted. Lowell and Parker have black marks on their records. Felter has to keep a low profile; a civilian cover for his intelligence ties means he isn't even identified usually as military. MacMillan is still a non-com at heart and will never master the bureaucratic skills a field-grade officer needs as much as, if not more than, battlefield ones.

The book has romantic stirrings, something Griffin tends to do in series installments when external events are in a lull. Lowell, whose roving has jeopardized his career, launches another affair, this with a prominent townsman's wife, and is found out. Greer's brand-new widow, Melody, scandalizes people when she starts seeing another man way too soon.

There's development of yet another new fighting branch – the Green Berets. Felter and Lowell's old CO from the Greek civil war, Hanrahan, has been given the unenviable mission of launching a special forces unit without visible support from higher up in authority. Felter, as Eisenhower's aide, possesses fearsome clout but can't run interference on this one...

One thing I like about this series is how well Griffin works in the Army's modernization of itself after World War II. Most of our characters distinguished themselves as tankers there or in Korea, then moved on to other fields such as paratroops. But the farsighted see that these won't figure much in upcoming wars. Gunships and special forces will. And Griffin lets us see, through his characters, how they develop and despite resistance from much of the brass.

The winds of war are brewing. Vietnam and the Bay of Pigs are just around the corner." [20-04]

Special Ops

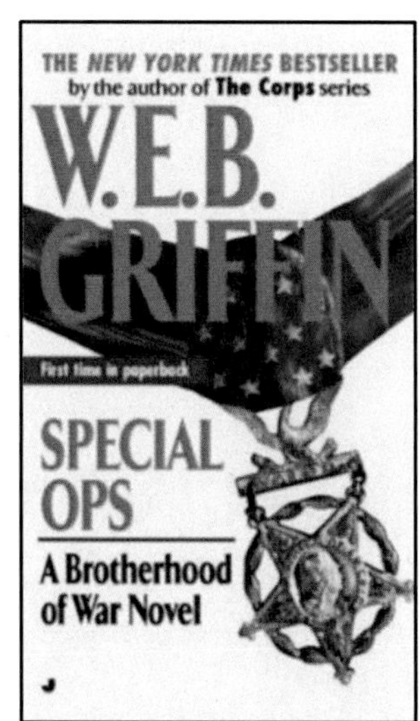

Cold War, Cuba, Congo

W.E.B. Griffin G. P. Putnam (2001)

In November 1964, Cuban revolutionary Che Guevara went to the Congo with two hundred men, intent on making it his first step in taking over Africa and South America.

He failed, thanks in large part to the efforts of an intrepid band of Green Berets. Licking his wounds, he retreated to Cuba to recruit more men and try the same thing in Bolivia.

He failed there, too.

In fact, he died there, and thus, despite his incompetence, became a glorious martyr to the cause. But who was trying to kill him, really—and who was trying to keep him alive?

The brotherhood is back—Craig Lowell, Sandy Felter, Jack Portet, Geoff Craig, Robert Bellmon, George Washington "Father" Lunsford, Master Sergeant Doubting Thomas—and their mission has never been more dramatic and deadly... [BC]

William Edmund Butterworth III (1929–2019), better known by his pen name, **W.E.B. Griffin**, was an American writer of military and detective fiction with 59 novels in seven series published under that name. See "The West Point Legacies" chapter for a more complete bio and other novels in this series.

Drums of War - Book #2 of "A Full Measure Trilogy"

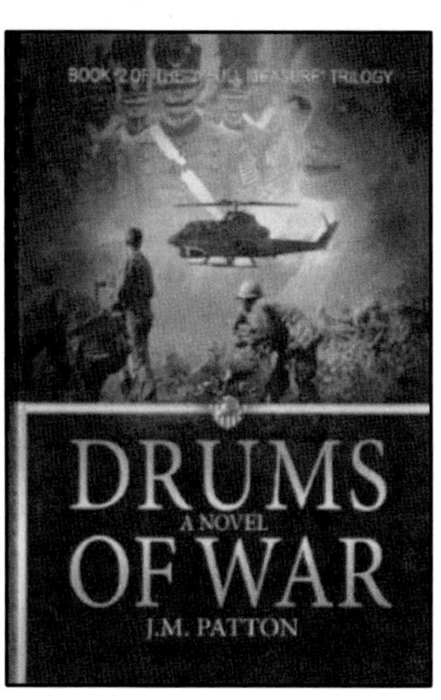

Aviation, Viet Nam, Cold War, WP Author

Joseph M. Patton PublishAuthority (2021)

Following a personal tragedy and their graduation from West Point, Jake Jacobs and Patrick McSwain don the army blue to fulfill their obligation to the United States Army by serving in the combat arms. Jake goes to the Green Berets at a time when Special Forces were resented by conventional units and near extinction. Patrick becomes a Huey Cobra helicopter pilot, risking his life to support troops on the ground with a weapon terrifyingly capable of tearing things up. Both young men arc dedicated warriors, and the women who love them find that Duty-Honor-Country has also become their way of life.

The Vietnam War is in its final throes of agony for the American military while another enemy, encouraged by the Cold War, forms a future threat that will test the resolve and adaptability of America to enemies foreign and domestic. As a Green Beret, Jake finds himself leading the last inland mission in South Vietnam and is quickly thrust into combat with terrorist hijackings and their death-dealing use of chemical weapons on American soil. A demoralized military makes for uncertain careers, shifting internal politics at the highest levels of command, and military families suffering the indignities of honorable military service out of public favor. [BC]

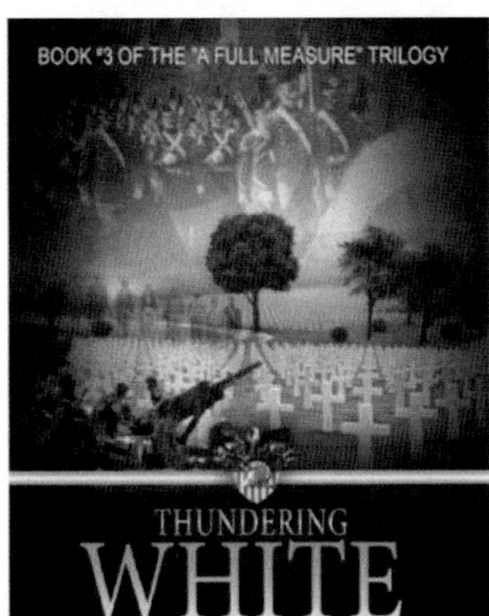

Thundering White Crosses - Book #3 of "A Full Measure Trilogy"

Cold War, WP Author

Joseph M. Patton PublishAuthority (2023)

Thundering White Crosses presents a set of complex themes with contemporary repercussions. When assigned back at West Point as an instructor, Jake Jacobs finds that the institution of his affection is changing, driven by the winds of political whims and a shifting national culture. Jake questions if the future of West Point can remain true to its mission and provide the nation with the same continuity of military leadership as it has in the past or will all the academies become a casualty of the Capital Beltway.

Rumors have circled for years of a high-level Soviet mole. If true, this mole is the most dangerous traitor the nation has experienced. A compulsion to find this mole is forced upon Jake. It is a duty, and it has become personal. Running parallel to the search, someone is vetting and assassinating corrupt politicians, labeling them as domestic enemies. Jake's search for the mole takes him to Afghanistan, to Operation Urgent Fury in Grenada, and to the most dangerous environment --- the halls of Capitol Hill. If the first two books of the trilogy were a rollercoaster ride, Thundering White Crosses accelerates that ride and exhilarates the reader with compelling twists and turns. [BC]

Joseph "Mike" Patton (1951–), after two years at New Mexico Military Academy, entered West Point with the Class of 1973. He was given a medical discharge after his yearling year. He continued his education and earned a degree in mathematics at Baylor University. After successful years with a large U.S. computer company, his career evolved to various management positions in finance, banking, and securities. All three novels in the "Full Measure" trilogy are included in this collection. [BC]

The Global War on Terror

September 2001 to the Current Day 2023

The war on terror, officially the Global War on Terrorism (GWOT), is an ongoing international military campaign initiated by the United States following the September 11 attacks. The targets of the campaign are primarily Islamic terrorist groups, with prominent targets including al-Qaeda and the Islamic State of Iraq and the Levant (ISIL).

The "war on terror" uses war as a metaphor to describe a variety of actions which fall outside the traditional definition of war that are taken to eliminate international terrorism. The 43rd President of the United States, George W. Bush, first used the term "war on terrorism" on September 16, 2001, and then "war on terror" a few days later in a formal speech to Congress. Bush indicated the enemy of the war on terror as "a radical network of terrorists and every government that supports them." The initial conflict was aimed at al-Qaeda, with the main theater in Afghanistan and Pakistan…

The Obama administration sought to avoid use of the term and instead preferred to use the term Overseas Contingency Operation. On May 23, 2013, Obama announced that the Global War on Terrorism was over, indicating that the U.S. would not wage war against a tactic but would instead focus on a specific group of terrorist networks. The rise of ISIL led to the global Operation Inherent Resolve, and an international campaign to destroy the terrorist organization.

The notion of a "War on Terror" was contentious, with critics charging that it has been used to reduce civil liberties and infringe upon human rights, such as controversial actions by the U.S. including surveillance, torture, and extraordinary rendition, and drone strikes that resulted in the deaths of suspected terrorists but also civilians. Many of the U.S. actions were supported by other countries, including the 54 countries that were involved with CIA black sites, or those that assisted with drone strikes. [20-05]

This obscure novel, *Autumn on the Hudson,* was certainly prescient – twelve years before 9/11. It is an exciting read, especially so for those who have attended a football game at Michie Stadium! This novel and the ones that follow, *Let Them Die at West Point* and *With Honor in Hand,* are the only ones in the collection depicting a terrorist attack on West Point.

Autumn on the Hudson

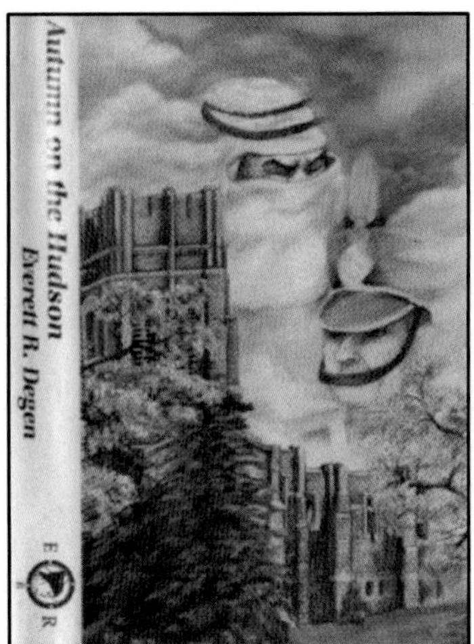

Global War on Terror, Sports, Crime

Everett R. Degen E&R Publishing (1989)

Ali Bengali is a soldier who has come out of the desert from a Middle Eastern country to accomplish a specific mission of revenge against the United States of America…

In the United States, it is the Fall of the year, the foliage at its peak in color. College football games are number one popularity among spectator sports, and for the first time ever the two leading candidates for the prestigious Heisman trophy play for the military academies. One is the wide receiver for Army, while the second contender is the quarterback for the Air Force team. The final game of the season will find the two cadets facing on the same playing field as the rival teams meet at West Point…

On the day of the game, the stadium at West Point is filled to capacity with fans, and there are important dignitaries among them. During the contest, while many of the fans at home are viewing the game over their lunch, Ali makes his move. The surprise of an unexpected attack witnessed on national television exposes a vulnerability that can only be compared to Pearl Harbor and its effect on the American people. Unlike Pearl Harbor, where the Japanese were immediately identified as the perpetrators, no one person or group steps forward to claim responsibility for the disaster at West Point. A shocked and angered nation has no one to retaliate against.

With his primary mission successfully completed, Ali decides to humble the authorities even more as he moves on to the alternative target he had been given if West Point proved an impossible task. He heads for the Air Force Base near Alamogordo, New Mexico, the home of the largest tactical fighter wing in the United States Air Force. [DJ]

Everett R. Degan (1941–2015) served in the U.S. Air Force as a flight nurse in Vietnam. He was awarded the Air Commendation Medal for outstanding airmanship and courage under hazardous conditions. Degan retired as a major and resided in Plattsburgh, NY. [20-06]

Let Them Die at West Point

GWOT, Mystery Intrigue

Carl Markowitz Self-Published (2022)

The United States Military Academy at West Point is scheduled to host a two-week mid-summer seminar For NATO security personnel and families. The opening dinner of the seminar will be attended by the President of the United States, the First Lady, the Joint Chiefs of Staff and their spouses…. It has, however, come to the attention of terrorists in four Middle Eastern countries who are jointly planning an attack on West Point.

The story follows Army Captain Casey Saint-Clair, an intelligence officer attached to the Pentagon, Navy Commander, Ramon Rodriguez, a SEAL team commander, and the Israeli Mossad, as they attempt to thwart the impending attack. [BC]

Carl S. Markowitz was raised in Hampton, Virginia, attended the University of Virginia and received his Juris Doctor from the College of William & Mary. He practiced law for 45 years in Norfolk, VA, before retiring. This is his second novel. [BC]

With Honor in Hand

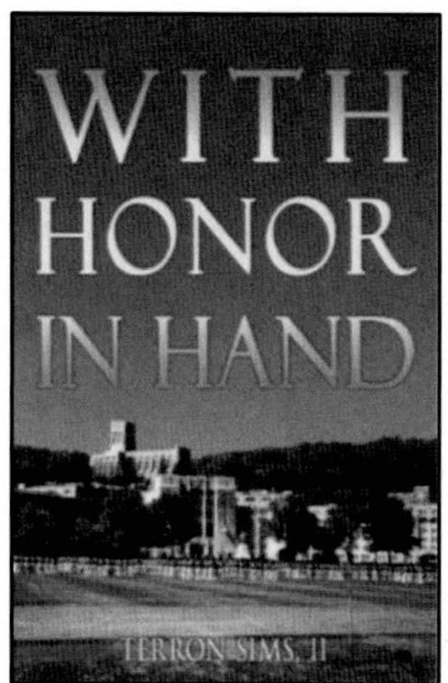

Black Cadet, GWOT, Intrigue, WP Author

Terron Sims II iUniverse (2010)

With *Honor in Hand* is the tale of two friends battling with a serious moral dilemma—a fight between the code of their profession vs. their code of honor. Mercenaries, the two friends, Douglas "Big Mac" Pollard and Amos "Man Killer" Stewart, are the truest of professionals and the best at what they do. They have never reneged on a contract, but now find themselves in a position where they wish they could exercise that option.

As *With Honor in Hand* progresses, the cold-hearted [Serbian] Colonel Drasneb unfolds his vengeful plan which strains Mac and Killer's moral fiber: destroying the West Point Corps of Cadets. Through the course of the explosive action, a newly tested hero emerges from among the chaos to save his brothers and sisters of the Corps. [BC]

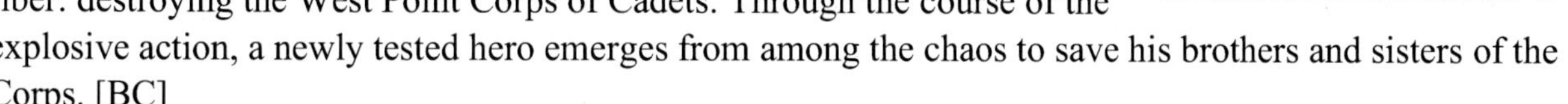

Hands of Honor

Black Cadet, GWOT, Intrigue, WP Author

Terron Sims II iUniverse (2011)

Friendship is a cherished and highly coveted quality, yet it is rarely ever properly expressed or truly put to the test. In Hands of Honor, the interlinking friendships of three men are put to the test when their friends—Marcos Bakoos, Major Johnson and Ben Irons——take off for a fun-filled and much-deserved New Year's vacation to Marcos's hometown of Beirut, Lebanon.

Before the festivities begin, suspected Islamic terrorists hijack their flight. Marcos, a lieutenant in the Lebanese Army and the son of Lebanon's president, is kidnapped and held for ransom. Major and Ben must use their skills acquired in Army Ranger training to free Marco. They reach out to a mysterious acquaintance from their past to pull off a daring rescue attempt.

Breaking with protocol and violating direct orders from their superiors, Major and Ben risk their lives for that of their friend, understanding that true friendship supersedes rules and regulations. During their mission, they realize their actions are tangled in a dangerous web with ancient ties. They discover the incident surrounding their actions is but one part of a grander plan—the outcome over which they have no control. [BC]

Terron Sims, II (1977–) graduated from West Point in 2000. An Iraq Veteran, he was key in helping establish Baghdad's local governments and was the Wasit Province primary military liaison officer. Terron currently Chairs the DNC's Veterans & Military Families Council. He lives in Arlington, Virginia. [BC]

Sword of Valor: Black Sabre Chronicles #5

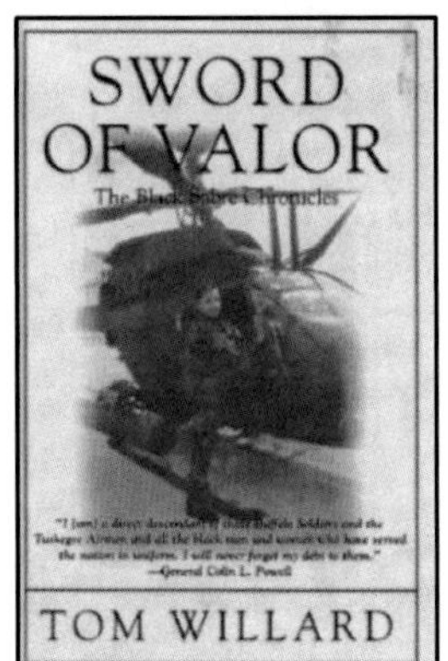

Gulf War, Female, Aviation

Tom Willard Forge (2003)

Tom Willard's critically acclaimed Black Sabre Chronicles trace the 130-year history of the Sharps military family from the time of the Western Indian Wars through the two World Wars, Vietnam, and, in this fifth and final novel, the Gulf War of 1990–1991.

Lieutenant Argonne Sharps is a West Pointer and the only black woman to pilot a Kiowa reconnaissance helicopter in the 101st Airborne "Screaming Eagles" division. She is assigned to the Persian Gulf in preparation for the 101st's deployment-to Saudi Arabia in Operation Desert Shield, and in its behind-the-lines assault into lraq in Operation Desert Storm.

Her valor in "extracting" Special Forces, officer Jerome Moody from Kuwait City, earns Argonne a Bronze Star citation and Moody's undying gratitude - and love. Argonne's experiences in the Gulf War impact her family at the Black Sabre Ranch in Arizona, where they confront feelings of pride and anxiety as their beloved daughter becomes the first woman, and the fifth generation of Sharps, to go to war.

Tom Willard's intimate knowledge of combat—earned in Vietnam—gives Sword of Valor a special ring of authenticity as the brief, high-tech war unfolds, and the Sharps family's history of military service reaches a dramatic climax. [DJ]

Tom Willard (1934–) authored five books in the Black Sabre Chronicles. See *"The West Point Legacies"* chapter for the other books in this collection.

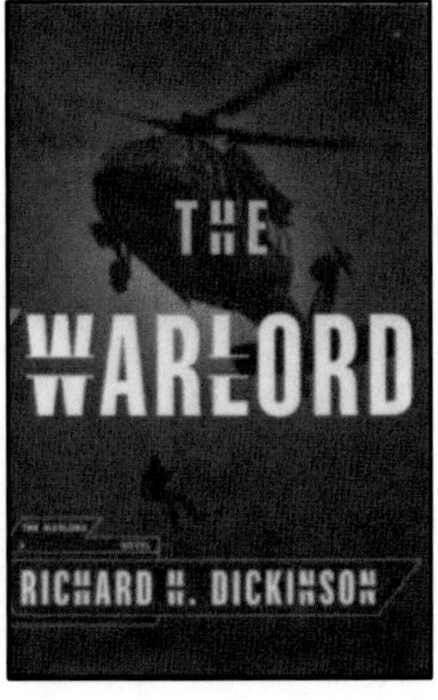

The Warlord: A Jackson Monroe Novel

Afghanistan, WP Author

Richard H. Dickinson Rugged Land Press (2004)

Meet three-star general Jackson Monroe, a character very much based on four-star general Colin Powell.

What would happen if a polished middle-aged man like Powell found himself shot down in the mountains of Afghanistan and surrounded by the enemy? Trying to make his way across hostile territory, evading, feinting, fighting, and then avenging, Monroe finally finds the commando he once was and the commander he always wanted to be. [DJ]

Acts of Honor

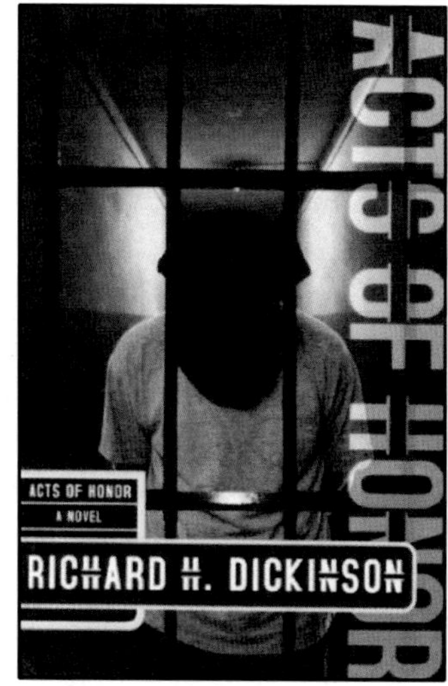

Iraq, WP Author

Richard H. Dickinson Book Surge Publishing (2008)

For Morgan Buckner, guard duty at Abu Ghraib prison turns deadly during the fall of 2003 when his only friend is murdered during a prison riot. The young soldier exacts his revenge in a manner that elicits valuable information from the murderous prisoner but violates the Geneva Conventions. When the information pays dividends that save American lives, General Robert Tannerbeck must decide whether to put the welfare of his men ahead of international law and his own personal honor. But when U.S. Marines capture an American journalist embedded with Sunni terrorists, the resulting chain of events leads to corruption at the highest levels of the military, within Congress, and at the U.S. Military Academy at West Point. Throughout it all, General Tannerbeck fights a losing battle to retain his honor, while Buckner comes to embrace the concepts of Duty, Honor, and Country. [BC]

Richard H. Dickinson (1951–) was commissioned from West Point into the U.S. Airforce, spending twelve years as a hurricane hunter and air traffic controller. [DJ] He has written several military thrillers which are included in the "Army Aviation" and "In the Far East" chapters, but Jackson Monroe only appears in one other of them....as a sniper in Vietnam!

Spirit Mission

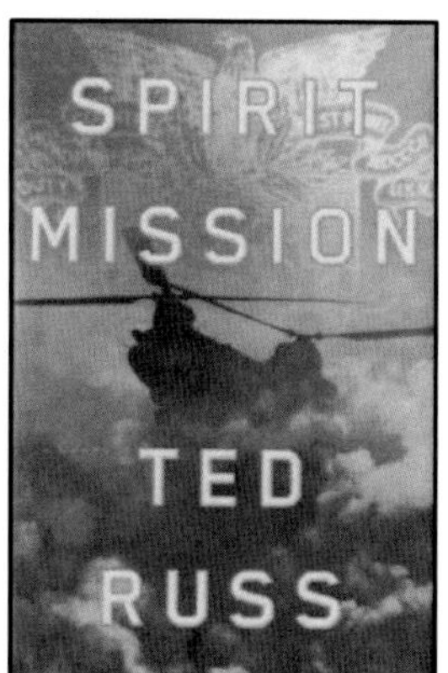

Iraq, WP Author

Ted Russ Henry Holt and Co. (2016)

To honor bonds forged twenty-five years ago at West Point, Lt. Colonel Sam Avery leads an illegal mission deep into ISIS-held territory.

An MH-47G Chinook helicopter departs formation in the Iraqi night. The mission is unauthorized. The objective is reckless. Success is unlikely. But to save a friend, Sam Avery and his crew of Night Stalkers have prepared for one last flight.

ISIS operatives in Tal Afar, Iraq, have captured American aid worker Henry Stillmont. Avery knows Stillmont as "the Guru," the West Point squad leader who twenty-five years ago taught the young cadet about brotherhood, loyalty, and when to break the rules. Sam will risk his career and his life to save him.

As they near their target, Sam reflects on his time in the crucible of the United States Military Academy. West Point made Sam the leader he is. But his fellow cadets made him the man that he is. The ideals of duty, honor, and country have echoed throughout his life and drive him and his comrades as they undertake their final and most audacious spirit mission. [DJ]

Ted Russ is a graduate of the United States Military Academy at West Point. He served as an officer and helicopter pilot ultimately with the 160th Special Operations Aviation Regiment. After leaving the Army in 2000, he received an MBA from Emory University and now lives in Georgia. [DJ]

Engagement

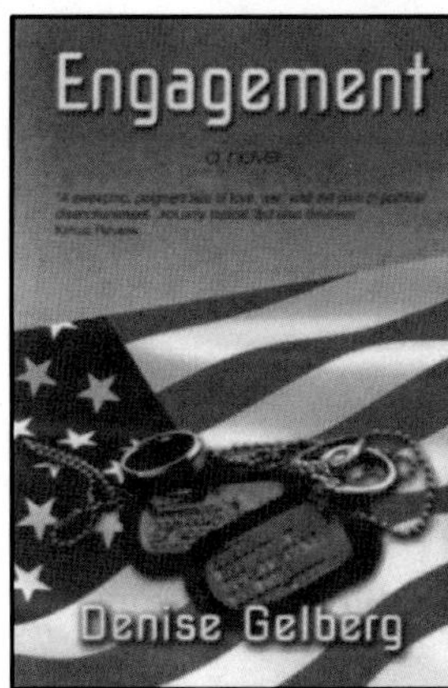

GWOT Iraq, Romance

Denise Gelberg Self-published (2016)

Engagement is the story of young lovers separated by war in the aftermath of the 9/11 terrorist attacks. As Tomas goes off to serve in Operation Iraqi Freedom, Sunny takes her first teaching job in a school that serves children from military families. Soon the future they envision is twisted by war's stark realities. It is a glimpse into the rationale and complexities of the Iraqi War as seen through the eyes of a conservative-leaning West Point cadet and his liberal fiancé. [BC]

Denise Gelberg is the author of *Fertility: A Novel,* and numerous articles on education. An advocate for children, Denise has written about the current state of education in the United States, including the book, *The "Business" of Reforming American Schools.* 20-07

In the Shadow Strike Series, David Rivers, West Pointer, an elite-level assassin and veteran operator who has served as a Ranger and a mercenary now leads a CIA contract team in covert action around the world to rout out terrorist threats. The David Rivers character can be found again in Jason Kasper's other series of books located in the "Mystery, Crime, and Intrigue" chapter.

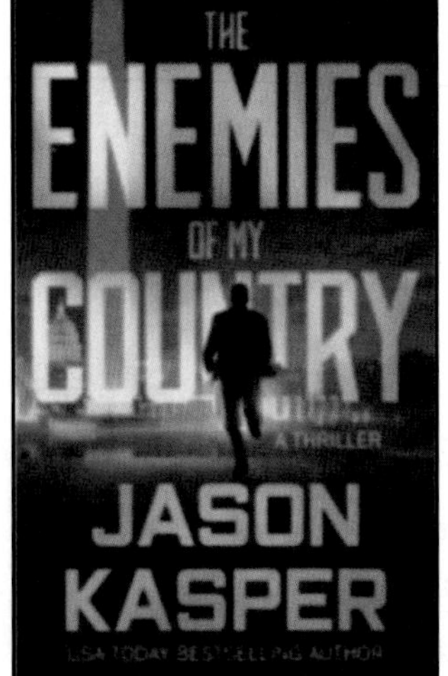

Enemies of My Country

GWOT, Intrigue, WP Author

Jason Kasper Severn River Publishing (2021)

David Rivers is an elite-level assassin. A veteran operator who has served as a Ranger, a mercenary, and now as a CIA contractor conducting covert action around the world.

In his secluded mountain home in Virginia, however, David Rivers lives the quiet life of a family man. His cover legend is so strong that even his wife doesn't know the true nature of his work.

Half a world away, on a mission to assassinate a foreign operative, Rivers uncovers intelligence pointing to an imminent attack on US soil. Now he must hunt down the terrorists before it's too late, but there was something impossibly chilling about this particular intel. The target is in his hometown…and David Rivers' wife and daughter are mentioned by name. [BC]

Last Target Standing

Severn River Publishing (2021)

After the largest terrorist attack in US history is narrowly foiled, the sole enemy survivor has only one name to provide his interrogators: Ghulam Samedi, a fugitive hiding in the rugged mountains of China's Xinjiang Province. [BC]

Covert Kill

Severn River Publishing (2021)

When American citizens in Nigeria are kidnapped and held for ransom, David Rivers and his team of CIA contractors find themselves enveloped in an international firestorm. [BC]

Narco Assassins

Severn River Publishing (2022)

David Rivers chases an elusive narco-assassin through the jungles of Colombia in this explosive assassination thriller… [BC]

Jason Kasper enlisted in the US Army in June 2001serving in Afghanistan and Iraq before attending West Point. Upon returning from his final deployment in 2016 as a Green Beret team commander, Jason began his second career as an author. [20-08]

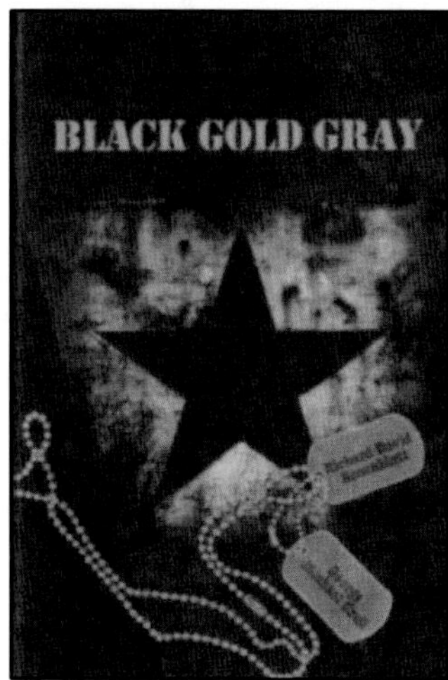

Black Gold Gray

GWOT, WP Author

Richard Rosenblatt & George Crall Maximilian Books (2008)

This saga is based on the composite actual lives of eight outstanding West Point 1949 classmates who survived WWII, the Korean War, and Vietnam, and then went on a secret mission in 2004. The action moves from Saudi Arabia to Iraq, through Germany and into Paris, down to Morocco, and into the Sahara. This exposé reveals conspiracies in Washington, London, and the Middle East and the reasons for American military involvement in Iraq. The authors assert that this story is fictional. The events and characters described are imaginary. [DJ]

Richard Rosenblatt (1926–2018) graduated from West Point in 1949 after serving in the Air Force during WW2. He later completed Air Force pilot training and served in Germany, France, and Morocco and as a linguist in those countries. In 1968, he founded a media advertising company and won four medals in the San Diego Senior Olympics at the age of eighty. [DJ]

George Crall (1923–?) He served in WW2 before attending West Point, graduating in 1949 and commissioned in the Marine Corps retiring years later from the reserve as a Colonel. He then entered the construction business later managing major industrial projects throughout Africa and the Middle East. Another of his works is included in the chapter "The World Wars." [DJ]

West Point Warlord

GWOT, Afghanistan, WP Author

Dr. Patrick D. O'Farrell   Dennis R. O'Farrell
CreateSpace Publishing

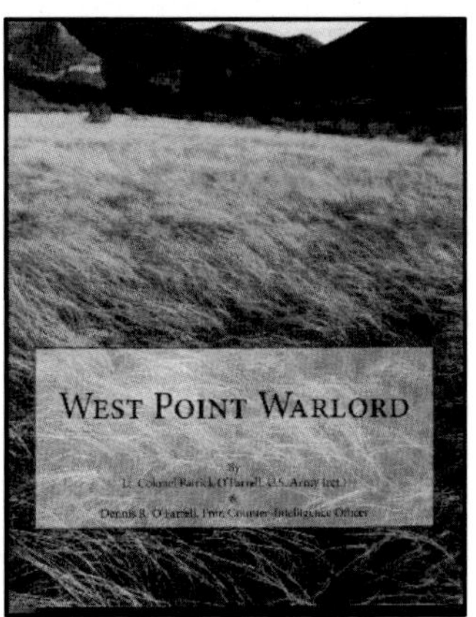

The author comments: "I have had the opportunity to fight various locations across the planet...places like Somalia, Afghanistan, Northern Iraq, Pakistan as well as other places U.S. forces are not supposed to be."

One of these places is well detailed in "West Point Warlord." Although the book is a work of fiction, it incorporates situations that have truly happened. It accurately depicts life in the combat zone, challenges faced by warriors in combat, humor -- in some cases, very dark humor, a camaraderie and love that is experienced daily by our soldiers, sailors, airmen, and marines. It is a fascinating story written via open source, unclassified sources detailing a West Point graduate's battle against an Al-Qaeda arch enemy. Qand Agha, an evil, murderous Afghan warlord attempting to disrupt American Operations in Afghanistan.

This novel gets its authentic feeling of true Army life based on the real life experiences of the authors -- an Academy graduate, career Army officers with combat experience in Afghanistan during the early days of Operation Enduring Freedom. It moves from the parade field at West Point along the banks of the Hudson River, to the attacks of September 11 at the Pentagon, to a combat deployment to Afghanistan. The story culminates in an exciting [battle] along the rugged mountainside of Northern Afghanistan. [DJ]

Dennis R. O'Farrell – A former U.S. Army Officer and University of Wyoming graduate with a degree in Journalism. Dennis is father to William and Patrick O'Farrell, both Army veterans with combat service in Desert Storm and Operation Enduring Freedom. **Patrick D. O'Farrell** (1960 –) West Point Class of 1982 is a career Army officer who served in Afghanistan during the early days of Operation Enduring Freedom, 2002-2003. Pat is an Airborne-Ranger and holds an MBA & Ph.D. He retired as a Lt. Col in 2004. 20-09

Chapter 21
Poetry, Drama & Film

Poetry

The earliest fictional references to West Point were poetic. General William H. Carter writing in a 1900 monograph on *West Point in Literature* observed:

> "West Point seated in the romantic Highlands, in the shadow of Cro' Nest, and guarding, as it were, the very throat of the majestic Hudson where it breaks through the mountain barriers on its way to the sea has been the scene of many historic incidents which have left an impression upon us who have lingered there. There is an old West Point tradition that the talented young author, Joseph Rodman Drake, conceived the quaint idea of "The Culprit Fay," as a result of a bantering wager in the Mess, that no tale of love without the human element could be made of interest. Whether this tradition is wholly true, the fact remains that young Drake received his inspiration under the shadow of Cro' Nest and his West Point elfins, goblins, sprites and fairies will live as long as American verse received the honor that is its due."

Poetry has regularly been offered up by West Point cadets, as we shall see in the pages that follow.

West Point Tic Tacs: A Collection of Military Verse

Poetry, Songs, Drawings

Bret Harte Homer Lee & Company (1878)

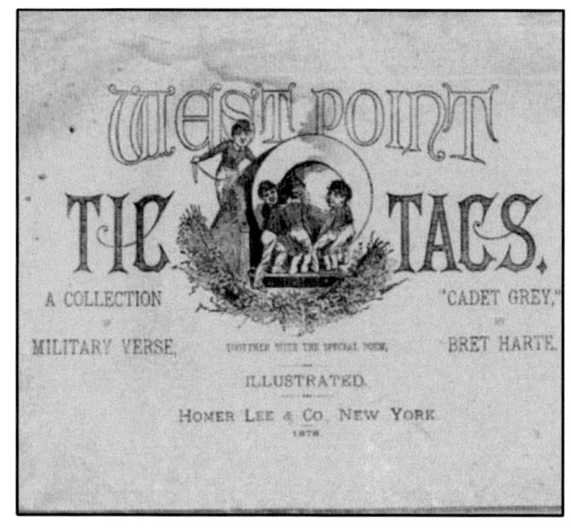

This large anthology was assembled by the American poet Bret Harte. It is more fully described in the chapter, "Remembering the Old Corps."

It is a very hard-to-find work in it original form, but re-prints are available.

The Culprit Fay

Poetry

Joseph Rodman Drake   Rudd & Carleton (1820)

“West Point, seated in the romantic Highlands, in the shadow of Cro’ Nest, and guarding, as it were, the very throat of the Hudson where it breaks through the mountain barrier on its way to the sea, has been the scene of many historic incidents which have left an impression on all who lingered there. There is an old West Point tradition that the talented young author, Joseph Rodman Drake, conceived the quaint idea of “The Culprit Fay” as a result of a bantering wager at The Mess, that no tale of love without human element could be made of interest. Whether the tradition be wholly true, the fact remains the young Drake received his inspiration under the shadow of Cro’ Nest, and his West Point elfins, goblins, sprites, and fairies will live as long as American verse receives the honor that is its due.”

From *West Point in Literature* by Brigadier General Wm. Carter, Lord Baltimore Press, 1909

TIS the middle watch of a summer’s night –
The earth is dark, but the heavens are bright;
Nought is seen in the vault on high
But the moon, and the stars, and the cloudless sky,
And the flood which rolls its milky hue,
A river of light on the welkin blue.
The moon looks down on old Cronest,
She mellows the shades on his shaggy breast,
And seems his huge gray form to throw
In a sliver cone on the wave below;

His sides are broken by spots of shade,
By the walnut bough and the cedar made,
And through their clustering branches dark
Glimmers and dies the fire-fly’s spark –
Like starry twinkles that momently break
Through the rifts of the gathering tempest’s rack.

‘Tis the hour of fairy ban and spell:
The wood-tick has kept the minutes well;
He has counted them all with click and stroke,
Deep in the heart of the mountain oak,
And he has awakened the sentry elve
Who sleeps with him in the haunted tree,
To bid him ring the hour of twelve,
And call the fays to their revelry;
Twelve small strokes on his tinkling bell –
(‘Twas made of the white snail’s pearly shell:)
‘Midnight comes, and all is well!
Hither, hither, wing your way!
‘Tis the dawn of the fairy day.’
....
It continues for 6 pages.

Joseph Rodman Drake (1795–1820) was a noted early American poet, belonging to the “Knickerbocker group” of New York writers, which also included, among others, Fitz-Greene Halleck, Washington Irving, and William Cullen Bryant. Born in New York City, he was orphaned at an early age, but as a child showed promise in writing poems. He was educated at Columbia College. Sadly, Drake died of consumption at the age of twenty-five. A collection of his poems, *The Culprit Fay and Other Poems*, was published posthumously by his daughter in 1835. [21-01]

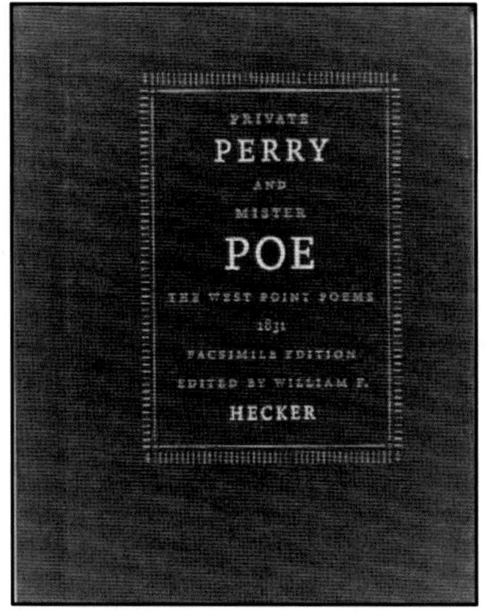

Private Perry and Mister Poe: The West Point Poems, 1831

Anthology, Poetry, WP Author, WP ex

Edited by Major William F. Hecker, Class of 1991 with contributions by Daniel Hoffman & Gerard McGowan LSU Press (2005)

Poems (1831) is a book of verse Poe dedicated "To the U.S. Corps of Cadets." Poe solicited among his fellows for funds to bring out the collection; they, accustomed to his light verse send-ups of their instructors, must have been surprised indeed to receive a work so different from their expectations. Its pages can still surprise the contemporary reader, who expects to find, in "To Helen," the familiar and unforgettable lines, "To the glory that was Greece / And the grandeur that was Rome," or, in "Sonnet: To Science," the concluding image of the poet's lost lyrical impulse, "and from me / The summer dream beneath the tamarind tree."

The reader will discover none of these lines in the 1831 volume. To read "The City in the Sea" we must turn instead to "The Doomed City," and finding other unfamiliar titles – "Irene," "A Paean" -- discover them to be the first incarnations of "The Sleeper" and "Lenore." Comparisons with the later final versions reveal how skillful a reviser was Poe, for in every case the changes are improvements. [EB]

Major William Hecker III, Class of 1991, taught English at West Point. He was killed in Iraq in 2005 when his HMMWV rolled over an IED. He is buried in the cemetery at West Point. [21-02]

Our Little Brown House: A Poem of West Point

Poetry, WP Author

Maria L. Stewart F. Kalkhoff Jr. (1880)

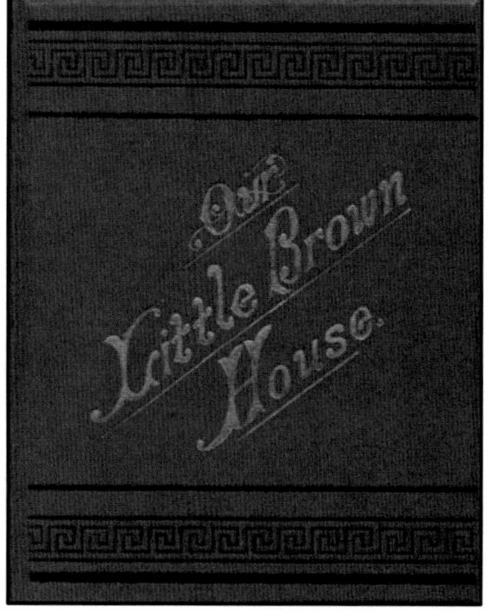

A book of poems written for the New Year's festival at the cadet's sabbath school at the Methodist Episcopal Church. They were compiled and published by Maria Stewart.

> "There's a little brown house just under the hill; It's not by the river, nor yet by a rill; It's not on the green-sward where the gay and proud meet, but it stands on the corner of Bandbarrack's street.

OUR LITTLE BROWN HOUSE;

A Poem of West Point.

WRITTEN FOR THE NEW YEAR'S FESTIVAL AT THE CADETS' SABBATH-SCHOOL OF THE METHODIST EPISCOPAL CHURCH.

JANUARY 1, 1879.

THE AUTHORESS, (M. L. S.)

NEW YORK:
PUBLISHED BY F. KALKHOFF, Jr.
1880.

This time-honored veteran, in armor complete, Has stood many winters the storm and the sleet— The early spring rains and the long summer heat, The wear and the tear of a great many feet.

It's a very small building, and plain in its way; No high-toned paintings, not a thing that is gay; It was built of the gun-house of Col Thayer fame, During the years of the Delafield reign.

Then came Captain B.—he thought it all wrong That such a small house should hold such a throng; So out went the walls, up went the roof, And thus it was altered and made large enough.

....

"But where are the loved ones we met here of yore? Their forms and their faces we'll see nevermore; Their loud, cheery laugh and swift-coming feet No more in the Sabbath-school ever to greet.

Some have launched out on the world's busy tide, Some have got married, some have died, Some on the frontier, wading through strife, With the musketry's rattle and the wild scalper's knife.

Some by the camp-fires, with their minds on the rack, Eating salt pork with a little hard-tack, Wading through snow or fording a river, Or asleep on the ground without any cover.

From the falls of Missouri, with its loud, maddening roar, To the slopes of Pacific, an ever-green shore, To the Atlantic Ocean, with a coast sand-bound, There some of my boys are sure to be found... [EB]

Maria L. Stewart (?–1883) was a resident of West Point. She and her husband are buried in the West Point Cemetery. [21-03]

Pegasus Remounts: Anthology of Cadet Verse 1928

Anthology, Poetry, WP Author

Charles D. Curran & Edward F. Shepherd Moore Printing (1928)

FOREWORD

Poetical composition is certainly not an important part of an Army Officer's training -- and the publication of a collection of verse may seem strange when coming from a school so rigidly conservative and so essentially practical as West Point.

However, ever since the arrival of Col. Lucius Holt at the Military Academy, this institution has shown a marked trend toward a broadening of its curriculum and, an increasing stress upon the cultural side of education.

The new movement has had its greatest manifestation in the English Department. Of late years a course in versification was inaugurated for the benefit of those cadets who showed special aptitude. Under the inspired teaching of Major A. W. Chilton, these men acquired not only a valuable appreciation of poetry but also a desire to try that form of composition for themselves. To that beginning we owe many of the efforts incorporated in our anthology.

At present time every cadet is given a short course in versification and increasingly great number are writing verse for their own pleasure.

With the assistance of Lt. Col. C. B. Hodges, Commandant of Cadets, Lt. Col. C. E. Wheat, Professor of English, and the instructors of the English Department we have been able to prepare this volume.

Pegasus Remounts is an anthology of poetry edited and published by **Charles D. Curran**, Class of 1928. Subsequent versions appear in 1929, 1931 and again in 1936 by the cadets at West Point. This diminutive volume (3" x 4") contains 103 poems by 22 cadets.

A.W. Chilton, mentioned in the above forward, authored the novel *A Cadet's Honor.* Also of interest is cadet Robert Wohlforth, Class of 1927, who contributed three poems to this collection. He later wrote *Tin Soldiers*, a controversial novel of cadet life. Those two novels are described in "The Cadet Experience" chapter.

Courtship at West Point

Poetry, WP Author

Harry de Metropolis William-Frederick Press (1952)

"American Beauty or
Courtship at West Point"
(To my beloved wife)

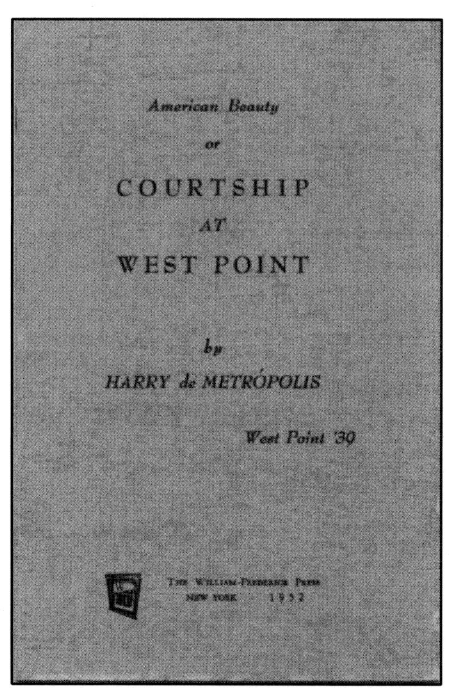

O tender maiden, pure and fair,
Whose arms hold me tonight,
Thy burning lips and hips so rare
Produce Supreme Delight!

Such love and passion uncontrolled
I swear come from some other world!
Thy sky-blue eyes and golden hair
Delicious love-light shed;

Angelic glow thou lent'st the air,
Sweet partner of my bed; With nodding
smiles we see why June
Is picked for lovers' honeymoon.

One week ago in sacred rite
The priest did us combine;
And Hymen in his book did write:
"A union most divine!"

Mine to love, honor and adore
As empress of my heart—and more!

"Convoy" is the lead poem in this anthology. Admiral Nimitz had it forwarded to the Officer-in-Charge of escorting ships, to be read to his officers and sailors. There are thirty-three poems in the collection.

Love and War

Anthology, Poetry, WP Author, WW2

Harry de Metropolis William-Frederick Press (1952)

"Convoy" -- Dedicated to the United States Navy with admiration and gratitude. It was composed in May, 1942, to prophesy the eventual victory of America over Japan and Germany.

Come here, my son,
I'll tell you a story
Of a breathless sea-trip
For God and Country.

'Twas in December,
Nineteen Forty-one,
When we weighed anchor
And followed the sun.

No friends, no loved-ones,
Came to see us off;
No bands, no ribbons
Bedecked the wharf.

And sleepless nights
In hot, suffocating holds
With blacked-out lights.

Our old and filthy ship
Did stink so high
That God drew heaven higher
And higher into the sky.

We cleared the harbor
For some unknown fate;
And our last look was
Of the Golden Gate.

Twenty ships loaded
With thirty thousand men
Comprised our belliferous,
Ocean-going caravan.

The first day out
We admired the ocean;
But Night stirred our hearts
With apprehension.

Then came endless days

I stepped down below
To inspect a hold,
What I saw there
Was Purgatory's hole:

Poor, human cargo
In frightened sleep,
Piled neat like cordwood
Four high, fifty deep;

Sad, precious fodder
For the maws of War,
That's what we mortals
Seem to be destined for:

[about 58 stanzas follow]

Thus we traveled
With fragile faith
Across the Ocean
Of the Shadow of Death.

SO SHALL AMERICA
IN HER DESTINED COURSE
EMERGE FROM THE WAR
SAFE, FREE, AND
VICTORIOUS!"

Harry de Metropolis (1913–1982), Class of 1939, rose to the rank of major in World War II serving in the Pacific theater. He was a poet at heart. His subjects were war, romance, foreign lands, and heroic figures. Both poetry volumes are dedicated to his wife Doris. They are buried together at West Point. [21-04]

This next slim volume of poems, *Shades of Gray*, carries with it a similar spirit as found in *Pegasus Remounts*. It was privately published in 1970 and includes poems written by 15 cadets.

Shades of Gray

Poetry, Anthology, WP Author

Michael D. Anderson (editor) M. D. Anderson (1970)

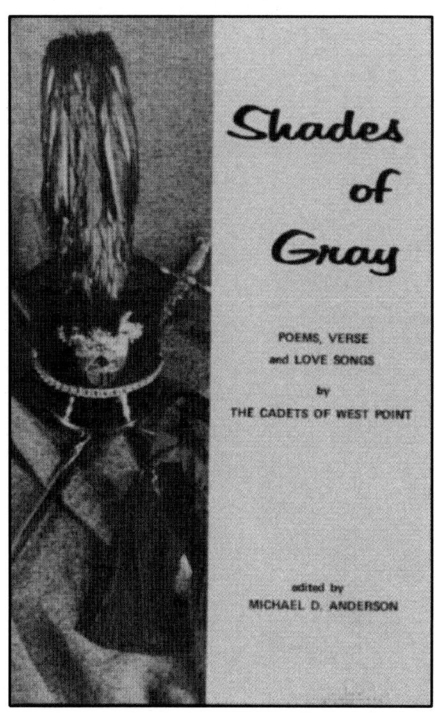

From the Forward:

"We're not sure there's any way you can understand these poems the way we do. It's not that the feelings and sentiments are unique to us. In fact, they are very common—we share them with you. It's the setting you can't feel. We live in a curiously time and space confined world, and in the hard, changing years of being in that world, we are shaped by those confines. To understand how we feel, you have to know some part of us—that we are carried in a cycle of experience tied to the seasons. We live almost all our days at West Point, and go home only for Christmas-Winters, Easter-Springs, Summer-Summers, and Labor Day-Falls. (Strangely, there are no Thanksgivings.) We learn early to feel at a distance and love closely in solar rhythms. If you look into these poems, you can see the marks our four years of tidal existence leave. The words of aloneness, of patient expectation, of loving briefly and intensely—they are all here. The years of separation have not removed us from the world. They have taught us to reach, touch, and carry more tenderly."

Michael D. Anderson (1947–) graduated with the Class of 1970, then served five years before leaving the Army to study medicine. He is a family doctor in Red Wing, MN, offering primary care services. [21-05]

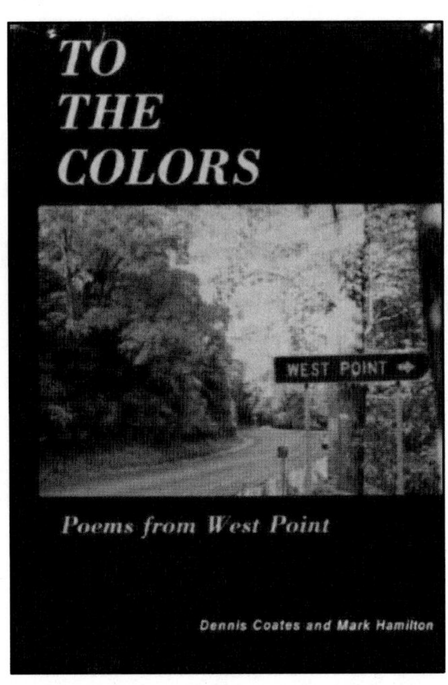

To the Colors: Poems from West Point

Poetry, WP Author

Dennis Coates & Mark R. Hamilton Vortex Pub. Co. (1975)

From the Forward:

Every cadet, soldier or visitor who has come to the U.S. Military Academy has been impressed by the natural beauty of the place. Many people are somewhat confused by their simultaneous perceptions of beauty and power, nature and architecture, vitality, and history.

The poets, Mark Hamilton and Dennis Coates, assure us that there is a splendid harmony at work among the images, a coherence to our impressions of this very representative American place. Their poems celebrate this orchestration and express the appealing essence of West Point.

This is an old place, set in an old place,
Flanked by a river older than tradition,
Reviewed by mountains whose memories trace
The echoes of retreat on to silence.
This is a strong place, this is a stone place,
Granite set in granite, cannon on the green.
The Hudson River rubs against the base
Of rocks so bare they starve themselves of green.
This is a cold place, a frozen place
When the pure wind whips through ruined trees
And everywhere the fixed gray faces,
Colder than flesh, command fields of snow.
Into this place Spring blares like reveille,
Young and warm, spreading its fresh, leafed filigree.

The poets organize their works by the four seasons at West Point, with each season having a chapter of poems.

The poets are both graduates of the Class of 1967, United States Military Academy and later were assigned to the Department of English at West Point. While serving in Vietnam in 1969, **Captain Dennis Coates** was awarded the Silver Star. In 1972, he received his Master of Arts degree from Duke University. As a cadet, **Captain Mark Hamilton** was the starting Army fullback for three years. He earned his Master of Arts degree from Florida State University in 1972. [DJ]

Thayer's Return: Early History of West Point in Verse

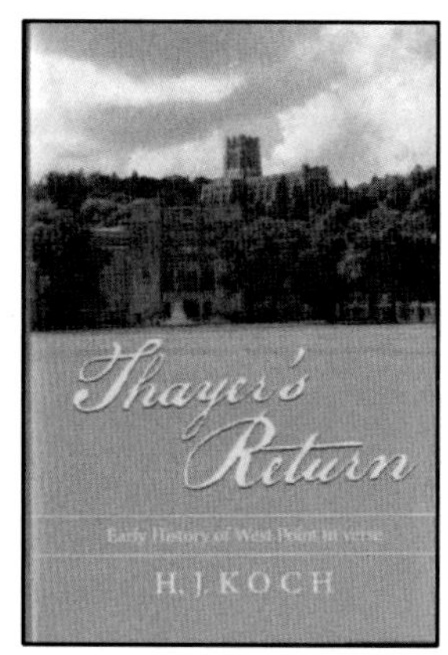

Poetry, Thayer, Supernatural

H. J. Koch Lulu Publishing Services (2019)

This compilation of verse, divided into four parts, provides a unique perspective on the early history of West Point. The Father of West Point, Sylvanus Thayer, has returned from the mist of history in the form of a ghost to seek an update on the Academy from a cadet. As the two men converse over a number of nights, they lyrically explore history of West Point founding in 1802 until World War I. [BC]

This book is further described in the chapter, "Revolution, War of 1812 & Sylvanus Thayer."

Athena Speaks: Thirty Years of Women at West Point

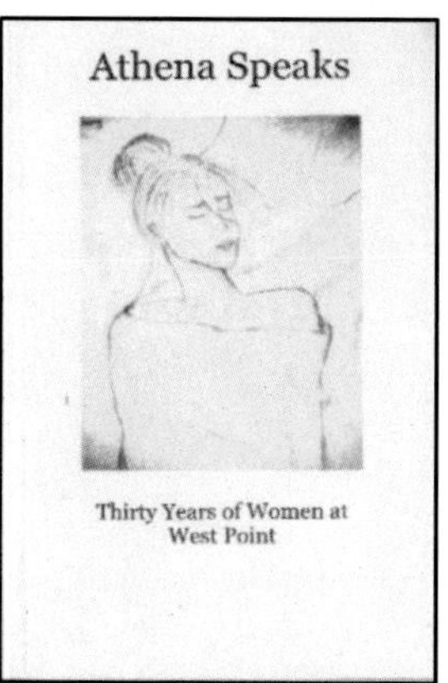

WP Female, Poetry, Cadet, WP Author

Abbey Carter & Marya Rosenberg, Editors
The Margaret Chase Smith Foundation (2009)

This book contains 80 poems, recollections and prints of women who attended West Point from 1977 to 2007. The book is described more fully in the chapter, "Women at West Point."

"Cold Feet"

Is America ready for me?
Ready to see my guts blown to bits?
Ready for the body bag to see?

Is it harder because I have tits?
Harder because I'm daddy's little daughter?
Harder because I'm the sweet girl-next-door ditz?

Or are you happy to have the butch slaughtered?
The bitch who tries to be tough and callous.
Do you care if that girl is martyred?

Assertive, aggressive, envious of a phallus,
"So go on and let her die like men do.
And then she can have her damn status."

But I am not that girl you keep referring to.
My name is Joanna—we are not the same.
Now am I getting too real for you?

Do you see the saint in my name?
Are you afraid that history might repeat?
Well you're right if you think I want someone to blame,

I am scared and starting to get cold feet.

Joanna Pietrantonio Hall, 1999

"Lake Frederick, Boys Wonder"

Smiley, the biggest perv
of all New Cadets in Echo Company
asks me what it's like,
the female shower time.
"It's...nice," I reply
and as he presses me for details
of asses and tits I can only think
that the shower and the shocks
of unseasonably frozen water
and the shrieks of voices still
high with laughter and the backs
covered with heat rash, shoulders
broad and hair dripping loose into
haphazardly remade buns
is the strength of my girls, is strength
for my heart, is strength which
no words could make
Smiley understand.

Abbey Carter, 2009

Abby Carter, Class of 2009, and **Marya Rosenberg**, Class of 2007, compiled and contributed poems to this anthology.

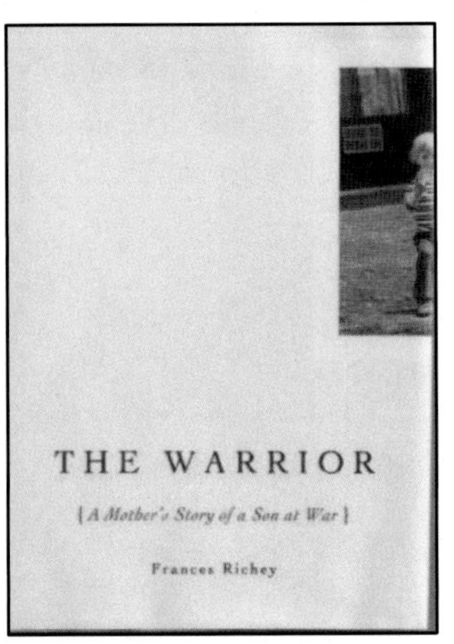

The Warrior: A Mother's Story of a Son at War

Iraq, Poetry

Frances Richey Viking (2008)

When Frances Richey's son, Ben, a graduate of the United States Military Academy at West Point and a Green Beret, went on the first of his two deployments to Iraq, Richey began to write. *The Warrior* is her urgent and intensely personal exploration of what a mother is feeling as her only son goes off to war, as she says good-bye to him, misses him, prays for him, and waits for him to come home.

At the heart of this memoir in verse lies a mother's love for her son—a son from whom she feels distant both literally and metaphorically, for she is opposed to the war but nevertheless realizes that she needs to understand and support the choices he has made.

The Warrior speaks to the world of those who wait while their loved ones are in combat or perilous situations. It is also concerned with the love and pain that constitute close relationships. These heart-wrenching and beautifully composed poems are born of necessity; they are for Richey a way of bridging the distance between herself and her son, of bearing witness to the act of waiting and to the life that her son was living with all of its dangers and mysteries. [DJ]

Frances Richey, a West Virginia native, graduated from the University of Kentucky. After working in the business world for almost two decades, she left to teach yoga and write. She is the author of *The Burning Point* (White Pine Press, 2004), winner of the White Pine Press Poetry Prize. She lives in New York City. [21-06]

DRAMA

There are West Pointers with dramatic talent. A testament to that is the enduring popularity of the Firsties' annual 100th Night Show. Also, who knew that we had a Civil War general who fancied himself a playwright?

West Point: A Comedy in Three Acts

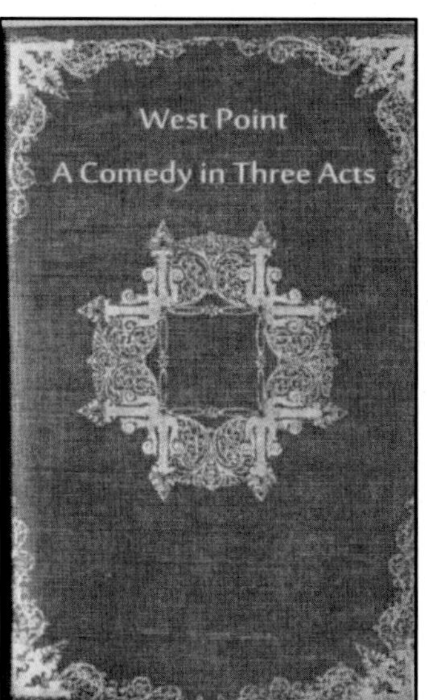

Poetry/Drama, Anthology

George A. Baker Frederick A. Stokes Co (1879)

CHARACTERS.

RANDOLPH PENDEXTER (411: Corporal B Co., 7th Reg. N. G. S. N.), age 24.
GRAF HEINRICH VON RODEN (Captain in the White Cuirassiers), age 23.
ROBERT WENDELL (U. S. Corps of Cadets), age 20.
FREDERICK CLAYTON (2nd Lieutenant 34th U. S. Infantry), age 23.
ALFRED CLAYTON (Lieutenant- Colonel US.A., retired), age 50.
MRS. RANDOLPH PENDEXTER (Widow of GENERAL RANDOLPH PENDEXTER, C.S.A), age 43.
MRS. LOUISE VAN ORDEN HUNT (Widow of BRIGADIER-GENERAL HIRAM HUNT, U. S. Volunteers), age 23.
NELLIE CLAYTON (Daughter of COLONEL CLAYTON), age 18.

ACT I. SCENE -- Grounds of West Point Hotel. Southwest corner of hotel piazza and steps.

Enter C0L. CLAYTON from hotel.

COL. C.: Ten o'clock, eh! And I was to be up for guard-mounting! Not I! It was a luxury to damn the morning gun and go to sleep again. Well, the old place doesn't alter much. I could almost imagine myself back in my "plebe" camp forty years ago nearly. "Plebe" camp was purgatory in those days, but it's nothing to looking after half a million of other people's money, and a third-class corporal cannot "haze" half as well as a good-looking young widow.

Enter LT. CLAYTON, R.

LT. C. My dear father-

COL. C. Eh, what! Why the devil don't you salute, sir?

LT. C. (Saluting) Colonel!

COL. C. (Returning salute.) Lieutenant! My dear boy! This is a surprise! I thought you in Wyoming with your command.

LT. C. I'm on leave. Got it unexpectedly, and I didn't write. I reached New York Monday afternoon, went to the house, heard you were at West Point.

George Augustus Baker (1849–1906) was a journalist, lawyer and author of novels and poetry. He graduated from City College of New York and Columbia Law School. His works include *Bad Habits of a Good Society* (1876). [21-07]

Allatoona: An Historical and Military Drama in Five Acts

Civil War, WP Author, Drama

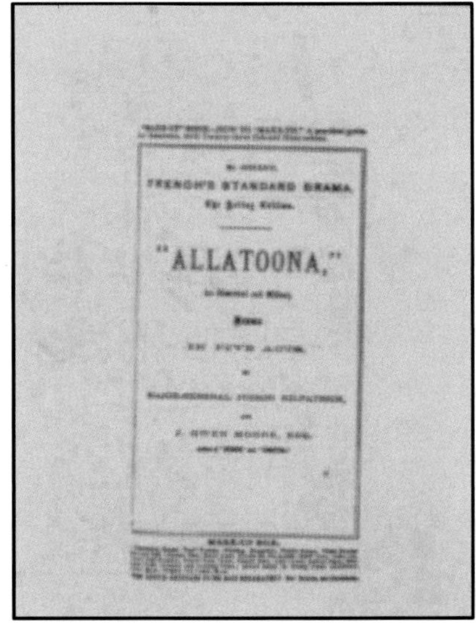

FRENCH'S STANDARD DRAMA

"ALLATOONA,"

Judson Kilpatrick and J. Owen Moore.
Samuel French (1875) (A modern reprint by Pranava Books, India)

This is a five act play about the battle of Allatoona Pass in 1864 near Rome Georgia.

It merges fictional characters with real Union and Confederate officers in the actual settings: West Point, New York City, and Georgia.

Act I

Scene 1: A barracks room at West Point – cadets discuss then argue about the fall of Fort Sumpter and future loyalties of the Corps.

Scene 2: On the Plain at West Point – Southern cadets fall out. Charles Dunbar, Georgia in lead.

Scene 3: A barracks room at West Point – northern cadets decide to confront southern cadets.

Scene 4: A barracks room at West Point – acrimonious confrontation between southern cadets led by cadet Dunbar and loyalist cadets behind cadet Estes.

Act II

Scene 1: Village hall at Knox Vermont – patriotic villagers fired up to volunteer for the Union

Scene 2: Knox VT outside a villager's house: husband and wife debate his decision to enlist

Scene 3: City residence in New York City: Observing regiments pass through to Washington

Act III (Three years later)

Scene 1: Residence in Rome Georgia: U.S General Corse discussing strategy to stop C.S. General Hood's advance, with his adjutant Colonel Estes who, when at West Point, was a former beau of Helen Dunbar.

Scene 2: Grounds of Union camp at Rome Georgia: Joshing among enlisted soldiers

Scene 3 Woodlawn Plantation – Home of the Dunbars. Yankees under General Corse and Col. Estes in seeking forage confront Helen Dunbar mistress of plantation. Her brother and other Confederates are concealed in cellar. After the Yankees depart, a plot is hatched to have Helen invite Corse to dinner, where Dunbar and his friends will take him prisoner. Helen objects but is convinced by her friend May that she must do it to prevent a battle and much bloodshed.

Act IV

Scene 1: Residence in Rome Georgia: General Corse making plans to stop General Hood when he receives an invitation to dine at Woodlawn Plantation. A negro servant overhears Dunbar's plan and informs the General's orderly, but the general as left to survey his defenses and Colonel Estes has already left for the dinner engagement.

Scene 2: In a grove near Woodlawn, Dunbar is waiting for the Yankee officers to appear. A fellow officer and regimental surgeon attempt to dissuade Dunbar, saying it is dishonorable and will bring terrible misfortune to his estate and sister. Dunbar refuses to change his plan.

Scene 3: Interior of Woodlawn: Col. Estes arrives with a small escort and is soon surrounded and attacked. Dunbar and Estes engage in sword dueling. Helen stands between them to stop their struggle. General Corse enters the room with escorts and takes Dunbar prisoner. At that point a dying rebel soldier is brought and indicates that Hood is on the march to Allatoona Pass. General Corse, alarmed, says he must move his troops quickly to prevent Hood's movement. The house has been set on fire by soldiers outside. All depart, Helen Dunbar in tears at the loss of her home.

Act V

Scene 1: Sherman's HQ in Atlanta: Sherman learns that Hood's forces have crossed the Chattahoochee River headed for Allatoona Pass. Colonel Estes rides in with a dispatch from General Kilpatrick that he and General Corse are fighting a delaying action, but need support. Sherman orders the Army to mobilize.

Scene 2: The battle of Allatoona Pass. Corse's troops in desperate defense pending the arrival of Howard's Corps. Estes has returned to report that help is forthcoming and then joins the fray. He discovers that Dunbar (somehow escaped) and is now leading rebel charge. Estes and Dunbar engage, but Dunbar is shot down. Howard's troops arrive to save the day.

Hugh Judson Kilpatrick (1836–1881) was a cavalry officer in the Union Army during the American Civil War, achieving the rank of brevet major general. He was later the United States Minister to Chile and an unsuccessful candidate for the U.S. House of Representatives. Nicknamed "Kill-Cavalry" for his tactics recklessly disregarding the lives of soldiers under his command, Kilpatrick was both praised for the victories he achieved, criticized for this personal licentious behavior, and despised by Southerners whose homes and towns he devastated. He is buried at West Point. [21-08]

No information on co-writer **J. Owen Moore** could be found.

Some fifty-six years later, Kilpatrick's and Moore's play was re-written and published by Christopher Morley. The characters in Morley's version are the same (save for Col. Estes), but the locations in Georgia are different.

The Blue and the Gray Or War is Hell

Civil War, WP Author, Drama

Judson Kilpatrick and Owen J. Moore
as revised by Christopher Morley Doubleday Doran (1931)

The Great Dramatic Triumph
THE BLUE & THE GRAY
OR War is Hell
REVISED AND EDITED BY
CHRISTOPHER MORLEY
From an OLD SCRIPT by
JUDSON KILPATRICK and J. OWEN MOORE
Straight from its record-breaking run
at the OLD RIALTO THEATER, HOBOKEN

MELODRAMA IN FOUR ACTS

ACT ONE

SCENE 1 Interior of Cadet barracks at West Point, April, 1861.
SCENE 2 A grove overlooking the river, West Point.
SCENE 3 The Parade Ground.
SCENE 4 The Barracks (same as Scene 1).
SCENE 5 Village Hall, Knox, Vermont.
SCENE 6 A Residence on Broadway, New York.

ACT TWO
SCENE 1 A Bivouac in the pine woods, near Rome, Georgia. Autumn, 1864.
SCENE 2 Grounds adjoining Corse's camp. Early morning.
SCENE 3 Interior at Guilford Plantation.
SCENE 4 Confederate rendezvous at Bass Ferry.
SCENE 5 Interior at Guilford Plantation {same as Scene 3).

ACT THREE
SCENE 1 The garden, Guilford Plantation
SCENE 2 Sherman's headquarters at Atlanta.
SCENE 3 General Curse's headquarters office in camp.
SCENE 4 Interior at Guilford Plantation (same as in Act Two).

ACT FOUR
The Battle of Kenesaw Mountain.
CHARACTERS
Cadets at West Point, later Federal and Confederate Officers
Taylor Cook & Charles Dunbar, Rhet Kingsbury & Reed Lamar
Annie May Blackman & Helen Dunbar.
Commandant, Superintendent of U. S. Military academy
Seth Green, of Knox, Vermont
Squire Cooly, Maria Green, Dr. Spencer
Mammy, an old negro woman. Ben, an old negro
Captain Chase, Quartermaster Corps
General Corse, General W. T. Sherman, General Slocum

Christopher Morley (1890–1957) was an American journalist, novelist, essayist, and poet. He also produced stage productions for a few years and gave college lectures. New York newspapers published a note he sent to his friends shortly before his death:

> "Read, every day, something no one else is reading. Think, every day, something no one else is thinking. Do, every day, something no one else would be silly enough to do. It is bad for the mind to continually be part of unanimity." 21-09

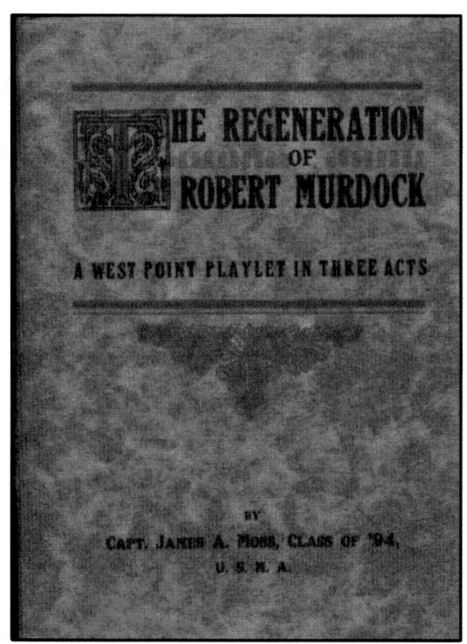

Regeneration of Robert Murdoch: A West Point Playlet

Drama, WP Author

James Moss Privately (1895)

The Regeneration of Robert Murdock, a West Point playlet in three acts, by Capt. James A. Moss, Class of '94, U.S.M.A., has just come from the press. The playlet was especially written for and produced at the reunion of West Pointers, held in Washington on March 30, 1912, which was the first reunion of West Pointers ever held in Washington, and at which 210 graduates and 25 guests were present. The story of "The Regeneration of Robert Murdock" is simple and beautiful, appealing, as it does, with force to the love of Alma Mater.

Robert Murdock, a lieutenant colonel of the General Staff, on duty in Washington, owes all that he is, all that he has, to West Point. However, he has strayed away from the fold, so to speak, but is induced by his classmate, Henry Thayer, to go up to West Point for their class reunion. Murdock witnesses the graduation parade, "hikes" up to old Fort "Put," takes a stroll on Flirtation Walk—he lives again in spirit his cadet days and is regenerated: hence the title, "The Regeneration of Robert Murdock."

The playlet made an impression on a number of graduates who willingly contributed the funds necessary to defray the cost of its publication. The booklet appears as an illustrated pamphlet that is a credit to the printer's art, and a copy is to be placed in the hands of every living graduate.

Lieut. Charles Braden '69, Highland Falls, NY, secretary and treasurer of the Association of Graduates, has charge of the distribution. Braden had his leg shattered by a bullet in the Yellowstone Campaign of 1873. He was forced to retire and took up teaching. He died in 1919 and is buried at West Point.

When Lt. Moss was first stationed at Missoula, MT, he was tasked by General Nelson Miles to evaluate the feasibility of bicycles for use by the cavalry. He led twenty "buffalo soldiers" from the 25th Infantry – accompanied by an army surgeon and a newspaper reporter from Fort Missoula to St. Louis, Missouri, on bicycles. The 41-day, 2000-mile trek was an experiment in the legitimacy of using bicycles in the Army. Although Moss reported favorably on the bicycles, they were not adopted by the Army for combat use, primarily because of the weight that had to be carried by a soldier.

The return to Fort Missoula trip was more rapid – they went by train. Moss is on the left of the second rank for soldiers. [21-11]

James Moss (1872–1941), Class of 1897, was the class goat. While serving in the Philippines, he was awarded the Silver Star Medal and commanded the 367th Infantry during World War I. Moss took up writing books during his Army career. By 1919, Moss had reached the rank of colonel. He decided to leave the Army and spent the next twenty years writing. His 37 books were exclusively manuals for the instruction of officers and soldiers. [21-10]

FILM

While the overwhelming number of works in this collection are novels and written stories, there have been a number of movies produced featuring West Point and its cadets. They first emerged in the golden age of film from 1927 to 1960. Very few since then.

West Point

Cadet, Romance, Cinema

Raymond L. Shrock MGM Pictures (1927)
Directed by Edward Sedgwick

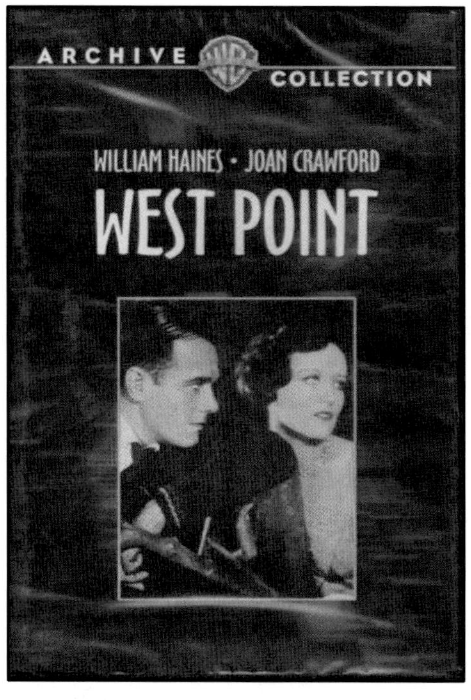

You have a 50-yard-line seat for the big game!

West Point. The pride of America, the home of glorious tradition — unless you're a hotshot plebe named Brice Wayne. Then it's just a backdrop to personal glory. William Haines stars as Brice and Joan Crawford plays the girl he loves in a comedy-drama about a brash young gridiron hero who puts himself above the corps, learns a bitter lesson in team spirit and charges into the Army-Navy game for a chance to redeem himself. That on-screen spark between Haines and Crawford was reflected in off-screen camaraderie. The two, who would be named male and female box-office champs in 1930, became devoted lifelong friends. [DJ]

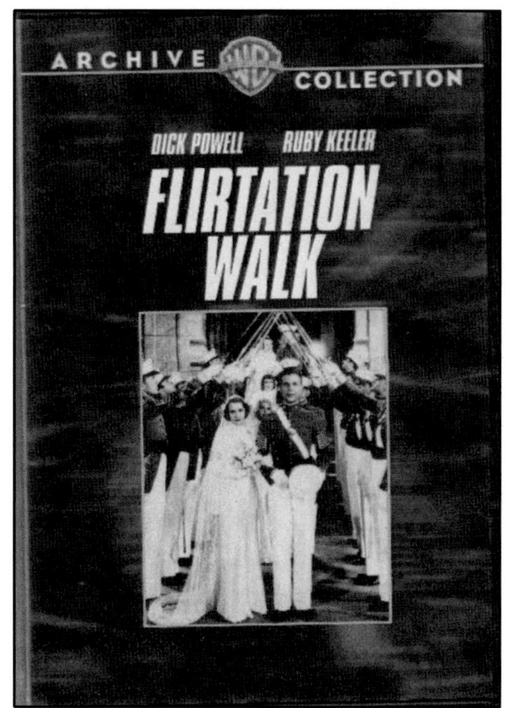

Flirtation Walk

Cadet, Romance, Cinema

Directed by Lou Edelmanirst National Pictures (1934)

When Dick Powell and Ruby Keeler, the irresistible he and she of *42nd Street* and *Gold Diggers of 1933* take a stroll down West Point's Flirtation Walk, it's clear to musical fans that their next trip is bound to be down the aisle. The stars play a cadet and general's daughter who once shared a Hawaiian fling — until she said aloha. But three years later they're cast together in the military academy's Hundredth Night Show, where sweet music and snappy rhythms work their romantic magic. Featuring catchy tunes, comedy and cheerful flag-waving, *Flirtation Walk* earned two Academy Award nominations. [BC]

Rosalie

Cadet, Romance, Cinema

W.S. Van Dyke, Director MGM Studios (1937)

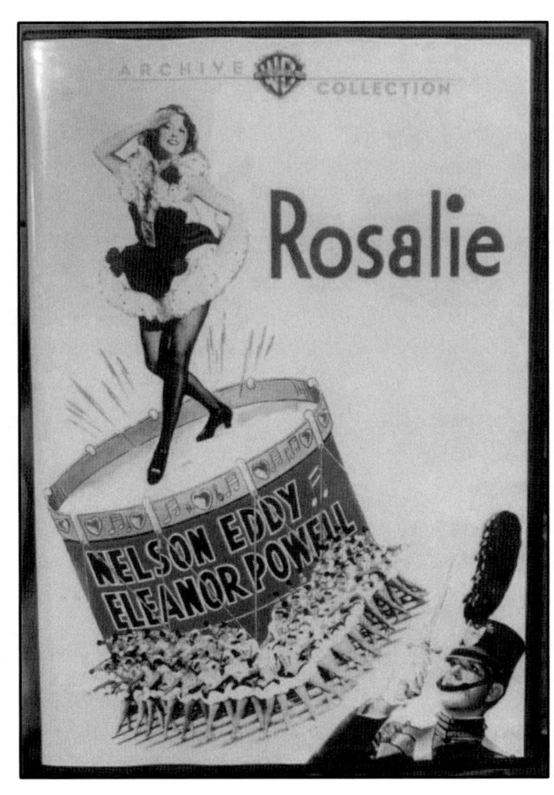

An adaptation of the 1928 stage musical of the same name, the film was released in December 1937. The film follows the story of the musical but replaces most of the Broadway score with new songs by Cole Porter. Dick Thorpe (Nelson Eddy) is a football star for the Army. Rosalie (Eleanor Powell), a Vassar student who is also a princess (Princess Rosalie of Romanza) in disguise, who watches an Army football game. They are attracted to each other and agree to meet in her country in Europe. When Dick flies into her country, he is greeted as a hero by the king (Frank Morgan) and finds Rosalie is engaged to marry Prince Paul (Tom Rutherford), who actually is in love with Brenda (Ilona Massey). Dick, not knowing of Prince Paul's affections, leaves the country. The king and his family are forced to leave their troubled country, and Dick and Rosalie are finally reunited at West Point.
21-12

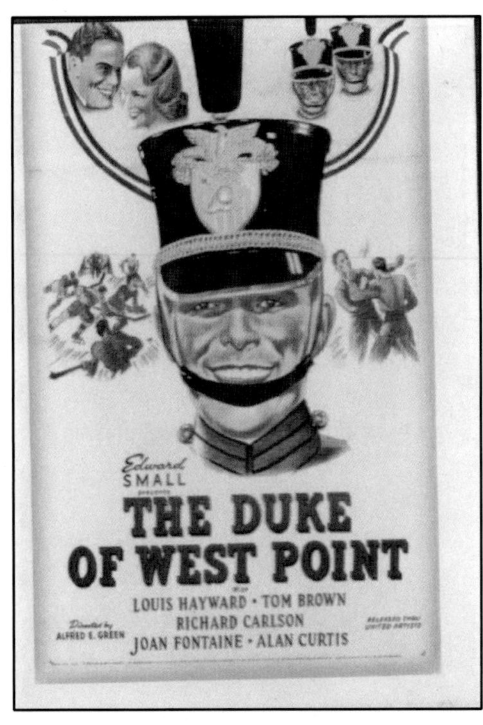

The Duke of West Point

Cadet, Romance, Cinema

Alfred Green, Director United Artists (1938)

Louis Hayward plays Stephen Early, "Duke", an American raised in England and school at Cambridge who goes to West Point out of family tradition. He's an insufferable snob with an infuriating tendency to always get his own way, and an ability to master any sport in seconds! He speaks like an Englishman, has a variety of bizarre idiosyncrasies, and succeeds as much at infuriating his fellow classmates as he does on the field. Over time he develops a friendship with his roommates who have their differences with the Duke and thinks he needs to be taught a lesson! [BC]

West Point Widow

Cadet, Romance, Cinema

Robert Siodmak, Director Paramount Pictures (1941)

A hospital nurse marries a West Point football hero. She soon gets pregnant, but this doesn't stop her from annulling the marriage so as not to interfere with her husband's military career. Though she keeps it a secret, her plan is to marry him again after he graduates from the academy, which forbids students to marry. She doesn't tell a soul about her pregnancy either. Trouble ensues when an enamored intern learns that she has a baby girl. He too keeps mum until her husband graduates. Unfortunately, by that time, the cadet is no longer interested in marrying her, so she ends up marrying the intern instead and happiness ensues. [21-13]

Ten Gentlemen from West Point

Cinema, Cadet, War of 1812

Henry Hathaway, Director 20th Century Fox (1942)

Among those who are fighting to have Congress re-establish the military academy at West Point in the beginning of the nineteenth century is a young Washington socialite, Carolyn Bainbridge. Congress resolves to revive the Academy on a one-year trial basis. Major Sam Carter, a martinet who doesn't believe a college can produce real fighting men, is made the Commandant, and determines to make soldiers - or failures - out of the small band of cadets, by enforcing stringent disciplinary action. Among the cadets are Howard Shelton, Carolyn's fiancée, and Dawson, a Kentucky frontiersman. There is bad blood between the two from the start, and matters are worsened when Dawson falls in love with Carolyn. Many of the cadets resign, under the discouraging conditions and grueling punishment that is part of Carter's plan to make the school hard and the exercises difficult, and the number of cadets left is down to ten. Word arrives that the Indian chief Tecumseh has gone on the warpath. Carter is ordered to take part in quelling the rebellion, and to include the cadets along with the regular troops. Shelton, on patrol, is shot at by an Indian, and leaves his post in pursuit. Dawson leaves to bring him back followed by Major Carter who is captured by the Indians. Using tactics learned at West Point, the small band of cadets attacks the much larger Indian force to rescue Carter and Dawson. The movie closes with the ten cadets receiving their Army commissions. [21-14]

The Spirit of West Point

Cinema, Cadet, Football

Ralph Murphy, Director Films Around the World (1947)

"No need for lengthy explanations about a film called Spirit of West Point, starring Glenn Davis and Doc Blanchard. It is a typical low-budget job which trades on the brilliant reputations of the Army's great football pair. Glenn and Doc show up at West Point, absorb the traditions of the place, get on the team and face the pitfalls, mainly math, of a cadet's career. Intercut with these dramatized experiences are flash backs to the homelife of the two and a generous assortment of news pictures of Army games in which the duo played. For those who are nuts about football these news reel reminiscences are worthwhile. And with the juvenile trade the shots of West Point and the rah-rah atmosphere will likely score. Furthermore, we will say this for the makers: They haven't loaded the story with slush about sweethearts, but rather have kept it in a fairly factual, masculine vein. However, Messrs. Davis and Blanchard, Mr. Inside and Mr. Outside, are no threats when it comes to acting before the camera, and the supporting cast is no great help. It is strictly a teenagers' drama that is showing on the Victoria's screen." [21-15]

This original full size theater poster from 1947 is in the collection.

Beyond Glory

Cinema, Cadet, WW2

John Farrow, Director Paramount Pictures (1948)

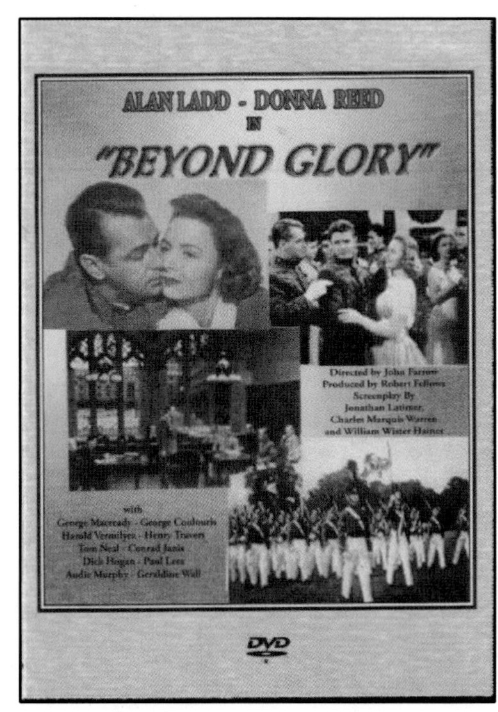

Beyond Glory is a 1948 American drama film starring Alan Ladd and Donna Reed. The film is about a former soldier who thinks he may have caused the death of his commanding officer in Tunisia. After visiting the officer's widow, they fall in love, and she encourages him to attend the United States Military Academy at West Point. World War II hero Audie Murphy made his film debut in the small role of Ladd's academy roommate, Cadet Thomas. [21-16]

The West Point Story

Cadet, Romance, Cinema

Roy Del Ruth, Director Warner Brothers (1950)

Yankee Doodle Dandy Academy Award® winner James Cagney puts on his dancing shoes again for this merry musical comedy packed with spirited star power and lively tunes by Jule Styne and Sammy Cahn. Cagney plays Bix Bixby, a Broadway showman/producer down on his luck yet full of hotshot ideas. Brought to West Point to stage the cadets' annual musical, the Hundredth Night Show, Bixby decides to make the show a candidate for a transfer to Broadway. But first, he must lure the show's talented lead (Gordon MacRae) out of the military. He's got just the right bait: a sweet-natured Hollywood star (Doris Day). Virginia Mayo and Gene Nelson also star alongside the irrepressible Cagney. [21-17]

Here is the third film in Universal-International's *Francis the Talking Mule* series. It stars Donald O'Connor, Lori Nelson, Alice Kelley, and Gregg Palmer. The distinctive voice of Francis is a voice-over by actor Chill Wills. The book on which the movie is based is reviewed in the "Mascots & Other Army Animals" chapter.

Francis Goes to West Point

Cadet, Animal, Cinema

Arthur Lubin, Director Universal-International (1952)

Bumbling former World War II serviceman Peter Stirling is sent to West Point as a reward for stopping a plot to blow up his government workplace. After enrolling and falling to the bottom of his class, he is privately tutored by his old army friend Francis, which gets him into trouble when he reveals that this tutor is one of West Point's very own mule mascots. [21-18]

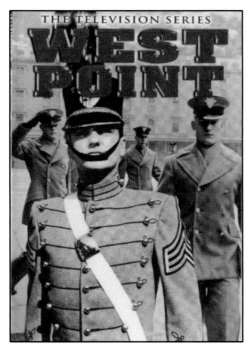

West Point: The Television Series

TV Series, Cadet

MGM Studios (1956)

From the annals of the U. S. Military Academy come authentic, dramatic stories of adventure and gallantry, starring the men who become future leaders in the defense of Freedom. Dedicated to the service of their country, the Cadets are the nation's pride, a part of a rich tradition. Young men from tenements and mansions, from farms and townhouses, from prep schools and city night schools, make up The Corps. WEST POINT is the story of young men and their experiences, adventures, hardships and triumphs.

A big exam, a major sports event, field maneuvers, romance on "Flirtation Walk," discipline and learning in classroom and on the drill field—forge the character of a career officer at WEST POINT. Cadets themselves—individually and in formation—appear in stories produced with the full cooperation of the U. S. Department of Defense, Department of the Army and the U. S. Military Academy. [DJ]

The Long Gray Line

Cadet, DVD, Romance

John Ford, Director
Sony Pictures Home Entertainment (2002)

This is based on the book *Bringing up the Brass.* See the chapter "Army Sports." The movie stars Tyrone Power and Maureen O'Hara.

Arriving from County Tipperary, Ireland, in 1898, Marty begins waiting tables. After two months he has nothing to show for it, because he is docked for every dish he breaks. When he learns that enlisted men only worry about the guardhouse, he joins the U.S. Army. Captain Koehler, Master of the Sword, is impressed with his fist-fighting and brings him on as an assistant in athletics instruction.

Fifty five years later, facing forced retirement, Master Sergeant Martin Maher goes to the White House to appeal to the Commander in Chief, President Dwight D. Eisenhower, who gives Marty a warm welcome and listens to his story.

The President tells General Dotson to call the Point and find out what the SNAFU is. Marty gives an aide a bottle of hair restorer for the President. Dotson tells Marty he is AWOL and flies him back to the Point, where the Superintendent and Dotson hustle him onto the crowded parade ground. The film concludes with a full dress parade in Marty's honor. [21-19]

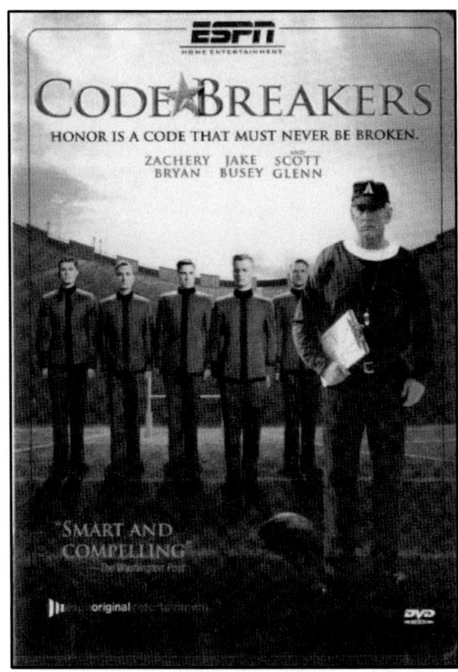

Code Breakers

Cinema, Cadet, Football, Scandal

Bob Holcomb, Director ESPN (2006)

Based on the first three chapters of the 2000 novel, *A Return to Glory* by Bill McWilliams, the movie chronicles the 1951 cheating scandal at West Point and its impact on Army's football team, which was forced to eject from the Academy virtually its entire squad. The film begins going into the 1950 Army-Navy Game, the Cadets football team was heavily favored, yet went on to lose to a weak Midshipmen squad, 14–2. The Academy and football team were then thrown into a scandal when 90 cadets, including 37 lettering football players, resigned in a cheating scandal which broke the Academy's Honor Code. The film follows the cadet Brian Nolan, who is led to a ring of cheaters when he is in need of academic help to pass. A serious piece of the film involves the relationship of Coach Blaik, played by Scott Glenn, and his son Bob Blaik, played by Corey Sevier. Bob, who was a cadet responsible for breaking the Academy Honor Code by cheating in academics deals with the guilt along with the other football players also involved. [21-20]

Have Gun - Will Travel

TV Series, Paladin

CBS Broadcasting (2004)

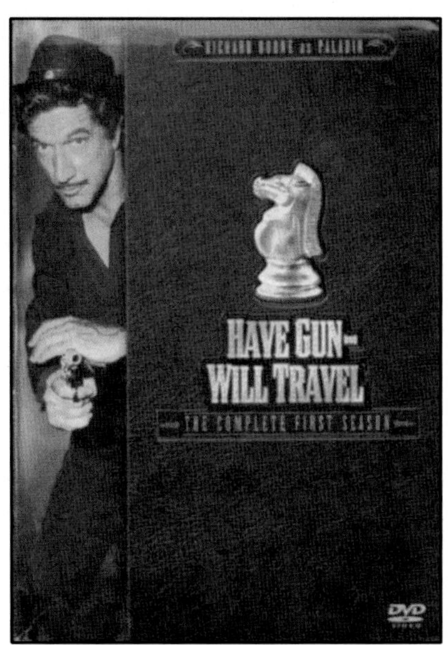

"Have Gun – Will Travel. Wire Paladin, San Francisco" It's the statement on a business card, adorned with a chess-piece knight, that heralds the professional services of Paladin (played by Richard Boone) in this wildly popular Western series from the Golden Age of Television [1950's & 60's]. Based at the Hotel Carlton in San Francisco and assisted by his manservant Hey Boy (played by Kam Tong), Paladin, a West Point graduate and former Union cavalry officer, is an intelligent but mysterious loner and a man of many talents, including detective, bodyguard, courier, sleuth, and bounty hunter. When the situation is desperate, Paladin is the man to wire. This premiere season showcases Boone and a number of eminent guest stars in a kaleidoscope of thrilling, action-packed adventures featuring the heroic man in black! [DJ]

Dress Gray

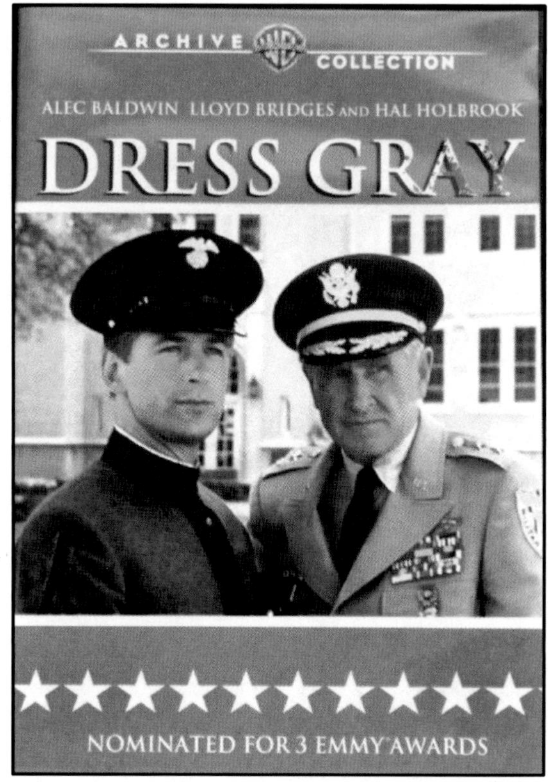

Cadet, Crime, TV Series

Glen Jordan, Director NBC (1986)

Dress Gray is a 1986 American television miniseries starring Alec Baldwin, Lloyd Bridges and Hal Holbrook. The program, about a cadet at a West Point-like military academy who investigates the murder of a fellow cadet, was adapted for the screen by Gore Vidal from the novel of the same name by Lucian Truscott IV.

Dress Gray is set during the era of the Vietnam War. A new class of cadets arrives at the Ulysses S. Grant Military Academy for its 100th anniversary. Ten months later one of those new cadets, David Hand is found dead, apparently drowned despite being a top swimmer. [21-21]

This drama was not filmed at West Point, but at the New Mexico Military Institute in Roswell, NM.

Chapter 22

Remembering the "Old Corps"

Here are some works from the 19th Century that speak to the customs and tradition of the "Old Corps." Originals of these books are quite rare, though all have been reprinted as the copyrights expired long ago. There are no color pictures in the books, but there are some wonderful illustrations.

Presented here are stories and poems from each of the books.

West Point Scrap Book: A Collection of Stories, Songs, and Legends

Anthology, Satire, Songs, Poetry, WP Author

Lt. Oliver Ellsworth Wood Van Nostrand (1874)

This is a collection of 19th century West Point lore in over 100 stories, poems, songs, and drawings gathered in one volume by a USMA graduate. The following four titles are a sampling of the works within. The individual authors are unknown.

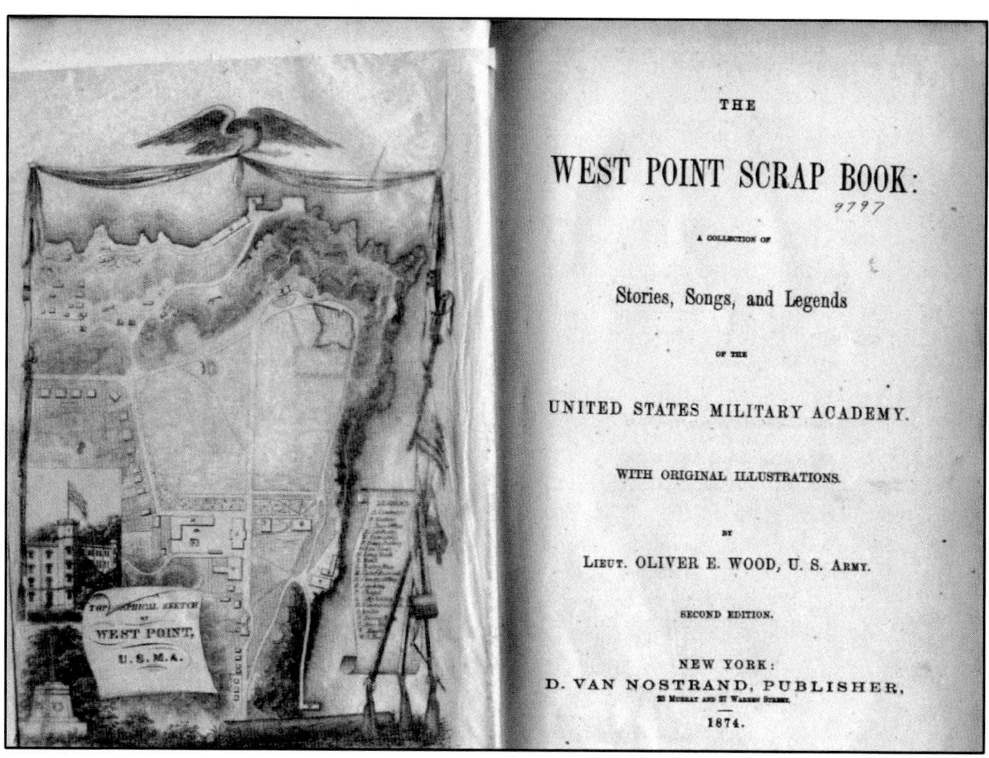

THE

WEST POINT SCRAP BOOK:

A COLLECTION OF

Stories, Songs, and Legends

OF THE

UNITED STATES MILITARY ACADEMY.

WITH ORIGINAL ILLUSTRATIONS.

BY

LIEUT. OLIVER E. WOOD, U. S. ARMY.

SECOND EDITION.

NEW YORK:
D. VAN NOSTRAND, PUBLISHER,

1874.

"Shoulder-Straps"

A discussion between mother and daughter

"Pray tell me, mamma, what the shoulder-straps mean,
That on the bluecoats of our officers' gleam,
You know they're so different, now why should it be,
That not even the uniform buttons agree?
I've noticed, for instance, a blank, and a bar,
two bars, leaves of silver, of gold, and a star,
Two stars, and an eagle, now what may it mean,
scarlet, or orange, light blue, or dark green?"

"Now, listen, my daughter, and pray take heed,
For the income and straps of a beau are agreed.
You may dance with a leaf, and flirt with a bar,
But reserve your best smile for the eagle and star.
And remember the fence with nothing within
Is the field of the stripling, whose spurs are to win,
A poor *Second Lieutenant*, perchance still in debt,
For the clothes he wore out as a West Point Cadet."

"And if on the field, a bar should appear,
your prudence, my darling, should lead you to fear.
For if left a lone widow, the pension's so small,
Your gloves and *first mourning* would swallow it all.
And e'en with your Captain, who flourishes two,
Don't prefer the gay Line to the Staff's sober blue.
For the difference per month, in the mutter of pay,
Not to mention the forage, quite wiles one away.

"Next in order are leaves, but here you reverse
Each value metallic in prose and in verse.
For though gold be a Major, the silvery hue
Marks the Lieutenant-Colonel, on scarlet or blue.
Then, over the forest, and 'neath the bright stars,
Soars the eagle - the lord of the leaves and the bars.
Besides, 'tis suggestive of eagles that fly,
When the wife of the Colonel her bonnets would buy.

"Above all, my darling, still honor the star,
Though it shines 'neath a silver-head, better by far
To catch some old General, than make him afraid,
And you won't be the first to command a brigade."
— "I've heard you, dear mother, and thought it all o'er,
My heart's with the lover who went to the war;
You knew the poor boy has not even a bar,
But I'd rather be his than the bride of a star!"

"The Attempt to Bombard the Superintendent's House"

A very serious prank.

"Under the flag-staff on the Plain, during the whole time I was at the Point, were two guns laid upon trestles, one a 12-pounder and the other a 24-pounder. The tradition accounting for the fact that they were thus dismounted, ran as follows:

Sometime previous to 1823, these guns were mounted on their carriages. Early one morning the 24-pounder was discovered directly opposite the door of the Superintendent's house, close to the road, and pointed at the window just over the door. Upon examination, the gun was found to be loaded with a full cartridge, and double shotted, with a thick wad. In the vent was found a long fuse, or slow match of the kind then used to fire large guns. The fuse had been lighted, and had burned nearly up to the vent, but the previous night had been very stormy, and the wind and rain had evidently extinguished the match. Had the gun exploded, the front wall of the house would have been battered down, and loss of life would have taken place. In consequence of this murderous attempt, the guns were afterwards dismounted."

"The Encampment"

Reminiscences of an Old Grad

"Between the 20th and 25th of June comes the annual marching into camp, this being pitched on the north-eastern portion of the plain. The examination being ended, the First Class having graduated, the old Third Class having gone on furlough, and all the classes having been duly promoted, then comes the flitting. Orders are published at parade to pitch the tents, and march into camp at a stated hour, vacating all the barracks-rooms, which orders provoke such a stampede of tables, buckets, chairs, trunks, mattresses, etc., to the now vacant recitation-rooms, that a first of May in Gotham is comparatively tame… Before breakfast, the campground is laid out, and the tents erected by the quickest diligence of their future occupants. At the indicated hour, the signal sounds, the companies are formed and marched into the parade ground, when the battalion, with the band playing, and colors unfurled, marches to its new home. The encampment consists of eight rows of tents, two to each company, opening on four streets, or company grounds; and a broad avenue runs down the center of the camp. The tents of the Company Officers, and of the Instructors of Tactics, are pitched opposite their respective companies and the Commandant's marquee is placed at the foot of the broad avenue. The guard-tents, six in number, are at the opposite end of the camp.

THE ENCAMPMENT

A chain of six sentinels surrounds the campground day and night. The guard consists of three reliefs, which walk post in turn, through the twenty-four hours, for which each guard is detailed. This detail is drawn as equitably as possible from the four companies, and guard duty recurs once from two to four days, making it really quite hard work for those not inured to it. That direful sound of the Corporal, pounding on the tent-floors with the butt of his musket, and bawling "Turn out! Second relief!" tears most frightful rents in the blessed garment of sleep, which settles down so gently on the poor, weary Plebe, while he dreams of home and mother. On waking to the hard reality, he rubs his eyes, snatches his musket, adjusts his cartridge box, and quickly takes his place among the six martyrs. When the relief is duly marshalled, it is marched by the Corporal around the line of posts, each sentinel challenging the long-looked for delegation with a fierce "Who comes there?" as though he thought them horse-marines at least. The Corporal responds, "Relief!" Once more the martial sentinel cries, "Halt, relief! Advance Corporal with the countersign!" which cabalistic word being demanded, the Corporal advances, and whispers it over the sentinel's bayonet-point; whereupon he so rises in the sentinel's estimation, that the latter quickly yields his post, and falls in at the rear of the relief. This round completed, the six patriots seek the solace of the tent-floor, stoutly hoping that the officer-in-charge will keep his distance, and not require a turn-out of the guard for moonlight inspection.

Walking post promotes meditation. To pace "No. 5" on a bright moonlight night, when shadows mottle the distant mountain slopes, and seem to sleep under the crumbling ruins of old Fort Clinton, when steamboats are rippling the glowing waters of the placid Hudson below, and locomotives are dashing wildly along the railroad across the river, when the white tents glow softly, and the quiet stars shine tremblingly; there is in all this enough to stir up whatever tender memories, high purposes, ambitious longings, and refined sensibilities may dwell in the sentinel's deepest nature. Or when a sultry day has rounded to close, and the storm-spirit has piled up his black cloud fleeces in the highland gorge, and on the crest of CroNest. When the rush of battle comes, and the glowing lightning fitfully reveals the snowy tents, wildly flapping in the rushing blast, as if terror-stricken at the deep rolling thunders, and the quick alternations of vivid light and solid darkness scarce can the soul of the sentry be so dead as not then to be moved and awed before sublimity so transcendent. To be roused by such storms from sleep under a tent to see the very threads of canvas flash into view, when the burning lightnings leap through the air above; and to fancy the electric arrow speeding to the bayonet point of the muskets standing at his head; this is among the cadet's magnificent experiences, and quite compensate for a wet blanket, or a deluged locker.

THE RETURN TO BARRACKS.

About the 28th of August the encampment is wont to be broken up, and the corps return to barrack-
An illumination of the camp usually takes place on the evening before it is broken up, and the convolutions of "stag dance" are exhibited in the parade-ground. With fervor and vivacity outdoing an Indian War-dance. This curious cross between the shuffle and the quadrille is frequent evening diversion of the Cadet Camp. It is performed by twenty or more cadets who gyrate among rows of candles stuck along the ground, cadencing their movements by the low, muffled rattle of a drum, presenting a very pandemonium-like picture. In the olden time the practice was for the corps to leave West Point during the summer season and make long marches into the adjoining States; but this usage has long since been relinquished, some say to save money, but others declare that the cadets were too prone to make merry and run riot during this periodical enlargement; perhaps both are right. The scene presented during the striking of tents is quite lively and picturesque. In the early hours of the day all private property of the cadets (their blankets, clothing, etc.) is carried by them to the rooms assigned them in the barracks, leaving in camp only their muskets and full dress. At the fixed hour "the general beats," and all fly to their tents, awaiting three taps on the large drum. At the first tap, all except the corner tent-cords are cast loose, and the pegs withdrawn; at the second, the corner-cords and pegs are loosed, and the tent gathered in to the tent poles, which are hoisted out and so steadied, that at the third tap, all the tents instantly go down in concert; and woe to any "unlucky Joe" who fails to complete the prostration at the moment. The tents are folded and piled; the companies are formed, and, taking their stacked arms, are marched to the parade; the Commandant then marches the battalion back to the barracks, and the encampment is no more."

"Recollections of the Riding Hall"

"If ye have tears, prepare to shed them now."

"The greater part of last year, while my class were learning to ride, I was confined to the hospital by sickness, and accordingly deprived of the advantages they were enjoying. Still, having been occasionally on horseback, I thought I should escape making any remarkable display of deficiency in that branch of our profession.

When I commenced riding at West Point, it was a very different matter from what goes by the same name elsewhere. Without stirrups, without often even a saddle, we were mounted on ungainly brutes, and trotted around until life was nearly extinct. When I came back from "Furlough," my class had ridden nearly a year, while I had ridden only a week or two. Nothing daunted, however, and trusting to fortune and my own powers, I buckled on a pair of rusty spurs, found myself securely fastened to an enormous sabre, with an iron scabbard, and sallied forth.

Dragoon brought me in a raw-boned, vicious-looking animal, which, after some preliminary difficulties, I succeeded in mounting. "Trot!" Horse started; so did I, half off my saddle. I had never been taught to keep my heels "well out;" accordingly my spurs "*went in;*" horse went in, too! Peculiar motion! Began to suspect I was losing my balance; saber flew out and hit the horse on the head; in plunged my spurs deep among his ribs; another jump; saber flew back and hit him on the flank; spurs worked convulsively among his bones; jump! thump! spur! horse reared; seized his mane! Horse reared up; I caught his ears and saved myself. It began to grow exciting.

Finally, horse started off, such a race! Pulling on his mane had no tendency to check his wild career; rather seemed to irritate him; had a good hold with the spurs but did not consider myself safe. Sabre flew up and hit me in the face; blind for a moment; heard something drop; looked up on the saddle, and found I was not there! Concluded that it must have been me that dropped. Horse standing near, wagging his tail, with a quiet twinkle in his eye, adding insult to injury!

All this time imagine the riding-master shouting: "Where are you going?" "Keep in ranks, sir!" "Keep your spurs out of your horse!" "Mr. B—! for--'s sake, take your hands off his ears," interlarding his remarks with an occasional expletive verging on the profane. Mounted once more, and, with the exception of the throwing, the previous performance was repeated an incalculable number of times, until, at the expiration of the hour, bruised, battered, and blinded, the ride was ended.

The next day I was reported for "spurring my horse cruelly!" "Inattention!" "Not keeping in ranks!" "Not starting off at the command!" "Not holding reins properly," etc., etc. For each of these reports I received the appropriate number of "demerit," and corresponding "extras." Went to my room and wrote an impassioned eulogy on the pleasures of pedestrianism, headed with the appropriate motto, "Walk up hill, and foot it down!" Since that day I have fallen down three flights of stairs, from stumbling over my saber; been kicked by my horse and incapacitated from performing military duty for six weeks.

Oliver E Wood (1844 –1910), compiler of this anthology, graduated with the Class of 1867 after serving in the Civil War as an artillerist. This collection was published in 1874 when he was a junior officer. He retired as a Major General in 1906. 22-01

West Point Tic Tacs: A Collection of Military Verse

Anthology, Poetry, Songs

Bret Harte Homer Lee & Company (1878)

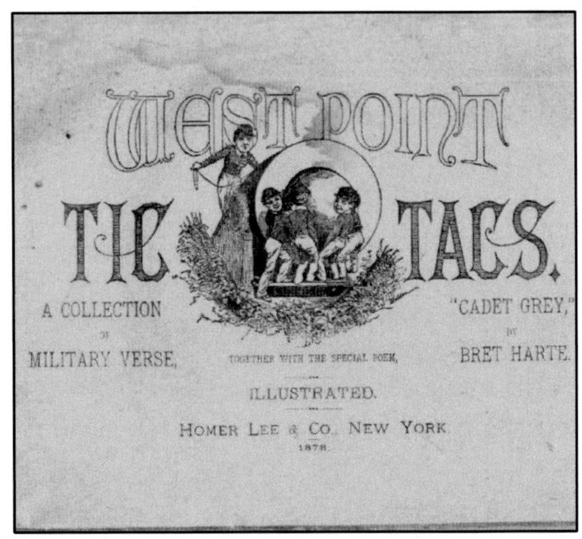

From the preface:

"More than half the book consists of new matter. "Cadet Grey," by Bret Harte, is the longest and most elaborate contribution to American poetry of its distinguished author. The structure of the verse is in the Spenserian measure and is in the narrative manner of Byron's "Childe Harold" and "Don Juan." The illustrations, which are from original pen drawings, were all made expressly for this collection by Thomas Nast, Weldon, Darley, Moran, Kelly, Hopkins, and others; and will be found, alike in conception and execution, far above any others ever attempted in a book of this character. It will gratify Mr. Nast's many Army friends to find that he has contributed to the illustrations; and our thanks are cordially rendered to him, as well as to Messrs. Harper & Brothers, for granting us his valuable aid, and for other courtesies."

"West Point, Canto II"

By Bret Harte

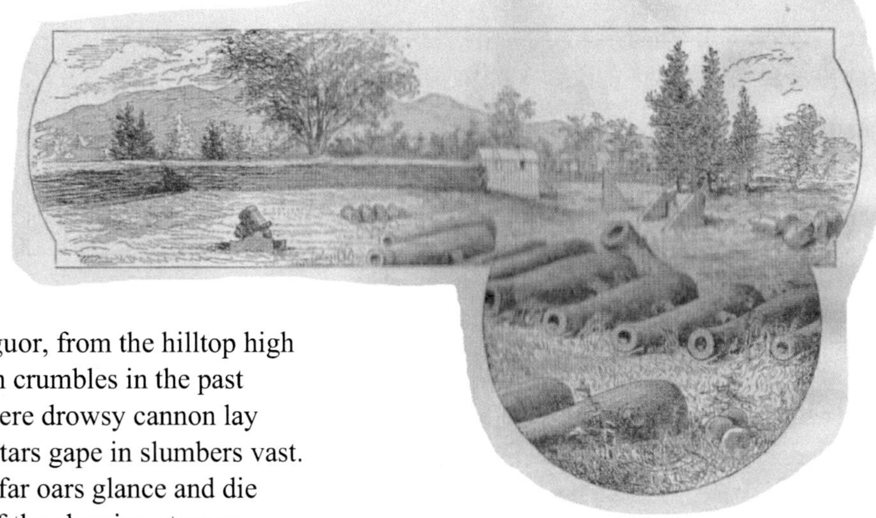

"All space breathes languor, from the hilltop high
Where Putnam's bastion crumbles in the past
To swooning depths where drowsy cannon lay
And wide-mouthed mortars gape in slumbers vast.
Stroke upon stroke, the far oars glance and die
On the hushed bosom of the sleeping stream;
Bright for one moment drifts a white sail by,
Bright for one moment shows a bayonet gleam
For on the level plain, then passes as a dream.

Soft down the line of darkened battlements,
Bright on each lattice of the barrack walls,
Where the low arching sallyport indents
Seen through its gloom beyond the moonbeam falls.
All is repose, save where the camping tents
Mock the white gravestones further on, where sound
No morning guns for reveille, nor whence

No drum-beat calls retreat, but still is ever found
Waiting and present on each sentry's round.
Within the camp they lie, the young, the brave,
Half knight, half schoolboy, acolytes of fame,
Pledged to one alter and perchance one grave.
Bred to fear nothing but reproach and blame,
Ascetic dandies o'er whom vestals rave,

Clean-limbed young Spartans, disciplined young elves
Taught to destroy, that they may 'live to save,
Students embattled, soldiers at their shelves,
Heroes whose conquests are at first themselves.

"On Flirtation Walk"

By Bret Harte

The night was June's, the moon rode high and clear,
"T'was such a night as this" three years ago
Miss Kitty sang the song that two might hear.

…There is a walk where trees o'er arching grow,
Too wide for one, not wide enough for three
(a fact precluding any plural beau),
Which quite explained Miss Kitty's company,
But not why Grey that favored one should be.

There is a spring whose limpid waters hide
Somewhere within the shadows of that path
Called Kosciusko's. There two figures bide,
Gray and Miss Kitty. Surely Nature hath
No fairer mirror for a might-be bride
Than the same pool that caught our gentle belle
To its dark heart one moment. At her side
Grey bent. A something trembled o'er the well,
Bright, spherical-- a tear? Ah! no, a button fell!
Grey bent.

Bret Harte (1836–1902) was an American short story writer and poet best remembered for short fiction featuring miners, gamblers, and other romantic figures of the California Gold Rush. In a career spanning more than four decades, he also wrote poetry, plays, lectures, book reviews, editorials, and magazine sketches. As he moved from California to the eastern U.S. and later to Europe, he incorporated new subjects and characters into his stories, but his Gold Rush tales have been those most often reprinted, adapted and admired. [22-03]

"Bivouac of the Dead"

By Theodore O'Hara

The muffled drum's sad roll has beat
The soldier's last tattoo;
No more on life's parade shall meet
The brave and fallen few.
On Fames eternal camping ground
Their silent tents are spread,
And Glory guards with solemn round
The Bivouac of the Dead.

No rumor of the foe's advance
Now swells upon the wind,
No troubled thought at mid-night haunts,
Of Loved ones left behind,
No vision of the morrow's strife,
The warrior's dream alarms,
Nor braying horn nor screaming fife
At dawn shall call to arms.

Sons of "the dank and dirty ground,"
Ye should not slumber there,
Where stranger steps and tongues resound
Along with headless air:
Your own proud land's heroic soil
Must be your fitter grave,
She claims from war her richest spoil-
The ashes of the brave!

Now 'neath their parent turf they rest,
Far from the gory field,
Borne to a Spartan mother's breast,
On many a bloody shield,
The sunshine of their native sky
Smiles sadly on them here,
And kindred eyes and hearts watch by the
The soldier's sepulcher.

Rest on, embalmed and sainted dead,
Dear as the blood ye gave!
No impious footsteps here shall tread
The herbage of your grave,
Nor shall your glory be forgot
While Fame her record keeps
Or honor paints the hallowed spot
Where valor proudly sleeps.

Yon faithful herald's blazoned stone,
With mournful pride shall tell,
When many a vanquished aged hath flown,
The story how ye fell,
Nor wreck, nor change, nor winter's flight,
Nor time's remorseless doom,
Shall mar one ray of glory's light
That girds your deathless tomb.

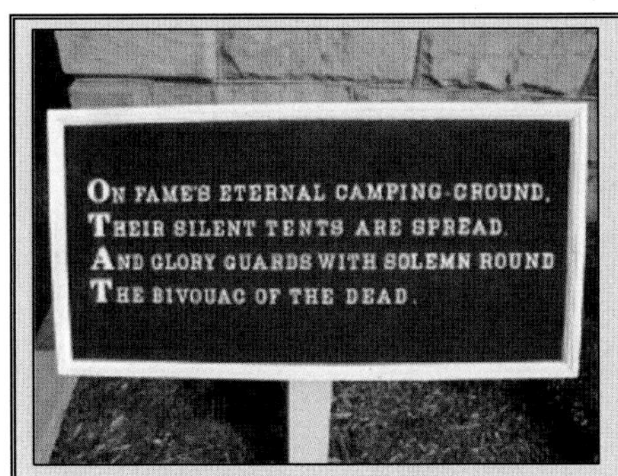
ON FAME'S ETERNAL CAMPING-GROUND,
THEIR SILENT TENTS ARE SPREAD,
AND GLORY GUARDS WITH SOLEMN ROUND
THE BIVOUAC OF THE DEAD.

Theodore O'Hara (1820–1867) served in the Mexican-American War. He wrote this elegy to remember his fellow Kentuckians who died in Mexico. Its verses are seen on plaques in many military cemeteries throughout the country. [22-02]

"Benny Havens, Oh!"

Author Unknown

From the book…

A song that is sung by the soldiers of Uncle Sam. And a drawing of the proprietor.

"BENNY" HAVENS, as all army men now living must know, was years ago a seller of contraband liquors and viands to the Cadets at West Point. At last, he tired out the patience of the officers of the Academy who felt that they could not any longer wink at his notorious infractions of the rule that no liquors should be sold on the Government reservation at the Point, and he was expelled from the grounds. But because he was ejected, he was not at all disposed to think that there should be "no more cakes and ale," and he opened a regular establishment a mile or two down the river, at Highland Falls, which soon became a favorite resort of the Cadets on convivial occasions, in most cases at the risk of dismissal.

The song which has carried the name of old BENNY around the world was originally composed by Dr. O'Brien, when a lieutenant in the Eight Infantry, on the occasions of a visit to his old friend Major Ripley A. Arnold, then a "first class man" residing in the old North Barracks at the Academy. They made many excursions to BENNY's. The song was composed by O'Brien and others then set to the tune of the "wearing of the Green." It soon became popular, and year after year additional verses have been composed by poets of succeeding classes, to suit certain events, as, for instance to commemorate the memory of a dead classmate, or to extol the names of heroes in war, until the original five verses have swollen to this size [28 in this 1878 volume].

Perhaps the greatest admirer the immortal BENNY had among the Cadets was the poet Edgar A. Poe, who was dismissed before completing his course. Poe was perfectly infatuated with the old joker and would steal away from the Academy and sit from morning until night conversing with the host and drawing out the old man's peculiarities of character. BENNY used to relate many interesting anecdotes of the poet and was a great admirer of the "Raven."

Here are the original five verses.

Come, fill your glasses, fellows, and stand up in row
To singing sentimentally, we're going for to go;
In the army there's sobriety, promotion's very slow,
So we'll sing our reminiscences of Benny Haven's oh!

> Oh! Benny Havens, oh! Oh! Benny Havens, oh!
> So we'll sing our reminiscences of Benny Havens, oh!

Now Roe's Hotel's a perfect "fess," and Cozzens all the go,
And officers as thick as hops infest "The Falls" below;
But we'll slip them all so quietly, as once a week we'll go
To toast the lovely flower that blooms at Benny Havens, oh!

Oh! Benny Havens, oh! etc.

Let's toast our foster-father, the Republic, as you know,
Who in the paths of science taught us upward for to go;
And the maiden, of our native land; whose cheeks like roses glow,
They're oft remembered in our cups at Benny Havens, oh!

Oh! Benny Havens, oh! etc.

To the ladies Of the Empire State, whose hearts, and albums too,
Bear sad remembrance of the wrongs we stripling soldiers do,
We bid fond adieu, my boys; our hearts with sorrow flow;
Our loves and rhyming had their source at Benny Havens, oh!

Oh! Benny Havens, oh! etc.

And when in academic halls, to summer hops we go,
And tread the mazes of the dance on the light fantastic toe,
We look into those sunny eyes, where youth and pleasure glow,
And think ourselves within the walls of Benny Havens, oh!

Oh! Benny Havens, oh! etc.

Showing how the weight of a plebe's gun increases as the march progresses:

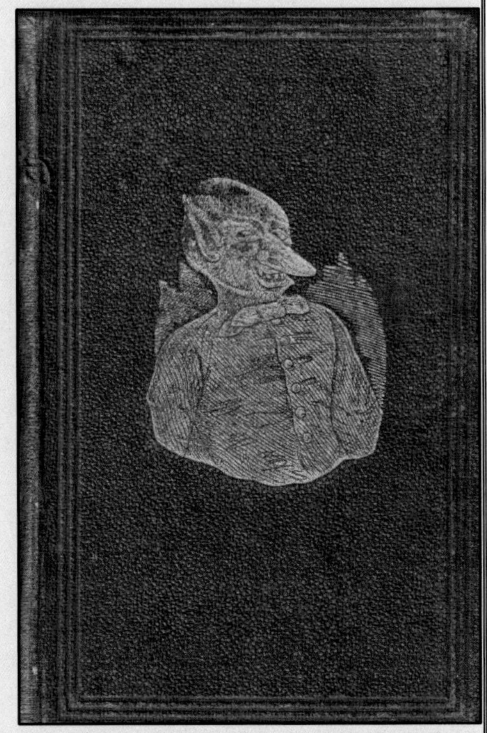

John Derby (Class of 1846) was chided by his superiors on the lighthearted and tongue-in-cheek tone of his dispatches. Posted to California following service in the Mexican-American War, Derby overcame boredom by composing comic essays, verse, and drawings under the pseudonyms of "Squibob" and "John Phoenix." He submitted these for publication in newspapers and magazines. Having exhausted his superior's patience, Derby was transferred back East after several years.

In 1856 *Phoenixiana* appeared -- a collection of Derby's journalistic pieces satirizing the body politic. Here is his Preface to the 12th edition appearing in 1866:

> "This book is merely a collection of sundry sketches, recently published in the newspapers and magazines of California. They were received with approval, separately, and it is to be hoped
>
> 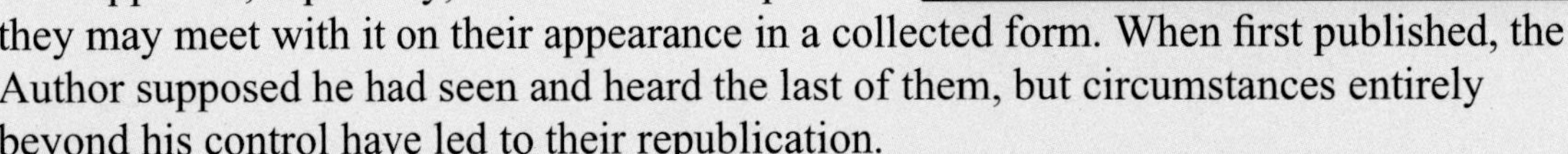
>
> they may meet with it on their appearance in a collected form. When first published, the Author supposed he had seen and heard the last of them, but circumstances entirely beyond his control have led to their republication.
> The Author does not flatter himself that he has made any very great addition to the literature of the age, by this performance; but if his book turns out to be a very bad one, he will be consoled by the reflection that it is by no means the first, and probably will not be the last of that kind, that has been given to the Public. Meanwhile, this is, by the blessing of Divine Providence, and through the exertions of the Immortal Washington, a free country; and no man can be compelled to read anything against his inclination. With unbounded respect for everybody."
>
> JOHN PHOENIX
> San Francisco July 15, 1866

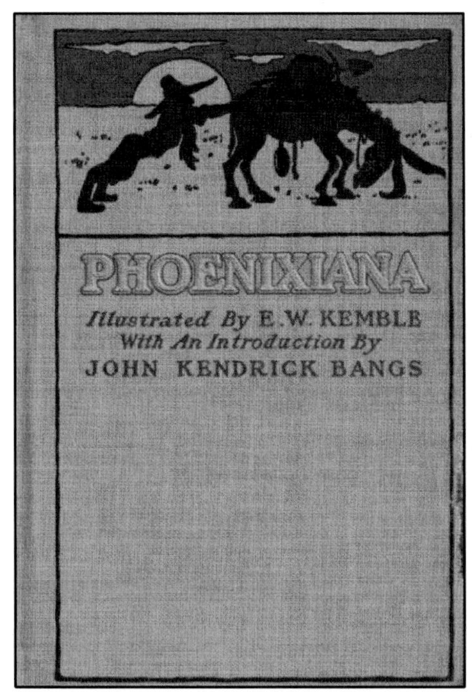

Phoenixiana* or *Sketches & Burlesques

WP Author, Satire, California

John Horatio Derby D. Appleton & Company (1903)

The opening story, an "Official Report," mocks the graft and corruption attendant to public works projects in San Francisco.

"OFFICIAL REPORT OF PROFESSOR JOHN PHOENIX, A.M., February 15, 1855"

Of a Survey and Reconnaissance of the route from San Francisco to the Mission of Dolores, made with a view to ascertaining the practicability of connecting those points by railroad.

[Note: Mission Dolores is a Spanish Californian mission, the oldest surviving structure in San Francisco, located only 2.5 miles from City Hall. Photo as it was in 1856.] [22-04]

"It having been definitely determined that the great Railroad connecting the City of San Francisco with the head of navigation on Mission Creek, should be constructed without unnecessary delay, a large appropriation ($120,000) was granted for the purpose of causing thorough military examinations to be made of the proposed routes. The routes [were the Northern, Central, and Southern]. Each of these proposed routes has many enthusiastic advocates; but the Central was, undoubtedly, the favorite of the public, it being more extensively used by emigrants from San Francisco to the Mission, and therefore more widely and favorably known than the others.

It was to the examination of this route, that the Committee, feeling a confidence (eminently justified by the result of my labors) in my experience, judgment, and skill as a Military Engineer, appointed me on the first instant. Having notified that Honorable Body of my acceptance of the important trust confided to me, in a letter, wherein I also took occasion to congratulate them on the good judgment they had evinced, I drew from the Treasury the amount ($40,000) appropriated for my peculiar route, and having invested it securely in loans at three per cent a month (made, to avoid accident, in my own name), I proceeded to organize my party for the expedition.

In a few days my arrangements were completed, and my scientific corps organized, as follows:

John Phoenix, A.M.	Principal Engineer, Chief Astronomer
Lieut. Minus Root	Apocryphal Engineer, 1st Asst. Astronomer
Lieut. Nonplus A. Zero	Hypercritical Engineer, 2nd Asst. Astronomer
Dr. Abraham Dunshunner	Geologist
Dr. Targee Heavysterne	Naturalist
Herr Von Der Weegates.	Botanist
Dr. Fogy L. Bigguns	Ethnologist
Dr. Tushmaker	Dentist
Henry Alfred Jenkins, R.A.	Draftsman
Adolphe Kraut	Draftsman
Hi Fun	Interpreter
James Phoenix (my elder brother)	Treasurer
Joseph Phoenix ditto	Quartermaster
William Phoenix (younger Brother)	Commissary
Peter Phoenix ditto	Clerk
Paul Phoenix (my cousin)	Sutler
Reuben Phoenix ditto . . .	Wagon-Master
Richard Phoenix (second Cousin)	Asst. ditto

These gentlemen, with one hundred and eighty-four laborers employed as teamsters, chainmen, rodmen, etc., made up the party.

For instruments, we had 1 large Transit Instrument (8 inch achromatic lens), 1 Mural Circle, 1 Altitude and Azimuth Instrument (these instruments were permanently set up in a mule-cart, which was backed into the plane of the true meridian, when required for use), 13 large Theodolites, 13 small [of the same], 8 Transit Compasses, 17 sextants, 34 artificial horizons, 1 side-real Clock, and 184 solar compasses.

Each employee was furnished with a gold chronometer watch, and, by a singular mistake, a diamond pin and gold chain; for directions having been given, that they should be furnished with "chains and pins," meaning, of course, such articles as are used in surveying—Lieutenant Root, whose "zeal somewhat overran his discretion," incontinently procured for each man the above-named articles of jewelry, by mistake. They were purchased at Tucker's (where, it is needless to remark, "you can buy a diamond pin or ring"), and afterward proved extremely useful in our intercourse with the natives of the Mission of Dolores and indeed, along the route.

Every man was suitably armed, with four of Colt's revolvers, a Minié rifle, a copy of Colonel Benton's speech on the Pacific Railroad, and a mountain howitzer. These last-named heavy articles required each man to be furnished with a wheelbarrow for their transportation, which was accordingly done; and these vehicles proved of great service on the survey in transporting not only the arms but the baggage of the party, as well as the plunder derived from the natives. A squadron of dragoons, numbering 150 men, under Captain McSpadden, had been detailed as an escort. They accordingly left about a week before us, and we heard of them occasionally on the march.

On consulting with my assistants, I had determined to select as one base of operation, a line joining the summit of Telegraph Hill with the extremity of the wharf at Oakland, and two large iron thirty two pounders [cannon] were accordingly procured, and at great expense imbedded in the earth, one at each end of the line to mark the initial points. On placing the compasses over these points to determine the bearing of the base, we were extremely perplexed by the unaccountable local attraction that prevailed; and were compelled to select a new location."

The story goes on another twenty pages describing the incompetent leadership and blundering of the crew. [EB]

"Venus"

VENUS AND VULCAN.

From Lectures on Astronomy:

"This beautiful planet may be seen either a little after sunset or shortly before sunrise, according as it becomes the morning or the evening star, but never departing quite 48° from the Sun. Its day is about twenty-five minutes shorter than ours; its year seven and a half months or thirty-two weeks. The diameter of Venus is 7,700 miles, and she receives from the Sun thrice as much light and heat as the Earth.

An old Dutchman named Schroeter spent more than ten years in observations on this planet, and finally discovered a mountain on it twenty-two miles in height, but he never could discover anything on the mountain, not even a mouse, and finally died about as wise as when he commenced his studies.

Venus in Mythology was a Goddess of singular beauty who became the wife of Vulcan, the blacksmith, and, we regret to add, behaved in the most immoral manner after her marriage. The celebrated case of Vulcan vs. Mars, and the consequent scandal, is probably still fresh in the minds of our readers. By a large portion of society, however, she was considered an ill-used and persecuted lady, against whose high tone of morals and strictly virtuous conduct not a shadow of suspicion could be cast. Vulcan, by the same parties, was considered a horrid brute, and they all agreed that it served him right when he lost his case and had to pay the costs of court. Venus still remains the Goddess of Beauty, and not a few of her protégés may be found in California."

John Derby (1823–1861) Class of 1846 served in the Mexican-American War and was severely wounded in a cavalry charge at Cero Gordo. After a half dozen years of service in California, Derby was transferred back east, where he succumbed to a brain hemorrhage at the age of 38. He is buried in the cemetery at West Point. [22-05]

The Spirit of Old West Point, 1858-1862

WP Author, Cadet, Memoir

Morris Schaff Houghton Mifflin Company (1907)

Schaff recounts his cadet experience immediately prior to the Civil War, paying particular notice to the personalities and demeanor of fellow cadets and the staff who were soon off to war.

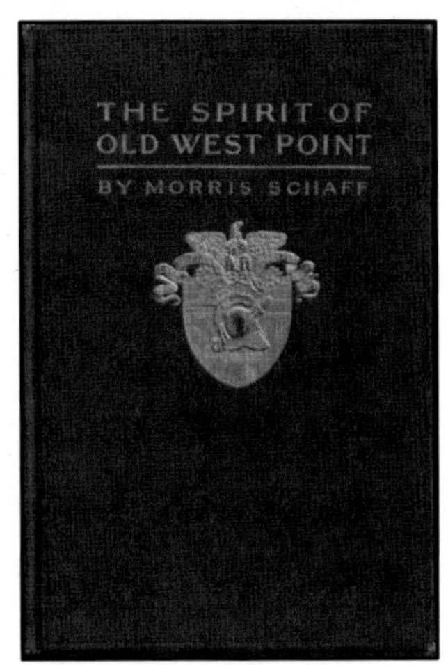

ON THE THRESHOLD

"Sometime during the winter of 1857-58, I received from the Hon. Samuel S. Cox, member of Congress from Ohio, representing the district composed of Licking, Franklin, and Pickaway, an appointment as cadet at West Point…

Never, I think, did fire burn as cheerily as ours burned that night, and somehow, I am fain to believe, the curling smoke communicated the news to the old farm; for the fields — how often had I wandered over them from childhood; oh, yes, how often had I seen the cattle grazing, — the corn tasseling, and their sweet pomp of daisies and clover and shocks of ripened wheat!— all seemed to greet me the next morning as I walked out to feed the sheep. We sat long round the fire, and read and re-read the entrance requirements, both physical and mental, as set forth in the circular accompanying the appointment.

This circular, prepared by Jefferson Davis, Secretary of War, himself a graduate of West Point, announced that only about a third of all who entered were graduated, and counseled the appointee that unless he had an aptitude for mathematics, etc., it might be better for him not to accept the appointment; thus, he would escape the mortification of failure for himself and family. In view of my lack of opportunity to acquire a knowledge of mathematics, or, for that matter, more than the simplest rudiments of an education in any branch, I wonder now that I dared to face the ordeal. But how the future gleams through the gates of youth!"

Here is his poignant recollection of Alonzo Cushing, hero at Gettysburg:

FINDING OUR PLACE

"Cushing, a day or so after reporting, saw me leaning, downhearted and lonely enough, against a post of the stoop. It was after dinner, and I was overlooking the crowd of yearlings who had assembled at the verge of limits. Their glittering brass buttons, jaunty caps, trim figures, and white pants still enliven for me the memory of that old drum-echoing area. Cushing fastened his eye on me and then asked, his prominent white teeth gleaming through his radiant smile, "What is your name, Animal?" - the title given by the third-class men to all new cadets. "Schaf'," I answered demurely.

"Come right down here, Mr. Shad," commanded Cushing. Well, I went, and had the usual guying, and subsequently was conducted over to a room in the second or third division, where I was ordered to debate the repeal of the Missouri Compromise with another animal by the name of Vance, from Illinois, whose eyes were so large and white as almost to prolong twilight…Vance, with great gallantry, helped to rally our lines in the face of Hood's heroic division on the battlefield of Chickamauga."

"I stayed over a month at Gettysburg after the battle, collecting and shipping the arms and guns left on the field, -- there were 37,574 muskets, -- and more than once I stood where the brave Cushing gave up his life, right at the peak of Pickett's daring charge. Oh, that day and that hour! History will not let that smiling, splendid boy die in vain; long her dew will glisten over his record as the earthly morning dew glistens in the fields."

Then 283 pages and a half century later:

"And now, dear old Alma Mater, Fountain of Truth, Hearth of Courage, Altar of Duty, Tabernacle of Honor, with a loyal and a grateful heart I have tried, as well as I could, to picture you as you were when you took me, a mere boy, awkward and ignorant, and trained me for the high duties of an officer, unfolding from time-to-time views of those ever-enduring virtues that characterize the soldier, the Christian, and the gentleman. All that I am I owe to you. May the Keeper of all preserve you; not only for the sake of our country's past glories and high destiny, but for the sake of the ideals of the soldier and the gentleman!"

Morris Schaff (1840–1929) graduated from West Point in June 1862 and was commissioned as a Second Lieutenant of Ordnance. Schaff served in multiple battles and campaigns during the U.S. Civil War, including the Rappahannock Campaign and the Richmond Campaign serving under generals Warren, Hooker, Meade, and Grant. He resigned from the Army in 1871 to pursue a business career. His wartime experiences greatly influenced the authorship of his early 20th century books and articles. [22-06]

Note: In 2014 Cushing was posthumously awarded the Medal of Honor. He is buried at West Point.

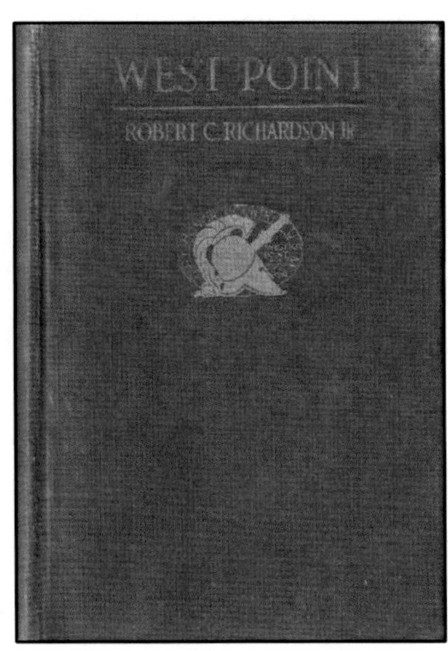

West Point: An Intimate Picture of the National Military Academy and of the Life of a Cadet

WP Author, Cadet, Memoir

Robert Richardson G.P. Putnam Sons (1917)

From the Preface:

"For many years the Military Academy was what its name implies, an Academy, but it has expanded from time to time until it is a military university, giving instruction for all branches of the service except the Medical Corps, and securing for each graduate a broad foundation which enables him to specialize in any direction by means of the various special schools for each branch. The glory of West Point, however, is in the West Point character, now well known in every civilized country in the world, with its reputation for fidelity, efficiency, discipline, and general uprightness. The standing army of the United States has always been too small for the tasks that have been laid upon it, and at every crisis it has had to train large forces of citizen soldiers summoned from civil life for the emergency. These citizen soldiers, as well as the Regular Army itself, rely upon the scientific education and high character of the West Point graduate to keep the art of war abreast, if not a little ahead, of the times, and for the initiative and informing leaven to permeate the mass and to cause the firm progress of discipline and uprightness throughout the whole. Shortly after the Mexican War a verse was added to the old West Point song of "Benny Havens, Oh!":

> "Their [graduates] blood has watered Western plains
> And northern wilds of snow,
> Has dyed deep red the Everglades,
> And walls of Mexico."

Since that time, they have shed it copiously in Cuba, China, and the Philippines, and they are now about to take their places with comrades from civil life fighting for liberty and democracy on the battlefields of France."

Hugh L. Scott, Army Chief of Staff

TABLE OF CONTENTS

XII. Spiritual Influences
XIII. The Spirit of West Point

While these chapters are not fictional, they are quite "story like" engaging the reader, transporting him back to a by-gone era. [EB]

Robert Charlwood Richardson Jr. (1882–1954) was admitted as a cadet at the United States Military Academy on June 19, 1900. His military career spanned the first half of the 20th century. He was a veteran of the 1904 Philippine insurrection, World War I, and World War II. He commanded the U.S. Army, Pacific (Hawaiian Department) during the height of World War II in 1943 until his retirement in 1946. [22-07]

Moving to the early 20th century, we find two interesting works which are definitely about the "Old Corps." The first book is quite fictional, while the second relates long lost stories of real individuals who made an impression during their sojourn at the Academy.

Postcard circa 1919

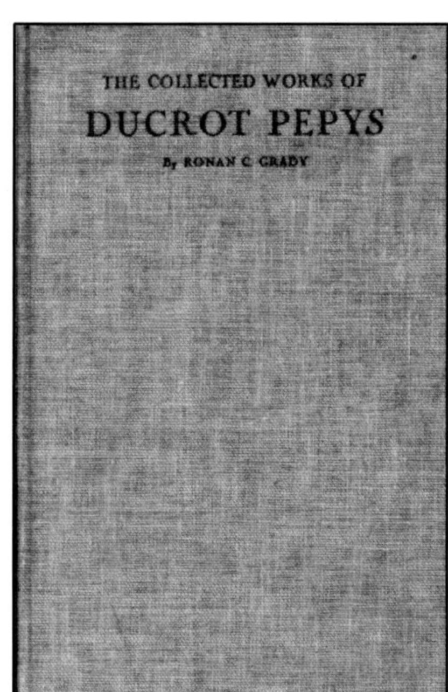

The Collected Works of Ducrot Pepys

Cadet, Anthology, Satire, WP Author

Ronan C. Grady Moore Publishing Co. (1943)

Compiled and edited by Roger Hilsman, Jr. Class of '43
Illustrated by Lewis F. Webster, Class of '43

From the Forward:

Yes, the life of a cadet is quite often trying, but, as it is with almost all difficult things, *la vie militaire* provides an opportunity for many a laugh. And this is what Ronan C. Grady has done. The man himself is gifted with a great creative sense of humor, and the impact on Grady and the "System" produces not a crash, but a wild, raucous laugh. Step by step through the years Grady has not recorded so much the products of his imagination, but the effect of the actual bewildering events that befall any cadet. The endless soireés, the eternal inspections, the hoped-for rain, the impartial, satanic justice of the Academic P's are all here in their reality. You see, this is not a book about West Point in its cumulative result, but a book about West Point as each little detail occurs. You see, a cadet does not get the big picture. All he sees is the little day to day events, which he calls soireés. Most cadets sigh and do their duty, Grady gets excruciatingly funny. For three years cadets have laughed 'til the tears came over Grady's diary of Ducrot Pepys, because not only was it funny, but amazingly, it was true!

The life of a cadet is to say the least, peculiar. To train the happy American college lad to be an officer capable of leading men into battle, discipline must be severe. At West Point, discipline is severe. For four years in normal times a cadet is closely confined within the grey walls of the Academy. His every move is watched over, guarded, and guided.

Plebe year, of course, is the worst, or best, depending on the square of the distance you are from it. The Fourth Classman not only has the many restrictions of the upper class cadet, but he has also the not-so-pleasant status of being a plebe. Every upperclassman is his superior and feels greatly the responsibility he has for bringing up the plebe right. For the plebe, it often means, a bewildering number of police calls, push-ups, and other interesting games.

The upperclassman is comparatively lucky; he has only the "System" with which to contend. However, this is often more than enough! To begin with, there is a special book of regulations published which the cadet must obey. Obviously, it is humanly impossible to do this completely, so the "System" provides certain interesting punishments such as confinement, walking the area, losing leave privileges, and so on. Then, add a long and difficult academic course, and you have the makings of an academy to train officers.

Excerpt from chapter: Plebe Year

"Dropped my rifle at parade but with great presence of mind fell down after it. Two first classmen knocked down in the rush of yearlings vying to aid me from the field....

Saturday inspection. My sane wife [old WP slang for roommate] in transports of joy that he received but two demerits...I received my usual seven...had qualifying bouts in boxing today. As I bleed quite easily, I got a good grade....

Tonight, I had to carve a leg of lamb that had been insufficiently killed. I checked a strong break for freedom by clubbing it with the milk pitcher....

"Clubbing it with the milk pitcher. . ."

Math Dept. seems to have a slight edge on the English Dept. [in failing cadets], but there is a fine competitive feeling between the two…"

. . . .

Later in the book…

TUESDAY. Today we rode horses. During the summer we spent two weeks riding on horses, and it was a pastime I did not enjoy. I do not enjoy it now. For some reason I seem to bring out the baser nature in every horse I meet...I am quite consciously afraid of horses and do everything I can to hide it from them and if I cannot fool a horse, I am indeed a failure in life. Usually, I swagger up to my beast, pat him on the part of his head farthest away from his teeth, and busy myself professionally with the large pieces of leather that are strewn over any horse. Then he bites me. From this point on it is open war between me and the horse, with me fighting a game but losing battle. If ever I attain the high place destiny has in store for me, there are several horses I know that are going to be torn to pieces between wild automobiles…

MONDAY. Early Graduation is still developing. Also, I note that a spirit not only martial but marital is developing among my classmates. They are continually bedecking some comely young lass with gems and making promises which, Lord help them, they intend to keep. This can lead only to unhappiness, Army brats, and someone getting trampled to death on the Chapel steps. One of my more feckless friends has already asked me to his wedding. A charming girl but I have doubts as to her abilities as a cook and I have none concerning his. There are probably compensating factors about which I know little but to a practical eye the outlook is gloomy. Nevertheless, I shall attend the wedding and choke down my fears and oceans of champagne and incidentally wish them joy. My other wife [roommate], praise be to Allah, has not shown any tendencies in the marrying line. This does not redound to his credit, however, as it is due less to his reasoning powers than to blunted reflexes. At any rate it's comforting to think that he will not be perpetuating his kind.

From a review by J. Phoenix Esq. on Amazon, 2007

"It was in the cadet-run POINTER magazine of 27 September 1940 that the diary of "Mr. Ducrot Pepys," a Plebe (freshman at West Point), first appeared. It was loosely based upon the diary of Samuel Pepys, an English diarist who chronicled London life during the years of 1660-69, making observations about people and events with an amazing eye for the telling detail…In all, 60 installments of the 'Ducrot' diary made it into print...

In actuality, Ducrot Pepys was **Ronan Calistus Grady** (1921–1992), a cadet. 'Grady,' as he was known to his friends, retired as an Army colonel, died in 1992, and is buried at West Point. Grady had agreed to revive Ducrot Pepys--most likely as an 'old grad'--for the 50th Reunion of the Class of June, 1943. Unfortunately, he died before he could accomplish the task."

West Point: Whistler in Cadet Gray and other Stories about West Point

Cadet, Anthology

Kenneth W. Rapp
North River Press distributed by Caroline House Publishers (1978)

Here are fourteen stories about the personalities of, and events which took place at the United States Military Academy. Some of the events are historically true, others are legendary. But all contribute to the reader's understanding of life at West Point.

Superintendent Richard Delafield, Major William J. Worth, and Captain George Derby are only a few of the many military figures who parade through the pages that follow. Humorist Mark Twain, British actor Sir Henry Irving, American painter James McNeil Whistler (then a cadet), and European ballerina Fanny Elssler are some of the non-military personalities you will find. [DJ]

The Table of Contents.

Kenneth W. Rapp was Assistant Archivist at the U.S. Military Academy. [DJ]

Chapter 23

West Point Candidates & Ex

This chapter is about "comings" and "goings" at West Point. The first section tells of lads who are seeking an appointment for a cadetship and how they achieved it (or didn't in one instance). The second half of the chapter has several novels about those cadets who left West Point before their graduation.

Arkie, the Runaway; or How He Got into West Point

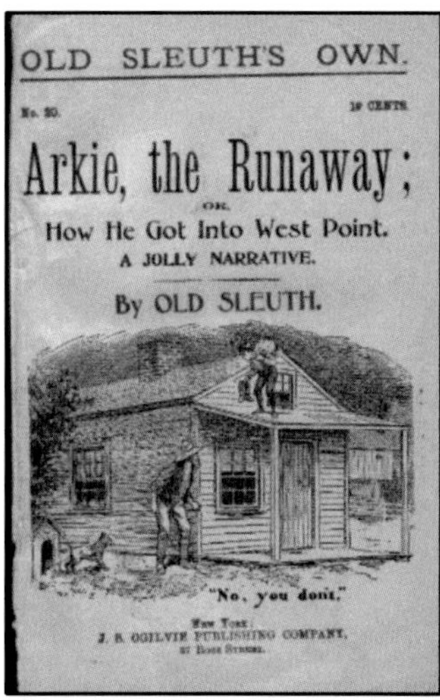

WP Candidate

Old Sleuth Ogilvie Publishing (1895)

Arkie Benton was a stepson. His widowed mother remarried to Farmer Kent but she passed away soon after. Arkie was an avid reader and educated himself with borrowed texts. The farmer treated Arkie as an indentured servant with no prospect of relief. Weary of the arduous life, Arkie fled the farm after reading how a farm boy in New York had taken a competitive exam for entrance into West Point and succeeded.

Adventures ensued. Arkie learned about the mean and dangerous life on the road as he worked his way East. He did befriend a couple of people
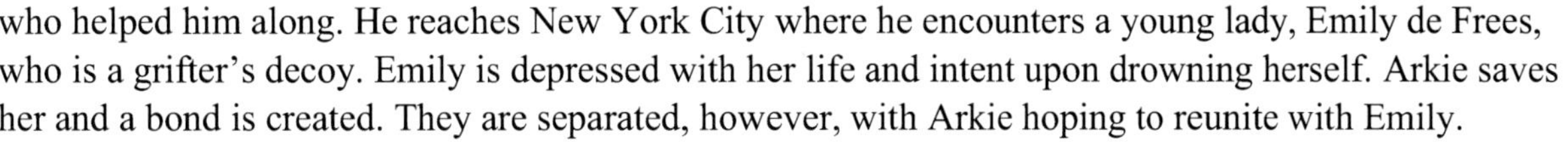
who helped him along. He reaches New York City where he encounters a young lady, Emily de Frees, who is a grifter's decoy. Emily is depressed with her life and intent upon drowning herself. Arkie saves her and a bond is created. They are separated, however, with Arkie hoping to reunite with Emily.

Arkie is industrious, makes contacts, all the while hoping for a chance to take the West Point entrance exam. In a year or so, he does take the exam and is accepted into West Point. He does well as a cadet rising to the rank of sergeant in the graduating class. At a Spring hop, he spies a most lovely young woman being escorted by a lieutenant. It is Emily in very fine attire. Her surname is now Kempton, after the well-to-do friend of her mother's that took her in after Emily's suicide attempt. Her guardian wishes her to marry an Army officer.

Emilie is staying at a hotel in Fort Montgomery. Arkie, in civilian attire, manages to meet her there and the acquaintance is renewed. He indicates that he is a "sergeant," but does not mention that he is within weeks of becoming a 2nd lieutenant. They part company for a bit, but later meet at an evening hop with Arkie in his full dress gray. A courtship ensues. [EB]

The Old Sleuth was the masthead of hundreds of detective and crime dime novels and magazines issued by various publishers from 1872 to 1920, in over fifteen different series. **Old Sleuth** was believed to be a pseudonym of **Harlan Page Halsey**. Very few of the quick-moving plots are available in an easy-to-read form today.[23-01]

The Eagles Brood

WP Candidate, Pulp Fiction

Lt. John T. Hopper Argosy Magazine (1928)

From the story:

"It was Jim's favorite walk. As he hiked along, his outward consciousness saw the fields, the sky, the low range of highlands which enclosed the Rowanee Valley; but his inner mind was dreaming -- dreaming of West Point.

Ever since Congressman Bill announced that he would give a competitive examination, the winner to have the coveted principal appointment to West Point, Jim's mind had been filled with nothing else.

Almost as far back as he could remember, Jim had wanted to go to West Point. During his boyhood days he had eagerly devoured all boy's books relating to West Point, and cadet days.

Jim's father was as anxious for Jim to go as Jim was himself. Mr. Briggs had just been able to keep his son at high school. To support him at an engineering college was out of the question. And Mr. Briggs wanted his son to have the chance he himself never had. Mr. Briggs felt that at West Point his son would receive an education, engineering and otherwise, inferior to none in the world.

As Jim walked along, his dreams took him farther and farther into the goal of his ambitions. West Point, that gray, stern citadel. Would he ever go there? Would he ever be one of those tall, straight, god-like creatures he had seen in the picture sections of Sunday newspapers? In his heart, he both hoped and doubted. There were so many obstacles to be overcome. First, he must stand highest in the competitive examination. That in itself was not easy, for the examination was to be given in all the towns and cities of the Congressional District of Louisiana in which he lived. No less than fifty young men hoped and were working as hard as Jim Briggs himself.

And, even if he did, by some great favor of chance, stand highest in that exam, he would still have before him the forbidding entrance examinations to West Point. For, winning the competitive examination only gave him the right to take these entrance examinations which were to be held in March. These, he had heard, were the most terrible and hardest of all examinations. Not only must he qualify mentally, but also, physically. Failing to do either would mean that West Point would still be barred to him...

As Jim walked on, he forgot all that stood in the way before he could even set foot on the United States Military Reservation at West Point, New York. He began now to dream that he was already there...

"Help!" It was a woman's shriek, loud and insistent.

"Help! Help! Help!"

Jim snapped from his dreaming…He saw a meadow entirely surrounded by a fence. A little way from him, just outside the fence, was a girl in white, waving frantically at him, and pointing at the same time to a lone tree which stood in the meadow. An angry bull shook his head and pawed the ground beneath the tree, which was small and scrubby.

Jim ran to the girl. "My father," she gasped breathlessly, "is up in that tree. The bull chased us. Father couldn't keep up with me, so he had to climb the tree…" [EB]

John T. Hopper (1903–1970) graduated from West Point in 1927 but resigned his commission in 1930 to pursue a writing career. See the "Army Sports" chapter for a more complete biography.

Red Randall, son of an Army Air Force officer, was scheduled to attend R-Day at West Point in June 1942. Red was was in Hawaii on the morning of December 7, 1941, when the Japanese attacked. He aspired to be an Army pilot, so when war came, Red was thrown into a series of adventures serving his country much sooner than he had hoped. All seven of Robert Sydney Bowen's "Red Randal" novels can be found in the "Army Aviation" chapter.

The Downward Path

WP Candidate, Okinawa

Cliff Towner Vantage Press (1954)

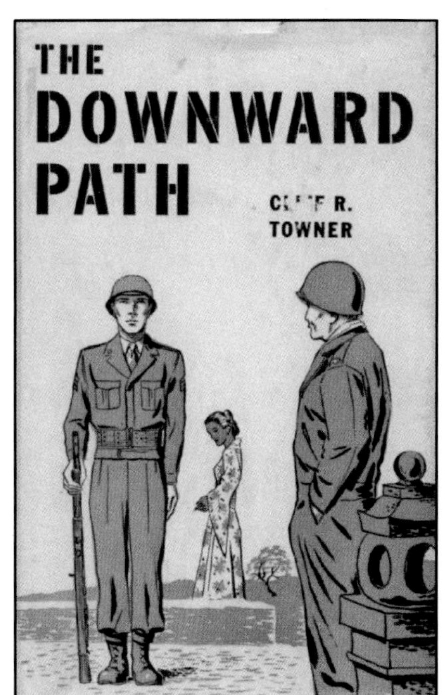

Tracy Carpenter wanted an Army career. He was studying hard for his West Point exams while on his first tour as a sergeant with the Okinawa occupational forces, after the close of World War II. Then the CO who had encouraged his ambition was replaced by Major Michael Craig. From that time forward, an evil star seemed to rule every move Tracy made. The inevitable result was disaster.

Accident, error, had luck, faulty judgment, wrong companions—all these contributed to Tracy's decline and fall, aided and abetted by Major Craig's obsessive malevolence and implacable hatred for the young enlisted man; yet, in every crucial situation, what Tracy did, seemed at the time the only thing he could do. When Major Craig refused him a furlough to take his exams, he reacted exactly as the sinister major had hoped. When the major denied him permission to marry Sutzico, the island girl he loved, he again strengthened his persecutors hand by going AWOL, in despair. Every path seemed to lead downward.

One stirring scene succeeds another; the movement never for a moment halts. Wild binges, furtive amatory affairs, a raid on a bootlegger's camp, a typhoon, and knock-down-and-drag-out fist fights all come alive… [DJ]

Cliff R. Towner of Elmira, New York, drew on his own experiences in Okinawa, in 1947, 1948, and 1949, as an enlisted man in the Signal Corps, for much of the material he has put into *The Downward Path*. The plot and characters, however, are his own creation. [DJ]

Introducing Parri

WP Candidate, Romance

Janet Lambert New York, Dutton (1962)

Fourteen-year-old Parri MacDonald, daughter of Penny Parrish and Josh MacDonald, attends private school and is quite lonely. After going to New York and charging an expensive coat to her mother's account, and auditioning for a Broadway show, Parri's parents realize that they haven't been very attentive to their daughter. While Parri is struggling with her problems, her cousin, Davy Parrish, son of Carrol and David Parrish and a victim of polio in his childhood, has difficulty passing the West Point physical. [DJ]

Janet Lambert (1893–1973) authored 54 young-adult fiction titles for girls from 1941 to 1969. She was the wife of an Army officer, so many of her stories revolve around military families. Other books and a biography are found in the chapter, "West Point Romances."

Inheritors of the Storm

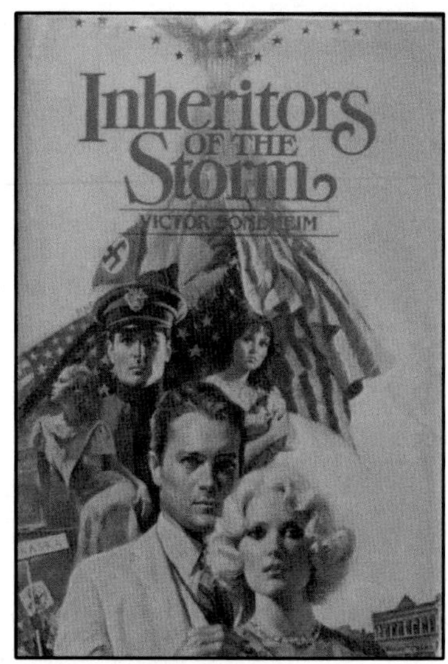

The Depression, WP Candidate

Victor Sondheim Dell Publishing (1981)

This is the saga of the Sinclairs, a wealthy family whose patriarch, Bradford Sinclair, Sr., committed suicide after the stock market crash of 1929. For the surviving widow and her children, the Sinclair legacy meant bankruptcy, disgrace, and broken-off lives. As the Depression grew deeper, they struggled not only to survive, but to make their mark on the rapidly changing world around them.

Brad, the eldest, with nothing but courage and a gifted tongue, rose high in the Roosevelt administration. Jeremy, with nothing but a writer's dream, became a first-rate news correspondent in Hitler's Germany. Pamela worked her way up as the most valuable employee of a Senate committee, engaged to Washington's most eligible bachelor. Young June Alice, tragically fated to live the life of a migrant farm worker; while Gordon scrambled to obtain an appointment to West Point, survived its four years of rigor, and was dispatched to Manchuria just prior to the Japanese invasion. [DJ]

Donald Moffitt (1931–2014), aka Victor Sondheim, was primarily a science fiction novelist. In the 1950s, Moffitt published approximately 100 short stories under many pen names while editing trade magazines by day. Moffitt later turned his attention to historical fiction such as *Inheritors of the Storm*. He notes on the dust jacket that he just finished a sequel, *Swimmers in the Tide*. It was never published and presumably resides with the rest of his papers in the Kansas University library system. [23-02]

How Far Would You Have Gotten If I Hadn't Called You Back?

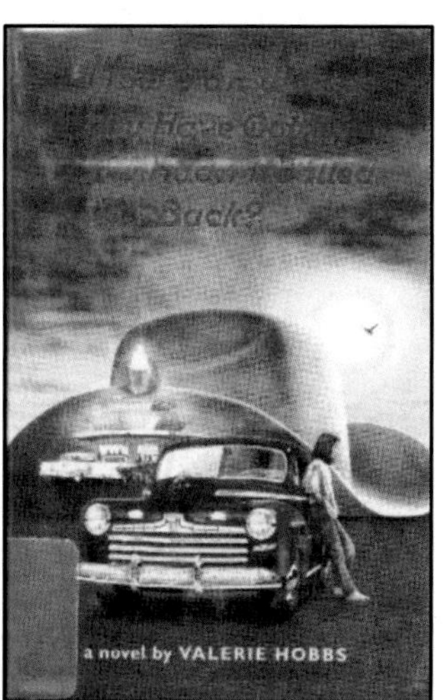

WP Candidate

Valerie Hobbs Orchard Books (1995)

This novel involves a young woman, Bron, growing up in California, her choice of boyfriends, one of whom is a candidate for entrance to West Point.

At school or at the local Frostee Freeze, Bron, is the "Girl From New Jersey," which her parents have fled because of a family crisis. They end up in Ojala, California, a dusty, tile-roofed town where the kids' teeth are all too white and school is "something you did between parties." If you weren't popular the main topic of interest is who has a new car or who's died in one.

Bron has neither a car nor a piano. Nor friends at first. But one day there's Lanie, Bron's age and beautiful and about to marry Jimbo despite his evil nature. There's J.C., the racer, who should be off limits but isn't. There's Silver, a '46 Ford that Bron can buy with tip money earned at her parents' restaurant.

And there's Will. She's heard her father tell him, when Will first shows up at the restaurant, "You'll have to check that, son," meaning the .45 in the holster slung on the boy's right hip. Will is a rancher, from outside the town and the man in his family at age eighteen. Nothing about him is what Bron thought she wanted; and there is the mystery. How could a piano and a pistol, a near-deadly race in Silver, and a sud den wind in the mountains all connect and cast such light across her life? [DJ]

Valerie Hobbs did not set out to write novels for young adults, but ever since critics praised her 1995 coming-of-age story, *How Far Would You Have Gotten If I Hadn't Called You Back*? she has been a respected author of fiction for teens. At the rate of approximately one book per year, Hobbs has crafted character-driven tales about young people on the verge of adulthood, forced to make serious decisions about the direction their lives will take. [23-03]

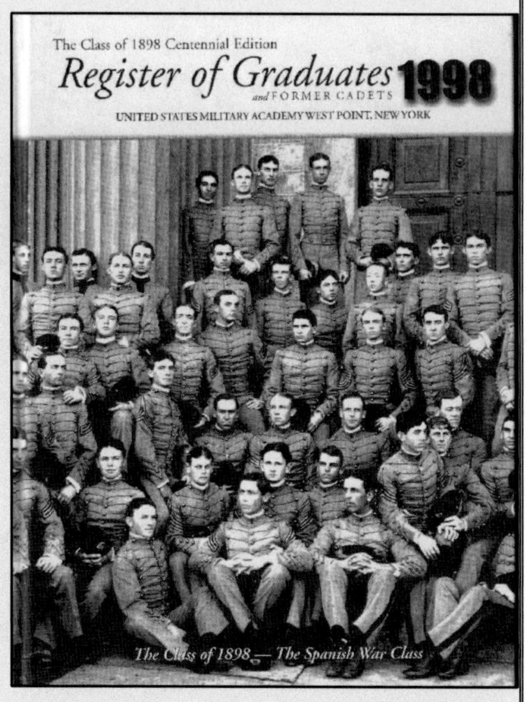

West Point and an Army career are not for everyone. There are young men and women entering the Academy, though carefully selected, who subsequently determine that their life goals lie elsewhere or who sustain injuries that preclude commissioning as an officer. There is no shame in their departure. For other cadets, circumstances dictate that they be separated from the Academy. Those that leave before graduation are referred to as "West Point - Ex."

A cadet may elect to leave the Academy up until the time he begins classes in the third year. He will not incur a service requirement before then.

The Academy maintains a remarkable public record of every individual who passes through its sally ports onto the Plain, whether they graduate or not. It can be found in the *Register of Graduates and Former Cadets,* which is updated annually.

The **Cullum number** is a reference and identification number assigned to each graduate. It was created by brevet Major General George W. Cullum (USMA Class of 1833) who, in 1850, began the monumental work of chronicling the biographies of every graduate. He assigned number one to the first West Point graduate, Joseph Gardner Swift, and then numbered all successive graduates in sequence…. From 1802 through the Class of 1977, graduates were listed by General Order of Merit. Beginning with the Class of 1978, graduates were listed alphabetically, and then by date of graduation. [23-04]

Here is a sample from the 1998 Register. Note the "x" and the class year beside the names of those who left before graduation. Others have their Cullum number assigned which points to a succinct (and cryptic) biographical record later in the book.

Hoblitzell, H A C	x1851	**Hoebeke**, Adrian L	9932
Hobson, Brian K	42237	Arnold J	12489
Eric M	52298	**Hoeber**, Adolph	x1878
George F	x1936	**Hoefer**, Fred S	x1922
James B	15826	**Hoeferkamp**, H R	20570
James M, Jr	4115	**Hoefert**, Richard A	32942
James W	x1972	Scott E	x1978
Joshua A	53253	Thomas E	32035
[2]Karen J	37494	**Hoeffer**, Henry J	8054
[1]Karen J Hinsey		**Hoefling**, John A	15811
Kenneth B	9433	**Hoege**, Howard H, III	51217
Michael W	29442	Howard H, Jr	28008
Ronald H	x1957	**Hoeh**, Daniel P	35650
Victor W, Jr	11944	**Hoehl**, Edward R	x1933
Walker E	4851	Francis R	9333
William H	5082	**Hoehne**, Fred N	48282
Hocevar, Bradley A	x1987	**Hoellerer**, Joseph	40293
Steven B	47312		

Incidentally, there are several novels in this collection written by West Point Ex's: Gus Lee, Joe Patton, Wayne Gundrum, and Keith Bush.

Shanghai Passage: Mutiny & Mystery on the Pacific

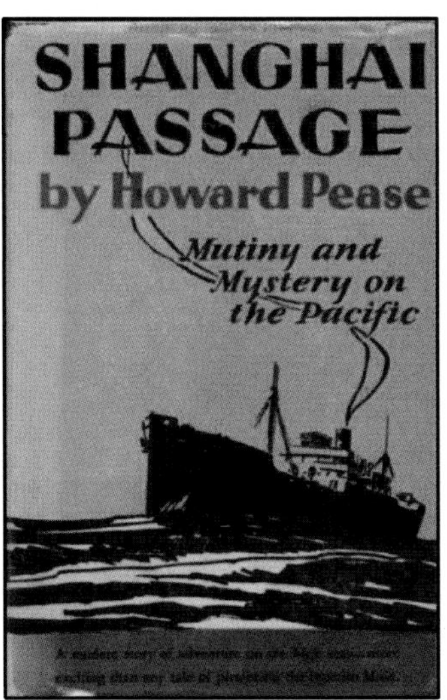

West Point Ex, Mystery, Intrigue

Howard Pease Sun Dial Press (1937)

MUTINY AND MYSTERY ON THE PACIFIC

Smarting from his expulsion from the U. S. Military Academy at West Point, Stuart Ormsby goes aboard the freighter "Nanking," outward bound for the China coast. Mystery, mutiny and the shadow of sudden death brood over the rusty decks of the old steamer. Strange figures are found among the riff raff crew: Wu Sing, the cook, gliding like a sinister shadow; Shark Bashford, the rascally mate; Toppy, the impudent cockney seaman; Swede Jorgenson, and Tod Moran, oiler—all of them involved in the mysterious dangers that threaten the "Nanking." [DJ]

Howard Pease (1894–1974) was an American writer of adventure stories. Most of his stories revolved around a young protagonist, Joseph "Tod" Moran, who shipped out on tramp freighters during the interwar years. The author knows the sea. He has shipped out of his home port, San Francisco; to American seaports from Seattle to Boston. [23-05]

I, James McNeil Whistler

West Point Ex

Lawrence Williams Simon & Schuster (1972)

Rarely have subject and style been so entertainingly fused as in this portrait of the incomparable, indomitable painter, James McNeill Whistler. Meticulously accurate and as wonderfully detailed as if the great master had really recounted it himself, this purported "autobiography" is charged with the same immense gaiety and élan that made Whistler such a fascinating and controversial personality of his time.

From Whistler's early artistic beginnings in Paris—he was an American expatriate whose intended military career had been cut short when he was discharged from West Point for failing chemistry—the book crackles with excitement. Caught up in the company of the great Impressionists (and keeping even closer company with his beautiful model-mistress), he soon moves on to his fantastic and swashbuckling career in London. Here, his unshakable confidence that he was always right (and his critics always wrong) won him even more notoriety than his frequent art triumphs. He had warm and admiring friends, like Rossetti; he had fierce enemies who despised his work, like the outstanding Establishment art critic of the day, John Ruskin.

The climax of the book is reached in the incredible lawsuit which Whistler brought and argued himself when it came to trial against Ruskin, who had mercilessly ridiculed his painting, "Nocturne in Black and Gold: The Falling Rocket." Whistler is nearly as well known for his performance in court on this occasion as he is for the almost accidental painting that earned him his greatest renown, "Arrangement in Gray and Black," known popularly as "Whistler's Mother." [DJ]

No biographical information could be found about this author.

Hailey's War

West Point Ex

Jodi Compton Shaye Areheart Books (2010)

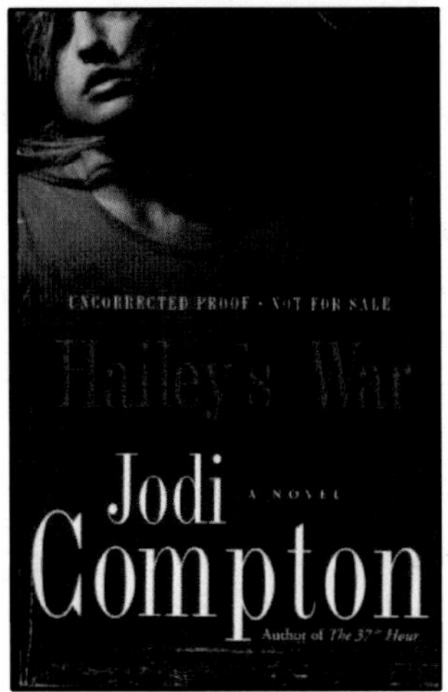

Twenty-four-year-old Hailey Cain has dropped out of a U.S. Military Academy for reasons she won't reveal. Now working as a hike messenger in San Francisco, Hailey keeps a low profile until her high school best friend Serena Delgadilio makes a call that will turn her whole life upside-down.

Serena is the head of an all-female gang on the rough streets of L.A. She wants Hailey to escort the cousin of a recently murdered gang member across the border to Mexico. It's a mission that will nearly cost Hailey her life, causing her to choose more than once between loyalty and lawlessness; and forcing her to confront two very big secrets in her past. [DJ]

Jodi Compton is from San Luis Obispo, California. She reports: "I'm the author of four mystery novels (I tend to use the term "crime novels," but either/or), with a fifth coming out through Amazon in 2021. I'm also a freelance book editor, and before coronavirus shut down most of live entertainment, I was getting some bookings as a stand-up comic." [23-06]

"Batwoman: Seven Years Ago"

WP Female, WP Ex, Comic Book, Crime

Greg Rucka
Detective Comics, Vol. 59 (Jan 2010) and Vol. 60 (Feb 2010)

This comic book series depicts the transformation of Kate Kane into Batwoman following her resignation from West Point. She chose not to lie about her sexual orientation. See the chapter "Paranormal, Supernatural, and Futuristic" for a more complete description and the author biography. [EB]

The most famous "Ex" from West Point is Edgar Allen Poe, who dropped out in 1834. Two novels about Poe at West Point are included in the chapter, "Mystery, Crime & Intrigue."

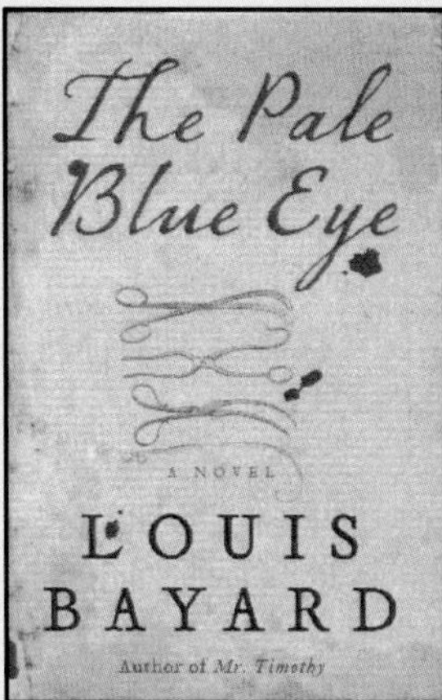

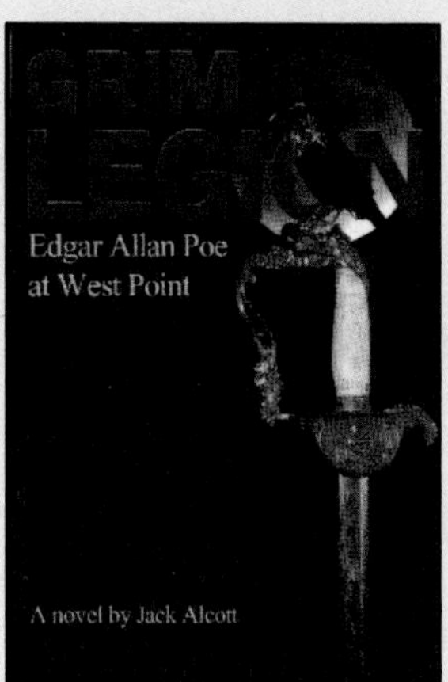

Two early novels tell of foreign cadets who left West Point because of exigent circumstances at home.

Get Your Man,
A Canadian Mounted Mystery

Ethel & James Dorrance (1921)
in "Mystery, Crime & Intrigue"

The Boy Scouts' Victory

George Durston (1921)
in "World Wars"

Chapter 24

Other Books by West Point Authors

A number of books and stories in this collection by West Point authors did not fit into one of the earlier chapters. They are, however, justifiably part of the West Point literary heritage. We begin with several works from the late 19th century.

The Wide, Wide World

WP Author, Adventure Abroad

Susan Warner Lamplighter Publish. (1852)

The Wide, Wide World is a sentimental work about the life of young Ellen Montgomery. The story begins with Ellen's happy life being disrupted by the fact that her mother is very ill, and her father must take her to Europe, requiring Ellen to leave home to live with an almost-unknown aunt. Very popular American novel in the mid-19th century. [24-01]

Susan Bogert Warner (1819–1885) was an American Presbyterian writer of religious fiction, children's fiction, and theological works. She is best remembered for *The Wide, Wide World.* [24-01]
From 1837 until the beginning of the 19th century, Susan and Sister Anna lived on a farm on Constitution Island across the Hudson from West Point. They were quite religious, published many books, and frequently invited West Point cadets to prayer meetings and to relax away from their post on a Sunday afternoon. Both sisters are buried in the West Point cemetery. Their home is preserved and may be visited by taking a boat from the dock at West Point. [EB]

My Official Wife

WP Author, Adventure Abroad

Richard Henry Savage Routlege Press (1892)

From a Moving Picture World synopsis:

"The marriage of Marguerite Lenox to a wealthy Russian, and her subsequent widowhood, occasions a trip to Russia by her father, Arthur Bainbridge Lenox. He is a handsome man in the early forties. The noble Weletsky family, into whom his daughter has married, have never seen either Lenox or his wife, but desire Lenox's cooperation in the settlement of his daughter's estates. The summons comes while they are in Paris. A passport for two, man and wife, is secured, but Mrs. Lenox is of delicate health and decides to let her husband take the journey alone.

The Nihilist, "Helen Marie," is also preparing a trip to Russia. Of unknown identity, her activities are yet notorious, and the police of Russia are warned. Knowledge of the passport is brought to her by a young Nihilist girl employed in Mrs. Lenox's services. Helene Marie has a just cause against the Russian aristocracy. When hardly more than a child, she saw her family butchered in cold blood. She carries through a ruse whereby Lenox permits her to cross the Russian frontier as his wife. Her charm begins to work upon his susceptible nature. The pair are continually brought into contact with personages and officials dangerous to Helene Marie.

Finally, at the hotel in St. Petersburg she reveals her identity to Lenox and dares him to betray her secret. She charms the rich aristocratic Weletskys and Sacha Weletsky falls in love with her. The strain on Lenox induces him to resort to a drug for sleep. He forestalls his daughter's contemplated journey to Petersburg (from the Russian provinces) and attempts to take "his official wife" back to western Europe. Her work in Russia has been completed. She would gladly go, but the Weletskys beg her to remain and attend a ball. She learns the Czar is to be in attendance. It is her one chance to become the Joan of Arc of the Nihilists. She refuses to go back with Lenox. Lenox therefore purposely misses the train. He returns to the hotel, finds his "official wife" being wooed by Sacha. But he accompanies her to the ball. During the evening his hand touches the pistol in the folds of her gown. He realizes her object is the Czar's assassination. He averts this tragedy by a sleeping potion which he gives to Helen Marie in a glass of punch. She collapses and he carries her home.

Meanwhile the secret service has sent a telegram to the real Mrs. Lenox in Paris which brings her to Russia. Lenox's secret is, however, protected by the police, because of his saving the life of the Czar, Helene Marie induces Sacha to elope with her in his yacht, which is fired upon from the forts and Helene reveals her identity. The young man renounces rank for love of her, but his yacht is sunk by the Imperial guns." [24-02]

The Midnight Passenger

WP Author, Adventure Abroad

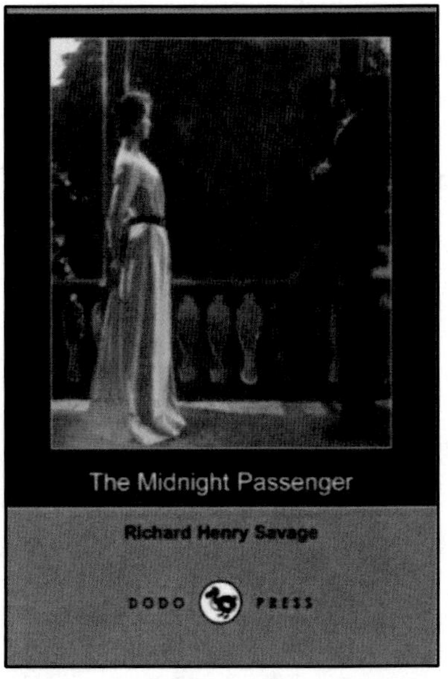

Richard Henry Savage Dodo Press (2007) Reprint

Randall Clayton was surrounded by enemies. His father's business partner had looked after him in the years since his father's death. But Hugh Worthington's motives were not altruistic – he had a secret to hide and a scheme to bring to fruition that would make him millions at Clayton's expense. Clayton's roommate, Arthur Ferris, had his own schemes, including stealing the affections of Worthington's daughter away from Clayton. Clayton worked for a pittance in New York, where he was watched day and night by Worthington's spies, and by the ruthless Fritz Braun, who plotted to rob Clayton of the large deposit that he daily carried for his employer. It seemed that Jack Witherspoon was his only friend, the only one he could trust. But Jack was sailing for Europe and neither man fully comprehended the danger that was closing in on Randall. [24-03]

Richard Henry Savage (1846–1903) was raised in California, studied law, then obtained an appointment to West Point. He graduated in 1868. He served in the Corps of Engineers and travelled abroad extensively, marrying a Russian noblewoman in Germany. Savage was appointed envoy to Rome and even served for a time in the Egyptian Army. In 1890 he was struck with jungle fever in Honduras. While recuperating in New York state he wrote his first book: *My Official Wife*. This very successful action-and-adventure story was followed by more, at the rate of about three per year. In 1903 he was run over by a horse-drawn carriage while crossing a street in New York City. Savage is buried in the cemetery at West Point. 24-04

But Yet a Woman

WP Author, Adventure Abroad, Romance

Arthur Sherburne Hardy Dodd, Mead, & Co. (1883)

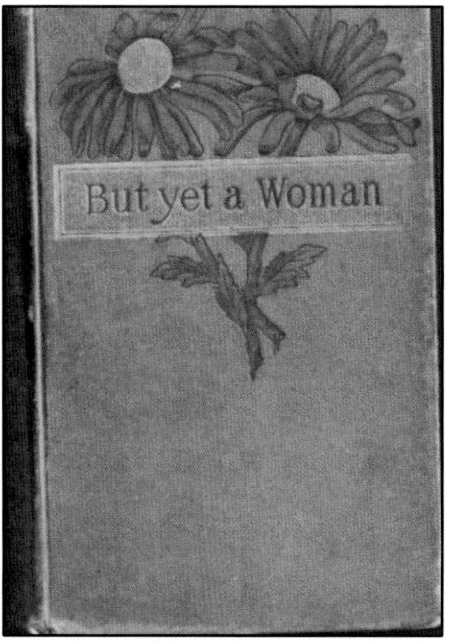

This "is a romance of real life, its scene laid mainly in Paris during the time of the Second Empire. Renée Michael, a fair young girl destined to be a *réligieuse,* shares the home and adorns the salon of her elderly bachelor uncle, M. Michael. They enjoy the friendship of M. Lande, and his son, Dr. Roger Lande. The four, together with Father Le Blanc, a kindly old curé, and Madame Stephanie Milevski, make up a congenial house party at M. Michael's summer home on Mt. St. Jean. Stephanie, the half-sister of her host, is the young widow of a Russian nobleman who has died in exile. She was associated with the eminent journalist M. De Marzac in the Bourbon restoration plot and became the object of his ardent though unrequited love. Her affection is for Dr. Roger Lande; but he loves Renée, and not in vain. Stephanie induces M. Michael to allow her to take Renée on a journey to Spain. Upon the eve of their departure, De Marzac, angered by Stephanie's continued denial of his suit, accuses her of taking Renée to Spain in order to prevent Roger from wooing her until the time set to begin her novitiate shall have arrived. The unraveling of this situation makes an excellent story. The book, published in 1883, is written with charming delicacy of treatment, and conceived entirely in the French spirit." [24-05]

No. 13, Rue Du Bon Diable

WP Author, Adventure Abroad, Crime

Arthur Sherburne Hardy   Houghton Mifflin Co (1917)

From the opening chapter:

"On the morning of Friday, the 9th of May, at twenty minutes past eleven, a messenger from the Crédit Lyonnais rang at No. 13, Rue du Bon Diable. Under his arm was one of those leather portfolios in which bank messengers are accustomed to carry drafts, bills of exchange, and like valuable papers. In this instance the portfolio contained thirty banknotes of one thousand francs each, destined for M. Janvier. The occasion for the withdrawal of so large a sum was the birthday of his niece Corinne. . .

On this 9th of May Corinne had reached her eighteenth birthday, and M. Janvier's affection, which had kept pace with the years, was rioting in prodigality. The fact is, Corinne possessed a charming neck and throat, and her uncle had conceived the idea of encircling it with a string of pearls."

This is a crime story set in Paris. We know the killer right from the start; the question is, will he be caught, and if so, how? [24-06]

Arthur Sherburne Hardy (1847–1930) was an American engineer, educator, editor, diplomat, novelist, and poet. He completed one year at Amherst College before becoming a cadet at the United States Military Academy in 1865. He excelled in languages graduating tenth in the class of 1869. Following the Civil War, there was little chance of advancement in the Army, so he resigned in 1870 to become a professor of civil engineering at Grinnell College and later Dartmouth College, where he served a year abroad. He published several highly respected books on mathematics during his academic career. After his academic/publishing career, Hardy was appointed as the United States ambassador to several countries including Persia, Romania, Serbia, and Spain. [24-07]

Donald's School Days

WP Author

General O.O. Howard   Lee & Shepard Company (1899)

From the Preface:

"In early life I was very much entertained and stimulated by Hughes's books for England, Tom Brown at Rugby" and "Tom Brown at Oxford." These pleasing stories of the sports and of boys and young men naturally led me to think of things corresponding in our New England life. *Donald's School Days* embraced my first effort to present to youthful readers a connected story which contained substantially biographical information about two boys whom I knew from babyhood, and who actually graduated from the farm, the school, college, and one of them from a theological seminary. As I have previously said, I attempted portraiture of youth for the benefit of youth, as I observed persons and things in our New England life, showing the actual training of boys (forty years ago) and how strong wills and hot tempers were brought under subjection. I followed one of the lad's work of life and gave touches of his successful beginnings.

The cordial reception by the readers, and the good results testified to the author in a multiplicity of individual instances, induce him to carry out his original promise to carry the younger of the boys into the Civil War, and give a recital of actual campaigns and battles. There is much evidence in my hand of the hold *Donald's School Days* has upon the public. The nature of boys is doubtless the same, though our country and our modes of living are undergoing rapid and wonderful changes. The new generation of children and youth which have come on the stage since the book was written will, I believe, give a hearty welcome to the volume when it shall appear in a new dress and with modern illustrations. Boys enjoy to a degree reading of what their fathers accomplished, and how they acted when of their own age; but what their grandfathers did has a curious and often stronger hold upon them. Perhaps a better reason for reissuing "Donald" with some proper alterations is that he ought to bear company with "Henry in the War," my model volunteer. This book my worthy publishers are now to present as a proper companion to the other. It will be remembered that the early life of Henry was carried on with that of his brother Donald in the first effort, where Donald was the principal character. In the new book, *Henry in the War*, Henry will, of course, become the hero of the story.

Oliver O. Howard (1830–1909) was a major general and corps commander in the Civil War. Howard wrote two novels for youth. *Henry in the War* was the other one. It is included along with a more extensive biography of General Howard in the "Civil War" chapter.

Moving to the 20th century, we encounter again one of the most prolific of West Point story tellers—John T. Hopper. Eighteen of his stories are included in this collection, but that is only a fraction of his pulp fiction output between 1927 and 1945. All but one of his stories that follow involve the Army and take place in Panama. The United States Army occupied the Panama Canal Zone from 1902 until the early 1990s. Protecting the Panama Canal was a paramount interest of the United States.

"Here Comes the Fleet"

Panama, WP Author

Lt. John T. Hopper Argosy Magazine (November 16, 1929)

When the Fleet is in, the Navy must be served — but that's not saying what sort of dish the Canal Zone Army defenders may concoct for the gobs!

Here comes the fleet! The shout was raised and carried along by a dozen voices, and finally penetrated the gun pit, where little Private Amos Dougherty was industriously polishing a bit of brass on one of the big guns that protect the Pacific entrance to the Panama Canal. The hand which an instant before had been rubbing so cheerfully and contentedly, halted, and began shaking as though its owner had suddenly become possessed with the palsy. [Amos had been courting Mamie, who was claimed by the heavyweight boxing champ of the fleet. The latter had vowed to destroy any soldier that messed with this girl in his absence.]

Panama City seemed buried in a blizzard of white. Shore leave for the fleet. Every narrow, dirty street, every bar, every blaring cabaret was jammed with sailors in white. There were thousands of them, drinking, dancing, fighting, loving. Here and there, the green of a lone soldier's uniform like a leaf on unbaled cotton.

It was about midnight in the bar of the Golden Dollar when Hank Mitzenberger, hairy-chested, heavyweight champ of the fleet, caught up with the quaking, diminutive Amos Dougherty. It was not one of Hank's traits to beat about the bush. Although he had never heard of mathematics, he believed that a straight arm was the shortest distance between nose and fist.

"Here y'are, ya little mutt!" was his greeting. "What's dis I hear 'bout yuh two-timing' me wit' me goil?" "Honest, I haven't, Hank!" whimpered Amos, cringing. "It's a mistake. It's another fellow that's been rushing her. No kidding, Hank. I've seen Mamie once, or maybe twice, but I was only trying to do you a favor, to tell her what a mistake she was making…" [EB]

"M.P. In the Canal Zone's Forbidden Area"

Panama, WP Author

Lt. John Hopper   Argosy Magazine (July 18,1931)

"Corporal Peters, of the thankless race of M.P.'s, normally had his hands full protecting his fellow soldiers from the thugs of Panama City's forbidden native quarter—but the trap he stumbled in this night was no normal one." [EB]

"Ninth Inning Nerve"

Sports, Panama, WP Author

Lt. John Hopper   Argosy Magazine (May 21, 1932)

This novelette in two parts covers an Army-Navy baseball game in the Panama Canal Zone.

"Lanky Devlin had his own reasons for not wanting the Army to know his real name, but he would pitch for them until the going was tough…" [EB]

"Failure Means Death: A Battle of Spies in Panama"

Panama, WP Author

Lt. John T. Hopper Argosy Magazine (Oct 10,1932)

TULLY'S STRANGE BUSINESS

Major General James W. Marshall, in command of the United States Army troops stationed in the Panama Canal Zone, sat back in his chair and puffed comfortably on his half-smoked cigar. The general was massive in build, hearty by nature and jovial of manner…The general wore the conventional military evening dress of the tropics; a white monkey jacket, ornamented by a knot of gold at each shoulder; civilian starched shirt with bat wing collar and black tie; and black cloth trousers.

The general's back was to the seaward railing of the balcony of the Union Club, Panama City. He was gazing with a little smile out upon the paved floor, upon which the feet of many dancers were going "shuff-shuff" rhythmically. In a corner, a Panama orchestra was playing a sobbing blues number…

The general smiled at the man beside him; They were the only persons at the table. All the others were dancing. The man returned the general's smile.

"Nice party you're giving, general," he complimented.

General Marshall took another leisurely puff at his cigar. "Pretty good, Tully," he nodded, "for an old bachelor like me, eh?"

Tully was an odd-looking character. He was dressed in civilian black. He was small in comparison with the general. There was about him the keen, quick, searching manner of the ferret. His beady black eyes were forever darting in and out among the dancers...

"You know, Tully," said the general good-naturedly, settling himself more comfortably in his chair, "I hate to see you around."

"Why, general?" asked Tully, raising his meager, gray eyebrows. His voice was dry, and not very strong. It gave the impression that it had not spoken with any great emotion for the past twenty years, or more. "We've known each other for a good many years, general, and have been good friends all that time, I hope."

"Yes," the general admitted. "All of that, Tully. But it's your blasted business! You never come around but what there are murders, killings, suicides, thievery, skullduggery, and whatnot. Just knowing you're down here makes me nervous. I don't know what to expect! Whenever you fellows in the Intelligence Dept come drifting around, there's something in the wind. What's up this time, Tully?"

Tully raised his slender shoulders slightly. "Who can tell, general? You know how this business is. But I guess it's nothing to be especially worried about. Washington just received information that there were some international spies seen down here, and so I was sent down to kind of nose around."

General Marshall snorted loudly. "You're, a damned spy yourself, Tully! . . ." [EB]

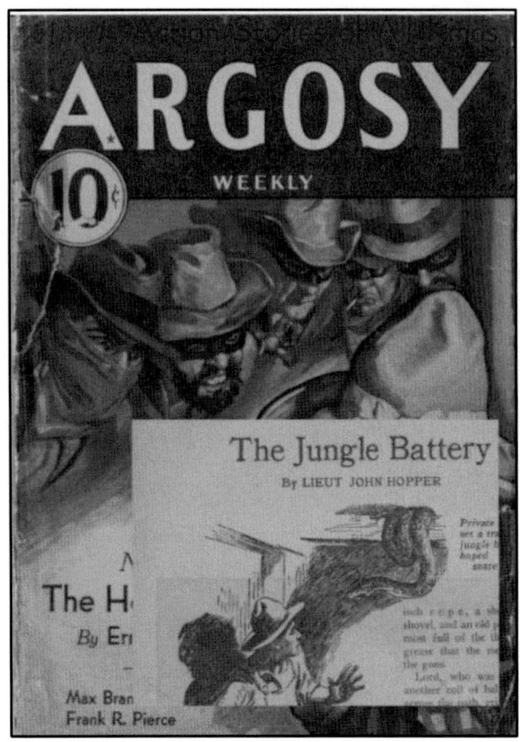

"The Jungle Battery: A Canal Zone Death Plot"

Panama, WP Author

Lt. John T. Hopper Argosy Magazine (April 1, 1933)

Private Philip Lord was constructing a trap to catch and kill a man, when Captain Bauer rounded a turn in the path and came upon him.

"What are you making here, Lord?" asked the officer. Curiously, he eyed the things in the path. There was an ax, a coil of half-inch rope, a short-handled shovel, and an old paint can almost full of the thick, brown grease that the men used on the guns.

Lord, who was unwinding another coil of half-inch rope across the path, grinned at his captain. "Aimin' to catch me a hog, sir. A wild hog. There's one that's been usin' this here path for his own private an' personal use ever since the new magazine's been built."

Lord wiped the perspiration from his forehead with his hairy, sun-reddened forearm. Of the two men, the captain looked much the cooler in the heat that pressed around them in the small patch of jungle.

This was a little odd, for the officer was in full uniform, compared with what the soldier was wearing. Shoes, leather puttees, breeches, shirt, black tie; and campaign hat made up Bauer's dress, while Private Lord was clad simply in his shirt, faded blue denim overalls, heavy quartermaster's brogans, and a battered campaign hat which was not even graced by the red cord of the artillery.

But then, Private Lord thought to himself, it was no wonder that he was sweating like a tin mess pitcher full of ice water. Only Captain Bauer did not know the real reason. Neither did Slick Henly know it. Slick who was Lord's fellow caretaker of the jungle battery, miles deep in the jungle that began beside the Pedro Miguel locks of the Panama Canal. Nobody in the world knew it except Private Lord himself. It was quite a thing to set a trap to catch a wild hog - and catch a human hog instead.

Captain Bauer looked interested. "A wild hog, eh" he said.

Private Lord smiled at him. "Has the captain ever ate a piece of wild hog, sir—No? Well, when I catch this one, I'll bring in a piece for you."

"That'll be too much trouble, Lord. It's a long trip into the fort from here. Thanks just the same."

Lord's eyes widened upon the officer. "I don't mind the trip, sir," he protested. "The captain really ought to have a taste of jungle hog before he leaves Panama."

Bauer smiled in the have-it-your-own-way-then fashion which army officers use when their men insist on giving them presents. He looked at the coil of rope that Lord had in his hands.

Noting the glance, the soldier grinned apologetically. "It's some of the rope we had in the tool shed, sir. It's been there quite a while, an' I thought the captain wouldn't mind if I used it for this."

"No. Go ahead. It's all right." The officer watched while the soldier pushed his way through the thick jungle shrubbery beside the path, unwinding the rope as he went. A moment later, Lord reappeared, perspiring more than ever. "I wonder if the captain'd mind givin' me a hand—little?" he began embarrassedly. "If it's too much trouble," he added hastily, "I can wait till Slick—er—Private Henly comes back from town, sir."

"No, that's all right," said Captain Bauer, just as Private Lord knew that he would. "What can I do?"

Private Lord felt his heart bumping beneath his perspiration-drenched shirt. Everything he had planned was going along with ridiculous smoothness. He had had nothing less than a touch of genius when he had thought of the idea of securing Captain Bauer's assistance in constructing a trap to catch wild hog. . . .

But having Captain Bauer help him was not the sum total of his smartness. There was the trap itself, a most marvelous and fearful contraption. Night after night, in the hot, heavy darkness of the little shed which the two caretakers shared together, Lord had lain awake, listening to and hating Henly's regular, peaceful breathing, while he tried to create in his mind the plan of a trap that would not fail and at the same time would leave him without liability for what it caught. [EB]

"The Vodka Boatman"

WP Author

Lt. John Hopper Argosy Magazine (September 5, 1931)

"Pal Reilly, U. S. N., went ashore at Vladivostok for a Labor Day celebration; but be had small cause for celebrating his encounter with that grim-faced woman commissar and her Soviet henchmen." [EB]

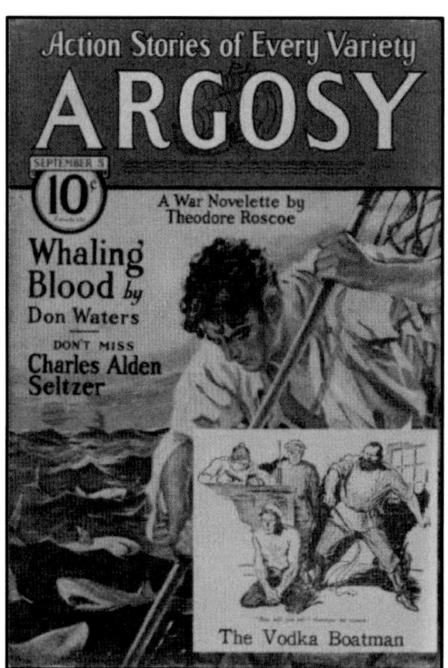

John T. Hopper (1903–1970) graduated from West Point in 1927 but resigned his commission in 1930 to pursue a writing career. We might presume that he spent a portion of his brief military career in the Panama Canal Zone. See the "Army Sports" chapter for a more complete biography.

"A Nickelodeon Childhood"

WP Author

Robert Wohlforth New Yorker Magazine (1934-1938)

Stories of the author's youth in the New York City - 1910s:

A Nickelodeon Childhood The Perils of Electricity
Down with Daylight Savings In and Out of "Birth of a Nation"

Robert Wohlforth (1902–1997) graduated with the Class of 1926. His one novel, *Tin Soldiers*, which is described in "The Cadet Experience" chapter was extremely controversial when published in 1934. It is also quite rare.

The remaining works in this chapter are from the late 20th century, mostly by authors whose works have appeared in other chapters within this catalog.

How Darkness Fell

Korea, WP Author

Col. R.A. Ellsworth Vantage Press (1974)

"Is it possible for the United States to destroy constitutional government and establish a socialist dictatorship? Are we contributing to the communist efforts to rule the world? The mistakes, blunders, wrong estimates, and poor management by our government since the creation of the Federal Reserve Bank and the graduated income tax in 1913 have brought this great nation to the brink of disaster. The fallacious Keynes economics of deficit spending, the Fabian Socialist influence, no-win wars, the advocacy of retreat and surrender, 'peace with convergence' and the welfare state has brought Uncle Sam to his knees.

This unique novel is about a mythical figure, Frank Rodriguez, a West Point officer who turns communist under a strange chain of events, then defects back to freedom and tells all. Frank's five classmates share his story and join him in a new vision of 'Technocracy City,' as a counter-utopia to the dread specter of communism." [DJ]

Robert A. Ellsworth (1899–1982) graduated with the Class of 1924 and served his career in the Field Artillery. During World War II, his service in the Pacific and in Europe was distinguished by many citations for valor. Among his decorations are three Silver Stars, the Legion of Merit, three Bronze Star Medals, the Air Medal, and the Purple Heart. He also received two awards of the Croix de Guerre. He was wounded in battle and retired with a medical disability in Palm Springs, California in 1946. This appears to be his only book. [24-08]

China Boy

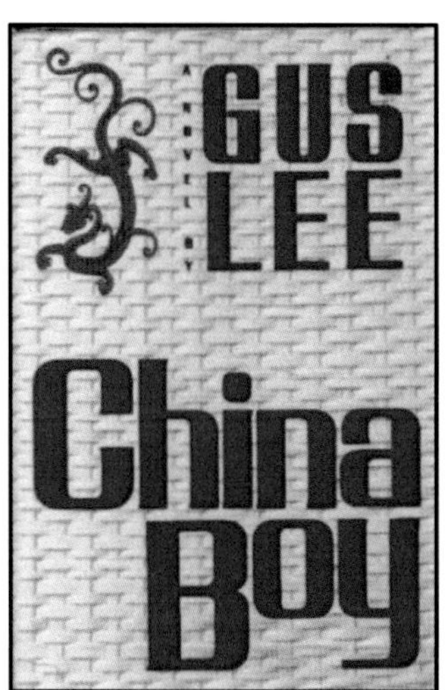

WP Author, California

Gus Lee Dutton (1991)

China Boy is a novel of family relationships, culture shock, and the perils of growing up in an America of sharp differences and shared humanity.

Kai Ting is the only American-born son of an aristocratic Mandarin family that fled China in the wake of Mao's revolution. Growing up in San Francisco's ghetto, Kai is caught between two worlds — embracing neither the Chinese nor the American way of life. After his mother's death, Kai is suddenly plunged into American culture by his new stepmother, a Philadelphia society woman who tries to erase every vestige of China from the household. [DJ]

Augustus Samuel Mein-Sun "Gus" Lee (1946–) entered West Point with the Class of 1968 but left before graduating. He has two other novels in this collection: *Honor and Duty* in the "Cadet Experience" chapter and *Tiger's Tale* located in the "*In the Far East*" chapter. A more complete bio can be found there.

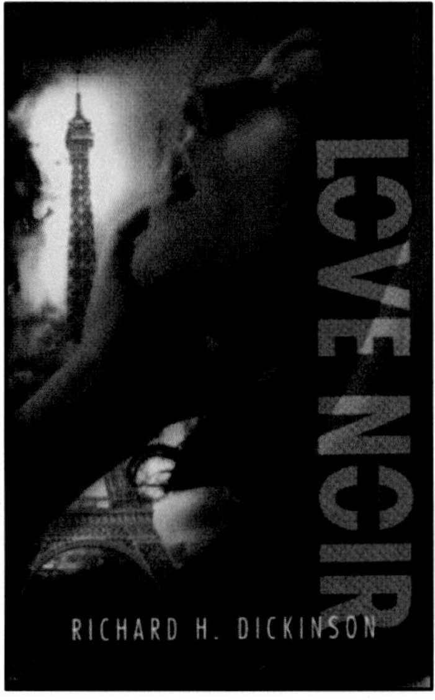

Love Noir

WP Author, Family Dysfunction

Richard H. Dickinson Ludlow Publishing (2010)

Would you die for love? In the case of Richard H. Dickinson's novel, *Love Noir,* perhaps a more likely question is: Would you kill for love?

Paris teenager Morgoux, who has suffered her mother's abandonment, turns to her politically powerful father, Eric Duval— for comfort and reassurance. A victim of his own weaknesses, the narcissistic Eric becomes his daughter's lover, entangling the child in a labyrinth of emotions which the angry child is incapable of handling. When her father submits to social pressures and remarries, Morgoux's emotions turn from rage to murder.

This is a novel about coverups and deceit, about amorality and love; a novel that explores the maturing of an unbalanced adolescent into a manipulative, psychotic woman who drops well-meaning people into her dark and secretive world. [BC]

Richard H. Dickinson, (1951–) West Point Class of 1973, has several other novels in this collection including military thrillers in the chapters "In the Far East" and "Global War on Terrorism." More biography information can be found in those chapters.

A Front for Murder

Crime, WP Author

Guy Emery McCrae Smith Co. (1947)

Just off the fashionable lobby of San Francisco's Sherwin Hotel, in assistant manager Bruce Morrow's office, lies the corpse of a man with a bullet hole in his chest. A thin thread of uncertain evidence is enough to focus suspicion on Morrow and involve Sheila Sherwin, the lovely daughter of the hotel owner.

The house detective's investigation and findings serve to complicate the situation when he uncovers a scandal surrounding the fascinating Mrs. Langlois, a guest whose strange past eventually connects explosively with the present.

Another chilling murder, and the pressure of mounting suspicion drives Bruce Morrow to fight back. Knowing that at the end of his sleuthing he must accuse—or be accused—Morrow brings about a surprisingly clever solution that promises to hold the reader in a new and different kind of suspense. [DJ]

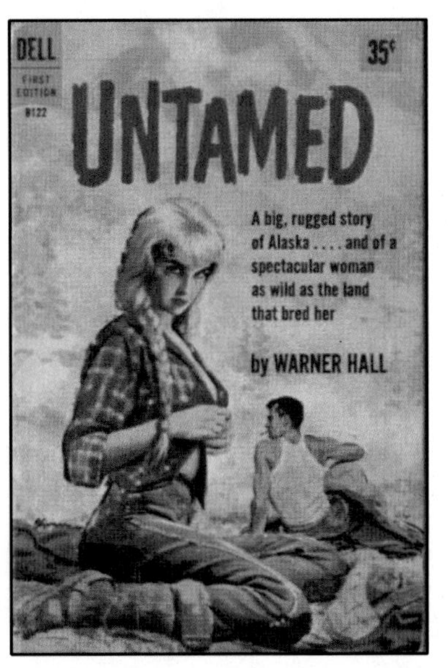

Untamed

WP Author, Crime

Guy Emery (writing as Warner Hall) Dell Publishing (1958)

The name was Crahan, a trouble-shooting engineer with a liking for strong drink, big jobs and full-grown women.

This Alaskan deal looked made to order. The Scotch was free flowing if you knew the right man. The job was to stake out a road through the virgin wilderness of the Mena Peninsula. And the woman -- she'd be his guide -- was a structural magnificence as challenging as the great mountains that loomed on the horizon. This was one assignment, Crahan decided, that would take some real engineering. He was looking forward to it. [BC]

"Home is the Warrior"

Pulp Fiction, Alaska, Homesteading, WP Author

Guy Emery Adventure Magazine (October 1946)

Anchorage, Alaska 1946 – brawling boomtown of cheechakoes and sourdoughs, pilots from Elmendorf Field and Aleuts from down the Chain – where pretty girls from the CAA and Base Engineer offices brushed parka skirts with Knicks from the reservation at Eklutna – and landgrabbers lay in wait behind every totem pole to dispute the Territory with any ex-GI who had taken Uncle Sam's offer to homestead in the North.

It was a last frontier – for fighters only – and John McQueen wanted no part of it. He'd had a bellyful of turmoil overseas, and now he was going to have a little peace and quiet – even if he had to start another war to get it! [EB]

Russell Guy Emery (1909–1964) graduated from West Point in 1930. His first book was published in 1940, *Wings Over West Point*, also in this collection. Following the war, he concentrated on his writing, published a mystery novel, *Front for Murder*, wrote many magazine sports stories, and a series of boy's books with West Point sports for plots. He is buried in the West Point Cemetery. [24-09]

The first chapter of this catalog opened with the observations of Major Aloysius Norton, USMA Class of 1944, in his Columbia master's degree thesis (1948) entitled "The Customs and Traditions of West Point in the American Novel." We conclude with a work written six decades later by a West Point English professor on the importance of studying literature at West Point. It is not fiction but certainly appropriate for a collection that celebrates the fiction of West Point.

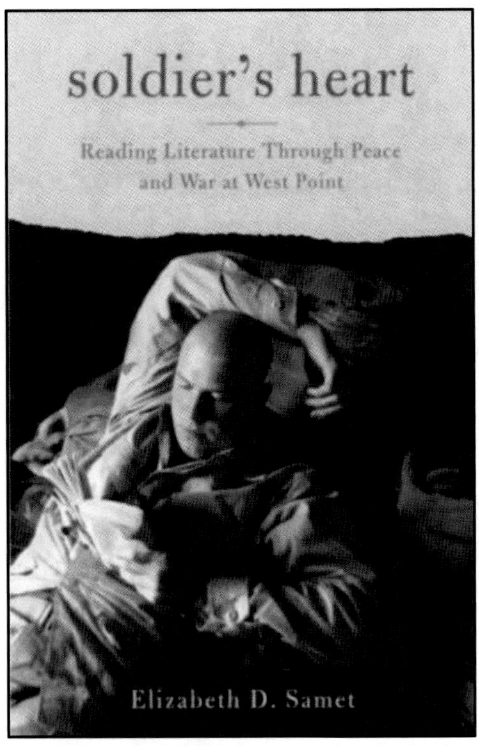

Soldier's Heart: Reading Literature Through Peace and War at West Point

Poetry, Literature, WP Author

Elizabeth D. Samet   Farrar, Straus and Giroux (2007)

Elizabeth D. Samet and her students learned to romanticize the army "through the stories of their fathers and from the movies." For Samet, it was the old World War II movies she used to watch on TV, while her students grew up on *Braveheart* and *Saving Private Ryan*. Unlike their teacher, however, these students, cadets at the United States Military Academy at West Point, have decided to turn make-believe into real life.

West Point is a world away from Yale, where Samet attended graduate school, and where nothing sufficiently prepared her for teaching literature to young men and women training to fight a war. Intimate and poignant, *Soldier's Heart* chronicles the various tensions inherent in that life as well as the ways in which war has transformed Samet's relationship to literature. Fighting in Iraq, Samet's former students share what books and movies mean to them—the poetry of Wallace Stevens, the fiction of Virginia Woolf and J.M. Coetzee, the 'epics of Homer, or the films of Bogart and Cagney. Their letters in turn prompt Samet to wonder exactly what she owes to cadets in the classroom.

Samet arrived at West Point before September 11, 2001, and has seen the academy change dramatically. In *Soldier's Heart*, she reads this transformation through her own experiences and those of her students. Forcefully examining what it means to be a civilian teaching literature at a military academy, Samet also considers the role of women in the army, the dangerous tides of religious and political zeal roiling the country, the uses of the call to patriotism, and the cult of sacrifice she believes is currently paralyzing national debate. Ultimately, Samet offers an honest and original reflection on the relationship between art and life. [DJ].

Elizabeth D. Samet received her B.A. from Harvard and her Ph.D. in English literature from Yale. She is the author of *Willing Disobedience: Citizens, Soldiers, and the Progress of Consent in America, 1776-1898*. Ms. Samet is an English professor at West Point. [DJ]

Acknowledgements

This volume is a product of many years of studying the literature of West Point and its graduates (plus spouses, mascots, ghosts and so on). The variety of topics is wide-ranging and fascinating. Even so, this work could not have materialized without the support of others.

Inspiration

The Class of 1998 was my guiding star for this project, especially my son Eric and his plebe roommates Bill Song and Nate Moore, who have offered me good cheer over these many years. Other '98ers welcomed me along the way: Jim Mullin, Michelle Robbins Lavicka and Rebecca D'Angelo Riordan.

Special kudos go to two Class of 1998 women who volunteered to design the cover of this catalog. Sarah Pollak Dudley responded to my request for a "mystical" concept. She diligently worked through a number of design iterations until we all agreed, "That's it!" My publisher and editor were picky! Kristi Mouw Ramsey developed the text design for the cover while cheerfully accepting input from the entire team. I am grateful to both for their commitment to the project and their creation of a dignified entrance for *Grip Hands Thru the Shadows*..

A tip of the tar bucket goes to Mark Weaver for updating the '98 Fund graphic of fallen classmates, and to Tessa Burns Snodgrass for permission to use her mule rider pose in the Army mascots chapter. Also, thanks to Ray Field, 25th reunion coordinator, who arranged a presentation ceremony at their 2023 gathering.

Our family is grateful to Lt. Colonel Eli Orm and wife Wanda for their friendship and Hawaiian hospitality over two decades. As a junior officer, Eli spent multiple tours prowling the front lines in the Global War on Terrorism. Very risky business. Enjoy your retirement, Eli!

Faculty and Staff

Almost all of the source material for this book came from outside the Academy, from books I owned and documentation I found through the internet. The one individual from within the Academy who provided critical support is Christopher Barth, Associate Dean and Director of the Library and Archives. He inspired my progress through every chapter over the three years it took to author this catalog. Chris has been instrumental in finding a welcoming home for this collection in the West Point Archives and suggesting I donate it in the name of a West Point class. Thank you to Dean Barth and here's to you, Class of 1998.

As publication date neared and packing the books for delivery to West Point began, Chris Barth introduced me to Jenn Chess, Communications & Marketing Librarian. She became my principal contact to other West Point offices. She is managing the planning & publicity for the November gift acceptance ceremony at the Class of 1998's reunion. Thank you, Jenn!

The Register of Graduates and Former Cadets

Two invaluable companions through the authoring experience were the 1965 and 1998 editions of **Register of Graduates and Former Cadets** which is updated annually. One cannot write about West Pointers and their careers without those treasure troves of data. With so many West Point authors to identify in composing biographies, these works were my starting point and/or they confirmed internet postings.

The Authors

I thank those authors who responded to my inquiries and endorsed this effort. Richard H. Dickinson (WP 1973), from Washington state, has five books in the collection on a variety of subjects from Vietnam to GWOT to aviation. Gus Lee (x1968) was one of my first "West Point reads" with *Honor and Duty.* James "Mike" Patton, (x1974) from New Mexico (three novels) and John Vermillion (WP 1970) from South Carolina (eight novels) have always been responsive and supportive.

Jason Kasper (WP 1981) paused in his very busy life – publishing a new adventur every few months – to review *Grip Hands*. Susan Spieth (WP 1985) with her four novels in the *Gray Girl* series, has been a regular correspondent offering me encouragement. Thank you both.

Please take the time to read their novels! I enjoyed them all.

The Editor

My deepest appreciation goes to Joyelle Soucier of *Proof & Pen LLC - Writing, Editing, and Proofreading Services* Harleysville, PA [Proofandpen.com]. It was by sheer happenstance that we connected in early 2022 and a fortunate one for me! Joyelle did a fine job of catching inconsistencies and restraining me as I charged off with another "what if..." or "how about…." (think choker collar on an eager Labrador retriever). We got it done and laughed often.

As we neared publication, Joyelle stepped forward to prepare an exceptional promotional brochure for *Grip Hands* and was the shepherdess evaluating my stumbling website development. Its remaining issues are mine alone, not hers. Taking the tasks to heart, Joyelle borrowed a couple of dozen books to read and also visited West Point for the first time to meet the library/archive staff. I expect that she will be joining us on November 10th at West Point for the formal gift acceptance. Thank you, Joyelle.

And to Wrap this Up

I thank our younger son, Jeffrey, for stepping forward at the eleventh hour to coach me through the "BlackGrayGold" website; advising us on printing the brochure; then do a final inventory of the collection before loading the 38 boxes for the trek to West Point. I would have preferred to pass through the Thayer Gate with an Army mule train pulling a wagonload of books but pleased to finally deliver them with Jeffrey in a U-Haul van.

About the Author

Ed Blomstedt's interest in West Point began as an Assistant Scoutmaster in Unionville, PA where he led camping trips to historic battlefields around the East. A favorite destination was the Hudson River Valley and West Point. The cemetery was always a great stop for the boys to lunch and explore, though some scouts found the nearby firehouse more interesting.

Ed was raised in Delaware and graduated with a degree in economics from Brown University, later earning a Drexel University MBA. He enjoyed a management career in several industries before retiring in 2013.

Ed and Mae, his wife of 50 years, have two sons and reside in Ambler, Pennsylvania.

In 1994, Ed's son, Eric, entered West Point. He graduated in 1998 with top honors in economics and social sciences and an East-West Fellowship to the University of Hawaii. Eric first deployed as an Armor officer in Korea, but switched to Signals Intelligence in 2001, subsequently serving two tours in Iraq. He retired in 2019 as a Lt. Colonel after several years with the Joint Special Operations Command. He is now employed by a defense contractor in northern Virginia. Eric and his wife, Janice, have two daughters.

Previous publications by the author:

Be Thou at Peace – The Cemetery at West Point, NY, A Resting Place for Warriors
Barton Cove Publishing (2013)

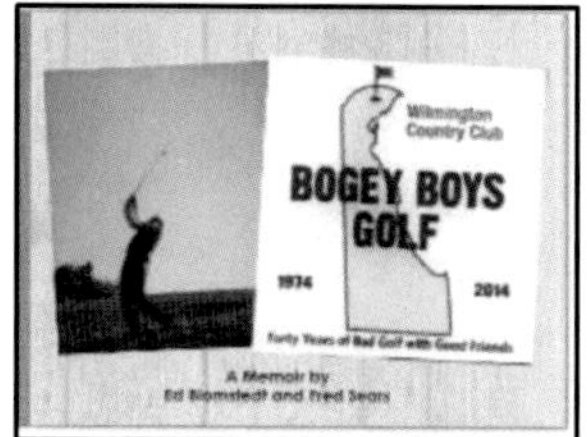

Bogey Boys Golf at Wilmington Country Club Forty Years of Bad Golf with Good Friends
Shutterfly (2015)

Contact the Author: eblomstedt@blackgraygold.com

Book website: www.blackgraygold.com

Source References

Chapter 1 – The Cadet Experience

1-01 Source: https://en.wikipedia.org/wiki/William_James_Roe

1-02 Source: https://en.wikipedia.org/wiki/Charles_King_(general)

1-03 Source: https://pennyspoetryfandom.com/wiki/Williston_Fish

1-04 Source: https://en.wikipedia.org/wiki/Anna_Bartlett_Warner

1-05 Source: www.findagrave.com/memorial/19387465/lemuel-de_bra Also, "The Experience Exchange," *The Writer*, Highland Falls NY April- 1926.

1-06 Source: https://stratemeyer.org/webster/

1-07 Source: https://wc.rootsweb.com/trees/234503/I00103/harveyking-shackleford

1-08 Source: https://www.goodreads.com/author/show/16118293.Walter_F_Eberhardt

1-09 Source: U.S. Military Academy Registry of Graduates – 1965

1-10 Source: West Point Association of Graduates Memorial, "Be Thou at Peace"

1-11 Source: https://en.wikipedia.org/wiki/Hugh_S._Johnson

1-12 Source: https://www.westpointaog.org/memorial-article?id=f3077a75-a118-42e5-825c-3c8af4826891

1-13 Source: https://www.af.mil/About-Us/Biographies/Display/Article/107170/brigadier-general-lawrence-mcilroy-guyer/

1-14 Source: Dust jacket of *Cadet Derry*

1-15 Source: https://www.westpointaog.org/memorial-article?id=e4bca736-a4b2-465c-b8e1-c0af2009a867

1-16 Source: https://military-history.fandom.com/wiki/Gus_Lee

1-17 Source: https://tawdrakandle.com/

1-18 Source: http://www.mikeconradart.com/PeterParsec.html

1-19 Source: http://www.mikeconradart.com/about.html

1-20 Source: https://stores.mikeconradart.com/grayboy-parody-issue-of-the-pointer-1979/

Chapter 2 – The Cadet Series of Books

2-01 Source: https://sf-encyclopedia.com/entry/lewis_henry_harrison

2-02 Source: https://en.wikipedia.org/wiki/Upton_Sinclair

2-03 Source: https://en.wikipedia.org/wiki/Paul_Bernard_Malone

2-04 Source: https://en.wikipedia.org/wiki/H._Irving_Hancock

2-05 Source: Author's forward in her books

2-06 Source: 1965 West Point Register of Graduates

2-07 Source: https://en.wikipedia.org/wiki/Russell_Reeder

2-08 Source: excerpted from the website – www.susanispieth.com

Chapter 3 – West Point Romances

3-01 Source: https://prabook.com/web/david.gilliam/3766614

3-02 Source: https://www.familyfiction.com/authors/al-and-joanna-lacy/

3-03 Source: https://evolvedpub.com/team-member/author/j-f-collen

3-04 Source: https://pennyspoetry.fandom.com/wiki/Williston_Fish

3-05 Source: https://en.wikipedia.org/wiki/Clara_Louise_Burnham

3-06 Source: https://www.hsp.org/sites/default/files/legacy_files/migrated/1899horstmannlippincottfindingaid.pdf

3-07 Source: https://en.wikipedia.org/wiki/Lilian_Bell

3-08 Source: https://en.wikipedia.org/wiki/C._N._Williamson

3-09 Source: *NY Times* Obituary, 1930

3-10 Source: https://www.goodreads.com/author/show/5813022.Siri_Mitchell

3-11 Source: www.Elizabethcamden.com

3-12 Source: https://en.wikipedia.org/wiki/Janet_Lambert. Picture from dustjacket *Myself and I*

3-13 Source: https://en.wikipedia.org/wiki/Elizabeth_Byrd

3-14 Source: Washington Post obituary, Feb 20, 2011

3-15 Source: https://en.wikipedia.org/wiki/Molly_Elliot_Seawell

3-16 Source: https://en.wikipedia.org/wiki/Emilie_Loring

3-17 Source: https://www.fictiondb.com/author/jo-calloway~1073.htm

3-18 Source: https://www.amazon.com/Roz-Denny-Fox/e/B000APBYYG%3Fref=dbs_a_mng_rwt_scns_share

3-19 Source: https://www.legacy.com/us/obituaries/timesunion/name/hansen-alexander-obituary?id=7619225

3-20 Source: https://www.findagrave.com/memorial/119846402/mary-alice-gernert

3-21 Source: http://wdgertsch.com/bio.html

Chapter 4 – Army Sports

4-01 Source: Northern Illinois Univ. https://www.ulib.niu.edu/badndp/patten_william.html?msclkid=0310579daeaa11eca815a1037eaa24e0

4-02 Source: https://www.amazon.com/Montrew-Dunham/e/B001IOH13Q?msclkid=adba22b0aeaa11ecbc6f6ef434b0660a

4-03 Source: https://dangutman.com/about-dan/

4-04 Source: http://www.philsp.com/homeville/fmi/p/p00502.htm

4-05 Source: https://www.threeinvestigatorsbooks.com/Graham_M_Dean.pdf

4-06 Source: https://www.westpointaog.org/memorial-article?id=f3077a75-a118-42e5-825c-3c8af4826891

4-07 Source: http://www.philsp.com/homeville/cfi/i00329.htm#A52

4-08 Source: Boston Globe obituaries, Dec. 14, 2007

Source: Picture: www.geni.com/people/Narcissa-Campion

4-09 Source: https://www.westpointaog.org/memorial-article?id=8e083646-5457-496c-abe6-19a1f9301c43

4-10 Source: Goodreads.com & ReshelveAlexandria.com & Bethlehembooks.com

4-11 Source: http://www.philsp.com/homeville/afi/n00226.htm#A111

4-12 Source: Texas Historical Association: Handbook of Texans & UT Texas Archival Retrieval Online

4-13 Source: https://www.feinsteinbooks.com/

4-14 Source: Sports Illustrated Article by Frank DeFord, Sept 1965

Chapter 5 – Mascots & Other Army Animals

5-01 Source: https://www.linkedin.com/in/scotty-autin-16473876

5-02 Source: https://en.wikipedia.org/wiki/Seymour_Eaton

5-03 Source: https://en.wikipedia.org/wiki/Army_Mules

5-04 Source: Photo courtesy of Tessa [Burns] Snodgrass, West Point Class of 1999

5-05 Source: https://en.wikipedia.org/wiki/Hugh_Troy

5-06 Source: https://pipiwiki.com/wiki/Howard_Allison_Sturtzel

5-07 Source: https://vtspecialcollections.wordpress.com/2017/04/27/illustrations-from-a-magnificent-character/

5-08 Source: http://www.philsp.com/homeville/fmi/i/i00904.htm#A2

5-09 Source: https://en.wikipedia.org/wiki/Phil_Stong#:~:text=Philip%20Duffield%20Stong%20(January%2027,a%20Broadway%20musical%20in%201996.

5-10 Source: https://en.wikipedia.org/wiki/Harold_Felton

5-11 Source: https://www.nytimes.com/2003/11/26/arts/david-stern-94-of-francis-talking-mule.html

5-12 Source: https://en.wikipedia.org/wiki/Patricia_Miles_Martin

5-13 Source: https://en.wikipedia.org/wiki/Fairfax_Downey

5-14 Source: https://www.findagrave.com/memorial/112657897/helen-watson

5-15 Source: https://horseracingsense.com/mule-horse-which-best/

5-16 Source: https://pabook.libraries.psu.edu/literary-cultural-heritage-map-pa/bios/Kjelgaard__James

5-17 Source: www.mcall.com/news/mc-xpm-1984-07-03-2437619-story.html

5-18 Source: www.findagrave.com/memorial/11260735

Chapter 6 – Paranormal, Supernatural & Futuristic

6-01 Source: https://knowledgenuts.com/paranormal-vs-supernatural

6-02 Source: https://www.army.mil/article/229265/the_supernatural_side_of_u_s_military_Academy_at_west_point

6-03 Source: www.TimothyRONeill.com

6-04 Source: https://en.wikipedia.org/wiki/Ed_and_Lorraine_Warren

6-05 Source: https://en.wikipedia.org/wiki/Thad_Krasnesky

6-06 Source: https://www.audible.com/author/Mr-Paul-Dellinger/B00LU3JS3Q

6-07 Source: http://www.cryptozoonews.com/cohen-obit/

6-08 Source: www.andrawatkins.com

6-09 Source: https://www.fantasticfiction.com/a/p-g-allison/

6-10 Source: https://en.wikipedia.org/wiki/Manly_Wade_Wellman

6-11 Source: https://sf-encyclopedia.com/entry/burks_arthur_j

6-12 Source: https://lovecraft.fandom.com/wiki/C._L._Moore

6-13 Source: https://en.wikipedia.org/wiki/Jack_Williamson

6-14 Source: https://en.wikipedia.org/wiki/Lee_Elias

6-15 Source: https://www.montreat.edu/academics/faculty/william-forstchen/, photo from Audible.com

6-16 Source: https://en.wikipedia.org/wiki/Kurt_Vonnegut

6-17 Source: https://en.wikipedia.org/wiki/Robert_A._Heinlein

6-18 Source: https://en.wikipedia.org/wiki/Buzz_Aldrin

6-19 Source: https://en.wikipedia.org/wiki/Tony_Daniel_(science_fiction_writer), photo from WorldswithoutEnd.com

6-20 Source: http://davidnickle.ca/

6-21 Source: https://en.wikipedia.org/wiki/Karl_Schroeder]

6-22 Source: www.vijayaschartz.com

6-23 Source: https://en.wikipedia.org/wiki/Greg_Rucka

6-24 Source: mikeconradart.com

6-25 Source: https://en.wikipedia.org/wiki/List_of_astronauts_educated_at_the_United_States_Military_Academy#cite_note-25

Chapter 7 – Women at West Point

7-01 Source: Dust jacket of 30th anniversary edition

7-02 Source: https://en.wikipedia.org/wiki/Juleen_Compton

7-03 Source: http://www.vakkur.com/bio.html

7-04 Source: https://www.findagrave.com/memorial/49321240/benjamin-alvord-spiller

7-05 Source: https://www.amazon.com/Amy-Efaw/e/B001H6SNA0

7-06 Source: https://www.jebandyauthor.com/about-the-author.html

7-07 Source: https://www.susanispieth.com

7-08 Source: https://www.susanispieth.com

7-09 Source: https://www.west-point.org/users/usma1965/25774/

7-10 Source: http://www.clairegibson.com/about

Chapter 8 – Army Life & Army Wives

8-01 Source: https://www.findagrave.com/memorial/39254634/margaret-irvin-carrington

8-02 Source: https://www.tshaonline.org/handbook/entries/boyd-frances-anne-mullen

8-03 Source: https://en.wikipedia.org/wiki/Elizabeth_Bacon_Custer

8-04 Source: *NY Times* Obituary, 1984

8-05 Source: https://sitkahistory.com/2015/09/letters-from-emily-2/

8-06 Source: HistoricPittsburg.org

8-07 Source: https://en.wikipedia.org/wiki/Brander_Matthews

8-08 Source: https://blackgrooves.org/tag/lavice-hendricks/

8-09 Source: https://en.wikipedia.org/wiki/Charles_King_(general)

8-10 Source: https://www.lva.virginia.gov/public/dvb/bio.php?b=Seawell_Molly_Elliot

8-11 Source: www.bjhoff.com

8-12 Source: *NY Times* Obituary, July 2017

8-13 Source: The Norman [Oklahoma] Transcript obituary, January 2021

8-14 Source: https://en.wikipedia.org/wiki/Katherine_Tupper_Marshall

Chapter 9 – Soldiers of Fortune, Paladins, Miscreants & Rogues

9-01 Source: https://en.wikipedia.org/wiki/Richard_Henry_Savage

9-02 Source: https://en.wikipedia.org/wiki/Richard_Harding_Davis

9-03 Source: https://en.wikipedia.org/wiki/C._N._Williamson

9-04 Source: https://en.wikipedia.org/wiki/John_Blake_(soldier)

9-05 Source: https://en.wikipedia.org/wiki/Ted_Berkman

9-06 Source: https://en.wikipedia.org/wiki/Have_Gun_%E2%80%93_Will_Travel

9-07 Source: https://en.wikipedia.org/wiki/Noel_Loomis

9-08 Source: https://jack-reacher.fandom.com/wiki/Small_Wars

9-09 Source: https://en.wikipedia.org/wiki/Lee_Child

9-10 Source: Photo from dustjacket

9-11 Source: Facebook Vintage Paperback & Book covers, November 18, 2018

9-12 Source: https://en.wikipedia.org/wiki/Ralph_Dennis

9-13 Source: http://donaldhonig.com/Welcome.html

9-14 Source: https://www.amazon.com/Memphis-Kingmaker-Cecilia-Hallman/dp/0977893006

9-15 Source: https://truewestmagazine.com/on-the-trail-of-custer/

Chapter 10 – Mystery, Crime & Intrigue

10-01 Source: https://en.wikipedia.org/wiki/Edgar_Allan_Poe

10-02 Source: From CivilizedBears.com, Jul 2021 Brian A. Burhoe

10-03 Source: https://pulpflakes.blogspot.com/2017/01

10-04 Source: https://en.wikipedia.org/wiki/Lucian_K._Truscott_IV

10-05 Source: https://nelsondemille.net/about/

10-06 Source: https://en.wikipedia.org/wiki/James_A._Michener

10-07 Source: https://en.wikipedia.org/wiki/Thomas_E._Ricks_(journalist)

10-08 Source: https://en.wikipedia.org/wiki/James_Patterson

10-09 Source: https://www.britannica.com/biography/Mary-Higgins-Clark

10-10 Source: https://en.wikipedia.org/wiki/Bob_Mayer_(author)

10-11 Source: https://www.west-point.org/users/usma1949/16939/MA.pdf

10-12 Source: https://us.macmillan.com/author/edruggero

10-13 Source: https://en.wikipedia.org/wiki/Louis_Bayard

10-14 Source: https://www.amazon.com/JackAlcott/e/B005HAE8RO%3Fref=dbs_a_mng_rwt_scns_share

10-15 Source: https://en.wikipedia.org/wiki/Richard_North_Patterson

10-16 Source: https://en.wikipedia.org/wiki/John_Grisham

[10-17] Source: https://en.wikipedia.org/ Brian_Haig

[10-18] Source: https://en.wikipedia.org/wiki/Knights_Templar

[10-19] Source: https://www.fictiondb.com/author/paul-christopher~39909.htm

[10-20] Source: https://jason-kasper.com/author/

Chapter 11 – Army Aviation

[11-01] Source: https://www.williamwhitson.com/

[11-02] Source: https://en.wikipedia.org/wiki/Henry_H._Arnold

[11-03] Source: https://www.westpointaog.org/memorial-article?id=8e083646-5457-496c-abe6-19a1f9301c43

[11-04] Source: https://www.newspapers.com/clip/3311845/death-of-louis-chilton-goldsmith/ and http://www.philsp.com/homeville/fmi/n02/n02945.htm#A193

[11-05] Source: https://en.wikipedia.org/wiki/Robert_Sidney_Bowen

[11-06] Source: https://jamesreasoner.blogspot.com/2020/04/forgotten-books-mantrap-duane-yarnell.html

[11-07] Source: Amazon Review from Library Journal: Copyright 1988 Reed Business Information,

[11-08] Source: www.noellesalazar.com

[11-09] Source: Amazon Review from Library Journal: Copyright 1988 Reed Business Information,

[11-10] Source: https://www.encyclopedia.com/arts/educational-magazines/dickinson-richard-h

[11-11] Source: http://wdgertsch.com/bio.html

[11-12] Source: https://wrt.tcu.edu/staff/cynthia-shearer/ and

https://www.mswritersandmusicians.com/mississippi-writers/cynthia-shearer

Chapter 12 – Army Medical Service Corps

[12-01] Source: https://seattlemysteryblog.typepad.com/seattle_mystery/2017/01/golden-age-gals- helen-wells.html

[12-02] Source: ackermanbooks.com

[12-03] Source: https://us.macmillan.com/author/sorayalane

[12-04] Source: https://www.goodreads.com/author/show/1319040.Virginia_B_McDonnell

[12-05] Source: https://en.wikipedia.org/wiki/Richard_Sale_(director)

[12-06] Source: https://www.encyclopedia.com/arts/news-wires-white-papers-and-books/seifert-Elizabeth

[12-07] Source: https://en.wikipedia.org/wiki/Frank_G._Slaughter

[12-08] Source: Source: mashfandom.com

[12-09] Source: https://www.dignitymemorial.com/obituaries/marblehead-ma/jules-seletz-5254583

Chapter 13 – Revolution, War of 1812 & Sylvanus Thayer

13-01 Source: https://en.wikipedia.org/wiki/Burke_Boyce

13-02 Source: https://honorsandawards.iu.edu/awards/honoree

13-03 Source: https://en.wikipedia.org/wiki/James_Thomas_Flexner

13-04 Source: *NY Times* Obituary, June 3, 2020

13-05 Source: https://www.lawrencefamhis.com/ancestors-o/g0/p285.htm

13-06 Source: https://en.wikisource.org/wiki/Author:Edwin_Irvine_Haines

13-07 Source: https://www.legacy.com/us/obituaries/cumberlink/name/james-wensyel-obituary?id=10152376

13-08 Source: https://dc.fandom.com/wiki/Ed_Herron

13-09 Source: https://www.findagrave.com/memorial/16136428/stephen-angus_douglas-cox

13-10 Source: https://en.wikipedia.org/wiki/Russell_Gordon_Carter

13-11 Source: https://imagecascade.com/anne-emery.html

13-12 Source: www.prabook.com

13-13 Source: http://phyllisawhitney.com

13-14 Source: https://en.wikipedia.org/wiki/Martha_Finley

13-15 Source: https://en.wikipedia.org/wiki/Henry_Bedford-Jones

13-16 Source: https://obits.mlive.com/us/obituaries/kalamazoo/name/leon-burgoyne-obituary?id=13198898

13-17 Source: https://en.wikipedia.org/wiki/Sylvanus_Thayer

13-18 Source: https://en.wikipedia.org/wiki/George_Fielding_Eliot

13-19 Source: "Institute News" Military Affairs Vol. 45, No. 2 April 1981

Chapter 14 – Manifest Destiny

14-01 Source: Williams-Mystic, Maritime Studies Program

14-02 Source: https://www.fantasticfiction.com/m/jason-manning/

14-03 Source: openlibrary.org/authors/OL25717A

14-04 Source: https://en.wikipedia.org/wiki/Noel_Gerson and Photo Saperebooks.com/authors

14-05 Source: https://wolfpackpublishing.com/robert-vaughan-author/

14-06 Source: https://en.wikipedia.org/wiki/Will_Cook_(writer)

14-07 Source: https://okjournalismhalloffame.com/1976/foster-harris/

14-08 Source: https://en.wikipedia.org/wiki/Charles_King_(general)

14-09 Source: https://pabook.libraries.psu.edu/literary-cultural-heritage-map-pa/bios/Kjelgaard__James

14-10 Source: https://en.wikipedia.org/wiki/William_R._Cox

14-11 Source: Historical Novels Review, Aug 2002

14-12 Source: https://www.nps.gov/articles/000/frederick-whittaker-civil-war-cavalry-officer-best-selling-author-controversial-custer-biographer.htm

14-13 Source: https://en.wikipedia.org/wiki/Fred_Chiaventone

14-14 Source: https://en.wikipedia.org/wiki/Michael_Blake_(author)

14-15 Source: https://www.simonandschuster.com/authors/John-Hough/17135450

14-16 Source: https://openlibrary.org/authors/OL4513958A/Anita_Melva_Anderson

14-17 Source: http://westernfictionreview.blogspot.com/search?q=john+wesley+howard

14-18 Source: https://en.wikipedia.org/wiki/Hamlin_Garland

14-19 Source: https://en.wikipedia.org/wiki/Edward_S._Ellis

14-20 Source: https://en.wikipedia.org/wiki/Molly_Elliot_Seawell

14-21 Source: Review in *The New York Times*, Oct 17, 1903:

14-22 Source: https://tvtropes.org/pmwiki/pmwiki.php/Film/OnlyTheValiant

14-23 Source: https://en.wikipedia.org/wiki/Charles_Marquis_Warren

14-24 Source: https://en.wikipedia.org/wiki/Henry_Wilson_Allen

14-25 Source: https://en.wikipedia.org/wiki/John_Edward_Ames

14-26 Source: The Fiction Mags Index philsp.com

14-27 Source: https://en.wikipedia.org/wiki/Paul_Horgan

14-28 Source: https://www.goodreads.com/author/show/600763.William_Hopson

14-29 Source: https://prabook.com/web/charles_newman.heckelmann/1669657

14-30 Source: https://en.wikipedia.org/wiki/William_Wister_Haines

Chapter 15 – The Civil War

15-01 Source: https://study.com/academy/lesson/what-is-historical-fiction-definition- characteristics-books-authors.html

15-02 Source: https://www.amazon.com/His-sombre-rivals-Edward-Payson/dp/1147838941

15-03 Source: https://www.goodreads.com/review/show/1597757812?book_show_action=true&from_review_page=1

15-04 Source: https://americanliterature.com/author/edward-payson-roe

15-05 Source: *The New York Times*, Obituary, 13-March-1974

15-06 Source: https://en.wikipedia.org/wiki/Oliver_Otis_Howard

15-07 Source: www.erbzine.com/king

15-08 Source: Monograph by Robert E. Miller, Missouri Historical Review, July 1991

15-09 Source: https://en.wikipedia.org/wiki/E._L._Doctorow

15-10 Source: https://*en.wikipedia.org/wiki/Simon_Hawke*

15-11 Source: https://en.wikipedia.org/wiki/J._T._Edson

15-12 Source: https://www.encyclopedia.com/arts/educational-magazines/potter-patricia-1940

15-13 Source: LinkedIn - Donald C Bowman

15-14 Source: https://pabook.libraries.psu.edu/literary-cultural-heritage-map-pa/bios/Abrahams__Robert_David

15-15 Source: https://en.wikipedia.org/wiki/F._Van_Wyck_Mason

15-16 Source: Obituary, *NY Times*: March 9, 1993

15-17 Source: https://www.amazon.ca/Rosemary-Eaton/e/B0193D0T46%3Fref=dbs_a_mng_rwt_scns_share

15-18 Source: https://en.wikipedia.org/wiki/Michael_Shaara

15-19 Source: www.jeffshaara.com

15-20 Source: https://en.wikipedia.org/wiki/Alden_Carter

15-21 Source: https://www.legacy.com/us/obituaries/cumberlink/name/james-wensyel-obituary?id=10152376

15-22 Source: https://en.wikipedia.org/wiki/Bob_Mayer_(author)

Chapter 16 – The World Wars

16-01 Source: https://www.librarything.com/author/durstongeorge

16-02 Source: www.fictiondb.com/author/clair-w-hayes~134365.htm

16-03 Source: https://www.williamwhitson.com/

16-04 Source: https://www.af.mil/About-Us/Biographies/Display/Article/107522/

16-05 Source: http://www.paperbackwarrior.com/search/label/Jack%20Pearl?m=0

16-06 Source: https://freshfiction.com/author.php?id=10226

16-07 Source: www.jeffshaara.com

Chapter 17 – General Officers

17-01 Source: http://www.mykeithfamily.com/index_files/Page2205.htm

17-02 Source: Source – *NY Times* Obituary, Sept 4, 1971

17-03 Source: Review by wmorton38 on LibraryThing.com, Aug 28, 2007

17-04 Source: https://en.wikipedia.org/wiki/Thomas_Dixon_Jr.

17-05 Source: www.amazon.com/Diane-Haeger/e/B001IGQHFC

17-06 Source: https://www.johnjdwyer.com/

17-07 Source: www.nytimes.com/1983/06/21/obituaries/elizabeth-seifert.html

[17-08] Source: https://en.wikipedia.org/wiki/John_P._Marquand
Photo: Boston Public Library Print Dept

[17-09] Source: https://www.af.mil/About-Us/Biographies/Display/Article/107522/

[17-10] Source: https://www.goodreads.com/author/show/10363.Stephen_Longstreet

[17-11] Source: https://en.wikipedia.org/wiki/Robert_Leckie_(author)

[17-12] Source: www.BobMayer.com

[17-13] Source: https://en.wikipedia.org/wiki/Treasure_Chest_(comics)

Chapter 18 – In the Far East

[18-01] Source: https://en.wikipedia.org/wiki/Richard_Ernest_Dupuy Picture: nytimes.com/1975/04/26

[18-02] Source: https://en.wikipedia.org/wiki/Paul_Cain_(writer)

[18-03] Source: https://en.wikipedia.org/wiki/Hugh_S._Johnson

[18-04] Source: *NY Times* Obituary, 1950

[18-05] Source: https://en.wikipedia.org/wiki/E._Hoffmann_Price#

[18-06] Source: https://www.goodreads.com/author/show/238876.Ed_Ruggero

[18-07] Source: www.guslee.net

[18-08] Source: SFFWorld.com 2017/06 interview

[18-09] Source: https://www.sarbonn.com

[18-10] Source: https://www.amazon.com/*Jason*-M.-*Morwick*/e/B004WNF1G4

[18-11] Source: Dan Berger, Amazon Review, on July 2, 2016

[18-12] Source: https://en.wikipedia.org/wiki/David_Halberstam

[18-13] Source: https://en.wikipedia.org/wiki/Josiah_Bunting_III

[18-14] Source: Dan Berger, from his review on Amazon, September 5, 2016

[18-15] Source: https://www.fantasticfiction.com/c/nicholas-cain/

[18-16] Source: https://freshfiction.com/author.php?id=10226

Chapter 19 – The West Point Legacies

[19-01] Source: https://freshfiction.com/author.php?id=10226

[19-02] Source: https://en.wikipedia.org/wiki/Brotherhood_of_War

[19-03] Source: https://en.wikipedia.org/wiki/W._E._B._Griffin

[19-04] Source: https://en.wikipedia.org/wiki/Rick_Atkinson

Atkinson Photo: By fourandsixty – Own work, CC BY-SA 3.0, https://commons.wikimedia.org/w/index.php?curid=42961284

Chapter 20 – The Cold War & Global War on Terrorism

20-01 Source: https://tomdavisauthor.com/about/

20-02 Source: https://en.wikipedia.org/wiki/Harold_Coyle

20-03 Source: https://us.macmillan.com/author/edruggero

20-04 Source: Daniel Berger: The Green Berets launch in the run-up to the Bay of Pigs and Vietnam. Review on Amazon, August 14, 2016

20-05 Source: https://en.wikipedia.org/wiki/War_on_terror

20-06 Source: https://www.brownfuneralhomeinc.com/memorials/major-everett-degen-usaf-retired/2279009/obituary.php

20-07 Source: http://denisegelberg.forpr.net

20-08 Source: https://jason-kasper.com/author/

20-09 Source: https://www.amazon.com/West-Point-Warlord-OFarrell-ebook/dp/B0793PS8XT

Chapter 21 – Poetry, Drama & Film

21-01 Source: https://en.wikipedia.org/wiki/Joseph_Rodman_Drake

21-02 Source: https://www.westpointaog.org/memorial-article?id=faf425e1-8c7a-4e18-8a16-7306f0c04eea

21-03 Source: USMA: Cemetery/Columbarium Locator Report

21-04 Source: http://defender.west-point.org/service/eulogies.mhtml?u=11623

21-05 Source: https://www.findatopdoc.com/doctor/3689620-Michael-Anderson-family- practitioner-Red-Wing-MN-55066

21-06 Source: https://books.google.com/books/about/The_Warrior.html?id=FJRPEAAAQBAJ& source=kp_author_description

21-07 Source: https://en.wikipedia.org/wiki/George_Augustus_Baker

21-08 Source: *Be Thou at Peace*, E. Blomstedt, Barton Cove Publishing, 2013

21-09 Source: https://en.wikipedia.org/wiki/Christopher_Morley

21-10 Source: http://bicyclecorpsriders.blogspot.com/2009/01/lt-james-moss.html

21-11 Source: pediment.com/blogs/news/lt-moss and indagrave.com/memorial/5902/james-a-moss]

21-12 Source: https://en.wikipedia.org/wiki/Rosalie_(film)

21-13 Source: https://www.amazon.com/West-Point-Widow-Anne-Shirley/dp/B00MDZ6NS8

21-14 Source: https://www.imdb.com/title/tt0035421/

21-15 Source: Review in *The New York Times*, October 3, 1947

21-16 Source: https://en.wikipedia.org/wiki/Beyond_Glory

21-17 Source: https://en.wikipedia.org/wiki/The_West_Point_Story_(film)

21-18 Source: https://en.wikipedia.org/wiki/Francis_Goes_to_West_Point

[21-19] Source: https://en.wikipedia.org/wiki/The_Long_Gray_Line

[21-20] Source: https://en.wikipedia.org/wiki/Code_Breakers_(fil

[21-21] Source: https://en.wikipedia.org/wiki/Dress_Gray

Chapter 22 – Remembering the "Old Corps"

[22-01] Source: Register of Graduates, U.S. Military Academy, 1968.

[22-02] Source: https://www.cem.va.gov/cem/history/bivouac.asp

[22-03] Source: https://en.wikipedia.org/wiki/Bret_Harte

[22-04] Source: By SMU Central University Libraries - Mission of Los Dolores. Uploaded by PD Tillman, No restrictions, https://commons.wikimedia.org/w/index.php?curid

=28510847

[22-05] Source: *Be Thou at Peace,* pg. 35. E. Blomstedt, Barton Cove Publishing 2015.

[22-06] Source: https://en.wikipedia.org/wiki/Morris_Schaff

[22-07] Source: https://en.wikipedia.org/wiki/Robert_C._Richardson_Jr.

Chapter 23 – West Point Candidates & Ex

[23-01] Source: https://www.movingpicturereprintseries.com/four-dime-novels-from-the-old-sleuth-1896-1898

[23-02] Source: https://www.penbaypilot.com/article/donald-moffitt-obituary/45290

[23-03] Source: https://www.valeriehobbs.com/

[23-04] Source: https://en.wikipedia.org/wiki/United_States_Military_Academy

[23-05] Source: https://en.wikipedia.org/wiki/Howard_Pease

[23-06] Source: https://medium.com/about-me-stories/about-me-jodi-compton-da55f9875427

Chapter 24 – Other Books by West Point Authors

[24-01] Source: https://en.wikipedia.org/wiki/Susan_Warner

[24-02] Source: https://www.imdb.com/title/tt0004369/?ref_=fn_al_tt_1

[24-03] Source: http://www.loyalbooks.com/book/Midnight-Passenger

[24-04] Source: https://en.wikipedia.org/wiki/Richard_Henry_Savage

[24-05] Source: https://www.bartleby.com/library/readersdigest/301.html

[24-06] Source: https://www.mobileread.com/forums/showthread.php?p=4151773#post4151773

[24-07] Source: https://en.wikipedia.org/wiki/Arthur_Sherburne_Hardy

[24-08] Source: https://www.westpointaog.org/memorial-article?id=cb4bb382-6044-4b21-8d04 e0800b3a384d

[24-09] Source: https://www.findagrave.com/memorial/136035796/guy-russell-emery

Emblem

The following emblem which appears at the end of each chapter features the sword and helmet of Athena, Greek goddess of war and wisdom. The original drawing is taken from the title page of ***The Spirit of Old West Point,*** by Morris Schaff, Class of June 1862. The book was published in 1907 by Houghton Mifflen Co. The graphic has been colorized for this catalog.

Grip Hands Author Index

Bold Type - West Point Author **T. Paperback - Trade Paperback**

Author	Title	Format	Chapter (Primary)	Pg #
Abbott, Tom J	Allie McCrae & the West Point Half-Blood	Hardback	Ch 14 Manifest Destiny	292
Abrahams, Robert D.	Uncommon Soldier, The	Paperback	Ch 15 Civil War	307
Ackerman, Sara	Lieutenant's Nurse, The	T. Paperback	Ch 12 Army Medical	228
Agnew, James B	Eggnog Riot: Mutiny at West Point	Hardback	Ch 13 Revo, 1812, Thayer	251
Alcott, Jack	Grim Legion	Hardback	Ch 10 Mystery, Crime	194
Aldrin, Buzz	Encounter With Tiber	Hardback	Ch 6 Para, Super, Future	125
Alexander, Hansen	From West Point to Watergate	T. Paperback	Ch 3 Romance	66
Allison, P.G.	Missy Goes to Annapolis: Missy Book 9	T. Paperback	Ch 6 Para, Super, Future	115
	Missy Goes to West Point: Missy Book 2	T. Paperback	Ch 6 Para, Super, Future	113
	Missy Makes Mayhem: Missy Book 5	T. Paperback	Ch 6 Para, Super, Future	114
	Missy More Adventures at Annapolis: Missy Book 10	T. Paperback	Ch 6 Para, Super, Future	115
	Missy the Werecat Series	T. Paperback	Ch 7 Women at WP	141
	Missy's First Mission: Missy Book 3	T. Paperback	Ch 6 Para, Super, Future	114
	Missy's Misadventure: Missy Book 4	T. Paperback	Ch 6 Para, Super, Future	114
	Missy Returns to West Point Book 11	T. Paperb5ck	Ch 6 Para, Super, Future	115
	The Fire Witch: Tracy Book 1	T. Paperback	Ch 6 Para, Super, Future	116
	Tracy Plays Demon: Tracy Book 2	T. Paperback	Ch 6 Para, Super, Future	116
Ames, John Edward	Unwritten Order, The	Paperback	Ch 14 Manifest Destiny	290
Anderson, A.M.	Comanche and his Captain	Hardback	Ch 14 Manifest Destiny	279
Anderson, Michael	Shades of Gray	T. Paperback	Ch 21 Poetry/Drama/Film	405
Anderson, Ruth	West Point Girl	Pulp Fiction	Ch 3 Romance	56
Annixter, Paul	Murders on the Range	Pulp Fiction	Ch 5 Mascots	90
Appel, David	Comanche: America's Most Heroic Horse	Hardback	Ch 5 Mascots	99
APUSA	As a Soldier Would	Hardback	Ch 3 Romance	51
Archibald, Joe	Special Forces Trooper	Hardback	Ch 18 In the Far East	365
	West Point Wingback	Hardback	Ch 4 Army Sports	81
Arney, Chris	Goatnapping Gladiators of West Point	T. Paperback	Ch 4 Army Sports	85
Arnold, H. H.	Bill Bruce Becomes an Ace	Hardback	Ch 11 Army Aviation	212
	Bill Bruce Flight Series	Hardback	Ch 11 Army Aviation	211
	Bill Bruce the Flying Cadet	Hardback	Ch 11 Army Aviation	211
	Bill Bruce on Forest Patrol	Hardback	Ch 11 Army Aviation	212
	Bill Bruce Becomes an Ace	Hardback	Ch 16 World Wars	325
	Bill Bruce in The Trans-Continental Race	Hardback	Ch 11 Army Aviation	212
	Bill Bruce on Border Patrol	Hardback	Ch 11 Army Aviation	212
	Bill Bruce Pioneer Aviators	Hardback	Ch 11 Army Aviation	211
Atkinson, Rick	Long Gray Line, The	Hardback	Ch 19 WP Legacies	381
Autin, Scott	Army Bears!?	Magazine	Ch 5 Mascots	87
Bailey, Anthony	Major André	Hardback	Ch 13 Revo, 1812, Thayer	237
Baker, George A	West Point: A Comedy in Three Acts	Hardback	Ch 21 Poetry/Drama/Film	409
Bandy Jr, J. E.	The Plebes: Guardians of Honor	Hardback	Ch 7 Women at WP	137
	The Yearlings: Guardians of Honor	Hardback	Ch 7 Women at WP	137
	Cows and Firsties: Guardians of Honor	Hardback	Ch 7 Women at WP	138
	Guardians of Honor Series #1 - #3	Hardback	Ch 2 Cadet Series	43
Barns, Glen M.	Only the Losers Win	Paperback	Ch 9 Paladins, Rogues	175
Bayard, Louis	Pale Blue Eye, The	Hardback	Ch 10 Mystery, Crime	194
Bell, Lillian	Underside of Things	Hardback	Ch 3 Romance	52

Author	Title	Format	Chapter (Primary)	Pg #
Benson, Leon, Director	West Point: The Television Series	DVD	Ch 21 Poetry/Drama/Film	419
Berkman, Ted	Cast a Giant Shadow: Mickey Marcus	Paperback	Ch 9 Paladins, Rogues	169
Bishop, Curtis	West Point Whirlwind - A Touchdown Outlaw	Pulp Fiction	Ch 4 Army Sports	82
Blake, Col. John Y	A West Pointer with the Boers	Hardback	Ch 9 Paladins, Rogues	168
Blake, Michael	Marching to Valhalla: Custer's Last Days	Hardback	Ch 14 Manifest Destiny	277
Bowen, Robert S.	Red Randal Flight Series	Hardback	Ch 11 Army Aviation	215
	Red Randall at Midway	Hardback	Ch 11 Army Aviation	216
	Red Randall at Pearl Harbor	Hardback	Ch 11 Army Aviation	215
	Red Randall in Burma	Hardback	Ch 11 Army Aviation	217
	Red Randall in the Aleutians	Hardback	Ch 11 Army Aviation	216
	Red Randall on Active Duty	Hardback	Ch 11 Army Aviation	215
	Red Randall on New Guinea	Hardback	Ch 11 Army Aviation	216
	Red Randall Over Tokyo	Hardback	Ch 11 Army Aviation	215
Bowman, Donald C.	Miss Mary's Honor Guard	T. Paperback	Ch 15 Civil War	306
Boyce, Burke	Perilous Night, The	Hardback	Ch 13 Revo, 1812, Thayer	235
Boyd, Mrs. Orsemus	Cavalry Life in Tent & Field	Hardback	Ch 8 Army Life, Wives	147
Boynton, Howard	Cadet Detective's Hot Hustle, The	Pulp Fiction	Ch 9 Paladins, Rogues	175
Bradley, Mary Quale	Advice to Ladies…	Other	Ch 3 Romance	62
Brenner, Barbara	Hemi: A Mule	Hardback	Ch 5 Mascots	94
Bunting, Josiah	Lionheads, The	Hardback	Ch 18 In the Far East	367
Burana, Lily	I Love a Man in Uniform	Hardback	Ch 8 Army Life, Wives	163
Burgoyne, Leon	Ensign Ronan: A Story of Fort Dearborn	Hardback	Ch 13 Revo, 1812, Thayer	248
Burks, Arthur J.	West Point of Tomorrow - the Planet Patrol	Comic book	Ch 6 Para, Super, Future	119
Burnham, Clara L.	Miss Bagg's Secretary: West Point Romance	Hardback	Ch 3 Romance	50
	West Point Wooing: Victorian Romance	Hardback	Ch 3 Romance	50
Bush, Keith A.	Ringknockers	Hardback	Ch 4 Army Sports	85
Byrd, Elizabeth	It Had to Be You	Hardback	Ch 3 Romance	61
Cain, George M.A.	Soldier's First Duty: A	T. Paperback	Ch 18 In the Far East	354
Callahan, Pete	Armored Corps #1	Paperback	Ch 18 In the Far East	361
	Attack by Fire: Armored Corps #3	Paperback	Ch 18 In the Far East	361
	Engage and Destroy: Armored Corps #2	Paperback	Ch 18 In the Far East	361
Calloway, Jo	Illusive Lover	Paperback	Ch 3 Romance	65
Camden, Elizabeth	Summer of Dreams	T. Paperback	Ch 3 Romance	57
Carlson, Floyd	Find the West Point Cadet	Magazine	Ch 10 Mystery, Crime	191
Carrington, Margaret	Ab-Sa-Ra-Ka	T. Paperback	Ch 8 Army Life, Wives	146
Carson, Sam	Major, Here's the Mules	Pulp Fiction	Ch 5 Mascots	91
Carter, Abbey & Rosenberg, Marya, Editors	Athena Speaks: Women at West Point	T. Paperback	Ch 7 Women at WP	135
	Athena Speaks: Women at West Point	T. Paperback	Ch 21 Poetry/Drama/Film	407
Carter, Alden R.	Bright Starry Banner	Hardback	Ch 15 Civil War	318
Carter, Russel Gordon	Patriot Lad at Old West Point, A	Hardback	Ch 13 Revo, 1812, Thayer	242
CBS Broadcasting	Have Gun, Will Travel	DVD	Ch 21 Poetry/Drama/Film	421
Cervus, G.I.	Cut: A Story of West Point	Hardback	Ch 1 Cadet Experience	2
Chamberlain, Wm.	Combat General: A Novel	Hardback	Ch 17 General Officers	344
	Forced March to Loon Creek	Paperback	Ch 14 Manifest Destiny	273
	Matt Quarterhill, Rifleman	Hardback	Ch 16 World Wars	328
	Miracle in Manila	Pulp Fiction	Ch 16 World Wars	328
	Trumpets of Company K	Paperback	Ch 14 Manifest Destiny	273
	Zone of Sudden Death, The	Paperback	Ch 16 World Wars	328

Author	Title	Format	Chapter (Primary)	Pg #
Chiaventone, Frederick	Moon of Bitter Cold	Hardback	Ch 14 Manifest Destiny	276
Chiaventone, Frederick J.	Road We Do Not Know, A: A Novel of Custer	Hardback	Ch 14 Manifest Destiny	277
Child, Lee	Midnight Line, The - Jack Reacher	Hardback	Ch 9 Paladins, Rogues	171
	Never Go Back - Jack Reacher	Hardback	Ch 9 Paladins, Rogues	170
	Small Wars - Jack Reacher	Hardback	Ch 9 Paladins, Rogues	171
Chilton, Alexander	West Pointer's Honor	Hardback	Ch 1 Cadet Experience	14
Christenson, George	Flames of War	Hardback	Ch 18 In the Far East	371
Christopher, Paul	Sword of Templars, The	Paperback	Ch 10 Mystery, Crime	204
	Templars Series	Paperback	Ch 10 Mystery, Crime	204
Clark, Mary Higgins	Nighttime Is My Time	Hardback	Ch 10 Mystery, Crime	189
Cline, Patricia Edwards	Corduroy Road, The	Hardback	Ch 13 Revo, 1812, Thayer	243
Cloos, Bert	Skirmish	Paperback	Ch 14 Manifest Destiny	267
Coates, Dennis	To the Colors: Poems from West Point	Hardback	Ch 21 Poetry/Drama/Film	406
Cohen, Daniel	World's Most Famous Ghosts	Paperback	Ch 6 Para, Super, Future	111
Collen, J F	Flirtation on the Hudson	T. Paperback	Ch 3 Romance	48
Compton, Jodi	Hailey's War	Paperback	Ch 23 WP Cand. & Ex	452
Compton, Juleen	Women in West Point	Manuscript	Ch 7 Women at WP	132
Conrad, Michael	Adventures of Peter Parsec, Space Cadet	Paperback	Ch 1 Cadet Experience	22
	Grayboy	Magazine	Ch 1 Cadet Experience	23
	Peter Parsec, Raiders of the Lost Dark	Paperback	Ch 6 Para, Super, Future	130
Cook, Will	Fort Starke/First Command	Hardback	Ch 14 Manifest Destiny	260
Cooley, John W.	Queen of Battle	Hardback	Ch 7 Women at WP	142
Coplin, Keith	Crofton's Fire	T. Paperback	Ch 9 Paladins, Rogues	167
Cox, Stephen A.	Dare Boys After Benedict Arnold	Hardback	Ch 13 Revo, 1812, Thayer	241
Cox, William R.	Warrior Breed	Pulp Fiction	Ch 14 Manifest Destiny	271
Coyle, Harold	God's Children	Hardback	Ch 20 ColdWar -GWOT	387
	Sword Point	Hardback	Ch 20 ColdWar -GWOT	385
	Trial by Fire	Hardback	Ch 20 ColdWar -GWOT	386
Crall, George	Hitler Invades England	Paperback	Ch 16 World Wars	334
Crandall, F.E.	Douglas MacArthur - Battlefield General Parts 1-4	Comic book	Ch 17 General Officers	347
Crary, Catherine	Dear Belle: Letters from a Cadet and Officer	Hardback	Ch 15 Civil War	298
Crocco, David	Of Honor and Dishonor	T. Paperback	Ch 1 Cadet Experience	20
Crockett, Lucy Herndon	Capitan - The Story of an Army Mule	Hardback	Ch 5 Mascots	90
Curran, Charles D.	Pegasus Remounts - Cadet Verse	Hardback	Ch 21 Poetry/Drama/Film	402
Custer, Elizabeth B	Boots and Saddles: Life in Dakota	T. Paperback	Ch 8 Army Life, Wives	148
	Following the Guidon	Hardback	Ch 8 Army Life, Wives	149
	Tenting On The Plains	Hardback	Ch 8 Army Life, Wives	148
Daniel, Tony	Metaplanetary: Interplanetary Civil War	Hardback	Ch 6 Para, Super, Future	126
	Superluminal	Hardback	Ch 6 Para, Super, Future	127
Daves, Delmer	Flirtation Walk	DVD	Ch 21 Poetry/Drama/Film	415
Davis, Richard Harding	Captain Macklin	Hardback	Ch 9 Paladins, Rogues	166
Davis, Tom	Conclave	T. Paperback	Ch 20 ColdWar -GWOT	385
	Empty Quiver	T. Paperback	Ch 20 ColdWar -GWOT	385
de Metropolis, Harry	Courtship at West Point	Hardback	Ch 21 Poetry/Drama/Film	403
	Love and War	Hardback	Ch 21 Poetry/Drama/Film	404
Dean, Graham	Herb Kent, West Point Cadet	Hardback	Ch 4 Army Sports	74
	Herb Kent, West Point Fullback	Hardback	Ch 4 Army Sports	74

Author	Title	Format	Chapter (Primary)	Pg #
Degen, Everett R.	Autumn on the Hudson	Hardback	Ch 20 ColdWar -GWOT	392
Deitrick, Jaquelin (Janet)	Johnny Mouse of Corregidor	Hardback	Ch 5 Mascots	101
	Parade Ground	Hardback	Ch 8 Army Life, Wives	159
	Tomorrow, The Accolade	Hardback	Ch 8 Army Life, Wives	159
Del Ruth, Roy, Director	West Point Story, The	DVD	Ch 21 Poetry/Drama/Film	419
Dellinger, Paul	Werewolf of West Point, The	Magazine (paper)	Ch 6 Para, Super, Future	110
DeMille, Nelson	General's Daughter, The	Hardback	Ch 10 Mystery, Crime	186
Dennis, Ralph	MacTaggart's War	Hardback	Ch 9 Paladins, Rogues	176
Denny Fox, Roz	Major Attraction	Paperback	Ch 3 Romance	65
Derby, John Horatio	Phoenixiana: Sketches & Burlesques	Hardback	Ch 22 Old Corps	435
Dickinson, Richard	Acts of Honor	T. Paperback	Ch 20 ColdWar -GWOT	395
	Hurricane Alley	Paperbook	Ch 11 Army Aviation	222
	Love Noir	Hardback	Ch 24 Oth. by WP Auth.	465
	Silent Men, The	Hardback	Ch 18 In the Far East	372
	Warlord, The	Hardback	Ch 20 ColdWar -GWOT	394
Dixon, John	Point, The	Hardback	Ch 6 Para, Super, Future	117
Dixon, Thomas	Victim, The - The Real Jefferson Davis	Hardback	Ch 17 General Officers	340
Doctorow, E.L	March, The	Hardback	Ch 15 Civil War	304
Dorrance, Ethel & James	Get Your Man - Canadian Mounted Mystery	Hardback	Ch 10 Mystery, Crime	183
Downey, Fairfax	Army Mule	Hardback	Ch 5 Mascots	94
	Cavalry Mount	Pulp Fiction	Ch 5 Mascots	98
	Mascots: Military Mascots	Hardback	Ch 5 Mascots	95
	Seventh's Staghound, The	Hardback	Ch 5 Mascots	100
Drake, Joseph Rodman	Culprit Fay, The	Hardback	Ch 21 Poetry/Drama/Film	400
Drille, Hearton	Tactics, Cupid in Shoulder Straps	Hardback	Ch 3 Romance	46
DuBois, E. James	Pathfinder, The	T. Paperback	Ch 18 In the Far East	374
Dunham, Montrew	Abner Doubleday: Boy Baseball Pioneer	Hardback	Ch 4 Army Sports	70
Dupuy, Ernest R.	Bucko, The	Pulp Fiction	Ch 18 In the Far East	353
Durston, George	Boy Scouts' Victory, The	Hardback	Ch 16 World Wars	321
Dwyer, John J.	Stonewall	T. Paperback	Ch 17 General Officers	341
Eaton, Rosemary B.	Of War and Hearts: A Time of War Book 3	T. Paperback	Ch 15 Civil War	312
	Of War and Hearts: Licking Valley Book 2	T. Paperback	Ch 15 Civil War	311
	Of War and Hearts: West Point Academy Book 1	T. Paperback	Ch 15 Civil War	311
Eaton, Seymour	Roosevelt Bears Visit West Point	Paperback	Ch 5 Mascots	88
Eberhardt, Walter F	Classmates	Hardback	Ch 1 Cadet Experience	11
Edson, J.T.	Devil Gun, The	Paperback	Ch 15 Civil War	305
Edwards, David	Ghost Watch at West Point	Paperback	Ch 6 Para, Super, Future	110
Efaw, Amy	Battle Dress	Hardback	Ch 7 Women at WP	134
Elias, Lee	Tommy Tomorrow of the Planeteers	Comic book	Ch 6 Para, Super, Future	122
Elias, Lee	Tommy Tomorrow the West Point of Space	Comic book	Ch 6 Para, Super, Future	122
Ellis, Edward S	Young Scout, The: Story of a WP Lieutenant	Hardback	Ch 14 Manifest Destiny	284
Ellsworth, R. A.	How Darkness Fell	Hardback	Ch 24 Oth. by WP Auth.	464
Emery, Anne	Spy in Old West Point, A	Hardback	Ch 13 Revo, 1812, Thayer	242
Emery, R. G.	Front for Murder, A	Hardback	Ch 24 Oth. by WP Auth.	466
	Gray Line and Gold	Hardback	Ch 4 Army Sports	79
	Home is the Warrior	Pulp Fiction	Ch 24 Oth. by WP Auth.	467
	Warren of West Point	Hardback	Ch 4 Army Sports	79

Author	Title	Format	Chapter (Primary)	Pg #
	Wings Over West Point	Hardback	Ch 11 Army Aviation	213
Farrow, John F., Director	Beyond Glory	DVD	Ch 21 Poetry/Drama/Film	418
Feinstein, John	Rivalry, The - Mystery at the Army-Navy Game	Hardback	Ch 4 Army Sports	83
Felton, Harold W.	Sgt O'Keefe & his Mule Balaam	Hardback	Ch 5 Mascots	92
Finley, Martha	Elsie On the Hudson	Hardback	Ch 13 Revo, 1812, Thayer	245
	Elsie Yachting With the Raymond's	Hardback	Ch 13 Revo, 1812, Thayer	245
Firstone, Alan (aka Arney, Chris)	Son of the Silvery Waters	T. Paperback	Ch 13 Revo, 1812, Thayer	246
Fish, Williston	Short Rations	Hardback	Ch 1 Cadet Experience	4
	Won at West Point: A Romance on the Hudson	Hardback	Ch 3 Romance	49
Fisher, Clay	Black Apache	Paperback	Ch 14 Manifest Destiny	290
Fleming, Thomas J.	Officers' Wives	Hardback	Ch 8 Army Life, Wives	160
	When This Cruel War Is Over	Hardback	Ch 15 Civil War	318
Flexner, James	Traitor and the Spy, The - Arnold & Andre	Hardback	Ch 13 Revo, 1812, Thayer	237
Ford, John	Long Gray Line	DVD	Ch 21 Poetry/Drama/Film	420
Ford, Norman R.	Black, Gray, & Gold, The - West Point Scandal	Hardback	Ch 4 Army Sports	84
	Ghostly Assemblage -Farewell to Honor	Hardback	Ch 13 Revo, 1812, Thayer	252
	Thayer of West Point	Hardback	Ch 13 Revo, 1812, Thayer	252
Fordyce, W.C.	Civil War Dragoon	Hardback	Ch 15 Civil War	303
Forstchen, William R.	Star Voyager Academy (Wing Commander)	Paperback	Ch 6 Para, Super, Future	123
Foster-Harris, William	Long Knives Ride, The	Pulp Fiction	Ch 14 Manifest Destiny	265
Frost, Meigs	Feud's End	Pulp Fiction	Ch 18 In the Far East	355
Frost, Thomas Gold	Man of Destiny, The - General U.S. Grant	Hardback	Ch 17 General Officers	338
Garland, Hamlin	Captain of the Gray-Horse Troop, The	Hardback	Ch 14 Manifest Destiny	283
Garrison, Lt. Frederick	Cadet's Honor: Mark Mallory's Heroism	Hardback	Ch 2 Cadet Series	28
	Off For West Point: Mark Mallory's Struggle	Hardback	Ch 2 Cadet Series	28
	On Guard: Mark Mallory's Celebration	Hardback	Ch 2 Cadet Series	28
	West Point Rivals: Mark Mallory's Stratagem	Hardback	Ch 2 Cadet Series	28
	West Point Treasure: Mark Mallory's Find	Hardback	Ch 2 Cadet Series	28
Garst, Laura	West Pointer in the Land of the Mikado	Hardback	Ch 9 Paladins, Rogues	168
Gelberg, Denise	Engagement	T. Paperback	Ch 20 ColdWar -GWOT	396
Gernert, Mary Alice	Mayor's Daughter - A Timeless Love Story	T. Paperback	Ch 3 Romance	67
Gertsch, W. Darrell	Lotus Redemption	T. Paperback	Ch 3 Romance	67
	Lotus Redemption	T. Paperback	Ch 11 Army Aviation	222
Gibson, Claire	Beyond the Point : a Novel	Hardback	Ch 7 Women at WP	143
Gilliam, David Tod	Rose Croix - A Story of Two Hemispheres, The	Hardback	Ch 3 Romance	47
Goldsmith, Louis C.	Fools Fly High	Pulp Fiction	Ch 11 Army Aviation	214
	You Can't Waste Pilots	Pulp Fiction	Ch 11 Army Aviation	213
Grady, Ronan C.	Collected Works of Ducrot Pepys, The	Hardback	Ch 22 Old Corps	441
Gray, Beverly C	Black Knights of the Hudson: Books I - VI	T. Paperback	Ch 19 WP Legacies	376
	Boots and Saddles: Black Knights of the Hudson Book II	T. Paperback	Ch 14 Manifest Destiny	273
	Changing of the Guard: Black Knights of the Hudson Book III	T. Paperback	Ch 14 Manifest Destiny	293
	Pershing's Eagles: Black Knights of the Hudson Book VI	T. Paperback	Ch 16 World Wars	323

Author	Title	Format	Chapter (Primary)	Pg #
	Shadow of the Flags: Black Knights of the Hudson Book I	T. Paperback	Ch 15 Civil War	296
	The Long Gray Line: Black Knights of the Hudson Book IV	T. Paperback	Ch 1 Cadet Experience	6
	War Clouds in the East: Black Knights of the Hudson Book V	T. Paperback	Ch 16 World Wars	323
Green, Alfred E. Director	Duke of West Point, The	DVD	Ch 21 Poetry/Drama/Film	416
Greenlee, C.L.	For Love through Tears	T. Paperback	Ch 3 Romance	68
Griffin, W.E.B	Aviators, The: Brotherhood of War	T. Paperback	Ch 11 Army Aviation	221
	Berets, The: Brotherhood of War	T. Paperback	Ch 18 In the Far East	368
	Captains, The: Brotherhood of War	Hardback	Ch 18 In the Far East	363
	Colonels, The: Brotherhood of War	Paperback	Ch 20 ColdWar -GWOT	388
	Lieutenants, The: Brotherhood of War	Hardback	Ch 16 World Wars	330
	Majors, The: Brotherhood of War	Hardback	Ch 11 Army Aviation	220
	Majors, The: Brotherhood of War	Hardback	Ch 11 Army Aviation	221
	Special Ops: Brotherhood of War	Paperback	Ch 20 ColdWar -GWOT	389
	The Brotherhood of War	Paperback	Ch 19 WP Legacies	379
Grisham, John	Reckoning, The	Hardback	Ch 10 Mystery, Crime	198
Gundrum, Duane	Absent Without Leave	T. Paperback	Ch 10 Mystery, Crime	199
	Deadly Deceptions	T. Paperback	Ch 18 In the Far East	362
Gutman, Dan	Abner & Me	Hardback	Ch 4 Army Sports	70
Guyer, Lawrence M.	French Leave - American Boy Magazine	Pulp Fiction	Ch 1 Cadet Experience	16
Haeger, Diane	My Dearest Cecelia: General Sherman	T. Paperback	Ch 17 General Officers	341
Haig, Brian	Capital Game	Hardback	Ch 10 Mystery, Crime	202
	Hunted, The	Hardback	Ch 10 Mystery, Crime	202
	Kingmaker, The	T. Paperback	Ch 10 Mystery, Crime	200
	Man in Middle, The	Hardback	Ch 10 Mystery, Crime	201
	Mortal Allies	Hardback	Ch 10 Mystery, Crime	200
	Night Crew, The	T. Paperback	Ch 10 Mystery, Crime	203
	President's Assassin, The	Hardback	Ch 10 Mystery, Crime	201
	Private Sector	Hardback	Ch 10 Mystery, Crime	200
	Sean Drummond Series	Hardback	Ch 10 Mystery, Crime	199
	Secret Sanction, The	T. Paperback	Ch 10 Mystery, Crime	199
Haines, Irvine	Exquisite Siren, The: Peggy Shippen & John André	Hardback	Ch 13 Revo, 1812, Thayer	239
Haines, William W.	The Winter War	Hardback	Ch 14 Manifest Destiny	294
Halberstam, David	One Very Hot Day	Hardback	Ch 18 In the Far East	366
Hallman, Cecilia A.	Memphis Kingmaker, The	Hardback	Ch 9 Paladins, Rogues	179
Hamilton, Alice King	Mildred's Cadet - An Idyl of West Point	Hardback	Ch 3 Romance	48
	Dick Prescotts First Year at West Point	Hardback	Ch 2 Cadet Series	32
	Dick Prescotts Fourth Year at West Point	Hardback	Ch 2 Cadet Series	33
	Dick Prescotts Second Year at West Point	Hardback	Ch 2 Cadet Series	32
	Dick Prescotts Third Year at West Point	Hardback	Ch 2 Cadet Series	33
Hardy, Arthur Sherburne	But Yet A Woman	Hardback	Ch 24 Oth. by WP Auth.	457
	No. 13, Rue du Bon Diable	Hardback	Ch 24 Oth. by WP Auth.	458
Harr, John Ensor	Dark Eagle: A Novel of Benedict Arnold	T. Paperback	Ch 13 Revo, 1812, Thayer	238
Harrington, Captain S. S.	Breaking into West Point	Pulp Fiction	Ch 1 Cadet Experience	7
	Soldiers Honor, A	Pulp Fiction	Ch 3 Romance	55
Harte, Bret	West Point Tic Tacs: Military Verse	Hardback	Ch 22 Old Corps	428
	West Point Tic Tacs: Military Verse	Hardback	Ch 21 Poetry/Drama/Film	399
Hauck, Phillip	Saga of Peter Huston, The	Hardback	Ch 14 Manifest Destiny	268

Author	Title	Format	Chapter (Primary)	Pg #
Hawke, Simon	Sons Of Glory #1	Paperback	Ch 15 Civil War	304
Hawkins, Edward	Prisoners of Devil's Claw	Paperback	Ch 14 Manifest Destiny	272
Hawkins, Jack	Blood Trails	Paperback	Ch 18 In the Far East	369
Hayes, Clair W.	Boy Allies with Pershing in France, The	Hardback	Ch 16 World Wars	322
Hazel, Harry	West Point Cadet, The or Young Officer's Bride	Pulp Fiction	Ch 14 Manifest Destiny	257
Heckelmann, Charles N.	Guns of Arizona	Paperback	Ch 14 Manifest Destiny	292
Hecker, Major William F.	Private Perry and Mister Poe	Hardback	Ch 21 Poetry/Drama/Film	401
Heinlein, Robert A	Revolt in 2100	Hardback	Ch 6 Para, Super, Future	124
Hendricks, LaVice	Black Torch of West Point: A Love Story	T. Paperback	Ch 8 Army Life, Wives	152
Herbert, Hugh F.	West Point Widow	DVD	Ch 21 Poetry/Drama/Film	417
Hobbs, Valerie	How Far Would You Have Gotten?	Hardback	Ch 23 WP Cand. & Ex	449
Hoff, B. J.	To Love and to Honor (The Dalton Saga #1)	T. Paperback	Ch 8 Army Life, Wives	156
	Whisper in the Wind (The Dalton Saga#2)	T. Paperback	Ch 8 Army Life, Wives	157
Holcomb, Bob, Director	Code Breakers	DVD	Ch 21 Poetry/Drama/Film	421
Honig, Donald	Ghost Of Major Pryor, The	Hardback	Ch 9 Paladins, Rogues	178
	Sword of General Englund, The	Hardback	Ch 9 Paladins, Rogues	177
Hooker, Richard	M*A*S*H	Hardback	Ch 12 Medical Corps	233
Hopper, Lt. John T.	Army's Ball	Pulp Fiction	Ch 4 Army Sports	72
	Blood Across Kansas	Pulp Fiction	Ch 14 Manifest Destiny	263
	Eagles Brood	Pulp Fiction	Ch 23 WP Cand. & Ex	446
	Failure Means Death: Spies in Panama	Pulp Fiction	Ch 24 Oth. by WP Auth.	461
	Here Comes the Fleet	Pulp Fiction	Ch 24 Oth. by WP Auth.	459
	Jungle Battery, The: A Canal Zone Death Plot	Pulp Fiction	Ch 24 Oth. by WP Auth.	462
	Last Game, The	Pulp Fiction	Ch 4 Army Sports	72
	M.P. In the Canal Zone's Forbidden Area	Pulp Fiction	Ch 24 Oth. by WP Auth.	460
	Masked Death -- A Fencing Story	Pulp Fiction	Ch 4 Army Sports	73
	Ninth Inning Nerve	Pulp Fiction	Ch 24 Oth. by WP Auth.	460
	Notre Dame to Beat	Pulp Fiction	Ch 4 Army Sports	72
	Puck Shy - A West Point Hockey Novel	Pulp Fiction	Ch 4 Army Sports	73
	Recognition	Pulp Fiction	Ch 1 Cadet Experience	11
	Texas Comes to West Point	Pulp Fiction	Ch 1 Cadet Experience	12
	Texas Joins the Army	Pulp Fiction	Ch 14 Manifest Destiny	266
	That Army-Navy Combination	Pulp Fiction	Ch 4 Army Sports	71
	Vodka Boatman, The	Pulp Fiction	Ch 24 Oth. by WP Auth.	463
	File Boner, The	Pulp Fiction	Ch 1 Cadet Experience	13
Hopson, William	Tombstone Stage	Paperback	Ch 14 Manifest Destiny	291
Horgan, Paul	Distant Trumpet, A	Hardback	Ch 14 Manifest Destiny	290
Hough, John, Jr	Little Bighorn: A Novel	Hardback	Ch 14 Manifest Destiny	278
Howard, General O. O.	Henry in the War	Hardback	Ch 15 Civil War	299
	Donald's School Days	Hardback	Ch 24 Oth. by WP Auth.	458
Howard, John Wesley	Easy Company	Paperback	Ch 14 Manifest Destiny	281
	Easy Company & the Suicide Boys #1	Paperback	Ch 14 Manifest Destiny	282
John Fielding Eliot	Sylvanus Thayer of West Point	Hardback	Ch 13 Revo, 1812, Thayer	250
Johnson, Hugh S.	Williams at West Point	Hardback	Ch 1 Cadet Experience	15
	Williams on Service	Hardback	Ch 18 In the Far East	354
Jones, H. Bedford	West Point Gray	Pulp Fiction	Ch 13 Revo, 1812, Thayer	247
Jordan, Glen	Dress Gray	DVD	Ch 21 Poetry/Drama/Film	422

Author	Title	Format	Chapter (Primary)	Pg #
Kandle, Tawdra	First Classman, The - West Point Tour of Duty	T. Paperback	Ch 1 Cadet Experience	22
Kane, Harriet T.	Lady of Arlington: Mrs. Robert E. Lee	Hardback	Ch 8 Army Life, Wives	149
Kasper, Jason	American Mercenary David Rivers Series	T. Paperback	Ch 10 Mystery, Crime	206
	Covert Kill: Shadow Strike Series	T. Paperback	Ch 20 ColdWar -GWOT	397
	Dark Redemption: David Rivers Series Book 3	T. Paperback	Ch 10 Mystery, Crime	206
	Enemies of My Country Shadow Strike Series	Hardback	Ch 20 ColdWar -GWOT	396
	Fifth Bandit: A Spider Heist Thriller	T. Paperback	Ch 10 Mystery, Crime	208
	Greatest Enemy: David Rivers Series Book 1	T. Paperback	Ch 10 Mystery, Crime	206
	Last Target Standing: Shadow Strike Series	T. Paperback	Ch 20 ColdWar -GWOT	397
	Manhatten Job: A Spider Heist Thriller	T. Paperback	Ch 10 Mystery, Crime	208
	Narco Assassins: Shadow Strike Series	T. Paperback	Ch 20 ColdWar -GWOT	397
	Offer of Revenge: David Rivers Series Book 2	T. Paperback	Ch 10 Mystery, Crime	206
	Sky Thieves: A Spider Heist Thriller	T. Paperback	Ch 10 Mystery, Crime	208
	Spider Heist Series	T. Paperback	Ch 10 Mystery, Crime	207
	Spider Heist: A Spider Heist Thriller	Hardback	Ch 10 Mystery, Crime	207
	Vengeance Calling: David Rivers Series Book 4	T. Paperback	Ch 10 Mystery, Crime	207
Kilpatrick, Judson	Allatoona: An Historical and Military Drama	Paperback	Ch 21 Poetry/Drama/Film	410
	Blue and the Gray, The	Paperback	Ch 21 Poetry/Drama/Film	412
King, Charles	Apache Princess, An: A Tale of the Indian Frontier	Hardback	Ch 14 Manifest Destiny	284
	Army Wife, The	Hardback	Ch 8 Army Life, Wives	152
	Between the Lines: A Story of the War	Hardback	Ch 15 Civil War	299
	Broken Sword, A: A Tale of the Civil War	Hardback	Ch 15 Civil War	301
	Cadet Days - A Story of West Point	Pulp Fiction	Ch 1 Cadet Experience	3
	Cadet Days - Serialized	Hardback	Ch 1 Cadet Experience	4
	Fort Frayne	Hardback	Ch 14 Manifest Destiny	269
	Found in the Philippines: A Woman's Letters	Hardback	Ch 18 In the Far East	352
	Garrison Tangle, A	Hardback	Ch 8 Army Life, Wives	153
	General's Double, The: Story of Army of the Potomac	Hardback	Ch 15 Civil War	302
	In Spite of Foes or Ten Year Trial	Hardback	Ch 14 Manifest Destiny	287
	Medal of Honor - A Study of Peace & War	Hardback	Ch 14 Manifest Destiny	286
	Norman Holt: the Army of the Cumberland	Hardback	Ch 15 Civil War	300
	Soldiers Trial, A -the Canteen Crusade	Hardback	Ch 8 Army Life, Wives	153
	To the Front - Sequel to Cadet Days	Hardback	Ch 14 Manifest Destiny	270
	Warrior Gap, The	Hardback	Ch 14 Manifest Destiny	269
	War-Time Wooing, A	Hardback	Ch 15 Civil War	301
Kjelgaard, Jim	Horses for the Cavalry	Pulp Fiction	Ch 5 Mascots	97
	Lieutenant's Horse, The	Pulp Fiction	Ch 14 Manifest Destiny	271
Koch, H J	Thayer's Return: Early History of West Point	Hardback	Ch 21 Poetry/Drama/Film	407
	Thayer's Return: Early History of West Point	T. Paperback	Ch 13 Revo, 1812, Thayer	254
Krasnesky, Thad	Fright to the Point: Ghosts of West Point	T. Paperback	Ch 6 Para, Super, Future	108
Lacy, Al & Joanna	Tender Flame	Hardback	Ch 3 Romance	47
Lambert, Janet	Candy Kane	Hardback	Ch 3 Romance	60
	Don't Cry Little Girl	Hardback	Ch 3 Romance	59

Author	Title	Format	Chapter (Primary)	Pg #
	Dreams of Glory	Hardback	Ch 3 Romance	58
	Glory Be	Hardback	Ch 3 Romance	58
	Introducing Parri	Hardback	Ch 23 WP Cand. & Ex	448
	Miss America	Hardback	Ch 3 Romance	58
	Star Spangled Summer	Hardback	Ch 3 Romance	57
	That's My Girl	Hardback	Ch 3 Romance	59
Lane, Soraya M.	Girls of Pearl Harbor, The	T. Paperback	Ch 12 Medical Corps	228
Laufe, Abe	Army Doctor's Wife on the Frontier, An	Hardback	Ch 8 Army Life, Wives	150
Lawrence, Edmond	Hazard of West Point - Part 2 of 3	Pulp Fiction	Ch 1 Cadet Experience	8
Leckie, Robert	General, The: The Saga of an American Warlord	Paperback	Ch 17 General Officers	346
Lee, Gus	China Boy	Hardback	Ch 24 Oth. by WP Auth.	465
	Honor And Duty	Hardback	Ch 1 Cadet Experience	19
	Tiger's Tail	Hardback	Ch 18 In the Far East	359
Lippincott, Bertha	Chevrons: A Story of West Point	Hardback	Ch 3 Romance	51
Longstreet, Stephen	General, The: A Novel	Hardback	Ch 17 General Officers	344
Loomis, Noel	Have Gun, Will Travel	Paperback	Ch 9 Paladins, Rogues	170
Loring, Emilie	Beyond the Cloud - A Girl in Love	Paperback	Ch 3 Romance	65
Lounsberry, Lt. Lionel	Cadet Kit Carey	Hardback	Ch 2 Cadet Series	27
	Captain Carey Fighting the Indians at Pine Ridge	Hardback	Ch 2 Cadet Series	27
	Kit Carey's Protégé	Hardback	Ch 2 Cadet Series	27
	Lieutenant Carey's Luck	Hardback	Ch 2 Cadet Series	28
Lubetkin, M. John	Custer's Gold	Hardback	Ch 9 Paladins, Rogues	180
Lubin, Arthur, Director	Francis Goes to West Point	DVD	Ch 21 Poetry/Drama/Film	419
Lyons, Kennedy	West Point Five, The	Hardback	Ch 4 Army Sports	76
	West Pointers on the Gridiron	Hardback	Ch 4 Army Sports	75
Maher, Marty	Bringing Up the Brass	Hardback	Ch 4 Army Sports	78
Maihafer, Harry J.	Oblivion - Mystery of WP Cadet Cox	Hardback	Ch 10 Mystery, Crime	191
Malone, Paul	Cadet Mark Mallory Series	Magazine (paper)	Ch 2 Cadet Series	28
	Plebe at West Point	Hardback	Ch 2 Cadet Series	30
	West Point Cadet	Hardback	Ch 2 Cadet Series	31
	West Point Lieutenant	Hardback	Ch 2 Cadet Series	31
	West Point Yearling	Hardback	Ch 2 Cadet Series	30
	Winning His Way to West Point	Hardback	Ch 2 Cadet Series	29
Manning, Jason	Long Hunters, The	Paperback	Ch 14 Manifest Destiny	258
Mano, Kevin R.	Days, The	T. Paperback	Ch 1 Cadet Experience	21
Markowitz, Carl	Let Them Die at West Point	T. Paperback	Ch 20 ColdWar -GWOT	392
Marquand, John P.	Melville Goodwin, USA	Hardback	Ch 17 General Officers	343
Marshall, Katherine Tupper	Together: Annals of an Army Wife	Hardback	Ch 8 Army Life, Wives	162
Mason, F. V. W.	Captain Redspurs	Pulp Fiction	Ch 15 Civil War	308
Mayer, Bob	Duty, Honor, Country - West Point to Shiloh	T. Paperback	Ch 15 Civil War	320
	Duty, Honor, Country - West Point to Shiloh	T. Paperback	Ch 17 General Officers	346
	Jefferson Allegiance, The	Hardback	Ch 10 Mystery, Crime	190
	Line, The	Paperback	Ch 10 Mystery, Crime	189
McCalls Magazine	Daisy McCall Comes to West Point	Pulp Fiction	Ch 3 Romance	63
McDonnell, Virginia RN	West Point Nurse	Paperback	Ch 3 Romance	60
			Ch 12 Army Medical	229
McNary, Herbert	I've Got Army in my Blood	Pulp Fiction	Ch 4 Army Sports	77

Author	Title	Format	Chapter (Primary)	Pg #
McNary, Herbert	West Point Bombardier	Pulp Fiction	Ch 4 Army Sports	77
Michener, James A.	Legacy	Hardback	Ch 10 Mystery, Crime	187
Mill, Robert R.	West Point Ring, The	Pulp Fiction	Ch 10 Mystery, Crime	184
Miller, Agnes	Lingernots & the Valley Feud, The	Hardback	Ch 13 Revo, 1812, Thayer	244
Mitchell, Siri	Flirtation Walk	T. Paperback	Ch 3 Romance	55
Montgomery, George	Ten Gentlemen from West Point	DVD	Ch 21 Poetry/Drama/Film	417
Moore, C. L.	Earth's Last Citadel	Pulp Fiction	Ch 6 Para, Super, Future	120
	Earth's Last Citadel	Paperback	Ch 6 Para, Super, Future	120
Moritz, Mike	General Paul B. Malone's West Point Series	Pamphlet	Ch 2 Cadet Series	29
Morrison, Paul R.	West Point First Classman	Pulp Fiction	Ch 2 Cadet Series	39
	West Point Fourth Classman	Pulp Fiction	Ch 2 Cadet Series	37
	West Point Second Classman	Pulp Fiction	Ch 2 Cadet Series	38
	West Point Third Classman	Pulp Fiction	Ch 2 Cadet Series	38
Morwick, Jason M.	Morning Calm	T. Paperback	Ch 18 In the Far East	363
Moss, James	Regeneration of Robert Murdoch	Paperback	Ch 21 Poetry/Drama/Film	413
Murphy, Ralph, Director	Spirit of West Point, The	DVD	Ch 21 Poetry/Drama/Film	418
Nemeth, MIke	West Point: A to Z	Hardback	Ch 1 Cadet Experience	24
Nickle, David	Claus Effect, The	Paperback	Ch 6 Para, Super, Future	127
Nolan, J.C.	Treason at the Point	Hardback	Ch 13 Revo, 1812, Thayer	236
Norton, Aloysius	Customs of West Point in American Novel	Manuscript	Ch 1 Cadet Experience	1
O'Farrell, Dr. Patrick D.	West Point Warlord	T. Paperback	Ch 20 ColdWar -GWOT	398
Old Sleuth	Arkie the Runaway	Pulp Fiction	Ch 23 WP Cand. & Ex	445
Olsen, Theodore V.	Mission to the West	Hardback	Ch 14 Manifest Destiny	258
O'Neill, Timothy R.	Shades of Gray	Hardback	Ch 6 Para, Super, Future	104
Patterson, James	Four Blind Mice (Alex Cross)	Hardback	Ch 10 Mystery, Crime	188
Patterson, Richard North	In the Name of Honor	Hardback	Ch 10 Mystery, Crime	195
Patton, J. M.	Drums of War: A Full Measure Trilogy	T. Paperback	Ch 20 ColdWar -GWOT	389
	Thundering White Crosses: A Full Measure Trilogy	T. Paperback	Ch 20 ColdWar -GWOT	390
	West Point - "A Full Measure Trilogy"	T. Paperback	Ch 1 Cadet Experience	21
Pearce, Dick	Impudent Rifle, The	Hardback	Ch 14 Manifest Destiny	259
	Restless Border, The	Hardback	Ch 14 Manifest Destiny	260
Pearl, Jack	Garrison's Gorillas - The Fear Formula	Hardback	Ch 16 World Wars	329
Pease, Howard	Shanghai Passage	Hardback	Ch 23 WP Cand. & Ex	451
Peterson, Donna	Dress Gray	Hardback	Ch 7 Women at WP	131
Porter, Donald Clayton	Seneca Patriots	Paperback	Ch 14 Manifest Destiny	259
Potter, Patricia	Soldier And The Rebel, The	Paperback	Ch 15 Civil War	306
Price, E Hoffman	One Step from Hell	Pulp Fiction	Ch 18 In the Far East	356
Rapp, Kenneth W.	West Point: Whistler in Cadet Gray	Hardback	Ch 22 Old Corps	443
Redula, Lori	Season of Change	T. Paperback	Ch 8 Army Life, Wives	156
Reeder, Russel	Attack at Fort Lookout	Hardback	Ch 13 Revo, 1812, Thayer	249
	Clint Lane - West Point to Berlin	Hardback	Ch 2 Cadet Series	42
	Clint Lane in Korea	Hardback	Ch 2 Cadet Series	42
	West Point First Classman	Hardback	Ch 2 Cadet Series	41
	West Point Plebe	Hardback	Ch 2 Cadet Series	40
	West Point Second Classman	Hardback	Ch 2 Cadet Series	41
	West Point Yearling	Hardback	Ch 2 Cadet Series	40
Richardson, Robert	West Point: An Intimate Picture	Hardback	Ch 22 Old Corps	440

Author	Title	Format	Chapter (Primary)	Pg #
Richey, Frances	Warrior, The: A Mother's Story of a Son at War	Hardback	Ch 21 Poetry/Drama/Film	408
Ricks, Thomas E.	Soldier's Duty, A	Hardback	Ch 10 Mystery, Crime	187
Roe, Edward Payson	His Sombre Rivals	Hardback	Ch 15 Civil War	297
	Original Belle, An	Hardback	Ch 15 Civil War	297
Roe, Frances M. A.	Army Letters from an Officer's Wife	Hardback	Ch 8 Army Life, Wives	146
Rosentblatt, Richard	Black Gold Gray	Hardback	Ch 20 ColdWar -GWOT	397
Rucka, Greg	Batwoman - Seven Years Ago	Comic book	Ch 6 Para, Super, Future	129
	Batwoman - Seven Years Ago	Comic book	Ch 23 WP Cand. & Ex	452
Ruggero, Ed	Academy, The	Hardback	Ch 10 Mystery, Crime	193
	Blame the Dead	Hardback	Ch 16 World Wars	334
	Breaking Ranks	Paperback	Ch 10 Mystery, Crime	192
	Comes the War	Hardback	Ch 16 World Wars	335
	Common Defense	Hardback	Ch 20 ColdWar -GWOT	387
	Thirty-Eight North Yankee	Hardback	Ch 18 In the Far East	359
Russ, Ted	Spirit Mission	Hardback	Ch 20 ColdWar -GWOT	395
Russel, Florence K.	Born to the Blue	Hardback	Ch 2 Cadet Series	34
	From Chevrons to Shoulder Straps	Hardback	Ch 2 Cadet Series	36
	In West Point Gray	Hardback	Ch 2 Cadet Series	35
	Woman's Journey Through the Philippines, A	Hardback	Ch 18 In the Far East	357
Salazar, Noelle	Flight Girls, The	T. Paperback	Ch 11 Army Aviation	219
Sale, Richard	Judas Tree, The	Pulp Fiction	Ch 15 Civil War	310
	Rebels are Coming!, The	Pulp Fiction	Ch 15 Civil War	309
	River Risin'	Pulp Fiction	Ch 12 Army Medical	230
	Swap for Stonewall, A	Pulp Fiction	Ch 15 Civil War	308
Samet, Elizabeth D.	Soldier's Heart: Reading Literature	Hardback	Ch 24 Oth. by WP Auth.	468
Saunders, Raymond	Fenwick Travers and the Forbidden Kingdom	Hardback	Ch 9 Paladins, Rogues	173
	Fenwick Travers and the Forbidden Kingdom	Hardback	Ch 18 In the Far East	356
	Fenwick Travers and the Panama Canal	Hardback	Ch 9 Paladins, Rogues	174
	Fenwick Travers and the Years of Empire	Hardback	Ch 9 Paladins, Rogues	173
Savage, Richard Henry	Captain Landon - A Story of Modern Rome	Hardback	Ch 9 Paladins, Rogues	165
	Midnight Passenger, The	Hardback	Ch 24 Oth. by WP Auth.	456
	My Official Wife	Hardback	Ch 24 Oth. by WP Auth.	455
Schaff, Morris	Spirit of Old West Point, The	Hardback	Ch 22 Old Corps	438
Schartz, Vijaya	Anaz-Voohai - Operation Pleiades	Paperback	Ch 6 Para, Super, Future	128
Schneider, Michelle	Paranormal at West Point	Magazine	Ch 6 Para, Super, Future	103
Schrock, Raymond L.	West Point - movie	DVD	Ch 21 Poetry/Drama/Film	414
Seawell, Molly Elliott	Betty at Fort Blizzard	Hardback	Ch 8 Army Life, Wives	155
	Betty's Virgina Christmas	Hardback	Ch 3 Romance	64
	Thru Thick and Thin	Hardback	Ch 14 Manifest Destiny	285
Seifert, Elizabeth	Army Doctor	Hardback	Ch 12 Medical Corps	231
	Homecoming	Hardback	Ch 17 General Officers	342
Seifert, Shirley	Captain Grant: A Novel	Hardback	Ch 17 General Officers	339
	Farewell, My General	Hardback	Ch 17 General Officers	339
Seletz, Jules M.	West Point's Sentinel Event	T. Paperback	Ch 12 Medical Corps	234
Sergent, Mary Eliz.	Freddy the Would-be Field Mouse	Paperback	Ch 5 Mascots	101
	Rufus the West Point Squirrel	Hardback	Ch 5 Mascots	102
	Wesley the West Point "Wabbit"	Hardback	Ch 5 Mascots	101

Author	Title	Format	Chapter (Primary)	Pg #
Tudbury, Moran	Army Brat -- A West Point Track Story	Pulp Fiction	Ch 4 Army Sports	81
Utermahlen, Brian	Pass in Review	T. Paperback	Ch 19 WP Legacies	377
	Pass in Review - COUNTRY	T. Paperback	Ch 18 In the Far East	372
	Pass in Review - DUTY	T. Paperback	Ch 16 World Wars	326
	Pass in Review - HONOR	T. Paperback	Ch 11 Army Aviation	220
	Pass in Review - HONOR	T. Paperback	Ch 16 World Wars	327
Vakkur, Mark	Matter of Trust	Paperback	Ch 7 Women at WP	133
Van Dyke, W. S. Director	Rosalie	DVD	Ch 21 Poetry/Drama/Film	416
Vandergroot, Roy	Satan Sounds Boots and Saddles	Pulp Fiction	Ch 14 Manifest Destiny	290
Vaughan, Robert	Blood on the Plains	Paperback	Ch 14 Manifest Destiny	262
	Yesterday's Reveille	Paperback	Ch 14 Manifest Destiny	263
Vermillion, John M.	Comfort Kills: Simon Pack #5	T. Paperback	Ch 10 Mystery, Crime	198
	Don't Call Me General: Simon Pack #2	T. Paperback	Ch 10 Mystery, Crime	196
	Evil in Disguise: Simon Pack #4	T. Paperback	Ch 10 Mystery, Crime	197
	It's Not Dark Yet: Simon Pack #3	T. Paperback	Ch 10 Mystery, Crime	197
	Just Pack: Simon Pack #7	T. Paperback	Ch 10 Mystery, Crime	198
	Matai: Simon Pack #6	T. Paperback	Ch 10 Mystery, Crime	198
	Pack's Posse: Simon Pack #8	T. Paperback	Ch 10 Mystery, Crime	198
	Simon Pack Series	T. Paperback	Ch 10 Mystery, Crime	196
	Supe - A Novel of West Point, The	T. Paperback	Ch 10 Mystery, Crime	196
Vonnegut, Kurt	Hocus Pocus	Hardback	Ch 6 Para, Super, Future	124
Waddel, Charles Cary	Girl of the Guard Line, The	Hardback	Ch 3 Romance	54
Wall, Judith Henry	Handsome Women	Hardback	Ch 8 Army Life, Wives	161
Warner Hall (R.G. Emery)	Untamed	Paperback	Ch 24 Oth. by WP Auth.	466
Warner, Anna B.	West Point Colours	Hardback	Ch 1 Cadet Experience	5
Warner, Susan	Wide, Wide World, The	Hardback	Ch 24 Oth. by WP Auth.	455
Warren, C.M.	Bugles are for Soldiers	Pulp Fiction	Ch 14 Manifest Destiny	287
	Only the Valiant	Paperback	Ch 14 Manifest Destiny	288
	Valley of the Shadow	Hardback	Ch 14 Manifest Destiny	287
Warren, Ed & Lorraine	Ghost Hunters	Hardback	Ch 6 Para, Super, Future	105
Warren, Larry	Killer from West Point, The	Pulp Fiction	Ch 9 Paladins, Rogues	181
Watkins, Amanda	Hard to Die	T. Paperback	Ch 6 Para, Super, Future	112
Watson, Helen Orr	Shavetail Sam. U.S. Army Mule	Hardback	Ch 5 Mascots	96
	Top Kick. U.S. Army Horse	Hardback	Ch 5 Mascots	97
	Trooper. U. S. Army Dog	Hardback	Ch 5 Mascots	100
Webster, Frank V	Tom Taylor at West Point	Hardback	Ch 1 Cadet Experience	9
Weldon, Col. J. Thomas	West Point Boys, The	Paperback	Ch 1 Cadet Experience	7
Wellman, Manley Wade	West Point 3000 A.D.	Comic book	Ch 6 Para, Super, Future	118
Wells, Helen	Cherry Ames, Army Nurse	Hardback	Ch 12 Medical Corps	226
	Cherry Ames, Chief Nurse	Hardback	Ch 12 Medical Corps	226
	Cherry Ames, Flight Nurse	Hardback	Ch 12 Medical Corps	227
	Cherry Ames, Veterans Nurse	Hardback	Ch 12 Medical Corps	227
Wensyel, James	Appomattox: The Passing of the Armies	Hardback	Ch 15 Civil War	319
	Martha's Easter Bonnet	Hardback	Ch 13 Revo, 1812, Thayer	239
	Petersburg - Out of the Trenches	Hardback	Ch 15 Civil War	319
Whitney, Phyllis	Mystery of the Haunted Pool	Hardback	Ch 13 Revo, 1812, Thayer	244
Whitson, William	Apprentice Warrior - Born for Flight	Hardback	Ch 11 Army Aviation	210
	Test of Battle: Born for Flight	T. Paperback	Ch 11 Army Aviation	210

Author	Title	Format	Chapter (Primary)	Pg #
	Test of Battle: Born for Flight	T. Paperback	Ch 16 World Wars	325
Whittaker, Frederick	Cadet Button, The	Paperback	Ch 14 Manifest Destiny	274
	Popular Life of Gen'l Geo. A. Custer, A	Hardback	Ch 14 Manifest Destiny	275
Willard, Tom	Black Sabre Chronicles #1 - #5	Hardback	Ch 19 WP Legacies	378
	Buffalo Soldiers: Black Sabre Chronicles #1	Hardback	Ch 14 Manifest Destiny	293
	Sable Dough Boys: Black Sabre Chronicles #2	Hardback	Ch 16 World Wars	324
	Stone Ponies, The: The Black Sabre Chronicles #4	Hardback	Ch 18 In the Far East	370
	Sword of Valor: Black Sabre Chronicles #5	Hardback	Ch 20 ColdWar -GWOT	394
	Wings of Honor: Black Sabre Chronicles #3	T. Paperback	Ch 16 World Wars	330
Williams, Lawrence	I, James McNeil Whistler	Hardback	Ch 23 WP Cand. & Ex	451
Williamson, C.N. & A.M.	Lady Betty Across the Water	Hardback	Ch 3 Romance	52
	Soldier of the Legion - Romance of the Desert	Hardback	Ch 9 Paladins, Rogues	167
Williamson, Jack	Dragon's Island	Hardback	Ch 6 Para, Super, Future	121
Wohlforth, Robert	Nickelodeon Childhood, A	Pamphlet	Ch 24 Oth. by WP Auth.	464
	Tin Soldiers	Hardback	Ch 1 Cadet Experience	18
Wood, Lt. Oliver E.	West Point Scrap Book: A Collection	Hardback	Ch 22 Old Corps	423
Yarnell, Duane	Coming in on a Prayer	Pulp Fiction	Ch 11 Army Aviation	218

Grip Hands Title Index

Bold Type - West Point Author T. Paperback - Trade Paperback

Title	Primary Author	Format	Chapter (Primary)	Pg #
7 Knights	Cox, Brian	T. Paperback	Ch 10 Mystery, Crime	205
Absent Without Leave	**Gundrum Duane**	T. Paperback	Ch 10 Mystery, Crime	199
Abner & Me	Gutman, Dan	Hardback	Ch 4 Army Sports	70
Abner Doubleday: Boy Baseball Pioneer	Dunham, Montrew	Hardback	Ch 4 Army Sports	70
Ab-Sa-Ra-Ka	Carrington, Margaret	T. Paperback	Ch 8 Army Life, Wives	146
Academy, The	**Ruggero, Ed**	Hardback	Ch 10 Mystery, Crime	193
Acts of Honor	**Dickinson, Richard H.**	T. Paperback	Ch 20 ColdWar -GWOT	395
Adventures of Peter Parsec, Space Cadet	**Conrad, Michael**	Paperback	Ch 1 Cadet Experience	23
Advice to Ladies…	Bradley, Mary Quale	Other	Ch 3 Romance	62
Allatoona: An Historical and Military Drama	**Kilpatrick, Judson**	Paperback	Ch 21 Poetry/Drama/Film	410
Allie McCrae and the West Point Half-Blood	Abbott, Tom J	Hardback	Ch 14 Manifest Destiny	292
American Mercenary David Rivers Series	**Kasper, Jason**	T. Paperback	Ch 10 Mystery, Crime	206
Anaz-Voohai - Operation Pleiades	Schartz, Vijaya	Paperback	Ch 6 Para, Super, Future	128
Apache Princess, An: A Tale of the Indian Frontier	**King, Charles**	Hardback	Ch 14 Manifest Destiny	284
Appomattox: The Passing of the Armies	**Wensyel, James**	Hardback	Ch 15 Civil War	319
Apprentice Warrior - Born for Flight	**Whitson, William W.**	Hardback	Ch 11 Army Aviation	210
Area Bird: Gray Girl Book II	**Spieth, Susan**	T. Paperback	Ch 7 Women at WP	139
Arkie the Runaway	Old Sleuth	Pulp Fiction	Ch 23 WP Cand. & Ex	445
Armored Corps #1	Callahan, Pete	Paperback	Ch 18 In the Far East	361
Army Bears!?	**Autin, Scott**	Magazine	Ch 5 Mascots	87
Army Blue	**Truscott, Lucian K.**	Hardback	Ch 18 In the Far East	370
Army Brat -- A West Point Track Story	Tudbury, Moran	Pulp Fiction	Ch 4 Army Sports	81
Army Doctor	Seifert, Elizabeth	Hardback	Ch 12 Medical Corps	231
Army Doctor's Wife on the Frontier, An	Laufe, Abe	Hardback	Ch 8 Army Life, Wives	150
Army Letters from an Officer's Wife	Roe, Frances M. A.	Hardback	Ch 8 Army Life, Wives	146
Army Mule	Downey, Fairfax	Hardback	Ch 5 Mascots	94
Army Wife, The	**King, Charles**	Hardback	Ch 8 Army Life, Wives	152
Army Wife, The	Smith, Mrs. R.D.	Magazine	Ch 8 Army Life, Wives	158
Army's Ball	**Hopper, Lt. John T.**	Pulp Fiction	Ch 4 Army Sports	72
As a Soldier Would	APUSA	Hardback	Ch 3 Romance	51
Athena Speaks: Women at West Point	Carter, Abbey & Rosenberg, Marya, Editors	T. Paperback	Ch 7 Women at WP	135
Athena Speaks: Women at West Point	Carter, Abbey & Rosenberg, Marya, Editors	T. Paperback	Ch 21 Poetry/Drama/Film	407
Attack at Fort Lookout	**Reeder, Russel**	Hardback	Ch 13 Revo, 1812, Thayer	249
Attack by Fire: Armored Corps #3	Callahan, Pete	Paperback	Ch 18 In the Far East	361
Autumn on the Hudson	Degen, Everett R.	Hardback	Ch 20 ColdWar -GWOT	392
Aviators, The: Brotherhood of War	Griffin, W.E.B	T. Paperback	Ch 11 Army Aviation	221
Battle Dress	**Efaw, Amy**	Hardback	Ch 7 Women at WP	134
Batwoman - Seven Years Ago	Rucka, Greg	…	Ch 23 WP Cand. & Ex	452
Batwoman - Seven Years Ago	Rucka, Greg	Comic book	Ch 6 Para, Super, Future	129

Title	Primary Author	Format	Chapter (Primary)	Pg #
Berets, The: Brotherhood of War	Griffin, W.E.B	T. Paperback	Ch 18 In the Far East	368
Betsy McCall Goes to West Point	McCalls Magazine	Magazine	Ch 3 Romance	63
Betty at Fort Blizzard	Seawell, Molly Elliott	Hardback	Ch 8 Army Life, Wives	155
Betty's Virgina Christmas	Seawell, Molly Elliott	Hardback	Ch 3 Romance	64
Between the Lines: A Story of the War	**King, Charles**	Hardback	Ch 15 Civil War	299
Beyond Glory	Farrow, John F., Director	DVD	Ch 21 Poetry/Drama/Film	418
Beyond the Cloud - A Girl in Love	Loring, Emilie	Paperback	Ch 3 Romance	65
Beyond the Point: a Novel	Gibson, Claire	Hardback	Ch 7 Women at WP	143
Bill Bruce Becomes an Ace	**Arnold, H. H.**	Hardback	Ch 11 Army Aviation	212
Bill Bruce Becomes an Ace	**Arnold, H.H.**	Hardback	Ch 16 World Wars	325
Bill Bruce Flight Series	**Arnold, H. H.**	Hardback	Ch 11 Army Aviation	211
Bill Bruce in The Trans-Continental Race	**Arnold, H.H.**	Hardback	Ch 11 Army Aviation	212
Bill Bruce on Border Patrol	**Arnold, H.H.**	Hardback	Ch 11 Army Aviation	212
Bill Bruce on Forest Patrol	**Arnold, H.H.**	Hardback	Ch 11 Army Aviation	212
Bill Bruce Pioneer Aviators	**Arnold, H.H.**	Hardback	Ch 11 Army Aviation	211
Bill Bruce the Flying Cadet	**Arnold, H. H.**	Hardback	Ch 11 Army Aviation	211
Black Apache	Fisher, Clay	Paperback	Ch 14 Manifest Destiny	289
Black Gold Gray	**Rosentblatt, Richard**	Hardback	Ch 20 ColdWar -GWOT	397
Black Knights of the Hudson: Books I - VI	Gray, Beverly C	T. Paperback	Ch 19 WP Legacies	376
Black Sabre Chronicles #1 - #5	Willard, Tom	Hardback	Ch 19 WP Legacies	378
Black Torch of West Point: A Love Story	Hendricks, LaVice	T. Paperback	Ch 8 Army Life, Wives	152
Black, Gray, & Gold, The - West Point Scandal	**Ford, Norman R.**	Hardback	Ch 4 Army Sports	84
Blame the Dead	**Ruggero, Ed**	Hardback	Ch 16 World Wars	334
Blame the Dead	**Ruggero, Ed**	Hardback	Ch 12 Army Medical Svc	280
Blaze of Glory, A	Shaara, Jeff	Hardback	Ch 15 Civil War	315
Blood Across Kansas	**Hopper, Lt. John T.**	Pulp Fiction	Ch 14 Manifest Destiny	263
Blood on the Plains	Vaughan, Robert	Paperback	Ch 14 Manifest Destiny	262
Blood Trails	Hawkins, Jack	Paperback	Ch 18 In the Far East	369
Blue and the Gray, The	**Kilpatrick, Judson**	Paperback	Ch 21 Poetry/Drama/Film	412
Boots and Saddles: Black Knights of the Hudson Book II	Gray, Beverly C	T. Paperback	Ch 14 Manifest Destiny	273
Boots and Saddles: Life in Dakota	Custer, Elizabeth B	T. Paperback	Ch 8 Army Life, Wives	148
Born to the Blue	Russel, Florence K.	Hardback	Ch 2 Cadet Series	34
Boy Allies with Pershing in France, The	Hayes, Clair W.	Hardback	Ch 16 World Wars	322
Boy Scouts' Victory, The	Durston, George	Hardback	Ch 16 World Wars	321
Breaking into West Point	Harrington, Captain S. S.	Pulp Fiction	Ch 1 Cadet Experience	7
Breaking Ranks	**Ruggero, Ed**	Paperback	Ch 10 Mystery, Crime	192
Bright Starry Banner	Carter, Alden R.	Hardback	Ch 15 Civil War	318
Bringing Up the Brass	**Maher, Marty**	Hardback	Ch 4 Army Sports	78
Broken Sword, A: A Tale of the Civil War	**King, Charles**	Hardback	Ch 15 Civil War	301
Bucko, The	**Dupuy, Ernest R.**	Pulp Fiction	Ch 18 In the Far East	353
Buffalo Soldiers: Black Sabre Chronicles #1	Willard, Tom	Hardback	Ch 14 Manifest Destiny	293
Bugles are for Soldiers	Warren, C.M.	Pulp Fiction	Ch 14 Manifest Destiny	287
But Yet A Woman	**Hardy, Arthur Sherburne**	Hardback	Ch 24 Oth. by WP Auth.	457

Title	Primary Author	Format	Chapter (Primary)	Pg #
Cadet Button, The	Whittaker, Frederick	Paperback	Ch 14 Manifest Destiny	274
Cadet Days - A Story of West Point	**King, Charles**	Pulp Fiction	Ch 1 Cadet Experience	3
Cadet Days - Serialized	**King, Charles**	Hardback	Ch 1 Cadet Experience	4
Cadet Derry, West Pointer	**Stanley, John Berchram**	Hardback	Ch 1 Cadet Experience	17
Cadet Detective's Hot Hustle, The	Boynton, Howard	Pulp Fiction	Ch 9 Paladins, Rogues	175
Cadet Kit Carey	Lounsberry, Lt. Lionel	Hardback	Ch 2 Cadet Series	27
Cadet Mark Mallory Series	**Malone, Paul**	Magazine	Ch 2 Cadet Series	28
Cadet's Honor: Mark Mallory's Heroism	Garrison, Lt. Frederick	Hardback	Ch 2 Cadet Series	28
Candy Kane	Lambert, Janet	Hardback	Ch 3 Romance	60
Capital Game	**Haig, Brian**	Hardback	Ch 10 Mystery, Crime	202
Capitan - The Story of an Army Mule	Crockett, Lucy Herndon	Hardback	Ch 5 Mascots	90
Captain Carey Fighting the Indians at Pine Ridge	Lounsberry, Lt. Lionel	Hardback	Ch 2 Cadet Series	27
Captain Grant: A Novel	Seifert, Shirley	Hardback	Ch 17 General Officers	339
Captain Landon - A Story of Modern Rome	**Savage, Richard Henry**	Hardback	Ch 9 Paladins, Rogues	165
Captain Macklin	Davis, Richard Harding	Hardback	Ch 9 Paladins, Rogues	166
Captain of the Gray-Horse Troop, The	Garland, Hamlin	Hardback	Ch 14 Manifest Destiny	282
Captain Redspurs	Mason, F. V. W.	Pulp Fiction	Ch 15 Civil War	308
Captains, The: Brotherhood of War	Griffin, W.E.B	Hardback	Ch 18 In the Far East	363
Cast a Giant Shadow: Mickey Marcus	Berkman, Ted	Paperback	Ch 9 Paladins, Rogues	169
Cavalry Life in Tent & Field	Boyd, Mrs. Orsemus	Hardback	Ch 8 Army Life, Wives	147
Cavalry Mount	Downey, Fairfax	Pulp Fiction	Ch 5 Mascots	98
Chain of Thunder, A	Shaara, Jeff	Hardback	Ch 15 Civil War	316
Changing of the Guard: Black Knights of the Hudson Book III	Gray, Beverly C	T. Paperback	Ch 14 Manifest Destiny	293
Cherry Ames, Army Nurse	Wells, Helen	Hardback	Ch 12 Medical Corps	226
Cherry Ames, Chief Nurse	Wells, Helen	Hardback	Ch 12 Medical Corps	226
Cherry Ames, Flight Nurse	Wells, Helen	Hardback	Ch 12 Medical Corps	227
Cherry Ames, Veterans Nurse	Wells, Helen	Hardback	Ch 12 Medical Corps	227
Chevrons: A Story of West Point	Lippincott, Bertha	Hardback	Ch 3 Romance	51
China Boy	**Lee, Gus**	Hardback	Ch 24 Oth. by WP Auth.	465
Civil War Dragoon	Fordyce, W.C.	Hardback	Ch 15 Civil War	303
Civil War in the East - Generals	...	...	Ch 17 General Officers	348
Civil War in the West - Generals	...	..	Ch 17 General Officers	349
Classmates	Eberhardt, Walter F	Hardback	Ch 1 Cadet Experience	11
Claus Effect, The	Nickle, David	Paperback	Ch 6 Para, Super, Future	127
Clint Lane - West Point to Berlin	**Reeder, Russel**	Hardback	Ch 2 Cadet Series	42
Clint Lane in Korea	**Reeder, Russel**	Hardback	Ch 2 Cadet Series	42
Code Breakers	Holcomb, Bob, Director	DVD	Ch 21 Poetry/Drama/Film	421
Collected Works of Ducrot Pepys, The	**Grady, Ronan C.**	Hardback	Ch 22 Old Corps	441
Colonels, The: Brotherhood of War	Griffin, W.E.B	Paperback	Ch 20 ColdWar -GWOT	388
Comanche and his Captain	Anderson, A.M.	Hardback	Ch 14 Manifest Destiny	279
Comanche: America's Most Heroic Horse	Appel, David	Hardback	Ch 5 Mascots	99
Combat General: A Novel	**Chamberlain, Wm.**	Hardback	Ch 17 General Officers	344
Comes the War	**Ruggero, Ed**	Hardback	Ch 16 World Wars	335
Comfort Kills: Simon Pack #5	**Vermillion, John M.**	T. Paperback	Ch 10 Mystery, Crime	198
Coming in on a Prayer	Yarnell, Duane	Pulp Fiction	Ch 11 Army Aviation	218

Title	Primary Author	Format	Chapter (Primary)	Pg #
Common Defense	**Ruggero, Ed**	Hardback	Ch 20 ColdWar -GWOT	387
Conclave	**Davis, Tom**	T. Paperback	Ch 20 ColdWar -GWOT	385
Corduroy Road, The	Cline, Patricia Edwards	Hardback	Ch 13 Revo, 1812, Thayer	243
Courtship at West Point	**de Metropolis, Harry**	Hardback	Ch 21 Poetry/Drama/Film	403
Covert Kill: Shadow Strike Series	**Kasper, Jason**	T. Paperback	Ch 20 ColdWar -GWOT	397
Cows and Firsties: Guardians of Honor	Bandy Jr, J.E.	Hardback	Ch 7 Women at WP	138
Crofton's Fire	Coplin, Keith	T. Paperback	Ch 9 Paladins, Rogues	167
Culprit Fay, The	Drake, Joseph Rodman	Hardback	Ch 21 Poetry/Drama/Film	400
Custer's Gold	Lubetkin, M. John	Hardback	Ch 9 Paladins, Rogues	180
Customs of West Point in American Novel	**Norton, Aloysius**	Manuscript	Ch 1 Cadet Experience	1
Cut: A Story of West Point	**Cervus, G.I.**	Hardback	Ch 1 Cadet Experience	2
Dare Boys After Benedict Arnold	Cox, Stephen A.	Hardback	Ch 13 Revo, 1812, Thayer	241
Dark Eagle: A Novel of Benedict Arnold	Harr, John Ensor	T. Paperback	Ch 13 Revo, 1812, Thayer	238
Dark Redemption: David Rivers Series #3	**Kasper, Jason**	T. Paperback	Ch 10 Mystery, Crime	206
Days, The	**Mano, Kevin R.**	T. Paperback	Ch 1 Cadet Experience	21
Deadly Deceptions	**Gundrum, Duane**	T. Paperback	Ch 18 In the Far East	362
Dear Belle: Letters from a Cadet and Officer	Crary, Catherine	Hardback	Ch 15 Civil War	298
Devil Gun, The	Edson, J.T.	Paperback	Ch 15 Civil War	305
Dick Merriwell's The Yale Nine at West Point	Standish, Burt L.	Pulp Fiction	Ch 4 Army Sports	69
Dick Prescotts First Year at West Point	Hancock, H. Irving	Hardback	Ch 2 Cadet Series	32
Dick Prescotts Fourth Year at West Point	Hancock, H. Irving	Hardback	Ch 2 Cadet Series	33
Dick Prescotts Second Year at West Point	Hancock, H. Irving	Hardback	Ch 2 Cadet Series	32
Dick Prescotts Third Year at West Point	Hancock, H. Irving	Hardback	Ch 2 Cadet Series	33
Distant Trumpet, A	Horgan, Paul	Hardback	Ch 14 Manifest Destiny	290
Donald's School Days	**Howard, General O.O.**	Hardback	Ch 24 Oth. by WP Auth.	458
Don't Call Me General: Simon Pack #2	**Vermillion, John M.**	T. Paperback	Ch 10 Mystery, Crime	196
Don't Cry Little Girl	Lambert, Janet	Hardback	Ch 3 Romance	59
Douglas MacArthur - Battlefield General Parts 1-4	Crandall, F.E.	Comic book	Ch 17 General Officers	347
Downward Path, The	Towner, Cliff R	Hardback	Ch 23 WP Cand. & Ex	447
Dragon's Island	Williamson, Jack	Hardback	Ch 6 Para, Super, Future	121
Drama	...	...	Ch 21 Poetry/Drama/Film	409
Dreams of Glory	Lambert, Janet	Hardback	Ch 3 Romance	58
Dress Gray	Jordan, Glen	DVD	Ch 21 Poetry/Drama/Film	422
Dress Gray	**Peterson, Donna**	Hardback	Ch 7 Women at WP	131
Dress Gray	**Truscott, Lucian K.**	Hardback	Ch 10 Mystery, Crime	184
Drums of War: A Full Measure Trilogy	**Patton, J. M.**	T. Paperback	Ch 20 ColdWar -GWOT	389
Duke of West Point, The	Green, Alfred E. Director	DVD	Ch 21 Poetry/Drama/Film	416
Duty, Honor, Country - West Point to Shiloh	**Mayer, Bob**	T. Paperback	Ch 15 Civil War	320
Duty, Honor, Country - West Point to Shiloh	**Mayer, Bob**	T. Paperback	Ch 17 General Officers	346
Eagles Brood	**Hopper, Lt. John T.**	Pulp Fiction	Ch 23 WP Cand. & Ex	446
Earth's Last Citadel	Moore, C. L.	Pulp Fiction	Ch 6 Para, Super, Future	120
Earth's Last Citadel	Moore, C. L.	Paperback	Ch 6 Para, Super, Future	120

Title	Primary Author	Format	Chapter (Primary)	Pg #
Francis Goes to West Point	Lubin, Arthur, Director	DVD	Ch 21 Poetry/Drama/Film	419
Francis the Talking Mule	Stern, David	Comic book	Ch 5 Mascots	93
Francis the Talking Mule	Stern, David	Hardback	Ch 5 Mascots	93
Fred Fearnot at West Point	Standish, Hal	Pulp Fiction	Ch 1 Cadet Experience	10
Freddy the Would-be Field Mouse	Sergent, Mary Eliz.	Paperback	Ch 5 Mascots	101
French Leave - American Boy Magazine	**Guyer, Lawrence M.**	Pulp Fiction	Ch 1 Cadet Experience	16
Fright to the Point: Ghosts of West Point	Krasnesky, Thad	T. Paperback	Ch 6 Para, Super, Future	108
From Chevrons to Shoulder Straps	Russel, Florence K.	Hardback	Ch 2 Cadet Series	36
From West Point to Watergate	Alexander, Hansen	T. Paperback	Ch 3 Romance	66
Front for Murder, A	**Emery, R. G.**	Hardback	Ch 24 Oth. by WP Auth.	466
Full Dress Gray	**Truscott, Lucian K**	Hardback	Ch 10 Mystery, Crime	185
Futuristic	...	...	Ch 6 Para, Super, Future	118
Garrison Tangle, A	**King, Charles**	Hardback	Ch 8 Army Life, Wives	153
Garrison's Gorillas - The Fear Formula	Pearl, Jack	Hardback	Ch 16 World Wars	329
General Paul B. Malone's West Point Series	Moritz, Mike	Pamphlet	Ch 2 Cadet Series	29
General, The: A Novel	Longstreet, Stephen	Hardback	Ch 17 General Officers	344
General, The: The Saga of an American Warlord	Leckie, Robert	Paperback	Ch 17 General Officers	346
General's Daughter, The	DeMille, Nelson	Hardback	Ch 10 Mystery, Crime	186
General's Double, The: Story of Army of Potomac	**King, Charles**	Hardback	Ch 15 Civil War	302
Get Your Man - Canadian Mounted Mystery	Dorrance, Ethel & James	Hardback	Ch 10 Mystery, Crime	183
Ghost Hunters	Warren, Ed & Lorraine	Hardback	Ch 6 Para, Super, Future	105
Ghost Of Major Pryor, The	Honig, Donald	Hardback	Ch 9 Paladins, Rogues	178
Ghost Watch at West Point	Edwards, David	Paperback	Ch 6 Para, Super, Future	110
Ghostly Assemblage -Farewell to Honor	**Ford, Norman R.**	Hardback	Ch 13 Revo, 1812, Thayer	252
Girl of the Guard Line, The	Waddel, Charles Cary	Hardback	Ch 3 Romance	54
Girls of Pearl Harbor, The	Lane, Soraya M.	T. Paperback	Ch 12 Medical Corps	228
Glory Be	Lambert, Janet	Hardback	Ch 3 Romance	58
Goatnapping Gladiators of West Point	**Arney, Chris**	T. Paperback	Ch 4 Army Sports	85
Gods and Generals	Shaara, Jeff M.	Hardback	Ch 15 Civil War	314
God's Children	Coyle, Harold	Hardback	Ch 20 ColdWar -GWOT	387
Gone for Soldiers	Shaara, Jeff	Hardback	Ch 14 Manifest Destiny	262
Gray Girl Series #1 - #4	**Spieth, Susan**	T. Paperback	Ch 2 Cadet Series	44
Gray Girl: Gray Girl Book I	**Spieth, Susan**	T. Paperback	Ch 7 Women at WP	139
Gray Line and Gold	**Emery, R. G.**	Hardback	Ch 4 Army Sports	79
Grayboy	**Conrad, Michael**	Magazine	Ch 1 Cadet Experience	24
Greatest Enemy: David Rivers Series Book 1	**Kasper, Jason**	T. Paperback	Ch 10 Mystery, Crime	206
Grim Legion	Alcott, Jack	Hardback	Ch 10 Mystery, Crime	194
Guardians of Honor Series #1 - #3	Bandy Jr, J.E.	Hardback	Ch 2 Cadet Series	43
Guns of Arizona	Heckelmann, Charles N.	Paperback	Ch 14 Manifest Destiny	292
Hailey's War	Compton, Jodi	Paperback	Ch 23 WP Cand. & Ex	452
Hands of Honor	**Sims II, Terron**	T. Paperback	Ch 20 ColdWar -GWOT	393
Handsome Women	Wall, Judith Henry	Hardback	Ch 8 Army Life, Wives	161
Hard to Die	Watkins, Amanda	T. Paperback	Ch 6 Para, Super, Future	112

Title	Primary Author	Format	Chapter (Primary)	Pg #
Haunting Hussar of West Point, The	Not stated	Comic book	Ch 6 Para, Super, Future	109
Have Gun, Will Travel	CBS Broadcasting	DVD	Ch 21 Poetry/Drama/Film	421
Have Gun, Will Travel	Loomis, Noel	Paperback	Ch 9 Paladins, Rogues	170
Hazard of West Point - Part 2 of 3	Lawrence, Edmond	Pulp Fiction	Ch 1 Cadet Experience	8
Heart of War	**Truscott, Lucian K.**	Hardback	Ch 10 Mystery, Crime	185
Hemi: A Mule	Brenner, Barbara	Hardback	Ch 5 Mascots	94
Henry in the War	**Howard, General O. O.**	Hardback	Ch 15 Civil War	299
Herb Kent, West Point Cadet	Dean, Graham	Hardback	Ch 4 Army Sports	74
Herb Kent, West Point Fullback	Dean, Graham	Hardback	Ch 4 Army Sports	74
Here Comes the Fleet	**Hopper, Lt. John T.**	Pulp Fiction	Ch 24 Oth. by WP Auth.	459
His Sombre Rivals	Roe, Edward Payson	Hardback	Ch 15 Civil War	297
Hitler Invades England	**Crall, George**	Paperback	Ch 16 World Wars	334
Hocus Pocus	Vonnegut, Kurt	Hardback	Ch 6 Para, Super, Future	124
Home is the Warrior	**Emery, Guy**	Pulp Fiction	Ch 24 Oth. by WP Auth.	467
Homecoming	Seifert, Elizabeth	Hardback	Ch 17 General Officers	342
Honor And Duty	**Lee, Gus**	Hardback	Ch 1 Cadet Experience	19
Horses for the Cavalry	Kjelgaard, Jim	Pulp Fiction	Ch 5 Mascots	97
How Darkness Fell	**Ellsworth, R. A.**	Hardback	Ch 24 Oth. by WP Auth.	464
How Far Would You Have Gotten?	Hobbs, Valerie	Hardback	Ch 23 WP Cand. & Ex	449
Hunted, The	**Haig, Brian**	Hardback	Ch 10 Mystery, Crime	202
Hurricane Alley	**Dickinson, Richard H.**	Paperbook	Ch 11 Army Aviation	222
I Love a Man in Uniform	Burana, Lily	Hardback	Ch 8 Army Life, Wives	163
I, James McNeil Whistler	Williams, Lawrence	Hardback	Ch 23 WP Cand. & Ex	451
Illusive Lover	Calloway, Jo	Paperback	Ch 3 Romance	65
Impudent Rifle, The	Pearce, Dick	Hardback	Ch 14 Manifest Destiny	259
In Spite of Foes or Ten Year Trial	**King, Charles**	Hardback	Ch 14 Manifest Destiny	286
In the Name of Honor	Patterson, Richard North	Hardback	Ch 10 Mystery, Crime	195
In West Point Gray	Russel, Florence K.	Hardback	Ch 2 Cadet Series	35
Indian Wars	...	...	Ch 14 Manifest Destiny	258
Indomitable	**Spiller, Ben**	Hardback	Ch 7 Women at WP	133
Inheritors of the Storm	Sondheim, Victor	Hardback	Ch 23 WP Cand. & Ex	448
Introducing Parri	Lambert, Janet	Hardback	Ch 23 WP Cand. & Ex	448
It Had to Be You	Byrd, Elizabeth	Hardback	Ch 3 Romance	61
It's Not Dark Yet : Simon Pack #3	**Vermillion, John M.**	T. Paperback	Ch 10 Mystery, Crime	197
I've Got Army in my Blood	McNary, Herbert	Pulp Fiction	Ch 4 Army Sports	77
Jefferson Allegiance, The	**Mayer, Bob**	Hardback	Ch 10 Mystery, Crime	190
Johnny Mouse of Corregidor	Deitrick, Jaquelin (Janet)	Hardback	Ch 5 Mascots	101
Judas Tree, The	Sale, Richard	Pulp Fiction	Ch 15 Civil War	310
Jungle Battery, The: A Canal Zone Death Plot	**Hopper, Lt. John T.**	Pulp Fiction	Ch 24 Oth. by WP Auth.	462
Just Pack: Simon Pack #7	**Vermillion, John M.**	T. Paperback	Ch 10 Mystery, Crime	198
Killer Angels, The	Shaara, Michael	Hardback	Ch 15 Civil War	313
Killer from West Point, The	Warren, Larry	Pulp Fiction	Ch 9 Paladins, Rogues	181
Kingmaker, The	**Haig, Brian**	T. Paperback	Ch 10 Mystery, Crime	200
Kit Carey's Protégé	Lounsberry, Lt. Lionel	Hardback	Ch 2 Cadet Series	27

Title	Primary Author	Format	Chapter (Primary)	Pg #
Of War and Hearts: West Point Academy Book 1	Eaton, Rosemary B.	T. Paperback	Ch 15 Civil War	311
Off For West Point: Mark Mallory's Struggle	Garrison, Lt. Frederick	Hardback	Ch 2 Cadet Series	28
Offer of Revenge: David Rivers Series Book 2	**Kasper, Jason**	T. Paperback	Ch 10 Mystery, Crime	206
Officers' Wives	Fleming, Thomas J.	Hardback	Ch 8 Army Life, Wives	160
On Guard: Mark Mallory's Celebration	Garrison, Lt. Frederick	Hardback	Ch 2 Cadet Series	28
One Step from Hell	**Price, E Hoffman**	Pulp Fiction	Ch 18 In the Far East	356
One Very Hot Day	Halberstam, David	Hardback	Ch 18 In the Far East	366
Only the Losers Win	Barns, Glen M.	Paperback	Ch 9 Paladins, Rogues	175
Only the Valiant	Warren, Charles M.	Paperback	Ch 14 Manifest Destiny	288
Operation White Star	**Sutton, Richard**	Hardback	Ch 18 In the Far East	373
Original Belle, An	Roe, Edward Payson	Hardback	Ch 15 Civil War	297
Our Little Brown House	Stewart, Maria	Hardback	Ch 21 Poetry/Drama/Film	401
Pack's Posse: Simon Pack #8	**Vermillion, John M.**	T. Paperback	Ch 10 Mystery, Crime	198
Paladins, The	...	...	Ch 9 Paladins, Rogues	169
Pale Blue Eye, The	Bayard, Louis	Hardback	Ch 10 Mystery, Crime	194
Parade Ground	Deitrick, Jaquelin (Janet)	Hardback	Ch 8 Army Life, Wives	159
Paranormal at West Point	Schneider, Michelle	Magazine	Ch 6 Para, Super, Future	103
Pass in Review	**Utermahlen, Brian**	T. Paperback	Ch 19 WP Legacies	377
Pass in Review - COUNTRY	**Utermahlen, Brian**	T. Paperback	Ch 18 In the Far East	372
Pass in Review - DUTY	**Utermahlen, Brian**	T. Paperback	Ch 16 World Wars	326
Pass in Review - HONOR	**Utermahlen, Brian**	T. Paperback	Ch 11 Army Aviation	220
Pass in Review - HONOR	**Utermahlen, Brian**	T. Paperback	Ch 16 World Wars	327
Pathfinder, The	DuBois, E. James	T. Paperback	Ch 18 In the Far East	374
Patriot Lad at Old West Point, A	Carter, Russel Gordon	Hardback	Ch 13 Revo, 1812, Thayer	242
Pegasus Remounts - Cadet Verse	**Curran, Charles D.**	Hardback	Ch 21 Poetry/Drama/Film	402
Perilous Night, The	Boyce, Burke	Hardback	Ch 13 Revo, 1812, Thayer	235
Pershing's Eagles: Black Knights of the Hudson Book VI	Gray, Beverly C	T. Paperback	Ch 16 World Wars	323
Peter Parsec, Raiders of the Lost Dark	**Conrad, Michael**	Paperback	Ch 6 Para, Super, Future	130
Petersburg - Out of the Trenches	**Wensyel, James**	Hardback	Ch 15 Civil War	319
Philippines	...	...	Ch 18 In the Far East	351
Phoenixiana: Sketches & Burlesques	**Derby, John Horatio**	Hardback	Ch 22 Old Corps	435
Plebe at West Point	**Malone, Paul**	Hardback	Ch 2 Cadet Series	30
Poetry	...	...	Ch 21 Poetry/Drama/Film	399
Point, The	Dixon, John	Hardback	Ch 6 Para, Super, Future	117
Popular Life of Gen'l Geo. A. Custer, A	Whittaker, Frederick	Hardback	Ch 14 Manifest Destiny	275
President's Assassin, The	**Haig, Brian**	Hardback	Ch 10 Mystery, Crime	201
Prisoners of Devil's Claw	Hawkins, Edward	Paperback	Ch 14 Manifest Destiny	272
Private Perry and Mister Poe	**Hecker, Major William F.**	Hardback	Ch 21 Poetry/Drama/Film	401
Private Sector	**Haig, Brian**	Hardback	Ch 10 Mystery, Crime	200
Puck Shy - A West Point Hockey Novel	**Hopper, Lt. John T.**	Pulp Fiction	Ch 4 Army Sports	73

Title	Primary Author	Format	Chapter (Primary)	Pg #
Queen of Battle	**Cooley, John W.**	Hardback	Ch 7 Women at WP	142
Rebels are Coming!, The	Sale, Richard	Pulp Fiction	Ch 15 Civil War	309
Rebound	**Emery, R. G.**	Hardback	Ch 4 Army Sports	80
Reckoning, The	Grisham, John	Hardback	Ch 10 Mystery, Crime	198
Recognition	**Hopper, Lt. John T.**	Pulp Fiction	Ch 1 Cadet Experience	11
Red Randal Flight Series	Bowen, Robert S.	Hardback	Ch 11 Army Aviation	215
Red Randall at Midway	Bowen, Robert S.	Hardback	Ch 11 Army Aviation	216
Red Randall at Pearl Harbor	Bowen, Robert S.	Hardback	Ch 11 Army Aviation	215
Red Randall in Burma	Bowen, Robert S.	Hardback	Ch 11 Army Aviation	217
Red Randall in the Aleutians	Bowen, Robert S.	Hardback	Ch 11 Army Aviation	216
Red Randall on Active Duty	Bowen, Robert S.	Hardback	Ch 11 Army Aviation	215
Red Randall on New Guinea	Bowen, Robert S.	Hardback	Ch 11 Army Aviation	216
Red Randall Over Tokyo	Bowen, Robert S.	Hardback	Ch 11 Army Aviation	215
Regeneration of Robert Murdoch	**Moss, James**	Paperback	Ch 21 Poetry/Drama/Film	413
Restless Border, The	Pearce, Dick	Hardback	Ch 14 Manifest Destiny	260
Revolt in 2100	Heinlein, Robert A	Hardback	Ch 6 Para, Super, Future	124
Ringknockers	**Bush, Keith A.**	Hardback	Ch 4 Army Sports	85
Rising Tide, The	Shaara, Jeff	T. Paperback	Ch 16 World Wars	331
Rivalry, The - Mystery at Army-Navy Game	Feinstein, John	Hardback	Ch 4 Army Sports	83
River Risin'	Sale, Richard	Pulp Fiction	Ch 12 Army Medical	230
Road We Do Not Know, A: A Novel of Custer	Chiaventone, Frederick J.	Hardback	Ch 14 Manifest Destiny	277
Rogues	...	...	Ch 9 Paladins, Rogues	174
Roosevelt Bears Visit West Point	Eaton, Seymour	Paperback	Ch 5 Mascots	88
Rosalie	Van Dyke, W. S. Director	DVD	Ch 21 Poetry/Drama/Film	416
Rose Croix - A Story of Two Hemispheres, The	Gilliam, David Tod	Hardback	Ch 3 Romance	47
Rufus the West Point Squirrel	Sergent, Mary Eliz.	Hardback	Ch 5 Mascots	102
Sable Dough Boys: Black Sabre Chronicles #2	Willard, Tom	Hardback	Ch 16 World Wars	324
Saga of Peter Huston, The	Hauck, Phillip	Hardback	Ch 14 Manifest Destiny	268
Satan Sounds Boots and Saddles	Vandergroot, Roy	Pulp Fiction	Ch 14 Manifest Destiny	290
Sean Drummond Series	**Haig, Brian**	Hardback	Ch 10 Mystery, Crime	199
Season of Change	Redula, Lori	T. Paperback	Ch 8 Army Life, Wives	156
Secret Sanction, The	**Haig, Brian**	T. Paperback	Ch 10 Mystery, Crime	199
Seneca Patriots	Porter, Donald Clayton	Paperback	Ch 14 Manifest Destiny	259
Seventh's Staghound, The	Downey, Fairfax	Hardback	Ch 5 Mascots	100
Sgt O'Keefe & his Mule Balaam	Felton, Harold W.	Hardback	Ch 5 Mascots	92
Shades of Gray	Anderson, Michael D.	T. Paperback	Ch 21 Poetry/Drama/Film	405
Shades of Gray	O'Neill, Timothy R.	Hardback	Ch 6 Para, Super, Future	104
Shadow of the Flags: Black Knights of the Hudson Book I	Gray, Beverly C	T. Paperback	Ch 15 Civil War	296
Shanghai Passage	Pease, Howard	Hardback	Ch 23 WP Cand. & Ex	451
Shavetail Sam. U.S. Army Mule	Watson, Helen Orr	Hardback	Ch 5 Mascots	96
Short Rations	**Fish, Williston**	Hardback	Ch 1 Cadet Experience	4
Silent Men, The	**Dickinson, Richard H.**	Hardback	Ch 18 In the Far East	372
Simon Pack Series	**Vermillion, John M.**	T. Paperback	Ch 10 Mystery, Crime	196
Skirmish	Cloos, Bert	Paperback	Ch 14 Manifest Destiny	267

Title	Primary Author	Format	Chapter (Primary)	Pg #
Sky Thieves: A Spider Heist Thriller	**Kasper, Jason**	T. Paperback	Ch 10 Mystery, Crime	208
Small Wars - Jack Reacher	Child, Lee	Hardback	Ch 9 Paladins, Rogues	171
Smoke at Dawn, The: A Novel of the Civil War	Shaara, Jeff	Hardback	Ch 15 Civil War	316
Soldier And The Rebel, The	Potter, Patricia	Paperback	Ch 15 Civil War	306
Soldier of the Legion - Romance of the Desert	Williamson, C.N. & A.M.	Hardback	Ch 9 Paladins, Rogues	167
Soldier's Duty, A	Ricks, Thomas E.	Hardback	Ch 10 Mystery, Crime	187
Soldier's First Duty: A	Cain, George M.A.	T. Paperback	Ch 18 In the Far East	354
Soldier's Heart: Reading Literature	**Samet, Elizabeth D.**	Hardback	Ch 24 Oth. by WP Auth.	468
Soldiers Honor, A	Harrington, Captain S. S.	Pulp Fiction	Ch 3 Romance	55
Soldiers of Fortune	...	...	Ch 9 Paladins, Rogues	165
Soldiers Trial, A -the Canteen Crusade	**King, Charles**	Hardback	Ch 8 Army Life, Wives	153
Son of the Silvery Waters	**Firstone, Alan (aka Arney, Chris)**	T. Paperback	Ch 13 Revo, 1812, Thayer	246
Sons Of Glory #1	Hawke, Simon	Paperback	Ch 15 Civil War	304
Special Forces Trooper	Archibald, Joe	Hardback	Ch 18 In the Far East	365
Special Ops: Brotherhood of War	Griffin, W.E.B	Paperback	Ch 20 ColdWar -GWOT	389
Spider Heist Series	**Kasper, Jason**	T. Paperback	Ch 10 Mystery, Crime	207
Spider Heist: A Spider Heist Thriller	**Kasper, Jason**	Hardback	Ch 10 Mystery, Crime	207
Spirit Mission	**Russ, Ted**	Hardback	Ch 20 ColdWar -GWOT	395
Spirit of Old West Point, The	**Schaff, Morris**	Hardback	Ch 22 Old Corps	438
Spirit of West Point, The	Murphy, Ralph, Director	DVD	Ch 21 Poetry/Drama/Film	418
Spy in Old West Point, A	Emery, Anne	Hardback	Ch 13 Revo, 1812, Thayer	242
Star Spangled Summer	Lambert, Janet	Hardback	Ch 3 Romance	57
Star Voyager Academy (Wing Commander)	Forstchen, William R.	Paperback	Ch 6 Para, Super, Future	123
Steel Wave, The	Shaara, Jeff	Hardback	Ch 16 World Wars	331
Stone Ponies, The: The Black Sabre Chronicles #4	Willard, Tom	Hardback	Ch 18 In the Far East	370
Stonewall	Dwyer, John J.	T. Paperback	Ch 17 General Officers	341
Stories of the Army	Not stated	Hardback	Ch 8 Army Life, Wives	151
Story of West Point, The	Not stated	Comic book	Ch 13 Revo, 1812, Thayer	240
Summer of Dreams	Camden, Elizabeth	T. Paperback	Ch 3 Romance	57
Supe - A Novel of West Point, The	**Vermillion, John M.**	T. Paperback	Ch 10 Mystery, Crime	196
Superluminal	Daniel, Tony	Hardback	Ch 6 Para, Super, Future	127
Supernatural			Ch 6 Para, Super, Future	113
Surgeon U.S.A.	Slaughter, Frank D.	Hardback	Ch 12 Medical Corps	232
Swap for Stonewall, A	Sale, Richard	Pulp Fiction	Ch 15 Civil War	308
Sword and Scalpel	Slaughter, Frank D.	Hardback	Ch 12 Medical Corps	232
Sword of Templars, The	Christopher, Paul	Paperback	Ch 10 Mystery, Crime	204
Sword of General Englund, The	Honig, Donald	Hardback	Ch 9 Paladins, Rogues	177
Sword of Valor: Black Sabre Chronicles #5	Willard, Tom	Hardback	Ch 20 ColdWar -GWOT	394
Sword Point	Coyle, Harold	Hardback	Ch 20 ColdWar -GWOT	385
Sylvanus Thayer of West Point	**John Fielding Eliot**	Hardback	Ch 13 Revo, 1812, Thayer	250
Tactics, Cupid in Shoulder Straps	Drille, Hearton	Hardback	Ch 3 Romance	46
Teenage Sports Stories: The Land Torpedo	**Strong, Paschal**	Hardback	Ch 4 Army Sports	76
Templars Series	Christopher, Paul	Paperback	Ch 10 Mystery, Crime	204

Title	Primary Author	Format	Chapter (Primary)	Pg #
Ten Gentlemen from West Point	Montgomery, George	DVD	Ch 21 Poetry/Drama/Film	417
Tender Flame	Lacy, Al & Joanna	Hardback	Ch 3 Romance	47
Tenting On The Plains	Custer, Elizabeth B	Hardback	Ch 8 Army Life, Wives	148
Test of Battle: Born for Flight	**Whitson, William W.**	T. Paperback	Ch 11 Army Aviation	210
Test of Battle: Born for Flight	**Whitson, William W.**	T. Paperback	Ch 16 World Wars	325
Texas Comes to West Point	**Hopper, Lt. John T.**	Pulp Fiction	Ch 1 Cadet Experience	12
Texas Joins the Army	**Hopper, Lt. John T.**	Pulp Fiction	Ch 14 Manifest Destiny	266
That Army-Navy Combination	**Hopper, Lt. John T.**	Pulp Fiction	Ch 4 Army Sports	71
That's My Girl	Lambert, Janet	Hardback	Ch 3 Romance	59
Thayer of West Point	**Ford, Norman R.**	Hardback	Ch 13 Revo, 1812, Thayer	252
Thayer's Return: Early History of West Point	Koch, H J	T. Paperback	Ch 21 Poetry/Drama/Film	407
Thayer's Return: Early History of West Point	Koch, H.J.	T. Paperback	Ch 13 Revo, 1812, Thayer	254
The Brotherhood of War	Griffin, W.E.B	Paperback	Ch 19 WP Legacies	379
The Fire Witch: Tracy Book 1	Allison, P.G.	T. Paperback	Ch 6 Para, Super, Future	116
The Long Gray Line: Black Knights of the Hudson Book IV	Gray, Beverly C	T. Paperback	Ch 1 Cadet Experience	6
The Plebes: Guardians of Honor	Bandy Jr, J. E.	Hardback	Ch 7 Women at WP	137
The Revoultionary War	...	..	Ch 13 Revo, 1812, Thayer	235
The Yearlings: Guardians of Honor	Bandy Jr, J. E.	Hardback	Ch 7 Women at WP	137
Thirty-Eight North Yankee	**Ruggero, Ed**	Hardback	Ch 18 In the Far East	359
Three Plebes at West Point	**Strong, Paschal**	Hardback	Ch 1 Cadet Experience	15
Thru Thick and Thin	Seawell, Molly Elliott	Hardback	Ch 14 Manifest Destiny	284
Thundering White Crosses: A Full Measure Trilogy	**Patton, J. M.**	T. Paperback	Ch 20 ColdWar -GWOT	390
Tiger's Tail	**Lee, Gus**	Hardback	Ch 18 In the Far East	359
Tin Soldiers	**Wohlforth, Robert**	Hardback	Ch 1 Cadet Experience	18
To Love and to Honor (The Dalton Saga #1)	Hoff, B. J.	T. Paperback	Ch 8 Army Life, Wives	156
To the Colors: Poems from West Point	**Coates, Dennis**	Hardback	Ch 21 Poetry/Drama/Film	406
To the Front - Sequel to Cadet Days	**King, Charles**	Hardback	Ch 14 Manifest Destiny	270
Together: Annals of an Army Wife	Marshall, Katherine Tupper	Hardback	Ch 8 Army Life, Wives	162
Tom Taylor at West Point	Webster, Frank V	Hardback	Ch 1 Cadet Experience	9
Tomahawk, The Frontiersman of West Point	Not stated	Comic book	Ch 13 Revo, 1812, Thayer	240
Tombstone Stage	Hopson, William	Paperback	Ch 14 Manifest Destiny	291
Tommy Tomorrow of the Planeteers	Elias, Lee	Comic book	Ch 6 Para, Super, Future	122
Tommy Tomorrow the West Point of Space	Elias, Lee	Comic book	Ch 6 Para, Super, Future	122
Tomorrow, The Accolade	Deitrick, Jaquelin (Janet)	Hardback	Ch 8 Army Life, Wives	159
Top Kick. U.S. Army Horse	Watson, Helen Orr	Hardback	Ch 5 Mascots	97
Tracy Plays Demon: Tracy Book 2	Allison, P.G.	T. Paperback	Ch 6 Para, Super, Future	116
Traitor and the Spy, The - Arnold & Andre	Flexner, James	Hardback	Ch 13 Revo, 1812, Thayer	237
Treason at the Point	Nolan, J.C.	Hardback	Ch 13 Revo, 1812, Thayer	236
Trial by Fire	Coyle, Harold	Hardback	Ch 20 ColdWar -GWOT	386
Trooper. U. S. Army Dog	Watson, Helen Orr	Hardback	Ch 5 Mascots	100

Title	Primary Author	Format	Chapter (Primary)	Pg #
Trumpets of Company K	**Chamberlain, Wm.**	Paperback	Ch 14 Manifest Destiny	273
Uncommon Soldier, The	Abrahams, Robert D.	Paperback	Ch 15 Civil War	307
Underside of Things	Bell, Lillian	Hardback	Ch 3 Romance	52
Untamed	**Warner Hall (R.G. Emery)**	Paperback	Ch 24 Oth. by WP Auth.	466
Unwritten Order, The	Ames, John Edward	Paperback	Ch 14 Manifest Destiny	289
Valley of the Shadow	Warren, Charles M.	Hardback	Ch 14 Manifest Destiny	288
Vengeance Calling: David Rivers #4	**Kasper, Jason**	T. Paperback	Ch 10 Mystery, Crime	207
Victim, The – The Real Jefferson Davis	Dixon, Thomas	Hardback	Ch 17 General Officers	340
Vietnam	...	...	Ch 18 In the Far East	365
Vodka Boatman, The	**Hopper, Lt. John T.**	Pulp Fiction	Ch 24 Oth. by WP Auth.	463
War Clouds in the East: Black Knights of the Hudson Book V	Gray, Beverly C	T. Paperback	Ch 16 World Wars	323
War of 1812	...	...	Ch 13 Revo, 1812, Thayer	246
Warlord, The	**Dickinson, Richard H.**	Hardback	Ch 20 ColdWar -GWOT	394
Warren of West Point	**Emery, R. G.**	Hardback	Ch 4 Army Sports	79
Warrior Breed	Cox, William R.	Pulp Fiction	Ch 14 Manifest Destiny	271
Warrior Gap, The	**King, Charles**	Hardback	Ch 14 Manifest Destiny	269
Warrior, The: A Mother's Story of a Son at War	Richey, Frances	Hardback	Ch 21 Poetry/Drama/Film	408
War-Time Wooing, A	**King, Charles**	Hardback	Ch 15 Civil War	301
Weekend Romance	Teeters, Peggy	Hardback	Ch 3 Romance	61
Werewolf of West Point, The	Dellinger, Paul	Magazine	Ch 6 Para, Super, Future	110
Wesley the West Point "Wabbit"	Sergent, Mary Eliz.	Hardback	Ch 5 Mascots	101
West Point - "A Full Measure Trilogy"	**Patton, J. M.**	T. Paperback	Ch 1 Cadet Experience	21
West Point - movie	Schrock, Raymond L.	DVD	Ch 21 Poetry/Drama/Film	414
West Point 3000 A.D.	Wellman, Manley Wade	Comic book	Ch 6 Para, Super, Future	118
West Point Bombardier	McNary, Herbert	Pulp Fiction	Ch 4 Army Sports	77
West Point Boys, The	Weldon, Col. J. Thomas	Paperback	Ch 1 Cadet Experience	7
West Point Cadet	**Malone, Paul**	Hardback	Ch 2 Cadet Series	31
West Point Cadet, The or Young Officer's Bride	Hazel, Harry	Pulp Fiction	Ch 14 Manifest Destiny	257
West Point Colours	**Warner, Anna B.**	Hardback	Ch 1 Cadet Experience	5
West Point Deep Cover	Thistle, Rik	Hardback	Ch 20 ColdWar -GWOT	384
West Point First Classman	Morrison, Paul R.	Pulp Fiction	Ch 2 Cadet Series	39
West Point First Classman	**Reeder, Russel**	Hardback	Ch 2 Cadet Series	41
West Point Five, The	**Lyons, Kennedy**	Hardback	Ch 4 Army Sports	76
West Point Fourth Classman	Morrison, Paul R.	Pulp Fiction	Ch 2 Cadet Series	37
West Point Girl	Anderson, Ruth	Pulp Fiction	Ch 3 Romance	56
West Point Gray	Jones, H. Bedford	Pulp Fiction	Ch 13 Revo, 1812, Thayer	247
West Point Lieutenant	**Malone, Paul**	Hardback	Ch 2 Cadet Series	31
West Point Nurse	McDonnell, Virginia RN	Paperback	Ch 3 Romance	60
			Ch 12 Army Medical	229
West Point of Tomorrow - the Planet Patrol	Burks, Arthur J.	Comic book	Ch 6 Para, Super, Future	119
West Point Plebe	**Reeder, Russel**	Hardback	Ch 2 Cadet Series	40

Title	Primary Author	Format	Chapter (Primary)	Pg #
West Point Ring, The	Mill, Robert R.	Pulp Fiction	Ch 10 Mystery, Crime	184
West Point Rivals: Mark Mallory's Stratagem	Garrison, Lt. Frederick	Hardback	Ch 2 Cadet Series	28
West Point Scrap Book: A Collection	**Wood, Lt. Oliver E.**	Hardback	Ch 22 Old Corps	423
West Point Second Classman	Morrison, Paul R.	Pulp Fiction	Ch 2 Cadet Series	38
West Point Second Classman	**Reeder, Russel**	Hardback	Ch 2 Cadet Series	41
West Point Story - A Board Game	Not stated	Board game	Ch 1 Cadet Experience	25
West Point Story, The	Del Ruth, Roy, Director	DVD	Ch 21 Poetry/Drama/Film	419
West Point Third Classman	Morrison, Paul R.	Pulp Fiction	Ch 2 Cadet Series	38
West Point Tic Tacs: Military Verse	Harte, Bret	Hardback	Ch 22 Old Corps	428
West Point Tic Tacs: Military Verse	Harte, Brett	Hardback	Ch 21 Poetry/Drama/Film	399
West Point Treasure: Mark Mallory's Find	Garrison, Lt. Frederick	Hardback	Ch 2 Cadet Series	28
West Point Warlord	**O'Farrell, Dr. Patrick D.**	T. Paperback	Ch 20 ColdWar -GWOT	398
West Point Werewolf	Stephens, L.C.	Paperback	Ch 6 Para, Super, Future	111
West Point Whirlwind - A Touchdown Outlaw	Bishop, Curtis	Pulp Fiction	Ch 4 Army Sports	82
West Point Widow	Herbert, Hugh F.	DVD	Ch 21 Poetry/Drama/Film	417
West Point Wingback	Archibald, Joe	Hardback	Ch 4 Army Sports	81
West Point Wins	**Strong, Paschal**	Hardback	Ch 4 Army Sports	75
West Point Wooing: Victorian Romance	Burnham, Clara Louise	Hardback	Ch 3 Romance	50
West Point Yearling	**Malone, Paul**	Hardback	Ch 2 Cadet Series	30
West Point Yearling	**Reeder, Russel**	Hardback	Ch 2 Cadet Series	40
West Point: A Comedy in Three Acts	Baker, George A	Hardback	Ch 21 Poetry/Drama/Film	409
West Point: A to Z	**Nemeth, MIke**	Hardback	Ch 1 Cadet Experience	22
West Point: An Intimate Picture	**Richardson, Robert**	Hardback	Ch 22 Old Corps	440
West Point: The Television Series	Benson, Leon, Dir.	DVD	Ch 21 Poetry/Drama/Film	420
West Point: Whistler in Cadet Gray	Rapp, Kenneth W.	Hardback	Ch 22 Old Corps	444
West Pointer in the Land of the Mikado	Garst, Laura	Hardback	Ch 9 Paladins, Rogues	168
West Pointer with the Boers, A	**Blake, Col. John Y**	Hardback	Ch 9 Paladins, Rogues	168
West Pointer's Honor	**Chilton, Alexander**	Hardback	Ch 1 Cadet Experience	14
West Pointers on the Gridiron	**Lyons, Kennedy**	Hardback	Ch 4 Army Sports	75
West Point's Sentinel Event	Seletz, Jules M.	T. Paperback	Ch 12 Medical Corps	234
When This Cruel War Is Over	Fleming, Thomas J.	Hardback	Ch 15 Civil War	318
Whisper Flight; A Glider Mission in Burma	**Stanley, John Berchram**	Hardback	Ch 11 Army Aviation	217
Whisper in the Wind (The Dalton Saga#2)	Hoff, B. J.	T. Paperback	Ch 8 Army Life, Wives	157
Wide, Wide World, The	**Warner, Susan**	Hardback	Ch 24 Oth. by WP Auth.	455
Williams at West Point	**Johnson, Hugh S.**	Hardback	Ch 1 Cadet Experience	15
Williams on Service	**Johnson, Hugh S.**	Hardback	Ch 18 In the Far East	354
Wings of Honor: Black Sabre Chronicles #3	Willard, Tom	T. Paperback	Ch 16 World Wars	330
Wings Over West Point	**Emery, R. G.**	Hardback	Ch 11 Army Aviation	213
Winning His Way to West Point	**Malone, Paul**	Hardback	Ch 2 Cadet Series	29
Winter War, The	Haines, William W.	Hardback	Ch 14 Manifest Destiny	294
Witch Heart: Gray Girl Book IV	**Spieth, Susan**	T. Paperback	Ch 7 Women at WP	140
With Honor in Hand	**Sims II, Terron**	Paperback	Ch 20 ColdWar -GWOT	393
Woman's Journey Through the Philippines, A	Russel, Florence K.	Hardback	Ch 18 In the Far East	357
Women in West Point	Compton, Juleen	Manuscript	Ch 7 Women at WP	132

Title	Primary Author	Format	Chapter (Primary)	Pg #
Won at West Point: A Romance on the Hudson	**Fish, Williston**	Hardback	Ch 3 Romance	49
Wonder Book of Air	Shearer, Cynthia	Hardback	Ch 11 Army Aviation	223
World War I	...	...	Ch 16 World Wars	320
World War II	...	...	Ch 16 World Wars	326
World's Most Famous Ghosts	Cohen, Daniel	Paperback	Ch 6 Para, Super, Future	111
Yesterday's Reveille	Vaughan, Robert	Paperback	Ch 14 Manifest Destiny	263
You Can't Waste Pilots	Goldsmith, Louis C.	Pulp Fiction	Ch 11 Army Aviation	213
Young Scout, The: Story of a WP Lieutenant	Ellis, Edward S	Hardback	Ch 14 Manifest Destiny	283
Zone of Sudden Death, The	**Chamberlain, Wm.**	Paperback	Ch 16 World Wars	328

Made in the USA
Monee, IL
24 August 2023

55243255-b928-4882-8a09-1e97738477ecR01